"All the News That's Fit to Print."

The New York Times.

EXTRA
6:30 A. M.

VOL. LXIV...NO. 20,923.   NEW YORK, SATURDAY, MAY 8, 1915.—TWENTY-FOUR PAGES.   ONE CENT

LUSITANIA SUNK BY A SUBMARINE, PROBABLY 1,260 DEAD;
TWICE TORPEDOED OFF IRISH COAST; SINKS IN 15 MINUTES;
CAPT. TURNER SAVED, FROHMAN AND VANDERBILT MISSING;
WASHINGTON BELIEVES THAT A GRAVE CRISIS IS AT HAND

SHOCKS THE PRESIDENT

Washington Deeply Stirred by the Loss of American Lives.

BULLETINS AT WHITE HOUSE

"Wilson Reads Them Closely, but Is Silent on the Nation's Course."

HINTS OF CONGRESS CALL

Loss of Lusitania Recalls Firm Tone of Our First Warning to Germany.

CAPITAL FULL OF RUMORS

The Lost Cunard Mail Steamship
X Where the First Torpedo Struck.   XX Where the Second Torpedo Struck.

SOME DEAD TAKEN ASHORE

Several Hundred Survivors at Queenstown and Kinsale.

"STEWARD TELLS OF DISASTER"

One Torpedo Crashes Into the Doomed Liner's Bow, Another Into the Engine Room.

SHIP LISTS OVER TO PORT

Makes It Impossible to Lower Many Boats, So Hundreds Must Have Gone Down.

ATTACKED IN BROAD DAY

Canard Office Here Besieged for News; Fate of 1,918 on Lusitania Long in Doubt

List of Saved Includes Capt. Turner; Vanderbilt and Frohman Reported Lost

Saw the Submarine 100 Yards Off and Watched Torpedo as It Struck Ship

Loss of the Lusitania Fills London With Horror and Utter Amazement

Only 650 Were Saved, Four Cabin Passengers

LUSITANIA

"Just when you thought they'd forgotten how to write intelligent, illuminating, and entertaining historical novels, along comes LUSITANIA to prove there's life in the old genre yet. There's so much life, in fact, that it . . . leaves the reader happily exhausted as the novel reaches its sad, bitter conclusion . . . LUSITANIA is entertaining, informative, and thoroughly engrossing—'popular' fiction of the very best kind."

LUSITANIA

"BRILLIANT . . . DAZZLING . . . FILLED WITH MEMORABLE CHARACTERS . . . A CONSISTENTLY EXCITING HISTORICAL NOVEL . . . AWESOME IN ITS TRAGIC POWER."

Publishers Weekly

"Packed with romance, extravagance, and political intrigue . . . a powerful World War I thriller . . . a terrifying fictional glimpse into the psychology of a nation."

Booklist

LUSITANIA

DAVID BUTLER

BALLANTINE BOOKS • NEW YORK

Library of Congress Catalog Card Number: 82-40139

ISBN 0-345-30514-0

This edition published by arrangement with Random House, Inc.

Manufactured in the United States of America

First Ballantine Books Edition: December 1983

FOR MARY

PROLOGUE

SHE WAS HIS.

He thought of her, sleek, aristocratic, so beautiful the very sight of her stopped his breath, and he could hardly believe it. So many men admired her and wanted her. And she was his.

None of his elation showed. He had learned to hide his feelings, especially from the desk men, the soft-palmed, smooth-faced men in their rooms of mahogany and brocade and polished leather. Years before, because he knew his life and career depended on their decisions, trying to talk to them had made him tongue-tied and clumsy. Now he nodded and said as little as possible, letting his record speak for him more convincingly than he ever could. And they had given her to him.

Square and solid, he sat in the Chairman's office of the Cunard Steamship Company in Liverpool. There were papers to be signed and while he waited, expressionless, his heavy hands folded in his lap, he remembered the first time he had been here. Twenty, no, more than thirty years ago. To have his appointment confirmed as third officer on the steamer *Cherbourg*, running between Liverpool and the Mediterranean. 1878 . . . God in Heaven, was it that long ago?

With a slight frown of surprise, he realized how young the present Chairman was, scarcely more than forty. That put a good twenty years between them. The younger man's career was mostly ahead of him, while his was nearly over, four years to compulsory retirement under company rules. Yet at least he was at the top now. This morning they had more or less admitted it. That was something.

Alfred Booth, the Chairman of the Board, had noticed

Turner's glance toward him and raised his head inquiringly, but if the Captain saw it, he gave no sign and did not respond. Booth was disconcerted for a moment, until he realized he had simply been dismissed from the Captain's mind. That, too, was disconcerting. He picked up his gold-nibbed pen and made a number of small, neat, completely unnecessary ticks on his memo pad beside the points they had discussed.

Booth was seated primly behind his mahogany desk, its highly polished surface all the more imposing for being entirely free of clutter. Clutter implied indecision and lack of efficiency and the qualities Booth admired most were precision and dispatch. Tall, alert, always impeccably dressed, he wore an old-fashioned cutaway coat and dark matching waistcoat over striped trousers, the uniform he felt he owed to his position. The impression he gave was of prissiness and self-importance, but it hid an astute and agile mind, ruthless and surprisingly imaginative. The ticks made, he replaced the top on his fountain pen, laid it down neatly by the pad and considered his visitor. Thank God for William Thomas Turner, he thought.

That morning he had reread Turner's bulging personal file and wondered what his predecessors had been thinking of, all those years ago. He could see that Turner was no courtier, but they weren't choosing him for the diplomatic corps. His quality leaped out of the file, his background and early training, list of voyages, commendations, testimonials from every master he'd ever sailed under. And then his amazing rise when his promotion was finally, reluctantly given, until ten years later he became a Commodore Captain of the Line.

Cunard's two famous sister ships, the fastest and most luxurious liners ever built, the *Lusitania* and *Mauretania*, had won back the Blue Ribbon for Britain. Turner had captained them both, breaking his own records on successive trips from Liverpool to New York. Last year he had done the same with the even larger *Aquitania*, on her maiden voyage. Thanks to the designers and him, Cunard was now the leading shipping and passenger company in the North Atlantic.

Yet looking at him as he sat, solid and unmoving, his head slightly lowered following his own private thoughts, Booth

2

was aware that he would never stand out in a crowd. To the casual eye there was nothing remarkable about him. Stocky, clean-shaven, grizzled hair. Handsome, one of the partners' wives had called him. Perhaps that square-jawed, craggy face might seem handsome to some women. Ashore, he seldom wore uniform and the high collar, dark suit and tie were serviceable, nothing more. Not ill-fitting, but not the dress of a man of means. The trousers were narrow and uncreased in the old style. The shoes were a disgrace. Thick-soled brogues, meticulously shined, but with hairline cracks across the uppers from long use.

Booth let his look travel upward again and had to suppress a start as Turner's eyes rose to meet his. That was it, the clue to this man. The eyes were direct and challenging, making one feel one had to prove one's worth, to justify oneself. I give you a clean bill, they said, let me see how you mark it up. Booth coughed. "These are difficult days, Captain. Difficult and—ah—dangerous days."

Turner nodded.

"As both you and I predicted, Lord Kitchener appears to have been right."

The war was entering its seventh month. In its opening stages the previous autumn, the forecast had been that it would be a short, sharp campaign, over by Christmas. But a few more clear-sighted men had balanced the small British Expeditionary Force and the antiquated unpreparedness of the French against the highly organized, superbly equipped German military machine and realized that the Allies would be lucky, in fact, if the conflict did not end in disaster. In particular, the Secretary of State for War, Field Marshal Lord Kitchener, had warned that, even if France could be saved, the struggle would last from four to five years. He had been laughed at and denounced as a scaremonger, yet the fighting went on with no possible ending in sight, and those who had laughed began to fear that even Kitchener's estimate might be too limited.

International peace and goodwill had been the theme that memorable summer of 1914, with Colonel House, the friend and special envoy of American President Woodrow Wilson, visiting the courts of Europe in a bid to end the state of armed truce which had existed between them all for so long.

3

His many influential friends in London agreed that the President's initiative for commonsense talks between the capitals was most timely. The British government was cautiously interested, then more responsive when they heard that the idea had been approved in principle by the German Emperor.

For many years, the peace of Europe had often seemed to hang on the whims and ambitions of one man, Kaiser Wilhelm II. Born in Prussia in the days of its great chancellor, Bismarck, he was brought up among dreams of glory. As a boy he had cheered and wept to see his father in a shining gold helmet lead the victory parade through Berlin, when his grandfather, the Prussian King, was proclaimed the first German Kaiser after the Franco-Prussian War. From that moment, Germany became the dominant military power in Europe.

Through his English mother, Wilhelm was also the grandson of Queen Victoria, that tiny, indomitable woman whose word was law over much of the world's surface. In his whole life, there was no one he so loved and respected.

With the unexpected death of his father, he became Kaiser himself in his early twenties. Suddenly he took precedence over all his relations, even his glamorous Uncle Bertie, the Prince of Wales. Over everyone except his grandmother, Victoria. Slim, handsome, mercurial, a brilliant linguist, inventor and designer, he was the idol of his people. In spite of an undeveloped and useless left arm, which his uniforms managed to disguise, he was a splendid figure on horseback, an enthusiastic sportsman who enjoyed winning. His Ministers were impressed by his quick grasp of political questions, especially of foreign affairs. His generals, like his Ministers, applauded, and his vanity, against which his grandmother had always cautioned him, grew ungovernable. Winning became a necessity, a matter of national and personal prestige. To take advice from anyone, even the wily old Bismarck, became irksome and, in a fit of pique, he dismissed him, assuming total personal responsibility for the well-being of the Reich, the All Highest.

It was a period of constantly increasing prosperity with a giant surge in population. Germany was desperate with the need to expand, and Wilhelm could see how simple it would be if only he possessed an overseas empire, like the

French and Belgians, and everywhere the British with their countless dominions, colonies and protectorates. He dreamed of taking what he wanted, but that would involve transporting a large number of soldiers by ship. Any hope of that was abruptly wiped out by his grandmother's Jubilee celebrations and the Naval Review at Spithead when mile after mile of massive warships steamed past with only a cable length between them, only a fraction of the Royal Navy and an awesome reminder to potential enemies of Britain's sea power. From then on he developed a new obsession, with the sea. German dockyards were set to work to produce battleships, destroyers and cruisers. Wilhelm wanted his own Naval Review.

During the South African War, he gave secret aid to the Boers, hoping England would be defeated and leave the southern tip of Africa within the German sphere of influence. Then, in the midst of a round of state functions to usher in the new century, the shattering news arrived in Berlin that Queen Victoria was dying. Terrified that he would be too late, Wilhelm hurried to England without his usual entourage, humble and penitent. In Victoria's final hours, he knelt by her bed, supporting her failing body with his good right arm.

After the funeral, he could not bear to leave. The English side of his nature, so long suppressed, responded to the warmth of acceptance and forgiveness that surrounded him. The family . . . the family . . . Any suggestion of a dispute between them was unthinkable.

Uncle Bertie had become King Emperor, as Edward the Seventh, and had begun to hope the slate had been wiped clean for a new beginning, but back in Germany, surrounded by his own military advisers again, Wilhelm saw his historic chance. Because of the hatred roused by the Boer War, England was the most detested nation in Europe, without a single ally. If he could split the alliance between France and Russia by putting pressure on his cousin Nicholas, the weak and unimaginative Czar, Germany would be undisputed master of the Continent. Victoria's death had released him. The opportunity had come to show everyone exactly what an Emperor should be.

However, the field had not been left as clear for him as

he thought. Troubled by the isolation of his country and the growing rivalry with Germany, the year after his coronation, Bertie decided to risk his standing in an attempt to change the international climate. Confiding not even in his own cabinet, he set out on a series of foreign state visits and talks, where his friendliness and deceptively simple speeches had an astonishing effect, prizing Italy away from her triple alliance with Germany and Austria, reminding the smaller nations of Britain's traditional role as their defender, and creating a new and friendly association with France, the Entente Cordiale. Almost overnight, Bertie became Edward the Peacemaker and London the diplomatic capital of Europe.

The world had watched and marveled, and outwardly Wilhelm was all congratulation, while inside himself he seethed with anger and jealousy. He launched into an orgy of brinkmanship, telling a cheering Reichstag, "We are surrounded by enemies, but we have always fought best with our backs to the wall. Germany cannot be denied her place in the sun!"

King Edward watched his nephew's efforts at first with amused exasperation and then with concern. With his most trusted aides, he began a reorganization of the British Army. At the same time, with the appointment as First Sea Lord of his friend, the unconventional Admiral Jacky Fisher, he began to overhaul the Royal Navy. Mighty as it was, kept at a strength equal to the fleets of any other two nations combined, many of the huge battleships were obsolete. The launching of Fisher's first dreadnought revolutionized naval warfare. Immediately, all other types of warship became vulnerable. In Germany, Wilhelm demanded his own fleet of dreadnoughts and there was panic when it was found that the Kiel Canal was not wide enough to admit their passage to the sea. The canal was widened, the docks were put on twenty-four-hour shifts, and the race was on.

To most people it was all an amusing, if hair-raising, game. War was impossible. The Edwardian sun shone and the world began to enjoy the more relaxed atmosphere and liberal attitudes of the new century. Then in 1910, worn out by a grueling load of work after many years of self-indulgence, Edward the Seventh died. International society of which he was the leader went into mourning. He was succeeded by his son George, George the Fifth, a former naval officer who still showed the stiffness and formal outlook of his early training.

At the funeral, Wilhelm wept and embraced his cousin George. Again he had only realized the true extent of his affection when it was too late. He had been often unnecessarily antagonistic in the past, he admitted, but only because he had had to think what was best for his own country. He promised that, from now on, everything would be different. Yet it was already too late.

Outwardly, little had changed. The diplomatic quadrille went on. In the United States, the idealistic, silver-tongued William Jennings Bryan reluctantly acknowledged the fact that the presidential tide had forever passed him by and accepted the office of Secretary of State in the government of Woodrow Wilson. There was still tea on the lawn and yachts still raced at Cowes. Jack "Li'l Artha" Johnson of Galveston, Texas, the first Negro heavyweight boxing champion of the world, escaped to France to avoid a prison sentence for taking his white wife across state lines before they were married. Ragtime music was becoming socially acceptable and fashionable couples danced the one-step and turkey trot, while the more adventurous shocked their elders with the sexually daring tango. The sentimental sang "Let Me Call You Sweetheart" and "Meet Me Tonight In Dreamland" and messenger boys whistled "Shine On, Harvest Moon." Picture theaters had begun their irresistible spread, Biographs, Bijous and Roxies, revolutionizing mass entertainment and, already, winsome Mary Pickford was beginning to resent being known only as Little Mary, while the stars of the legitimate stage had their names in lights, Maude Adams, Ethel Barrymore, Mrs. Patrick Campbell and Ellen Terry. The motorcar had become an essential means of transport, forcing local authorities everywhere to improve road surfaces and street lighting. The airplane had made astonishing progress and new aircraft were capable of altitudes of two and three thousand feet and speeds of nearly 100 mph. Amundsen conquered the South Pole on skis and, a month later, Captain Scott reached it on dog sleds only to die heroically with all his party on the return to base. Pablo Ruiz, known as Picasso, and Georges Braque

7

created a sensation with a modern approach to art, which they called Cubism. People were reading *Howard's End*, *Tono Bungay* and *The Forsyte Saga*, *Pollyanna* and *Tarzan of the Apes*. Czar Nicholas II had been forced by massive uprisings to agree to the formation of a representative parliament, the Duma, with advisory authority. At the same time, he left more and more decisions on internal affairs to his strong-willed wife, who had come under the influence of the mystic adventurer Rasputin. In America, the baseball league disputes were being settled and the Boston Red Sox bought Babe Ruth from the Baltimore minor league team with whom he had just started his professional career. In Britain, cricket and football were uppermost in the minds of the masses, with Burnley holders of the F.A. Cup. That April of 1914, King George and Queen Mary paid a state visit to Paris.

June 28 was St. Vitus's Day, a Serbian national holiday. In Sarajevo, capital of Bosnia, the Archduke Franz Ferdinand, heir to the Austro-Hungarian empire, rode with his pretty wife in an open car. A pale and undernourished nineteen-year-old youth, Gavrilo Princip, mingled with the sullen crowd in the streets. In his pocket, he gripped the butt of a loaded Browning revolver. When the royal carriage passed, he ran forward and fired twice, the first shot tearing open Franz Ferdinand's jugular vein, the second drilling into the Archduchess Sophie's stomach. Nothing could be done to save them. Princip was seized and taken for interrogation.

The news of the assassination caused little interest in the rest of Europe and hardly a ripple in the United States. Sarajevo was barely a name, as was Franz Ferdinand, nephew of the autocratic old Austrian Kaiser, Franz Joseph. The unrest in the Balkans had gone on for so long no one paid much attention any more. While Europe basked in its fine weather, the Austrian political police checked out information that the assassination had been planned on the orders of the government of Serbia.

Colonel House, President Wilson's special envoy, was a highly gratified man. His ambition was to have the President accepted as the successor to King Edward as the world's peacemaker and already he had been favorably received both in Berlin and in London. But even as the Colonel sailed home to report in person to President Wilson, an Austrian ultimatum was delivered to Serbia and Czar Nicholas mobilized the Russian army to support the Serbs.

There was a flurry of diplomatic activity. As Russia's ally, France was involved and war fever mounted in Paris. Great Britain was morally bound to support France, although there was no offensive treaty. The great unknown was Germany, Austria's ally. Woodrow Wilson cabled, calling for restraint and arbitration, but his urgent communication did not reach Kaiser Wilhelm, who was cruising in the Norwegian fjords. The British Foreign Secretary, Sir Edward Grey, a sincere pacifist, begged Vienna and St. Petersburg to demobilize before it was too late. But Austrian troops were already marching against Serbia.

Wilhelm arrived back in Potsdam, anxious and haggard, hoping that a display of firmness would make Russia back down. The Czar, too, was eager for a negotiated settlement and telegraphed, "It would be right to give the Austro-Serbian problem to the Hague Conference. Your loving Nicky." Wilhelm's advisers dismissed the suggestion and convinced him that he must issue the order for general mobilization. That very evening, Wilhelm cabled to "dear Georgie" in Buckingham Palace, "On technical grounds my mobilization, which had already been proclaimed this afternoon, must proceed against two fronts, East and West, as prepared. I hope that France will not become nervous."

He felt that he was being rushed by his generals and that control was slipping out of his hands. He had a recurring nightmare of being attacked on one side by Russia and on the other by France, backed by England. He had never forgotten the review at Spithead. Yet he took heart when his Ministers advised him that the British had no intention of fighting and Admiral von Tirpitz assured him that the German Navy could more than hold its own. In any case, his Chiefs of Staff agreed, the British fighting force could be routed by one division of their armies, which now stood at 850,000 men at the peak of preparation. In the event of war on two fronts, France would be wiped out by a lightning strike before England had time to react. Then, with the Austrians, they would advance on the defenseless Czar. Glory beckoned to Wilhelm, and on August 1, Germany declared war on Russia.

There were almost identical scenes of patriotic fervor in

Berlin and Paris as the two nations were called to arms. From London, Sir Edward Grey urged last-minute talks. "What terms would Britain require for remaining neutral?" asked the German Chancellor, Bethmann Hollweg. Britain's neutrality, Grey said, depended on neither side opening hostilities and on Germany undertaking to observe the integrity of Belgium, which Britain was pledged to defend.

True to his nature, Kaiser Wilhelm wavered and ordered his Commander-in-Chief, General von Moltke, to proceed only against Russia. Von Moltke protested that if the plan were changed now the result would be disaster. Wilhelm conceded at last that the main advance must still be in the West. But certain units were to be held back to avoid giving too much impression of a threat. It was strategic madness, and von Moltke returned to his quarters dejected and disillusioned. All evening Wilhelm read and reread the communications from Wilson and Colonel House, from his cousins George and Nicky, from Grey and from his own ambassadors and advisers. All waited for him to make the final move, or to step back. He had used Germany's strength as a bluff, but it had been called.

At eleven at night, von Moltke was summoned again to be told that, again, Wilhelm had changed his mind. "I have reconsidered. Advance as arranged." Von Moltke was relieved, although his confidence in the Kaiser had been rocked and would never fully recover. On August 3, Germany declared war on France and the first field-gray columns swept into Belgium.

That evening, Sir Edward Grey was standing at a window in the Foreign Office, watching the streetlamps being lit outside. "The lamps are going out all over Europe," he muttered. "We shall not see them lit again in our lifetime." The next day Parliament was in session to debate the crisis when Grey entered and read a telegram from Albert, King of the Belgians, asking for aid against the invaders of his small country. Against all his beliefs, but to the wild cheering of the House, he announced that Great Britain was now at war with Germany.

The German High Command's plan for the invasion of France had been worked out years before by their most brilliant strategist, General von Schlieffen, a feint toward

Alsace-Lorraine, followed by a mighty pincer movement sweeping in through Belgium and along the West Coast through the Flanders plains to swing in on Paris. Complete in all its details, the Plan predicted total victory in forty days.

It worked at first exactly as von Schlieffen had promised. Despite the heroic resistance of the Belgians which gave the British Expeditionary Force time to land unopposed, the German advance past the Belgian forts and down through northwest France was spectacular. Yet the "contemptible little" B.E.F. held on in the west, although pushed further and further back, while the French Commander-in-Chief, "Papa" Joffre, hurled the bulk of his army at the German center where machine guns mowed them down by the ten thousand in their dashing red and blue uniforms.

It seemed that nothing could save Paris, but just as the government was preparing to flee, von Moltke blundered. Worried by Russian successes in East Prussia, he ordered two corps and a cavalry division from his right wing to the Eastern Front. Deprived of essential troops, the sweep had to take the shorter route to the east of Paris, instead of encircling it. Though outnumbered by six to one, the despised Expeditionary Force had managed to delay the advance long enough to save the capital. Joffre with a hastily formed new army came up on the British left and launched a desperate flank attack. By an apparent miracle, the Germans were smashed back from the River Marne. To try to save the situation, three German cavalry corps were sent racing west through Flanders to cut off the Channel ports, but at each stage they were outstripped by Allied units, who immediately dug rifle pits, blocking the way south. The Schlieffen Plan had failed and the campaign of swift advances, sweeps and countermaneuvers was over. Before the end of the year, the Western Front stretched from Switzerland to the Belgian coast, both sides spread out along endless miles of waterlogged trenches, facing each other across barbed wire and the narrow strip of earth between, no-man's-land, scythed by machine gun bullets, plowed and pounded by heavy bombardments until not a living or growing thing remained, nothing but mud and corpses rotting in the shellholes, uncollected.

There had been silence for some moments in Alfred Booth's office. He reproved himself mentally for being tactless. "Of course, you have a son out there," he said.

Turner nodded. "Royal Artillery." His boy, Norman, was an officer in a front-line regiment. Out there. It was a hard thought to bear, sometimes. The descriptions in the papers weren't too pretty and must leave out the worst. Hundreds of thousands dead in senseless charges and retreats over the same two or three hundred yards, all that bitter winter. Norman had been home once on leave and wouldn't talk about it. He had taken the dog for a walk, slept, but most of the time he sat by the fire, silent, as if he'd never be warm again.

A secretary brought in the forms, waited until Turner had signed them, and left again. Booth smiled with satisfaction. "Well, now she's in your hands, Captain. None better."

Turner shrugged very slightly. "I'll have to look her over."

"Naturally," Booth agreed. "Naturally. We want her to be at her best, as much as you do. These days especially. She's more important now than ever. But I don't have to remind you of that." He hesitated and rose, ending the interview. Not to make it seem too abrupt, he came round the desk to shake hands. "Well, I wish you luck. Not that you'll need it. You could always get more out of her than anyone."

Chapter 1

WALTHER SCHWIEGER CAME AWAKE WITH A START.

He had propped himself up and one hand was raised to protect his head. He knew he had cried out. He was naked and he felt a slick of sweat round his eyes and in the crease of his chest. He had had the dream again.

As he lay back, he became conscious of a warm pressure on his thigh and remembered the girl. She was naked like him, sprawled on her face beside him, one arm flexed under her neck, the other thrown up over the pillow. Her head was turned away and all he could see was a tangle of dark auburn hair. He could hear her breathing softly, a snuffling sound, through her half-open mouth. Mercifully, she had not woken up.

The pressure on his thigh was from the curve of her hip and his skin felt fused to hers by a moist warmth. He eased himself away carefully and she still did not wake, although she murmured and shifted in her sleep at the loss of contact.

He lay quietly, controlling his own breathing. His lips were dry and his throat thick with the aftertaste of too much brandy. He was not thinking clearly yet and his mouth was drawn back, the muscles of his neck tight with the effort to stop the heaving of his chest, the panted sound of his fear.

Fear. It was not something he could ever admit to, an obscene blemish. Give way to it and you lost all respect, all power to command. Yet it was there. He had to confess it to himself, with a self-disgust that was almost despair. The dream proved it. It had come every night for weeks, always the same. He was in the fish, and young Bibermann was singing *Die Lorelei*.

He forced it out of his mind. Think of something else. Anything. This room, close and unfamiliar, with its smell of violets, a sweet, cheap scent of violets. Not like the oil and sweat and stale breath smell of the fish. Something else! This girl—Dora. No, that was the other one. Anneliese. Red hair, a wide mouth, plump but not fat, a surprisingly small waist above full, firm hips. No use—he knew too little about her and the dream was still too vivid. He could still hear Bibermann's high tenor voice singing that damned sentimental old song, whatever his mind turned to. Every night it became harder to drive away.

He sensed the tremors of panic growing, his breath coming jerkily again. How could he fight it? You defeated an enemy by facing him, standing up to him. Either you stood up, or you ran away. He had no choice, for the dream returned however deep he thought he had buried it. He had to pull it out into the light and go through it with his eyes open for once, whatever happened. He lay still, letting the memory of the singing fill his mind and bring the other memories that began so peacefully, so reassuringly.

He was in the fish, and it was Christmas, that first Christmas of Armageddon. He had hoped to be given leave, to go home to Berlin to see his family, his mother and sisters who were so proud of him, hiding their anxiety. They would fuss over him and pamper him, but when he tried to wear an old suit or his hunting clothes to relax, they would make him put on his uniform to impress the neighbors and his father's friends and clients. Instead, Fregattenkapitän Bauer, commander of his flotilla, had sent him out on patrol.

He was in the messroom behind his own quarters. It was swelteringly hot, filled to bursting with officers and men in noisy high spirits. Amongst all the songs and laughter, someone called for the machinist's mate, young Bibermann, to sing. No, that's too soon. Step by step, that's how to take it. Everything in order and perspective.

In the early hours of the morning of Christmas Eve, the U 20 had chugged out on its diesels from its Emden base, past the booms and shore batteries with their huge, quick-firing guns, skirting the island of Borkum and out into the North Sea. After scanning the horizon, they submerged to test the engines and controls before beginning their patrol backward and forward on the seaward side of the long line of islands that guarded the mouth of the Ems. All day the slow sweep had continued, sometimes at periscope depth, sometimes on the surface, with no sign of an enemy warship. Schwieger had shared lookout with the engineering officer, the quartermaster and his new watch officer, Leutnant Zentner, either on deck or in the conning tower. The crew became more and more subdued as the hours passed, thinking of their families and the parties just starting on shore. He was not the only one who had wanted leave. He had had to turn down several requests, including one from squat, barrel-shaped Lippe with his straw-colored spade beard, but the petty officer of the torpedo room had been unable to spare him. Lippe was the ship's joker, a former fisherman from East Prussia, always chuckling, telling outrageously bawdy stories even in action. It was a joke itself, the idea of him getting married. But during one of his deck watches, he was disturbed to see Lippe sitting hunched and alone at the stern rail, trailing a fishing line, avoiding everyone. His resentment added to the general depression of the crew. A hell of a way to celebrate Christmas.

They spent the night on the surface, recharging their electric batteries, without incident. When the cook woke him just before dawn, he pulled on his gray leather trousers and jacket over his thick sweater and drawers. Slinging his binoculars and scarf round his neck, he took his cap and gloves and went up through the rear hatch to the deck. Zentner was standing near the hatch, on lookout. A tall, thin young man with bright red hair and a long, pale, anxious face, he had transferred from a destroyer and had just completed his underwater training. This was his first official cruise. He came to attention and saluted, reporting that nothing had been sighted throughout the four hours that Schwieger had slept. After a short hesitation, he added the compliments of the season. Schwieger thanked him and returned the compliments. The other members of the watch, ratings stationed fore and aft, stared stolidly out to sea.

Christmas Day. There was little mist and the sun was rising over the dark landmass in the distance. The sea was almost motionless. As the sky cleared, the somber, leaden surface of the water was touched with faint glimmers of light, serpents of silver writhing toward them and vanishing as soon as they were seen, but slowly growing in number, becoming brighter, until suddenly the sun leaped free of the land and flushed the eastern sky, and the water sparkled all round them, every tiny ripple glittering and shimmering, incandescent with reflections of rose and gold. Then the angle of the sun crept higher. The radiance faded, and it was morning. The U-boat pitched gently in the surface swell.

Schwieger breathed out. He took up his binoculars and traversed the horizon. As Zentner had reported, no sign of anything. He stamped his feet on the deck plate, glad of his fur-lined boots and his scarf, for the air was fresh, with a nip of frost in it. He saw Zentner eyeing his scarf and his padded gloves. The scarf was pure wool, a grayish blue, knitted for him by his youngest sister. Zentner did not wear one, and his gloves were thin, his leathers shiny and stiff with newness, not softened and scuffed like his. "You should wear a scarf," Schwieger said.

"I don't have one, sir," Zentner explained. "I didn't think I'd need one."

"It gets damned cold up here. And when we're submerged for any length of time," Schwieger told him. "You can borrow mine for your next watch."

"Thank you very much, sir," Zentner said, and smiled. Schwieger was startled. The smile was wide, splitting Zentner's narrow face nearly in half under the long hook of his nose. A whimsical but open-hearted smile, and Schwieger caught himself beginning to smile back. He turned it into a nod.

All that day the patrol went on as ordered, a ceaseless sweep backward and forward along a forty-mile path, without spotting a single craft, either friendly or enemy. As darkness fell, Schwieger was again on deck with the U-boat hove to. Behind him, he heard the engineering officer say something and Zentner reply, then laugh quietly, ruefully. He could imagine what had been said. They were alone in the immensity of the ocean, everyone else had wisely stayed at home. Through the forward hatch, he heard someone whistling below. He had been thinking about his crew, fine fellows who worked hard and fought well. They had the least comfortable life and the least chance of staying alive of anyone in the navy. Strange, that up till very recently patrols only went out by day. It was considered impossibly dangerous because of foul air and the risk of poisonous gases escaping from the batteries to spend even one night submerged. He had been a junior officer on one of the six submarines which took part in the daring experiment of December 1912, surviving an endurance test of six whole days at sea. True, they had spent most of the time anchored to buoys in the Heligoland Bight, but what a sensation it had caused! Only two years ago. How extraordinary, when you thought of what was taken for granted now. At night there was certainly less danger underwater than on the surface, with the possibility of being rammed in the darkness. The crew had done its duty. Schwieger moved to the conning tower, climbed the three or four rungs and swung his leg over to descend. "Close the hatches for diving," he ordered.

There was no emergency and the crew carried out the maneuver with routine efficiency. The engines throbbed. A hiss of air as the ballast tanks filled. As the U 20 gained speed, the horizontal rudders tilted and her nose dipped. Broken water creamed round the rail and a wave washed along her deck to slap against the hump of her conning tower, foaming round it and the stubs of her twin periscopes as she sank out of sight, leaving only a rush of eddies, a concave swirl on the surface that closed, spuming and bubbling for a moment, and then was erased by the swell. The U 20 slipped effortlessly down into the unlit depths and settled smoothly on the mud of the sea bottom with her gauges at sixty feet.

Schwieger was in his tiny commander's cabin immediately behind central control. He heard the tramp of feet as the crew went past, obeying the order "All hands to the mess room." A voice, it was Lippe's, muttered, "What now?" Seconds later there were exclamations of surprise, followed by silence. It was time. He took off his leather jacket and cap, pulled back the green cloth curtain that was his door and went out into the passageway.

The miniature mess room was more crowded than it had ever been before, with four officers and thirty-two men crammed into it. Zentner had done wonders in the few minutes available to organize the cook and his assistant. A circular life buoy had been hung at the far end, with a length of green cloth twisted round it to turn it into a wreath.

Colored and checkered signal pennants had been looped along the walls and strung across under the low ceiling. The crew stood pressed together shoulder to shoulder and looked toward the bulkhead door, puzzled, as Schwieger came through, his hands behind his back. "Well, gentlemen," he said, "now we can celebrate Christmas."

The crew stared as Schwieger brought his hands round in front. He was holding two bottles of rum. Zentner grinned at the gasp which sounded like a bass note in the confined space. Lippe smiled his first smile for two days, and the men broke out into cheers, for Christmas and for Schwieger. They respected and trusted their young Commander and had known that, somehow, he wouldn't let them down.

The cook had mounds of sausages already on the boil and savory dumplings and a fry of chopped potatoes, eggs and onions. There were tins of sauerkraut and pickles and red cabbage, and other tins of syrupy fruit, pears, peaches, pineapples. The men found places to sit, under the table, between one another's legs, on the bunks, since the mess room also acted as quarters for most of the crew, where they slept in shifts. Mugs were passed round, hot tea spiked with rum, and toasts were drunk, first to the Kaiser, then the Fatherland, the Navy, the Submarine Service and the U 20. Schwieger was concerned in case the drink ran out, but if he knew Quartermaster Wendt, he'd have schnapps or brandy on board somewhere. He was right. Wendt had both. And there were more toasts. To Admiral von Tirpitz, to Kapitänleutnant Schwieger and his officers. Then, each progressively bawdier and less respectful, to the petty officers and their sections in turn, and the cook. There was a roar at one to Lippe and his torpedoes, and his own special torpedo he kept for the ladies.

For that night there were no distinctions between ranks. Jokes and reminiscences sparked across the room and the laughter was nonstop. In that tiny, sealed chamber inside a cigar-shaped iron fish on the sea floor there was good fellowship, and nothing beyond existed.

When the remains of the food were being cleared away, Zentner remembered the ship's mascot, a little wirehaired dachshund called Hansel. While he was being fetched, the leavings were all scraped onto one tin plate, a heap of sweet and spicy scraps that sent him frantic, when he was hoisted up onto the table. Hansel was the best turn of the evening, running round and round the tabletop, skittering and sliding on his short legs, his droopy ears flapping, barking with excitement, until he stopped to eat his Christmas dinner with his tail wagging like an overwound metronome. Lippe began to sing a sailors' song in time to it, his blue pebble eyes scrunched up with delight and his huge chest heaving under his beard, and others joined in, trying to catch up.

The musicians in the crew brought out their instruments, a mandoline, a fiddle, and Lippe's concertina, which he played like a virtuoso. Led by them, the choruses went on, songs of the service and of the High Seas Fleet, roared out full-throatedly. The iron hull rang with music and laughter. Then someone called for the machinist's mate, Bibermann, to sing.

It was a popular choice and he couldn't refuse. Although some were still talking and laughing, or trying to sing themselves, they all fell silent after the first few notes. Softly, in a high, clear tenor, he began the old ballad of the Lorelei. In the hush, listening to that pure voice, Schwieger felt his mind drift away from the mess room to a holiday he had spent in his boyhood, in the mountains. He could smell the freshness of the air, the scent of the pine forests under the immensity of the open sky. Space and freedom to move all round him, and peak rising beyond peak to the limit of sight. With a shudder, he was brought back to the crush of the mess room and the stench of mingled sweat and oil fumes and stale breath. He found he was holding his own breath as his lungs reacted against it. It was the song that had called him back. He had heard it so often before, he had been listening to the melody, not the words. Suddenly he became aware of them, the story of the beautiful Rhine-maiden who lured poor sailors to death by drowning, and for the first time since his very first dive he was conscious of the water all round them, millions of tons of it pressing down on the metal shell of the submarine. If the hull cracked, they would be squashed flat. Suppose the motors failed? They would never reach the surface again, but swallow their tongues, choking in their own foul breath. He had seen men panic and recognized the symptoms in himself, even as he fought the urge to shout orders to start the engines. It was a hard fight to control himself, but he won it, although it left him exhausted, his body prickling with icy sweat.

The damned song was nearly over.

He was leaning against the wall by the entrance bulkhead and still holding a tin mug, which he had gripped so tightly that the handle was nearly twisted off, the edge biting into his finger. He winced as he relaxed his hold, and looked round quickly, afraid that his men had seen.

No one was looking at him. The song had affected them all in their own ways, reminding them of home and other, gentler times. Most heads were lowered. Many had their eyes shut, some wet with tears. The atmosphere had changed and, when Bibermann finished, the applause was subdued. The silence that followed stretched on, until Schwieger nodded to the musicians to play something else. The violinist, judging the mood, played the opening bars of the carol they all knew and, slowly, they all joined in. "Silent Night, Holy Night," they sang, the rough voices hushed and tender. It was deeply touching, but exactly what Schwieger had not wanted. A homesick, unhappy crew was vulnerable and soon lost efficiency and any will to fight. There was a greater risk. If any others had felt the same nausea as he had, the same need to escape, the rot could spread.

He saw Lippe shift uncomfortably where he sat at the other end of the room, his concertina lying loose in his lap, and guessed that part of his discomfort was because of the solemnness. Lippe could neither read nor write. He was a creature of instinct and liked to laugh all the time because it did away with the need for thought. Schwieger caught his eye and made himself smile. Lippe grinned back and was puzzled for a moment when Schwieger moved his hands together and apart; then he understood and beamed. He picked up the squeezebox very gingerly and, suddenly, played a loud, jangled chord that startled everyone and made Hansel jump up barking. Some of the crew protested, but he only chuckled, his fingers rippling over the keys as he sang, "O Josephine, my little Josephine." The tune was catchy and the song highly indecorous, but very funny, about a pretty little girl from East Saxony who went to Hamburg to make her fortune as a dancer. She danced the waltz with her left leg, the polka with her right, and between them made a very good living. Most of the crew were laughing, joining in, their feet tapping. It had become a party again.

Schwieger saw his new watch officer, Zentner, smiling to him across the room with appreciation. He looked back expressionlessly, beginning to realize that the red-haired lieutenant was nobody's fool.

The dream was in two parts. That was the first.

He was glad of the light that was starting to filter in round the edges of the bedroom curtains, even though he was calmer, more in control of himself now. He glanced at the sleeping girl and wondered what he would have said or done if his crying out like that had wakened her. Would he have been able to hide his fear? Could she sense it now, if she woke?

What he was doing was too much of a gamble. He should only have tried it when he was alone. Some other time. His eyes went back to the chill light that framed the curtains. But already that was not what he was seeing. He couldn't stop it. Already he was in the conning tower.

From Zentner smiling, the dream always jumped to the forward conning tower port and the pale green water beyond the thick glass. The U 20 was running submerged at minimum speed, just under the surface. They were returning through the English Channel from their first longer distance mission, down the coast of France, past the Channel Islands and Brittany and into the Atlantic for the first time. "Now you're really baptized," Schwieger had told the crew. They had done well and had four more pennants to fly when they sailed into home base, having sunk a light Birmingham class cruiser with two torpedoes, and two steamers and a large schooner carrying grain to Le Havre with the other four.

They had just entered the Straits of Dover, the narrowest gap between France and England with much Allied traffic crossing and recrossing under the protection of destroyers, which was why they ran submerged. There was every chance of meeting an enemy warship, even a battleship, and Schwieger cursed under his breath that all his torpedoes were used up. Fuel stocks were low and he had called Hirsch, the engineering officer, up from Central Control, sending Zentner down to take his place. As Hirsch and he discussed the optimum speed at which they could reach their base in good

21

time and yet save a small reserve of fuel for an emergency, he was standing at the periscope, looking through the eye-piece, his hands on the grips while he swiveled slowly, scanning the area ahead. The rudders held them steady at fifteen feet, so the top of the asparagus was about three feet above the surface. At their low rate of knots, its wake would scarcely show.

Schwieger's eyes were strained from long watching and he rested them for a moment. He glanced automatically at the window and the green dusk outside it, filled with bubbles. "If we're past Calais by 18:00 hours and then make six knots, we should be home by two or three in the morning," Hirsch was saying. He paused and smiled. "Of course you might prefer to lie offshore tonight and come in with the morning tide."

Schwieger considered it. On his left, the head of the helmsman at the rudder controls was tilted, listening. Come in by daylight, Schwieger thought. Why not? The men deserved it. Seeing the four pennants for the kills made on the voyage, the sailors and dockworkers at Emden would give them a rousing welcome. Good for morale, both on board and ashore. "Very well," he nodded. "All things being equal, we'll take the morning tide." The helmsman's back straightened with pride. He was a middle-aged family man, graying, dependable, and now would have something to boast about.

Schwieger smiled slightly to Hirsch and turned back to the periscope. He leaned forward and, when his eyes adjusted, he tensed in shock. The sea had been empty before. Now there was something in the water, approaching them just off to starboard. No, it was they who were approaching. The object was stationary, round and metallic, painted a dull red. With the miniaturizing effect of the lenses, it was hard to judge its size. He had chosen this route carefully, because the Straits were littered with minefields. Twisting lanes had been left through them, along which Allied shipping traveled under naval pilots, but German Naval Intelligence already had maps of most of these lanes and copies were issued to every U-boat commander. This area was much used by French coastal vessels and should be safe. In any case, the British had made a ridiculous error of reckoning and hung their mines too close to the surface, for which the entire Submarine Flotilla thanked them daily in their prayers. Detecting a minefield, you only needed to dive to a comfortable depth and glide safely by underneath it.

Of course, there were always accidents with rogue mines. On the very day war was declared, the German navy had sown hundreds of them outside all the North Sea ports in England and Scotland. Many of those and others from the Channel had broken free and you had to keep an eye out for them. Touch one anywhere and it would explode, and just one was enough to split a submarine open like an overripe banana.

Schwieger breathed out. The object he had spotted was not a mine. It was some kind of large buoy, and would pass harmlessly by off to their starboard beam. Nevertheless, as he swiveled the stick, he was careful not to miss anything. And the glass picked up what could be another of the buoys some way off to port. It was puzzling, and experience had taught him not to take unnecessary chances. He called down the speaking tube to Zentner, "Buoys ahead. Trim her down to fifty feet."

Hirsch was already hurrying down to central control. The helmsman, Lembeck, looked round. "Steady as she goes," Schwieger said quietly.

The hum of the motors became louder as they increased speed for diving. Schwieger pressed down the lever to retract the periscope and locked it off. He moved to the forward window and peered through. There was still just enough surface light to make out the taper of the upper deck toward the bow, but nothing beyond. They might never know what function the two buoys had, if any. The entrance to a fishing lane? He half turned to check the course with the helmsman.

At that moment, there was a loud clang and the U 20 shuddered all along her length, as her prow hit something. Schwieger staggered and clutched at the rim of the port to steady himself. For a few seconds, there was a hideous sound, a deafening metallic grating as though giant chains were flailing at the U-boat and scraping along her frame and the shudders continued, then her stern bucked violently and, as sharply, plunged. The helmsman screamed. Schwieger was hurled backward, smashing onto the shaft of the periscope and cannoning off it to hit the side of the conning tower with his left shoulder. He felt a searing pain and crumpled to the deck. His head had struck the periscope and he was dizzy. Almost by reflex he grabbed for a stanchion with his right hand and hooked his arm round it to pull himself up.

And the lights failed.

Half-sitting, he lay in the impenetrable darkness, clinging to the stanchion as the shaking and battering went on. Trapped, but with her propeller still trying to drive her on, the U 20 had gone crazy, swaying and pitching wildly, nearly rolling over, corkscrewing with her bow raised high above her stern. And all the time he knew instinctively that they were sinking. Some enormous weight was dragging them down. It was the minutes of nightmare he had gone through on Christmas night become a reality and he heard himself moaning, moaning with sheer, blinding terror.

Then the stern struck bottom with a jarring crash that jolted him free of his hold and he sprawled across the tilted deck. He lay spread-eagled, with his face pressed against the iron floor, waiting for the rending collapse of the hull, the bursting lungs, the obliterating inrush of water.

He held his breath for so long that he choked, bringing up bile, and the sharp, sick taste made him retch. As he spat out the thin vomit, the lights flickered and came on. Dim at first, then brighter. The scraping sounds from outside continued, only more subdued, with less force. He began to make out other sounds, shouting and cries for help from below.

Miraculously, the U 20 had landed right way up. But stern down, at a sharp angle. Something must be supporting her prow. In spite of his fear, his mind began to work again. They were on the bottom, but at what depth? And what had caused it?

Cautiously, as if the slightest wrong move might start the bucking and plunging again, he raised his head and looked round. His binoculars lay quite near him, the lenses shattered. As he looked at them, the submarine trembled and they slithered down to join the debris piled up behind him. He turned his head. The helmsman lay doubled over his wheel, wedged between it and the bulkhead. From the angle of his head he could tell that his neck was broken. Very

24

carefully, he began to inch up the inclined deck toward the forward window. His left arm was useless and hurt abominably, but he had only one thought, to reach the window. Somehow, it was unthinkable to die without knowing why.

He reached the space under the window and rested for a while, before pushing himself up to kneel. He had to lean his head back, but all he could see was his own reflection in the glass, bloodied down his right cheek where it had scraped on the deck. Beyond his reflection, he was puzzled by what looked like a thick strand of weed outside. He caught the lower edge of the window and drew himself to his feet, bending forward to peer through the glass. At lower depths, the light from the conning tower extended only a few feet. He moved his head to let as much shine past him as possible, and his eyes opened wide in surprise. What he had taken to be weed was chain! The sounds had been exactly what they suggested. Through the port all he could see were loops and festoons of heavy steel chain, wrapped round and round the frame of the submarine, which had been caught in the giant meshes just like the fish it counterfeited.

He heard footsteps stumbling up the ladder from central control and glanced round. Zentner came climbing up. He had lost his cap and his face was streaked with blood from a long gash under his hairline. He was wild-eyed and trembling. "What was it?" he called. "What was it, sir?"

"A net," Schwieger said numbly. "A bloody great chain net. The buoys were supporting a section of it. It's wrapped all round us."

Zentner had seen the helmsman. "Lembeck?"

"Dead, poor devil," Schwieger told him. Even as he spoke, he thought, but he may be the lucky one.

Zentner clambered, slipping, up the sloping deck to join him at the window. He looked out and, at the sight of the shadowy links and spans of the huge net that enfolded them, he became deathly still.

In the silence, Schwieger became aware of new sounds, a faint creaking and grating, for which he had been waiting, the hull of the U 20 protesting at the strain that was being placed on it. "What's our depth?" he asked.

Zentner's head jerked round. His face was drained of color and he stammered. "I—I don't know, sir. The gauges failed at a hundred feet—but that was minutes ago." They were deep, really deep. Schwieger nodded, listening, and now Zentner heard the sounds also, as the strange creaking grew more pronounced. "What is it? What's that noise, sir?"

"It's the hull," Schwieger said. "The pressure. The pressure's forcing the plates apart."

Zentner stared at him in horror. It was not a question of waiting until the air ran out. They did not have that amount of time. He heard Hirsch call up to him from below, "Captain! Captain?" He was conscious of Zentner gazing at him, begging him with his eyes to do something, to save them. Did none of them realize he could not work miracles? With icy detachment he looked out at the killer chains which held them ensnared. The terrible fear had liberated him, purging him of all human feelings. The moment had come, as he had known it would. He was dead already, only waiting for the death of the U-boat to make it final.

Zentner turned with him and together they watched the meshes that were motionless now. The flailing had ceased, and the din of the chains battering and dragging on the hull. Yet just when everything seemed to have settled, the whole length of the submarine vibrated when something heavy struck it near the prow. A few seconds later, the tremor was repeated and the chains round the forward section were ground down against the deck. Watching, Schwieger could just see something bouncing down toward him along the steep angle at which the U 20 lay. In spite of its size and weight, the arcs it made when it hit the chains and rebounded were lazy in the high density, a large, black pineapple, its iron sides bristling with the projecting horns of its detonators. Zentner gave a whimpering gasp beside him, as the mine's leap brought it straight for them, looming larger and larger until the curved metal and detonator spikes seemed to fill the window. Inches from them, it collided with the chains swathed round the conning tower, mashing them against it with a jarring crash that knocked Zentner off his feet.

His mouth open in a silent scream, Schwieger saw the mine bounce back from the chains and lift, a length of its broken tether trailing from a ring in its side. It hung for a moment, then spun slowly over the top of the conning tower.

Zentner was on his knees, struggling to rise, but trembling so uncontrollably he could hardly stand. Schwieger caught his arm and held it tightly, steadying him. They stood without breathing, listening, hearing the slither and scrape of the trailing chain on the stern deck and waiting for the explosion that would send them to oblivion.

That was where the nightmare ended, in a choking agony, the scream tearing out at last from his throat and his arms raised to hold off the inrushing waters. So he had woken every night since, until he was afraid to sleep, even to close his eyes. To go on board the U 20, to make himself sail in her, was a triumph of willpower. Not courage. More rightly, the fear of revealing his fear. Yet he knew it could not go on. He would crack like others had, those who were never mentioned, and remembered only with embarrassment. There was no forgiveness, no treatment for loss of nerve, and only from thinking through what had happened, he was panting, his body running again with sweat.

Panic was close and he struggled against it. In God's name, why had he deliberately put himself through this? To face it, to face up to it for once before his nerve went completely. Step by step, he had said. So . . . The dream always ended with the mine. But that had not been the end, or he would not be lying here on this bed. Then, what had happened? He forced his mind back to that moment of terror.

Zentner and he had waited in the conning tower for long heartbeats, but nothing came. The red-haired lieutenant had never stopped shaking and Schwieger stood holding his arm tightly, listening. There was silence again. The mine had either been deflected and landed on the soft mud of the seabed or had regained its buoyancy and was floating back up to the surface.

In the hush, Schwieger realized two things, that he was still by some miracle alive, and that the creaking of the plates whose riveted edges were being pried open by the pressure of the water was louder. The U 20 was still fighting back, while he had given in. His men believed in him, and he had failed them.

With no conscious thought, his training and his pride took over. He released his grip on Zentner's arm. "Man the wheel," he told him. He wiped the blood and trickle of vomit from his mouth with the back of his wrist, slid to the ladder hatch and climbed down one-handed, his left arm hanging uselessly by his side.

Central control was a shambles. Everything movable was strewn about and smashed. Bibermann, the machinist's mate, lay unconscious in an angle of the deck. One man was on his knees, praying. The other six or seven technicians watched Schwieger with blank, shocked eyes. Hirsch alone was working, checking the controls and the connections to the banks of dials and gauges with a ferocious concentration. Haupert, the navigation lieutenant, stood by him willing to assist, but ignored.

The forward bulkhead doors were shut. Shouts for help were coming from the stern section and, glancing round, Schwieger saw men crowded into the corridor watching him. One, the youngest member of the crew, was sobbing like a child. Lippe had his arm round the boy's shoulders.

Schwieger allowed himself only a few seconds to observe conditions. Certain actions had to be taken quickly. He moved to the kneeling man and tapped his shoulder. They needed someone's prayers, but this was the medical orderly and his skill was even more essential. "Put Bibermann in my cabin," Schwieger told him. "Then find the boatswain. If there are any other wounded, they're to be brought to midships."

Hearing his voice, Haupert snapped to attention and Hirsch looked round with relief. Schwieger turned to them. "How badly is she damaged?"

"Difficult to tell, sir," Hirsch reported. "Several of her gauges are either blocked or out of kilter—speed, depth . . ."

"How deep do you reckon we are?"

"I'd guess about two hundred feet, sir," Haupert said, worriedly. "Maybe nearer two hundred and fifty."

Schwieger nodded. That agreed with his own estimate.

"The electric motors are working," Hirsch said. "But there's no response from the horizontal rudders, nor the propellers. If there's chain wrapped round them . . ." He did not need to go on. If steel chain was snagged round the propellers, being forced to turn, they would either twist out of shape or snap. Then, without power, they would really be finished. "I've emptied the ballast tanks," Hirsch added, "but she didn't rise an inch."

Schwieger nodded again, his mind racing. The U 20 was well and truly trapped, unable to move in any direction. Long before the air ran out, she would have lost her fight against the pressure on her hull and caved in. The horizontal rudders were controlled from down here. He had seen for himself the chains that immobilized them. He moved to the speaking tube and called up, "Zentner? Are you at the helm?"

Zentner's voice came back. "Yes, Captain."

"Try the wheel."

The waiting seemed like minutes until the lieutenant's voice came again. "It won't budge, Captain! Only an inch either way. It won't turn any further."

"Very well," Schwieger said. "Don't force it. Stand by."

He stayed by the tube, quite motionless, evaluating. The U 20 had just picked up speed to begin her dive when she hit, at about twenty, at most thirty feet. The net must have been slung low in the water to allow fishing smacks and surface craft free passage above it. So it was designed specifically to catch submarines. To be any use, it would have to go down at least a hundred feet. The U 20 had rammed it fairly near the top edge and sunk, striking the bottom stern first. From the angle at which she lay, something was propping up her bows. It could be rocks. Or . . . it could be the bulk of the huge net piled up underneath her, giving a slight chance that the chains were coiled only around the section forward from the conning tower. That would account for the horizontal rudders being disabled. He remembered how the mine had bounced over him and the sound of its broken chain scraping along the stern deck. Directly on the deck, with no obstruction. Yet Zentner had reported the main rudders jammed, as were the propellers. There could be another reason for that. The stern had struck bottom with a jarring impact that he could still feel. Supposing it was partly buried, the thick mud would clog the screws as effectively as chain . . .

They would have to take a gamble, a desperate gamble against a hideous certainty. Turning to Hirsch, he saw everyone watching him with alarm, having taken his momentary withdrawal for despair. Well, they'd soon have something else to think about. Thank God the mechanism for the ballast tanks was operational. "Fill the forward tanks,"

29

he ordered Hirsch. The engineering officer was puzzled, but went straight to the levers.

Schwieger had seen the boatswain helping to carry a wounded man into his cabin. As he made for him, he told Haupert, "Open all the forward doors, and lock them back."

The boatswain and the medical orderly had laid the wounded man on the floor of the commander's cabin and were coming out to make room for Lippe, who was supporting the young crewman who had been sobbing. Schwieger apologized mentally to the boy when he saw that his elbow was smashed. The boatswain, a stolid Bavarian, stood to attention. "Get all hands forward," he told him.

"How far forward, sir?"

"Right into the torpedo room," Schwieger said. "And move!" He turned back to the central station, calling, "All of you—get up to the bows!"

Behind him, the boatswain was shouting, "All hands forward! All hands forward! To the torpedo room!"

Haupert had opened the doors and, above the shuffle of feet as the crew filed up the sloping corridor, Schwieger heard the hiss of compressed air from the filling ballast tanks under the bows. Seeing the men troop past, Hirsch had understood what he was trying and pressed down on the levers, as if he could force more water into the tanks.

The boatswain had also understood and was shouting, "Lively! Come on—step lively!" pushing the men, packing them into the forward officers' quarters and the narrow torpedo room, that was lighter and had more space now its torpedoes had all been fired. They stood pressed together, their heads bent and stifling in the hot, close air, wondering what the hell was going on.

Schwieger waited with Haupert and the boatswain by the door of the centeral station. He was not sure what he had expected, but nothing happened. "Get them aft," he said. "Then all forward again, and running."

"Everyone aft!" the boatswain ordered. "Let's be having you back to the mess room!" He cursed the crew under his breath as they went by, thrusting them on. "Move—get moving, you dozy bastards! This tin can's going to split open all round us, if you don't shift your arses!" He followed the last men down to the mess room, his hands on their backs, shoving them into the ones in front. "You'll listen for my order!" he called. "On the command, you'll run like buggery for the bows. I'll have the balls off the last man there!"

Schwieger nodded to Haupert. "Go with them," he said and, as soon as the lieutenant reached the waiting men, gave the signal.

The boatswain shouted, "Run!!" and led the charge for the bows himself. The crew raced past Schwieger and Hirsch, slamming into the forward section, and the U-boat shuddered at the sudden shift of weight. "Back!" Schwieger cried. "Again!" And the maneuver was repeated, the crew now realizing what it meant and hurling themselves into it with all their strength.

Schwieger was gambling that the U-boat's prow projected beyond whatever was supporting it, at least enough to give some leverage, to set up a seesaw effect through the abrupt dispersals of weight. At each charge, the hull shuddered and trembled more, the needles and level indicators of the dials oscillating. Again and again, panting and sweating, the men raced backward and forward, cannoning into one another in the tapered bows, shouldering and pushing one another further forward. Among them, Schwieger saw the boy with the smashed elbow running, white-faced, his teeth set, holding on to Lippe. It reminded him of the pain from his own injured arm forgotten in the stress and he gritted his teeth like the boy, joining in on the end of the next charge.

It could not go on indefinitely. The men were tiring and the atmosphere was becoming heavier as their violent exertion used up oxygen. He was glad that only Zentner and he had seen the mine. All the time he was conscious of it, perhaps suspended just above them or lying against their side. And where there was one, there must be others somewhere in the tangled section of the net underneath them. He prayed to God, to Thor and Odin, to Jesus, the Virgin. I'll build you a shrine, a temple . . . for every one of you! he vowed. Only help us!

As if in answer, when he threw himself one last time into the packed mass in the forward section, hunching with his right side, the U 20 gave her most convulsive shudder yet, her stern slewed in the mud and tore free of its sucking grip. Under the impulse of the empty rear tanks and the

31

weight in the bows, the stern leaped up, stopping short as the shackles round her prow held tight and jerking them all to the deck. Schwieger bit off a scream as someone landed on his arm. He was hazy with pain, yet still aware that something had happened to the lights.

He shook his head to clear it and saw that they were burning steadily. It was the flicker of the lights and the threatened loss of power that had cut off the crew's elation at what they had done. Now they were picking themselves up, chuckling and beginning to surge forward.

"Stay where you are!" Schwieger ordered. "Nobody move!" He inched toward the entrance to central control.

Hirsch had been holding on to a fixed swivel chair and had spun round with it, winding himself against the worktop shelf. Doubled over, he looked for the level indicator. The bubble was almost horizontal. "We're level, Captain," he reported. "Nearly on . . . even keel."

Schwieger moved cautiously round the bulkhead to the speaking tube. "Zentner!" he called. "Do you hear me, Zentner?"

Zentner's voice answered. "I'm with you, sir."

"Try the wheel."

There was an agonizing pause, then Zentner's voice came again, excited. "She's responding! The rudder's responding!"

The crew could not be held back any longer and broke into a ragged cheer. Schwieger let himself smile back, nodding to them. Fine fellows, he'd always said so. He beckoned to Haupert and the machinist to help Hirsch, and while they did what was needed, slowly equalizing the fore and aft ballast tanks, he and the boatswain sent men aft in ones and twos, counting them off to keep weight evenly distributed along the keel.

It took time, since everything had to be done properly. Yet time was fast running out. He had sent the boatswain's mate to check on damage and the man came back, ashen, reporting sea water seeping through the seams in half a dozen places.

The control personnel were all in position. "Reverse engines," Schwieger said. "Gently. Very gently."

Haupert switched the engines to reverse. Hirsch glanced round, then fed them minimal power. Schwieger was straining to listen and echoed the sigh of relief that ran down the corridor at the faint churning of the screws as they began to revolve, slowly but freely.

"Increase power," Schwieger said.

When the screws bit into the water, the clangor and rasp of the chains started again, with the meshes clutching and wrapping tighter while the U 20 strove to back out.

All at once, Schwieger held up his hand. "Stop engines!" he ordered. And repeated it, when they hesitated in surprise, "Stop engines!"

Hirsch cut the power. In the hush as the noise of the engines faded and the net stilled again, they all heard the sound Schwieger's experienced ear had picked up, the thrum of propellers directly above them. Not just of one vessel, but several, crossing and recrossing. Not the low-pitched drone of cruisers or the whir of minesweepers. Schwieger had recognized it at once, the sharp, wasplike buzzing of destroyers. They must have been lying in wait and the agitation of the buoys supporting the net must have signaled a major catch.

"*Liebor Herr Gott,*" Hirsch muttered hoarsely, "haven't we boon through enough?"

"Reverse, full power," Schwieger said quietly. All submerged sailing was done blind, on the gauges, and he was not certain which ones he could still trust. Yet they indicated the U 20 was backing, dragging the net with her. As she reached full power, there was an ear-splitting screech and crunching and she rocked suddenly, her prow yawing rapidly from side to side. She had torn free of the net!

Schwieger clawed for the speaking tube and shouted up to Zentner, "Hold her! Try to hold her!" In less time than he would have thought possible, she steadied and lay still in the water with only the protesting creak of her seams to show that anything had ever troubled her.

As soon as she had escaped from the net, Hirsch had cut the power. The temptation now was to blow her tanks and shoot straight up to the surface. The destroyers were still circling, however, in a tight area and Schwieger knew the instant her conning tower appeared, they'd put a shell into it or ram her. Yet the damned depth gauge was out of order . . . "Trim her up," he told Hirsch. "As slowly as you like. If we break surface, we're done for." He was still at the speaking tube and called up to Zentner, "Did you hear? Keep a lookout for light. The first sign of natural light, sing down!"

Gradually the U-boat rose toward the surface. He had no way of knowing how far or how fast, only that the graduated expulsion of the water from her ballast tanks meant she was going up. He counted off the minutes, five . . . ten . . . fifteen. Was Zentner going to sleep up there? Then his voice called down, "Light! It's getting lighter!"

Hirsch stopped the ascent immediately, without waiting for an order. "Very well," Schwieger said. "Trim her down at the same rate. For one minute." This time he counted off the seconds and at sixty the tanks were locked off.

The sound of the destroyers was much louder and they seemed to be closing in on their exact position. An illusion, he knew. One thing, the U 20 had withstood the terrific pressure and the grinding of the plates had ceased. But that did not guarantee that some of the weakened seams might not blow at any moment. Water was still seeping in and the greatest danger now was of it reaching the storage cells of the batteries, where it would interact with the sulfuric acid, producing enough chlorine gas to kill every man on board. The worst inflow came from the forward ventilator, which must have been ripped away by the chains. They would need to surface soon, to change the air and make what repairs they could.

First, they had to get away from the destroyers. Running blind, any course he selected would be another gamble, but the safest was their original one. Provided they had not drifted too far, they should pass through the gap they had made in the net. He checked the old course on the chart, relayed the directions to Zentner and sent the quartermaster up to spell him at the helm.

Twenty minutes later, traveling at a fair speed, they had obviously slipped through the anti-submarine net. Yet disturbingly, the destroyers were still above them.

By now, they must be well past Dunkirk and the zone of minefields. He considered making for the U-boat base at Zeebrugge on the Belgian coast, yet that would mean he'd have to feel his way through the German minefields, without even being able to use his periscopes. The first priority was to lose the destroyers.

He dived lower and put on speed, turning to port. But the angry buzz of the propellers stayed on his tail. He took the risk of diving even lower, wheeled to starboard and cut all engines. No possible sound nor movement could tell the destroyers where he lay, yet they remained almost exactly above him.

"How do they know?" Hirsch asked tensely. "*How* do they know?" Normally a calm, methodical man, his nerves showed signs of fraying.

Schwieger had no answer. Any leakage of oil or flotsam must have been left behind long ago. "Full ahead," he ordered, and called up the tube, "hard round!" The U 20 surged forward and almost banked with the tightness of her turn. She fled west-southwest, in a direction Schwieger hoped was parallel to the net and minefields. But at her submerged speed she was no match for the destroyers and the whole crew could hear their propellers circling and swooping on either side and one that kept to a fixed distance just abaft her stern. Somehow they were able to pinpoint her precise position. They knew that sooner or later in her damaged state and running out of air, she would have to come up. They were waiting and ready for the kill.

Schwieger had gone as far as he dared in a fixed line and turned again to starboard, trusting that they were heading into the open North Sea. He could ask no advice or assistance from Haupert, who was helpless without his compass which, at this stage, had lost all significance. With the weakened hull and with no depth gauge, he couldn't dive. He couldn't stop and sit it out. He could only run, for as long as the motors and the air held out.

Zentner had been relieved and came down to central control. He saw him watching, then speak to the medical orderly, who approached and saluted. Schwieger waved the man away. Because of fatigue and the intense pain from his shoulder, he knew he could not relax his concentration for a moment or he would collapse.

Veering, dodging, tacking, wheeling about, the deadly game of cat and mouse went on. All nonessential personnel were ordered to keep silent and make no movement, to

35

conserve oxygen. Yet still the air grew more difficult to breathe and the reek of oil fumes more nauseating. Men were stationed in the battery compartments to detect the first whiff of gas. One of the injured moaned continually, stretching all nerves beyond sympathy, until Zentner made the orderly feed him a massive dose of morphine that knocked him out.

Incessantly, in whatever direction they turned, however fast or slowly, the sound of the destroyers' propellers remained above them, the high-pitched buzz that Schwieger had come to hate more than he had ever hated any other sound. For over four hours the hunt had gone on. The crewmen were forced to breathe shallowly now, their mouths permanently open. Occasionally someone retched dryly at the fumes. Zentner was standing beside him. He suspected ready to catch him if he dropped. Hirsch was conferring with the machinist and came to them. "I'm sorry, Captain," he panted. "We can't go on much longer. The batteries are almost exhausted."

Schwieger nodded, but had scarcely heard him. For some minutes he had been conscious of a change in the pattern of the whirring propellers that dogged them. Those out to the side had become more erratic, swooping out wider and cutting back, as though searching more anxiously for their quarry, while the devil that had ridden all the time on their tail had fallen back. Here he came now, spurting to catch up.

"Hard to starboard!" Schwieger ordered instinctively and, as the U 20 turned, "full ahead!"

"We'll use up the last of our power!" Hirsch objected.

"Full ahead, damn you!" Schwieger insisted, and the U 20's screws churned faster, driving her on. After a few minutes, he felt the stirring of a wild hope and saw it reflected in the faces of all those around him. For the first time, the sound of the destroyers had dropped behind. Had they won clear of them at last? No! Here they came, the bastards! "Hard to port!" he shouted.

The U 20's motors coughed on the turn, but picked up again and she sped on. Again the destroyers were left behind, growing fainter and fainter, until they could no longer be made out. They had finally given them the slip. Schwieger let his eyes close briefly in relief. He opened them to see Hirsch watching him, pleading, and nodded. "Reduce speed to half."

He was bone weary and faint with the pain that threatened to unman him. Zentner turned to congratulate him, and they both heard it. The furious hornet's buzz of a destroyer heading from starboard straight for them. Schwieger stood frozen with despair as it passed right over them, then looked questioningly at Zentner, when it kept on going, fading into the distance. Was it a fluke, sheer chance? But no. Another was coming from port, crossing at speed just in front of their bows and, like the first, plowing on without stopping. Dimly, a mile or so on either side, they caught the sound of the rest of the swarm spread out and searching. Somehow, they had lost sight of whatever had been betraying the U 20's position. What was it, and what direction could she now take that would not lead her to one of the circling hunters? All at once, to Zentner's surprise, Schwieger murmured, "I'm an idiot!" He had just realized the time. At nearly 18:00 hours, up on the surface the sun had set and their pursuers were casting about, looking for their trail in the dark.

"We're going up," he decided. The others were alarmed, but he gave orders to commence a gradual ascent, exactly as they had risen from the depths. "We don't want to pop up out of the water like a cork, right under their noses," he warned. "And be prepared to crash-dive." He would never reach the conning tower on his own and he took Zentner's arm. "Help me."

With his watch officer supporting him, he managed to clamber up. The conning tower had been roughly set to rights, the helmsman's body removed, and the quartermaster was still at the wheel. He saw that his shattered binoculars had been replaced on their hook. They were beyond repair. The shutter had been bolted over the forward port and he unfastened it. The water outside was an inky, opaque black without any trace of greenness. Night covered the face of the earth. Dear God, let it shield us, he prayed.

As they crept slowly upward, he noticed how much less bright the electric lamps had become. Hirsch was not being overcautious about the motors. Their power was draining fast.

Zentner had taken his position behind him to operate the lever that raised and lowered the periscope, and immediately discovered a fresh problem. The main periscope was out of action, either smashed or jammed. Schwieger moved to the smaller stick, the little finger periscope, only two inches in diameter, and saw that Zentner's fingers were crossed as he tested it. By luck, it was still working. He ran it back down and they waited, watching tensely for any change in the blackness of the water outside.

At last it came, although perhaps only sight as keen and as trained as Schwieger's and the quartermaster's would have noticed it. Zentner could see no difference, but the order was passed down to halt the ascent. The U 20 lay motionless in the dark water. "Too calm," Schwieger said, and they crept up another estimated fifteen feet. Now there were definite signs of movement, the tug and sway of turbulence above them. The tiny eye of the periscope probed up, and up, and broke surface. Zentner relayed the information that they were at periscope depth.

The little asparagus was only two feet above the surface, its view obscured by the waves of a heavy swell. Through the lens, Schwieger saw that it was dark with scattered cloud throwing patches of deep shadow on the moonlit water. He swiveled slowly, and tensed when the lens registered a flash of light. He zeroed on it, straining to see, and just made out the outline he was expecting, a destroyer steaming in hunting diagonals, her searchlights playing on the water. Beyond her were the lights of another, and far off to the side another two. They had been robbed of their prey and now were ravening, unwilling to give up. He turned the eye back to the first he had sighted, the nearest, only half to three-quarters of a mile off his beam. It was a British H class destroyer, perhaps the very one that had buzzed above his stern all afternoon. In this light and this sea, his approach would never be spotted and he regretted bitterly that he had used the last of his torpedoes on that grain schooner. Just one simple bow shot would have given him the most intense satisfaction and taught that damned hornet an unforgettable lesson in vertical navigation.

Instead, he completed his careful scan with the periscope and, setting a course for north-by-east, stole off into the dark. At periscope depth, the U 20 could make better speed for less power and soon the lights had faded and vanished, miles behind. He brought her to the surface in the cloud shadow at the edge of a broad stretch of moonlight.

Zentner was first up the ladder and opened the hatch, climbing out. The air that flooded in was freezing cold, but sweet as honey. The boatswain and Lippe were standing by with axes and followed Zentner out. Schwieger went up after them and stood on the ladder, leaning on the rim of the hatch. He watched his lieutenant and the two men walk carefully on the wet, heaving deck, checking for any damage that might be dangerous. The bow rails had been mangled by the chain net and the funnel of the forward ventilator torn away, leaving only a jagged stump. The retractable masts had gone and the main periscope beside him had been snapped off, as easily as the stalk of asparagus it resembled. There were deep gouges in the plates of the deck and lengths of chain still wrapped round the conning tower. But what was it that had continually given away their position?

"Was zum Teufel?" Lippe shouted.

It was the boatswain who had found it. Snagged round one of the stanchions of the portside stern rail was the end of a length of thinner chain. He knelt and pulled at it, in case it was fouling the rudder. Instead of coming away, it snaked up in the water. Following its line, they saw that it was attached to a large, round object bobbing in the waves about a hundred feet from their stern. Schwieger's heart missed a beat. But it wasn't the mine. It was one of the red marker buoys that had supported the section of anti-submarine net they had rammed . . . All the hours they had twisted and turned, trying to escape, unable to dive to a safe depth, that infernal buoy had been dancing along behind them. How those English must have laughed! The easiest sport they had ever had. With two fierce blows each of their axes that drew sparks in the moonlight, the boatswain and Lippe severed the chain and it slipped over the side.

Schwieger's head was throbbing and he knew he had to climb back down. He fell the last few rungs of the ladder. What happened next he could never recall clearly. He vaguely remembered the quartermaster trying to lift him, then Zentner and the medical orderly holding him, while Lippe took a grip on his left arm with its dislocated shoulder and wrenched it.

The next he remembered was coming awake in his cabin. His shoulder still ached, but it was tightly bandaged and the pain was duller. His arm was in a sling. From the crispness of the air and the thrum of the diesels, he could tell they were on the surface, traveling at speed. He sat up, draped his leather jacket round his shoulders and got to his feet. He was puzzled at what had become of the injured crewmen, and even more puzzled when he saw from his watch that he had slept for five hours. He drew aside the curtain and went out.

The injured men were lying on mattresses in central control. Zentner, as senior lieutenant, had taken command and set a course direct for the mouth of the Ems. He was nervous, until Schwieger assured him he would have done exactly the same. On the surface, the U 20 made her fastest speed and it was the best way to recharge the batteries in case of emergency. Most of the collision damage had been tidied up. The machinists and Hirsch had stripped the malfunctioning gauges and were working on them. Everything was in order and proceeding as normal and the night run passed uneventfully. Except that Schwieger was disturbed to realize that the crew tended not to look at him.

They arrived at their home waters in time to sail in, as Hirsch had suggested, on the morning tide. And got the reception they had hoped for. Seeing the U 20's battered superstructure and the pennants hanging from a jury mast at her prow, all the vessels she passed saluted her, their sirens whooping and hooting. Sailors on the other ships and the workers in the base cheered and waved as she turned in to dock.

It was not a bad result, Schwieger was thinking. For all they had done, one man dead, Bibermann concussed and three others with broken legs or arms. Not too bad. The men had been dispersed and he was coming down the gangplank alone, when he stopped short abruptly. His whole crew and their officers were drawn up in two lines at the foot of the gangplank. As he came ashore, they took off their caps and cheered him. He walked slowly down the avenue they made, feeling honored and embarrassed, because they did not know he was a fraud.

Chapter 2

HE LAY ON HIS BACK, REMEMBERING THAT MOMENT. HIS breathing had stilled and he felt surprisingly calm. The dream usually left him shaking for an hour.

But then, he had never followed it through. It always ended with the terror of suffocation and tearing flesh when the mine exploded. But the mine didn't explode. By a miracle. And he had not choked to death on his own swollen tongue, as he dreamed. The thought of it still terrified him— yet it had not actually happened. He was here, in a neat bedroom in Wilhelmshaven, at his ease. He could never have imagined that, in the conning tower of the U 20 with the net grappled round her prow like a great, metallic squid. This would have seemed like a dream. Perhaps it was, and the other was real. Perhaps he had really died then.

This was certainly borrowed time. By all the laws of chance, the U 20 should still be lying trapped on the bottom or have been blown to twisted wreckage. Yet she had survived, and he with her. He'd been given the Iron Cross, First Class. He was ashamed to wear it, knowing he was a coward. Why was he so afraid? Of death? Death was the logical end. As a serving officer, he had accepted it as possible, almost inevitable. When it came, it could not be worse than he had gone through. The important thing, the most important, was not to give in. You fought harder, better, knowing you were already dead. You fought not to save yourself, but your men and your ship. But first you fought to defeat the enemy, wherever you found him.

His thoughts were incoherent, yet somewhere inside him he knew there was truth. He told himself again, why fear death, when you are already dead? Each time he repeated it, he could feel his fear receding further, shriveling inside himself. It was like a liberation.

41

The girl beside him murmured and shifted, moving closer. He looked at her, but she had not woken up. Her head was still turned away and all he saw was her tumbled auburn hair, glowing a richer copper in the brighter light that was warming the room.

He had met her through Zentner. Rudolph, who had become a friend. He had always avoided intimacy with members of his crew. Rudolph was different, though, a true companion. Conscientious on duty, amusing, irreverent and high-spirited ashore. He always knew where to find girls. Schwieger with his punctilious, upper-middle-class Berliner background was a little shocked by the swift relaxation of morals brought about by the war, although he accepted the reasons for it. Casualty figures on all fronts were appalling and life seemed too short suddenly, too uncertain. The long process of old-fashioned courtship especially had lost its meaning. "You don't go calling with flowers for a month nowadays, Walther," Rudolph had laughed. "They're all for the taking." Schwieger had shaken his head. "Believe me. More than any soldier, more even than the Zeppelin pilots, they appreciate us. As soon as they see the U-boat flashes on the uniform, the battle's won."

While the U 20 was being refitted, he accompanied Schwieger on an official visit to Wilhelmshaven. "So it's official," Rudolph said. "You're going to stand to attention for the Kaiser. That doesn't prevent us from having a little fun."

Wilhelmshaven had expanded rapidly with the boom in civil and naval shipbuilding and was now the Reich's principal base on the North Sea. Over the past twenty years, theaters, hotels and restaurants had sprung up, and blocks of elegant houses. As the headquarters of the High Seas Fleet, the navy was the city's lifeblood, and everywhere naval men were made welcome. None more so than the new heroes of the popular press, the men of the Submarine Flotilla.

In the evening, they put on their best uniforms and dined early, then took in a music hall, where the show was bright and slightly risqué. Afterwards, they found a pleasant wine cellar with a small orchestra. It was fairly late and the atmosphere was cheerfully convivial, groups at the long tables

42

singing and clinking their glasses. They chose a smaller table to the rear. It had been a full and highly enjoyable day, and Schwieger was content, willing to return to the hotel whenever it was agreeable, but Rudi muttered restlessly at their lack of success. "I don't understand it! Girls everywhere, sweet and pretty, and all with someone else. It's like walking through a rose garden and not being allowed to smell the blossoms." He considered it a defeat to visit one of the brothels and, in any case, Schwieger would not have gone with him. They ordered brandy. Asbach, not French brandy out of principle. "What do you think?" Rudolph asked.

Schwieger looked round. Two young women were sitting by themselves at a table to the side. One had striking auburn hair and the other was a lively brunette. They were well-dressed, animated, modishly made up with eyeshadow and lip salve. "You know I don't like bought women," he said quietly.

"They're not on the game," Rudolph insisted. "Otherwise they wouldn't just be sitting there. And obviously they don't object to company, or they wouldn't have come here." He considered them. "The redhead's prettier. You'd better have her."

Schwieger was amused. "Why?"

"Well, look at me," Rudolph grinned. "Two red heads on a pillow, it's a disaster. In affairs of the heart, contrast is everything." Before he could be stopped, he was up and crossing to the other table.

Schwieger watched him bow and present himself. Slim in his dark uniform, with his merry face and manner, he was fairly irresistible. The young women made a token resistance and gave in gracefully. He beckoned. Schwieger rose and joined them, and was introduced to Rudolph's new friends, Dora and Anneliese.

They were in their twenties. Anneliese's dark copper hair, looped fashionably over the ears and piled up loosely at the back with a thick braid wound round it like a coronet, framed a rather wide face with slightly slanted, hazel eyes and a full, generous mouth, challengingly attractive. Dora, the brunette, wore her hair short with tiny bangs on her forehead. She was slighter, slimmer, with dark, cheeky eyes, a tilted nose and pointed, minx's chin. They were singers in

a touring Viennese Operetta company, playing Wilhelmshaven for three weeks. They both had small parts in *A Gypsy
Baron* and *One Night in Venice* and understudied the female
leads.

"I'd like to see you perform sometime," Rudolph said.

"I'd have to know you a lot better," Dora smiled, teasing.

Rudolph glanced across at Schwieger in a way that said
"Promising. Very promising."

The waiter found them with their brandies and they ordered another round, for themselves and the girls. "I was
just telling them that we only have a few days," Rudolph
said, "before we go back to sea. And since we know hardly
anyone here, it's wonderful to share a moment or two in
such delightful company."

Schwieger nodded. He sat still and smiling, hoping they
could not guess that this kind of flirtatious small talk made
him acutely uncomfortable.

"You're not stationed here, then?" Dora asked Rudolph.

"No."

"So what are you doing in Wilhelmshaven?" Anneliese
asked Schwieger. Her voice was low and soft.

He hesitated. "I'm not sure I'm permitted to tell you."

"How very diplomatic!" Dora teased.

"Careless talk." Rudolph nodded. "You're both beautiful
enough to be very dangerous spies."

"Spies?" Dora giggled.

"Leading us on. Tempting two poor U-boat men with your
feminine wiles. In certain circumstances, I could see myself
forced to reveal everything."

They laughed. Dora's laugh was a quick, high ripple,
Anneliese's quieter, more in the throat.

They had both noticed the ribbon of Schwieger's Iron
Cross and Anneliese asked him if he had met Hersing and
Weddigen, the submarine aces. When he said they were
friends of his, their eyes widened with excitement. He always preferred not to talk about himself and what he did,
or had done. Some of it was secret, most of it boringly
repetitious, in conditions of such squalor and discomfort that
only those who had experienced it could appreciate. The
moments of action, thrilling to hear about and imagine death
breathing down your neck, were fearsome and gut-churning

44

to live through, and to remember. There was much he chose not to remember.

The girls waited eagerly for him to go on, and were disappointed. When Rudolph told them, however, that they were from the U 20 and that Schwieger was the commander, they perked up again. The U 20? Surely they'd read about it? Kapitänleutnant Schwieger . . . Of course! How many thousand tons of ships had he sunk? He was high on the list of aces! Dora seemed to want to reach out and touch him, to assure herself he was real. It made him even more uncomfortable and withdrawn. Rudolph made up for him with stories of submarine life, nothing too indiscreet or gory, just enough to keep them titillated.

Schwieger was only half listening. He felt ashamed. They had mentioned Weddigen and Hersing, and thought of him as the same. They were paladins, cool and daring. He longed to be like them. The mask he wore for the sake of his crew was modeled on them. He should have protested that they were much more worthy of admiration. He wanted to explain that what he did was all training and the obligation to do his duty. He was not a hero. Yet would they understand, if he confessed the fears that tortured him every time he gave the order to dive? What good would it do, either him or them?

Rudolph was telling them how demanding the life was and about barrel-shaped Lippe, without mentioning names, who had been refused leave to get married. "Poor man," Dora pouted. "Yes," Rudolph nodded. "And when we docked again, there was a letter from the fiancée to say it was too late. The baby had already been born." Dora squealed and covered her mouth.

Anneliese smiled, relieved to see that Schwieger was smiling, too. "Didn't he resent it?" she asked him.

"Uh—no. He said it was a blessing. Now there was no reason to get married."

They laughed. "I can see you don't like to talk about it," she said, "but wasn't it the U 20 that escaped from the net?"

"Many have," he said.

"And many haven't," Rudolph added. Dora shivered deliciously and he took her hand. With the other, he signaled for more drinks.

"What's it like?" she asked. "What does it feel like, when you look out of the window, or that periscope thing, and see you're completely surrounded by mines?"

He shook his head. "I can't tell you."

"Surely that can't be secret!" she protested.

"No, it's not secret. But if I'd seen that, I wouldn't be here." She grimaced at him, giggling, and pretended to draw her hand away, making him hold it more tightly.

"You haven't told us much about yourselves," Schwieger said to change the subject. "Is your tour going well?"

"We're getting very good houses," Anneliese said. "Everybody thought it was crazy to present light opera just now, but it's what people seem to want."

"It's rubbish," Dora objected. "Don't let's speak about it."

"Please," Schwieger smiled. "I think it's fascinating."

"What's fascinating about wearing big earrings and awful skirts and prancing about the stage, pretending to be gypsies?"

"Depends who's wearing them," Rudolph chuckled.

"There you are, you see!" she exclaimed. "You think women are only there to dress up and look pretty. You men are the only ones allowed to do anything interesting. Even in the war! Everyone's needed, they keep telling us. But what do they let women do? Nothing! They won't let us join the army, or the navy."

"Or the submarine service."

"Why not? I'm sure we could be useful."

Rudolph's long face creased in thought. "I'm sure the crew would think of quite a few uses for you," he said slowly.

She seemed genuinely annoyed for a moment, then laughed. "Oh, you! It's no use trying to talk seriously to you."

"No use at all," he admitted.

Schwieger was beginning to relax, now the conversation had moved from dangerous ground. It was partly the brandy and partly Anneliese's smile to him. It was warm and lazy and said, I know, I understand. "You still haven't told us about the net." Dora was speaking to him, and he went cold.

"He won't," Anneliese said quietly.

"Well, Rudi, then! Come on."

Rudolph made a good story of it, painting in the details, making the girls wince and bite their lips. Again Schwieger tried not to listen, but he was trapped. His palms grew moist

46

and he slipped a napkin from the table, pretending just to hold it. It was strange hearing his own nightmare through someone else's memories, almost hypnotic, yet he managed to look detached, while his mind flooded with images and he fought the sensation of choking. The succubus of fear that fastened on him every night hovered over him. Please, God, don't let it show! he begged.

Rudolph had reached the point when the mine bounced slowly toward them and passed over their heads. "So you did see one that close!" Dora gasped. "What did you do?"

"I pissed myself," he said.

The girls squeaked with shock, laughed and were embarrassed, all at the same time. He smiled back and shrugged, totally candid. Dora wrinkled her nose in distaste. "You didn't!" she said, and turned to Schwieger. "It's not true."

"Of course it is," he confirmed. "We all did. It's a natural reaction in the circumstances."

They laughed. He had meant only to help Rudolph, yet wished he had not spoken when they all looked at him with a respectful admiration. They insisted on regarding him as a hero, even his friend. What he had said they'd interpreted as "I can perceive and make allowance for weakness in others, although there is none in me."

"I really don't think it should be me telling this story," Rudolph said, apologetically.

"And I refuse to," Schwieger said. "We reversed engines and pulled ourselves out. That's all there was to it. Now, this time we do change the subject." Annehese smiled to him. Of them all, she was the only one who appreciated his embarrassment at being praised beyond his merit. It was odd. He felt close to her already, without any of the touching and flirting of the other two. He clicked his fingers at the waiter, who hurried for more brandy.

To their surprise, the wine cellar was almost empty. Time had passed quickly and it was late, nearly two in the morning. Of the orchestra, only the pianist and violinist remained. There were several couples and a last drunken group at one of the long tables. The emptiness caused a slightly awkward pause for a minute, until the old waiter returned, bowing so deferentially to Schwieger that he nearly let the glasses slide off the tray.

Dora giggled. It had reminded her of a performance of

47

Die Fledermaus, when the servant in the party scene dropped the tray holding all the champagne glasses and the cast carried on, trying to ignore the crunching under their feet and toasting one another with nothing. "Drink, darling, drink with me," she sang softly, raising her hand, the fingers curled. Rudolph imitated her and they bumped their fingers together. Schwieger and Anneliese copied them and the backs of their hands stayed together for several heartbeats as they touched for the first time.

Anneliese laughed, more vivaciously than she had all evening. As though she had been restrained by his reserve and took his touch as a sign that he really liked her.

"Ah, the Mona Lisa not only smiles—she can laugh," Rudolph murmured.

There was a loud chord from the piano and a scattering of applause. They looked round to see the violinist closing his case.

"Would you care for another drink?" Schwieger asked Anneliese.

She refused, smiling. "No, thank you. I've already had as much as I usually have in a week." She breathed out and brushed her fingertips over her forehead.

"Me, too," Dora agreed. "I'm not sure I'll be able to get up."

"Well . . . I suppose we ought to be going," Rudolph said.

"Do you have to get back to barracks or something?" Dora asked casually. He smiled to her and she lowered her eyes.

Coming up the steps outside, Anneliese took Schwieger's arm. "This fresh air's making me dizzy," she shivered, and pulled up the fur collar of her coat. The brandy had gone to her head.

There were no taxis or carriages, although there were still people about in the street, lights in other cafés and beer cellars, snatches of music. "Why don't we walk?" Dora suggested. "It's not far."

They both had rooms in a house quite near the theater. When they reached it, Schwieger hesitated. "It's been a lovely evening," Anneliese thanked him. "Can I—can I make you some tea or coffee?" Rudolph was already helping Dora to unlock the door.

The house had not been electrified and the hall was lit by

a small gas mantle, turned down very low. "Are you sure it's all right?" Rudolph whispered.

"You don't have to whisper," Dora told him. "The landlady's old and very deaf and doesn't mind what visitors we have."

"She must be unique," he grinned. Dora had a room on the third floor. She said good night to Schwieger at the door, coquettishly, a hint of bravado. Rudolph bowed and followed her in.

Anneliese's room was above, on the top floor. It was comfortable, with brown flock wallpaper, a tasseled rug over the table and a brass bedstead. She lit the gas and he helped her off with her coat. The walk and climbing the stairs had made him aware of how much he had drunk, all day since midmorning. "It's cold," Anneliese said. "I'll light the fire."

But she did not move. She was near him, looking at him. "I'm frightened of you," she said quietly.

"Of me?" He was startled.

"The way you look at me, at everyone. As if we hardly exist." That's not true, he wanted to say. "I suppose what we do, what everyone else does, seems so trivial to you."

"No. Not at all," he muttered.

"You face death and danger every day. You're used to it. I've—I've never met anyone really brave before."

Schwieger was shocked. He had thought she understood, that he only did his duty as best he could, forcing himself at times and nearly failing. But going on. Instead, she thought of him just as the others did, some impossible tinsel figure, a fearless knight. She did not see him at all.

She was flushed and trembling. "I wanted you the moment I saw you. Is it wrong of me to say it?"

It was not him. It was the uniform and ribbon she had seen. Just as Rudolph had predicted and promised . . . It was humiliating. He had to get away. "I don't—don't—" he began.

She swayed and seemed about to fall and he caught her. At once, her arms were round him and her mouth was searching up for his. The warmth of her body in the chill room made his react, in spite of himself. She was muttering against his lips, "Please . . . please . . . " and he kissed her.

Somehow she had undone the buttons down the front of his uniform. Her hands moved on his chest and held his

49

waist, then she stepped away, reaching for the fastenings at the back of her dress.

In his whole life, orderly and conventional, he had never experienced such headlong passion in a woman. She was completely possessed. Yet as he watched her, immobile, something made her hesitate and she turned to the fireplace. He glimpsed her deeply indented back in the gap of her dress as she switched off the gas lamp. Her clothes rustled and she was naked, coming back to him. Her figure was a pale glimmer, that narrow waist and high, full breasts. She was touching him, helping him, making him, undress. And they were in bed.

Her hair was coming undone and drifted over his face. Her breath was hot and the warm musky smell of her body attacked him when she pressed herself against him. Murmuring, constantly moving, she kissed his throat and the side of his neck and his mouth. But the stir of desire he had felt had gone. Her nearness and movement had no effect on him. He did not even hold her. If he had touched her, it would have been to push her away.

"What—what's wrong? What is it?" she muttered. Her voice was slurred. "Mh? What is it? Don't you want to?"

Just as he could not touch her, neither could he speak. Or am I afraid to? he asked himself. He felt shame for them both. For her abandon, for his own stupidity in letting it happen. His lack of response. He had degraded her and exposed himself as less than a man.

He expected her to be angry, to scorn him and turn on him. He would have had no defense. Instead, with his stillness and silence, she quieted herself, lying heavily on him, one leg thrown over his. "Mh? What's the matter? Don't you want to?" she repeated. The energy the brandy had given her was almost used up, he realized. It was as if he could feel it ebbing from her. She murmured again, but drowsily. Her body, soft and warm, squirmed slowly against his and settled by his side. Her hand slid from his shoulder to lie on his breastbone. "Hold me. Just hold me," she murmured, twisting her head so that her cheek was against the curve of his shoulder.

They had both fallen asleep. And the dream had wakened him.

He had been lying in one position too long and needed to

stretch, but did not want to risk waking her. It was not something he looked forward to. She had every right to be offended and resentful. Rudolph and he had made the running, offered themselves to the girls, that's all it had been. Anneliese had obviously been assessing him, just as he had tried to appraise her. They had little to go on except appearances, and she had taken him at the value of his rank and uniform. She'd been flattered and drunk too much, and lost all inhibitions in that sudden rush of passion. And his body had rejected her. No, not his body, that was an evasion. He had no wide experience of women, but he was not physically incapable. It was his fastidious and guarded mind, too used to controlling every reaction. And lately, obsessed with concealing his fear. It had even robbed him of his manhood.

The darkness was receding and he had begun to make out objects in the room. Early morning light glowed through the curtains, revealing their spiraling, flower pattern. He was aware of being more at ease than for some time. In the human animal, the vital force was said to be at its lowest just before dawn, after that the spirits lifted. But it was more than that. He would have to think of moving. He had his appointment at Headquarters later in the morning, full dress and highly secret. It would be best to get up quietly, dress and be gone, without any embarrassment or recriminations.

Although the girl, Anneliese, would never understand, he was grateful to her. It had been a cathartic night. The drunkenness and sick humiliation, and the dream worse than ever. Yet perhaps it had been meant. His limp incapacity even with such stimulation had compelled him to admit to himself how deep his fear went, how far into him its rot had spread. And he had faced it. He was not fully certain how, but he knew it was not so strong any more. It had been like a presence. He had been unable to think of anything, anything at all, without it intruding. Now its power over him was gone. His naked confession of it, reliving it and refusing ever to submit, was that the reason? Or was it his final acceptance that whatever lay in store for him could not be escaped? One or all of them, it didn't matter. Only that he was whole again. The fear had shown that it could be controlled.

He should get up and dress. Just for another few minutes,

though, it was pleasant to enjoy the feeling of being at ease. He filled his lungs and breathed out slowly.

"Are you awake?" Anneliese asked quietly.

It was so unexpected that he tensed. She had not moved. Her head was still turned away from him, her hair tumbled on the pillow.

"I wonder what time it is," she said.

"Still very early."

Hearing his voice, she shifted round slowly to face him. Strands of copper hair veiled her face and she drew them aside. He had forgotten her eyes, hazel flecked with amber, widely spaced and slightly slanted. Involuntarily, he glanced down to where the top of the quilt was tented by her bare shoulder, drawn by the crescents of her plump breasts.

She tucked the quilt up to her chin and, for a moment, they could not look at each other.

"It's embarrassing, isn't it?" she said softly.

"A little."

He wanted to say it was no fault of hers. She saw his faint smile and looked away again. "I'm sorry."

"Sorry?"

"For last night," she said hesitantly. "I—I let you down." He was grateful for her kindness. "I disappointed you."

He was not sure whether she was being kind or genuinely didn't remember. She was waiting and he had to say something. "Not at all. You didn't disappoint me in any way."

"But nothing happened." She was puzzled.

"I—well, that was really my fault," he told her, although it was difficult. "I couldn't. Nothing—I just couldn't."

She surprised him again, by smiling. "Didn't you find me attractive?"

"That's not a question that needs an answer. You're very desirable. It was me . . . I'd drunk too much, I think."

She was relieved. She had only a confused memory of arriving at the house and concentrating hard not to trip going up the stairs. She had wished he'd put his arms round her waist, like Rudi's was round Dora. Two brandies and maybe a glass of wine were usually her limit. It was not good for the voice. And last night she'd had six or seven. She could remember him helping her off with her coat. Then . . . the hardness of his body, and being in bed, and fighting against a wave of dizziness and tiredness that washed over her as soon as she lay down. She had been desperately afraid she'd be no use to him and that she'd be sick. There was his shoulder. She had laid her cheek against it, and that was the last she remembered. And all the while he'd probably been feeling exactly the same. That was why she smiled.

His broad shoulders were bare above the quilt. He was lying with his head turned to her, and that faint, strange smile of his. A frown made creases between his eyes. He was so handsome . . . Blond hair, light blue eyes, clear and direct, not piercing, more sensitive. His mouth was straight and well-shaped, the upper lip a little fuller. With his rounded chin it gave him a boyish look, although he must be about thirty. She was proud he had chosen her and not Dora. Yet she could tell he was troubled by what had happened, or hadn't happened. And not just that his body hadn't responded. She wanted to put her hand up and smooth away the creases from between his eyes. "You think too much," she said.

He smiled quickly, more openly. "I've just finished telling myself that."

They were silent again.

Her eyes went back to the broad slope of his shoulders. "Are you cold?" He shook his head. "I'll make a pot of coffee in a minute."

"Thank you. I have an appointment this morning I can't be late."

"Of course not," she said.

She was lying facing him. She shifted to make herself more comfortable and the front of her thigh touched the side of his. It was like an electric shock. She stopped moving at once, but did not draw back. He could feel his flesh tingle where her thigh just nudged it. All her caresses the night before had not had such an effect.

Anneliese's throat was dry. "We're here till the end of the week, then we move to Dresden," she said. He nodded. "How long will you be in Wilhelmshaven?"

"Another few days."

She realized. "You're staying for the naval review?"

"Yes." He wondered if she could sense the tension in him. From her casualness he doubted it.

She hesitated. "Will I see you again?" she asked, so softly that he scarcely heard her.

He had not meant to. A mere ten minutes ago, he had been ready to slip away. Now . . . "If that would please you," he said carefully.

"Oh, yes." She stretched out her hand and laid it on his flat stomach. "I want to make it up to you," she whispered.

The mingled perfume of violets and of her skin was heady. Her fingers opened, circling lower. This time, the reaction of his loins was fierce and immediate. She smiled suddenly. He rolled over toward her, trapping her hand between them. Her body yielded and welcomed. His arms were round her and she gasped at his strength, as he bore down.

Her mouth was open and hot under his.

Chapter 3

WILL TURNER CAME OUT INTO WATER STREET FROM THE
Cunard offices. It was a blustery day and the March wind
had a bite in it, whistling straight in from the river. He
was glad Mabel had made him take his warm overcoat.
There were few people about and the street seemed unnaturally empty, almost as if expecting a siege, with sand-
bags piled up to window level at the lower end where it
opened out to the docks. He thought of finding a little restaurant for an early lunch, but decided against it. He knew
himself. He would only be putting off the moment he saw
her, to savor it a while longer. He felt like a boy on his way
to visit his best girl after a year's voyage. Best girl? You're
going soft in the head, Will, he told himself. Yet he had to
admit he was eager to see her. He turned his face to the
wind and headed briskly toward the Mersey, a squarebuilt,
stocky figure in an anonymous dark overcoat and bowler
hat.

The air was even keener as he came out of the windbreak
of the high buildings, but it was how he liked it, clean and
fresh. The river was quite choppy and he could see the
shorefront houses of Seacombe far away over on the left
bank quite clearly. Two sailboats were just passing each
other in mid channel and a coasting steamer heading in toward the Half Tide Dock. The New Brighton ferry was
getting ready to cast off.

He had come out near the south end of the Landing Stage,
a huge floating quay nearly half a mile long, supported by
hundreds of iron pontoons and connected to the shore by
eight bridges, in the center of the Liverpool Docks. The city
owed its existence to the river and the docks that bordered
it for all of seven miles. Even the promenade on which he

was standing in front of the tall Liver Buildings had once been an old dock basin, now filled in. The Mersey with its long, wide estuary partly enclosed by sandbanks at its mouth had made Liverpool into England's principal seaport and second largest city.

Here at the south end of the Landing Stage, the ferryboats came in. He walked round their ticket offices and waiting halls to the Pier Head, the broad, open space between the Liver Buildings and Prince's Dock. He could remember it choked with hawkers, gin booths and bumboat women, stalls selling seamen's gear, four-wheelers and heavy carts loaded with crates and barrels for the warehouses. Now it was a terminus for electric trams, rattling and clanking in by the minute, their tinny bells clinking and the overhead wires sparking as the drivers shifted the connecting rods with their hooked poles. And the passengers spilled out, children and sightseers clattering down from the upper decks, tripping over the tramlines set in the cobbles, housewives with bulging shopping baskets hurrying for the ferry booking halls, businessmen making for the quayside offices. There were more uniforms to be seen nowadays, navy blue and khaki. A small platoon of Argyll and Sutherland Highlanders, colorful in their kilts and sporrans, their bonnets cocked high at the side, waited by their kitbags, winking and signaling to the younger women, as their sergeant looked for the Transport Officer who had been supposed to meet them.

Turner crossed the Pier Head unnoticed and passed the Riverside Station, built right by the Landing Stage and only used by Atlantic passengers, for the north end of the Landing Stage was where oceangoing steamers and the Transatlantic liners tied up. He walked on unhurriedly down Prince's Dock Parade, keeping his eyes on the Customs Hall or the shoreward buildings, until he came to the first of the north end's bridges.

A sign of the times. There was a barrier across the bridge, a single, wooden arm with a helmeted policeman by its counterweight. Two soldiers stood on guard with rifles, wearing flat-topped caps, khaki uniforms and puttees. A great comfort to know they're there, Turner thought dryly, if Tirpitz comes steaming up the Mersey in an armored battleship. As one of them stepped forward to ask for his identification, the policeman saluted smartly. "A very fine day, Captain," he said.

"It is, indeed," Turner nodded. He touched the brim of his bowler to the two soldiers, who came raggedly to attention as he went past them on to the bridge. Halfway across, he looked up for the first time.

And there she was.

Towering over the quay, her sleek, black side was nearly eight hundred feet long. Above her brilliant white superstructure, her four giant funnels, a stark black now with the identifying red bands of the Line painted out, soared to a height of a hundred and fifty feet above her keel. Not even taking into account her two masts at fore and aft which rose two hundred feet, she dwarfed everything else in sight. Yet she was not simply a colossus. From the clean, vertical knife-edge of her prow to the delicate undercurve of her stern, the line was exquisite. Her designer had given her grace to match her power, as her height balanced her slender length. The *Lusitania*, Greyhound of the Seas.

His footsteps clanging hollowly on the iron bridge, Turner walked on with no change in pace, although his breath had caught for a moment as he had known it would. Greyhound of the Seas. He had won that pet name for her himself, coaxing her to an astonishing 25.88 knots and a record Atlantic crossing. That's what she had been built for, to snatch back the Blue Ribbon from Germany for Cunard and Great Britain, as she had done. The government had subsidized her construction, to Admiralty specifications for speed and strength. Her hull throughout was of steel, with a cellular double bottom and a floor at every frame, sixty inches thick on the center line and deeper where it supported the engines. Her length was divided by twelve watertight compartments, specially toughened, while down her sides ran a second hull enclosing all her vital machinery and forming two immense longitudinal compartments, which gave extra buoyancy and protection against collision damage, making her a ship within a ship. Her safety was proverbial, with each of these great sections capable of being subdivided, to create one hundred and seventy-five smaller watertight compartments at the touch of an electric switch.

John Brown of Clydebank, the only shipyard big enough

to construct her, had made history by fitting her with six huge turbine engines, four for ahead and two for astern, the first time they had been installed in an oceangoing liner. Her power was unimaginable, twenty-five enormous boilers fired by a hundred and ninety-two furnaces providing the steam for her turbines, whose three million blades at Full Ahead could produce 70,000 horsepower. With her boiler rooms, engines and controls out of view below the waterline, to the world she was a floating palace, a vast, sumptuously decorated luxury hotel with accommodation for over two thousand passengers and a crew of nine hundred. Nothing like her had ever been seen before.

She was Turner's first love, in spite of all the other queens of the Line he had captained. She had been his greatest challenge and his greatest success. He was not a fanciful man, but if ships had a soul, as some said, he had felt hers respond to his, a locking of his strength and will with whatever spirit was formed out of her metal and wood and electrical circuits and pounding engines. Not a thought he could communicate to any other living being, but a feeling he had known deep in himself, reluctantly admitted and never forgotten. All other ships were vehicles, mechanical, insensible, inanimate. To him, she was alive.

Cunard owned her and the government continued to pay a yearly subsidy for her running costs and the carrying of mail to and from the United States. But there had been a condition. In the event of war, all the ships of their merchant fleet were to be placed at the disposal of the Admiralty to meet the threat of Germany's armed cruisers. Already some of Cunard's smaller vessels had been withdrawn from service, partially armor-plated and fitted with 4 1/2-inch guns. The *Mauretania* and *Aquitania* were being converted to troop transports. The *Lusitania* herself was diverted for a month to Canada dry dock for conversion, but the success of the Royal Navy in bottling up the German Fleet in its home ports had given her a reprieve. Quietly, she had been returned to normal service, the only major liner still making the Liverpool to New York run, and for months had been driven backward and forward across hostile seas with makeshift crews and inadequate maintenance.

Dockworkers on the Landing Stage manhandled crates and packing cases, building them up into temporary stacks, and loaded smaller cases and packages into open trucks and onto haulage wagons as the last of her cargo was hoisted ashore. Turner made his way through them, heading for the service gangway. He noted a slackness in the stern hawsers. They'd have to be tightened before the tide turned.

Junior Third Officer Harry Robson was assisting Second Officer Hefford with the unloading. To aid the war effort, on each trip the *Lusitania* brought back from New York large consignments of supplies, raw materials and small arms ammunition, but she had not been designed as a cargo ship and, with only two small holds below the forward section of the lower deck, extra stowage space had been provided by transforming the forward compartments of the four decks immediately above into additional holds. With no winches or hatches for them, it meant that every case and crate had to be shifted by hand either to the foredeck or the lowest cargo deck. It was hot and dirty work and Robson wished he could wear a sweater like the seamen instead of his double-breasted uniform coat. He unbuttoned it and pushed his peaked cap back from his forehead. A fair-haired, still pink-faced young man, Robson owed his promotion to wartime conditions. Part of the Admiralty's interest in Cunard had been the Line's potential value as a training ground for junior officers and Able Seamen.

He had been up to report the refrigerated hold cleared and to check the manifest. Hurrying back down, he paused for a moment, looking out over the rail of the shelter deck, halfway down but still a dizzying height above the quay. He felt the breeze chill the perspiration on his skin and ran a finger round inside his starched collar. They were nowhere near finished. Another two or three hours, he thought. At least, damn it!

There was a girl from Sefton he had met just before this last trip. Pretty and easy to talk to, not too tall, just right, with very, very light, astonishingly light, blue eyes and taffy-colored hair. Not a beauty, but the eyes made up for it, and her figure was promising. More than just promising as he had discovered in a hectic twenty minutes in the back seat of the deserted upper deck of the Sefton tram the night before he sailed. She worked at the Dock Board Office, one of the new female secretaries they were trying out to release men for service. She hadn't been so thrilled to see him again as he had expected, but she had agreed to let him take her out, if he was waiting when she finished for the day. At this rate, he would miss her, or arrive a sweaty wreck with as much chance of a conquest as a Lascar in a nunnery.

He tapped the rail and carried on down. As he passed the service gangway, he glanced to the side and stopped. A man was starting up it, a civilian in a dark overcoat and bowler hat. He'd just come through the activity on the quay without anyone challenging him. The night before they sailed back into the Mersey, the Chief Officer had warned them that, even in their home port, they would still have to be on constant watch. The Kaiser's spies were everywhere. The man heading up the gangway was not anyone Robson had seen before. There was no sign of the masters-at-arms and no one to back Robson up, yet he had no choice. The man was stepping onto the deck and Robson moved forward. "Yes?" he asked.

Turner's eyes flicked toward him, taking in his youth and his earnest, determined expression. He nodded and made to walk on, but the junior officer blocked his way.

"Is there something I can do for you?" It was not so much a question as a demand for identification.

Turner considered him. The young man was a bit hot and bothered, and none too sure of himself under the officious pose. "You can do up your buttons and put your hat on straight," he said flatly.

As an answer, it was so completely unexpected that Robson blinked. There was a tone about it that was unmistakable and he felt he ought to respond, but was not sure how. Nor could he think of any follow-up questions.

While he hesitated, Frank Tower, an oiler, came out of one of the third-class lavatories near them. He stopped abruptly, recognizing Turner. Bloody 'ell, he thought, it's Bowler Bill! He closed the door very quietly behind him, but Turner had seen him.

"It's Tower, isn't it? Mr. Bryce on board?"

60

"Inspectin' Number Two boiler room, Cap'n Turner, sir."

"Trouble?"

"Routine inspection, Cap'n, sir." Tower saluted and made off smartly before anyone decided to ask why he wasn't down below, where he should have been. He spent his whole life down below, in the self-contained world of the engines below the waterline. In port, when there was a chance he wouldn't be missed, he liked to slip up and have a walk around, to fill his lungs with fresh air away from the fumes and see how the other half lived. It was a revelation, although he had never got as high as the promenade or boat decks. On days like these, provided you stepped out lively and looked as if you'd been sent on a definite errand, you could have a decent stroll, get a fair amount of exercise and none of the officers you passed ever thought to question you. But fancy nearly bumping into Bowler Bill like that . . . He'd been lucky, for old Bill always wanted to know what everyone was up to.

Robson had jerked his cap visor down and frantically done up his buttons. I've blown it, I've blown it, he told himself, got across the Old Man the minute he comes on board. As soon as the oiler had spoken, he had recognized Turner. If someone like him took favorable notice of you, you were made. Sod it. He drew himself up and saluted. "I . . . sorry, sir," he stammered, "I wasn't expecting you."

"No reason why you should be," Turner said. "You were quite right to stop me. What's your name?"

"Robson, sir. Junior Third Officer."

Turner nodded. "Is the Chief about, Dobson?"

"Mr. Hefford is, sir. Second Officer. He's with the Pier Superintendent."

"Well, let him know I'm on board, Dobson. I'll see him when he's free. And tell Mr. Bryce I want him on the bridge in ten minutes."

"Aye aye, sir." He saluted. "Robson, sir." Turner nodded again and moved on, leaving Robson faintly puzzled. The Commodore had almost had a hint of a smile. He cheered up. It was only when he put his hands in his pockets that he found he had missed the top button of his coat and fastened it all crooked.

Turner went straight to one of the two electrically operated elevators at midships. Another of the *Lusitania*'s innovations, they ran the height of the six upper decks. He reached the boat deck in seconds and went up the outside ladder to the navigating bridge. If the engine room was the heart of the ship, the bridge was the brain, controlling her whole life, her movements and reactions. As well as the controls, the bridge housed the chartroom and the first and second officers' quarters.

Quartermaster Johnston was on duty in the main control room, known as the wheelhouse, with its eleven high, forward windows and a long, uncovered observation wing sweeping out to either side. Hearing footsteps on the ladder, he glanced round and was surprised to see Turner's familiar bowler appear through the side windows. His immediate reaction was one of exhilaration. A veteran seaman of many years experience, he had been less than happy at the way the *Lusy* had been handled on her last few voyages. The responsibility of command was always a strain, doubly so in wartime, but her captain, Daniel Dow, had clearly been heading for a nervous breakdown. "Fairweather Paddy" Dow, they called him. Even the sight of a rising sea made him jumpy and the constant threat of submarines and enemy raiders had been the straw that broke the camel. As soon as the *Lusy* had docked on this last trip, the Board had ordered him ashore to rest for an indefinite period. The rumor had gone round that Bowler Bill might be given command, but Johnston hadn't credited it. It was too much to hope for, wishful thinking. Yet here he was. He stood to attention and saluted as Turner rolled back the starboard door and came inside.

Turner raised a finger to the brim of his bowler. He was used to being saluted as a token of respect, but he had noticed that these days it happened more frequently. Another sign of the times.

He was pleased to see Johnston, whom he remembered well. A good man, as much a part of this wheelhouse as the helm and the engine room telegraph. Everything was the same, the same dials and brass and mahogany fittings and polished softwood deck. So like a dozen or so other wheelhouses he had known, and yet unique, with its own special feel. He walked over to his usual place in front of the portside forward windows, looking downriver past the halyards of the foremast and over the raised tip of the prow. Automatically, he put his hands behind his back, clasping them loosely, and even as he did so, he realized it was a gesture, confirming to himself that she was now his, that he had taken command. He turned as the door slid back and Archie Bryce came in.

In his fifties, Chief Engineer Archibald Bryce had worked for Cunard almost exactly the same length of time as Turner. They were out of the same mold. Bryce's father had served as engineer on one of the Line's first paddle steamers and he had quite naturally followed the same career, with no thought of any other. A tall, top-heavy man with dark, friendly eyes and a bulbous nose over a beetling mustache, the skin of his face was tanned like old cowhide from over thirty years of furnaces and boiler-room heat. He was still wearing his loose cotton working jacket and overtrousers, crumpled with use and permanently stained with old grease runs and patches that even the ship's steam laundry could not remove. He had paused only to wipe his hands with a cloth and settle his narrow-brimmed cap more squarely on his head before hurrying up to the bridge, the moment he heard the new captain was aboard. There were some who'd have had to wait until he had finished his engine checks. He drew himself up to his full height and saluted.

Great God, they're all at it, Turner thought. Might as well be in the blessed Navy. He tipped his bowler in reply. "Not taken you away from anything important, I hope, Mr. Bryce?"

"Nothing that couldn't be put by for a while, sir." Bryce's accent was a rich, unmistakable Geordie inherited from his keel-boat ancestors on the Tyne.

"Good. Very good." There were questions Turner wanted answers to as soon as possible, but he was conscious of Quartermaster Johnston listening. He nodded to him and went out through the door Bryce had left open. Bryce followed him, and together they walked across the observation wing to the far rail.

They stood for a moment in silence, looking down at the shifting pattern of movement on the quay, where the unloading still went on. They had sailed together often before, most recently on the *Aquitania*, but the closeness of their

63

friendship could never be guessed from their formality in public. "It's good to see you, Archie," he said.

"Mutual, Will."

When Archie Bryce smiled his quick, confidential smile, the ends of his mustache popped up in two little bow waves that disappeared under the overhang of his cheeks. It always amused Turner. He glanced back at the wheelhouse. They were well out of earshot. "What's been going on?"

Bryce also glanced round before answering. "How d'you mean?"

"Oh, come on! Paddy Dow. The Board says they've ordered him ashore to rest. What's the story?"

"It's worse than they're letting on," Bryce told him quietly. "I doubt if he'll ever take a ship out again."

Turner grimaced. Although they were very different, Paddy was an old and valued friend. "As bad as that?"

"His nerves have gone to blazes. Well, you know, he's always been a bit windy." Dow was a popular captain with passengers. His notoriously queasy stomach had made him an expert at avoiding rough seas and at judging course to give the smoothest sailing available. "He never got over that business right at the start of the war."

Turner nodded. It was a story he had heard Paddy tell himself, and seen how his hands trembled as he told it. On the very day war broke out, the *Lusitania* had begun a trip home from New York under Paddy's command. Only an hour or two out, while Paddy was still discussing Admiralty instructions on signals and potential minefields with his senior officers and arranging a system of double watches, a warship was sighted on the horizon. By the time she had been identified as German, she had already changed course on an angle to intercept. Paddy had thought he had several days to adjust his mind to being at war, and suddenly it was steaming straight toward him. He had no doubt he could outrun the warship, but had no means of guessing the range of her guns. By sheer luck he spotted a low-lying fog bank to the south and swung the *Lusitania* at full speed toward it. Driving on through the fog, as soon as he estimated he was below the warship's horizon, he turned hard round and raced north. Safe again, with the enemy warship searching the empty sea far behind him, he took up his original eastward course and docked in Liverpool, warmly congratulated, but a badly shaken man. "He always worried too much," Turner said. "He could show anything a clean pair of heels, with the *Lusitania*'s speed."

"It's not what it was," Bryce said, and explained as Turner looked at him in surprise, "I've had to shut down six boilers."

"What in hell's name for?"

Bryce shrugged. "Economy. Not enough passengers, so the Company's losing money. The powers that be won't let them scrub the New York run, so the only way they can break even is by saving on nonessentials, like coal."

"I don't consider fuel a nonessential!" Turner snapped.

"Neither do I, Will. Paddy and I argued till we were blue in the face, but we got our orders—reduce fuel consumption by a quarter. We're running on three boiler rooms, instead of four."

"So what's her top speed now?"

"Down from twenty-six knots to twenty-one."

"Cruising speed?"

"Eighteen."

Turner's head swiveled back to the quay, but his eyes registered none of the movement as he calculated. A loss of five knots at maximum speed? She was still faster than most of the German High Seas Fleet, except for the biggest battleships and the top class cruisers. The Navy had most of them penned up in their home ports, afraid to show their noses. Most, but not all. Some of the fastest were acting as lone raiders. At twenty-one knots he doubted if the *Lusitania* could outdistance them. Maybe, but not their guns. He grunted. "I'll have a word with the Chairman."

"You'd be wasting your breath," Bryce said. "The crew's been reduced by nearly a third as well. I'm short of about ninety men in the engine room. I couldn't manage the other boilers even if you got permission."

Turner had wanted to know the worst. So far he had not heard one thing he'd liked.

"You can imagine the effect of it all on Paddy," Bryce went on. "That and the Boche submarines—their bloody U-boats."

There was a bitterness in his voice that Turner had never heard before. He could understand it. In these last months all sailors had come to fear the new and terrible weapon, the submarine. Undersea boats, as the Germans called them.

Purely defensive and of strictly limited operational value, the naval experts had said. Submarines were severely restricted by their short range, the unreliability of their motors and low speed underwater, which made them hard to maneuver. German successes in the North Sea and English Channel during the first weeks of the war were put down to luck, but a shudder went through the navy when, in the early morning of September 22, 1914, the antiquated, kerosene-burning U 9 torpedoed and sank three British armored cruisers inside an hour, with the loss of over a thousand lives. Shortly after, further sinkings off the north of Scotland and the coast of Ireland, even out in the deep Atlantic, confirmed intelligence reports that the Germans had developed a more advanced, diesel-driven type of U-boat, more heavily armed and with a greatly increased range. That winter saw the start of a more deadly form of warfare than any ever experienced before in the history of the seas, with the crews of battleships and liners, cargo vessels and tramp steamers, learning, often too late, to keep an unceasing watch for the track of periscopes and the sudden white slanting wake of a torpedo.

Paddy was partly in trouble because of his last eastward crossing, when, having received a warning of enemy submarines in St. Patrick's Channel, he had promptly hoisted the neutral American flag, shot across the Irish Sea without even stopping to take on a pilot and into the Mersey, still flying the Stars and Stripes. "What's the story of the Yankee flag?" Turner asked.

Bryce shrugged. "I wasn't on the bridge. But we were carrying three or four hundred Americans, and the U.S. mails. So I suppose it was legitimate."

Turner nodded noncommittally. Archie was only echoing the official explanation of the incident to Washington. It was a white lie. Like all Merchant Captains he had been sent secret instructions to fly a neutral flag in an emergency. Yet it shouldn't have been necessary in this case. The *Lusitania* was still twice as fast as any U-boat. And in spite of some tales he'd heard, they'd never come to sinking unarmed passenger ships, carrying no contraband.

Although he had not been consciously registering the activity down on the quayside, for some time he had been aware of one group that made a different pattern from the others. While most movement was busy, but random, theirs was tighter, almost disciplined, as they loaded a line of heavy, enclosed trucks. The thought niggled at him. "What's that lot, Archie?" he asked.

"Which?"

"The ones by the closed trucks. Who are they?"

Bryce lowered his voice. "Soldiers from the Depot, in mufti. Every trip we bring back a thousand or so cases of ammunition, crates of shrapnel. And God knows what else. Of course they have to keep it quiet."

Too bloody true! Turner thought. He felt a shiver of cold. All his calculations had just been thrown out of the window. No wonder Paddy was nervous.

There was a clatter on the ladder from the boat deck, as Second Officer Hefford came hurrying up. He spotted Bowler Bill and the Chief over by the rail and hurried toward them, remembering halfway to stop and salute.

Turner recognized him and raised a hand in acknowledgment.

"I understand you've assumed command, sir," Hefford said.

"The assumption is correct, Mr. Hefford," Turner told him.

Hefford could not understand why the Chief laughed. It only made him more flustered. "Do you have any instructions, sir? Anything you want to see?"

"Well, I'd like a look at the log," Turner said. "And to have a tour of inspection—when you're free."

"Unloading's fairly automatic, sir. I'm more or less free now. What sections do you wish to see?"

Turner considered him, tall, stiff, a bit plodding. It was common knowledge in the Line that, the year before the war, the *Lusitania* had been withdrawn from service on the orders of the Admiralty and placed in dry dock for extensive secret modifications. Then, immediately following the outbreak of hostilities, she had spent that month in Canada dry dock, presumably for conversion to an auxiliary cruiser, until someone decided she'd be more useful carrying on as she was. Still, the modifications had been made and Turner meant to see for himself exactly what they were.

"Any particular sections, sir?" Hefford repeated.

Turner's eyes flicked down to the quay and back, as the first of the disguised army trucks moved out. "All of her, Mr. Hefford," he said evenly, "from top to bottom. I don't intend to sail her out until I've checked every rivet."

Will Turner had completed his inspection, accepted a lift from the Pier Superintendent to the Exchange Station and taken the electric train home to Crosby. He had been unusually silent, with much to think about.

The pubs were just opening and, instead of going straight home, he stopped at the Blundell Arms and got himself a pint of beer. Ashore he was a more gregarious man, but he had no wish for company. He sat at a small, marble-topped table in a corner of the saloon bar, avoiding the other early customers, as he cut a square of dark plug tobacco, shredded it carefully in the palm of his hand and filled his pipe, with the pint untouched in front of him.

They'd had a go at her, all right. She still looked trim enough, her paintwork shining, brass fittings winking, a matchless luxury liner. But it was as well the demand for accommodation on her had fallen. The Admiralty had stripped the whole lower deck, the one immediately above the boiler rooms, and shut off the forward sections of the main, upper and shelter decks, losing many passenger cabins, the second-class smoke room and third-class dining room and ladies' room, to make space for extra cargo. Her entire length on both sides, from twenty-six feet above the waterline up to the shelter deck, had been armor-plated, and the forward section of the shelter deck itself was bolted and barred on Admiralty orders. What it contained or was ready to contain he guessed at as he checked back along the deck and discovered revolving rings for six-inch guns concealed under removable panels in the teak planking. The spacing suggested six guns to each side, with further gun-rings sited on the afterdeck and forecastle. Without Admiralty authorization, he had no means of opening the secret forward compartment on the shelter deck to find out what was stored there, but discovering that the large coal bunker forward of No. 1 boiler room had also been sealed off and that Bryce had a key, he insisted on it being unlocked. As he suspected, it had been converted into a magazine, with racks for six-inch shells and electrical apparatus to lift them up to the guns. At least there were no shells, which argued that the guns themselves had not been stored on board, either, since the Admiralty had changed its mind about the *Lusitania*'s function. That was something. But a major technical problem remained. With the lower deck, almost on the waterline, having been stripped and armor-plating sheathing the upper and shelter decks, she was now top-heavy and her careful balance destroyed. There was no saying how she would handle. Presumably as well as ever on her way back from New York, with her bunkers and cargo space full. But on the way out . . . ? He cursed the bright naval minds that had planned her conversion, and he cursed the need for it, the war that had mutilated her. As it threatened his sons, and millions of other sons.

Holding his pipe unlit, he raised his glass and drank deeply, adding a silent toast. God damn the Kaiser, he thought. And all who sail in him.

Chapter 4

WHILE HE WAITED, GRAND ADMIRAL ALFRED VON TIRPITZ glanced at the huge map of western Europe and the British Isles mounted on the wall to the left of his desk. All the land masses, channels, bays, harbors, capes and islands, he knew them as well as he knew the shape of his own blunt hands. It occurred to him it was one map he could probably draw blindfolded, he had studied it so often in the fifty years he had been a sailor.

Half a century . . . Since he had joined the Prussian navy as a cadet at fifteen. It had been no more than a coastal defense force then. He'd aimed them at the young Kaiser's imagination, those memoranda he had written on the need for a national battle fleet, and in 1897, the year of old Queen Victoria's Diamond Jubilee, Wilhelm had appointed him Minister of Marine. Out of that the High Seas Fleet was born. Even the panic caused by the launching of the first British dreadnought turned to his advantage when he realized that what mattered now was armor, speed and firepower, not numbers, and that in building his own superbattleships he could almost match the rate of his rivals. Germany suddenly ranked as a naval power second only to Great Britain, much superior to the smaller forces of the United States, France and Italy. It was a stupendous achievement, brought about as Tirpitz had promised in less than twenty years.

And yet . . . the day war broke out, without even consulting him, the Kaiser ordered all units of the Imperial Navy to return to base. No attack was made on the transports carrying the British Expeditionary Force. When he protested, von Moltke told him it was immaterial whether the B.E.F. landed or not, as the Army would have completed the total defeat of France within six weeks. When Tirpitz

70

appealed to the Kaiser, Wilhelm told him he had no desire to put his fleet in danger unnecessarily. As days went by and his most urgent pleas were unanswered, it became obvious that the unthinkable had happened and the Kaiser had lost his nerve.

It was only when he was ordered to join General Headquarters at Koblenz that Tirpitz discovered he had been bypassed. The jealous members of Kaiser Wilhelm's Naval Secretariat had convinced him that the Grand Admiral was too old to hold a key operational command, while the Chancellor, Bethmann Hollweg, argued that he was too dangerous. To his despair, Tirpitz had seen others appointed and a chain of command established which effectively cut him out. Intrigues and personal malice had muzzled him just when his bite was most needed.

Yet his personal influence was still powerful and, when the Army's dream of instant glory was shattered at the Marne and reached stalemate on the Western Front, the Naval War Staff had begun to listen to him. The cautious Commander-in-Chief appointed instead of him was under threat of dismissal. This time he must take part in the choosing of the replacement.

The map . . . He had grown to loathe it, with its unalterable contours. For all its inland size, the Reich had only a hundred and eighty miles of western coastline, much of it useless, another few to the north in the Baltic. Even the Rhine turned south at the last moment, so that its enormous estuary became part of Holland. Yet, more significant, more fundamental than all—just as Borkum and the other islands protected Emden and as Heligoland sheltered Cuxhaven and Wilhelmshaven from the North Sea, so the long, irregular triangle of the British Isles lay like a massive breakwater between Germany and the ocean. Only two exits to the Atlantic. One to the south, guarded now by minefields and the Channel Fleet, and the broader passage to the north, with the vast natural harbor of Scapa Flow in Scotland where the British Grand Fleet waited, ready to pounce. And not a German patrol anywhere in the North Sea. It was shameful!

He glanced at his visitor, who was still reading. Tall and broad-built, Schwieger reminded him of himself when he was younger. Though he had been even broader. On his deep-chested six-foot frame, Tirpitz was built like a bull. With his bald head, penetrating eyes and divided beard that stabbed down to his chest in two thick gray forks, his appearance was intimidating. His voice gruff, his manner direct and abrupt, he could be ruthless, even fearsome, yet there were many who had seen the other side of him, jovial and unpretentious, an old saltwater sea dog.

He was passionately attached to the navy he had created. Unlike most high-ranking officers he did not entirely trust to the view from his desk and departmental reports. In every branch there were promising junior officers whose opinions he valued and whom he consulted confidentially on problems and developments from the practical viewpoint. Walther Schwieger was his touchstone in the submarine service. Tirpitz saw him as no-nonsense and experienced. A U-boat man since before the war, he was not in it just for the excitement and did not court public admiration like some of the others, yet his record was one of the finest. He was standing in front of the desk, frowning as he finished reading.

"Well?" Tirpitz asked.

"It's disturbing, sir," Schwieger said, "if it's official."

"It's official," Tirpitz confirmed. "And true. Hersing took them from the captain of a British steamer just before he sank her."

Schwieger looked again at the papers he was holding. They were the log, cargo manifest and sailing instructions of the Scots freighter *Ben Cruachan*. Among them was a copy of Admiralty orders to the captains of all British merchant vessels, instructing them to paint over their names and ports of registry. In future it was forbidden to stop when challenged by a submarine. The procedure was, if armed, to open fire at once and, if unarmed, to attempt to ram. Legal proceedings would be taken against any captain who surrendered his ship. A further note advised masters not to fly the red ensign in home waters, but to sail under the flag of a neutral nation.

Reading the orders again, Schwieger felt his throat tighten. Always up to now, U-boats like warships had observed the internationally agreed Cruiser Rules. The custom, if the ship was believed to be unarmed, was to surface and board it.

Neutral vessels not carrying contraband were allowed to continue. Those owned by or trading with the enemy were taken over by a prize crew or, if circumstances did not permit, passengers and crew were given time to get clear in the boats and the ship was torpedoed or blown up with an explosive charge. These had been the principles of civilized naval warfare for hundreds of years.

"Well?" Tirpitz asked again.

"If British ships obey these orders," Schwieger said, "it will change the entire nature of the submarine war."

"You could not go on as you have?"

Schwieger paused. "Always—as often as not—I've let neutrals go by. Torpedoes are too valuable. I try to keep them for warships and armed merchantmen." Tirpitz grunted and nodded for him to continue. "It's often hardly possible to tell if a freighter is armed or not. She could have a small covered gun on her forecastle or after deck, not visible from the angle of the periscope. You come up in a welter of water and for a minute you can't see anything. You're neither submarine nor surface craft. It takes minutes to get up speed and more minutes to dive again, if you have to."

"And that's when you're most vulnerable."

"Exactly, sir."

Von Tirpitz's right hand lay on the desk. His fingers had clenched. He uncurled them slowly and rapped his knuckles on the wood. "So . . . it's become a war against merchant shipping. You object to that?"

Schwieger gave himself a moment before replying. "It is not my choice, sir. I don't think any of us enjoy attacking civilian ships. And yet . . . their Blockade, in a way, is an attack on our civilians. Should we have any scruples about retaliating?"

"None whatsoever," Tirpitz said flatly. "We are engaged in an all-out war, a total war. Their Blockade is slowly strangling us, and if we go for their windpipe in return, it's only self-defense."

"Yes, sir." Schwieger was still holding the papers. He laid them carefully on the desk. "There is another factor raised by these. Perhaps the most important. The instruction to British merchant vessels to fly a neutral flag on entering the war zone."

Good man, Tirpitz thought. That might indeed be the most important factor, although not the most obvious. "So?"

"It's always a tricky business stopping and boarding neutrals. As I said, we tend to leave them alone. One merchantman is much like another and, unless you get really close, you have to trust the flag. If we can no longer do that, if any number of them might be sailing under false colors . . ." He shook his head. "If they're too big to risk challenging, we'd either let them pass or sink them without warning. Now, much of England's trade is with the United States. If we sink a suspected ship that's flying the Stars and Stripes and afterwards find it was a bona fide American freighter—that could cause enormous problems in reparations and diplomatic protests and—"

"It's not your place to meddle in politics!" Tirpitz rapped out. "Your function is to obey orders, to see to the wellbeing and efficiency of your crew and to carry out whatever missions are assigned to you, regardless of any other consideration."

Schwieger stood to attention. "Sir."

Tirpitz, however, was not nearly so displeased as he seemed. The boy was shrewd and had gone straight to the heart of the matter. Undoubtedly, the great problem was the position of the United States. "Having made that clear," he said, and surprised Schwieger by waving to him to stand at ease, "I'd be most interested to hear your comments."

Schwieger was in two minds as to how to answer. The safest tack would be a simple assertion of loyalty and willingness to perform his duties unquestioningly. With some senior officers that was the only attitude permitted, yet he sensed that if he took refuge in the conventional attitude the Grand Admiral would be disappointed. And rising in him, he felt the pride that he and all his comrades took in their flotilla, so despised until now when it was needed. It wasn't the usual opinion on some operational or technical problem the Grand Admiral wanted, but something more. Hersing and Weddigen and Max, he was accountable to them all in his mind, and unless he spoke the truth, he would fail them. "You will forgive me, sir, if I tell you that I accept your definition of the duties of a naval commander, yet point out, with respect, that it cannot apply one hundred percent to the U-boat Flotilla." He saw von Tirpitz's eyes narrow. "There has never before been a weapon like the submarine. We ourselves have only very recently begun to realize its full potential. Until only a few months ago, it was rated as an auxiliary craft of use as an instrument of observation, or in defense as a kind of mobile mine."

Von Tirpitz grunted, reminded of his own past descriptions of the role of submarines. Well, Weddigen put an end to that conception, assisted by one or two others, including Schwieger.

"But that's all old history," Schwieger went on. "Yes, it is true that the U-boat commander has the same duties and obligations as the captain of a destroyer or a corvette, with the distinction that the powers of destruction he has available are infinitely greater. I do not need to give examples. The U-boat, properly handled, is virtually indestructible— barring accident—and virtually undetectable. No doubt in time methods will be found to trace and attack it underwater, but at the moment there is no effective defense against it. Our only limitations are technical, and they are rapidly being solved. To sum up, nothing that sails on the surface can wholly be protected from us. For the foreseeable future, we are the masters of the sea."

The fingers of Tirpitz's hand curled and uncurled slowly as he listened. With everything the younger man said, he was forced to agree, although it struck chill to his heart. It was a violation of his whole career, everything for which he had worked. He had been a fool not to have realized the capabilities of those iron fish long before, but then no one had. No navy could accept its own obsolescence, not with a fleet of new ironclads, invincible leviathans. But vulnerable . . . vulnerable to those little gray sharks. He had grudged every Reichsmark spent on them, while he had lavished millions on his dreadnoughts. And Germany had entered the war with only twenty-nine U-boats fit for service, ten of them more or less obsolete. And only another fourteen of the newer model on the stocks. Blindness. He tapped the papers lying in front of him. "Now, be so good as to sum up the effect of these orders from the British Admiralty."

"I have not had time to consider them, sir. I could only give you a first impression."

"That's what I want." Tirpitz could order any number of surveys written by experts. None would tell him as much as he had already learned from the flush that had darkened Schwieger's throat as he read. "Not an analysis," he said. "Just your reaction."

"Anger, sir. Sheer blind anger at the way those English manipulate the rules to suit themselves, always protesting that they are the perfect gentlemen and always trying to put us in the wrong. And why? Because they're an island and more dependent on sea routes for their war supplies than anyone. So on the one hand they denounce us as barbarians and pirates and, on the other, issue instructions like these—offense under the law to stop, commands to open fire or ram on sight, to fly an illegal, neutral flag!—that can only lead to the discarding of the Cruiser Rules."

His voice had become harder as he spoke. Tirpitz had always met him in formal surroundings, an educated, well-balanced, Christian officer. He had a sudden image of him in a combat situation, intent and deadly. It was illuminating. "That's taking it rather too far, isn't it?" he said with deceptive mildness.

"It's either that or the end of the submarine campaign, sir," Schwieger stressed. He saw the Grand Admiral's eyebrows rise.

Tirpitz appeared to be examining his fingers as they uncurled. "You are not in favor of discontinuing the campaign, I imagine. So what would be your solution?"

The answer was so self-evident, Schwieger was surprised he had been asked. "To excuse any and every action they take, the British have warned neutrals entering the war zone that mistakes are liable to be made. We should do the same and leave the decision whether to sink or not to the commander on the spot. British merchant ships will know what to expect. If we can possibly save their crews, we shall do so." He paused. "If we cannot . . . then it cannot be helped."

The silence, when he finished, stretched on. Schwieger could have sworn the room was soundproofed, yet it was so quiet that in the distance he could make out the ringing of a telephone and, a moment later, beyond the windows, the impudent whoop of a tugboat at the end of the huge quay.

He had been carried away, he knew, indiscreet, and began to think the Minister was so incensed he could not trust himself to speak.

Von Tirpitz sat with his head tilted, his brows under the pale dome of his forehead slightly drawn together, gazing up at the gilded rope and acorn cornice that linked the high walls and ceiling. "When you shoot rabbits in moorland, it's a different sport from stalking deer in rough country," he said, inconsequentially. "Say you're at a partridge shoot. There are hundreds of them and the beaters drive them straight across your sights. There's no way the birds can retaliate. You're not pitting your courage and your strength against them, only your skill, to see how many you can bring down. If there are enough guns in the line, very few get through." His head swiveled and he looked directly at Schwieger. "It's a different kind of sport. But extremely satisfying."

Schwieger stood dead-still, held by the gaze of those clear, unblinking eyes.

The knock at the door was soft and rapid, a little louder than the one a moment before which Tirpitz had ignored. He glanced round irritably and rapped, "In!"

His senior aide opened the door and bowed, too used to him to be daunted. "Many pardons, sir, but a messenger has arrived from the Admiralty War Staff, Berlin."

"Well?"

"He says it is very urgent, sir. And personal."

At a nod from Tirpitz, the aide left. Schwieger wondered if it was his cue to withdraw also, but the Minister made no sign. A young man was coming in, tall, slim, the same rank as Schwieger. The posture of his body was relaxed, his features finely chiseled, but strong, his uniform impeccably cut. Everything about him suggested breeding, and Staff, that indefinable touch of superiority, conscious or unconscious. He even had a hint of a smile as he came to attention and saluted.

"Franz!" Tirpitz exclaimed with genuine pleasure. He pushed himself to his feet and moved round to the end of his desk. Both younger men were tall, but he still bulked over them. "I'd no idea they'd send you!"

"Why not, sir?" The young man stepped forward and Tirpitz wrung his hand, pressing his forearm with his left. "If someone has to bring the dispatches from Berlin, why not me? Gives me a chance to watch the Review."

Tirpitz realized it was meant for Schwieger's benefit, and nodded. "I don't think you've met Kapitänleutnant Schwieger, Franz."

The young man turned, smiling. He took off his peaked cap, tucking it under his arm. The click of his heels was slight, like his bow. "Von Rintelen," he said, presenting himself.

Schwieger clicked his heels and bowed in return, more precisely. "Von Schwieger." He did not often use the prefix, but it came out.

Von Rintelen was smiling more openly. "This is a moment to treasure. I have enjoyed reading your reports immensely."

Tirpitz could see that Schwieger was puzzled. "Franz is . . . attached to the Admiralty. He reads everything that comes in."

Von Rintelen sighed. "Everything. Memos, despatches, cables, complaints, requests—everything. But your reports, Commander Schwieger, are a model of conciseness, yet more informative than most others. I congratulate and thank you."

Schwieger was guarded. The Staff appointment, what was it—Naval Intelligence? The newcomer had something of the air of an aristocratic dandy, yet there was hidden steel inside. "You flatter me."

"Not at all. I assure you I have followed the career of the U 20 with great interest. I trust you got the deck-mounted gun asked for?"

An encyclopedic memory as well? Not many secrets could be withheld from this one. "On my last refit," Schwieger confirmed. "A 4.5. It's been very useful."

"I'm sure of it," von Rintelen smiled.

"All operational submarines are now being fitted with deck guns," Tirpitz said. "I can't imagine why they weren't standard equipment before."

"War has a way of accelerating improvisation," von Rintelen said. "Hostility is the mother of invention."

Tirpitz chuckled.

"It means we don't have to waste our torpedoes nor risk a boarding party to sink an arrested ship. Two shells below the waterline are usually sufficient. And in areas where there's a danger of enemy patrol boats, it's much quicker," Schwieger said. "In future, of course, that may become an even more important factor."

"Quite so," von Rintelen drawled. He glanced from Tirpitz back to Schwieger, and changed the subject. "Do you know, Commander, I am really very envious of you? I would happily exchange my desk and ten years seniority to have a command like yours. Or serve with you."

It was a statement that Schwieger heard fairly often from inactive and shorebound officers. Easily said, and frequently he doubted its sincerity. He did not, however, in this case, as his smile certified. He bowed, rather than insult von Rintelen with the conventional reply.

Tirpitz moved forward, taking Schwieger's arm. "Now, my boy, you'll forgive me," he rumbled. "It's been more than interesting, and I'm grateful." He steered him toward the door, and paused. "Continue your fine work. Always remember, however hard your task, the service and the nation are proud of you, all of you." Schwieger stepped back and saluted. "Thank you again. Now, not a word. This was between us."

Schwieger bowed and went out, and von Rintelen watched the Grand Admiral, who stood for a few seconds in thought. "Splendid fellow," he said. "Though not as tough as I'd pictured, with that soft chin and those baby blue eyes."

Tirpitz chuckled, heading back to his chair. "If you think he's angelic, you should see some of the others. But it's not like you to be deceived by appearances. The U-boat flotilla is too small and too essential to be trusted to weaklings. They're all carefully selected, highly trained. They're leaders, resourceful, competitive. And they're all killers." He sat with a grunt and flicked the points of his forked beard to each side in an automatic gesture.

Von Rintelen laid his cap on the desk. "I meant it, you know," he said. "I'd give anything to be one of them."

Tirpitz considered him. "Yes, you could be. You'd slot in as neatly as another bullet in a magazine."

Von Rintelen shrugged. "It's the years of training I'd object to. I want to see action now. I volunteered for the Naval Corps at the Front."

Tirpitz nodded. "So I'd heard. But fortunately, even those dunderheads on the War Staff realized you're too invaluable where you are."

Von Rintelen raised his hands and parted them, with a turn of the wrists. A small gesture, yet very eloquent. He was by a chair, highbacked with wooden arms, at the side of the desk, and glanced at the Grand Admiral.

"Of course, of course," Tirpitz growled. Not another junior officer in the whole of Germany would have dared to sit, but Tirpitz had known him since he was a child and was fond of him and his family. Von Rintelen was highly born, with connections throughout the entire ruling class. His birth would have been enough to guarantee his success, if he had not also been gifted with good looks, charm and a striking intelligence, which he had the wit to conceal behind the enjoyable guise of a self-indulgent young man about town. But in the mass of information that passed daily through the Admiralty offices, his logical mind had a knack of fixing on features which needed to be followed up. Decisions often had to be taken quickly and he took them, with little reference to the titular head of his department. His success rate in several distinct fields of counter-espionage was remarkable. Yet Tirpitz sympathized. It was not the physical action that his other side, the born fighter, longed for and needed.

"How is Marie-Luise?" he asked.

Von Rintelen brightened at once, as he had calculated. The deepest passion of Franz's life was his enchanting little daughter, the product of a marriage that had been dynastic. "More delightful every day," he smiled. "You know, last week she told me, 'Daddy, I think I love you more even than sugared almonds.' In view of her addiction to them, that is the greatest compliment I have ever been paid." Tirpitz laughed. "The only sadness is the amount she misses me when I have to be away. As I miss her. She was only reconciled to my coming to Wilhelmshaven when I said I might see you. I am commanded to give you a specially big hug. Which I trust, sir, you will take as delivered."

"Indeed I do," Tirpitz agreed. "You should have brought Marie-Luise with you. She'd like all the ships " He paused. "Do you have anything else to tell me!"

"Yes," von Rintelen said. "It has been decided."

Tirpitz sat erect, his excitement showing for once. "And what was decided?"

"The Naval War Staff has agreed—yes."

"And the Army?"

"Has no alternative. They need all the help they can get. On a quiet day, over five thousand men are killed on the Front Line, more than half of them by shells and bullets imported from America. If we cannot stop it at source, we can at least disrupt the traffic."

Two out of four. At last! Tirpitz had laid his hands flat on the desk to control a nervous tremor that not even his iron will could master. "And the government—Zimmermann, Bethmann?"

"The Foreign Ministry is bleating about some new, mysterious approach from Washington," von Rintelen said, with a grimace. "But Bethmann—our sources tell us a Treaty of London will shortly be signed, pledging each of the Allied Powers not to make a separate peace agreement with us. Bethmann has taken it to mean the end of his unrealistic English policy. He has no further reason to disagree and, although he has no conception of what it will mean, he also says, 'Yes. Do as you think best.' "

A vast and terrible elation filled the Grand Admiral. Watching, von Rintelen thought that he seldom resembled the caricatures of him in the radical and foreign press, the ogre, the fork-bearded demon of the sea, but he did at this moment. Marie-Luise would neither recognize nor like him.

The Army had bungled its promised victory. The Navy, his own creation, was being given the chance to smash the deadlock and force the enemy to their knees. The jealous, the schemers, had been outmaneuvered. Even the fainthearted were behind him. His gaze traveled across the room and von Rintelen could see where he was looking, at the dominating bronze bust of Kaiser Wilhelm on its plinth under the old flag of the Far Eastern Division.

"Now there's only one man left to convince," Tirpitz said.

81

Chapter 5

THEY MADE AN INCONGRUOUS COUPLE, PAGE THOUGHT, ONE so tall and bulky, the other slight and thin-spun, one forcefully dynamic, the other almost deliberately colorless. Hoover and House, like a vaudeville duo. Not that there was anything comic about them, except the contrast. Each in his own way was profoundly serious.

Ambassador Walter Hines Page had been discussing the problems of Belgian relief with Herbert Hoover when the Colonel arrived. Hoover, an Iowa-born mining engineer, tall and energetic, seemed to many the physical embodiment of American know-how. Page had first heard of him some fourteen years ago in reports from China during the Boxer Rebellion. Cut off like many others, young Hoover had set up and supervised relief for the besieged foreigners. An even greater problem arose after the invasion of Belgium. The English and French had opened their doors to hundreds of thousands of refugees, but the question remained of the seven million Belgians who had become virtual prisoners in their own land.

Food supplies were quickly exhausted and it became apparent that the German army of occupation had no intention of replacing them. Belgium faced starvation and needed urgent aid, which could only be provided by a neutral organization, completely independent of the warring nations. Everything hinged on the choice of a director for such an organization. It had to be a man of prodigious energy and intelligence, willing to give all his time to work that would be full of frustrations, unpaid but crippling in its demands. Dr. Page, the American Ambassador in London, was consulted and remembered Herbert Hoover. Hoover had accepted without hesitation and, in the last five months, as

Chairman of the Commission for Relief in Belgium had done wonders.

It was appropriate that Colonel House should meet him, Page thought. Edward Mandell House was a man of medium height, with a small, neat mustache, high cheekbones and prominent ears. The first impression he gave many people was of a mouse, a quiet little gray mouse. Born in Houston, Texas, there was still the trace of a Texas drawl in his soft, carefully precise voice. Colonel was an honorary title, given to him in gratitude for political assistance, behind the scenes. He was the Democratic tactician who more than any other had won the White House in 1912 for the scholarly, progressive Governor of New Jersey, Woodrow Wilson. A private American citizen of independent means, with no official post, no position in the administration, the Colonel had more political influence at home and abroad than anyone except the President, his closest friend. After the failure the previous year of his mission to prevent the war, he had now returned to Europe as Wilson's personal representative to see if terms could be worked out to end it. To protect Secretary of State Bryan's fragile pride, and to keep him from becoming involved in these secret negotiations, the President had let it be known that he was sending House to Europe to investigate the war relief situation.

"It's a matter of sheer volume, Colonel," Hoover was saying. "Every month we have to import into Belgium eighty million kilograms of foodstuffs." Supplies were bought mainly in the United States, Canada and Australia, and shipped to Europe. "And we daren't miss a month or many will die. I had to set up a whole distribution system through our Ambassador in Brussels and the Belgians themselves, and a team of American volunteers. I couldn't have done any of it without them."

"There's been a great response at home," Colonel House agreed. "You must have an enormous sum at your disposal."

"A remarkable feature of the C.R.B., which Mr Hoover may be too modest to tell you," Page said quietly, "is that its expenses and administrative costs, thanks to him, add up to less than one percent of all the moneys paid out."

House smiled. "I can only add my admiration to Dr. Page's."

"I don't ask for admiration, Colonel," Hoover said. "You

83

save it for the young men and women who've come out to join me. And for the clubs and churches and private individuals, rich and poor, who've given as much as they can afford. And the children who've sent us their pennies. Our people have seen that little country lying in ruins and blood and there has never been such a spontaneous outburst of national generosity. I have never felt so humble or so proud to be American." He hesitated, embarrassed by the unaccustomed show of feeling. "Good day, Colonel. I expect I'll see you again during your stay in London." They shook hands and Hoover left.

House watched Page move to his desk. Page was a liberal and humane man, one of Mr. Wilson's New Democrats, a publisher before accepting this appointment. He had published the President's own works, come to think of it. He was seated now, unlocking a drawer in the desk. Not a handsome man, with graying hair receding from a high forehead and that bulbous nose overshadowing his mustache, but his sincerity and social ease had made him an ideal choice for the Court of St. James. Considering his literary background, it was natural for him to respond to England's heritage and liberal traditions, the bond of the common language. House could sympathize. Yet there were dangers. "It is essential at these delicate stages of the President's peace initiative," he said, "that we do not fall into the trap of seeing this war as one of enlightened democracy versus military despotism. The issues are not nearly so simple."

Page was quite still. "I am perfectly aware of that, Colonel. I approach no question except in the light of what is best for our country and in line with my instructions from the President." He had taken a letter from the drawer. "This has come for you. It's franked by the Foreign Ministry in Berlin."

House took the letter eagerly. It was from the Under Secretary, Zimmermann, welcoming the Colonel's proposed visit to the Reich. It was not, however, the positive invitation House had hoped for, and he was disappointed.

Page suggested that he should explain his difficulties to Sir Edward Grey. That might go some way to allaying the feeling in England that the President was pro-German. "It's the effect of those notes of his," Page said, "and the protests of the State Department against the British Blockade."

House was equally serious. "You know how much he longs to play a decisive part in ending this conflict, yet he has to maintain a position of total impartiality and noninvolvement."

"Just exactly why?" Page asked. "I find it hard to see beyond the tens of thousands of young men being killed in Europe every month."

"It is a sobering thought," House agreed. "Yet . . ." He paused. "It cannot have escaped your notice that there is an election coming. Now, while many Americans wish us to become involved on one side or the other, many, many more hold the opinion that the President has no mandate to entangle us in the affairs of Europe. Sincerely and quite passionately they insist this war is none of our concern. If the President alienates those, it could be a disaster for us all."

"Then what is the answer?" Page asked at last.

"We must face the realities of the situation." House looked up at a sudden thought. "Do you know? I think I must make it part of my mission to discuss the freedom of the seas with Sir Edward, as a practical concept. Put to them properly, the British government might respond." He permitted himself a slight smile, a quirking of the corners of his mouth that gave him an oddly impish expression. "No, I don't accept there is any need for despair, Doctor."

Freshly painted, the lines of its prow and bulwarks picked out in gold, the pinnace danced over the waters of the bay. Its handling like its appearance was faultless, as they had to be with so many eyes on them. A Commodore stood at the helm and each member of the crew was a senior naval officer, proud to serve as an ordinary seaman on this day.

The bay was part of the estuary of the river Jade, a huge, heart-shaped basin fully ten miles across. Much of the perimeter became a tumbled waste of sand at low tide, but a navigable channel of four to six miles always remained in the fairway. As now at high water, the bay was like an inland sea, its surface barely ruffled, protected from the breakers of the North Sea by the long, encroaching sandbanks at its narrower entrance, dotted with sailing boats and sightseeing paddle steamers, ferries, fishing and pleasure craft. Today they swarmed round the northwest arm of the fairway, the deepwater basin in front of the great quays

85

and docks of the naval base at Wilhelmshaven. The sky had cleared since morning, only a few high clouds studding its pale blue. Kaiser's weather, the watchers told one another.

Drawn up at perfect intervals, filling the wide basin, were rank upon rank of warships, steel-clad dreadnoughts, battleships, cruisers, destroyers, spreading out to squadrons of torpedo boats, minelayers and minesweepers and the auxiliary fleet of converted passenger liners, armored turrets and the long, telescopic muzzles of their guns projecting from their shelter and promenade decks. All the ships were gala dressed, paint sparkling, trimmed with flags from bows to stern, with their crews in their best uniforms lining the rails. The pinnace had an escort of a double column of sleek, needle-pointed torpedo boats and, as it weaved in and out of the lines, the twelve-inch guns of the dreadnoughts dipped and crashed out in salute, bands played and the rows of massed ratings cheered, flourishing their caps in the air.

On the raised stern deck of the pinnace, Kaiser Wilhelm took the salute with his admirals. In his cocked hat and long-skirted, dark blue uniform, draped in gold braid but modestly free of medals for once, he had stood at the rail for two hours, his hand rising to acknowledge the tribute of each unit as he passed. His lifted head and the heightened color the emotions of the afternoon had brought to his cheeks gave him from a distance the appearance of youth. At fifty-five, however, his jawline had thickened like his body and the finely molded planes of his face had spread and grown heavier. His hair was streaked with gray and the upswept ends of his mustache no longer rose in arrogant waxed spikes, but were left fuller.

After six months of war, he had recovered his nerve and no one could suspect the occasional doubts which swept over him. He advised and still had his power of veto, but the omnipotent military machine which he had helped to construct had turned him in practice into a figurehead. He understood his role. He was the symbol of the courage and determination of the German people. All looked to him, the All Highest, to lead them to triumph and the place in the sun which he had so often promised.

Wilhelm was affected by the atmosphere. He had surrendered to the spell of the continuous chords of the anthem mingled with the cheering and the unending thunder of the guns. The sharp smell of cordite drifted over the water and pricked his nostrils, suggesting vistas of battle and glory. But a thought was rising, a memory which he tried to suppress but could not, for it was too strong. Another thunder, deeper, reaching further into the smoke-filled distance, and the huge gray shapes passing at his grandmother's Jubilee Review. And another thought came. If Grandmama were still alive, this hideous conflict would never have happened . . . It distressed him and jolted him back to the present.

Admiral von Pohl, Chief of Naval Staff, was beside him at the rail, leaning toward him. "For nearly two decades the people have been taxed so that we could spend millions on ships," he was saying. "They look at us now and ask, what use was it? Why is this mighty fleet we made sacrifices to build lying at anchor, unused? Your Imperial Majesty, there is not an officer or man in your navy who does not feel ashamed!"

What was he talking about? Impertinent, irrelevant. Wilhelm saluted as they passed under the shadow of the dreadnought *Kaiserin* and the salvo roared out. But the surge of emotion was held back, the uplift checked. Wilhelm caught himself up angrily, his right hand tightening its hold on the rail. The gloved hand of his undeveloped left arm rested on the hilt of the ceremonial dagger at his side.

Wilhelm blotted out the nagging voice again. As they passed the dreadnought's bridge he saluted and the cheers swelled. He saw and heard none of it consciously.

Georgie . . . where was Georgie? At Buckingham Palace or Windsor? Perhaps at Sandringham, walking in the park with his gun under his arm. That would be it. A fine shot. And May, so serious and conscientious, waiting at the tea table. With Aunt Alix, beautiful still in age. What did they think of him—if they thought of him?

War . . . Bungled plans and muddled execution. The casualty lists sickened him, the senseless, brutal bombardments and bloody skirmishes of the Front. No longer a tactical war, the generals told him. Slogging it out in unimaginable filth and horror, and the last man left alive the winner . . . Yet only by persevering might the impossible come to pass and victory, at least a truce with honor, be snatched from the fire. Not through standard methods of warfare would it come, the generals said, the breakthrough, but through terror, frightfulness, a policy of *Schrecklichkeit*, to quell the hearts of the enemy with the ferocity of the German onslaught on land and sea. Leaving what? Devastation. Pray God it would not come to that!

"Diplomatic protests mean nothing," Pohl was saying. "We are being robbed of victory!"

Yes . . . all depended on victory. On the breakthrough, the turn of the tide, before Germany faltered and the invincible machine ground to a halt from lack of supplies and raw materials. That was the crux, the paramount need to ensure an uninterrupted flow of supplies.

As if echoing his thoughts, Pohl's voice broke in. "Armaments, Your Imperial Majesty, oil, shrapnel, clothing, everything conceivable!" Wilhelm looked at him. The Chief of the Naval Staff was tense, his voice hoarse with the determination to make his point. "We began the war with absolute superiority in equipment and material. But our stocks are being used up inexorably, while theirs are constantly replaced."

"Yes, yes," Wilhelm said, impatiently. "We have discussed this again and again in Council."

Von Pohl glanced round. In a few moments, they would swing toward the flagship, their final destination. "The point is, sir," he said, "that we are agreed, all of us, that the war can only be won in the West. That being so, we must also accept that if we cannot make the breakthrough, the Entente Powers with their ever-increasing supply of armaments may be the ones to do so."

Wilhelm's head jerked. No one had yet dared to put that supposition so openly. "Nonsense! Long before they could be ready, we shall have hurled them back."

"Not this year, sir. And the opinion of our planners is that the enemy offensive will be ready and mounted some time between June and September."

Wilhelm saluted the *Derfflinger*'s bridge. "Then what is your alternative—surrender?"

The pinnace left the shadow of the cruiser and turned toward the flagship. "There is one step we can take, Your Imperial Majesty," von Pohl insisted. "Our main fleet would not be hazarded, but the British lines of supply would be seriously damaged. If not cut completely." He had Wilhelm's whole attention. "We should proclaim our own War Zone, in the North Sea and round the British Isles, including the Western Approaches. Within that zone, all enemy merchantmen will be liable to be sunk on sight. And neutrals must accept the same risk, if they trade deliberately with the enemies of the Reich."

It had been arranged carefully, Wilhelm could tell. Even the Review had been utilized. In the wide space between the last of the battle cruisers and the huge flagship *Friedrich der Grösse*, the place of honor had been given to the Submarine Flotilla. The pinnace was drawing abreast of the first of the line of U-boats, low in the water, their stepped conning towers open, crews drawn up along the center rails. "If we proclaim our own War Zone," Wilhelm muttered, "we shall be as much in breach of international law as the enemy.

"You are perfectly aware that what you are proposing is a counter blockade, a Submarine War!"

"Our U boats would police the War Zone, in the same way as British patrol boats and destroyers."

The Kaiser's mind was in turmoil. He recognized the determination in von Pohl and that he must have powerful backing. The suggestion of an all-out U-boat war had been made before, after the first spectacular sinkings had shown the new weapon's capabilities, but had been rejected out of hand. No civilized Power would unleash such terror on defenseless merchantmen.

Again as though interpreting his thoughts, von Pohl cut in. "In battle, when a soldier's rifle is empty, he stabs with his bayonet. When the bayonet is blunted, he swings the stock like a club. When the stock is shattered, he fights with his bare fists. We must use the only weapon left to us—not as feeble as our bare fists nor as limited as a rifle, but so resistless, so devastating, that within six weeks the enemy will be brought to his knees!"

His conviction was so total that Wilhelm felt himself catching fire from it. It was dangerous and he glanced away. One of the smaller submarines had been given pride of position in the center, an old kerosene-burner fitted with a tiny two-inch gun. Even before he saw the large 9 painted above the waterline at her gray prow, he recognized her. The U 9, Weddigen's U 9. On the chest of every man on her curving deck was the Iron Cross. He had presented them himself! He stood to attention as he saluted her flag and the answering roar of her crew moved him as no other moment in this long day. Although he knew now her placing was deliberate, that von Pohl, perhaps the whole Naval War Staff, had planned this. "I am not alone in my reservations," he warned. "Any such proposal would require weeks, perhaps months, of discussion and the consent of every civil and military department before it could be accepted. Nothing can be decided now."

Von Pohl drew himself up. "Sir, I have to report that approval of the proposal to declare a German War Zone has been obtained from the General Staff and Commander-in-Chief, the Admiralty and Naval War Staff, the Chancellor, the President of the Reichstag and the Foreign Ministry. Only Your Imperial Majesty's consent remains to be given." Wilhelm stared at him, his mind spinning. "I should inform Your Imperial Majesty that the consent of each department was obtained separately to avoid needless discussion, in view of the urgency of the situation and the necessity for immediate action."

And all without my knowledge! Wilhelm raged. Because they are afraid I shall refuse! The best hope of removing or restricting the British Blockade is still to work for strong diplomatic protests from the United States! All at once he saw his escape. He had one potent ally whose views the Navy would be forced to accept. "How can I give my consent until I have consulted the Minister of Marine?" he asked. "My decision will depend upon his."

For a second von Pohl could not hide his satisfaction and Wilhelm instantly realized the trap that had been laid for him. Von Pohl had not mentioned Tirpitz in his list. "The Grand Admiral has already notified his agreement to the proposal, Your Imperial Majesty," he said.

"How can that be?" Wilhelm exclaimed. "He has always been amongst the strongest opponents of submarine warfare!"

"Opinions change with altered circumstances, sir," von Pohl said smoothly. "I can assure you Grand Admiral von

Tirpitz deeply regrets his former attitude and in fact is waiting with a suggested form of declaration for the Imperial consent and signature."

On the foredeck of the giant flagship S.M.S. *Friedrich der Grösse*, the ship's company was drawn up, with bands and a large detachment of marines, facing the huge muzzles of her forward twelve-inch guns. Some distance in front of them, in two rows parallel to the line of the guns, were the captains of the Submarine Flotilla. Schwieger stood in the front row, between his close friend Max Valentiner and Otto Hersing. They were all in Number One uniform, with decorations and black silk stocks under their wing collars.

For hours the cheering and reverberations of the guns had echoed across the water, growing louder and fading again as the pinnace sailed up and down the lines. Every now and then Max had muttered, "Why can't we fall out? Go on—ask Bauer if we can fall out for a glass of beer." Schwieger stifled a smile and glanced at the broad back of Fregattenkapitän Bauer, commandant of the Third Submarine Flotilla, who stood in front of them, his hands clasped firmly behind his waist. But Max was silent now in the expectant hush that had fallen.

Then came the rising note of the whistle and Schwieger braced himself with the others, at the same moment as the resounding stamp of the ship's company springing to attention and the slap as the marines presented arms. The bands began the Imperial anthem and Schwieger chanced another look to the side. There was a stir among the flag officers and suddenly they were saluting and von Tirpitz was stepping forward. And the Kaiser himself appeared. Everyone else, even Tirpitz, was dwarfed by the power of his personality. Schwieger could feel it from where he stood, in the rush of excitement and involuntary racing of his pulse. He heard Max breathe out beside him and knew he felt it, too.

Seeing the Kaiser moving toward them, the crew's emotions spilled over and, without waiting for orders, they burst into spontaneous cheers. Their officers' shouted commands were drowned by the music and the roaring voices. Not a man broke rank, but they hurled their caps in the air and opened their throats, until the officers gave up and joined them, cheering the hope and inspiration of the Reich.

At the naked display of affection and loyalty, Wilhelm paused. The cheers became louder when they saw him smile and blink the wetness from his eyes. Many were sobbing as they cheered, and Prince Heinrich stood aside to let his Imperial brother go on alone.

His pace even, Wilhelm strode past the beetling gray turret of the forward guns, and stopped still when his view of the foredeck widened. There in front of him, young, alert, erect as ramrods, were his U-boat commanders. His young hawks, his seahawks. Hersing he saw and, at the end of the front row, retiring, boyish Weddigen. And Schwieger he recognized. And Kophamel, who had served in the U 1, the very first. And Hansen who captained the newest, largest of all submarines, the U 41. And all the others whose faces he knew, whose hands he had shaken and of whom the Fleet and the Fatherland were so justly proud. There was only one gesture he could make and the tumultuous cheering redoubled as he saluted his hawks.

Chapter 6

THE TENSION THAT FILLED THE FLAG OFFICERS GROUPED IN the Commander-in-Chief's cabin was almost tangible.

Von Müller, the Naval Secretary, his lips compressed, stood with Prince Heinrich, who had withdrawn from the whole affair. Müller's bitterness increased. He had been duped, he knew, outmaneuvered and outgunned. With the whole Secretariat, he had thought Tirpitz safely under control. Now Müller realized that all the time he had appeared to accept it, the Grand Admiral had been quietly strengthening his influence over the key policymakers, until today. With no official appointment, simply through manipulation of events and opinions and the consent of his supporters, he had virtually taken command of the entire Navy.

Tirpitz and von Pohl were nearest the desk with Admiral Bachmann opposite them, watching Kaiser Wilhelm, who was seated reading a single typewritten sheet of paper.

Wilhelm read slowly, checking and weighing each word of the draft. His excitement and determination had intensified after a short conference with Pohl and Tirpitz. The bold stroke, the throwing down of the gauntlet, appealed to him, but it must be presented to the world in exactly the right manner, a plain statement of firm intention.

1. The waters surrounding Great Britain and Ireland, including the whole English Channel, are hereby declared to be a war zone. On and after the 18th of February, 1915, every enemy merchant ship found in the said war zone will be destroyed without its being always possible to avert the dangers threatening the crews and passengers on that account.
2. Even neutral ships are exposed to danger in the

war zone, as, in view of the misuse of neutral flags ordered on January 31 by the British Government and of the accidents of naval war, it is impossible to avoid attacks being made on neutral vessels in mistake for those of the enemy.

3. Northward navigation around the Shetland Islands, in the eastern waters of the North Sea and in a strip of not less than thirty miles width along the Netherlands coast is in no danger.

VON POHL
Chief of the
Naval Staff

Bachmann took the ebony pen from its stand, dipped its nib in the inkwell and tendered it to Kaiser Wilhelm, for him to countersign.

The U-boat commanders were summoned to the main wardroom. Schwieger had recovered from the climactic emotions of the review, which, like him, none of the others was ashamed to acknowledge. "I don't mind admitting," Max had said, "it makes the whole damn bloody thing worthwhile." No one had disagreed, and each had been conscious of the additional honor as they entered the presence.

Yet they had not been summoned to a reception, they realized at once. The flag officers in front of them were not smiling and welcoming, but grave. The first surprise was the announcement by the Fleet's Chief-of-Staff, Admiral Scheer, that the present Commander-in-Chief of the High Seas Fleet had been replaced by Admiral von Pohl, with Bachmann taking over the Naval Staff. Shortly after, the Kaiser joined them, with Tirpitz on his right and Pohl on his left. Schwieger watched Tirpitz to try to judge his expression, but the old man's face was inscrutable, his eyes hooded, as they took their position in the center of the line of flag officers. Kaiser Wilhelm was carrying a sheet of paper, which he read out. To be sent to all foreign governments, it was the declaration of the German War Zone.

The declaration caused a sensation, breaking even the disciplined calm of the submarine officers as a feeling of disbelief was followed by elation, then a deep seriousness. Schwieger's gaze was fixed on Tirpitz, understanding at last the reason for his recent interview. The Grand Admiral, by whatever bitter and tortuous path, had been brought to change his opinion on the lawfulness and permissibility of an unrestricted submarine war. Perhaps it was his sense of outrage at these orders issued to merchant captains by the British Admiralty that led to his conversion. But he had needed to learn Schwieger's reaction to estimate how the orders would be received by the Flotilla . . . Schwieger's breath shortened and a wave of dizziness passed over him at the dreadful, overpowering sense of responsibility. Many lives, many, would be lost and the seas become a graveyard. If his reaction had been different? The Grand Admiral's head had turned imperceptibly and he was looking back at him.

"There are grave problems," the Kaiser went on. "There is the question of neutral vessels, and the right to fire on them. I say to you, solemnly, it is not your concern or your government's responsibility but their own if they do not heed our warning that they proceed through these waters at their own risk." He looked slowly round the silent wardroom. "The enemy has left you no alternative but to sink without warning. Undeniably, this will mean considerable loss of life in his merchant service. Although technically belligerents, they are still human beings. And I know you will do what you can to save them." He began to turn away as though he had finished, yet hesitated, wrestling with a thought. His voice was low. "The counter blockade is the first priority. If you cannot save them . . . then it cannot be helped."

Schwieger's whole body stiffened. He had heard himself speaking, his very words to von Tirpitz. The Grand Admiral was still watching him with what might have been compassion; then it was replaced by a trace of a smile which said as clearly as if he had spoken, "Well done, my boy. Thank you."

With several others, when he left the flagship, Schwieger went to the garrison church. He had seldom felt more in need of a few minutes of quiet. He did not pray, for no forms of prayer seemed appropriate. Yet the calm of the little building had its effect, isolated in its grounds from the noisy hilarity of the public holiday and the crowds in the streets.

His thoughts were jumbled. Principally they were of the coming campaign. No one could guess what it would mean. The proclamation would begin to operate in exactly two weeks time, when the war zone came into being.

It had not escaped him that, if the campaign was successful, he was a made man. The Grand Admiral was not ungenerous and had already taken an interest in his career. It was not enough merely to work hard and to wait for promotion as one's seniority increased with the years. In wartime, one could take sudden strides. Especially if one was already in favor.

He had always been ambitious, for his own sake and his family's. And what point was there in being in the service if one did not make one's mark in it, leave a name? But he had to confess this preoccupation with promotion was more recent, as recent as yesterday and the day before. It was not something he wanted to think about here, in the chapel, but like all thoughts he tried to drive away, it only became more insistent.

Anneliese. It was pure animal instinct, perhaps for both of them. But she was seldom far from his mind. Yesterday she had missed her afternoon rehearsal to be with him and, in the evening, he had made an excuse to Rudolph and met her again after the theater, alone. They had both been anxious in case Rudi turned up, looking for Dora. It would have been difficult, embarrassing to refuse an invitation to join them. Instead they had hurried back to her top-floor room. She had food and wine prepared, but they touched none of it. They had made love at once, not even reaching the bed, and lain in each other's arms all night, not sleeping. Dozing, and loving again, unable to exhaust their passion.

His feelings for her were as confused as his thoughts. She was not from his world. They had little or nothing in common. In the intervals, the moments of languor, they had talked. Trivia. Of her home and parents, childhood. Singing lessons and the unglamorous, tawdry reality of the theater. Yet she wanted no other life. He had not offered her one, hardly spoken of his, and not at all of his family. It was a despicable evasion, an insult to her that he could not. She neither noticed nor seemed to mind. Part of her appeal was that everything for her existed in the present, little past and certainly no future. Now. And that was what he needed, in a handful of days stolen from the war.

Yet even more despicable was his envy when she spoke of others. Lying beside him, holding him, she talked of his friends and comrades with such devotion, such awe, as though she were reaching out to them through him. He had never before been conscious of his fifth or sixth place in the list of aces, hardly thought of it. Hersing had his picture splashed across every front page after each kill. And Hansen and Weddigen only had to sink a trawler to be— He stopped himself, disgusted by his automatic envy. He would not let himself think of their courage and skill in such cheap terms! But they were ahead of him. He was judged by it. Many things were affected by it, promotion, the pride of his crew. All ships in the navy competed to be best, to be first, so why not submarines? How many you could bring down, Tirpitz had said, a different kind of game, and the open season began in two weeks time.

Anneliese would be—where did she say?—Dresden, then Münster, Oldenburg and Bremen. He would be God knows where, the Irish Sea, the Hebrides, south of the Channel. The U 20 was more demanding than a woman; only by thinking of her, he was back on board, and the full meaning of what he had heard today swept over him. The counter blockade was no less than a direct challenge to England's rule of the seas, and it was to be undertaken not by another fleet filling the horizon with warships, but by a tiny flotilla of U-boats, his flotilla. His sense of comradeship stretched out to all his friends, all his superiors and those who served under him. No group counted only in hundreds had been given such a responsibility since Leonidas and his Spartans held the pass of Thermopylae against the full might of the Persians.

He had promised to spend the late evening and the night with Anneliese, but she would understand. The wolfpack gained strength and courage from drawing together. He needed his comrades-in-arms around him. The fear that had nearly destroyed him had receded, replaced in the front of his mind by the warmth and fulfillment of Anneliese's body, yet it was still somewhere, waiting, like a spider in the darkest corner of its web. How could he feel envious of Weddigen and Hersing? So much of his courage was inspired by theirs, their devotion to duty and disregard of danger, and he honored them. As he hoped they honored him.

Some of his friends had left, others were leaving. He rose, bowed his head toward the altar and followed them.

* * *

Alfred Booth had often heard of Captain Turner's obstinacy, which was legendary, but had never personally come up against it. It was exasperating in the extreme. He had an early evening train to catch, to take him to London for a very important meeting tomorrow at the Board of Trade, and here he was arguing, *arguing*, with a Company employee! He fixed Turner with a look that usually ended opposition in the boardroom at once, but the Captain merely gazed back with that maddeningly dogged expression unchanged. They were in the spacious day cabin of the Captain's quarters immediately under the *Lusitania*'s bridge. He had thought it would save time and prove his willingness to cooperate if he came here rather than hold the meeting at the Cunard offices; instead it had given Turner the moral advantage. "I'm aware there undoubtedly are problems," Booth said. "It is only to be expected under present conditions."

"Nothing that can't be taken care of," Turner said.

Booth saw with irritation that he had taken up his blackthorn pipe and was patting his pockets for matches. His manners were as blunt as his accent, with its flat, northern vowels. "It may not be quite so simple," Booth told him. "Just what exactly do you find wrong?"

"It was in my report. There's various things, but most important, the Chief Engineer has discovered a malfunction in the low pressure turbine. And the standard of seamanship of the crew, from what I've seen, is deplorable."

"It is very difficult to get experienced men these days."

"Granted," Turner nodded. He put his pipe in his mouth and opened his matchbox. "But you can't sail a vessel this size properly with a two-thirds crew and half of them not even Able Seamen."

"We're making every effort to give you the best men available," Booth said, exasperatedly. "As I promised. Those other matters are not essential defects. They can be dealt with at any time."

"Best if it's done now."

"Good Lord, Captain," Booth protested, "don't you know there's a war on?"

Turner was about to strike a match. He paused and took the pipe from his mouth. "Well now, I've been chased into Queenstown by U-boats," he said quietly. "I have a son in France waiting to get his head blown off by a shell. Another in the Merchant Marine waiting to get his arse blown off by a torpedo. I'd say I was as aware of the war as the next man."

As soon as he had spoken, Booth knew he had made a mistake. He was more conciliatory. "I'm sorry. I take that back, Captain. There's been a lot of pressure on us lately." He lowered his voice. "We have a great responsibility at this time, all of us. The *Lusitania*, as much as any other ship in our fleet, is essential to the war effort. We must maintain delivery of supplies."

"That's very true," Turner agreed. He had struck a match and sucked on his pipe as he lit it. "I've been looking at the cargo manifests. I'm not surprised Captain Dow was uneasy on his last crossing, not with her bottom pumped full with a hundred thousand gallons of diesel oil, and his passengers sitting on top of it."

"There was absolutely no danger," Booth said.

Turner blew out his match. "I wouldn't like to have lit my pipe down there . . . And what all that liquid sloshing about did to her stability I hate to think. Then there's the ammunition, a couple of thousand cases of it."

"Again, no danger," Booth assured him. "It is nonexplosive in bulk. That was all checked and double-checked before it was allowed to be transported by rail in the United States. Besides, think of the contribution it's making."

"Very considerable, I'm sure," Turner said. "But you see, all these matters are your concern, Mr. Booth. Naturally I'm sympathetic to the war effort, but my first concern has to be my passengers. That's our boast, and our promise to them—that we've never lost a ship. It's a promise I honor and live by. The moment they step aboard my ship, they become my responsibility, not just to see them comfortable and fed and entertained, but above all to set them down safely at their destination. That's our duty, if you like, the only reason we're here. And it still must be, war or no war." It was an unusually long speech for him, and he tossed his

99

head almost in apology when he finished. He frowned at the bowl of his pipe and took out another match.

"Yes, of course, you're completely right, Captain Turner," Booth admitted. "We have a tradition to maintain, since we have decided to keep the *Lusitania* in service."

"What about the element of risk?"

"They calculate it as minimal," Booth said. "She can outstrip any surface raider the enemy has and, if you think how she's constructed, she has little to fear from submarines. Torpedo damage in any section can be isolated, without affecting her sailing ability in the slightest."

Turner nodded. Unlike the unlucky *Titanic*, which had sunk on her maiden voyage, filling with water when her side was gashed by a giant iceberg, damage to any section of the *Lusitania* could be contained at the touch of an electric switch and the other watertight compartments would keep her afloat. "Still," he pointed out, "with passengers' lives involved, we don't want to take even the least extra risk."

"Absolutely not," Booth agreed. Even as he said it, he realized the argument had come back to the beginning and that he had made another mistake. From the tilt of Turner's head, he knew that the Captain was aware of it, too. Booth sighed and gave in. "Very well. I'll do what I can to get you some more experienced men. And you'd better carry out what repairs and checks are needed."

"Very good, sir," Turner said, as though it had been Booth's suggestion all along. He rose with Booth and helped him into his dark overcoat.

Booth picked up his hat and briefcase from the table. "Only the most essential, mind," he warned. "Anything that can't be completed within seven or eight days must be left to another time. We have government contracts to fulfill, you know. Now, if you'll forgive me, I have a train to catch."

Turner was not fully satisfied, but could tell he had got all the concessions he was going to for the moment. He stood his pipe against the holder in the ashtray and moved to the door. Hanging on a stand beside it was his white-topped cap with gold braid on the visor, next to his bowler hat. He took the bowler.

Good God, Booth thought, so it's true! Bowler Bill. Turner had been given the nickname because of his custom of wearing the bowler and not his cap, except when he was on the bridge. Set squarely on his head, it looked fairly odd above his long-skirted, double-breasted uniform coat with the four broad bands of gold round each cuff.

As they walked toward the lifts, Booth could not help noticing that already the *Lusitania* was looking sprucer and more like her prewar self. Turner had put every available man to work on the decks and superstructure, cleaning, painting and polishing. They could start taking pride in her again. "I'm glad she's looking so well," Booth said approvingly. "We may be carrying a smaller number of passengers, but among them there's probably a higher percentage of really important ones."

They had reached the lifts. The captain's steward had gone ahead and was holding one open for them. As they went down, Booth saw Turner frown. "Is there something wrong?" he asked.

Turner shook his head. "Not exactly. I was just thinking, with so much more to worry about, extra watches and so on, I'll have less time to spend on the passengers. I'll have to leave a fair amount of the socializing to the First Officer."

"Is that unavoidable?" Booth queried.

"I'm afraid so. There's fewer of us on the bridge, so we'll have to double up, take longer spells."

"I see." Booth was thoughtful. It was petty, of course, in the circumstances, yet many passengers would feel slighted if they thought the captain was avoiding or ignoring them. "There are bound to be complaints. What can we do?"

A lot of damned nonsense, Turner thought. He smiled. "What we need is a deputy, an assistant captain to take care of the social side." To his surprise, he saw Booth look at him with a touch of new respect.

"A deputy," Booth said, weighing it in his mind. "What a splendid idea! There'd have to be no doubt who was in command, of course. We'd call him a—a Staff Captain. Yes. I'll see if I can come up with the right man. You'd have to approve him, after all."

I've made his day, Turner told himself. If he finds the right diplomatic type with polished manners and a proper accent.

* * *

101

The Naval Officers' Club was usually well attended, but on the day of the review most ships held parties and dinners in their mess rooms, and the U-boat commanders had the club's main salon more or less to themselves. The earlier solemnity had given way to a sense of excitement and animation. There were few opportunities for so many of them to be together like this and the atmosphere was stimulating, an impromptu celebration, although there were some who still stood silent and apart, preoccupied.

Schwieger found Max Valentiner by the long side table. Max had become impatient with the waiters and was popping the cork from a bottle of champagne with his thumbs. Schwieger smiled. "I thought you were longing for a glass of beer?"

"Beer?" Max laughed. "Not today, young Walther. Today the enemy is delivered into our hands, saith the All Highest, and we drink only champagne." The cork flew off with a bang and he poured the spouting wine into a triangle of glasses he had placed ready, scarcely spilling a drop, to applause from other friends round them. "Here, young Walther. Waldemar. Here, Karl." He handed out the glasses.

"A toast," someone suggested. "What shall we drink to?"

Max was sniffing his tall glass, savoring the flick of moisture as the bubbles burst under his nose. "Here's first to the Kaiser." He sipped. "And to the Navy and the Flotilla." Another sip. "And here's to us!" He tilted his head and upended his glass into his open mouth. The others copied him, choking and laughing as the champagne bubbled back, soaking their cheeks and chins.

"What do you think, Max?" Schwieger asked.

"Very little," Max said. "Mainly about fried potatoes, feather beds, plump women and wine." He saw that Schwieger was serious. "Of course that's wishful thinking. And it's going to get even more wishful in the next few months. We're going to have our work cut out, young Walther." He shrugged. "Maybe, just to survive."

Fregattenkapitän Bauer was passing and stopped while a white-tunicked waiter topped up Schwieger's glass. "Not too much of that, now," Bauer warned, only half joking. "I expect you back and fit tomorrow."

Schwieger was brought up short. "Tomorrow? That could be awkward." He had sent a note to the theater for Anneliese, promising to make up for this evening by spending the next day with her.

Bauer frowned. "You have a meeting?" he asked. "Official?" He was one of the few people who knew of the occasional interviews at the Ministry.

Schwieger saw the Fregattenkapitän's mistaken assumption and hesitated. "It would be difficult to get out of," he said carefully.

Bauer nodded. "All right. I'll get Rosenberg to take first patrol." He lowered his voice. "See if you can put a word in for us, eh? Time some of those newer boats were steered in our direction." He smiled and moved on.

One of the others called to Max. As he turned away, Schwieger looked round the salon, recognizing nearly everyone, although some of the old faces had gone, victims of ramming or of the nets and mines. Claus Hansen waved and came to join him. Popular, with his baby face and sunny manner, he already had his own special place in U-boat mythology. The week after Weddigen's spectacular exploit four months ago, Hansen had achieved another, of a different kind but just as epoch-making. In one of the old kerosene burners with a top speed of fourteen knots on the surface and eight submerged, he had set off across the North Sea and along the English coast on an endurance test that lasted for fifteen days and covered an incredible 1,700 miles, in a voyage right round the British Isles. Between them they had alerted the naval authorities to the undreamed-of capabilities of their underwater craft. A whole new school of tactical planning, all the rapid developments of the last four months had come from them. And from Hersing, who had sunk the first British ship, a 3,200-ton cruiser, in the opening days of the war.

"You're still with us, then," Hansen smiled.

"Just."

They moved on together toward the corner by one of the high windows, where a group had formed round Otto Hersing, schoolboys round the school captain. He was slim and very self-contained, his face narrow, more than any of the others like the hawk of the Kaiser's imagination. Stocky Karl Georg was saying, "So it was you who brought back those British Admiralty papers? Where'd you pick them up?"

"In Liverpool Bay." It was said casually, and some might

have done so for effect. But not Hersing. Where most commanders operated in the North Sea or just south of the Channel, he took his U 21 all the way round England to a position outside her main port.

"Which route did you use?" Schwieger asked.

"Through the Channel and round the south coast." Hersing paused. "Thanks for the warning about the net."

"It gave you no trouble?"

"I located two sets of buoys," Hersing told him. "Then I waited for low tide at night and went through between them, on the surface."

There was laughter.

"Did you get into the Mersey River?" Hansen asked.

"No," Hersing smiled. "I was tempted—but I didn't have a British pilot."

Georg chuckled. "They couldn't have had any idea you were there."

"I sent them a warning."

"How?"

Hersing paused. "I was reconnoitering, having a look at the coast farther north, and came to a promontory with a narrow island in front of it, a place called Barrow."

"I remember it," Hansen said. "There's some docks."

"Yes," Hersing confirmed, "quite extensive, with an airfield beside them. There were flying machines on the ground and in the air, freighters loading and unloading at the quay. All very peaceful, no one on guard or expecting a visitor. I thought I ought to leave a calling card. So I surfaced and gave them a few rounds with my deck gun."

Schwieger laughed with the others. "That stirred them up, I imagine."

"A bit," Hersing admitted. "I could still hear their batteries and machine guns when I was miles away."

"And then you picked up these orders," Georg persisted.

"Yes."

"What did you make of them?" Hansen asked.

Hersing clearly did not wish to be drawn. "Same as you, I should think. Or any of you."

"It's a question of morality," Georg insisted.

"Morality doesn't come into it," said a quiet voice.

Schwieger looked round and saw Weddigen just behind

him. "Hello, Otto," he smiled. Weddigen touched his arm and pressed it as he stepped to beside him in the circle, a slight, good-looking man, composed and alert. The quality one was most quickly aware of in him was his economy of movement, his stillness.

"What do you mean, it doesn't come into it?" Georg demanded.

"You've read those British orders," Weddigen said. "They change everything. And we've been given our own orders— to fight the Blockade by sending as many of the enemy to the bottom as possible."

"It's not really so clear-cut, though, Otto," Lepsius, one of the older commanders, argued quietly. "There's still a question of personal responsibility."

"Oh, come on, we're not country gentlemen!" Hansen broke in. "You'll be saying next, we don't shoot sitting ducks."

The laughter was uneasy.

"I know what he means," Weddigen said. "It's against one's sporting instincts to go for the helpless, unsuspecting targets when there's bigger and more dangerous game."

"Unfortunately, the bigger game is staying too close to its lair nowadays," Hersing commented. "We have to take the only targets that offer themselves."

"The thing is, we won't know what we're shooting at any more," Georg said, uncomfortably. "When you board a ship, if it's carrying contraband, you sink it. Sinking without warning, it could be medical supplies, books, children's toys, for heaven's sake, we just won't know."

"Innocent cargo this time, contraband the next," Schwieger said. "The important thing is to knock out the ship."

There was a murmur of agreement. The group had grown, with more from the rest of the room joining in, listening.

"My query is, it will cause a great deal of bitterness against us. Will its value to us be worth that?" Feldkirchner asked. Commander of the U 17, he had sunk the first merchant vessel of the war. "I mean, we started with twenty-eight U-boats and we've lost six or seven. Say, we now have twenty-one in service. At any time, a third are in dock for repairs and overhaul. Another third are on coastal defense. That leaves a third for distant patrol. Seven boats—that's all that will be in operation at any one time in all the thousands of square miles of this war zone."

The commanders looked at one another in silence for a moment, sobered by the odds.

"There's another fourteen of the new model on the stocks!" Hansen protested. "In the next month some will be launched!"

"All right," Feldkirchner conceded. "Instead of seven, in a month eight or ten boats will be available to patrol the war zone, and that's our whole counter blockade. What can it achieve?"

"Everything!" Schwieger had spoken before he could stop himself. The others were surprised by his certainty, and he explained quickly, "I've been expecting something like this, so I've been thinking about it."

"Thinking what?" Hersing asked.

"At the present rate, each boat on patrol accounts for five to ten ships," Schwieger said. "Attacking without warning, torpedoes for larger vessels, the deck gun for smaller ones, the rate of sinking would be enormously increased. Each patrol lasts twenty to twenty-five days. One cannot guarantee to sink a ship a day in that period, but at a conservative estimate, in an unrestricted campaign, the rate of sinking for each patrol should be at least doubled."

The others were gazing at him, gripped by his precise analysis.

"Lieber Herr Gott," Hansen breathed. "Walther's right."

Weddigen had taken Schwieger's arm again and leaned on it to ease the weight on his leg. "Of course he is," he agreed. "Eight to ten U-boats on patrol, each taking care of sixteen to twenty merchantmen. That's a hundred and sixty sunk in a month. There's not that many being built to replace them anywhere in the world. Inside six months we could destroy the entire British Merchant Fleet!"

"All the cargo ships of any size, at least," Hersing added. "In place of the stranglehold the English have tried to put on us, we'll have a double nelson on them."

The laughter was quick and free and Schwieger could sense the new excitement round him. All it had taken was to point out the obvious. The old Grand Admiral had guessed correctly. The hunt, the thrill of the chase, he could feel the anticipation infecting him as it had the others. Hersing was smiling to him, his narrow face alight.

"Understand me," Georg was pointing out, "I don't give a fart what happens to any English, but if there's doubt about a vessel's neutrality, we must still challenge."

One of the others said, "The government's announced to everyone that the declaration will come into effect in two weeks time. That's all the warning they'll get as far as I'm concerned."

On Schwieger's other side, Hansen was thoughtful. "Who'll be the first to chalk up a hundred ships?" he wondered, and grinned at the reaction. "I'll tell you one thing, we'll need proper gun crews now. And deck drill. When I come up, I'll want my deck gun manned within thirty seconds and loaded and firing in under a minute."

Weddigen noticed that Lepsius and Georg were still troubled. "Don't look so serious," he smiled. "It won't all be one-sided. The odds may be slightly in our favor, but there's still nets and mines, and they'll be sending out destroyers and torpedo boats to hunt us and protect their sea lanes. That will be the challenge. We'll have to take our chances at slipping past them."

Schwieger remembered his earlier thought. "Like wolves raiding the sheepfolds," he murmured.

"Like a wolfpack," Hersing agreed, smiling. The idea and the word appealed to him and he raised his glass. "To the Wolfpack!"

The others took it up and also raised their glasses. "The Wolfpack!"

After the toast, they began breaking up into smaller animated conversations. Weddigen rested his weight on his left leg and released Schwieger's arm. His expression was almost dreamy. "It's a challenge, a real challenge this time."

Hersing had moved nearer them and said, "I saw you limping, Otto. What's wrong?"

Weddigen shrugged. "We were tossed about a bit on my last trip, a couple of stray mines. I twisted my knee."

"Is it bad?"

"Bearable. I was going on leave, but . . . it won't be possible now."

"Did I hear you'd been transferred from the U 9?"

"Yes—more's the pity," Weddigen smiled. "They've given me one of the latest, the U 29, wider ranging, faster, more heavily armed. I pretend to be grateful, but I'll miss the old U 9. She was a lucky boat for me."

Lucky to have you as her commander, Schwieger thought. There's no one to compare.

"I'm glad to have a word with the two of you," Weddigen went on. He tapped his leg. "Having this made me think. In the Flotilla, we're allowed physical wounds and that's all. Yet the worst are the ones no one can see. We all know men, good men, who've cracked up a little and been dismissed."

"Makes me angry, that," Hersing muttered.

Schwieger had become taut. Were they talking about him? Had something been reported and were they warning him?

"I'm amazed it doesn't happen more often," Hersing continued. "And one thing is certain, the strain is going to get worse. More will crack up."

"Through no fault of their own," Weddigen stressed. "The human body and mind are just not meant to exist at such pressure. I'm thinking of submitting a report, a recommendation if you like, that all U-boat crews and commanders should be granted an official period of rest after every three or four tours of duty. And if at any other time commanders are aware of strain beginning to affect their efficiency, they should be able to apply for a rest period, to be granted as soon as practicable, with no disgrace. It's the only way to stop ourselves going to pieces. I was hoping to get some other people to support the recommendation."

"I'll sign it," Hersing promised. "It's the best idea I've heard in a long time."

"Thank you," Weddigen said. "What about you, Walther?"

"By all means," Schwieger assured him, and hesitated. "I agree particularly with the suggestion of an official rest period . . . since many would be reluctant, ashamed to admit there was anything wrong by applying for one."

"That's very true," Hersing said. "You can bear anything if you know it's not forever. Above all, there must be no disgrace attached."

"Yes," Weddigen answered. "Yes, I'll concentrate on that. Thank you both."

Lepsius and Hansen were trying to attract their attention.

Hersing moved to join them. Weddigen held back. He glanced up at Schwieger, half turned away, with an odd, almost wistful expression. "I envy you, Walther," he said quietly "I envy your certainty, your resolution."

He moved on and Schwieger stood still, watching him, then dropped his eyes to his empty glass to hide his shock. *Weddigen? Envied him?* The thought at first was disorienting, as if a rudder had suddenly snapped and he was adrift in strange currents. *Envied his certainty?* There was only one thing it could mean, and he did not want to accept it. He looked up and round the group, slowly. Were they all the same, all of them, even Hersing? All hiding an instability and fear they were afraid to admit? At least his screen was secure, since even Otto Weddigen had not seen behind it. Perhaps they had all developed their own protective screens, just like his. He realized that the thought, instead of alarming him as it might have, was curiously steadying. What they were asked to do was more than human and they needed an ideal, an inhuman ideal, to live up to, a pattern to follow. He looked at his fellow commanders, his comrades, for possibly the first time as individuals and marveled at the reserves of determination and gallantry they had found inside themselves, to seem and to become what they were. He felt released, nearly lightheaded, at the thought that he was not alone, that he was one of them. Weddigen envied him . . .

It was growing dark outside. Stewards came to draw the long curtains at the windows. He looked round and saw that Rudolph Zentner had come in and was making for him.

"Hello there," Rudolph smiled. "I thought you'd be here."

"Where have you been?" Schwieger asked.

"Out in the streets, enjoying the celebrations. They've all gone mad out there. Every U-boat man is a hero today."

"They cheered you on your way?"

"It was a triumphal progress," Rudolph told him, and they laughed. "By the way, I ran into Dora. You remember? The little singer, Anneliese's friend."

"I remember," Schwieger said casually. "How was she?"

Rudolph grinned. "Very welcoming, in the expurgated version. Briefly, their company is giving a party tonight on stage after the performance, and we're invited."

Schwieger shook his head. "I don't think I can come."

"Why not?" Rudolph objected. "It'll be the best fun in town. Besides, I promised. You don't want to disappoint them, do you?"

Schwieger had said he would have dinner with Max and Otto and one or two others. Rudolph could join them. Tonight was for his friends and he had put Anneliese out of his mind. Yet the thought of how easy it would be to be with her, of her perhaps waiting for him, was enticing. He must have dinner with his friends—but afterwards? "We'll see, Rudi," Schwieger said.

There was laughter farther down the room. Waldemar Kophamel and Max Valentiner had built a pyramid of champagne glasses, tiers of them tapering up from a base about three feet wide. It was exactly under one of the electric chandeliers and stretched up the full height of a man. Max was standing on a chair and they moved to the edge of the crowd round him to see what he was doing. He was holding a magnum of champagne.

"What is it?" Rudolph asked, fascinated.

"Watch," Feldkirchner told him. "Kophamel bet he couldn't do it and, if he does, has to pay for the champagne."

Georg unhooked a gold-hilted ceremonial sword from a wall display and passed it up to Max. He saluted Kophamel with it, then brought it down and with one slash severed the neck of the bottle. The commanders nearest him laughed and ducked as champagne spouted over them. Max handed back the sword and began to pour very carefully into the topmost, single glass. As it filled, the champagne spilled over and ran down the sides into the three glasses below. Just as they began to overflow, the magnum ran out, but Kophamel had uncorked another magnum and passed it up, taking the empty one.

"Keep it coming, keep it coming!" Max insisted.

More commanders took up bottles and opened them, holding them ready. There was a breathless, excited tension. The champagne was trickling over the fourth tier and into the one below, like a small fountain. Max began to pour more quickly and the stream became more constant, trickling, splashing, bubbling down and filling layer after layer as it spread out. The sparkle in the wine caught and reflected more sparkles from the chandelier, until the fountain almost seemed alight itself, a glittering, jeweled cascade of champagne, utterly artificial and unimaginably beautiful.

It reached the lowest tier of all, oozing over into it and filling the glasses standing on the floor. Everyone in the circle cheered and applauded, and Kophamel raised both arms in surrender.

Max lifted the topmost glass from the pyramid and presented it to him with a bow. "You're paying for it, Waldemar," he reminded him, grinning, "so you might as well have the first drink."

Schwieger and Rudolph moved in with the others, laughing. "I meant to ask," Rudolph said. "This war zone—the declaration, what will it mean?" He was handed two glasses and gave one to Schwieger, who did not answer at first. Rudolph looked at him and was puzzled to see him gazing at the wine in his glass. Then Schwieger raised the glass and smiled.

"It means we're going to have some sport," he said.

Chapter 7

WOODROW WILSON HAD HAD MISGIVINGS ABOUT THE MEETing before it began and now the faint churning of his stomach proved that his presentiment had been a true one. His dyspepsia had developed over the last five years, since he resigned as President of Princeton to plunge into the more turbulent world of politics, and had accelerated with the cares of office, until now his digestion was as sensitive as a barometer, reacting to tension in the air.

William Jennings Bryan, his Secretary of State, sat opposite him, upright and massive, his face as pale as the bust of an ancient Roman senator, craggy and clean-shaven. His large hands lay in his lap, joined at the fingertips, the whiteness of the tips betraying the force with which he pressed them together, although he strove to appear relaxed.

Watching them from the side was the State Department's Counsellor, Robert Lansing. An expert in international law, he was a handsome, cultivated man in his early fifties, with dark eyes and carefully groomed iron-gray hair. He waited deferentially for a moment for the Secretary to continue, then leaned forward. "I am sure Mr. Bryan is correct in his assessment of public opinion," he said in his precise eastern accent. "The fact is, Mr. President, that many people, especially in the business fraternity, take great exception to the British interpretation of 'stop and search.' "

"American-owned and American-chartered vessels have an inalienable right to sail and trade wherever they wish on the surface of the globe, without let or hindrance," Bryan growled. Even when he spoke quietly, his voice was resonant, rich with the accents of the Midwest, the voice of an orator.

Wilson refused to rise to the implied criticism. "That is a

right we have maintained," he said. "And shall still maintain with the utmost determination."

"Yet the British go their own self-centered way!" Bryan insisted. "They issue their sanctimonious answers to our Notes, promising to correct their abuses, promises they never intend to keep. Protests, Mr. President? We might as well go whistle down the wind!"

"Is it or is it not a fact," Wilson pointed out, "that the British authorities have not yet confiscated a single American cargo of any kind without making full payment?"

"It matters not!" Bryan declared. "Their money cannot blind us to their obvious twofold aim, to wage war on hapless women and children inside Germany by denying them the necessities of life, and at the same time to cripple our overseas trade!"

Wilson coughed. "The first of your assumptions appears to be a regrettable fact, Mr. Secretary," he said with surprising mildness. "The second, I would consider hardly tenable. Take, for example, the adverse effect of the Blockade on our cotton exports. Now, although raw cotton is not only of use in the manufacture of clothing, but also an essential ingredient in the making of explosives, as soon as Colonel House informed the British Foreign Secretary of the serious loss to our economy of our cotton sales, Sir Edward gave us his assurance, his categorical assurance, that it would never be placed on the prescribed list. And Britain now allows the free import of raw cotton into Germany. An example of magnanimity and fair dealing between nations."

At the mention of House's name, Bryan had stiffened and looked away. He bitterly resented the President's reliance on the Colonel as his guide and confidential adviser on all questions, internal and external, particularly his employment as Mr. Wilson's roving peace ambassador to Europe. Everyone knew of House's "secret" mission, even as they knew of the failure of Bryan's own peace initiatives. The pleas he had made to the warring nations to cease fighting while their dispute was settled by arbitration had either been turned down or ignored, and his own proposed trip to Europe to appeal to the heads of governments in person had been vetoed by the President, on the grounds that he could not be spared. Yet he was a man torn by his convictions and the desire to be fair and statesmanlike. He fought manfully against the resentments inside himself, and in his long nightly prayers pleaded for enlightenment.

His heavy, lowered head revealed none of his thoughts, no clue except a tightening of his thin-lipped mouth. Wilson and Counsellor Lansing waited some moments for his reaction, and again Lansing stepped in. "The cotton guarantee is most welcome, Mr. President," he said slowly, "yet in real terms it amounts to very little, since most shippers already have Allied contracts and the rest don't choose to take the risk of something going wrong. In view of the danger of mines and submarines, no company will insure freight that has to cross the British war zone."

Wilson nodded and cleared his throat, which felt constricted. A dull ache was building up in his left side.

The simple fact was that the United States possessed virtually no Merchant Marine. Millions of tons of shipping, but all plying coastal and inland waters. Incredible though it was, her actual number of ocean-going vessels was less than twenty, and more than half of them passenger liners. Nearly all her vast overseas trade was carried in foreign ships, far the largest percentage of them British. Before August 1914, German merchant ships had called regularly at American ports also. On the day of the declaration of war, many were loading and unloading, everywhere from Boston to New Orleans, including liners provisionally armed as cruisers. The liners had been interned automatically under international law, while the rest were trapped, unable to return home because of the British warships waiting for them just outside U.S. territorial limits. Theoretically they could load up with goods and sail off, taking their chances, but as Lansing said, few shippers could be found who were willing to risk it.

"None of this would have happened if my proposal for an embargo had been adopted last fall," Bryan observed pointedly.

"Well, it was not!" Wilson snapped. "And harking back to it is neither helpful nor relevant."

Bryan's fingers slipped together and clenched. Mr. Wilson could not help his waspish, schoolmasterish tone after so

114

many years of academic life, he knew, but it was hard not to feel resentment.

Wilson had been unable to prevent himself from showing his irritation. William Jennings Bryan was an uncomfortable bedfellow, and becoming increasingly so. Yet the only way to coexist was to treat him with unfailing courtesy. The Bryan Democrats were a powerful subsection of the party. "I'm sorry," he said.

Lansing said, "We cannot prevent the British from carrying out whatever action they deem necessary. We can only hope that good sense will prevail."

Wilson was silent for a time, thinking. Only last night, lying in bed unable to sleep, searching for a solution, he had realized that the war between the United States and England during the Madison administration had its origins in an almost identical situation, the blockade of Europe by the British fleet during England's struggle against Napoleon and the indignation of America at interference with her shipping. "It occurred to me," he told them, "that Madison and I are the only two Princeton men who have become President. The circumstances of the War of 1812 now run parallel. I sincerely hope they will not go further." He paused again and his voice was so low they could scarcely hear it. ". . . I hope I shall be wiser."

Joe Tumulty was waiting when the meeting broke up. The President's private secretary was a burly, fair-haired young man, with a round Irish face and blue eyes. Tumulty admired the President, just short of idolatry, although not blind to his occasional intolerance and waspishness. He knew that behind the public aloofness was a shy, engaging man, devoted to his family. The President had stopped in the corridor for a final word with Counsellor Lansing. Tall and spare, he kept his left hand pressed lightly against his side, which meant his dyspepsia was troubling him. Which meant the meeting hadn't gone too well. It was disturbing. As a supporter of Irish nationalism, Tumulty had no objection to the spectacle of the English getting their come-uppance, but not at the cost of American neutrality.

The President was coming toward him, his long face creased in thought. He stopped and took off his noseglasses and rubbed with his finger and thumb at the small indentations

115

they left on the bridge of his thin, prominent nose. "Anything, Joe?" he asked.

"Nothing that can't wait, sir," Tumulty told him. "There's a light lunch ready for you, if you'd care to have it now."

Wilson shook his head. "No, thank you. I'll have something, maybe a bit later. I'm going up for a while."

Tumulty walked with him to the private stairs. He only ever entered the First Family's domestic quarters by invitation.

Wilson patted his arm. "You mind the store, Joe," he said, with a slight smile. "I need time to think, to sort things out in my mind. I don't know how long, so I don't want to be disturbed. On no account. Understand? No calls, nothing."

Tumulty watched him go up. The President's posture was normally erect and braced, but his shoulders were beginning to stoop with tiredness. As his gray eyes had been tired. It was not rest he was going for, although he needed it. It was prayer and long hours of thought. Only the ignorant could ever envy him his position.

In his first days in the White House, Woodrow Wilson had seen it as a haven of peace, with its hundred rooms and spacious grounds where a man could think calmly and rationally at last, untroubled by passing clamor. The good wishes and hopes of the whole nation would flow there, encouraging and stimulating the Man at the center in his quiet endeavor to work for the advancement of the commonwealth.

It had not worked out that way. Nowhere in the whole mansion was safe from intrusion and interruption and he had slowly retreated from the historic rooms, making his own private bastion in a small study on the top floor. No one was permitted there except Colonel House, infrequently. He had filled it with mementos of his parents and family, of his early years in Virginia and Georgia, and his teaching days at Bryn Mawr and Princeton. Everywhere there was something to remind him of where he had come from, what he stood for and who he was.

He closed the door behind him with a sense of relief. The quietness and familiarity were immediately soothing. It was an overcast day and the room was fairly dark, its little windows looking out on to trees and the park.

He stopped as he reached the chair by the desk and went

down on his knees, as was his custom, his hands clasped under his bowed head, and asked for guidance in his thoughts and the blessing of continued peace for the people of America. He could never forget his boyhood in Georgia during the Civil War. His father's churchyard had been turned into a stockade for captured Yankee soldiers and the church itself into a hospital for the wounded. The blood and the screams of the maimed and dying. He prayed God that such scenes would never be repeated and that he might be spared to steer his country safely through the currents that constantly impelled it toward the maelstrom of war.

He rose, helping himself by leaning on the arm of the chair. At fifty-eight, his joints were beginning to stiffen. Not good. He'd have to take more exercise, make time for golf and walking.

As he sat, his eye caught the framed photograph of his wife. Ellen, dearest Ellen, her sensitive, sweet face. He was eternally grateful that at least for a year he had been able to make her First Lady.

His eyes were wet, remembering. Not a day passed but he longed for her. Everything was so much harder without her presence, and her sensible advice. And he had needed her at times to remind him he was only a man, and not infallible. He could still hear her voice at the dinner table, when he had been carried away, laying down the law to their guests, "Oh, Woodrow, you don't mean that." There was no one left to say that.

He had never made friends easily and, apart from his family, was a lonely man. There were few he could consider companions. Walter Page, but he was in England now. Tumulty was another, though much younger. And Mac. William Gibbs McAdoo, his son-in-law, the Secretary of the Treasury. He had been Wilson's campaign manager, tall and serious, a widower with adult children. He had made his name by forming the company that built the Hudson railroad tunnels under the North River. Wilson was shaken when Ellen had told him their daughter Eleanor had fallen in love with Mac, who was old enough to be her father. But they had married last spring and were devotedly happy. And Wilson had been glad of his son-in-law's understanding support in his own widowhood.

And there was Colonel House. No one except Ellen had

ever meant so much to him. They had first met when he had called on House at his New York hotel, as someone whose advice might be useful in the coming Presidential campaign. They had been staggered even at that first meeting by the similarity of their interests and outlook. He had sent House to Europe in the knowledge that any talks would be conducted as if he were there himself. But he missed him, his candid advice and the friendly admiration that was so much more reassuring than other people's flattery. Please God his efforts would be crowned with success.

Wilson's ambassadors, Page in London and Jimmy Gerard in Berlin, were cautiously optimistic and would give the Colonel any assistance needed. They were good men, the best, and any career diplomats who sneered at his choice of them for these demanding posts should learn of the wonders they performed daily in watching over U.S. interests. Their loyalty was unquestioned, and their obedience to his call for strict neutrality in thought and action.

He had to examine his own conscience on that. Could there be such a thing as pure and absolute neutrality? His father had been Scots-Irish, his mother English. His mind had been formed by Shakespeare, Scott and Dickens. He had never forgotten his first visit to England as a cure for overwork, a bicycling holiday to all the places he had read about. And that other holiday ten years later with Ellen and the girls, when they had taken a little house in the English Lake District to spend a magic summer in the countryside immortalized by his favorite poet, Wordsworth, worshiping in the church that contained the poet's tomb and drinking beer and gossiping in the local inn with the country people. It was hard to resist the appeal of those influences. Yet he also admired the industry, progressive advances and artistic genius of the German nation, and tried his utmost to show no favor.

The whole sickening business of the war exasperated him often. He could sympathize with those who said, let them get on with it. Let the corrupt old empires finish one another off, and good riddance. Walter Page had calculated that by the nineteen-thirties America would be the dominant world power. Now it was clear that, through the destruction of her only rivals, that position would be thrust upon her much sooner. And that responsibility. He prayed that she would be not only economically but morally ready to bear it.

But what if the United States was sucked into the war? All those young lives and all those millions of dollars that could be used for schools and hospitals, for better standards of living, they would all be poured away in armaments and uniforms and war machines. And the eyes of the nation were on Port Arthur and that one steamer sailing for Germany that could light the fuse.

Page wrote from London to tell him he was considered there to be pro-German. And the Berlin newspapers denounced him for allowing the sale of munitions to the Allies! He had accepted Lansing's advice that to refuse to sell supplies to either side would be a breach of neutral impartiality. He had to stand by that, whatever Secretary Bryan argued. At least, Bryan was one hundred percent American, unlike some of the pro-German senators. Or the pro-British ones, for that matter. It was a maze of thorns and pitfalls.

He had cabled to Walter Page at the London Embassy to use whatever influence he had with Prime Minister Asquith to urge restraint, yet it had to be coupled with the warning that America could permit no insult to her flag, her sovereignty or her honor. An impossible situation, and the anti-British Hearst press whipping up indignation, when what was needed was calmness and forbearance.

The knock at the door was so unexpected that he was startled for a moment. It was repeated, louder. One of his daughters? "Well, come in!" he called crossly.

The door was opened, to his surprise, by Joe Tumulty, who stood embarrassedly in the opening. "I'm sorry, Mr. President," he began.

"I told you I was on no account to be disturbed," Wilson said severely.

However, Joe was standing aside to make space for the taller, long-necked figure of William McAdoo to come past him. Mac nodded and Joe went out again, closing the door.

Wilson had gone cold. He immediately thought something must have happened to Eleanor, his daughter whom Mac had married. His son-in-law was looking so serious, his deeply lined face even more drawn than usual.

"I'm sorry to barge in," Mac said. "I've just been having lunch with Bill Flynn."

Wilson's eyebrows rose. Flynn was head of the Secret Service, a friend of McAdoo's. "Yes?"

Mac reached into an inside pocket. "Something had just come in." He took out a folded sheet of paper. "A report from one of our people in Berlin. Apparently, this is going to be announced at any moment."

Wilson took the paper and read it. The source had been deleted, but it was an advance warning of the declaration of the German war zone and the coming unrestricted submarine campaign. A note from Flynn confirmed that the source was reliable and, so far, accurate.

Wilson turned the paper back over into its fold and pressed it down. Germany had been on the point of winning herself a partner, but once again had changed the rules of the game. And he was not at all sure that he could honorably accept them. "I'd better have a word with Mr. Bryan," he said.

Chapter 8

"THEY ARE SUCH IDIOTS, THESE YANKEES," FRANZ VON
Papen muttered. The military attaché sat low in a leather
armchair, his long legs stretched out in front of him and
crossed elegantly at the ankles, so as not to spoil the knife-
edge crease in the narrow-cut trousers of his dark suit. "Of
course, one must remember how comparatively recently they
climbed down from the trees."

Boy-Ed laughed quietly. He was the naval attaché, assigned like von Papen to the German Embassy in Washington. Both were tall and faultlessly dressed, but unlike von
Papen, who was slim and intense, with haughty, patrician
features and prominent ears, Karl Boy-Ed was strongly built
and handsome, his expression frank and deceptively open.
Both men were educated, witty and well-bred, but the naval
attaché was a more welcome guest at the many clubs and
social evenings to which they were invited, in the capital
and in New York, their more usual base, since von Papen's
wit was often a little too biting and he was not so adept at
hiding his natural arrogance.

They met once a week in the luxurious captain's cabin of
the steamship *Vaterland*, interned at the Hamburg-Amerika docks at Hoboken. There they could report progress and
agree on any combined action, safe from prying eyes and
ears, for in addition to their social and liaison work at the
Embassy, they each controlled a section of the German intelligence service. Boy-Ed was largely responsible for sabotage and information-gathering at American ports and naval
installations, and for the secret coaling and provisioning of
German surface raiders in the Pacific and Atlantic through
U.S.-based freighters. Von Papen handled military fact-
gathering, the large-scale purchase of munitions and sup-

121

plies, sabotage of factories and railway lines, particularly those connecting the U.S. and Canada, and was commander of the huge number of German and Austro-Hungarian Americans who had volunteered for duty, if called upon, as reservists.

Boy-Ed was seated at the circular table, a large number of reports of cargo shipments loaded or waiting to be loaded on Allied merchant ships spread out in front of him. The reports were mainly from the crews of German ships stranded in New York Harbor, who kept watch for him on all docks and wharves. It was organized by the dock superintendents of the Hamburg-Amerika Line and merchant captains, as was the similar operation in all other U.S. ports.

Across the table from him, a young man was standing rigidly to attention. He was Richard Stegler, a Prussian naval reservist who had settled in New York. He had applied for his first citizenship papers just before the outbreak of war, but was still on the German reserve list and received orders to report to Captain Boy-Ed, to be informed that, since he could not get back to Germany, he was now a member of the espionage organization. He was employed in collecting and analyzing the cargo reports.

Von Papen levered himself up and moved to the side table to pour another drop of cognac into his coffee cup. One compensation for the tedium and squalor of the trip to Hoboken was that the captain's steward on the *Vaterland* made decent German coffee. "There's no problem about getting a passport for him," he said. "Ruroede or Wedell can arrange it. It will cost a hundred dollars."

Boy-Ed watched von Papen as he sipped his coffee. They worked well together, both having only one aim, victory by whatever means were necessary. Although military and naval attachés, their training was more for diplomatic and intelligence work. Boy-Ed was by far the more subtle and, although he admired his colleague's organizational abilities, there were many aspects of his own work which he kept to himself. As little as possible on paper and whatever might be incriminating locked up in the Embassy safes in Washington, technically German territory and invulnerable. He only hoped that von Papen was as careful.

Von Papen was taking up his light, stylish overcoat and bowler hat. "I shall leave first today," he said.

Von Papen came down the steamer's gangway and paused at its foot. His men were in place and one lit his pipe, as a sign that nothing suspicious had been noticed. He turned and walked round the dock, passing groups of apathetic German sailors and two or three longshoremen in caps and baggy lumberjackets watching some boys fishing.

Von Papen checked the ferries to see if there was one about to leave, and decided instead to take an electric car back through the river tunnel to New York. He climbed on and shouldered his way to a seat near the exit. Shortly after him, one of the longshoremen also boarded the car and stood holding a strap morosely, his head lowered, anonymous. He was Federal agent Frank Burke and, with frequent changes of appearance, he had been shadowing von Papen for days.

Richard Stegler was holding his glass tightly to stop his hands trembling. He had suspected nothing. Captain Boy-Ed had been friendly and complimentary, and it had taken him a few moments to realize what he was being ordered to do. Under the false name on the passport with which he would be provided, he was to book a passage on the British liner *Lusitania* for her next departure from New York. "To go where, sir?"

"To Liverpool," Boy-Ed told him. "You will stay there for ten days, to list the warships stationed in the Mersey River, the amount of munitions being unloaded on the Liverpool docks from the United States, and make a detailed note of all merchant ships in harbor and their sailing dates. Because of a new naval campaign which is about to begin, this information is highly important to us."

"Yes, sir." Stegler managed to keep his voice steady. "Suppose I'm asked what I'm doing there?"

"I expect you will be," Boy-Ed smiled. "You will travel as an American citizen, bidding for contracts to deliver food and clothing. From Liverpool you will proceed to London. You will spend another seven days studying and detailing the shipping in the Port of London and the Thames, then you will cross to Holland, where you will report to our nearest Embassy. Arrangements will be made to send you immediately to Berlin. You understand?"

"Yes, sir." Stegler took a sip of cognac, but his throat was so tight he had to force himself to swallow. He was thinking of his young wife, an American girl, and how difficult it was to hide what he was doing from her. How could he explain a trip to London?

He came ashore from the *Vaterland* a seriously worried man, and did not notice that he was followed all the way to his home in Jersey City by another of the longshoremen, Federal agent Albert Adams.

Frank Burke had changed cars with von Papen, stuffing his cap in the pocket of his lumberjacket, which he took off and carried under his arm. Now they were on foot, and he tagged him on a diagonal line from across the street. Von Papen walked briskly and purposefully, heading up Sixth Avenue, and Burke wished he had a back-up man so they could leapfrog, as occasional crowds at intersections made it hard to keep him in sight all the time.

Once he thought he had lost him. A streetcar and an unloading truck obscured his view, and when the military attaché should have appeared beyond them, he didn't. Burke dropped back, but couldn't see him. He hurried on, but there was no sign of the tall figure in the tight, serge coat and bowler hat anywhere. A policeman had stopped the traffic and Burke slipped in among the people waiting and crossed over with them. He worked quickly back down the sidewalk he had been watching, and nearly ran into his quarry standing in a group outside the window of a dry goods store, where a young man was undressing the wax mannequins. Burke had to carry on and walked to the next corner before turning and going back.

Von Papen was coming straight toward him. And passed within two feet. Burke reached the rubberneckers outside the window and paused, risking a look back. Von Papen had stopped to buy a newspaper, then went into the corner cigar store. Burke hurried across the road, dodging the traffic, and took up a position at the side of a telephone booth.

He waited, watching the cigar store, and as the minutes passed began to realize he had made an elementary mistake. He has assumed because of the purposeful walk that von Papen was making for somewhere definite and would carry on uptown. Stopping to look at the half-dressed mannequins should have warned him. It was uncharacteristic behavior. He hurried back across the avenue to the cigar store. As he had suspected, there was another door to the side street. The military attaché had vanished.

Franz von Papen was still smiling as he let himself into 60 Wall Street and rode in the elevator up to the twenty-fifth-floor office which was his secret headquarters. He had been aware of the broad-shouldered dockworker from the moment he had boarded the first car and remembered him, much more presentably dressed, sitting alone at a corner table in the Indian grill-room of the Hotel Astor at lunch, the day before. It was enjoyable to choose the exact point at which he would give him the slip.

It would never do to be followed to Wall Street today. His assistant, Wolf von Igel, was waiting with Wachendorf, Busse and the Irishman, Ryan. Tauscher, the Krupps agent, had arranged for the delivery of the automatic pistols and for two cases of dynamite from the Dupont Powder Company. Today was the final briefing for the mission to blow up the Welland Canal, the waterway that ran round the Canadian side of the Niagara Falls. With the Canadians forced to hold back valuable troops to guard their frontier, instead of sending them to France, over the next week the Intelligence Service would more than justify its existence.

Her legs were not very long, but they were trim and shapely and she flexed them prettily as she drew the stockings up her smooth thighs. Her name was Emilie and she was the wife of a stout, self-important, senior official at the Swiss Embassy.

Franz von Rintelen lay on the bed, watching her. The silk stockings were a light blue that matched her eyes. Her straw colored hair had been swept up into an elegant double roll, but the rolls had loosened and gleaming wisps and coils slipped free to dangle round her head like the serpent hair of Medusa, little golden serpents. One hung over her eyes and she blew at it, brushing it aside, as she checked that the openwork clocks of her stockings ran up straight over her slender ankles and the swell of her calves, before fastening garters round the darker bands at the top. The garters were ruched, white satin with black rosettes covering the clips. Apart from that, all she was wearing was a fine white linen chemisette, sleeveless, held up by narrow straps over the shoulders. Very fetching, but von Rintelen for once had scarcely done justice to her charms. He had too much on his mind.

She glanced up and, seeing his eyes on her, twitched her legs together and pushed the chemise down over the slight pout of her belly and the darker blond fuzz. It was involuntary and, when he laughed quietly, she laughed back. "Well . . ." she smiled, and shrugged.

She was sitting on the stool of the dressing table and swiveled her head to look in the mirror, making a moue at the ruin of her hairstyle. Her face was fresh and pretty, heart-shaped. The tinted salve had nearly all been kissed from her mouth and she touched the corners with the tip of her little finger, then licked her lips and stood up. The embroidered chemisette was fitted to her slim waist and stopped there, and she knew very well the picture she made as she bent, running her hands from the knee to each stocking top and adjusting the garters. She slid her toes into her mules, straightened and turned toward him.

Von Rintelen was lying naked on the floral coverlet and, seeing the effect she had had on him, she smiled slightly. She took two slow steps toward the bed, and stopped. "You're the one who insisted you had to get dressed," she said coolly. "So why don't you?" She lifted her chin and turned back to the dressing table. She picked up her brush and comb and went into the bathroom.

She is cross. Even the flirt of her little pink behind is cross, von Rintelen thought, as she clicked the glass door shut. He knew what would happen next and nodded when he heard the swish of the water taps. She was very modest in the bathroom. Modest, hygienic, very Swiss. Although, in the bedroom, she had that deliberate, exciting immodesty of a woman who has only newly been sexually liberated. He had met her at the Schröder mansion in the Tiergartenstrasse, where the Baroness held her popular, political salon. "Just your type, Franz'l," the Baroness had whispered wickedly. "And you'd be doing her a favor. Her husband is so boring." She clasped his hand and led him across. "Emilie, my dear, I want you to meet the most delightful young man in Germany. He's very shy—but I'm sure you can draw him out."

Von Rintelen still smiled, remembering his surprise at being described as "shy" and how sweetly Emilie had tried to "draw him out." Through her he had met Major Langhorne, the American military attaché, who had been worth his weight in gold dollars. In conversation one night he had complained about having to send all his confidential communiqués to Washington via London, where he was sure they were copied and read. Von Rintelen agreed that it was disgraceful. There was, however, the German-built radio station at Sayville, Long Island, which had recently been completed and was now in direct communication with the station at Nauen. Generously, von Rintelen offered to have Langhorne's dispatches transmitted for him. The attaché was grateful, although cautious. The dispatches would have to be sent in code, he insisted. "But naturally," von Rintelen agreed. "That way they will be perfectly safe."

The trusting Langhorne gave him the first long telegram and von Rintelen rushed it straight to Erzberger, head of the International Intelligence Bureau. Within two hours, cipher experts had broken the American code. Von Rintelen was able to decipher the dispatches himself and to doctor them. Almost at once the German position began to be reported more advantageously in the U.S. press, and he rewrote the dispatches even more favorably. Through the military attaché they were able to glean nearly everything that the Americans thought and decided. It was invaluable. Unfortunately, however, Major Langhorne had been abruptly summoned back to Washington, much to his surprise, for showing a distinct, pro-German bias in his communiqués. And the new attaché had politely refused the offer of the German radio transmitter. Pity.

Emilie came from the bathroom and crossed to the dressing room without looking at him. She had fixed her hair again in its lustrous twin rolls. Her chin high, stockinged thighs scissoring, her offended march made her delicate breasts bounce under the thin chemise.

He should get up and dress, as he had said, but he had at least half an hour before his secret meeting with Grand Admiral Tirpitz. After a strong protest from President Wilson and a plea from the German Chancellor, Bethmann, Kaiser Wilhelm had abruptly vetoed the cancellation of the unrestricted U-boat campaign. Von Rintelen had intercepted the order. To protect Tirpitz' entire strategy and to preserve the loyalty of the Navy in the face of such a retreat, somehow the Kaiser had to be induced to change his mind again. It was likely to be explosive. Danger and excitement acted on von Rintelen like a stimulant. And the sight of Emilie's pink and white semi-nudity was the only other urge he needed. He slid from the bed and rose, stretching. He had at least half an hour before he would have to leave.

Stockily pugnacious, with his snub nose and reddish hair, Winston Churchill was brooding in the window recess. He stood apart from the other dinner guests in Sir Edward Grey's salon. Nearest him were Walter Page and Hoover with the high Tory Lord Curzon, former Viceroy of India. When Curzon signaled to him, a typical and imperious flick of his index finger as though summoning a waiter, Churchill pretended not to notice. They would only want to talk about the Dardanelles.

When Turkey entered the war, hurling her army at the Russians in the Caucasus, the Czar had appealed to his allies for help to reduce the new pressure on his flank. Churchill, as First Lord of the Admiralty, had devised a plan for a massive naval bombardment to knock out the forts guarding the Dardanelles, the narrow Turkish straits giving access to the Black Sea from the eastern end of the Mediterranean. Only warships and marines were to be used. If the straits were forced, they would occupy the northern side, the Gallipoli peninsula. Whatever happened, Turkey would have to withdraw troops from the Caucasus to defend Constantinople. With her capital threatened, she might even sue for peace. Russia could be supplied and reinforced and the Central Powers would be caught in a continent-wide pincer movement. A special feature of Churchill's plan was that, as a purely naval action, it could be broken off and the ships retire at any time, if the forts proved more difficult to deal with than expected. It was the first truly imaginative proposal put forward at the War Council and was enthusiastically received.

He had not reckoned, however, with the jealousy of the service chiefs. Reluctant at first to accept a strategic suggestion from a politician, they had soon seen how it could end the stalemate of the war. The direction of it was taken out of Churchill's hands. The army insisted on being involved, which meant troopships and more battleships to protect them, and the proposed scale of the assault kept increasing until gradually the navy's Dardanelles bombardment had become the army's Gallipoli campaign.

Yet he could not shrug off responsibility. Many were going to die on those beaches, many more than he had ever bargained for. And all because he had thought of the damned idea in the first place. His thoughts were interrupted. Grey, the British Foreign Secretary, was showing in the principal guests of the evening, Colonel House and his wife, Loulie.

The Colonel caught sight of Churchill glowering in the window alcove and hoped they would not be seated near each other. He did not really like him, nor any member of the so-called jingoistic War Party. He was more pleased to see friendly faces among the other guests. Sir Edward led Loulie and him forward, and he noticed Churchill crossing to meet them. He made himself smile. "Ah, my dear, I don't believe you have met Mr. Churchill, First Lord of the Admiralty," he said.

Churchill bowed to Mrs. House, Loulie. She was beautiful, one of those genuine Texas beauties. At least he's done one wise thing, he thought, to choose such a wife. Churchill almost regretted that he had decided not to stay. He chatted briefly and amusingly, made his excuses that he had to catch a boat-train to Paris and left with their host.

As they went down the stairs, Grey said, "I'm sorry you have to leave, Winston. I think you rather charmed Colonel House, to his surprise. I'm grateful. He's fairly important."

"He makes me puke," Churchill said. Grey paused, startled. Churchill looked up at him. "There are women having their breasts cut off. Civilian atrocities. Prisoners bayoneted. A million men condemned to certain death in the trenches, and for what? So that a few Prussian generals can dictate the future of Europe. And all he can propose is his 'Freedom of the Seas' for all shipping. It will protect us from U boats, he says—and it will allow unlimited supplies and ammunition into Germany so that they can continue the butchery indefinitely! That's not just blindness, it's a betrayal of civilization. I've less and less time for such uninvolved neutrals. If they're not for us, they're against us." They had reached the foot of the stairs and he took his hat and coat from the butler, who was waiting.

Grey was troubled. "But don't you think their very lack

129

of involvement might be essential for the future?" he said. "We have all been touched by a kind of madness. Their place in the scheme of things may be to preserve the memory of normalcy, of sanity in a world that's run amuck."

"Tell that to the widows," Churchill said.

He did not go to the boat-train, but straight to the Admiralty and the closely guarded offices of Captain Reginald Hall, Director of Naval Intelligence. Although it was late, Room 40 was busy.

Captain Hall, a fine-looking man, his hair prematurely gray, was hunched over his desk, writing abstracts of the day's reports by the light of a shaded lamp. When his door opened after the stamp as the sentries outside presented arms, he looked up and started to rise, but Churchill waved him down. He threw his hat and coat on a chair as he crossed to the desk. "Any developments?"

"Nothing too significant, sir," Hall told him. "The day's analyses are just coming through. There are more indications of a Boche build-up on the Russian Front. Meanwhile, there's a report of a split in the High Command." Churchill grunted, interested. "It looks as if Hindenburg and Ludendorff are pushing one plan, while the Commander-in-Chief, Falkenhayn, favors another. There's been some pretty violent rows among them."

"Let's hope they shoot each other, then," Churchill muttered. Hall smiled briefly. "Any more news from Constantinople?" He took out his cigar case and held it out to Hall, who shook his head.

"Nothing to speak of," Hall said. "They know we're coming, of course—thanks to the Army signaling orders all over the place." Churchill grunted again and clipped the end of his cigar. "But they've no idea how soon or exactly where we're going to hit them."

"Well, that's something," Churchill said. He drew on his cigar in short, staccato puffs as he lit it, turning the largest of the wall charts, showing Western Europe and the British Isles. The chart was split up into squares by fine grid lines, and the position of every vessel in the British, French and Russian navies was indicated by a colored pin, the color and size of the pinhead denoting the class of ship. Also marked was the last known location of every ship in the German

Navy, from the Baltic to the Belgian ports. What interested Churchill most were three large, square-headed pins, painted red, with pivotal white arrows on top. Two had been placed high in the North Sea, the third nearer the English Channel. A fourth red square with a white diagonal was just southwest of Land's End.

The grid was an unwitting but extremely valuable present to Room 40 from the High Seas Fleet. A Yarmouth trawler had fished up in its nets some papers from one of the ships sunk in action at the Dogger Bank. They were sent to Naval Intelligence, where it was realized with great excitement that among them was a copy of the official grid devised by the German Admiralty to locate and keep track of the exact positions of all their units. German raiders never understood how, whenever they tried to slip through the North Sea patrols, the Royal Navy knew precisely where to find them. The grid was part of the answer and its possession was extremely secret.

"So they've come out again," Churchill growled.

"Three days ago. They're the ones who'll start the unrestricted campaign." Hall rose and came round to join him by the chart.

"How many U-boats in this patrol?"

"Impossible to say, sir. He's the only one who's been sighted—U 29." Hall pointed to the red square with the diagonal. "I should change that pin to a positive. He sank a three-and-a-half-thousand-ton steamer, bound for Falmouth with a cargo of engine parts."

"Without warning?"

"Cruiser Rules. They're playing it very correctly, just for now." Hall indicated the other red squares. "These are the ones whose positions we got by radio. The arrows show the course they were on, but they could be anywhere by now. And there might be any number of others with them, only not equipped with radio."

"The sooner every U-boat in that damned flotilla is fitted out with radio, the better," Churchill muttered. "Of course they don't always give their positions, do they?"

"No, sir, unfortunately," Hall said, then smiled. "But Marconi's working on it—a system of radio direction finding. As soon as our listening stations pick up a signal, they'll be able to tell exactly where it comes from."

"Is that possible?" Churchill asked. "How soon will it be ready?"

"In about another month, he reckons."

"I'll get on to him," Churchill promised. "It can't come quickly enough." Every day was precious now. The public had not been told, but already the U-boats had become a serious threat to British shipping. Supplies of every sort were scarce and submarine attacks were making many things difficult to replace. Shortage of shells and of rifle and machine gun ammunition caused the greatest anxiety. Allied factories could not produce anything like the quantity needed. Four or five times more was shot off every day than anyone had estimated and stocks were dangerously low.

Hall looked again at the wall chart. "Well, they've sent out their sharks. I'd give a lot to know what they're up to."

Churchill nodded. "Yes. And I'd give even more to know what that old forkbeard shark Tirpitz is up to."

Chapter 9

RUDOLPH ZENTNER STRUGGLED UP OUT OF SLEEP. HIS HEAD was buzzing and felt as heavy as a wooden tub. His whole body ached with tiredness and was stiff all down the front of his right side where it pressed against his sleeping partner. He had rolled over and was clasping it with his right arm, his cheek against its cold, slick metal surface. He pushed himself away and fell onto his back.

He was in his cramped bunk in the U 20, in the forward battery compartment which served as quarters for the officers. The demands of the new campaign meant that all available space was used to store shells for the deck gun and the temporary stowing of one of the spare torpedoes in the officers' quarters had become permanent. Rather than keep stepping over it or having it suspended from the low ceiling, he had it strapped along the outside of his bunk. He had been nervous at first, with a hundred and sixty pounds of TNT in the warhead next to his feet, but his nature was to look on the bright side and he soon learned to appreciate how snug it kept him when the U 20 tossed about on the surface at night and others were thrown out of their blankets onto the deck.

Still, its copper casing was undeniably cold and hard. For a moment he remembered Dora, the little minx-faced singer, with her hot, nervous thighs wriggling and clenching in her soft goosefeather bed. They had built up so much heat under that heavy quilt, he had thrown it off. He smiled, remembering how she had squealed and clutched herself in embarrassment, twisting over onto her stomach. Funny to be so coy, after what they'd just been doing. But she had laughed and struggled when he held her down, smacking her pert little buttocks, until she grabbed him where it hurt most and nearly finished their games for the night. Well . . . she was far away now.

He was still half asleep and at first did not react to the sound of footsteps hurrying past him. Then all at once he realized that the buzzing was not inside his head but was the bell for Action Stations. He came fully awake instantly and, quick as a cat, slid over the torpedo to the deck and pulled on his boots. He snatched his cap from the rack and ran through into Central Control.

Hirsch and his technicians were all in position and the new gunnery officer, Weiser, was standing by at the foot of the ladder. Zentner glanced at the dials and saw they were already at periscope depth. The bell had stopped and now he could hear what had caused the alert, the throb of powerful propellers, loud and very close.

Schwieger was at the periscope, swiveling it carefully in the direction of the sound, and Zentner hurried to help him, seizing the lever with both hands in case he had to bring the stick down fast. "Sorry," he said, "I'd only just got to sleep."

Schwieger did not answer. He was bending forward, gazing intently into the glass, holding the handgrips on either side so tightly that his knuckles shone white. "Damn . . ." he swore softly. "Damn, damn, damn!" He released the grips reluctantly and stood back.

"What's wrong?" Zentner asked. Schwieger nodded curtly toward the eyepiece and Zentner moved round, taking his place. At first he was puzzled, because he could see nothing except a dirty, brownish darkness. Then it seemed to shiver and dissolve and he had a glimpse of swelling green waves before wisps of the darkness curled round the lens of the periscope again. "Oh, Christ, no," he muttered. "Fog!" He straightened in disgust. The deep thrum of the screws was moving rapidly away from them.

"There's fog as thick as cabbage soup up there," Schwieger told Hirsch and the others. "We might as well try to shoot blindfolded."

"Did you catch sight of her, sir?" Hirsch asked. "What was it?"

"Yes, I saw her, just for a second," Schwieger said tightly. "An armored cruiser."

There were gasps of disappointment and Schwieger nodded, agreeing with them. Zentner shared his feeling of frustration. For months they had not even had a glimpse of a warship, no naval craft except fast, submarine-hunting torpedo boats and destroyers which they had learned to leave well alone. Others had reported sighting battleships, but only behind screens of zigzagging destroyers that made attack impossible. The British had no intention of exposing their capital ships to U-boats. This cruiser must have been returning from some station in the Atlantic and was running through the new German war zone for Plymouth or Portsmouth at very nearly full speed. For it to cross their path was a chance in a million—and they'd missed it!

"Couldn't we chase her, sir?" Weiser asked eagerly.

Schwieger stopped himself from snapping back. The gunnery lieutenant was a fresh-faced lad straight from Heidelberg. Brave too, if the ritual dueling scar high on his cheek was anything to go by, but a gosling underwater. "It would be a waste of fuel," Schwieger explained. "She's half as fast again as we are. We'd never catch her." He could have added that any captain who raced his submarine at top speed through fog had no right to his stripes and would be better employed pushing an ice cream cart, but he knew it would make the others laugh and bit it back. "You'll get some gun practice in soon enough. Don't worry," he said.

Zentner and the others did laugh, but it was kindly. Weiser flushed and smiled.

Schwieger turned back to the eyepiece. "Ahead, three knots," he ordered. "The fog might be local. Let's see if we can run out of it."

For the next twenty minutes they forged steadily ahead. Haupert, the navigation lieutenant, double-checked their course on the new gyroscopic compass and searched his charts for any sunken reefs or obstructions. Zentner raised the asparagus another two feet and stayed by the lever while Schwieger never took his eyes from the box, turning it slowly, searching for any break in the fog.

The U-boat was unnaturally silent, all ears straining to pick up any noise, especially propellers, for the danger of accidental ramming was very real. Zentner could see Schwieger's profile, set and intent. It had become more drawn over the last weeks and Zentner sometimes worried about him. Something had happened to Walther, ever since that review at Wilhelmshaven. It was not just the extra tension and excitement they all felt under the new conditions, something more personal. Ever since that secret meeting he had at the Grand Admiral's headquarters. Whatever it was, there was no guessing. Walther was one to keep his problems to himself. On days when there was no sinking, he prowled Central Control or stayed up in the conning tower on watch for hours on end. Everyone knew the flotilla was faced with a great responsibility and the hunting was more serious now. Their tally of kills mounted swiftly, but never swiftly enough to suit Walther. Yet there were days, too, when he was his old self, relaxed and friendly.

At last Schwieger stood back and rubbed his eyes with his fingertips to ease the strain. He shook his head. "No use. It's not a single bank, it's widespread. If we keep on, we'll soon be outside our area. Take her down to forty feet and we'll wait a while." Zentner lowered the periscope and locked it off as the U 20 began her dive.

Hansel, the little wirehaired dachshund, was sitting quietly in a corner as he had been trained to do. He sensed immediately that the alert was over and ran to Schwieger, yapping happily and frisking round him, jumping over the toes of his boots. Schwieger smiled and crouched, tickling Hansel gently just behind the ears. The little dachshund stopped barking at once and went rigid, his neck arched, tail pointing, with only the faintest tremor in his half-raised right front paw, the picture of ecstasy. Zentner chuckled and Schwieger glanced up. "Why don't you try to get some more sleep?"

"What about you?"

"I'm fine." Schwieger said. He ran his hand down Hansel's back, patted his rump and moved to join Haupert at the chart table. Zentner went back to his bunk.

"Churchill!" Kaiser Wilhelm spat out the name with bitter distaste. "When they sue for peace, I shall insist on him being hanged as a war criminal!"

They were pacing in the private garden of the Royal Palace in Berlin, a small enclosed space with a patch of lawn running down to the bank of the River Spree. Wilhelm was in plain gray uniform, carrying a cane. His dogs ran frisking in front of them. Tirpitz walked at his right, while Admiral Bachmann at his left stayed a respectful pace behind.

Tirpitz went on, "Then he said, 'This pressure of the gag shall not be relaxed until Germany gives in unconditionally.'"

"Never!" Wilhelm swore. He stopped and jabbed the point of his cane into the ground. "We shall smash the Blockade by every means in our power!"

Tirpitz bowed. "Your Imperial Majesty's resoluteness is an inspiration to us all. Our U-boats must of course be allowed to operate without those restrictions, which only benefit the enemy."

Wilhelm was brought up short. He had granted permission for an interview with a member of the Naval War Staff, he assumed to report on the opening of the British action in the Dardanelles. He had expected Bachmann, but as soon as he saw Tirpitz towering beside him, he knew his changed orders to the submarine flotilla were to be questioned. He had been on his guard, but Tirpitz had not mentioned U-boats, only Russia, Belgium, this inflammatory speech by Churchill, until Wilhelm had flown into a rage. He had dug a pit for himself and fallen into it. He jerked his cane out of the hole it had made. "There are complications," he grated. "International complications—if we harm neutral ships."

"Neutrals trading with the enemy are our enemies, in everything but name," Tirpitz pointed out. "And we have warned them that they enter the war zone at their own risk."

Wilhelm knew the Grand Admiral was right. Yet he had also known that Bethmann was right. He had searched for a point of balance between the two poles, but could not find one. "If we cannot police our war zone effectively, it will be worse than useless."

Tirpitz gestured to Bachmann, who came forward nervously. "Twelve new submarines go into commission this month, your Imperial Majesty," he said. "And the keels of fifty more are already laid down. In a very short time, we shall have the largest undersea fleet in the world."

Wilhelm's eyebrows rose. "And I suppose, Admiral, you guarantee that England will surrender within six weeks?"

Tirpitz tensed. It was a mocking reference to the generals' claim before the attack on France, but Bachmann did not notice the sarcasm. "Perhaps not six weeks, sir," he answered seriously, "but they certainly could not last more than a few months."

Wilhelm was impressed by his conviction. All the arguments of the past crowded in on him, but he still hesitated, troubled. "I have already issued orders canceling the campaign," he said.

Tirpitz's expression was bland. "By a strange oversight, your Imperial Majesty's orders were not received until after the first unrestricted patrol had left. Regrettably, few of them could be contacted."

"And what about the others?" Wilhelm demanded. "Have they been told?"

"I did not judge it advisable," Tirpitz said. "I knew that, undoubtedly, in view of the British offensive in the Dardanelles, you would not wish a change of orders to be announced."

So even the Navy has begun to question my commands, Wilhelm thought bitterly. They bow and scrape, but what have I become in my own kingdom? A rubber stamp! His bitterness was tempered by the realization that, strategically, Tirpitz and his supporters were right. If the Blockade was to be broken and any help given to Turkey, the U-boat campaign could not be halted. Even at the risk of war with the remaining neutrals. He caught sight of his wife, Dona, fair and plump, waiting for him on the terrace. He would spend the evening quietly with her, listening to music, perhaps, and forgetting that decisions were now being made with or without him. He would have to give in, but Tirpitz could wait.

The Grand Admiral was shaken when Kaiser Wilhelm whistled to the dogs, turned and strode back toward the terrace. "Come along, gentlemen," Wilhelm said. "The Kaiserin will wish to say hello."

The fog lay dank and heavy for nearly three hours over the U 20's patrol sector before it began to disperse; then a stiff breeze blew up out of the west, scattering the last, tattered streamers. Just as Walther Schwieger was feeling grateful, however, the intensity of the wind changed and soon had nearly reached gale force, whipping up waves as high as the Brandenburg Gate. He had no choice but to submerge again, and even at sixty feet they could feel the clashing turbulence of the surface.

He had used the first three hours making the torpedo crews run through the procedure for fast reloading underwater, a new technique calling for perfect communication and split-second timing in both the control and torpedo rooms. In an encounter with a heavily armed, attacking enemy it could mean life or death, and he had them repeat the technique over and over until they matched Weddigen's record time and could have carried it out blindfolded.

Most of the crew were exhausted by the end, yet buoyed up by his quiet praise and their pride in themselves. To Schwieger it was merely a weak substitute for action, a device to keep the men busy and practiced. Being prevented by the fog from firing even one shot at that cruiser still preyed on his mind. He took it too personally, Rudi had said. It was true, but he had good reason. Of all the commanders, he probably realized most clearly how much depended on them.

He had argued for all available boats to be concentrated on the main channels leading to British ports, where the sea lanes converged. It was the most dangerous plan because of coastal destroyers and the submarine-hunting Auxiliary Patrols, but the one least likely to let anything of any size slip through. Instead, the flotilla had been ordered to its usual spread-out stations, to attack in depth. The U 20 patrolled an area about two hundred miles south of Land's End in the southwest corner of England, to intercept freighters coming from West Africa and South America. So far the catch had been reasonable, just above average. It was partly luck, he knew, yet he envied Hersing, Rosenberg and the others who had been given St. George's Channel and the Irish Sea, and Hansen who had a roving commission in the North Sea. To be here was like being sent to watch for skirmishers on the edge of the battlefield.

For the crew's sake, he allowed none of his resentment or frustration to show. He let Hirsch think his curtness was due to the enforced, though unavoidable, wastage of electrical power in their motors, while young Weiser thought he was still secretly not too happy with the performance of the torpedo rooms. They were both relieved when the storm lessened and the U 20 put her nose above water for the first time that day.

Schwieger came out onto the conning tower platform and checked automatically that there were two sailors on lookout at the bows, another pair at the stern. It was late afternoon and the sun was already quite low. It would set in less than an hour. The wind had lessened to moderate and the U 20 pitched sluggishly in the surge of the long waves.

He filled his lungs with clean, cold air as he looked all round. From the top of the conning tower the depth of vision on a clear day was approximately thirty miles, and in all that expanse there was nothing that moved. Far to the south a low haze merged sea and sky. As he trained his telescope on it, traversing the horizon, he heard Zentner climbing up the ladder. Heading to and from the forward torpedo room, he had passed Rudi's bunk several times and seen how exhaustedly he slept. He let him have his full six hours and had just sent Boatswain Kurtz to wake him, beginning the watch himself. He returned his salute with a smile. "Feeling better?"

"A new man," Zentner said gratefully. "When did the fog lift?"

"Two hours ago. We've had a storm since then."

Zentner whistled and leaned back against the rail, taking out his cigarette case. "Sorry. I didn't feel a thing. You should have had me called."

"And spoil your beauty sleep? There was nothing anyone could do." Schwieger finished scanning the southern horizon and swung his glass to the northwest sector.

"Cigarette?" Zentner offered.

Schwieger smiled. "Fresh air's too much of a luxury." With the telescope extended, it was difficult to keep it fixed on any one point and he frowned as he adjusted the focus.

"Not working properly?"

"It's probably me," Schwieger admitted. "I'm not used to it. I still miss my old binoculars."

"The man at the shop thinks they're past repair," Zentner said, and bit off the last two words.

140

Schwieger looked at him in surprise. "What do you mean? I throw them out."

Zentner had spoken before he could stop himself. "Well . . . I rescued them," he said hesitantly. "A kind of keepsake. Do you mind?"

"No," Schwieger said. "Not if you want them." He was touched, and raised the telescope again to cover his embarrassment.

"You kept me sane and stopped me being a coward, that day with the net," Zentner told him quietly. "I'll never forget it."

"We were all a little crazy that day," Schwieger answered shortly.

Zentner lit his cigarette with one of the double-headed storm matches he kept in the pocket of his leathers. Afterwards, he held it cupped in his hands, enjoying the warmth of the flame on his palms. "Funny life we lead, altogether," he murmured. "One thing I never expected is how randy it makes me."

Schwieger lowered the telescope again. "Randy?"

"Every time we're out on patrol, I can't stop thinking about it," Zentner confessed. "Cooped up down there. And the dreams I have— If I could patent them, I'd make a fortune." Schwieger laughed. "No, seriously. Sooner or later, I'll end up making advances to that torpedo of mine."

"As Captain, I suppose I could solemnize the union," Schwieger smiled.

"Don't tempt me!" Zentner grinned. "Hey, do you know who's been featuring in my latest fantasies, one of the stars?— though God knows there are dozens. Dora. The little singer we met in Wilhelmshaven, when you had her friend, what was her name? Anneliese. You remember?"

Schwieger had been thinking of Anneliese just before Rudolph came up to join him, wondering where and how she was, and how you could miss someone so much after knowing her for only a few days. The pangs of parting had been painful for both of them. Anneliese had wept and clung to him. She would not see him off at the train, in case she shamed them both by breaking down. It was only after he had left that he realized he had made no promise, no arrangements to see her again. Perhaps it was better.

141

"Yes, I remember," he said.

"I'm afraid I got the best of the bargain there," Zentner smiled. "I mean, Anneliese was a bit heavy going."

"Captain!" one of the lookouts at the bows called sharply. He was pointing to the south.

They could just make out what he had seen, a dark speck emerging from the haze on the horizon. Schwieger trained the telescope on it.

"What is it?" Zentner asked.

Schwieger was silent for a moment, then grunted, "Can't make it out." He passed the glass to Zentner.

"I can't—no, I can't make it out, either," Zentner said. "High and square . . . What the hell is it?"

"Secure hatches for diving!" Schwieger shouted to the seamen on deck. Zentner was already sliding down the conning tower ladder.

Submerged, the U 20 headed on an angle to intercept and came to periscope depth again about half a mile from the point of contact. Schwieger was at the eyepiece. Haupert had fetched the copies of the British annuals *Jane's Fighting Ships 1914* and *The Naval Annual 1914*, which had been issued to each U-boat to make identification easier. They had the extra advantage of listing many of the cargo ships that had been armed. Haupert stood thumbing them.

"You can put these away," Schwieger said. He sounded disappointed.

"Why, sir?" Zentner asked.

For answer, Schwieger stood aside to let him look. The approaching vessel was in the eye of the periscope now, a three-masted sailing ship, square-rigged, making good speed in spite of her broad beam and obvious weight in the water. Zentner swore under his breath. "She looks fully laden, though," he said.

Schwieger nodded. "Can you see any guns?"

"No. And she certainly can't ram us, once she's stopped."

When the U-boat surged up out of the water a quarter of a mile to starboard on her line of route, the sailing ship yawed wildly as the helmsman lost control. At once the U 20's hatches were thrown open and Weiser's gun crew raced up onto the wet deck, slithering and sliding as they unplugged and loaded the gun. A detail of seamen followed and filed out on either side with rifles to cover them. Schwieger and Zentner came out onto the conning tower platform. The Petty Officer of the gun crew cursed his men for incompetence as they swiveled the deck gun and he sighted on their target, but Schwieger was well pleased. Young Weiser had trained them superbly.

In the minute and a half it had taken the U-boat to reach her attack state, the sailing ship had been brought back under control and was veering off to port. "Warning shot across her bows!" Schwieger ordered.

The deck gun was quickly elevated and the Petty Officer jerked the lanyard. At the crash of the shot, the gulls following the squarerigger rose squawking and wheeling into the air. The $4 \frac{1}{2}$-inch shell plowed into the water just beyond her bows and her captain must have realized at once that flight was hopeless, for her mainsail fell almost immediately, with most of the others soon after so that she was hove to, wallowing in the swell.

"Reverse, four knots," Schwieger called down the tube and the U 20 backed slowly to the sailing ship, which Weiser kept covered all the time with the reloaded deck gun. Unlike some of the other Commanders, Schwieger had had his gun mounted on the stern deck, to present as narrow as possible a target in case of concealed armaments on the ships he challenged and to allow a faster crash dive away from them.

Even now he was cautious, but finally halted the U 20 at about a hundred yards from the sailing ship when it could be clearly seen she was harmless. She showed no flag and, according to British instructions, her name and port of registry had been obliterated. The seamen were dark-haired with light brown skins and could have been Spanish or North African. They stood at the bulwarks gazing in terror, some appealing to the captain and his officers who were up on the bridge.

Schwieger took the speaking tube and shouted across, asking for the ship's name and nationality, cargo and destination. An excited jabber broke out in an incomprehensible language, increasing when Schwieger repeated his questions, until he could hardly hear himself. "Fire a shot in the air!" he ordered.

One of the riflemen pulled his trigger and, with the shot, all sound cut off. "That's better," Schwieger said. He called over again, this time in French, but even as he was speaking two of the brown-skinned seamen panicked and jumped over the side of their ship into the freezing water. "Damned idiots," Schwieger muttered, "they'll get themselves drowned!"

The foreign captain was pleading now and gesticulating, alternately pointing to the water and holding his arms above his head. Some of his men were throwing life belts down to the two in the water, jabbering again. It was becoming farcical.

"For pity's sake!" Schwieger muttered, half amused, half exasperated, and called down, "Does anyone speak Spanish?" The sailors on the U 20's deck were grinning. No one answered. "English?"

"I speak English," Zentner said, and shrugged when Schwieger looked at him in surprise. "My mother was American."

"Your mother?"

Zentner smiled. "Do you want me to sing 'Alexander's Ragtime Band'?" He took the megaphone and hailed the sailing ship. One of the officers on her bridge cupped his hands, answering. She was the *Maria de Molenos* out of Lagos in Portugal with a cargo of hides and phosphates, bound for Bristol.

Portugal was England's oldest ally and the cargo was illegal. Schwieger shook his head. Zentner shouted back, "You have entered the German War Zone and what you are carrying is contraband! Prepare to abandon ship!" As soon as his words were translated, the crew of the *Maria de Molenos* began to run about, some disappearing below, others unfastening the lifeboats. The captain was at the rail, his arms outstretched, pleading. "Do they have enough boats?" Zentner asked.

"More than enough," Schwieger said, then he frowned. "What the hell are they doing?"

On the Portuguese ship, one of the officers had sent some men aloft to reef the remaining sails. Zentner raised the megaphone again. "You have no time for that! Lower your boats and stand clear—we give you two more minutes!" He winked to Schwieger.

In what seemed like seconds, the ship's four boats were swung out and lowered, the seamen in them clutching bundles and bottles. The two men already in the water were dragged on board. The captain seemed to have fainted and his officers lifted him into the last of them. Leutnant Weiser watched from beside his gun as the Portuguese seamen sweated at the oars to get away.

"As soon as those boats are clear," Schwieger said. Zentner turned with him to look right round the horizon. This was the moment when they were most vulnerable, when another ship could bear down on them out of nowhere or an enemy submarine pick them off. British submarines had only one periscope, flattened at the top, unlike the German sticks, the four-inch and the two-inch finger, which were topped by an arched window. All U-boat sailors were trained to recognize them. "Keep a sharp watch there!" Schwieger ordered the men on lookout.

"He'll do it in one," Zentner predicted.

Schwieger glanced at the thick-ribbed squarerigger and shook his head. "Two at least."

"A dinner at Fat Margo's it doesn't take more than one," Zentner grinned. Weiser had heard and was smiling up at them. "Right, Fritz?"

Schwieger looked at the lifeboats. They were well clear now. Some of the crew were standing up, cursing and shaking their fists, while others tried to pull them down. Schwieger nodded to the gun crew.

The gulls had taken back their usual perches on the stern rail and halyards and flew up screaming in alarm when the gun crashed out again and the *Maria de Molenos* shuddered all along her frame. The shell burst toward her bows, tearing a jagged hole in her side just above the waterline. Smoke poured from the hole and small flames could be seen crackling in its darkness. She listed slightly to starboard, but steadied.

Some of the Portuguese in the lifeboats cheered to see their ship still afloat.

"Fritz . . ." Zentner complained, spreading his hands. "How could you do this to me? More than two and the dinner's on you."

"This is taking too long," Schwieger said quietly. "Get on with it."

145

The Petty Officer sighted the gun himself. The second shot smashed into the sailing ship below the waterline, just behind and below the first. Almost at once she began to settle by the bows. The cheering had stopped and the gulls wheeled protesting high above her. Smoke belched suddenly from her midships companionway and flames burst through the tarpaulin of her main cargo hatch. In a few minutes, she would have been ablaze, but she was keeling over too quickly. Waves washed over her deck, extinguishing the fire in a spout of steam and blacker smoke. She struggled as if trying to right herself and was swinging back nearly to an even keel, when all at once she plunged by the head. Her stern had risen, showing her iron rudder encrusted with barnacles, but was borne down and vanished. For a few seconds she seemed to hang in the water, suspended by her masts and shrouds; then slowly they sank out of sight and the sea closed in, swirling over where she had been.

There was a long silence after she disappeared.

The Portuguese had begun rowing again, putting as much distance as possible between them and the U-boat. The surface of the water was littered with flotsam and debris, spars, wooden crates, bits of rigging. Amongst them Schwieger saw something rearing and floundering. It was a cow the crew had shipped with them for fresh milk. "For God's sake," he ordered sharply, "someone put that beast out of its misery!"

One of the riflemen fired. The cow's head bucked and it slid beneath the water.

Schwieger breathed out slowly. There was fierce excitement at a sinking, a kind of sensual pleasure mixed with guilt, followed as soon as it was over by a sense of emptiness. He could only explain it as the loss that every true sailor feels at the sudden death of a ship. In these past months, he had learned that nearly everyone felt it, except the most unthinking. Like a post-coital sadness.

He heard a strange sound and looked round to identify it. Someone was weeping. He saw Lippe, the squat, spade-bearded torpedoman, standing by the conning tower. His massive shoulders were heaving as he sobbed. Surely not because of the cow? "What is it, man?" he said.

146

Lippe's head turned. Tears were streaming down his face. "The little dog . . . the little dog . . ." he whispered.

Others had seen it and were pointing out to the flotsam. Amongst it, a wooden box rocked in the waves. Clinging to it with its front paws, its snout supported on the lid, was a little black dog. The crew began to call out to it, encouraging it, telling it to swim toward them. Schwieger had also noticed it and, when Zentner looked a question at him, glanced quickly round the horizon again and nodded. The U 20 turned slowly and moved forward. Lippe hurried to the bows and, with the Boatswain's Mate holding him, leaned over the side and scooped the dog out of the water. It was a miniature black dachshund, almost a double of Hansel, only smooth-haired while he was wiry. Lippe hugged and kissed it and held it up for them all to see. He chuckled as he made a discovery. "It's a little girlfriend for Hansel!" he shouted. All the men were laughing. "We ought to call her Gretel, eh? What do you say, Captain?"

Schwieger was smiling. "No, that's too obvious," he said. "She's off the *Maria de Molenos*. We'll call her Maria."

The sailors laughed and applauded. Lippe held the dachshund up again for them all to see her, then took her down below through the forward hatch to dry her off and introduce her to Hansel.

Five minutes later when Schwieger came down into Central Control, he saw the two small dogs examining it together, then trotting off down the passage side by side, stopping to sniff at every interesting smell, for all the world as if Hansel were showing her round. The large torpedoman followed them, chuckling paternally. "Now, then, Lippe," Schwieger said, "they're your responsibility, remember?"

Lippe's barrel-shaped chest swelled with pride as he stood to attention. "With pleasure, sir," he boomed.

Schwieger had left Zentner on watch and come down to write up his log. It was growing dark and the U 20 was beginning her night patrol on the surface to recharge her batteries. The cook brought him a mug of tea and he carried it into his tiny cabin.

It was a relief to take off his cap and to sit down. Perhaps Rudolph was right in one way, he thought, about him taking it too personally. He ought to rest more. But the nights had become busy lately, with more British merchant ships trying to run for home under cover of darkness. They were learning to sail blind, too, blacking out all their lights. But to do that they had to stick to the sea lanes, where the U-boats lay waiting.

Hunting had been fair so far. Even today hadn't been wasted, thanks to that Portuguese squarerigger. Yet it was not sport, as the Grand Admiral had said. There was not a man on board who did not hate those fat-bellied freighters carrying food and shells and bullets to England while Germany's docks lay idle and lines grew longer outside her food stores.

His eye caught the photograph of his parents and sisters on the shelf at the head of his bunk. Even his mother's pretty little garden, that she'd been so proud of, had been dug up to plant vegetables. Like other gardens all over Germany. Only a small thing, but a sign of worse to come. Unless the sinkings went on, day and night, relentlessly, bringing England to her knees. He had never imagined it possible to hate people he had never seen with such intensity. The few he had met in the past seemed pleasant enough and polite. Perhaps it was not them, not the people, but their leaders, those hypocrites who had schemed for fifty years to deny Germany her true place in the world, as the Kaiser had so often warned. Next to his parents' photograph was a newspaper picture of Kaiser Wilhelm in uniform at the naval review, which he had cut out and pinned to the shelf. Just to see it was to recall the emotion and uplift of that day.

Unconsciously, the thought of Wilhelmshaven made him remember Anneliese, her head on his chest and her voice breaking as they said goodbye. He had tried to school himself not to think of her, but he could not trust his mind to obey him. It kept playing him false with little glimpses of her, memories of her touch, things she had murmured as her slanted hazel eyes glowed up into his.

He wrenched his thoughts away from her. She had gone from his life, vanished, as surely as that ship he had just sunk.

148

He pulled the logbook toward him and opened it. Think only of your patrol, your mission and your crew, he told himself. Nothing exists outside the U 20.

Peter Fletcher came silently round the screen of bushes. He walked very carefully, avoiding the patches where a film of ice covered the grass and might crackle under his shoes.

He crouched when he came into the open, but need not have worried. She was in plain sight, but had her back to him, all her attention on two gray squirrels playing in the bare branches of a maple. She was lower down the hillside, where it began to level out, and had not seen him as he circled up round her. It was not a long throw, yet he knew if he missed her he would not get another chance. He crept slowly down toward her, sideways, making sure he did not slip.

Her head was tilted and the peak of her red knitted hood hung down her back, nearly as long as her long, dark hair. Her hands were thrust deep in the pockets of her blue coat and she was laughing, high, girlish laughter, which she held back so as not to startle the squirrels. The smaller of the two was really cheeky, teasing the bigger one and darting away, dropping from branch to branch and climbing again in a scrambling spiral up the trunk. In shadow, they were quite difficult to make out against the ridged dark gray bark.

His foot slipped and he had to dig his heel in to stop himself sliding down, but she was so absorbed she did not hear. Even the low sun helped him, throwing their shadows back up the hill. He was much closer and steadied his breathing, making not a sound as he came right up behind her. Her shoulders twisted and he tensed until he saw she had only ducked slightly to follow the helter-skelter race of the two squirrels over and under the lowest branch. Her laughter covered any noise as he drew the hatchet from his belt.

He had been wondering exactly where to strike. Now her hair had fallen away, exposing an inch of white skin at the side of her neck where it dipped into her collar. His lips drew back in a snarl as he swung the hatchet above his head and brought it down.

When she felt the edge of the blade touch her neck, Diana squealed and leaped in the air, spinning round. Her hood nearly fell off and she grabbed it with both hands. The squirrels chittered sharply in alarm and vanished with a whisk of their tails.

He was grinning at her in triumph. "You're dead," he said.

"No, I'm not!" she protested. "You sneaked up on me. That's not fair, Peter!"

"Of course it is. I'm an Indian."

"No, you're not!"

"Yes, I am!" He shook the painted wooden hatchet at her. "I'm Louis Riel and you're a redcoat—and you're dead! Dead."

"It's not fair," she sniffed. "I'm always the redcoat." And she burst into tears.

"Aw, for Pete's sake!" he exclaimed disgustedly. "What are you crying for?"

She would not give him the satisfaction of knowing she'd been frightened. "You—you chased the s-squirrels away."

"You weren't supposed to be watching squirrels," he explained indignantly. "You were supposed to be hunting me. So if you get scalped, it's your own fault." It only made her wail louder, her small features dissolving in misery. In the distance he could hear their mother calling and winced. If Diana was still crying when they got home, he'd be given another lecture about the responsibility of being the older brother. Sometimes he thought she just cried out of spite. He hadn't even hurt her. "Oh, come on, Diana, stop crying. It's just silly. Look—tell you what. I'll race you to the paddock." She had given up wailing, but she still sobbed, her shoulders jerking. "I'll give you a start."

"How much start?" she sniffed suspiciously.

"From that elder tree down there."

Diana looked round, wiping her cheeks with her heavyknit woolen gloves. The big old elder was quite a way down. It was more than fair. She began to trot toward it.

"And wait for me to say Go!" he shouted after her.

Livvy Fletcher wrapped her arms round herself. Although most of the snow had melted, it was still cold, especially coming straight out of a warm kitchen. And the wind seemed to whistle round the porch. "Diana!" she called. "Peter! Where are you?" She could see that the bar was in place across the doors of the old hip-roofed barn, so they weren't in there. And they weren't in the paddock orchard.

150

If she knew Peter, they'd be up in the woods playing Sioux and Mounted Police, or Louis Riel the rebel and the militia. Oneidas, Mohawks, Delawares, Hurons, he knew the names of more Indian tribes than there were hairs on Bess's tail. But it would be dark soon and she didn't want them up in the woods when the light faded.

"Peter! Diana! Come in now—tea's ready!" she called. Bess, their collie, whined softly and stiffened like a pointer, looking toward the hillside beyond the paddock. She knows they're there, Livvy thought. "Go on, Bess," she said. "Go and fetch them." The collie jumped down from the porch and raced off, squeezing under the paddock fence and heading straight for the first line of trees.

Olivia Fletcher was a fine-looking woman with dark chestnut hair, which she wore tied back in a simple knot on the nape of her neck. Her grandmother once told her, "You're like me. With that bone structure, you won't ever have to worry about growing old." Now at thirty she looked at least five years younger, and in spite of having had two children, her figure was still slim and supple.

She was born in England and lived for her first twenty years with her parents just outside the little town of Winchelsea, near Rye in East Sussex. Her father was a country doctor with a prosperous practice, mainly among farmers and the retired people who settled in Winchelsea, on its hill overlooking the English Channel, for the gentle charm of its small, old streets and houses, a quiet backwater. She was educated at a local girls' school and afterwards, quite naturally, took over some of her mother's work in the dispensary attached to her father's consulting room.

At the end of the last war, the Boer War, two companies of Royal Engineers set up camp in the fields between the hill and Winchelsea Beach, to spend the time before they were demobilized repairing the old canal that the army had built a hundred years before, to link the harbors along the Sussex coast during the struggle against Napoleon. The officers were billeted in houses in the town, and her father, Dr. Gurney, had willingly offered the use of their spare bedroom.

Their guest was a young lieutenant, Matthew Fletcher. A Canadian, newly qualified as a mining engineer, he had volunteered for the British Army and served in the Transvaal. He was lucky to have landed up at Dr. Gurney's, since he had a shoulder wound that had never properly healed. Her father treated it and she dressed it at first twice a day, then once, then once a week, until the torn flesh knitted together leaving only a long, puckered scar. She thought him very big and shy, with a strange, but oddly attractive accent. In the two and a half months he stayed with them, she got to know him very well. Sometimes they walked together along the windy pebble beach and up over the headland toward the coast guard station at Fairlight. She showed him Romney Marsh and the ancient marsh churches. Once or twice he took her to one of the tea shops in Rye. He told her a lot about Canada and life there, and it sounded very exciting, such a huge country and so much of it just being really discovered. She was quite safe with him. He never said anything that worried her, or tried to kiss her or hold her like some of the young men she met at dances. When his orders came through and he went home at last, he left them all very tasteful little presents. Hers was a gold locket. And she couldn't understand herself, for she cried when she opened it and saw there was no photograph inside.

The next year was the unhappiest she had ever known. He wrote occasionally to her father, including messages for her and asking to be kindly remembered. The letters were from places with strange names, like Saskatoon and Moose Jaw and Cobalt. He was obviously working very hard at his career and had nearly forgotten her. But she found herself remembering moments of every day she had spent with him, the way he had smiled to her when she dressed his wound, although at first it must have hurt terribly. Once she nearly went frantic when she could not remember the cadence of his voice and sat in her room, her eyes tightly shut, until it came back, as clear as if he were talking to her. And many times she thought of the afternoon they were caught in a violent summer storm, with drenching rain and sheet lightning bowling over the fields around them. She had been unable to run because her shoes clogged up in the sudden mud, and he had lifted her, running with her to the shelter of a broken-down mill, where they had waited out the storm. The memory of how she had been pressed to his chest and the feel of his arm round her back and the other under her thighs as he carried her, his solid, male strength, warmed her, making her almost ashamed of her animal reaction.

She told no one what she felt or how much she missed him, and no one noticed anything, although her mother thought she had become very quiet and was losing weight and should go out more, to meet some nice young men. On her twentieth birthday, she had taken medicine to a poor family down by the crossroads and was walking back up the steep hill toward the Strand Gate, the medieval twin towers with the arch between them spanning the road into the town, when she saw someone come through the postern arch at the side and stand looking at her. It was Matt.

She could not move and he strode down the hill toward her and took her in his arms and kissed her, without saying a word.

She was smiling and crying at the same time, holding him at last, feeling his arms around her so tightly she felt she would be crushed into him. Then he drew her up the rest of the hill, through the gate to the lookout point, secluded and set back from the road. He had nothing to offer her when he left, he said, but now he had a position with an expanding firm, and good prospects. He did not know how he had lived through the last eighteen months without her and never wanted to be without her for another day of his life.

Her parents were more than a little surprised, but gave in when they saw Matt's determination and Livvy's total happiness. The three weeks it took to arrange the wedding seemed almost as long as all the time they had waited already, although her mother was sure there would be talk at how quickly it was taking place. They were married in Winchelsea's ancient parish church and sailed two days later on the small liner *Victorian* of the Allan Line for Montreal.

For the next five years Livvy had seen a lot of Canada, traveling with Matt on all his projects from Cobalt to Labrador and back west to Northern Saskatchewan, a makeshift, sometimes rough life in areas just being opened out. For two of those years she was carrying and nursing Peter. When they learned Diana was on the way, they decided it was time to find somewhere more permanent, even though it might mean Livvy having to stay at home with the children while Matt was gone for long weeks at out-of-the-way sites. He was in demand as a consultant engineer now, in many different areas of mining during those days of rapid expansion to the west. He took the challenge of helping to plan and tear a route through the Rockies for the Grand Trunk Pacific, joining Winnipeg and Prince Rupert, the last and toughest link of the transcontinental railway.

They found a house a few miles outside Calgary in the new province of Alberta. It had been built as a small ranch house, wooden-framed, painted cream and green, with a dark green roof. It had three bedrooms, a study den for Matt, a summer and winter kitchen and a long, wide living room, and was their first real married home. Livvy adored every stick and stone.

She had removed the winter screens from the southwest corner of the porch and was thinking she must get Matt to take the rest of them down when he came home at the weekend. From where she was standing, the view was breathtaking. On summer evenings after the children were in bed, she could sit, often for hours, watching while her mind drifted over the few problems and the great, enfolding happiness of her life. Above the foothills, seeming near although they were at least fifty miles away, rose the towering wall of the Rocky Mountains, range behind range, their peaks white and starkly pure in the pale sky, except occasionally at sunset when the eternal ice glowed red and the whole vast crest seemed on fire.

It was a wonderful place for children to grow up, free and healthy, with so much space around them. She often thought of her own childhood and the quietness and neatness of everything, the little fields and villages, the woolly marsh sheep. She missed her parents, particularly her father, who had just retired, but it was a small price to pay. Though she'd have liked Peter and Diana to know them.

She worried about her parents, if the Germans invaded, and was proud of the thousands of Canadians who had volunteered and gone to England for training. Yet she was relieved that Matt and the kids were so far away from it. She shivered and rubbed her arms with her crossed hands, glad that the milder weather was coming. It would be an early spring.

She heard Diana shrieking and looked round. She was racing across the paddock, her hair streaming, holding her hood with one hand in case she lost it. At five, she was slimming down, her legs lengthening, and already could run nearly as fast as Peter, who was two years older. He was pounding along after her and shouted as he pitched forward and sprawled on the hard ground, tripping over Bess, who had darted in front of him. Livvy was anxious for a second, but he was up again almost immediately.

Diana slammed into the fence, yelling, "I've won! I've won!" She scrambled through between the bars and came running over the track and up the lawn toward the house. Peter was climbing the fence behind her, shouting to her to stop. Livvy laughed and called, "Come on, you two! Tea's nearly on the table!"

As the children came tumbling into the house, Livvy noticed blood on the left knee of Peter's pants. The denim was torn and muddy. He had done it when he fell, only he had been too angry to realize it. She helped him off with his plaid jacket and sat him on one of the spoke-backed wooden kitchen chairs, kneeling to unlace his shoes. "Here, Diana," she said, "put those outside on the mat, when you take off your own."

She lifted him up to stand on the chair, told him to undo his belt and helped him to peel off the pants. He must have landed on a stone, for the knee had a nasty gash. After one quick glance at it, he stood looking straight ahead at the calendar of English country scenes his mother had hanging on the wall. For March, there was a colored painting of Salisbury Cathedral, and he thought the tall spire was just like a stone tepee. Livvy kept iodine and cotton wool in the kitchen cupboard. She fetched them and poured some of the boiling water for the tea into an enamel bowl. "This is going to hurt a bit," she warned him. "So you can shout a little if you want to."

"Redskins don't cry," he said.

Livvy crouched and, as gently as possible, washed away the dirt and grit from around the gash. It was not so bad as it had seemed, yet was still quite deep, and she had to wipe firmly along the cut to clean it. He caught his breath sharply, the only sound he made. She looked up at his small, determined face, the square jaw, the straight, blunt nose, so like Matt's, dark hair falling over his forehead, just like

155

his, and wanted to hug him. She poured some iodine on a piece of cotton wool. "Now this is really going to sting," she said. "But if you grit your teeth and count up to thirty, the worst'll be over."

He nodded, and gasped as she dabbed the cotton wool along the wound, wiping it and the skin on either side with the dark brown antiseptic. She saw his hands grab the spokes of the chair behind him and hold on tight, but he did not cry out.

"There we are, Chief," Livvy smiled. "Now, you just sit there while the squaws finish laying the table." As an extra treat, she brought out the last pot of her raspberry jam and the slab of chocolate cake she had been saving for tomorrow. She made the tea while Diana buttered the scones. As she lit the kitchen lamp, she heard a car rattling and bumping up the track toward the house. Who can that be? she wondered. Diana ran through to look out of one of the living room windows. There was silence and they heard her shriek, "It's Daddy!"

Peter started up and winced at the pain in his knee. Livvy set the lamp down carefully. "Rest your leg, Peter," she said. "We'll just stay here." She wanted to hurry out like Diana, but it would not be fair to leave him alone. She found her hands were trembling as she adjusted the wick.

She heard the car stop by the barn and Bess barking with excitement, then the sound of Diana opening the front door to the porch and the deep rumble of Matt's voice as he scooped her up. There was a thump as he dumped his case on the living room floor and he was in the kitchen door, seeming to fill it, with Diana held in the crook of one arm, his hair tousled and falling nearly to his right eyebrow. "I dunno," he laughed. "I've built roads over most of Canada, blasted holes through the Rockies. You'd think I could have laid one decent little bit of track up to my own house."

He set Diana down, kissed the top of Peter's head and rumpled his hair, and was coming toward her. She had got out another plate, cup and saucer and was holding them. He leaned down and kissed her cheek gently. "Hello, honey."

"Why are you home so soon?" she asked. It wasn't what she meant to say. It just came out. "Is something wrong?"

"No, no," he grinned. "But I have to see McIver at the

156

office in the morning, so I thought I might as well get back this evening. Disappointed?"

Before she could tell him it was the nicest surprise she'd had all year, he turned away, concerned. Peter had drawn his dressing gown aside and sat with his bandaged leg thrust out, trying to look as if it weren't deliberate. "What's happened to your knee?" Matt asked. "Did you hurt it?"

"You'll hear the whole saga while we have tea," Livvy said. "You're just in time."

"It was hurt bad, Daddy," Diana told him. "All bleedy. But he didn't cry, not one little bit."

"I'm an Indian," Peter said. "Indians don't cry."

Chapter 10

LIVVY WOKE UP WITH HER HEAD STILL ON MATT'S SHOULDER and his arm around her. She felt completely contented and rested, as she always did when they fell asleep after they had made love. After ten years, their response to each other was as passionate as ever, and she was sorry for the wives she heard complaining about the staleness of their marriages. Maybe it was because Matt spent those long weeks away, but she was still as eager to see him as she had been when she was a girl and found his touch as exciting. More. Even more exciting, for they had learned long ago that their needs were the same and had lost any sense of embarrassment or coyness with each other.

Waking up slowly, so relaxed, was almost a sensuous pleasure itself. Her body felt supple and fluid, defenseless yet protected by his solidity against her and the thickness of his arm around her. For such a strong man, he could be so gentle. Yet she had seen him nearly tear apart a hulking Russian miner who had insulted her at a camp up near Great Bear Lake. And the times when they both were carried away and he lost his control, demanding and forcing reactions from her, were when she felt most wholly a woman.

Yesterday, as soon as she heard Diana shouting and realized who it was, she had been excited. She was even more excited than the children to have him home for an extra two nights, although she had not shown it. After tea, he fixed the washing machine, securing the loose handle that drove the paddles inside the wooden tub, then sat with the children, admiring Diana's writing book from school and Peter's colored drawings of wigwams and braves and ponies. At bedtime he thrilled them with a story of how once in the Klondike he had been hunted for a day and a night by a huge grizzly bear, after the bullets in his rifle had frozen solid with the cold. Peter guessed he was making it up, but grinned and said nothing, not to spoil it for Diana.

Livvy had felt almost guilty, for she caught herself resenting his concentration on the children. All through tea and the hours till supper, she could think of nothing except how soon she could be alone with him. They had talked quietly about little things until the children were asleep and then had gone to bed themselves. She hadn't even remembered to ask him what he had to see the area manager about.

For the past eight or nine months, Matt had been working at the Lawson Valley site where there were hopes of a major oil strike. The valley was among the foothills south of Calgary, where the old-time ranches were gradually being split up and converted into dairy farms. Geologists had argued that there must be oil waiting to be discovered in Canada and, just before the war, one of the ranchers became obsessed with the idea that Lawson Valley was the place. He had convinced Matt and Bill Elder, an American engineer, by lighting the natural gas escaping from a crack in the ground and frying eggs and bacon over it in a tin plate. The first probes had confirmed there were supplies of oil and gas there somewhere and they had started the tricky and backbreaking work of sinking the first trial shafts. It would be Canada's first oil field and could be vital, if the war lasted much longer.

Livvy was conscious of the heaviness of her head on Matt's right shoulder and eased aside, in case his arm had gone to sleep.

"Don't move," he said.

She looked round, surprised. "Are you awake?"

His eyes were shut, but he nodded. "M'hm."

"Why didn't you say something?"

He grinned. "I just did." His hand moved up from her side and cupped her right breast, squeezing its fullness softly. Her nipple erected at once, pushing against the cotton of her nightdress. He passed the ball of his thumb over it and she murmured, snuggling closer to him. "Did I ever tell you how much I miss you?" he whispered.

"You don't need to." She lifted her head to kiss him and settled it on the curve of his arm again. "It was a marvelous

159

surprise when you walked in. I was anxious in case you couldn't get back this weekend at all."

"Why?"

"There's a dance at the school tomorrow night."

He laughed. "And you want me to take you? I'm not much of a dancer."

"I'm on the committee," she explained. "We're raising funds for medical supplies to send to France."

He looked quite serious for a moment, then he smiled. "Well, I guess that's worth a dance."

"You haven't told me why you have to see Mr. McIver."

"Oh—just that there's been a little hitch with the pipeline. The section over Moose Ridge came adrift."

"How?"

"Cattle, probably," he smiled. "There's still some roaming wild up there." His fingers reached for the warm fork of her thighs.

"I—I have to make breakfast," she whispered, her breath catching.

"M'hm." He smiled and nodded, and the arm that was round her rose, swinging her up effortlessly to face him. As she shifted her legs to suit the new position, his hand slid over her hip to draw her to him. She melted, pressing in against him, smiling as they kissed.

"I thought you were asleep," Diana said. Their heads swiveled and they saw her standing at the door, watching them, in her pink dressing gown and moccasin slippers. "Are you going to get up, Daddy?" she asked.

"I was just trying to," Matt said.

Livvy giggled and punched him on the chest. When she eased away, he caught her and they struggled in fun, laughing.

"Stop playing with Daddy, Mummy," Diana said crossly. "It's breakfast time and I'm hungry!"

As they were finishing breakfast, Dan Connally drove up in his Model T. He was one of their nearest neighbors and had seen Matt's gray Willys Overland go past the previous evening. Matt went out to have a word with him and brought him in for a cup of coffee. Livvy liked him a lot. He was a good-looking, fair-haired young man about her own age, a dependable friend, who kept an eye on the place while Matt was away.

160

He had brought some real news. Before leaving with the expeditionary force for England, one of his cousins had worked out a family code to beat the army censors and, in his latest letter, sent word that the Canadian units were leaving for France.

"Did he know what sector they were going to?" Matt asked.

"I doubt it," Dan said. "Most likely they won't find out until they're there. Anyway, the code's only for general things. He can't send names." Dan was a bachelor and worked in his family's store in town. It was no secret that, if his father had not been near retirement, Dan would have left with the volunteers.

"They've just missed some pretty heavy fighting over there, then," Matt said. "Around Neuve Chapelle."

Livvy shivered. "All those men killed, just to recapture one little village."

"That's the way this war's turning out," Matt said. "You have to push them back one village at a time."

"And hope you don't lose it again," Dan added. "One thing, at least the Hoinies have proved they can really fight."

"They've also shown they can be beaten," Matt said.

Peter was playing up his sore knee, wincing as he hobbled around. Livvy suspected it was mainly because Matt was home, but they decided to keep him off school anyway. Diana's face crumpled and it looked as if there was going to be a storm until Dan offered to drop her off at school on his way to work. She liked that, since he always let her ride in front with him and work the horn. And he always had a paper bag of mint candies on top of the dashboard.

After they had gone, Peter's injured knee gave no more trouble and he was able to help Matt with the chores. They took down the rest of the winter screens and he held the ladder while his father refixed some loose slates on the roof of the barn. Then Matt sawed down some old logs and Peter wheeled them in the barrow over to the lean to by the kitchen door, stacking them carefully.

Livvy watched them through the window while she got on with her baking, and realized more clearly than ever how alike they were. It was not just the physical resemblance, although already Peter was becoming his father in minia-

161

ture. It was in their seriousness and total concentration on their work and in how they both stood as they thought something out, with their legs slightly apart and braced and their heads tilted noticeably to the right. Perhaps Peter had copied it from Matt, even the frown, yet it was part of him now, too. Their daughter was more like her, but their son was all Matt.

When they came inside to wash, Matt asked her if she wanted to come into town with them. "I'd love to," she said. "But I've promised these things for the cake stall tomorrow night. Are you taking Peter?"

"I reckon it'll just about complete the miracle cure on that knee of his," Matt smiled. Peter blushed and started to limp again.

When they were ready, Peter hurried out to the car. He had forgotten his scarf and Livvy took it out to him. She found Matt standing by the woodpile, looking out toward the paddock and the woods with the oddest expression on his face. "I was thinking how happy we'd been here," he murmured.

"We always will be," she said. He smiled and kissed her.

She was anxious that they would not be gone too long and relieved when he told her his business with McIver shouldn't take more than an hour at most. "That's if he's in the office. If not, I'll just leave a note. Either way, we'll be home before lunch."

Peter felt very important, driving in the big open tourer beside his father. The Overland was 30 horsepower with a 110-inch wheel base and an electric self-starter, speedometer and headlamps, and brass kerosene carriage lamps attached to the sides. It cost nearly a thousand American dollars and was Matt's one extravagance. But he needed something really reliable to carry him over some of the trails he came across and he was making four thousand dollars a year now, so he could afford it. He had folded back the mohair hood and, even with the swivel windshield, Peter could feel the wind in his hair, giving the illusion they were traveling much faster than they really were. Matt drove hard but very surely, avoiding most of the bumps and potholes in the track.

"Can we go even faster?" Peter asked.

"Who do you think I am?" Matt smiled. "Eddie Ricken-backer?" Peter laughed.

As they came into town, Matt was wondering what Peter and Diana would make of Winchelsea, the little place their mother came from. It was so different from Calgary, a sprawling cow town of wide streets with frame houses, many of them with false fronts still at the upper stories. Although even that was changing, with larger, brick houses and stores and factories, and industry becoming almost as important as the annual cattle drives. The hitching posts for horses were disappearing and there were more men in blue overalls in the streets than cowpunchers nowadays. "Funny to think," he said, "that twenty years ago there was only a fort here and buffalo roved where we're driving now."

"Buffalo?" Peter repeated, startled.

"M'hm," Matt nodded. "Of course that was before the roads and the railways came. So I guess you could say I've helped to make a city."

They parked in the company's back lot, but instead of going inside, Matt led Peter down to the drugstore on the corner "I might be a little while," he explained.

Carlo, the middle-aged Italian behind the counter, bowed with mock deference when he took Peter's order of a rasp-berry soda and a glazed, cream-filled doughnut. "Now you look after him, Carlo," Matt cautioned. "He can have any-thing he wants."

When he had gone, Carlo went to the magazine rack and laid out a selection on the counter. Peter chose *Buffalo Bill Weekly*, because it had a picture of Bill's fight with Yellow-hand on the cover. He was soon absorbed and only looked up when Carlo slid a slice of blueberry pie onto his plate. He was about to start reading again when he saw something across the street. His father was walking along with Ser-geant Mackenzie. They seemed to be talking very seriously.

Phil Mackenzie was tall and sandy-haired, a sergeant in the Royal Canadian Mounted Police, unmistakable in his scarlet tunic. "The Captain was inclined to believe you were imagining things, Matt," he said, "but the pipeline was bro-ken again last night."

"Where?"

"Just where it comes out of Benson's Creek. We were

lucky again. Some fisherman spotted oil coming down with the water and reported it. We got an emergency team up there right away to repair it." Mackenzie paused. "You're sure the first break wasn't caused by cattle?"

"Cattle might bend it or trample it," Matt told him. "They wouldn't unscrew the junction of the pipe first. It was deliberate, all right."

They were opposite the company building and stopped. "But why?" Mackenzie asked.

"The why's easy. We're not getting too much oil out of the valley yet, but every drop's invaluable. With those two breakages we've probably lost several thousand barrels."

"Sabotage, you mean?"

"Without any doubt," Matt said.

Mackenzie glanced round and lowered his voice. "Just between us, there's been reports of attempted sabotage back east, at the Welland Canal and some railway bridges. So it's not something we can ignore." He saluted as an army car went past. "You say there are three of them?"

"At least three," Matt told him. "I've seen them and a bald-headed man drive through the oil field about four times lately. Once when they'd stopped to have a look, I went to talk to them, but they jumped back in and took off."

"Is there no security at the field?"

"None. It's all spread out, open," Matt said. "Some people use the tracks as a shortcut across the valley. But those men were kind of mapping it out."

"I see," Mackenzie frowned. "So what are they after?"

Matt was very serious. "Something big. I believe they're planning something that's going to happen before the new well goes into operation."

"When's that?" Mackenzie asked.

"It's scheduled for Monday," Matt said. "That's why I came to fetch you. I don't think we have much time to lose."

Will Turner liked to walk up Broadway. His American friends were amused by that, he knew. But then they never walked anywhere if they could avoid it. Occasionally in the park, or from their offices to their clubs. They seldom took the opportunity just to walk about their city and look at it. He found New York fascinating.

While the *Lusitania* was in dock, there were so many

things to attend to that he did not always have the chance, himself. On this trip, however, with Staff Captain Anderson handling most of the loading and unloading, he had a little more leisure time.

He came off the Rapid Transit Subway at the 23rd Street station and walked briskly up to Madison Square, where he slowed down. He had over an hour before he had arranged to meet her, so there was no hurry. He liked the square with its nicely laid-out garden and statues. The first one he passed was of Roscoe Conkling. Every time he saw it he reminded himself to ask someone who Roscoe Conkling was that he should have a statue put up to him, but he always forgot. The one he admired most was the bronze of Admiral Farragut in the opposite corner. Farragut, who had wiped out the pirates in the West Indies and later captured New Orleans from the South. He remembered him visiting Liverpool just after the Civil War, and crossed over to pay his respects. Broad and solid, Turner considered the statue as he tamped down and lit his pipe. With its striking pedestal, it did the old boy justice. There was nothing finer in the whole city.

He came out of the square where Broadway crossed Fifth Avenue and looked back at the intersection filled by the Fuller Building, known as the Flatiron. Yes, it was like that, yet even more like a great ship steaming majestically up the Avenue. With its height and bulk, it was just how the *Lusitania* would look, if some mighty hand could pluck her up from her berth and set her down in the midst of the city. He chuckled to see how unsuspecting women grabbed their hats and clutched at their fluttering skirts when they reached the corner. The Flatiron had the odd effect of increasing wind velocity, so that it was not unusual on a really blustery day for people to be flung right off the sidewalk.

Just opposite was the Hoffman House, where he often had dinner in the roof garden restaurant in the right season. He continued on his way uptown, coming to the start of the theater section, Weber's Music Hall, Daly's Theatre and Wallack's. Music was the second passion of his life. For a plain, seafaring man he had a surprising number of musicians and theater people among his friends. They liked him as a "character," blunt, yet sympathetic and appreciative.

He turned right into Herald Square past the statue of

Horace Greeley, and stood for a moment, looking up Sixth Avenue, its long prospect ruined by the west side elevated railway that ran all the way along it to Central Park. Across from him on the corner of 34th Street was Macy's huge Departmental Store. He could buy her a little present there, something tasteful, except he had no idea what she would like. Better leave it till later.

The traffic cop was signaling and he crossed with other pedestrians under the El and went round the two-storied concrete building of the *New York Herald*, and was back on Broadway. Over on the west sidewalk was the stretch his theater friends called the Rialto. All the out-of-work actors met there, exchanged gossip, saw their agents, looked for engagements. There was the Knickerbocker Theatre and the Casino, with its summer concerts in the beer garden on the roof. So much of New York life seemed to be conducted on roofs, or underground. There was no place like it. Opposite, between 39th Street and 40th Street, was the Metropolitan Opera House where he had heard Nellie Melba. No, that was at the Manhattan. He had heard Emma Eames at the Met. He preferred Melba.

On impulse, he went into Brummell's, the confectioner's. He had to take something, but the array of creams, chocolates and bonbons was bewildering, so he asked the girl behind the counter just to give him one of their assorted boxes. As he paid for it and collected it, he remembered the last time he had bought one of these selections. It had been for his wife. He had not seen her, not once since their separation, and did not like to be reminded. He hoped Mercedes wouldn't ask about her. She would surely have more tact.

He was still early and had a look at the photographs of Ethel Barrymore outside the Empire in a play called *The Shadow*. She was a very pretty girl, straight and no nonsense, and he decided to see it, if it was still playing on his next trip. He went past 42nd Street to the intersection with Seventh Avenue, from which many interesting old buildings had been cleared away to open up Longacre Square. Because of the terracotta and pink granite bulk of the *New York Times* building that stood in the middle, most people knew it as Times Square. The enormous 700-room Hotel Astor rose beyond it. There were more theaters, but for him

166

that marked the end of Broadway, most of it from there taken up by automobile stores and apartment houses. He turned back and went down West 42nd Street to the New Amsterdam.

Mercedes was waiting for him outside the stage door, looking a little anxious, but very pretty in a tan ankle-length skirt and a long, loose matching jacket with a high fur collar over a ruffled cream blouse. Her hair was swept up and drawn over her dark curls was a soft velvet cap, peaking above her left ear with a flourish of osprey feathers like a fleur-de-lis. She seemed relieved to see him. She ran to meet him and kissed him delightedly.

"You're as pretty as a picture, my dear," he told her. "I'm not late, am I?"

"No," she smiled. "Only, I was so excited I couldn't keep still. Then I started thinking, maybe you'd get lost or something."

He chuckled. "I'm not likely to do that." He gave her the chocolates. "Here. For you."

She saw the Brummell wrapping paper and made a face. "Oh, no . . . I'm trying to lose weight!"

"Ridiculous! You're just perfect," he told her. "Still, I can always give them to someone else."

"Don't you dare!" she laughed, and tucked her arm through his. "Now, where are we going to lunch?"

"I thought of Lüchow's," he said. "But is there somewhere nearer you'd like, somewhere your theater friends go, maybe."

"If you're sure," she said, doubtfully. She wanted to have a relaxed and happy time with him, not for him to feel out of place. "There's the Shanley. Or Sherry's, just a block down. But it's a bit pricey, Uncle Tom."

She was hugging his arm. Turner smiled. "If you don't mind, I certainly don't." Uncle Tom . . . He was Tom to his family, Will to his friends. There weren't many left who called him Tom. It was strange to hear it, oddly comforting. And he had to admit, he was reaching the age when it was flattering to be envied for the pretty girl on his arm, even if she was only his niece.

Sherry's was an attractive and fashionable restaurant, with elegance in its deliberately restrained decor. It was already filling for lunch and Mercedes was afraid they would not get in, but her uncle had a quietly authoritative manner, she discovered, and they were shown to a side table at the lower end. Not the best place to be noticed oneself, yet perfect for watching the other tables and who else came in.

As a young and not very highly paid actress, she had only been here once before and was very excited. She knew it would not mean much, if anything, to her uncle, although she was grateful to him for bringing her and hoped she was not making him spend more than he had intended. She took off her warm jacket, fluffed out the puff sleeves of her blouse and smoothed up her hair at the back as her eyes darted from table to table. She had never seen so many of her idols at one time. Otis Skinner, Florence Reed, William Gillette, Marie Tempest. It was as if they were all gathered for some purpose. The exquisite Marie Doro. And . . . "Look!" she whispered and touched his arm. "Uncle Tom—look over there. It's Ethel Barrymore."

Turner glanced across and recognized the young star, beautiful in spite of her broad forehead and slightly blunt nose. It was her expression, charming and serious, the grave eyes above a wide mouth ready to smile, that gave her such distinction. "Yes, it is," he said. He looked back at Mercedes and thought how very lovely she was herself, flushed and animated, her eyes sparkling.

She bit her lip to prevent her mouth opening too wide. "Look . . . look!" Turner looked, and saw two men coming in together. Everyone was looking at them. "It's Charles Frohman and David Belasco!" Mercedes whispered, excitedly. "They're two of—*the* two most important producers. They used to be partners and great friends, but then they had a row about something, some actress, and they haven't spoken to each other for the last twelve years! C.F.—that's Frohman—he's been very ill and everybody thought he was going to die." Her tones became dramatic. "Then one day a few weeks ago Belasco went round to see him . . . and from that moment he started to get better!"

"Well, well, now," he murmured.

She laughed. "I know it sounds like a story, but it's perfectly true. And it's just happened. Everybody's talking about it, though nobody's seen them together yet. Isn't it exciting?"

Turner nodded, smiling. Frohman and Belasco were both short men, with great presence. Belasco, slight and handsome, with a shock of white hair, had reached his early sixties. Frohman was younger and dark, but a massive chest over spindly legs made him seem squat and top-heavy. He walked with obvious difficulty, leaning on a cane. Both of them were smiling, replying to greetings, enjoying the effect they had created. It was one of the first of their public appearances to demonstrate their reunion. Some of their intimates had been in the know and were as delighted as they by the sensation as they strolled down the restaurant, pausing for a word or two at nearly every table.

"Which is more important?" Turner asked.

Mercedes thought. "C.F., I suppose. Oh, yes, if he takes you up, you're— He's made so many stars! Maude Adams, Pauline Chase, Ethel—Gillette—Billie Burke. Oh, dozens!" She saw that Turner was rising in his chair and waving. She gasped. Frohman was coming away from a table where Nat Goodwin and Otis Skinner sat with Florence Reed. He had noticed the wave and was frowning. Turner waved again. "No, Uncle Tom!" she whispered fiercely. "Please—please!" To her dismay, she saw Frohman move toward them.

She blushed furiously, then went white and looked down at her hands. She clenched them, fighting the impulse to hit her uncle. He was a dear, dear man, but he didn't realize what he had done. She had never felt so hideously embarrassed, and everyone would see them being snubbed. She prayed the ground would open up and swallow her, she said later.

She glanced up as Charles Frohman reached them, but could not think how to apologize for intruding. His face was squat like his body, froglike, with heavy-lidded eyes and full lips, made forbidding by his frown. However, the frown was a sign of pain and his sudden smile had immense charm, lighting up his eyes, as he held out his hand with genuine pleasure. "How very nice to see you, Captain Turner," he said warmly. "All the nicer for being so unexpected."

Turner had risen again and they shook hands. "It's an even greater pleasure to see you so much better, Mr. Frohman," he said.

"Oh—better?" Frohman shrugged. "Let's say, I'm a little

169

less unwell. I don't believe you've met my wife. We're inseparable." He chuckled and raised his cane to display it.

When he smiled down to her, Mercedes had only just managed to regain her composure and had to resist the impulse to stand herself, as before royalty. She had grabbed the underside of the tablecloth and was twisting it, although she looked composed and pretty, and shy, which suited her.

"And I don't believe you've met my niece, Miss Mercedes Desmore," Turner said.

"I have not had the honor." Frohman bowed. "But I have heard of her, and am prepared to become an admirer."

"Thank you. How do you do?" Mercedes managed to say, in a very small voice.

"She's rehearsing at the New Amsterdam Theatre," Turner said.

Frohman nodded. "Yes, indeed. The Henry Arthur Jones play, isn't it? I look forward to seeing it." He lowered his voice. "I shan't come round afterwards, Miss Desmore, because I still cannot walk very far. But if I really like you, I shall send round a piece of paper with a cross on it. If you get that, you come and see me the next day."

"Yes, Mr. Frohman," Mercedes whispered. His voice was deep and soft, a beautiful voice, and she could not imagine how she had ever thought him ugly.

"I had intended to travel back with you on this trip, Captain," he said. "However, unfortunately. Or"—he chuckled—"fortunately, rather, I'm about to open a new production myself, with David Belasco. So I shan't be able to, until your next voyage."

"That'll be something for *me* to look forward to," Turner assured him.

"Till your next trip, then." Frohman smiled and bowed to Mercedes. "And don't forget, Miss Desmore."

As Frohman limped away, Turner sat again. He was amused by Mercedes' deliberate lack of self-consciousness, even though she knew that many people were now looking at her.

"You beast!" she whispered. "Why didn't you tell me you knew him?"

"I didn't get much of a chance," Turner chuckled. "Well, it may help you a bit."

She could never remember what she had for lunch that

day. Only that she had come in almost completely unknown and, when she left, many people she idolized were smiling to her. She had taken the first step into a charmed circle.

Turner saw her back to the theater, where she hugged him as tightly as she used to when she was a little girl, and almost waltzed in through the stage door. He was still chuckling when he hailed an electric taxicab to take him to the Cunard Offices.

By the time he reached State Street, however, his good humor had largely been eroded by the remembered problems. While he paid the driver, he noticed two men, stolid seamen by their dress, watching him. One wrote something in a little notebook. Great God, Turner thought, they become more blatant every day. He went inside and straight up to the office of the General Manager. The secretary told him that Mr. Sumner was not in, but he said he would wait a few minutes, in case he appeared. She was dismayed when he marched through into the inner office, but did not dare to stop him.

Sumner was not at his desk. However, a second desk had been moved in and a young, very good-looking man whom Turner recognized was sitting at it. He was Captain Guy Gaunt, Naval Attaché at the British Embassy. From his clothes, a dark, well-cut suit and tie, he could have been a cultivated and successful man about town. An Australian by birth, his manner was easy and relaxed, and partly concealed a considerable intellect. The Navy had the pick of the career men and Gaunt had some very special talents. Like his counterparts, von Papen and Boy-Ed, he was more than he seemed, and was one of the chiefs of British Intelligence and Counter-Intelligence in the United States. Like them, too, he was technically based in Washington, but spent much of his time in New York, where he was a popular member of society. "Good afternoon, Captain Turner," he said. "Looking for me?"

"No. Sumner, actually," Turner grunted. He was annoyed at missing the manager. It was best to confront them when you had a bit of steam up.

"Nothing wrong, I hope?" Gaunt asked.

Turner shook his head. "No, no. Or everything, really. This whole damned war." Gaunt agreed silently. "We've just had a diabolical crossing. Now I know how a penny

171

feels when it's used for pitch and toss. It's the first time I've ever seen passengers seasick on the *Lusitania*."

"Ah, yes," Gaunt smiled. Turner, of course, had his own ideas about what was really important.

"On the *Lusitania*," Turner repeated. "It's sailing west with those damned new cargo spaces mostly empty. And not even a full supply of coal. It doesn't matter that we've lost one boiler room. I want Sumner to make sure we have the maximum supply on the eastbound voyage so the bunkers will only need topping up at Liverpool. It's the only real ballast we've got."

"Yes," Gaunt said. "Of course you'll have a full load of cargo on the journey home." Turner grunted. "You've seen the manifest?"

"The official one," Turner muttered.

The situation was extraordinary. Because of the President's insistence on strict neutrality, American manufacturers were prohibited from selling war materials direct to the Allied and German governments. They could, however, sell them to private businessmen, and a whole network of buyers had grown up. For the Allies, it was greatly simplified by most of the operation being taken over by the Morgan Bank, yet there were difficulties when it came to shipments of obvious contraband. And no vessel could be given a clearance to sail until the Collector of Customs had received an attested copy of the manifest. The subterfuge developed by Gaunt and accepted by the Collector of Customs for New York, Dudley Field Malone, was to provide a sworn manifest, which would be published, then a supplementary one several days after departure, which could be quietly ignored.

"The supplementary manifest is even more important," Gaunt said seriously, "now we've learned that the Germans send details of the cargoes on individual ships to their submarines."

"That's only to be expected," Turner commented. "I spotted two Jerries on my way in. They're not even pretending to hide any more."

"No," Gaunt said. "They're becoming desperate, so less predictable and more dangerous." He had men watching the offices of the Hamburg-Amerika Line, just as they had their men outside here.

"We'll all probably be desperate soon," Turner said. He made for the door and paused. "What are you lining up for my supplementary list this time? Another hundred thousand gallons of diesel oil?"

"Not quite so much," Gaunt smiled.

"But there'll be boxes of cartridges too, no doubt," Turner frowned. "It's an eerie feeling to know you've got that kind of lethal mixture stowed under your passengers' feet."

"There's absolutely no danger," Gaunt insisted. "The State Department won't allow any explosives to be carried on passenger ships. They are all nonexplosive in—"

"In bulk," Turner finished for him. "I keep being told that. They tested a whole load of cartridges and bullets by lighting a fire under them and they only spluttered a bit. Well, that's fine in the case of fire. But it occurs to me that if you hit a bullet hard enough on the end, it will go off. Now, why should a thousand bullets, hit even harder, refuse to go off just because they're 'in bulk'? However . . . ours not to reason why." He tipped his bowler hat and went out.

Chapter 11

JUST BEFORE DARK, MATT FLETCHER DROVE INTO BLACK Sapphire, the main township in the valley. Lights were coming on in some of the windows. He stopped outside the oil company's office, but instead of going in, he walked across the street and back down to the bar next to the hotel.

Squatting on the boardwalk with his back against the wall, wrapped in his blanket, was a very old Stoney Indian known as Harry Hightree, the nearest anyone could come to his real name. If Lawson Valley belonged to the oldest inhabitant, it would have been Harry's. Matt paused beside him and lit a cigarette. "You seen them?" he said through his cupped hands. The shake of Harry's head was so slight it could have been a tremor of age. "They been through town any time today?" The old man's head shook again. Matt dropped the pack of cigarettes and the box of matches on the edge of his blanket and went into the bar.

There were a few shift workers at the tables and some of them waved. Matt nodded back and went straight to the bar, where the short, dark-haired barman was already reaching for the Scotch. "No, thanks, Louis," Matt said. "I'm just looking for someone, a big fellow with cropped hair and a scar just here, on his left cheek."

"Oh, that one," Louis sniffed. "I don't see him for three four days."

"You sure?"

"Sure, I'm sure," Louis said. "He a friend of yours?"

"Don't know him from Adam," Matt smiled. "I have to see him on a matter of business."

"Then you take care, huh, Matt?"

"Why?"

"I don't know," Louis shrugged. "He's some kind of phony. Trying to make like one of my people. Sure, he speaks French

174

good, very good, but like a Frenchman, eh? He's no *habitant*, no *Canadien, tu comprends*?"

Matt nodded. "Did he have anyone with him?"

"I think so. Bald, flat nose. But he don't say nothing."

"Okay, thanks, Louis," Matt smiled. "Maybe I won't do business after all. Give me a beer, will you? To take out."

Matt came out from the bar and paused again by Harry Hightree, who was more invisible than ever in the shadow by the door. Matt held the bottle of beer down by his side. "Keep your eyes peeled, Harry," he said. The old Indian's hand moved quicker than a mosquito and the bottle vanished under a fold of his blanket.

The oil company's local manager was relieved to see Matt. "I thought I was going to have to go up there with them. It's not my sort of . . . you know," he apologized, and led Matt through into his office.

Sergeant Mackenzie was there already, with six other Mounties. Even in plain work jackets, sweaters and boots, like Matt, from their size and alertness no one could mistake them. McIver, the company's area manager in Calgary, was a large man too, but running to fat. He had taken the chair behind the desk and he was sweating, wiping the puffy skin under his eyes and the sides of his neck with his hand. "This is a desperate business, Matt," he muttered. "Desperate."

"Could be," Matt agreed. He looked at Mackenzie. "Where are the rest of you?"

"This is us," Mackenzie said, with a smile. He saw that Matt was troubled. "Well, you said there were only three of them. And the Force is kept pretty busy at weekends."

"There's only three I'm sure of," Matt said. "But there's at least two more."

"What makes you think so?"

"We have five wells in operation. They cover quite an area. Then there's the trial shafts, the tanks and separators, and the pipeline. Just at the field, itself, we're going to be spread out over more than a mile."

Mackenzie had stopped smiling. "What size crews do you have?"

"At night there's only a maintenance team," the local manager told him. "And there's the site engineer, or his deputy. There's an emergency crew on standby."

"Look, we can use them," McIver said. "And all the other

175

workers in town. We can throw a ring around the whole field and keep those people out, or scare them off."

"That's just what we don't want," Matt said. McIver blinked at him, startled, "It's no use scaring them off for a night."

Mackenzie nodded. "Besides, we don't know they're going to try anything tonight. They could just lie low till everyone's gone away again. It's best if everything looks normal. We have to find out what those birds are after, and catch them at it."

"What if you don't?" McIver asked.

"Then there's going to be one hell of a bang," Matt said.

Sadie, the plump blond office secretary, had been told the meeting was to discuss how to strengthen the pipeline after the two recent breaks, but suspected it was something even more serious. She brought in a tray of coffee and, seeing the way everyone fell silent, became anxious. Matt winked to her reassuringly as he took his mug.

"Well, we'll—uh—check out the Moose Ridge section in the morning, then," the office manager mumbled. "Thanks for hanging on, Sadie. You might as well get off home now."

From his shiftiness, Sadie knew there was definitely something up. She glanced at Matt. Just so long as nothing happens to that big stiff, she thought. One of the other men was holding the door open for her. "Here's your hat and what's your hurry," she grinned. "I'll just tidy up."

When she had gone out, McIver set his mug down hard on the desk. His hand was shaking so much he had nearly dropped it. "So . . . if everything's supposed to go on like normal," he muttered, "what do you want the three of us to do?" He included Matt and the local manager with himself.

"Nothing at all," Mackenzie told him. "In fact the Captain said we were to avoid getting civilians involved."

"I suppose that's right," the manager agreed quickly. "I mean, that we don't get mixed up in it."

"So who's going to stop me?" Matt asked.

"Not me," Mackenzie assured him. "We need at least one person who knows his way around out there." He pulled a .44 automatic from inside his jacket and held it out. Matt shook his head. "Don't be crazy," Mackenzie said. "If those birds are what we both think they are, you're going to need it."

176

Matt took the automatic. It was too bulky to go in his side pocket and he stuck it into the belt at his waist. It made him feel self-consciously like Peter playing cowboys.

They drove out to the field in three separate cars, with ten minutes between them. Phil Mackenzie went with Matt in the Overland. As Matt got behind the wheel, the butt of the automatic prodded him sharply under the ribs. He took it out and laid it on the floor between his legs.

It was a cold and dark night. The lighting stopped abruptly at the edge of town and Matt drove on his sidelights to let their eyes become used to the darkness. The road was only a paler gray strip in front of them. They were watchful and silent, until he pointed out the first of the derricks, its tall, skeletal shape glinting dimly in the faint glow of four gas lamps, hung on poles that formed a square working area around it. The shapes of two smaller, abandoned test wells could just be made out behind. "Aw, Jeese . . ." Mackenzie muttered. And again, when Matt pointed off to the left some minutes later, to the second well. "Aw, Jeese . . ." He went on repeating it under his breath like a litany. He was a religious man and it was the first mild profanity Matt had ever heard from him.

"I told you," Matt said quietly. The plan was for them to cover the center area, while the local manager dropped three of the Mounties at the far end of the field and McIver dropped the others off at the near end. Then they were to spread out, with one man from each team watching the road while the other two kept a shadow patrol on the wells. It had taken Mackenzie less than half a minute to realize it was a job for three or four times the number of men he had brought.

The main road had a good, made-up surface, but when they swung off on the side track, the tourer bumped and rattled so much there was no hope of making a quiet approach. "Well, it's early yet," Mackenzie said. "We've a long, cold night ahead." He looked back toward the road, but any sign of it had already disappeared. "You mentioned something about tanks and separators?"

"It's the kind of field this is," Matt explained. "We drilled down thousands of feet in various places and found nothing. Then one day we struck a pocket of natural gas. The pressure was so great we couldn't control it. It wrecked the derrick and ignited, a monstrous column of fire. We were lucky we didn't blow ourselves to kingdom come."

"I remember reading about that," Mackenzie said. "But where does the gas come in? I thought you pumped oil up out of underground lakes?"

"Not around here," Matt told him. "This is all porous limestone. It holds the oil like a sponge holds water. It's the gas pressure that brings it up, then the mixture is piped to separators, where the oil particles and gas are, well, separated and channeled to storage tanks. The pipeline carries the oil to the refinery and the gas is used for lighting and cooking all over this part of the Province."

In front of them was the black outcrop of a massive spur projecting from the valley wall. The track swerved to skirt it and rose over the lower end of the spur. As the Overland swung round, Mackenzie gasped and grabbed Matt's arm. "What's that?" Ahead and to the right, the sky glowed red and they could hear the dull roar of flames.

"Don't worry," Matt laughed. "That's the burn-off I told you about." The sergeant still did not understand. "To control the pressure, before a new well can be connected to the separators, we have to burn off the first rush of naphtha and gas." They topped the rise and could already feel the heat. On the floor of the fold beyond the spur, a plume of fire towered into the sky, a golden white shot with coral and pink as it climbed, turning to somber crimson and belching clouds of thick pitch-black smoke. The track passed within three hundred yards of it and the heat became intense. Both men had to screw up their eyes against the glare. They could just make out the framework of a tall derrick behind it.

Once they were past, it was as if they had been blinded. The dark ahead of them seemed impenetrable and Matt had to switch on the headlamps until he could see normally again.

"Is all that just wasted?" Mackenzie asked.

"In a way, I guess," Matt said. "But it's no use to us. We can't harness it. It'll be ready to be capped by Monday. Then we'll have our new well."

They drove on for another quarter of a mile, passing several trial sites and the third and earliest of the wells in operation. Beyond it, the track forked and the narrower side road which they took opened out into a wide gravel parking space. Three or four cars of the night-shift workers were already there and a covered two-ton delivery truck. Matt drew in beside the truck and pointed out the huts of the engineer and site foreman and the long, low administration building. All the pipes of the field were overground and converged on the bulky shapes of the separators behind the huts. More pipes led to the huge oil storage tanks and, off some distance to the side, to the even larger telescopic drums of the three main gas-holders.

Matt cut the headlights and the carriage lights, and they gave themselves a moment to accustom their ears and eyes to the silence and the darkness again. There was a scarcely audible hum from the separators and a distant, muted chunking from the well across from the fork in the track. It was all much quieter than Mackenzie had expected. A single gas lamp illuminated the middle of the parking lot. There were three or four more lamps by the separators and the tanks. A lamp above the door of the engineer's hut cast a strictly defined pool of light and more light streamed in a shaft from its window. The administration and foreman's huts were unlit.

"The other two wells are on the hillside over there," Matt said, pointing ahead.

"You produce enough gas here to service the whole of Alberta," Mackenzie complained. "Why don't you use a little more of it to light up the oil field?"

"I guess none of us ever thought of sabotage," Matt said.

"That's a fact," Mackenzie grunted.

They got out and Mackenzie came round the bonnet. Matt lowered his voice. "I ought to have a word with the engineer."

"Yeah, he'd better know what's going on," Mackenzie agreed. "Can you get in touch with the men at the rigs?"

"They're all linked by telephone."

"Okay," Mackenzie said. "Better tell them, too. But they're not to do anything except call the engineer if they notice anything suspicious. You'll be there to take the calls." Matt made to protest. "That's what we decided."

"Yeah, I know," Matt said. "But you've seen it now. There's too much for one man to check out."

Mackenzie hesitated and gave in. "All right. You take a look at those separators and the oil tanks, then get back to the hut. I'll check the gas-holders and move higher up the hillside." He squinted up at the sky. The heavy clouds were thinning and breaking up and the valley floor was clearer in the brighter, patchy moonlight. "If those clouds don't close up again, I should be able to spot anything that moves down here."

"If we're lucky," Matt nodded.

"If we are," Mackenzie agreed. "Like I said, it's early yet. For now, we're just having a look-see."

"Right."

"I'll check with you in an hour." Mackenzie started to move off, and paused. "If there's trouble, don't try anything heroic. Okay?"

"Okay," Matt said. "And good luck." Mackenzie did not answer and Matt watched him cross the parking space, keeping out of the cone of direct light from the lamp, his boots crunching on the icy gravel. Suddenly, as he reached the grass beyond it, Mackenzie vanished. Moving silently like a woodman, he blended into the shadows and was gone.

It had become intensely cold. Matt shivered and drew his fleece-lined jacket tighter round him as he made for the engineer's hut. A deep frost had settled on the ground and sparkled in the moonlight. Left alone, he felt at last the full tension of what they were doing here and, quite naturally, his movements became purposeful but watchful, as if he were out hunting. It was exactly the feeling he remembered, creeping up out of the mists for a dawn raid on a Boer commando. A startled, bearded sentry had risen from the ground at his feet, stabbing with a bayonet for his heart. The point of the blade was deflected by the buckle of his bandolier and twisted up, ripping through his left shoulder. His shot killed the sentry and signaled the main attack, and he had fought all through it without realizing how badly he had been wounded until it was over. His shoulder was throbbing now in the cold.

He pushed open the door of the hut and went in. The heat from the gas-fired stove seemed almost to suck him through the door. The lamps were lit, but there was no one in the room. "Sam? You there, Sam?" he called. There was no answer and he crossed to the door of the small sleeping room at the far end. It was empty, but Charlie Hewitt's blue

180

worsted overcoat lay across the bed. Charlie was the young deputy and must be on duty. He can't have gone far without his coat, Matt figured.

He turned back into the main room, sorting out his priorities. First, he had to warn the night crews to be on their guard. The telephone receiver was off its hook. He picked it up, cranked the handle and dialed the number for No. 1 Well. There was no reply. He tried it again, then No. 2 and No. 3 and had no response from any of them. Abruptly he thought of a reason why. The lines had been cut. Perhaps Charlie had been speaking to one or trying to call one when the line went dead, and had gone to investigate.

Matt moved quickly to the door, switched off the outside light and went out, stepping immediately to the side. He stood for a full minute without breathing, listening and looking slowly in a full arc around him. There was nothing to be seen or heard.

He eased round the corner of the hut into the darker shadow behind it. His new arc of sight covered the distant oil tanks and the nearer separators. There was still nothing to be seen. He moved cautiously along the rear wall of the hut toward them, pausing as his feet stumbled against something. Glancing down, he saw the pale glimmer of a face.

He crouched. It was Charlie Hewitt, lying on his stomach, his right cheek on the ground. Matt shook his arm. "Charlie!" he whispered urgently. "Charlie!" He rolled him over, cradling his head with one hand. The back of his head was wet and spongy and, when Matt held his hand up to catch the moonlight, it was covered with blood, nearly black in the pallid light. Charlie was dead.

Matt looked swiftly round toward the gas-holders and the hillside behind. It was too far to shout for Mackenzie, even if he could hear. Even if he was still able to. It had begun sooner than anyone had considered likely or possible. The unknown enemy could be all round them.

He wiped the palm of his hand on the frosty grass, then on Charlie's jacket, and stood up, revising his priorities again. How many of the night shift had been put out of action already, dead or unconscious? He had to assume most or all of them. The Mounties at the top end of the field would scarcely be in position yet, and the ones McIver was taking to the lower edge were too far away. The first thing was still to check the tanks and separators to see if they had been damaged. If the saboteurs were still up by the storage tanks, he would have the slight advantage of surprise.

The clouds were overlapping again under the high moon and it was black night as he started for the giant separators, guided by the gas lamps ringing them. All his senses were alert, probing the darkness round him. He was on concrete now and had to walk carefully on the ice-slick surface. The hum of the generators and processors was louder, enough to cover the slight slipping sound of his boots. Every five or six steps he paused, checking the space ahead.

The pipes from the valley wells were beginning to converge, some heading straight for the separators, others meeting at the connectors to the main pipes. Not to become snarled up in them, Matt circled to his left. There was still no sign of anyone moving between him and the lights, which caught the frost on the pipes and turned them into glittering diamond ribbons as they arrowed in. He stepped over one and ducked under another. Moving on, he glanced along it and stopped, noticing something. Something had disturbed its glistening surface, the marks showing up as dark smudges. It must have been recent, for the frost had only covered them since nightfall.

As soundlessly as possible he ran toward the marks at a half crouch, skidding to a halt when he came nearer and saw what had made them. His heart lurched in his chest. From his crouched position looking up, he saw four sticks of dynamite strapped to the thick pipe with broad bands of adhesive plaster. Shuffling closer until he was under it, he could make out a small timing device tied to the sticks, attached by wires to their detonator caps.

He had no idea how long he had, or whether the detonators were fixed to go off if they were tampered with, but he had to take the chance. It was only when he reached for the clasp knife in his pocket that he remembered he had left the automatic lying on the floor of the tourer. What the hell? he thought. What does it matter now? He opened the knife.

He supported the dynamite with one hand under the timer. With the other he slipped the smaller, sharper blade of the knife under the sticking tape and sliced carefully along, pressing the blade against the pipe. The bundle of dynamite sticks swung free and he changed his position, cutting the tapes that held it at the other side of the pipe. Still crouching and holding the timer firmly so that it would not be shaken, he tilted the end of the sticks toward him and unscrewed the detonator caps very cautiously, placing them one at a time on the ground beside him. Two sets of wires had fallen away. He eased the others off the nipples and cut the strings fastening the timer to the bundle. Without the detonators and wires, the dynamite was harmless and he laid it aside.

His hands were perfectly steady, but began to shake as soon as he put the sticks down, and he found he had held his breath for so long he was nearly choking. In spite of the cold, he was prickled with sweat. He gasped in air, getting control of himself, and rose, holding the timing device up to the light. As he suspected, it was very simple, made out of a cheap little travel alarm clock. Its face had been against the bundle of sticks and now he could see it was set to go off in one hour and twelve minutes.

It had probably been set originally for two hours, the time it would take the saboteurs to plant their bombs and get clear. How many more of these babies were there, strapped to the gasometers, the separators and the giant oil tanks? He had to steady himself again. It was the time that was most important. He could not spare a minute to go looking for anyone to help him. He was alone. But was there any possible way he could locate all the bombs and defuse them before one of them went off? Even if they had all been set to detonate at the same moment? He had to try or there wouldn't just be a big bang, there would be the biggest bloody bang since Krakatoa.

It was freezing hard now and he pulled down the flap at the back of his thick wool cap to cover his neck. If he checked out the separators first, he could throw the emergency switches and cut off the flow from the wells. He ducked through the tangle of pipes and ran for the next main group that came in from the northwest sector. He stopped again suddenly. His eye had caught a flicker of movement off to the side, between him and the brighter lights round the oil storage tanks.

You damned fool, he told himself, how many mistakes can

you make? It was obvious. If the timing devices had been set for two hours or less, the chances were that whoever was planting the bombs had not yet finished.

He could make out a figure quite distinctly now, crouching by the main pipes to the storage tanks. By coming out into the open, he had no doubt that he had been spotted himself. There was only one way to play it. He walked straight toward the crouching figure, making no noticeable attempt at concealment, but keeping as much as he could to the denser patches of shadow. He stuck his hands in his pockets. In one were his cigarettes and the timing mechanism he had put there without realizing it. In the other were his matches and the bone-handled clasp knife.

The clouds were splitting up again. Above them the moon was so full and bright it sent down shafts through the gaps in the cloud cover like the sun. One swept across the tanks and the end of the main pipes, revealing the figure beside them for a few seconds. It was the bald, fleshy man with the flattened nose. He was wearing a muffler wrapped up round his chin and a heavy ankle-length overcoat. He had been attaching a bundle of explosives to the nearest pipe and paused, leaning on it, peering toward Matt. His right hand held a revolver. "Goltz?" he called hoarsely. "Is that you, Goltz?"

"Uh-huh," Matt grunted, trying to sound like someone who wanted as little talk as possible. Without the automatic, he felt more exposed than ever. He was working the blade of the clasp knife open inside his pocket.

The man had straightened slightly, but was still not certain and had not lowered the revolver. "We've nearly finished," he said. "Who was that, then? Where are they?"

Matt walked steadily toward him. With luck, he might not shoot until the last moment. But he was becoming suspicious again, waiting for an answer. Matt had to speak. As he opened his mouth, something crashed against the side of his head. There was searing pain and a roaring in his ears, and he fell to the ground.

He lay crumpled, unable to move. By a miracle, he had not lost consciousness and could still fight against it. He knew he should be dead, but the padded earflaps of his cap were tied together over the top of his skull and had absorbed some of the force of whatever hit him. He heard the bald man give a startled shout and run toward him, then stop again as he exclaimed, "What the devil—?! I thought it was you!"

The man he had called Goltz was standing over Matt. "Put that gun away!" he rapped, his accent guttural, yet clipped. "*Du blödsinniger Ochse!* Don't you know any better than to shoot here?"

Matt heard the bald man come closer. "It's that snoopy bastard you thought was watching us!"

"Leave him," Goltz ordered.

Matt felt another intense pain as the bald man kicked him viciously in the ribs, and this time passed out.

It was the pain in his side that he was first aware of when he started to come round. Then of the strong fingers kneading the muscles at the nape of his neck. He gasped and tried to rise, but the fingers and another hand on his shoulder held him down easily. "Don't move. Not move," a deep voice told him. "Breathe deep." Matt could only lie still while the fingers searched out and soothed the pain in his head and, like magic, when he breathed in, his sight gradually cleared. When he tried again to sit up, the hands helped him.

His head hurt to turn, but he forgot the pain when he saw Harry Hightree kneeling beside him. "You walk now or you freeze," the old Indian said. Matt knew he was gaping at him. "You got one damn thick skull," Harry said admiringly.

It was a day of surprises, for Matt had never seen Harry smile before. "What are you doing here?" he muttered.

"Look for you."

Matt's wits were still slightly scrambled and he could not work it out.

"Your missy," Harry told him. "Missy Sadie. She sent me." Matt was struggling to get to his feet. The cold from the ground lanced through him and he was shivering violently. Harry had taken off Matt's cap and set it again on his head, drawing it down gently. "There now," he said. "I see motor and man with scar. I wait, but you don't come. I go to office and Missy Sadie tells me you left already, for oil wells."

"But how did you get here?" Matt asked.

"I ran," Harry said simply.

Six or seven miles? Matt thought. How long had it taken him? That thought was the impulse he needed and his mind clicked back into gear. He took the timer from his pocket. It was still working and he saw that over twenty minutes had gone by since he had first seen the bald man. That meant there were less than fifty left.

He pulled himself to his feet, leaning on Harry's arm, and they began to walk, to warm him up and restore his circulation. He wavered and swayed at first, but soon it was not so difficult and he could talk. "Thanks, Harry. I'll say it properly some other time," he gasped. "Right now, I want you to—want you to do something else for me." Harry nodded. "I need help—need it quick. Sergeant Mackenzie, you know him?" Harry nodded. "I have to know what's happened to him. He's up on the hillside somewhere. He may be hard to find."

"I found him," Harry said. "Behind some rocks, like you."

Matt stood still. "Is he dead?"

"No. Sore head like you. Maybe worse. Not so thick." The old man chuckled.

"Can you get him?" Matt asked. "Can you get him on his feet and down here?" He broke off, hearing something. It was the sound of a car, and he could see its lights approaching along the track. "Thank the Lord . . ." he breathed. He pushed himself off Harry's arm and managed to stand on his own. "Tell the Sergeant bombs, Harry," he said. "Tell him time bombs. And get him down here."

He set off at a stumbling run. His legs were weak and his feet slipped on the ice, but he drove himself on. He had to stop the car and get whoever was in it to come and help. With the jolting movement, his head began to pulse with pain again. He could feel his legs growing stronger, though, and he regulated his breathing to match his running stride, bringing himself under control like a machine.

He was afraid he would reach the road too late, but with excitement saw the car turn in toward the parking space. He increased his speed and arrived at the limit of the space as the driver switched off his engine and climbed out, a bulky man, balding, in a long, dark coat. Matt snarled like an animal and threw himself at him without a thought of the risk, slamming him against the car and spinning him round.

With his fist raised to smash down, he just managed to stop himself, recognizing McIver.

The area manager was winded, his eyes bulging with fear. "What—? Christ Awmighty . . . Matt!" he got out.

Matt released him and stood back, panting. "Sorry, Mack. Sorry, I thought you were someone else."

McIver's legs gave way and he slid down to sit on the running board. "Hell and dammit," he spluttered. "I come out here— You didn't give me a chance!"

"I wouldn't have if you'd been who I thought," Matt told him. "There's people been killed here tonight, Mack. Charlie Hewitt, maybe more." McIver stared at him. "What are you doing here?"

"I—I got to thinking," McIver muttered. "I was ashamed of myself. And came out to see if there was anything I could do."

"You're all right, Mack," Matt said. "Just the man."

"But what about Hewitt? What—?"

"Later," Matt told him. "Did you pass anyone on your way here?"

McIver was rising. "Yeah. Yeah, a limousine nearly pushed me off the track. It was going at a helluva lick. And there was a truck without lights. I almost ran into it."

Matt's head turned quickly. The two-ton truck beside which he had parked the Overland was gone. Now that he thought of it, he had never noticed it in the valley before.

McIver added as an afterthought, "It's parked on the track over there, by the cut-off to Number One Well."

Matt tensed. Ten to one the bald man had used the innocent-looking truck to bring in the dynamite. While the other one drove the limousine. He had a fast decision to make. Let me get it right just this once! he begged. There were the bombs back at the storage area, and the night crew at the well. If they hadn't been killed already, they would be when the derrick blew up. He took out the little alarm clock with the trailing wires. Thirty-six minutes left. He gave it to McIver.

"What is it?" McIver asked.

"It's a timing device. For time bombs." McIver nearly dropped it, but Matt grabbed his hand. "There's bombs planted round the separators and storage tanks. They're going to go off in half an hour. If you want to help, get up there and unscrew the detonators."

"Me?" McIver trembled. "I mean—for Chrissakes, Matt."

"And don't worry about them going off by accident. They're not booby-trapped."

". . . Not booby-trapped," McIver repeated mechanically. He was aware of his trembling, but could not stop it. "Holy Mother . . ."

"For a start, there's one on the main pipes near the oil tanks," Matt told him. McIver closed his eyes. "But there's others and they could be anywhere. With any luck, Sergeant Mackenzie should come to join you. Show him that and he'll know what to do. You'll have to be quick."

"Quick," McIver muttered. He opened his eyes and nodded.

The sound of the truck's engine starting up carried clearly to them in the night's stillness. Matt ran at once for the Overland. He jumped into the front seat, switched on and pressed the starter. Thank God for electric ignition, he thought, when the engine turned over at the first touch.

McIver had hurried after him and was holding on to the top of the door. "Matt!" he shouted. "Matt, what if we don't find them all in time?"

"You'd better hope that you do," Matt said. He shoved McIver's hand away. "Get going!" As he backed and turned, McIver began to run toward the oil tanks.

The tourer came out onto the track and Matt could see the truck's tail lights disappearing ahead of him. His instinct was to thrust his foot down and race after it, but this time he was sure of his priorities. He slewed the Overland round in a skidding curve and left the track, making directly for No. 1 Well.

Like all the other installations he had seen that evening, it seemed deserted when he drew up beside it. He found the first maintenance man lying on the perimeter near one of the gas lamps. He was partly conscious and could even stand, with help. He was too dazed to speak and Matt half lifted him across to the small site hut. The second man was lying over the threshold of the open door, much more badly injured. Evidently, he had put up a fight and been hideously battered for it. One of his hands was still thrown up to protect his head and the fingers had been mangled. Whatever kind of club or stick the man called Goltz used, it had a fearsome effect. Matt carried both of them inside the hut and closed the door against the cold.

Knowing exactly what he was looking for was a help. He found one bundle strapped to the side of the pump housing and defused it. With so much volatile gas around, it was more dangerous to dispose of the sticks of dynamite. There was a large bucket outside the hut, filled with water. He smashed the ice on the top with his heel and lowered the whole bundle carefully into it. It had been timed for thirty minutes.

He looked round for anything out of place or unusual. There was an upturned wooden crate by one of the main supports of the derrick. He climbed onto the crate and saw the second bomb, attached to one of the cross girders. He defused it and laid it in the bucket with the first. A thorough though rapid search of the site uncovered no others, although loose sticks of dynamite had been laid between the smaller wells to go off when the first two bombs exploded. The bald man was hurrying things up.

Matt's palms were damp. As he wiped them on his jacket, he thought of McIver. He could go back and help him. Or he could go on. He calculated another ten minutes had passed. If he could make it to the North Spur, there might just be a chance of saving the new well. He would have to take the shortest possible route.

He had left the Overland's motor running and gave himself a few seconds to rev up the engine before he moved off. His scalp was sticky with blood and he pulled off his cap to let the cold air dry it and dull the pain. The moon rode high, but its bland light was deceptive, making the ground ahead look smooth and level, when in reality it was pitted with holes and ditches, uneven, with stretches of loose shale and jagged outcrops of stone that could rip his tires to shreds. He would have to trust the keenness of his eyesight to avoid them. He released the brake and let in the clutch. "All right," he told the tourer. "Now's when we see if you live up to your name."

He took off, gaining speed as fast as he could change up, slewing when the tires lost their grip in turn in runnels of ice, swerving to miss half-concealed rocks, heading straight

189

for the distant spur. It was crazy and exhilarating. The Overland raced faster and faster, shaking and jouncing, sometimes with all four wheels off the ground as it launched itself over the top of an incline and thudded down onto the slope that fell away beyond. Twice he crossed the track and careered along it until it looped away and he left it again, cutting off bends and corners.

His nearside headlamp cracked and went out. The exhaust pipe was flattened and once or twice he was sure it would be torn off as the undercarriage scraped over rocks, but the tourer raced on with no loss of power. The glow had become a fiery radiance, lighting up the sky beyond the slope he was making for, when the tires suddenly struck a broad expanse of smooth stone and skidded on its film of ice. The tourer spun round and round, its tires screaming. He steered into the skid, straightened out and tore up the slope. Then the Overland breasted it and was streaking down the other side for the heat and the light of the burn-off.

At the sight in front of him, Matt nearly jammed his foot on the brake. On that surface, it would have been fatal. He killed his lamps, eased back on the throttle and braked as soon as he had slowed, shuddering to a halt. He had come out above the track, looking down into the fold of the valley in which the new well was sited. The limousine, a long, powerful Packard, was drawn up on the track. Between it and the ravening column of fire was the covered truck. A tall, well-dressed man, very erect, was standing arguing with the bald man and four others. The white incandescence of the well picked them out as sharply as with a spotlight.

The tall man was the one with the cropped hair and the scarred left cheek, and must be Goltz. He was leaning on a walking stick or cane sheathed in leather. It was not notably thick, yet Matt knew the leather was to hide the fact it was made of some heavy metal, or perhaps a wooden casing filled with lead shot. Goltz gestured angrily with it toward the burn-off, and the derricks and pumps behind it. Obviously, the others were afraid to take the dynamite too near to the blazing heat. Two of them were holding bombs, trying to explain the danger, and one turned away defiantly, laying his bundle of explosives in the back of the truck. Goltz would have gone for him with his cane if the bald man had not stepped in front of him.

190

Matt could see the whole plan now. They had started at the top end of the field, hitting the hillside wells and cutting the telephone lines. Then they had knocked out the administration and storage areas. The bald man and two helpers had been left to plant their bombs round the storage tanks and separators while Goltz dealt with the crew at Number 1 Well and dropped the other two here to deal with the new well. Then he would go back and check that his men were finished at the storage area and Number 1. They would pick up the other two and hit both wells at the lower end of the field on their way out. The bombs were all set for different intervals, to go off at approximately the same time, leaving them about thirty minutes to get clear. But somehow they had fallen behind schedule. Maybe when they reached the burn-off, they found the men left there had been too scared to approach the installations behind it with their bombs. Now the bald man was arguing they should cut their losses and get the hell out.

Matt felt for the automatic and put it back in his belt, where it should have been all the time. He slid the clutch in and took his foot off the brake. The roar of the fire drowned the sound of the tourer's engine as it began to roll forward.

The driver of the truck was going round to his door and Matt put on speed, aiming the Overland at the group, which was being given its last orders by Goltz before breaking up. Matt opened the throttle and the Overland tore down the long slope, but he was too intent on the scene below him. He saw the gully too late, the shallow bed of a small stream, just as the bonnet of the tourer dipped sharply. He had only a split second to brace himself before the nose slammed into the bank on the far side of the trough, buckling one of the front wheels. The Overland lurched violently to the side as its rear bucked, then crashed back down, crazily tilted but still upright.

Matt had taken the first impact with his arms, then been thrown round, his right shoulder smashing into the dashboard and his head against the passenger door. His neck felt as if it had nearly snapped and his left arm as though it had been wrenched from the socket. He pushed himself up groggily. His first hazy thought was to get out, in case the car burst into flames; then he remembered the group.

They had heard the crash and were staring up the slope.

191

At its tilted angle, the tourer was fully visible apart from the hood. Goltz and one of the men were already hurrying for the Packard. The bald man was shouting, taking out his revolver, and Matt ducked as he fired. The bullet smashed the brass carriage lamp beside him. Others began shooting, and bullets whined past into the hillside and thudded into the padded upholstery of the rear seats.

Matt kicked his door open and dived out into the shallow gully. The small stream that had made it was frozen solid and he squirmed along the ice away from the tourer. The sudden need for action wiped out all memory of pain, although the torn muscles in his left shoulder nagged at him cruelly as he hauled himself up the bank to look over.

The shooting had stopped. The Packard was already pulling away. The bald man was standing at the open passenger door of the truck with one foot on the running board, gesturing to the others who were scrambling up into the back. The bald man climbed in and slammed the door.

You're not getting away, you bastard! Matt swore. As he came up over the bank, he jerked out the automatic. He fired twice at the speeding Packard, but could not tell if he had hit it, for it turned a bend to go up the far slope and passed out of sight. He could hear the engine of the truck whirring, and whir again as the driver tried frantically to start it, and ran down toward it.

He stopped when the truck began to move off. Slowly, at first. It was facing away from him and Matt aimed carefully. He didn't want to hit the dynamite. He fired low, for the rear tires, but his shots went wide. He dropped to one knee and steadied his wrist on his left forearm. The truck was picking up speed and turning toward the road. His first shot sent the radiator cap whirling off. The next ricocheted off the hood and shattered the windshield. The truck leaped forward and Matt's third shot hit the front offside tire.

When it blew out, the truck veered wildly and began to spin, just like his skid on the ice. He had a glimpse through the side of the cabin of the bald man scrabbling at the driver who was slumped over the wheel, as the truck spun round and round, heading for the burn-off. Suddenly, the hood, the cabin and the tarpaulin cover blistered and smoked, crackling with small flames. Even above the thunder of the raging shaft of fire, Matt could hear the screams of the trapped men.

He flung himself flat on his face and the world exploded. His ears were blasted and the earth shook under him. There was a searing wave of heat and debris spattered all round him.

He lay nearly stunned for over ten minutes, until he could raise his head. God knows how much dynamite had still been in the truck. It had completely disappeared, leaving only a scarred black crater in the ground. The burn-off roared on, unaffected, unchanged.

After another ten minutes, two of the Mounties watching the lower end of the field came running up the track. They had seen nothing in their section; then the Packard had gone racing past for the main road and they had heard the explosion. They discovered Matt sitting, dazed, and helped him up. He pulled himself together and explained roughly what had happened. One patrolman had been sent to cover the new well. Matt had not seen him. They searched and called, but he had vanished.

Amazingly, the axles of the Overland were not broken. They heaved it out of the gully onto the slope and replaced the buckled wheel with the spare. One of them drove while the other sat in the back, supporting Matt, although he kept saying he was fine. They drove slowly and carefully in case of a breakdown and, from what he had told them, they were tense as they reached the cut-off, expecting the whole storage complex to dissolve in front of them in one vast, glaring ball of flame.

They stopped and listened. Everything was normal. The lights were on in the long administration hut and they found McIver and Harry Hightree in the main room with Mackenzie and the rest of the Mounties. Mackenzie's head was bandaged and he was relieved to see that Matt was able to walk, but made him sit down. One of his men was fixing the telephone wires to call for a doctor and ambulances. They were all subdued and quiet. It seemed incredible to them that the valley could still be in one piece.

The patrolmen who had gone to the hillside wells had found the crews unconscious, one man dead. They had located and dealt with the bombs, then hurried down to the storage area, arriving just as Harry brought down Mackenzie. Between them they searched out the twelve bombs planted in and around the complex. The last one had been spotted with only three minutes to go.

It was McIver who had defused it and he was still shaking. "I need a drink," he said.

"We all do," Sergeant Mackenzie agreed. "But first we'll say a wee prayer."

Chapter 12

THE U 20 HAD BEEN SHADOWING HER FOR OVER AN HOUR, and for most of that time the crew had been at Action Stations. They were all tense and silent and Schwieger could sense the tension almost like a physical force pressing in on him as they waited for him to decide.

The steamer they were tracking was large, between five and six thousand tons, he estimated, with one high, angled smokestack behind her stepped bridge and radio shack, and heavy cargo derricks on her stern and forecastle decks. Although Haupert and Zentner had searched the manuals, they could not identify her positively, but had found several very similar outlines, all of armed merchantmen. Haupert and Weiser were for attacking at once without warning. Rudi had not argued outright against it, yet had misgivings.

The moment of decision, Schwieger told himself, bitter and inevitable, when he would open fire on unsuspecting civilians. He thought he had reached it once already, during the night. He had been asleep when the watch officer woke him with the news that something was approaching, something big. He raced up to the open conning tower to find the ocean as still as a lake all round them, silvered by the moonlight. The approaching ship was already above the horizon, on a southwesterly course. In that light it was impossible to make her out clearly, yet she was a considerable size and steaming fast, fast enough to be a cruiser like the one that had escaped in the fog. Swinging on an angle to intercept, he had ordered Full Ahead on the surface for as long as he dared, then dived to periscope depth. There were anxious moments, in case the U 20's wake or her submersion had been spotted, but the sound of the cruiser's engines grew louder and louder. She had seen nothing.

Schwieger had stayed in the conning tower and Zentner came hurrying back up to report both bow tubes ready. It was foolish to risk only one torpedo, which might damage, but not penetrate, the cruiser's armor plating. Zentner grinned with nervous excitement as he raised the finger periscope very cautiously. Schwieger bent to the eyepiece, adjusted the direction, and the muscles of his stomach knotted in shock. What the lens picked up was not a cruiser. Even at the angle of approach, he could make out the huge crosses painted on her side.

Zentner was giving the order to stand by both tubes. Schwieger would need confirmation for his log and eased back, gesturing to him to take his place. Zentner knew how little time they had and moved in eagerly. He looked up, white-faced, and shook his head.

"Stand by to fire," Schwieger said tonelessly. For a second, he thought Rudi would refuse, but he turned to the firing buttons and placed his hands over them, although they were not quite steady.

Schwieger resumed his position at the eyepiece. He could not spare even two seconds to explain. For now he had made up his mind. By her course, the ship coming into his sights was heading away from England, from Liverpool, Bristol or Portsmouth, and so, in spite of her markings, could not be carrying wounded. Most likely she was not a hospital ship at all, but a transport or a disguised freighter taking supplies to the warships bombarding the Dardanelles. She had no right to immunity.

"Both tubes . . . fire!" he ordered.

The range was less than a thousand yards. Even so, he knew at once by its erratic track that the starboard torpedo would never reach its target. Its twin broke surface, plunged again and sped true. Even by moonlight, seen through the tiny lens, its white wake was distinctly visible.

Provided its internal mechanism functioned properly, the torpedo was an almost perfect weapon. Driven by its own propeller, it had great speed, accuracy and explosive power, and could be set at any depth from six to twenty-two feet. It was unsuited for close attack, because of the danger from shock waves to the craft which launched it, yet even that was an advantage, since the further a U-boat could keep from its prey, the less likelihood there was of being spotted, and torpedoes themselves needed distance to settle to their preset course and depth. In the first two or three hundred yards after they were fired, they plunged, then rose, sometimes clear of the surface, before diving again to their proper depth. The latest models had a range of nearly two miles and even at the extreme limit, provided his quarry's course and speed remained constant, Schwieger was one of the commanders who could almost guarantee a hit.

At a thousand yards, the port torpedo would take exactly one minute and two seconds to reach its target and, as he watched, his eyes fixed on the box of the periscope, he wondered at himself and at the answers the next few minutes would bring. Total war, the Grand Admiral had demanded. The judgment of the Commander was everything. Now Schwieger had committed himself, the U 20 and his whole future.

Yet he would never know what the Red Cross ship carried. At the last moment she changed direction. Nothing sudden or dramatic. Not evasive action. Someone merely adjusted her course very slightly by a point, even half a point, to starboard and the torpedo, instead of striking her hull square on and detonating, tore along her side in a flurry of white foam until it was deflected out into the empty sea. The Red Cross ship steamed on, unaware that her belly had nearly been ripped apart.

Schwieger slammed up the grips of the periscope and swore under his breath. The emotions which had been coursing through him, as his determination struggled against a mixture of dread and guilt, exploded in a single burst of frustration and anger. He glared round the conning tower at the boatswain, the helmsman and Zentner in turn, and not one of them dared to speak. He was ashamed of himself and managed a shrug and a half smile as he punched the air with his fist. "Well, we missed," he said. "We all have to miss sometime. She escaped by sheer chance."

"Or perhaps by the hand of Providence," Zentner murmured.

Later, in the quietness of the Commander's cabin, he took that back, yet Schwieger was conscious of him now, watching and waiting for him to make up his mind. The sea was choppy and there was little risk of the periscope being sighted. "We'll go in closer," he decided, "and make absolutely certain."

It was early morning, just after six, and the sky was heavy with the threat of rain. At five hundred yards, the bulk of the steamer filled the lens and there was no mistaking the dark silhouette of the two guns, one mounted at the stern and the other at the bows beyond the booms of the cargo masts. The U 20 stole ahead to the classic attack position on her bows. Zentner reported both stern tubes ready and set, as Schwieger had ordered, for fifteen feet with deflection for ten knots.

Everything now depended on how accurately Schwieger had estimated the steamer's speed and his skill as he maneuvered the U 20 in the next few minutes for her shot. He had decided to use only one torpedo, holding the other in reserve. As he called precise changes in direction to the helmsman, he had no doubts left whatever about his right to attack without warning. The big merchantman was armed, with her name and port of registry blacked out, so was not neutral.

Zentner had unscrewed the cover of the first stern tube firing button and kept his right thumb poised over it while he held the lever that controlled the elevation of the periscope with his left hand.

"Steady as she goes," Schwieger ordered.

"First stern tube ready," Zentner reported, taut.

"Torpedo . . . fire!"

Zentner pressed the firing button to make the electrical contact. At the same moment, he hauled on the lever to bring down the periscope and shouted into the speaking tube to the stern torpedo room, "First torpedo fired!"

They could feel the lurch of the U 20 as the long torpedo shot out of its tube and Hirsch instantly compensated for the lost weight by taking on more water as ballast, so that her stern would not bob up. Zentner held the lever of the asparagus down tightly, as though assuring himself that the eye was not above the surface. It was now that the torpedo's wake might be sighted and the guns of the steamer open fire.

Schwieger stood erect, his head raised, thumbs hooked in the pockets of his leather jacket, as they listened, counting off the seconds. At one minute and twenty-four seconds, they heard the distant, muffled crump of an explosion. "Out periscope!" Schwieger ordered.

It had been a perfect bow shot, striking the steamer midway between her prow and her bridge and tearing a jagged hole twenty to thirty feet across at her waterline. Already she was starting to list badly. Smoke poured from the hole and from the forward section of her superstructure, damaged by the explosion. The lifeboat directly above had been smashed to pieces.

There was no need to fire again. She was losing way rapidly and sinking by the bows. The order to abandon ship had evidently been given, for her boats were being lowered. The first boat to be swung out was at midships and her tackle had been damaged. A pulley snapped and the lifeboat dropped at one end, although still held at the other, hurling the crewmen in it down into the sea. The other four boats were launched successfully, though the one from nearest the bows was in trouble, sitting low in the water. Schwieger gave the order to surface and for the gun crew to stand by.

"You're going up?" Zentner queried, startled.

"Stand by to assist the wounded," Schwieger said, expressionless.

Zentner had misjudged him, and flushed. He came to attention and saluted.

When the U 20 broke surface, Schwieger was the first out of the conning tower. He winced, hearing what he had feared, and Zentner who had followed him gave a gasp of horror. Some of the men in the water nearest the steamer were screaming. Although she had lost speed, for some reason her engines had not been stopped and her propellers were still turning. The men were swimming desperately, yet being swept irresistibly along her side and sucked into the churning terror of her screws, which minced them one by one to strips. Nothing could be done to save them.

The U 20's hatches were open and lookouts slithered along her pitching deck to bows and stern. Weiser followed them out with the petty officer and gun crew, quickly manning the gun. Apart from helping survivors where necessary, Schwieger had to establish the ship's name, destination and cargo. If she took too long to sink, a party would have to be sent on board under Weiser or Zentner to place bombs in her holds and engine room. The waterlogged lifeboat was making toward them. "Reverse, half engines," Schwieger called down the speaking tube.

As the U 20 began to back toward her on one reversed propeller, there was a flash and a report from the gun at the forecastle of the stricken ship. Some heroic fool was trying to make a fight of it. Inexpertly aimed, the shell plowed into the water halfway between them. The men in the boats were shouting, some of them standing holding up their arms, but Schwieger had no option. A lucky hit could sink or disable the U 20. "Commence firing! Stop engines!" he ordered.

The deck gun roared immediately and its shell blew away part of the rail at the steamer's bows. Whoever was at her gun managed to loose off another three shots, each one creeping nearer to the U 20 and one capsizing the boat that had been making for her, until a direct hit from the deck gun exploded on the steamer's forecastle gun's protective shield, toppling it over and putting it out of action. Weiser went on shooting, accurately and systematically destroying the steamer's bridge and charthouse, radio shack, funnel and stern gun.

"Cease firing!" Schwieger called down, and the gun crew reluctantly stopped what had become target practice.

In the silence that followed, Schwieger realized that the seamen in the water who were being sucked into the steamer's propellers were no longer screaming. Two were being helped into one of the lifeboats. The others had all disappeared.

As the U 20 backed again toward them, the seamen in the boats began to row away frantically. "What are they doing?" Schwieger wondered.

"They think we're going to kill them," Zentner said quietly.

The boat that had been capsized lay upside down in the water. Seven or eight men, some of them wounded, hung desperately to her sides. One, who might have been an officer, had both arms blown off and they had managed, somehow, to push him up until he was half lying across her keel. When he saw the U-boat approaching, he cried out in fear, tried to rise and rolled off the keel. Although those nearest him in the water tried to grab him, he vanished at once.

The others watched the U 20 loom over them in dazed terror, becoming puzzled.

On orders from Schwieger, three of the riflemen covering the gun crew had laid down their Mauser Gewehr 98s and fetched lines and grappling hooks. They yelled and gesticulated at the men in the water to swim away, but they did not understand until Zentner shouted down, "For God's sake, get away from that boat! We're trying to help you!"

The grappling hooks splashed into the water on the far side of the upturned boat and were drawn back like fishing lines. At the first throw, two of them caught on the boat's gunwale and the third caught at the next throw. More of the U-boat crew joined in, hauling on the lines and flinging ropes out to the seamen who were in danger of drowning. Beyond them, the large steamer was slowly foundering, but all attention was on the lifeboat as the U-boat men fought to turn it over. When Lippe and Boatswain Kurtz added their muscles to the group straining on the lines, the heavy boat at last began to swing up. It righted itself suddenly with a great smack and an impact that drenched all the men who had been on the lines. Their laughter and cheer were echoed by the men in the water.

Who can explain it? Schwieger thought as he laughed with the others. A few minutes ago we were enemies. Now nothing is as important as saving their lives.

The lifeboat was tight against the U 20's side. The seamen were all clinging to ropes now and were pulled in, too. Sailors kneeled, leaning down and helping them up into the boat, which was partly waterlogged, yet seemed seaworthy. Other sailors had fetched mess tins and a bucket to be used as bailers, which they handed down. Lippe had got a loaf and some slabs of chocolate from the galley, which he threw down to one of the seamen. The two of them were grinning to each other like old friends.

Schwieger's attention was still on the boat when he heard one of the bow lookouts shout, "Sir! Captain!" He turned quickly at the note of panic in the man's voice.

"Jesus Maria!" Zentner muttered beside him. Others of the crew shouted out.

The conning tower of a British E-type submarine had broken the surface less than 250 yards from them. Even as

Schwieger opened his mouth to call an order to Weiser, the bows of the British submarine lunged up out of the water, and immediately he saw the wake of a torpedo heading straight toward them. The order was cut off before it could be uttered. Everyone was frozen, staring at that creamy, fizzing wake. Abruptly he could see the torpedo itself and hear it. There was no escape.

In the seconds before it reached them, he had only time for one coherent thought—how ironic . . . How damnably ironic!

The hissing line of bubbles from the compressed air that drove its propeller was louder and he glimpsed the seventeen-foot steel cigar as it rose to the surface. Then suddenly, its force thrust it completely out of the water, its screws whirring angrily. Schwieger's eyes were fixed on its blunt nose with its projecting striker. There was a moan from the sailors on the deck of the U 20 as it leaped through the air toward them like a monstrous rocket, cleared the deck by no more than inches, smashing the bow rail as it plunged over the other side and raced on.

Two thoughts flashed across Schwieger's mind. The first, that they had been saved by a miracle. The second, that the British submarine had dived and, having missed, would be circling for another shot. "Crash-dive! Action stations!" he roared.

The survivors in the lifeboat were pushing themselves desperately away from the side of the U 20. He had no time to consider them now. His men were pouring down through the hatches. He saw Weiser and the petty officer of the gun crew trying to gather up loose shells and yelled at them, "No time for that! Get below!" He thrust Zentner ahead of him down the ladder, took one last swift look round and dropped down himself, slamming the conning tower hatch shut behind him.

He could hear a babble of voices from the speaking tubes as all sections reported hatches secured. Hirsch was waiting for final orders. Schwieger shouldered Zentner aside and called into the tube, "Listen, Hirsch! Full Ahead, fifteen feet! And grab hold of something!"

"But, Captain—" Hirsch began.

"Full Ahead, damn you!" Schwieger shouted. "Now! And keep her at fifteen feet!"

Hirsch geared in the motors much faster than was safe. As the U 20 shot forward and sank under the surface, Schwieger wrapped his arms round the shaft of the periscope. The others in the conning tower were staring at him and he ordered them sharply to brace themselves.

They barely had time to obey him. In that last second's glance before they submerged, he had seen the British submarine's periscope begin to probe the surface immediately ahead of them. Cleverly, her commander had maneuvered her back nearly to her original position, knowing the U 20 would think that the one direction that might be safe. But Schwieger had called his bluff and now he would be giving frantic orders to submerge.

The grinding crunch as they collided was momentarily deafening and the impact hurled the unprepared members of both crews to the deck or sent them cannoning against bulkheads and instruments. Schwieger at first was the only one who knew what had happened. The side of his face had smashed against the piston-like shaft of the periscope and he was dizzied for a minute, blood trickling from his mouth where his teeth had cut the inside of his cheek. But he knew exactly what had occurred.

The British commander had started his dive the instant he was certain the U 20 was heading directly for him. Schwieger had gambled either on ramming him with his steel-clad prow or forcing him to crash-dive and lose his tactical advantage. Instead, the British submarine had reacted slower than he expected and had only commenced her dive when the U 20's prow had struck the top of her deck and sliced across it at an angle, her side colliding with the E submarine's conning tower.

There were shouts and cries from below and he heard Hirsch calling up in a quavering voice to find out what had happened. Schwieger stumbled to the speaking tube and told him. "But we've lost most of our buoyancy, sir," Hirsch reported, "and we don't seem able to move."

Zentner was on all fours, shaking his head slowly from side to side. Every second was vital and Schwieger kicked him sharply in the thigh. Zentner cried out and looked up, his head clearing. "Get on the tube!" Schwieger told him curtly. He took Zentner's hand, pulled him to his feet and turned to the conning tower window. Unbolting the cover, he swung it aside and peered out. He could see nothing in the darkness of the water beyond the thick glass.

"Captain!" Zentner called. He was gray-faced, holding himself upright with difficulty. "Hirsch reports we're going up." His puzzlement echoed the engineer officer's.

It was not possible! But even as Schwieger turned back to the window, he understood. "Get below!" he said sharply. "The senior man in each section to watch for leaks. Any sign! They're to report every minute!" Zentner was already moving to the ladder and Schwieger bent to the speaking tube. "Hirsch! Are you there?"

"Captain?"

"Flood all tanks!"

There was the briefest pause, but instead of acknowledging the order, Hirsch protested, "Captain! The British submarine could be right below us!"

"Of course she is!" Schwieger snapped. "What do you think's pushing us up? Now flood the tanks! We must get deeper!"

The sound of screeching metal that began the moment Hirsch started to fill the U 20's main ballast tanks proved that Schwieger was right. In ramming the other submarine and grinding along her back, the U-boat's prow had become lodged in her deck plates. If the British submarine's skin was pierced, the U 20's keel might still be partly sealing the gash, but her only hope would be to reach the surface as soon as she could.

The U 20's bows heaved and she rocked as if she were being shaken by the nose. "Dive, Hirsch! Get us down!" Schwieger shouted. He pulled himself to the forward window and held on to the sides tightly, gazing out. The British commander had been easing his boat up, carrying the U-boat up with it. Now, feeling the increasing pressure above him, he had blown his ballast tanks and it had become a struggle of one to rise and the other to force them both down.

Locked together, the two boats bucked and shuddered, vibrating all along their hulls as they strained against each other, rocking from side to side. Schwieger had a sudden memory of an illustration in a magazine when he was a boy, of two sea beasts, a great blue whale wrapped in the arms of a giant squid, fighting to the death in the unimaginable deeps of the ocean. "Deeper, Hirsch! Deeper!" he shouted.

It was repeated by Boatswain Kurtz, who had clawed his way to the speaking tubes without being told.

He's a U-boat man, Schwieger told himself, a real U-boat man! He tried to remember the fight of the sea monsters, to concentrate on them, and not to think of the other men, somewhere below them, and the other commander who was fighting to save his boat. "What's our depth?" he called.

Kurtz relayed the question. "Twenty-seven feet."

Not enough! Not enough! How bad were the leaks in the other submarine? Were they filling her—weighing her down?

The buffeting and shaking went on and Kurtz called again, "Fifteen feet, Captain!"

Schwieger clung to the bolts of the window, pressing forward against the glass. The water was still murky outside, but, incredibly, was growing lighter. Squinting down to starboard, he could just see something looming out of the darkness, and in a moment made out the slender, oval shape of the E type's conning tower. Something, perhaps one of the U 20's hydroplanes, had sheared off its periscope. Maybe down there, just as he was looking down, the other commander was gazing up. Were his men cheering? Was he congratulating himself? And what would happen when they reached the surface, a scramble to open the hatches and fight hand to hand on the decks?

He turned to send an order down to Weiser, and Kurtz said tensely, "Twenty feet, Captain."

Schwieger swung back to the window. He could no longer make out the enemy conning tower and the vibration in the hull had ceased. "Thirty feet, Captain," Kurtz said, and seconds later, "forty feet."

The creaking and grinding below them began again, and an even more violent shaking, as the British submarine's rudder was pushed hard round in a desperate attempt to tear her free of the U 20. What was it? Schwieger thought. Had the leaks in her deck plates become too severe to be stopped? Was she being inundated, the seawater pouring over her batteries and filling her with gas? Whatever it was, her commander had to free her and take the terrible gamble that she would reach the surface before she flooded. With a final rending screech she broke away.

"Sixty feet," Kurtz said.

Schwieger could hear the enemy submarine's engines laboring as she reversed. For a minute she scraped and bumped under the U 20's bows; then they lost contact. He ordered the U 20's descent and engines stopped and listened intently. The other engines were fainter, not rising, but sinking away below him. He saw that Kurtz was also listening, his head cocked, his mouth twisted in an expression that was not abhorrence, not distress, but a combination of them.

"They've gone," Kurtz muttered.

Schwieger was thinking of the enemy commander. You tried to kill us, the U 20. If you'd had more experience, you would have. I made an elementary mistake, staying by the wreck too long, and nearly paid the full price for it. If you'd attacked from fifty yards further off, you'd be sailing home in glory. If you'd reacted quicker, not been so cautious, I could never have rammed you and you'd still be out there somewhere, hunter or hunted. I'd have got you in the end, but it would have been a cleaner fight. Total war. Schwieger realized he felt very cold.

He saw Kurtz cross himself, his lips moving. Requiescat, he thought, and turned again to the window, although he knew there would be nothing to see. Yet there was something, after all. The glass was covered with a film of thick black oil.

Schwieger went down to Central Control. There was no jubilation in the crew. They were all thinking of those other men sinking far below. Zentner reported quietly that there was no sign of leakage. The U 20 was apparently undamaged. Hirsch, however, was still concerned by the loss of buoyancy and the forward horizontal rudders seemed to be jammed.

Central Control came back to life as the technicians and machinists were set to work, but after half an hour they could only report that the damage was not mechanical. The U 20 rose with great difficulty and had to be alternately coaxed and forced.

When they reached the surface again, the large cargo steamer had long since sunk. Wreckage from her had been spread for over two miles by the waves. The four lifeboats were nowhere to be seen.

* * *

Sweat was running down the faces of the two fiddlers. The piano was against the side wall and they were between it and the big iron stove. They had been glad of it at the start of the evening, but now the heat in the corner was sweltering. Carlo, who was playing the accordion, had taken off his jacket and undone his celluloid collar, one half of which stuck up nearly to his left ear. Moe Jackson, the pianist, looked as neat and precise as he did behind the counter of his agricultural goods store and seemed hardly affected by the heat at all. Carlo leaned both arms on top of his accordion and grinned from him to the fiddlers, who were playing the last dance before the supper break, a vigorous Schottische, which was not in his repertoire.

Livvy was dancing with the Pastor, an earnest young man who danced as he preached, well but very seriously. She tried not to smile to him as they hopped and spun, because it seemed to make him so embarrassed. The desks had all been moved back against the walls in the main room of the schoolhouse. The floor was crowded with couples and everyone else stood round the walls or sat on the desks, but Matt was not among them.

She had been worried when Mr. McIver drove him home in the morning with his left arm in a sling and a nasty cut by his right eye. Then when she was hanging his jacket up, she found his cap in the pocket, all stiff inside with dried blood. His thick hair hid the swelling, which was angry, the skin broken and discolored, when she made him show her. The doctor at Lawson Valley had cleaned it up and painted it with something, he told her.

She had only drawn the story out of him bit by bit. The car was in the company garage being overhauled. Apparently he had been parked too near the burn-off and there had been a blow-back, some kind of explosion. He was lucky. Two other men had been killed. It was awful and the thought of what might have happened was worse. Dan Connally took her over to the schoolhouse with the things she had made and she brought the kids with her to let Matt rest. He was still asleep when they got back and she had wondered if he ought not to stay at home. He laughed and said he only had a touch of a headache. Coming out would fix it. Now she couldn't see him anywhere.

207

The Schottische ended in a final, hectic spin that left even the Pastor panting. All the couples bowed and curtsied, as if they were in a ballroom back east, and the Pastor led Livvy courteously to the side, looking round a little anxiously for Matt or his wife. Livvy spotted her by the stove, excused herself and went to help her.

The Pastor's wife, Ursula, was a Scandinavian girl, as plump and jolly as he was thin and solemn. She was trying to lift the large copper pan that had been left on the stove to boil water for the tea. Livvy took the other handle and helped her to fill the three great enamel teapots. "Did you enjoy dancing with Erik?" Ursula asked.

"Very much," Livvy told her.

"I can't," Ursula chuckled. "He makes me laugh too much."

They carried two of the teapots down to the trestle tables at the end by the door. Miss Jessop, the teacher, brought the other. "Just like those men," she said crossly. "All standing around. None of them offering to help."

Livvy was kept busy for the next ten minutes, serving sandwiches and pouring tea. In one pause, she noticed a man who had just come in. Tall and broad-shouldered, in a brown tweed suit, he seemed familiar. It was Sergeant Mackenzie. She had not recognized him at first, out of uniform.

"You look worried," Ursula whispered.

"No," Livvy said. "I was just wondering where Matt had gone to."

"He'll be with all the other naughty boys," Ursula laughed. "In the back room."

One by one, during the last two dances, some of the men had sneaked into the teacher's room at the back, where the coats had been hung. Most of them had bottles or hip flasks which they passed round, keeping a wary eye out for Miss Jessop or the Pastor. Matt was in one corner with Dan and another friend, Barney Ferguson, a young farmer, sharing a half bottle of whiskey. Matt had a scarf tied round his neck to support his left arm. His shoulder was still pretty painful, although he had played it down for Livvy's sake. The doctor had told him he would have to rest the arm for at least three weeks.

"I don't understand it," Barney was saying. "Just to sit

in holes in the ground throwing shells at them. Why don't they storm the German trenches and push them right back to the Rhine?"

"It's not so easy," Matt said. "There's a lot more of them, and they're well dug in. Barbed wire, light artillery. And they have a lot more machine guns, apparently, than we have."

Lew Jensen and old Sven Nyquist came across to them. "Hey, Matt, you don't look so good," Lew said, concerned.

Matt smiled. "I'm okay, Lew."

"I heard it was a pretty bad accident down there at the Valley."

"A gas feedback or something. Just one of those things."

Old man Nyquist was holding out his flask. "Here, Matt, you take some of this." Matt knew what was in the flask. Old Sven's Special. Nyquist made it himself out of juniper berries up in the hills behind his farm. He had been bitten before and shook his head. "Come on, take," Nyquist said.

Matt grinned. "I want to be able to walk out of here." They laughed. Behind them he saw Sergeant Mackenzie open the door and look round. "Hi, Phil!" he called.

Mackenzie hung up his coat and came over. He turned down Dan's offer of the whiskey, but old man Nyquist was more insistent, although Jensen gave him a warning glance. "You gotta try this, Sergeant," he said. "Special brew."

Mackenzie sniffed suspiciously at the flask and took a sip.

"It's Norwegian," Nyquist said blandly. "Norwegians make it."

Mackenzie handed back the flask. "Don't anybody light a cigarette near that," he warned. They laughed and he touched Matt's arm. "Excuse us a minute." As he led Matt away, he winked. "Maybe I ought to break up that old rascal's still. He could turn somebody blind."

"Not the Norwegians," Matt smiled. "They're weaned on it."

Mackenzie grinned briefly. "How's the arm?"

"So-so. How's the head?"

"Same as yours. I'm walking." Mackenzie glanced round. "Your people have cooperated very well. We've been able to keep all news of the attempt out of the papers."

"So I see. Though not why."

"It's not up to me, Matt," Mackenzie said. "Not even to the Force. It's Security." He hesitated. "I might as well tell you. They say they're going to give me some kind of medal after the war's over."

"Great," Matt grinned.

"Oh, come off it!" Mackenzie protested. "We both know I didn't do much. You're the one it should go to."

"I don't want it," Matt said. "If you want rid of it, tell them to send it to Harry Hightree."

Carlo had started to play some Italian melodies during the supper break and they could hear the accordion more loudly when Livvy opened the door, looking for Matt. "There you are," she said. "I'm surprised at you, Sergeant Mackenzie, encouraging him."

"I don't think he needs much encouragement, Mrs. Fletcher," Mackenzie smiled.

Livvy laughed. "I don't suppose so. Now come along, all of you. Your wives are waiting at the supper table and there are some girls without escorts."

"Just lead me to them," old man Nyquist beamed.

"Outrageous!" Miss Jessop shrilled from the doorway. "This is my office and you've filled it with cigarette and cigar smoke, and alcohol fumes! It smells like some low barroom!"

It was very evident that old Sven had had a drop too much from his flask, when he bowed to her. "What you got against barrooms, Miss Jessop?" he asked. "You sure enough pretty, but you got one helluva sharp tongue."

Matt and Livvy and the others were still chuckling as they finished their sandwiches. The music started up again and couples began to form sets on the floor. Livvy was swaying. "Is my husband going to dance with me?" Matt smiled ruefully and tapped his arm in its sling. "Any excuse," she murmured. "Well, then, what about you, Sergeant?"

Mackenzie looked trapped and held his cup and saucer between them as a barrier. "Be a privilege, Mrs. Fletcher," he assured her. "Only I don't want to get the Force a bad name. I dance like I was wearing snowshoes."

Livvy laughed and was tempted to insist, but Dan Connally moved in and bowed. "If no one else is going to, may I have the honor?"

"You're the only gentleman here, Dan," Livvy said. She

took his arm and he led her out to join a set that needed another couple.

Moe Jackson was standing on his chair and called, "Address your partners—corners address—join your hands, go 'way to the west!"

With Livvy's firm hand in his and her body moving lithely beside him as they stepped and turned and spun, linking their elbows, Dan felt ten years younger and a foot taller. She was the most beautiful woman in the room, in the whole province, probably, and he cared for her more tenderly than he had thought it possible to feel for another human being.

Matt stood with Phil Mackenzie, watching them. He knew that Dan had a warm and troubled admiration for his wife and that she had a close regard for him. But he also knew them both too well to take it wrongly.

"Dance to the center—and dance to the wall," Moe was calling. "And all turn round, and promenade all!"

Livvy liked Dan very much as a friend, and enjoyed being with him. She laughed as they whirled and smiled to him as they sashayed back down the room, but she was aware of another pair of dark eyes watching. She was dancing for Matt.

It was nearly two in the morning when Dan drove them home, and old Granny Connally had nodded asleep in her chair. "The children? No trouble at all," she told them. "Diana woke up once and I gave her some milk, but she was asleep before she could finish it, the wee darlin'."

Matt and Livvy came out onto the porch to wave goodbye when Dan took his grandmother back to her little house a mile down the road. Livvy turned to go inside and Matt put his good arm round her, stopping her. It was a frosty night, with the stars sharp and bright in the limitless black vault of the sky. Livvy felt the tingle of cold on her cheeks and warmth all down her side, where she stood pressed against him. "I'd have died if anything had happened to you," she whispered.

"No, you mustn't say that," he told her, and kissed the side of her head. "You'd still have the children." When she tried to explain, he hugged her tighter. "Anyway, you're not getting rid of me so easily. I'm still in one piece."

"I thank God," she said. "I don't thank Him often enough, I know. But I really mean it."

They went inside. He built up the stove and she thought they would be going to bed. Instead, he said he'd like some coffee and sat at the kitchen table while she put on the pot. When she was lifting the cups down, he said, "I'm not going back to the Valley, Livvy. At least not for a while."

She was surprised. "Why not? I thought your work there was so important."

"It is," he nodded. "Or it could be. Once we've developed the proper equipment."

Livvy was setting the cups down on the saucers. "So what are you going to do?"

"I'm not quite sure yet." He smiled. "They've given me three months leave to decide."

Livvy was glad she had already put the cups down or she would have dropped them. "Matt!" she squeaked. "Three whole months?" She ran round the table to hug him.

"Hey, my arm!" he laughed.

"Oh, darling, sorry! Sorry." She crouched beside his chair, stroking his left arm with its torn shoulder muscles gently. "I was so excited. Three whole months? To have you at home—all of us together. Aren't you excited, too?"

"Pretty excited," he said, smiling and drawing her closer to kiss her.

"I can hardly believe it," she breathed. "Twelve lovely weeks. A quarter of a year! We'll have to do something special."

"I've been thinking that," he told her. "You know? I think it's high time the kids saw their grandparents."

He could only mean her mother and father. His own had died in a cholera epidemic when he was twelve. "Bring them over here, you mean?"

"Not exactly," he said. "I was kind of wondering what Diana and Peter would make of Winchelsea."

She was gazing at him. "Go home? I mean, *my* home. England—is that possible?"

"I don't see why not. We've talked about it often enough. Your folks are always saying how much they want to see the kids, and we don't want to keep putting it off, then find it's too late."

"Of course not." Livvy was more excited than ever, although also slightly perturbed, and bewildered by the suddenness of it. "Matt, is it possible?"

212

"I can't think why not."

She laughed. "Home . . . It would be wonderful! But—well, there's the war and everything. We'll have to think about it very carefully."

"That we will," he agreed. "Only not just now."

"Why not?"

He grinned. "Because the coffee's boiling over."

The next day, they took the children to church in the morning and after lunch went for a long walk in the woods, where the children had a rare adventure. Matt had often told them stories about an old, nearly blind raccoon that lived there and they half suspected he had made them up. But all at once, there was the furry, browny-gray raccoon padding down the path toward them. Matt whispered to them to stand still and be very quiet and the old raccoon with his sharp snout and bushy, ringed tail came almost right up to them, sniffed, wrinkled his nose and scuttled off into the leafless bushes. Diana was disappointed that he was not wearing the waistcoat, mittens and scarf that Matt said he always wore in cold weather, and Matt explained that they had probably got wet in the snow and he had hung them up somewhere to dry. Only, he was such a forgetful old fellow he had more than likely forgotten where and had come out now to look for them. Peter laughed and said, "I expect so." Even though they helped Diana to look very hard all the way home, they could not find them, either.

They had tea over at the Fergusons', where Matt had promised to meet Barney and three or four other friends, and after supper and the children's baths, he had a kind of delayed reaction to the last two nights and more or less went straight to bed, so Livvy did not have a chance to discuss the trip in any more detail with him. They had agreed not to mention it to the children, for the moment.

On Monday morning, with Peter and Diana at school and Matt gone to the office in Calgary, Livvy filled the washing machine and set up the mangle. It was dry enough to hang the sheets and pillowcases outside, although she draped the children's washing over the clotheshorse in the kitchen. Her mind was not on it, and when Matt came home in the middle of the afternoon, having been given a lift to the end of the track, she said, "I've been thinking and thinking about this trip. You know I'd love it in many ways, but—apart from anything else, there's the expense. We really have to discuss it seriously."

"But it's all settled," Matt smiled. He dropped onto the settee and stretched his legs out in front of him. "Oh, I'm stiff all over. I really need that time off."

Livvy sat beside him. "You still haven't explained. What do you mean, it's all settled?"

He took her hand. "Well, it appears some Anglo-Belgian company has developed a new type of drilling rig that could be just what we need. The Board would be very interested in me going over to have a look at it. And if I do, they are prepared to pay half my expenses."

"Matt!" She answered his smile, but still frowned. "And you agreed?"

"Well, like I said, it'll take me a week or two to clear things up. Then another few days, just pottering around here and having a rest. Then I thought the four of us could have a holiday for a couple of weeks, say—in New York." He smiled at her gasp of surprise. "Would you like that?"

She was biting her lower lip in excitement, and laughed. "I'd adore it!"

"Fine." He kissed her hand. "And we can sail from there about the end of April."

Chapter 13

THE NIGHT WAS INKY BLACK AND SO STILL THEY COULD HEAR the faint rustle of the wind among the trees on both sides of the inlet.

Walther Schwieger stood in the open conning tower, his eyes searching the darkness, his ears straining to hear, as the U 20 crept forward on the surface. Haupert was at the stern, giving whispered instructions to the helmsman who was steering by the hand-wheel. Weiser and his crew stood by the loaded deck gun. At the point of the prow, Zentner crouched with a three-man team to handle the Maxim machine gun on its tripod. On either side of him were men with plumb lines, taking nonstop depth soundings, which were passed back by silent-footed runners to the conning tower and the stern. All round the deck, all the available men were kneeling, armed with rifles, watching the slick glimmer of the water intently for any sign of mines. Already it was too shallow for the U 20 to submerge fully and Schwieger had turned her into a surface fighting ship.

He had little choice. The damage to her buoyancy tanks had not corrected itself and her forward hydroplanes were still jammed, after ramming the British submarine. She could only submerge slowly and erratically, while the buckled hydroplanes gave her a lurching, seesawing movement underwater, even at periscope depth. A near miss from being sighted by three patrol boats from the Scilly Isles had convinced him that positive action would have to be taken. After an hour's solitary thought in his cabin, he called his officers together.

Hirsch confirmed that he and his team had done all that was possible. He could make no effective repairs in mid-ocean. Zentner and the others were grave. They could see no alternative but to try to limp home, traveling by night, lying at periscope depth during the day. That would be hazardous and painfully slow, Schwieger told them. There was another choice. They could make for neutral Spain, which was nearer. However, if they reached it, they would be interned. So he told them what he had decided.

Twice in the past six months, they had rendezvoused with a small boat at night off the west coast of Ireland, once to pick up and deliver sealed packets of letters and once to land a German army officer who was to liaise with the Irish Nationalist Army. The boat and the unknown man who rowed it came from a narrow inlet on the coast of County Kerry. Their charts showed the rocks and shoals in great detail and the doglegged creek gently shelving, with no marks of habitation. Because the Irish rebels obviously considered it safe, Schwieger had decided to gamble that it was unguarded and uninhabited, and to give Hirsch a few hours to see what he could do in more stable conditions.

All the previous night, they had crept toward Ireland, heaving and wallowing in the long Atlantic swell, keeping far out from land. During the day, half submerged, they had eased in closer, lying all afternoon off the Skellig Islands. At nightfall they surfaced and moved past Bray Head, across the mouth of Dingle Bay to cut between Great Blasket and Inishbeg, past Cape Sybil and Smerwick Harbour to come in to the coast south of Ballydavid. Conditions were ideal, as if they had been ordered. Not too much sea running and the moon a silver crescent in a cloudless sky, giving only the faintest light.

In the conning tower, Schwieger had unbuttoned the flap of his holster and stood with his right hand on the rounded butt of his Mauser. The U 20 was turning slowly to port, following the bend in the creek. The bed was only eighteen feet below her keel now and shelving more rapidly. He began to hear the soft throb of the diesels more loudly as the steep banks closed in. They were high and precipitous, like most of this wild coastline, with no soil for cultivation or grass for sheep. Another blessing.

The whispered message came that the depth below them had shrunk to thirteen feet. He had just given the instruction to stop engines, when Zentner came back to report that he could see something ahead, a short quay or jetty.

"Any buildings?" Schwieger asked quickly.

"None in sight."

Schwieger could make out the shape of the landing place himself now, a pale finger slanting out into the water. "Ahead, dead slow," he called down softly.

The U 20 stole forward, invisible in the darkness and almost completely silent apart from the faint splash of the sounding leads. Twelve, ten, eight feet. At eight feet, the bottom leveled and the U-boat could inch ahead until her bows nudged the jetty, which turned out to be made of rough stone. At once, Zentner leaped down onto it, his Mauser in one hand, an electric torch in the other, followed by Boatswain Kurtz, Lippe and Bibermann with rifles. Schwieger checked his watch and saw by its luminous dial that it was just after midnight.

Zentner gestured to Kurtz and Lippe to scout the shore. As they set off, there was a splash in the water on the other side of the jetty. Zentner started forward and nearly tripped over a rope tied to an iron ring. He switched on the torch and saw a narrow rowboat with someone in it, a man cowering to stay below the level of the stones. He had been trying to cast off the rope from the prow of his boat. Zentner pointed his Mauser quickly and pulled the trigger, but the safety catch was on. As he fumbled with it, Lippe leaned over, seized the man by the collar and hauled him up.

Schwieger heard the murmur of voices and the sounds of a struggle. He swung himself down, raced along the deck and jumped onto the stone jetty. "Thank God I didn't shoot," Zentner muttered to him. In the beam of the torch, the person they had caught was shown to be a boy of fourteen or fifteen, with dark, tangled hair, dressed roughly in some kind of sleeveless, hide jerkin over a knitted sweater and patched trousers, barefoot. He was still struggling, but Lippe held him easily from behind by the upper arms.

"Kill the light!" Schwieger ordered. When Zentner switched off the torch, the boy began to yell. Lippe rapped him once on the back of the skull with his knotted fist and he sagged. "Who is he? What was he doing here?" Schwieger said.

"I don't know," Zentner answered. "I asked him, but he wouldn't tell us."

Schwieger took the torch, shaded it with his hand and played it down on the boy's boat. It was something like a long canoe, its thin walls coated with pitch or tar. The center to the bows was stacked with lobster creels. Another of the canoes was tied up beyond it and a wooden rowboat drawn up on the shore.

"Captain!" Kurtz called hoarsely.

Schwieger switched off the torch. As he turned, he saw what the Boatswain was pointing toward, a glow of light halfway up the hillside, a square, reddish glow as from a window. It shone for a half a minute, then went out when a shutter or curtain was pulled across it. "Put him on board," Schwieger ordered, and Lippe handed the unconscious boy up to the men on the U 20's deck. Schwieger touched Zentner's arm. "Come with me. Kurtz, Lippe, ahead and spread out. Bibermann, stay here."

At the end of the jetty was a cleared space with more wicker pots, baskets, a tangle of nets. Beyond it, the slope in one area was slightly less steep and up it ran a stony path. It led up to where the light had been. Kurtz and Lippe, their rifles cocked, moved quietly on the thin turf at the sides of the path. Schwieger followed them, with Zentner close behind him.

Halfway up, the hillside leveled even more and they could see the outline of a small, white-painted cottage with the rectangle of its one, curtained window. There was a narrow triangle of the reddish glow where the curtain did not cover one corner. Noiselessly they moved forward, stopping at once when a dog began to bark inside the cottage. A voice spoke harshly. There was a yelp and the barking cut off. Schwieger motioned with his pistol for Kurtz to watch the door and Lippe to check the back. There was no sign of any other building on the hillside. He eased forward to the chink of light, freezing as soon as he could see inside.

The cottage seemed to consist of only one room, although there was a small second door in the rear wall. It was fairly bare, painted white inside as out. He could see a wooden cupboard and table with two chairs. On the table was a little oil lamp, but most of the light came from a large, open hearth where blocks of some form of turf were burning. A woman, a girl, sat sewing on a stool by the fire. A man sat at the table, older, weatherbeaten and round-shouldered. He was reading a newspaper folded into a thin strip, tilting it toward the lamp.

Schwieger moved aside to let Zentner see in, but Rudi had barely moved forward when a black and white dog came out from under the table, barking loudly. The man swore and kicked a foot toward it; then the girl said something and he began to rise. Schwieger gestured sharply to Kurtz and he kicked the door open.

The man and the girl stood up quickly, startled, when Kurtz burst in. Their mouths opened as Schwieger and Zentner followed him. The dog had stopped barking, but began to growl, a low, threatening snarl, slinking forward, its fur bristling. The girl saw the muzzle of Kurtz's rifle swing to the dog and she hurried to it, catching it and pulling it back, kneeling behind it.

"Stand still! Put up your hands!" Zentner ordered in English. The girl looked at him blankly, but the man raised both hands above his head. "How many of you are there?" Zentner asked. "Come on, quick!"

The man found his voice. "The two of us. Just—just the two of us, sir."

His accent was so thick that Zentner had difficulty in understanding. He translated and Schwieger gestured to the other door. The dog growled when Kurtz moved, but the girl kept a tight hold. The door opened into a small storeroom for more nets and creels, with some jars and sacks on the shelves.

"It's only a storeroom," the man said. "A bit of a larder, sir." He paused, evidently confused. "Ye're not . . . That is, are ye—are ye, be chance, Germans?"

Zentner translated what he had said. Schwieger considered the man for a moment, then nodded. He glanced at the girl, who seemed frightened. Not the man, however, who appeared more curious. Schwieger decided on another gamble. There had been a password, when he delivered the letters and his passenger, two words in the Irish language. "Sinn Fein," he said.

"Holy be . . ." the man gasped. He began to smile and lower his arms, but stopped when Kurtz jabbed his rifle toward him. "Don't go joltin' that trigger now, me boy," the man warned. "Not till I've remembered the reply." His eyebrows knitted, then climbed as he smiled again. "*Gott strafe England* . . . Is that right, now? I'm not just sure how to say it."

Schwieger put his pistol in its holster and closed the flap.

The man's name was Patrick Kevin O'Dowd and, although he seemed to be only a simple peasant fisherman, he had a confidence and a quick intelligence that warned Schwieger not to underestimate him. He was a widower who lived here with his son and daughter, he told them. The boy was fifteen, the girl nearly eighteen.

"No one else?" Zentner asked. "No village?"

"Where would yes build it, sir?" O'Dowd laughed. "Ah, there were two other families, but they're long gone. The life's too hard." His hands were scarred and calloused, his face ruddy with working outdoors, deep lines running down from the broad nostrils. His hair was dark brown and curly, beginning to recede, no clue to his age which could have been anything between thirty and fifty. He wore a bottle-green sweater, crew-necked, with the frayed band of a collarless shirt showing above it and, over it, a moleskin waistcoat, open round his bulging stomach and held loosely together by a span of pinchbeck watch chain. His heavy corduroy trousers were tucked into a pair of cracked gumboots.

The girl, like the boy had been, was barefooted. She was slim but well-made. The leather belt round her waist emphasized its neatness, above the fullness of her rough, calf-length skirt. She was wearing a coarse gray collarless shirt like her father's and the knitted shawl round her shoulders was a dark green like his sweater, the ends folded and crossed in front, threaded under her belt. She was still crouching by the dog, holding it back.

When he glanced at her again, Schwieger was surprised. She was composed now, watchful, her eyes on the rifle pointing at her father. And she was beautiful. The oval of her face was out of a storybook, as proud and pale as a young queen, her nose and lips finely chiseled. Her eyes were black and widely spaced under high arched brows. There was a small umber mark, a natural beauty spot, under the right corner of her mouth and her hair was as dark as her father's, tumbled over her forehead and falling down her back in thick, uncombed waves that reflected a hint of auburn from the firelight. "Ask her if what her father says is true," he ordered quietly. "That there's no one else here "

When Zentner put the question to the girl, she gave no reaction and went on watching Kurtz. O'Dowd seemed embarrassed. "Yes'll have to forgive her, sir," he apologized. "Megeen doesn't have the English, d'ye see."

At the mention of her name, the girl looked at him and he spoke to her, a few words in a strange, liquid tongue. Zentner shrugged to Schwieger. She glanced at them and spoke, herself, her voice soft and lilting. When they did not understand, she smiled slightly, shyly, the smile softening and lighting up her features. Great God, that's a dangerous smile, Schwieger thought.

"I know yes have to ask, but ye can trust me," O'Dowd was saying. "There's only us here, and the boy. Seamus."

"I think we met him," Zentner said. "Down at the jetty."

O'Dowd stiffened. "Is he . . . ?"

"He's all right," Zentner assured him. "We took him on board."

Schwieger looked round. There was a bed in the far corner. On the floor against the wall beside it and the wall opposite were two palliasses and blankets. On a corner shelf above the bed stood a highly colored reproduction of a picture of Jesus, holding open His chest to display an idealized, jewel-like heart. A small nightlight was burning on the shelf in front of it.

O'Dowd had lowered his arms. "On board?" he echoed, puzzled. "I'm sorry, I still don't follow. Ye're off a submarine, now is that not so? But what are yes wantin'?"

Zentner translated for Schwieger, who nodded. "Our boat is tied up down there," Zentner said. "We need to make repairs."

"Holy Mother . . ." O'Dowd breathed. He spoke quickly to the girl, who rose in surprise. He slapped his hands against his thighs and laughed. "That I should live to see the day!"

Megeen smiled, reacting to his amusement. Then her head turned swiftly, her hearing sharper than any of the others. There was the scrape of a foot on stone outside and Kurtz swung his rifle to cover the door.

It was Lippe who came in, his width blocking the door for a second as he stepped through. He lowered the butt of his rifle to the floor carefully and saluted. "No one else round here, Captain," he reported. "There's another cottage higher up, but it's a ruin, empty." His eyes flicked to O'Dowd and the girl.

Zentner holstered his pistol as Schwieger rattled off a list of questions to him. He turned, to see O'Dowd heading toward the storeroom. "What are you doing?"

"Fetching us a drink," O'Dowd said.

Schwieger shook his head. "We have no time for that!" Zentner called.

O'Dowd reached into the storeroom and brought out an unlabeled bottle. "Well, now, I'm afraid yes'll have to make time," he told them. "Ye're the first strangers to cross my threshold this year, and ye must taste the hospitality of the house. It will be a blessing on us all."

Schwieger smiled and gave in. "Very well," Zentner said. "We thank you, but first tell us. Are there any guards stationed nearby?"

"Guards?" O'Dowd chuckled. "I'd not still be here if there were. No, there's a lookout at Ballydavid, three mile up the coast. And a post at Smerwick Harbour, southwest of us. But they're no trouble to us."

"They must keep a watch on this place."

"If ye'd call it that. Coast guard Feeny comes by twice a day from Ballydavid. That's if it's not rainin', though. He's not carin' to ride his bicycle in the wet." O'Dowd smiled. "He was here before sunset, so he'll not be back till mornin'. By then ye should be far away." Megeen had fetched the only three glasses and two teacups from the cupboard.

"What about lights?" Zentner asked. "If we have to use them, can they be seen?"

"Only by us and the angels," O'Dowd assured him.

Boatswain Kurtz was watching disapprovingly as he filled the cups and glasses. "Kurtz," Schwieger said, "get back down and tell Mr. Hirsch he can start. Set guards. Two armed sentries to the top of the hill. And no unnecessary noise."

Kurtz came to attention and left quickly.

"Ah, now," O'Dowd protested, "he hasn't had his drop!"

"He doesn't drink," Zentner told him.

O'Dowd sighed. "Oh, the poor man." He passed two of the glasses to Schwieger and Zentner and the third to Lippe.

Lippe shifted uncomfortably. "With the Captain's permission?"

"Of course," Schwieger smiled. "And you can propose the toast."

Lippe's head lowered in embarrassment as he thought. *"Zu . . . zum Sieg!"* he blurted.

When Zentner said it in English, O'Dowd raised his cup. "To victory," he repeated, standing erect. "To the success of German arms, and a free Ireland!" He drank the cup off in one swallow.

"Prosit," Schwieger toasted. The liquor in his glass was like a darker schnapps. He sipped it cautiously, expecting it to burn his throat, as it did, a harsh fire with a taste like bitter whiskey mixed with wood cinders.

Zentner had taken a larger swallow and coughed. *"Heilige Scheisse . . ."* he muttered.

Lippe had downed his drink in one, like O'Dowd, and stood holding his empty glass, smoothing the spread of his beard, his tongue clicking slowly in appreciation. O'Dowd picked up the remaining cup and offered it to him. Lippe hesitated, half turned away from Schwieger, who still caught the wink between them.

Schwieger smiled to Zentner. "I don't think I can finish this. Thank Mr. O'Dowd, will you? We must get back down."

"We have to leave now," Zentner said. "Perhaps you'd come with us, Mr. O'Dowd?"

"Surely. Surely, sir," O'Dowd muttered. He smiled to Lippe and nodded, and crossed to the bed to fetch his patched jacket. "I wonder yes brought him up here, when there's repairs needed down there," he chuckled. "What was it ye said wanted doin'?"

"The—uh. It's the—" Zentner could not translate. "We've damaged the horizontal rudders at the bow that help us to submerge and rise again."

"I see."

"And something's wrong with one of our ballast tanks. But with luck, it should only take two or three hours."

O'Dowd paused in putting on his jacket, then shrugged himself into it quickly. "Did ye say hours? But surely—I thought ye'd know."

"Know what?"

"The creek's tidal." O'Dowd came back to them, tugging the watch from his waistcoat pocket. He checked it worriedly. "If ye're not finished in under two hours, yes'll be grounded! Ye won't get off till midmornin'."

As soon as he heard, Schwieger turned to the door. "Come! Lippe, you'll stay on guard." He looked back. "You're only here in case the girl tries to run away. No nonsense."

Lippe was hurt. "I wouldn't, Captain! You know I wouldn't!" But Schwieger had gone.

O'Dowd was taking his cap from a nail behind the door. He stopped, realizing that Lippe was to remain, and glanced from him to Megeen. She was standing by the cupboard, motionless, watching them.

"She'll be quite safe," Zentner said. "You can trust us, too."

"I know I can," O'Dowd answered quietly. "If I didn't, I'd have shot ye while yes were drinkin'." He pulled back his waistcoat. A pouch was sewn on the inside and protruding from it was the handle of a flat Italian automatic. "Just so we understand each other."

Lippe faced them, wringing his hands. In someone so large it might have been comical, if his embarrassment had not been so genuine. He could not dare even to look at Megeen. Both of them had caught the sense of what her father had said, if not the words. "Will you tell him, sir, please?" he asked Zentner. "Please, would you tell him that I'm a fisherman myself, from East Prussia? So it's all right. He doesn't have to worry."

Sweat prickled on Schwieger's back as he hurried down the path. Below him, the U 20 lay at the jetty. Emergency lights had been rigged up on wires from her generator and strung on her forward jury mast, which had been hoisted, and from her bow rail. She stood out sharply against the blackness of the water, a perfect target. He knew it was childish, yet he could not drive out the thought of mortar shells bursting round her and machine guns opening up from the hillsides. Afraid again? he asked himself. More terrors, things that go bump in the night? If they're not there, you'll invent them.

Yet he knew it was not imagination. It was only too possible. A stray fisherman, someone walking in the hills might raise the alarm. He could not be one hundred percent certain they had not been spotted on the way in. He trusted O'Dowd instinctively, though he was positive he was not the man who had rowed out with the letters. However, even if he wanted to betray them, he would do nothing with his daughter in the cottage and his son on board.

Haupert was standing at the bows with Hirsch kneeling beside him, gazing down over the side. Three of his assistants had stripped off and were going down into the water one at a time, holding on to ropes tied to the deck rail in case of being attacked by cramp in the extreme cold. They could only stay under for about a minute at each attempt, and as each came up, he was hauled back onto the deck and given a mouthful of brandy, then wrapped in towels and blankets while he reported, until it was his turn again. They were already nearly exhausted and had not been able to gain a true estimate of the damage.

Hirsch rose as Schwieger climbed upon to the bows. "The ballast tank's no trouble," he said. "The corner of a deck plate from the English submarine is jamming the outlet. We only have to knock it out and test the shutter. Half an hour at most."

"What about the hydroplanes?"

"Just one," Hirsch told him. "On the port side, there's no damage. But the one to starboard seems completely buckled. That's the only problem."

"Not the only one," Schwieger said. He shouted to the men at midships to cast the plumb lines for a sounding.

"Seven feet, Captain!" And a voice called from the stern, "Seven feet!"

Haupert was the first to realize. "We had eight under our keel when we tied up! If the tide's going out, we'll have to get going!"

Schwieger shook his head. He had also realized something. "It's already too late. You remember that bar, shingle or whatever it was, just when we turned at the bend of the inlet? We couldn't clear it now, even if we left this second." Haupert started for the nearest hatch and he grabbed his arm. "Stay here! You'll panic the men."

"I wanted to look at the charts," Haupert explained. He stepped back. "It's my fault, Captain," he said bitterly. "I should have checked the tidal flow."

"I did," Schwieger told him. "It's not marked. So it's no

one's fault." He saw that Hirsch had taken off his cap and leather jacket and was unbelting his trousers. Schwieger was worried. "There's no hurry. We'll be here for hours."

"I have—have to see what's down there," Hirsch muttered, beginning to shiver.

It was illogical. He was blaming himself for the damage and for not having repaired it. Schwieger lowered his voice. "Hirsch, don't be a fool. You're not young enough for this game."

Hirsch was listening to the report of the last man who had been down. "You can't see," the man coughed. "It just— just felt badly bent."

"I have to know how badly. In what shape?"

The man's teeth were chattering violently and they gave him another swig of cognac. "I'm sorry, sir," he panted. "Couldn't make it out. Your hands go numb in seconds down there."

Hirsch turned away from him. "You see, Captain? I'm the only one who can tell what I need to know." He pulled his sweater over his head.

"Hirsch, listen to me!" Schwieger urged. "If anything happens to you, we're finished. Wait till the water level drops. We have time."

"You may need it, Captain," Hirsch said. "You may need to be ready, the minute the tide turns." He was stripped to his woolen vest and drawers and two crewmen helped him over the side, holding him until he had passed one of the ropes round his back and under his armpits. He lowered himself, gasping when his feet slid into the icy water, then took several deep breaths and slipped out of sight.

Schwieger and Haupert waited at the rail, gazing down. The lights made the surface into a mirror, reflecting their silhouettes, the images breaking up with the ripples as the taut rope jerked in the water. Schwieger was counting silently. At fifty, he began to be anxious and cursed himself for not having forbidden Hirsch to attempt it. In less than an hour, the U 20 would be stranded. Was it worth letting his Engineer Officer risk himself to save an hour? Sixty. After a count of another fifteen, he leaned over and felt the rope. It was still taut, but had not moved for the last six seconds. "Get him up!" he snapped. He hauled on the rope,

226

grunting at the dead weight on it. Haupert grabbed hold of it to help and the rope snaked back up through the water with no weight on it at all.

The three machinists were dropping the blankets from round themselves and rising, even as Schwieger shouted. They swarmed over the side, lowering themselves. "One of you stay at the surface!" Schwieger ordered.

Two of the machinists vanished into the blackness and the third hung on his rope up to his waist in the water, watching. In moments, the surface swirled and the other two reappeared, supporting Hirsch's inert body between them. The third man looped the slack of his own rope round Hirsch and tied it. At once, the crewmen began to heave them both up the U 20's steep side, the machinist supporting him, doing his best to keep his limp body from being scraped by the rivets of her plates. More crewmen crowded in to lift them over the rail and help the other two who were climbing up behind them.

Hirsch was quickly wrapped in blankets. "Turn him over," Schwieger said. Hirsch was rolled onto his face and Schwieger knelt beside him, putting one knee in the small of his back. Water was trickling from Hirsch's slack lips. The crewmen were silent as he took Hirsch's shoulders and pulled them strongly up, then dropped him, forcing his knee sharply into his back. About a pint of water spewed from Hirsch's mouth, and another gush when Schwieger wrenched his shoulders up and dropped him again.

Schwieger swung him over onto his back and pressed hard on his stomach. More water bubbled out, but not so much. When Schwieger bore down on Hirsch's chest, released it and pressed again, Hirsch spluttered and coughed, drawing in a ragged, wheezing breath. Schwieger pressed and released twice more and Hirsch's mouth gaped wide, gasping in air. He had begun to breathe on his own and Schwieger sat back.

The crew's silence broke and they started to cheer. Schwieger looked up quickly. "That's enough!" he rapped. "Not too much noise! You three, get below and keep warm." The three machinists were helped to the hatch.

Haupert was cradling Hirsch's head. The Engineer Officer's eyes had opened and he was trying to focus them as he coughed and spat out the last of the water from his lungs. "Captain . . . Captain?" he whispered, his voice harshly slurred.

"You're fine," Schwieger told him. "Everything's fine. Don't try to talk."

Hirsch put up his hand, searching. Schwieger took it, holding it firmly. "Must . . . must report," Hirsch croaked. "The hydroplane . . . bent back on itself . . . and twisted."

"I've got that," Schwieger said. "Rest now."

Hirsch's fingers gripped his tighter. His eyes were clearing. "Time . . . the time," he gasped. "Need time to detach it . . . beat—beat it back into shape . . . somehow. Take hours."

"Understood," Schwieger said. The men round them were muttering and, for their sake, he added loudly, "We have hours. That's good." He freed his hand from Hirsch's. "Haupert, get him below and into dry clothes. Put him in his bunk." Hirsch was trying to protest. "Strap him in, if you have to." Haupert and some others lifted Hirsch and carried him to the forward hatch.

Schwieger followed after and went to the chart table. The chart of the area of coastline was still in place, held by the elasticized straps. There was only a general indication of tides and a warning not to sail submerged too close to shore, because of hidden reefs and shoals. What O'Dowd had told them agreed with his memory of the chart, but he checked again.

The nearest town or village was nearly three miles away and there was no made-up road from it. Only the winding line of a track along the coast. From the contours, it must be a stiff gradient at places, hugging the side of the cliffs. No other track or path was noted, but, then, neither was this landing stage nor the cottage above it. Beyond the inlet, the headland jutted out in a series of jagged points, until it curved back round to the wider bay and harbor on the other side of the mountains. Two miles as the crow flies, yet again no mark of passes or paths. From his own climbing, he knew that paths would exist, but of the type that would add many miles of difficult walking to the journey. There was virtually no likelihood of anyone using them at this time of year. The inlet was as safe as it could be. Yet there was no point in advertising their presence or in wasting power. "Kill those outside lights," he ordered.

Bibermann pushed up a switch. There was a yell of indignation from the deck, and someone shouted back that it was Captain's orders.

All we can do for the moment is wait, Schwieger decided. Even as he thought of the rocks that O'Dowd had warned him about, lying next to the jetty, the U 20's prow crunched down on something that gave and she shuddered. The grinding under the bows continued for half a minute, then stopped. According to the gauge, her prow was at a slightly higher level than her stern. Schwieger tapped the chart table and smiled.

The cook was watching him from the door of the galley. "Brew up some tea now," Schwieger said. "We'll feed the crew in relays over the next hour. Whatever you can make in the time."

O'Dowd's son had scrambled round the periscope shafts and was gazing at him, worried by the grinding sounds he had heard. The dachshunds licked his hands, trying to remind him to fondle them. Schwieger was suddenly ashamed of keeping him here and signed to him to follow. He went through to the forward hatch, climbed the rungs and called to Zentner to tell the boy he was free to go ashore. He climbed up on deck, with Seamus behind him looking out of the hatch.

After a pause, O'Dowd himself spoke to his son in the language he had used with Megeen. Seamus shouted back, sounding reluctant. Schwieger heard O'Dowd and Zentner laughing, and O'Dowd said, "He wants to stay on board, sir. He doesn't want to come out."

Fifty minutes later when Schwieger ordered the emergency lights switched on again, the U 20 was completely stranded. He had sent the crew outside in batches as soon as they had eaten and they lined the jetty and the space at its end. They forgot their grumbles at the coldness of the night. Some of them moved closer to one another, worried, whispering. Even the armed guards spread out along the hillside could look at nothing else.

"Be the Holy," O'Dowd muttered to Zentner, "he's the lad, your Captain."

The tide had gone fully out. Haupert had scouted, reporting back that it had retreated as far as the bar of shingle at the bend, and the jury-lights revealed the naked bed of the creek, mud, shingle and small rocks, with a few shallow pools of water. But everyone was looking at the U-boat. Not one of them had ever seen her like this.

She sat high and dry, the gray paint with which she was coated scarcely reflecting the light. Living and working in her, she seemed so cramped, every possible inch taken up by the engines, batteries, controls and the torpedo rooms, with hardly any space left for the human beings who sailed in her. Beached, she seemed so much larger. Two hundred feet from her sharp prow to her streamlined stern. With a beam of only twenty feet, the length was emphasized by her narrowness, a slim gray shark with the oval hump of the conning tower on her back. She had settled at an angle, her stern on a ridged patch of mud and her bows six or seven feet higher, propped up on a rampart of rounded boulders heaped up along the outer wall of the jetty.

O'Dowd said something in Irish that Zentner did not understand, then chuckled admiringly, "And there was me after warnin' him! I see what he was up to. She's as snug as she'd be in any dry dock ye could find."

Already, teams directed by Haupert and Weiser were bringing down small trees from the hillside. There was the chunk of axes as the branches were lopped from them. The U 20's height was less than her narrow breadth, yet Schwieger did not wish to risk any chance of her rolling while work was carried out on her. Squads of crewmen wearing waders carried the timbers down to the bed of the creek, driving the bases into the shingly mud and wedging the points under the curve of her hull, as though she were on the slipway of a shipbuilder's yard.

Schwieger had jumped down onto the rocks by the jetty with the Engineer's Mate and the machinists. As he had hoped, the hydroplane was at a height where it could be worked on with ease. He detailed two men to deal with the outlet shutter on the damaged tank and to check the others.

The hydroplane was twisted exactly as Hirsch had described, the heavy iron plates crumpled like tinfoil. The Engineer's Mate swore softly under his breath as he examined it. "Can you repair it?" Schwieger asked.

"Take some doing, Captain," the Engineer's Mate answered, worriedly. "It's not just the 'plane itself. The linkage mechanism is twisted as well."

"Can it be straightened?"

The man was doubtful. "It's a question of how much stress has been put on it. Trying to bend it back, we might snap it off."

"Why don't they just get rid of the thing altogether?" O'Dowd asked. "Ye have another one on the port side."

"If we did that," Zentner told him, "we'd keep circling to port every time we tried to submerge or to rise again."

Near them, Lammeier, a member of the gun crew, was squatting at the edge of the jetty, watching intently. Bull-necked and muscular, he had been a blacksmith in a farming district in Silesia before the war, and Boatswain Kurtz had ordered him to stand by in case he was needed. Schwieger called up to him, "What do you say, Lammeier?"

Slow thinking, Lammeier scratched his chin, then shook his head. "It's the leverage, Captain."

"What do you mean?"

"You can't get the right leverage, not where it is," Lammeier said. "Specially if you don't want to break off the swivel arm. You have to bend back those folds before you can beat them flat, you see. And for that, you'd need something solid underneath."

"Like the jetty," Schwieger nodded. He turned to the Engineer's Mate. "Can you detach it, the whole thing?"

The Engineer's Mate grimaced. "We could try. I'd need two men to open her up inside, and we'd have to have some sort of scaffolding out here to bear the weight."

"Scaffolding? With that you could do it?"

"Probably, although it will take time."

Schwieger looked at his watch. It was already after two. He climbed the rocks and Lammeier and Zentner helped him up onto the jetty. "Did he say what time it gets light here?"

"Just before six," Zentner told him. "And the tide starts to come in again about eight-thirty, so we won't be afloat till ten at the earliest."

"That's what I calculated," Schwieger nodded. He saw the young gunnery lieutenant with a squad of men down in the creek. "Weiser!" he called. "Sort out any wood that could

231

be used for scaffolding and bring it round here. Quick about it!"

Zentner was behind him. "Captain," he said, "O'Dowd thinks he can help." He translated as the Irishman spoke eagerly, pointing to the hillside. "He has some timber stored . . . and, uh, pieces of tackle, landing gear . . . from the days when this creek was used by larger fishing boats."

"Where is it?" Schwieger asked.

"In the shed."

Schwieger was not surprised he had not noticed the shed. It was dug into the hillside, lined with stone, and covered with turf. Inside were various lengths of planking, chains and assorted wooden pulley blocks. The ropes had rotted and some of the metal parts were rusted with age, but Weiser was excited when he saw what there was. Some of the planks had already been drilled to take wooden pegs and the U 20's ropes would fit the pulleys.

Using the planks as main supports and thick saplings as cross beams, fixed by a mixture of pegs and lashings, a scaffolding began to take shape under the damaged hydroplane. O'Dowd supervised its construction. The framework looked rickety, but he knew what he was doing and it was strong and stable. At the same time, Weiser revealed a surprisingly inventive mind by rigging up a wooden derrick on the jetty with the pulleys and trimmed pine trunks, like the skeleton of a dinosaur.

But another hour slipped away. Schwieger watched and waited, feeling his impatience growing. He could not show it. Most of the crew were involved in the work. To keep telling them to hurry up would only distract them. He walked down the jetty to the landing space, where the Maxim gun was set up on its tripod, manned by three of the gun crew.

He warned them to stay alert, then went out along the hillside to check the guards set by the petty officer. Walking back, Schwieger paused, looking out over the creek at the shadowy hills beyond it, formless and mysterious because they were unknown. Although the night was cold, the little valley was sheltered from the stronger wind that had risen. The sky was clear, the stars and great, wheeling constellations distinct against its velvet blackness. All at once, the strangeness of what he was doing and where he was came

232

to him. Surely he had been mad to bring the U 20 here, and strand her on enemy soil? Any chance sighting in the next six and a half hours and the exit from the creek would be blocked by British coastal torpedo boats. Army units would encircle them in the hills and he would have no choice except surrender, to prevent his crew from being wiped out. He had no one to blame but himself.

He looked down at the U 20, naked and defenseless in the brightness of the jury-lamps, men swarming round her bows and Weiser's homemade derrick leaning over her. One thing he could do. He could plant explosive charges all along her keel on the inside and blow her up, before he would let her be taken.

When he arrived back at the landing space, he found that the hydroplane had been detached and swung onto the jetty on Weiser's derrick. "You're a good team," he told them. "You see how well you get on when I go for a walk?" They laughed, pleased with themselves and with him. O'Dowd was chuckling, watching his son Seamus, who was helping the cook and his mate, carrying a tray with mugs of hot soup and wearing a seaman's flat, brimless cap with the words on the ribbon round it, *Unterseeboots Flottille.*

The buckled hydroplane lay on the large, flat stones of the jetty. It was easier now to see how badly its plates had been bent out of shape, the leading corners of the rectangle folded nearly back on itself like an envelope and the whole thing humped into a cup shape in the center. It had been turned over and the narrower trailing edge was immobilized by a heavy boulder, while Kurtz and Lammeier, the ex-smith, prized and levered at the bent corners with crowbars. Lammeier was stripped to his singlet and trousers in spite of the cold, sweating and straining at the thick iron sheets. He paused to catch his breath.

"Well, Lammeier?" Schwieger asked.

"It's a bitch, Captain," Lammeier panted. "If you'll pardon the expression."

Schwieger saw that Kurtz had also stopped to rest. "I'll have Lippe brought down."

"It's not brute strength that's needed," Lammeier said. "Trouble is . . . there could be a fracture, could be all cracked inside the fold. We have to be careful." He signaled to one of the other men to come and add his weight to the end of the crowbar. A second man moved in to help Kurtz.

Schwieger heard O'Dowd mutter something and Rudi reply. They laughed. "What was that?"

Zentner grinned. "He said he'd never seen anyone work so hard as our crew. I told him we all enjoy a little shore leave."

Schwieger smiled. "As long as it doesn't go on too long. Ask him how many other people fish from this creek."

"I already have. He says four or five, but none of them regularly."

"What about weekend anglers?" Schwieger asked. "It's Saturday. How soon might someone turn up tomorrow?"

"It's not Saturday now, Captain. It's Sunday," O'Dowd corrected. "And there'll be not a soul fishin' this mornin'— or Father Shaunessy would set about them with his stick. He's a man with a great power of persuasion."

Zentner translated and added, smiling, "I like the sound of him."

"That coast guard he mentioned. When will he come?"

O'Dowd spat over the side of the jetty. "Feeny. Not till after second mass, between eleven and midday, say. He'll be hopin' for a cup o' tea and a look at Megeen."

"Are they—?" Zentner left it unfinished.

"The Divil they are!" O'Dowd swore. "That crawlin' dog's spittle! I'd break his slimy fingers off if he so much as touched her."

With two men on each of the crowbars, the twisted metal was beginning to give. Schwieger felt his spirits lifting, but there was still a small thought which niggled at the back of his mind. "Tell him we're grateful for what he has done to help us and that we trust him," he said to Zentner. "But I heard the voice of the man who brought out the letters, the same man who was waiting for Captain Wachendorf. It was not O'Dowd's voice. Where is that other man?"

When Zentner passed on the question, O'Dowd tensed. He stared at Schwieger for a moment, his mouth pressed into a hard slit, his eyes shrouded. He turned away abruptly, looking out past the faint line of the hills to the stars that spangled the dark sky. "It was my brother," he said quietly. "Liam. He came here to live and work with me after my wife died. It was him that was in the Movement. I only—

only helped him, when he needed me. Prayed for him." When Zentner had passed on what he said, O'Dowd turned to face them again. He made to speak, and stopped, then shrugged. "He was caught runnin' guns into Limerick. They hanged him last month at Dublin Castle."

It would be an intrusion to comment, and clearly he did not want it. As they stood in silence, there was a loud crack like a pistol shot from behind them. Schwieger spun round. Kurtz and the man helping him were staring in stupefaction. The whole corner they had been levering up had snapped off and they could hear it rattle as it hit the smaller stones on the far side of the jetty.

Lammeier had stopped working at once and scrambled over to look at the jagged edge that was left. He knelt and peered along the fold of his own corner, shaking his head. Bibermann sat on the edge of the jetty, turned and lowered himself, dropping to the stones. In a moment he was back, reaching as high as he could, holding up the heavy, broken section of hydroplane with both hands. Kurtz and the other man were almost distraught. "I'm sorry! Sorry, Captain!" Kurtz blurted. "But it—it just gave. Just flew away!" All the crewmen standing round were dismayed. Others came running up to see what had happened.

"Don't worry, Kurtz," Schwieger told him. "I don't think it was your fault."

"That it wasn't," Lammeier confirmed, angling the broken corner to the lights. "What I suspected. All fractured along the inner fold. And I'll bet that other bitch of a corner's fractured, too. If you'll parden the expression, Captain."

"I'll pardon it," Schwieger said. "What happens now?"

Lammeier shook his head doubtfully. "Nothing good. That other bi—, eh, other corner's bound to break off, too."

"There's no way you can stop it?"

Schwieger's question came too quickly and Lammeier was flustered. "Well . . . no. I mean—if I had a smithy, a forge, enough heat and some bellows—I mean, maybe I could bend it back and weld it together—maybe. But . . ." He looked round hopelessly at the emptiness of the little valley. While he waited for Schwieger to say something, he turned the corner of the hydroplane over and over apologetically, unable to face the others, who had been depending on him.

Zentner felt sorry for Lammeier, who was shivering as

235

he became aware of the cold. Unable to practice his skill, the man seemed lost. He picked up Lammeier's jacket and draped it over his shoulders.

Schwieger stood silent and withdrawn. He glanced at his watch. 4:18. Where had the time gone? Failure, he admitted to himself. It was only to be expected. The crew must be made to realize it had always been a gamble. It just hadn't come off. There was no disgrace in— He remembered something. "Mr. O'Dowd?" he said. The Irishman's head jerked at the sound of his name. "Ask him—didn't he say three families used to live here? We've seen two cottages. Where was the third?"

"Just over there," O'Dowd told them, pointing to beyond the landing space. "But there's little enough left of it. Nobody's lived there for twenty years."

The cottage was old, perhaps hundreds of years old, roofless, tumbledown. It was only a shell, the thinner side walls mainly crumbled away and a high mound of earth piled against one end. Schwieger and the guards had passed it several times, but never imagined that those heaps of unshaped stones had once been a building.

Schwieger stepped through the gap that had been the door. He played his torch over the scattered rubble covering the floor to the end wall with the earth piled against it outside. It was cracked and bulging inward. When he swung the torch to the other end wall, Lammeier, who was behind him, gave a gasp of surprise. They climbed over the rubble, followed by Zentner and O'Dowd. Haupert and Kurtz stayed at the doorway.

The deep stone fireplace was partly blocked by fallen debris. Lammeier kicked some of it out and crouched in the hearth, looking up the chimney at the square of stars visible through its open top. Schwieger flashed his torch up the shaft and they could see that it was nearly intact. They could hear the wind whistling in it and as Lammeier felt the rush of the natural draft on his face, he beamed. "There! Look!" Zentner exclaimed. He was shining his torch on what was left of the rear wall. Against it was an ancient bed platform made of one solid stone slab, two feet high by almost five wide.

"Well, Lammeier, here's your forge," Schwieger said. The

smith was already throwing loose stones out of the hearth. "Kurtz, send some men to clear this rubble!" Schwieger called. "And Haupert, see if Weiser and you can think how to get that hydroplane over here."

"He's the lad, all right," O'Dowd chuckled.

"Would you tell him I'll need wood, dry wood or coal, sir?" Lammeier asked Zentner. "Lots of it."

"Yes'll have better than that," O'Dowd promised. "Turf. It gives a grand blaze." He led them out and round to the mound at the opposite end. When he kicked at the side of it, what had seemed to be earth broke off in flattish blocks about a foot square.

"Good," Lammeier nodded approvingly. "Very good." The same kind of bricks cut from old peat bog deposits were used as fuel in parts of Germany.

The fireplace, the stone bed and the area between them were cleared and a fire was blazing in the hearth by the time Haupert and Weiser came with some of the gun crew, carrying the hydroplane on an improvised litter. It was slid onto the bed. Kurtz had fetched the crowbars and hammers and a pair of long-handled pincers, and lanterns were perched on the ruined walls.

Lammeier had tied his leather jacket round his waist like an apron. A rubber mat from the torpedo room hung from his neck as a bib. He had built a high horseshoe shape of stones in the fireplace and sited his fire inside it. He was feeding the flames with pieces of the driest turf blocks. "Not too much, not too little," he said. "A steady heat's the thing. As long as we can increase the temperature when we need to." He was happy again. "We'll do our best, Captain."

"I'm sure you will," Schwieger smiled.

Lippe had been relieved at the cottage and brought down to lend a hand. In the cramped space of the fireplace, there was room for only a few men to work and his strength was needed to shift the hydroplane.

Schwieger watched Lammeier and him, with Kurtz and O'Dowd, shuffle to the hearth under the weight of the hydroplane. The smith had decided that, before anything else, they must flatten the main plates, which had been warped into a cup shape. As they settled the hydroplane on the stone horseshoe with its bulge toward the flames, there was a murmur from the crewmen gathered outside the broken walls. "Where are their rifles?" Schwieger snapped to Weiser. "Every man who is not working must go armed! If they have nothing else to do, detail half of them as extra guards. The others can get some rest." In moments, the men were dispersed, and he sent Zentner to turn off the U 20's exterior lights again and make sure her hatches were blacked out. They must not forget where they were and the ever-present danger. He checked his watch. It was almost five o'clock.

He had to force himself not to count the long minutes as they crept by, each one taking them closer to morning and a greater chance of being discovered. At last Lammeier signed to the others and they moved in. The gloves O'Dowd was wearing and the pads of leather wrapped round the hands of the others smoked and gave off a stench like burning flesh when they lifted the hydroplane, which was glowing white in the center. Even though they were prepared for it, the heat was agony, and Lammeier kept gasping "Careful! Careful!" as they stumbled back to the stone slab. To drop it would have been disastrous and they were all sweating, faces contorted with pain, when they lowered it at last onto the slab, tilting it over to lie with the bulge uppermost.

As soon as it was laid down, Lippe grabbed one of the sledgehammers, but Lammeier stopped him from striking and showed him how to position the head on the curved metal, while O'Dowd held it steady with the pincers. Then the smith tapped it with his own hammer, using it as a punch. They had covered only a small arc of the surface when he stepped back.

"What's wrong?" Schwieger asked.

"Can't rush it, Captain," Lammeier said. "We could crack the plates, or drive a hole right through them."

Schwieger could tell by the man's tension that he was making him nervous. "Yes," he nodded. "All right, you're the expert. Just carry on."

O'Dowd was building up the fire. Again the four of them carried the hydroplane back to the hearth, and Schwieger made himself turn and leave, walking out of the light and past the mound of turf blocks toward the landing space. He felt himself beginning to shiver, not from the cold, but with his own tension. He had thought he had his nerves so completely under control now that it shocked him.

His arm brushed the rough bark of an old tree stump and he leaned against it while his legs steadied. Thank God no one can see, he told himself. In the welter of his thoughts he heard Weddigen saying, "The human body and mind are just not meant to exist at such pressure." And Hersing's voice, "You can bear anything, if you know it's not forever." If only that were true . . .

He lit his first cigarette for days. His hands were steady again. He was tired, he told himself. Naturally. He had not slept for the last thirty-eight hours.

Inevitably, he thought of Anneliese. She would be asleep. Alone? She had given herself to him so eagerly, so easily. She said she had never behaved like that before, never felt so passionate, so quickly. Could he believe her? He wondered at himself, because he realized that he wanted to believe her, more than anything.

He had almost forgotten his surroundings, but gradually became aware of them again. What was it? What was nagging at him? Something his conscious mind had not yet registered. Then he saw that the sky had turned from cobalt to silver. He looked up the winding valley of the creek. The line of the hills was clearer against the eastern sky. Not yet! Surely not yet? He checked his watch, and relaxed. It was the false dawn. It would fade soon, that illusion of brightness in the sky. But soon it would be no illusion and the morning would be on them. Behind him, the sound of the hammers began again.

It was even colder before the dawn and a thin mist stole out of the air, shimmering round the glow from the ruins. The walls were beginning to take shape through it. This time there was no mistake. It was morning.

He pushed himself away from the stump, against which he had been half lying for over an hour. His whole body felt stiff and chill, his face and hands numb. There were things he knew he should have done, written up his logbook, gone round the guards. The time had passed in a kind of daze, the silences broken by the clang of the hammers. The last bout of hammering had gone on longer than any of the others. Now there was silence again. A bird, a thrush, sang on the far side of the creek and was answered by another, higher up. He stamped his feet to warm them, and could no longer resist the temptation of the fire.

The four men had stopped working and were standing in front of the hearth, chatting. He felt a surge of anger when he saw they were passing a bottle among them. Lammeier turned with a start as he came toward them, but Schwieger bit off the words he had been about to say when he saw Lippe unwind the strips of leather from his hands. His fingers were seared and blackened. Lammeier's looked raw and bleeding. He was streaked with grime like the others and up his right forearm was the long, angry weal of a deep burn. But the man was smiling. "We've done it, Captain," he said. "We've straightened the bitch. Rough and ready, but I think she'll do."

Schwieger moved to the stone slab. The hydroplane lay on it, right way up, and he could see that it was back in shape, dented and battered, but back in shape. "There's only the linkage arm and the brace left to do," Lammeier told him.

As Schwieger looked at them, he saw Lippe wipe the neck of the bottle on his wrist and give it to O'Dowd. O'Dowd grinned and held it out. Even Kurtz smiled when Schwieger took it.

"Here's to you," Schwieger said. "All of you. Well done."

Chapter 14

VON RINTELEN LOOKED FRESH AND SPRUCE WHEN HE PRE-
sented himself just before eight at the Villa Corneau, Kaiser
Wilhelm's forward headquarters in the captured French town
of Charleville. The Kaiser seemed preoccupied this morning,
although he was pleased to see him. They rode out from the
stables in silence, followed at a slight distance by a mounted
equerry and an escort of cavalry. Wilhelm had had a private
road cut through Lécuyer Woods to the group of farms where
his riding track was laid out, complete with gallops, jumps
and obstacles to suit his mood. Guards were stationed in the
woods and at the farms and on every bend in the road. He
made a special point of saluting every French pedestrian
they passed, but von Rintelen noticed that many of them
did not acknowledge it or trouble to return the gesture. That
takes some courage, he thought; even in a plain gray uniform
they must know who he is.

Wilhelm remained preoccupied until they were among the
trees. He glanced back to make sure his escort was at the
regulation distance. "Have you heard that our last fortress
in Galicia has fallen?" he muttered.

"I had heard, sir, yes," von Rintelen told him.

"Many seem to have known last night," Wilhelm said. "But
I was only informed when I read the dispatches this morning."

Von Rintelen could see that not being among those told
at once was rankling. "I believe it was only confirmed during
the night," he answered carefully.

"Is that so? It could be so. It must be," Wilhelm decided.
"Well, the loss is a grave setback. But only temporary, I
understand, eh? In a matter of weeks, we shall have recon-
quered the whole of Galicia."

"General Falkenhayn is preparing a great victory for you,
sir," von Rintelen said.

241

"And about time!" Wilhelm barked. "It will be an even greater victory if it puts an end to this constant wrangling among the High Command. I will not have it!" They rode on in silence for a minute. Court etiquette insisted that von Rintelen could not raise a topic of conversation, only carry on one introduced by the Kaiser. "And you are off to America, I read, Franz," Wilhelm said. "Will you enjoy that?"

"I don't think 'enjoy' is the word I would use, All Highest," von Rintelen replied. "However, if it adds in any way to the success of our arms, I accept it willingly."

"And I honor you for it," Wilhelm declared. "You have my personal word, Franz, that your standing will not be adversely affected—in fact, will be enhanced by this mission. Which I am given to understand is absolutely vital. Otherwise I would not have agreed to it."

"And I only accepted in the hope that thereby I could serve Your Imperial Majesty."

Wilhelm flushed with pleasure. So many of the people with whom he was now surrounded forgot the niceties in a kind of military brusqueness. He urged his horse into a canter as they reached the Aiglemont Road and headed for the farms at Vivier-Guyon.

When they came out of the woods by Charleville, they saw a group of small French schoolchildren in their pinafores being taken for a walk. It was a very pretty sight and Wilhelm smiled as he rode up to them. *"Bonjour, mes enfants!"* he called gaily. The children looked at him, then turned as one and ran away, back to the town, followed by their lady teacher, who tried without success to make them return.

Von Rintelen saw Kaiser Wilhelm's face darken with anger, before it set into an expression of such hurt sadness as he had never seen before. The group rode back to the villa in silence, uneasily aware of Wilhelm's depression. They dismounted again at the stables, but instead of going indoors where hot drinks were waiting, he headed for the garden. Von Rintelen followed him.

They walked along the formal paths for some minutes, aimlessly. Wilhelm's favorite basset hound escaped from the house and came running to them, sniffing at von Rintelen and barking until Wilhelm bent down and patted it. When it licked his hand, he smiled briefly and said, "Yes, I've missed you, too." Satisfied, it barked again and trotted ahead of them happily as they went on, again in silence.

Behind the bushes by the wall, two of the Secret Field Police were watching them. Others were positioned throughout the grounds, half hidden, distinct in their felt hats and half-belted jackets, a parody of a gentleman's country dress. They had made themselves notorious with their night raids and interrogations of civilians. How distasteful, to live always under the eye of such people, von Rintelen thought. He was becoming anxious about the time and looked unobtrusively at his watch.

"You still have forty minutes before your train," Wilhelm said. The silence had been broken, but it was another minute until he spoke again, his voice so low von Rintelen could hardly hear. "Their parents teach them that I am a monster," Wilhelm said. "Did you know that? I am a monster . . ."

"It is only ignorance, sir," von Rintelen replied quietly.

"Yet a whole generation is growing up, believing that. And they will tell their children, and their children's children." Wilhelm was supporting the hand of his atrophied left arm with his right, both hands pressed back against his lower chest. The jovial mood created during the ride had been wiped out. He was hunched and withdrawn.

In spite of the difference in their age and rank, von Rintelen felt sorry for him. "When we have won," he said gently, "when all this area is part of Greater Germany and the fighting is over, they will see you as you really are. They will learn their mistake."

Silence fell between them again. Kaiser Wilhelm was grateful, yet the comfort that von Rintelen's words brought could not dispel the dark thoughts which so often came to plague him. "But how long? How long until we win?" he said, almost to himself. "How many more trainloads of corpses shall we see going past, on their way home? It haunts me day and night." His head rose and he looked up beyond the trees to where a flight of returning swallows wheeled and dived. "How pure the sky is . . . Yet only a few miles from here the air is filled with the stench of death. All Germany is ringed by that stench. And so it has come about, that famous encirclement I warned of. Did you ever meet my uncle Bertie?"

It took von Rintelen a moment to realize he meant King Edward of England. "Once, sir. You presented me at Kiel Regatta."

"I remember," Wilhelm nodded. "He admired your wife's hat. He always noticed those things." He paused. "There has never been anyone I so loved and hated at the same time. He plotted to keep our empire from expanding, you know. I could not allow that. Well, he's dead. And yet . . . while Germany is encircled by enemies, as he planned, he is still stronger than I am—I who am still alive."

As the gun crew carried the repaired hydroplane back across the landing space, Walther Schwieger saw Hirsch coming down the jetty toward them, leaning on the shoulder of the boy Seamus. Zentner was with them.

"He's a very bad patient," Zentner grinned.

Hirsch drew himself up and saluted. "I wish to report myself fit for duty, Captain," he said.

Schwieger could see that he was not quite steady. "I ordered you to your bunk," he reminded him.

"But I feel fine now!" Hirsch protested. "A little stiff, that's all. I felt much worse lying there, wondering what was happening." He paused. "Besides, I wanted to thank you for saving my life."

"Next time you try a silly trick like that, I'll let you drown," Schwieger warned him, then smiled. "But it's good to have you on your feet again."

When the hydroplane was carried past them, Hirsch made the men stop so that he could examine it. "But you've done it!" he exclaimed. "It's all done!"

"Here's the hero of the hour," Schwieger said.

Lammeier was following the litter with Kurtz and O'Dowd and his chest swelled with pride. "We did what we could, Captain," he answered modestly. "But I'm sorry. That other corner that's bent over, I was afraid it might break off, too. So I just had to hammer it flat."

"The best thing you could have done," Hirsch approved. "If that leading edge was completely cracked, the pressure when we submerge would force the plates apart and split the whole thing wide open."

Schwieger let Hirsch take over when they reached the

end of the jetty where Weiser and his team were waiting by the makeshift derrick. Undoubtedly, with the Engineer Officer able to oversee it, the work of re-installing the hydroplane would go much more quickly. It was already after eight o'clock and the sun had been up for nearly two hours. The tide was due to start coming in again in less than thirty minutes, according to O'Dowd, and they had to be ready to leave as soon as possible. In the daylight, everyone was aware of the hills and the eyes that might be watching them.

O'Dowd had come down with the others to see the hydroplane put back in place, "To follow it through," as he told Zentner. But the torpedoman, Lippe, had not come with them. He had picked up his rifle and thought about it, then decided against it.

He had enjoyed helping Lammeier, in spite of the heat and occasional pain. Helping to flatten that bitch, as Lammeier called it, had given him a primitive satisfaction. And he liked O'Dowd. The Irishman was his type, fisher people, turn their hands to anything. Yet he had been unhappy when he was relieved from his guard at the cottage. It was not a feeling he could put into words, but guarding that girl, that delicate creature, had made him feel somehow special. They had sat for a time, after the others had gone, and she had got on with her mending. He had the strangest sensation of being at home, and when Megeen glanced up and smiled to him, he had spoken to her quite naturally and she had replied. When they both realized that neither could understand what the other was saying, they had laughed so much . . . Then he saw that she was tired. He stood up, pointed to the bed, bowed to her and went outside with his rifle. A few minutes later, the light had gone out. Although the night was cold, he was not conscious of it and for three hours had paced slowly round and round the cottage, guarding the treasure within. It never occurred to him he had been stationed there in case Megeen tried to leave.

He did not like to think of anyone else taking his place and climbed back up the hill. Siegel, one of the electricians, was squatting on his haunches, propped up on his rifle, half asleep. Lippe told him he had come to relieve him and, without even saying thanks, Siegel yawned and nodded and went off down the path.

Lippe wondered if Megeen was awake. He expected she would be, for fisherfolk were early risers, but there was no smoke from the chimney. As he thought of her, he could not resist knocking on the door, just to say good morning. He could imagine her smile. It was worth staying up all night for. As he crossed to the cottage, he saw that the green curtain had been drawn back from the window. He stopped and looked in. The dog was lying asleep in front of the hearth, where a fire had been laid but not lit. Lippe looked the other way, and his heart seemed to turn over.

Megeen was standing by the bed, completely naked. There was a tin bowl on the floor beside her and she was drying herself after her Sunday morning wash. Her back was to him and she was partly in shadow at the unlit end of the room, but he had never seen anything so lovely. Her body was strong, though slimmer than he had thought, her legs and thighs well-shaped, curving to the swell of her firm hips and buttocks, the deep indentation of her spine. Her hair hung halfway to her waist, which seemed impossibly small. He could have spanned it with his two hands. She was drying her stomach and loins.

He felt guilty and ashamed of himself for watching her, yet he could not move away. There's no harm, no harm, he told himself. If she turned round, that would be different. It would be indecent to spy on her then, although he wanted her to turn. He nearly jumped back when she dropped the piece of towel, but she still did not turn. She picked up her coarse gray shirt from the bed and slipped it over her head. He was puzzled for a moment when she knelt, facing the corner above the bed. Then he saw what she was doing. Having covered herself, she was saying her morning prayer to the Sacred Heart of Jesus.

Lippe stepped back silently from the window. He was disgusted by himself, spying on her while she made herself ready to pray. And his hands shook at the realization of how shocked she would have been, how hateful she would have thought him, if she had turned and seen him watching. He moved further from the cottage, turning to look out over the valley. The buds were all breaking out on the bushes that lined it, the new leaves uncurling on the trees. Birds were singing everywhere and the sun, after the coldness of the night, seemed to be from a different season. The valley of the creek, just coming into spring, was untouched and beautiful, but he was still remembering the ivory of Megeen's body. The other women he knew, the ones he laughed and sported with, sailors' women, they were carthorses compared to her. He saw O'Dowd coming up toward him and stood to attention.

With the hydroplane almost back in position, Schwieger walked with Zentner and Haupert along the side of the creek to its bend. It was past nine o'clock and he wanted to check on the state of the tide. The water was just lapping at the top of the bar of shingle.

"Another good hour," Haupert said tensely.

Schwieger nodded. "At least."

"This is going to be the most difficult part," Zentner told him. "The waiting. The crew's getting nervous."

Schwieger nodded again. The crew had behaved well, obediently and efficiently, but now was more aware of the danger. He was tense himself. They had been lucky, damned lucky, but sooner or later someone from outside was bound to come and the U 20 was still stranded. They waited at the bend until they saw two long arms of water reach out round the hump of shingle, running further into the creek at each surge of the tide. Hurry up, damn you! he wanted to shout, but the tide was at no one's bidding and would take its time.

They turned and walked slowly back along the bank. He bent down and picked up a cigarette butt, then another three where one of the guards had been smoking. "I want every man, except those working with Hirsch, out on the hillside and round that landing space. They are to pick up everything that has been dropped during the night," he told Haupert. "It's for O'Dowd's sake, and ours if we ever have to use this as an anchorage again."

Haupert hurried back to the U-boat, glad to have something positive to do. Zentner understood Schwieger's methods by now. Keep the men busy, doing something useful. That's how to stop them brooding, he agreed. He just wondered if he would have thought of it.

They heard barking and, to their surprise, saw Hansel and Maria running down the slope from O'Dowd's cottage. Hansel was so excited and so unused to being ashore that he kept tripping on clumps of grass and rolling over and over, while Maria scampered round him, barking. O'Dowd's bigger dog was with them, eager to join in, prancing stiff-legged beside them as if afraid of stepping on them. Then they saw Lippe come to the edge of the level area and look down, chuckling. The torpedoman must have brought Hansel and Maria out for some exercise. The scene was so joyful that Schwieger did not have the heart to reprimand Lippe, but he would have to get them back on board soon.

"Well, well," Zentner murmured. "Beauty and the Beast."

Megeen had come to beside Lippe. Next to his barrel-chested bulk, with his great spade beard and thick arms, she seemed tiny. She was laughing, too, at the antics of the dogs. Then Lippe and she smiled to each other and turned, going back to the cottage.

Schwieger had almost forgotten the girl and felt an irrational touch of jealousy at Lippe's familiarity with her. Zentner had felt it also. "I don't know how he does it," he said. "Can't think what they see in him. And a girl as rare as that one— Can you imagine them together?"

"Not a pretty thought," Schwieger agreed.

Zentner laughed. He was looking down at the U 20. "What about Weiser's derrick? It'll blight his young life if he has to take it apart."

Schwieger considered. "O'Dowd could have made it, I suppose. We'll ask him if he wants it left."

They cut across and up to the cottage. The door was half open and O'Dowd sat, nearly asleep, in his chair. He started awake when they knocked. "Oh! . . . Yes'll forgive me. I'd nodded off." When Zentner told him why they had come, he was amused and delighted. "Now, that's what I call a keepsake! Me own crane . . . It could be more than useful. Will ye thank your Captain, Lieutenant? I'd be honored to have it."

Outside, they heard someone calling for the Captain and Lippe shouting back from lower down. One of the lookouts from the top of the path ran to the door. "Captain!" he said urgently. "There's someone coming!"

Schwieger hurried out, followed by Zentner and O'Dowd. He glanced down at the U 20. The tide was much further in and water swirled round her stern, but was less than two feet deep yet. He ran with the others to the top of the path, crouching as it began to level out to go over the brow.

The man still on lookout pointed. "There, Captain! On the far bend!"

The shoulder of the hill was rocky and narrow, with a sheer drop on its outer edge. The path became a wider track beyond it, cut into the face of the cliffs and twisting away in a series of loops, vanishing and reappearing at each bend, each one lower until it joined the longer stretch of a road that sloped up over the distant headland. For a second Schwieger glimpsed a man on a bicycle pedaling down the road; then he was gone behind the first of the bends.

"It's Feeny, the coast guard," O'Dowd said.

Schwieger recognized the name. "I thought he said he wouldn't come till later today?"

"He must be thinkin' Seamus and I will be at the lobster pots, or workin' down along the creek," O'Dowd said. "He'll be hopin' for a minute or two with Megeen." He spat to the side.

They ducked their heads as the man came into view again on the curve of the bend, pedaling slower as the track rose. Schwieger decided. "Tell Mr. O'Dowd I'm sorry. We'll have to grab this man when he comes. We'll take him with us on the U 20, but it will mean that questions are bound to be asked about his disappearance."

When Zentner translated, O'Dowd looked troubled. "No, wait," he said, "I have a better idea. Megeen usually leaves in a little while for twelve o'clock mass. She can set off now."

"What difference will that make?" Zentner asked.

"She'll meet him on the track," O'Dowd muttered. "I know Feeny. He won't be able to resist walkin' back with her to Ballydavid." He eased back, rising, and ran down to his cottage.

The man on the bicycle was in sight again on the next bend and Schwieger motioned his men back from the crest. Below them, the path to the jetty ran between some high boulders. "Get behind these. If she doesn't manage to stop him, jump him when he comes down." The men hurried to hide themselves.

Schwieger looked at the cottage. O'Dowd had come out with Megeen. He was speaking to her urgently and she seemed reluctant, although she was holding a white cotton scarf to wear over her head in church. He kissed her and she started up the hill. Good girl, Schwieger thought. "Rudi, tell O'Dowd we're grateful," he said. "I'll stay on watch." Zentner went down the path and tipped his hat to Megeen as they passed each other.

She paused for a moment, glancing back at the U 20. Come on! Schwieger urged silently and, as though she heard, she came up toward him. She paused again when she reached him, and smiled shyly. She was nervous, running her fingers along the folds of the scarf, and Schwieger disliked having to use her, knowing what it cost O'Dowd, but he made himself smile back and nod confidently. She went on up the path.

He crouched and ran to a slightly higher point before dropping to the ground and inching forward. Megeen was crossing the shoulder, shaking out the scarf. As she raised it to lay it over her head, a gust of wind flicked it out of her fingers. He nearly shouted to her to leave it, but she ran after it, scrambling over the flat stones, and caught it before it fluttered over the edge. She turned to go on and the coast guard appeared round the last corner at the same time, almost standing on the pedals as he forced his bicycle up the steep track. He stopped in surprise when he saw her, and waved. Megeen hesitated as though she had not noticed him and the man shouted her name, "Megeen!"

He moved on out of sight again on the inward curve, pushing his bicycle. Megeen glanced round at where she had last seen Schwieger. She was uncertain, but did the only sensible thing and walked toward the track. Yet it's over now, Schwieger thought. Having come so far, even if the man decided to go with her, he was sure to take one look at the creek before they left. Only a few steps across the shoulder and he would catch sight of the U-boat lying at the jetty. As he slid his Mauser from its holster, he saw Megeen sit on one of the flat-topped boulders near the top of the track. Schwieger was puzzled for a second, then told himself admiringly, she's as bright as her father. The man would stop to talk to her, have time to become used to the idea of accompanying her and, when she rose to leave, might just go with her without the risk of meeting O'Dowd. It would depend on how keen he was, but it could still work.

Coast guard Feeny was smiling as he came up the last few yards of the stony track. He had been thinking about Megeen all the way here. In fact he had woken up this morning thinking about her and wondering if he would meet her, or if her blackhearted devil of a father would be at the door of the cottage, letting him have only a glimpse of her over his shoulder. And here she was on her own.

Feeny had been watching Megeen grow up for the last five years, since she was a gawky, wide-eyed thirteen. Watched her turn into a young woman of grace and beauty, a wildflower blossoming unseen in this Godforsaken backwater, where not even the local fisherboys or the troopers from the army post had learned to come sniffing round. One way or another, sooner now than later, he was going to have her. Even if it meant standing with her in front of that damned old priest to make it legal.

Feeny was a self-important man in his thirties, well-made, though running to seed. His stomach bulged the black barathea of his tunic, held in by the webbing belt for the holster on his hip and the Webley which he had been issued in the first week of the war. A lanyard round his neck ran down to a ring in the butt of the pistol, and he fancied it gave him a jaunty, martial air. He wore a flat hat with a black visor and a white linen cover.

Megeen composed herself when she saw him lean his bicycle against the stony bank at the end of the track. She had not met him too often until these last six months, when he had started to come out to the creek at least twice a day on patrol. Seamus had laughed and said it was really for a sight of her and it had made her father angry. She was not such a child that she did not know why. It made her uncomfortable, the way Feeny's slightly bulging eyes followed her even when he was talking to her father. He was always laughing and smiling to her, as if to prove to her how nice he was. But the way he often looked at her was not nice.

He was coming toward her. His face was red and wet with exertion; even the bristles on his bushy mustache were damp. He wiped the back of his hand over it. The bottoms of his trousers were folded round and fastened with bicycle clips above the tops of his boots, and made his ankles seem too thin for his weight. He's like a sack of potatoes tied in the middle, Seamus had said, and she smiled, remembering.

251

Well, that's more promising, Feeny thought. Usually she was so solemn and shy. Maybe she was different when she was really on her own. The only times he'd seen her by herself at the cottage, it had been awkward, not knowing when O'Dowd might turn up. If only he could talk to her properly. He smiled back, catching his breath. "Good morning, Megeen. How are you this morning?" She said something in reply, but had stopped smiling. She was so lovely and delicate it made him nervous, and he had to remind himself she was only a wild, backward little thing who couldn't even speak the King's English. "Whatever you said, my dear," he grinned. "I'm sure you're as fine as ever." Her slender feet were crossed and he looked from them up the swell of her calves that showed under the hem of her skirt.

Megeen felt her flesh creep as his eyes moved over her, but she made herself smile again and pointed along the track, showing him the scarf.

That's it, he thought. Of course she's going to mass. "Ballydavid, is it?" he said. She smiled and nodded. What a stroke of luck! She was off on her own, not even that sniggering brother of hers with her. It would mean turning and going straight back, but it would be worth it. She was even early, so there was no need to hurry. He'd have a good hour and a half with her by themselves. He pointed to himself and her, then to the track, meaning he would come with her, if she liked. She hesitated and nodded. He could swear she was pleased. Progress, indeed . . . But God, it was like trying to talk to a foreigner, and he chuckled. He'd make damned sure she learned a civilized language before she was much older.

He heard dogs barking over the brow of the hill, down toward the creek. For a moment, it meant nothing to him; then he frowned. The O'Dowds only had one dog, a white and black mongrel that yapped at him. "Do you have visitors, then?" he asked. Megeen looked at him blankly. He could hear the dogs quite clearly, at least two, maybe three. There was a yelp, as though someone had kicked one of them, or caught one up. It was annoying. He did not want to be seen by O'Dowd, but he was supposed to report any strangers he came across along the coast.

As Feeny moved toward the path, Schwieger eased up

the safety catch on his pistol. He had realized something. Stupidly he had placed his men too far down the hill and the coast guard would spot the U 20 long before he reached them.

Feeny heard Megeen rise behind him and glanced round. Damn it, she was leaving. "Hang on!" he called. "I'm coming with you." The dogs had stopped barking. Most likely, it was just someone out for a morning's walk. He moved back to Megeen.

She had folded two opposite corners of the scarf together and was tying it round her head. "Don't cover up your pretty hair, darlin'," he protested. She did not understand and said something, questioning. Feeny was exasperated. "Why can't you—?" he began; then his scowl cleared at a sudden revelation. She really could not understand. "I'd like to—to touch your hair," he said. "Run my fingers through it." Her head tilted slightly. "I'd like to see it loose on your shoulders, your white shoulders." He smiled, feeling a power growing in himself. It was exciting and he wetted his lips, still smiling. "I'd like to take off that shawl and open your shirt, darlin'. And—and play with your little breasts."

Megeen was disturbed. She did not know what he was saying, but from his expression, she was sure his words did not match his fixed smile.

"Play with them and kiss them, the pretty little doves." He laughed, and she smiled uncertainly. "Yes, you'd like that, wouldn't you? And other things, too, eh? A good screw—would you like that? If I was to screw the little arse off you?"

Schwieger could hear the man laughing and see the girl's tautness even from where he was lying. She'd been clever to stop him like that, but now something was wrong. He was so intent on them, he did not hear Lippe coming until it was too late. The torpedoman squirmed up to lie beside him, peering down the slope. Schwieger gestured angrily to him to get back, but Lippe paid no attention.

Although she did not understand the words, Megeen did not want to listen any more. She could see that Feeny was excited. At least as they walked along the cliff track, she would not have to look at him. She turned away, hoping that he would follow her, and was surprised when he caught hold of her arm. "No, no. There's no hurry," he said. She

253

jerked at her arm, but he only held it more tightly. "No, you don't, darlin'," he laughed. "You don't get away, until you give me a kiss." He pulled her close, pressing against her, his arms round her. When he tried to kiss her, she twisted her face aside and shuddered as she felt his wet mustache scrape her cheek.

Lippe growled like an animal and started to rise, but Schwieger grabbed his shoulder, holding him down.

With her body against his, Feeny could feel her shivering, and her hands pushing him away both added to his excitement and made him angry. Her trembling roused him sexually, but he was cursing himself for a fool. After all those years of careful waiting, he was throwing it away in a moment of rashness. He knew that now he would only get this one chance with her. She was innocent and untouched. He had to rouse her too, make her respond, so that she felt bound to him, or ever after she would hide from him, never letting him near her to try again.

He caught her by the back of the head, forcing her face round to kiss her properly. She was making little whimpering sounds like a puppy, yet something was preventing her from crying out or screaming. He had a wild hope. Was she starting to feel it? Did she want it? His hand tore at her shirt, reaching inside. As his mouth searched for hers, hot and open, he felt her lips tightly shut under his. Her face was contorted, her eyes filled with revulsion and her knees jabbed up at him by instinct, hurting him. "Push me away, would you? Fight me off, you slut?" The anger exploded in his mind. He hurled her to the side by the hair.

Megeen landed badly, but rolled over and pushed herself up. She was scrambling forward and rising when Feeny caught her, before she could run. He whirled her round and threw her down violently. Her back and head hit the hard, stony ground and she was dazed. The hem of her skirt had flown up. Feeny dropped to his knees between her parted legs and pushed the skirt up higher. He was scrabbling at the belt of his trousers.

Schwieger had been struggling to hold Lippe down. The big torpedoman was trembling and moaning. When Feeny first threw Megeen to the side, he tore himself out of Schwieger's grasp, as Schwieger released him to go to the girl's aid. Lippe was up first. In a moment he was out of cover and charging down the slope.

Feeny's hat had fallen off. He had undone his trouser belt and the first four buttons of his fly, when he heard the sound of running steps and looked up to see a huge, bearded sailor racing toward him. By reflex, he ducked to the side to avoid being kicked and Lippe's boot, instead of catching him in the guts, struck him on the hip and sent him rolling over and over. Lippe staggered and stopped himself from falling. He turned to Megeen. She was coming round. Her eyes were open and she was trying to sit up, which somehow made her posture all the more obscene. He stooped and drew the skirt down carefully to cover her.

Feeny was rising, wincing at the pain in his hip, as he stared at Lippe in terror. It's a German! A bloody German! He clawed at the flap of his holster and pulled out his revolver. He had never actually fired it and it felt so heavy that he had to hold it with both hands. As he raised it, he saw another man running toward them, a man in a leather uniform, carrying a pistol. He wavered for a second, trying to decide which to shoot at.

It was all the time Lippe needed to cover the distance between them. He grabbed the Webley, wrenching it out of Feeny's hands. The jerk of the lanyard round his neck brought Feeny's head forward and Lippe's elbow rammed up into his face, smashing his nose. Feeny screamed in agony and his knees buckled. Dimly Lippe heard the Captain shouting an order to take the coast guard prisoner, but the blood was roaring in his head.

Schwieger had reached the girl, who was sitting up, and together they watched in amazement as the torpedoman lifted Feeny and, for all his size, raised him above his head. He was going to slam Feeny down onto the ground, as he had done to Megeen. Feeny was kicking and struggling, begging for mercy in a high, bubbling voice. Only one hand could reach Lippe and it beat at him and scratched at his face. A fingernail snagged in Lippe's right eye and tore at it, ripping the lower lid. The torpedoman bellowed in rage and heaved Feeny away from him. He had forgotten they were so near the edge of the cliff.

Feeny plunged over the edge and they could hear his thin

scream, until it ended in a crunching thud as he hit a projecting spike of stone. A moment or two later, they heard the crump as his body landed. Schwieger had helped Megeen up. He left her and ran forward to look down. There was no need to make sure. Long, razor-backed ridges of rock angled in toward the foot of the cliff, not yet masked by the tide. Feeny lay over one of them. His head was pulped and the sharp rock had nearly split him in two. Schwieger put his pistol back in its holster and turned away.

Lippe's mind had cleared and the events that had happened clicked through it in a series of vivid images, like magic lantern slides. He had never been a violent man and he was holding his hands in front of him, staring at them, as though unable to believe what they had done. Streamers of blood trickled down from his torn eyelid. Megeen was moving toward him. She had pulled her shirt together. When she reached Lippe and saw his anguish of mind, she took his hands, drew them to her and kissed each of them in turn. His whole body gave one convulsive tremor. Still holding him by one hand, she led him toward the path down to the cottage, where she could bathe his face and stanch the bleeding.

Schwieger watched them leave. He had been going to reprimand Lippe, but not now. Maybe he should even recommend him for a medal. Feeny's cap was lying on the ground. He picked it up and sent it skimming over the edge. There was the bicycle. He took it a short distance down the track and wheeled it back up, leaning on it heavily to make a rut in the pebbles. He turned the front wheel toward the edge and pushed it over. Its wheels were still spinning as it fell, toppling over and over, until it splintered on the rocks.

It was after eleven before the water in the creek was deep enough for the U 20 to leave safely. Once again, the Maxim gun was at the prow and Weiser's team was manning the deck gun, while crewmen with rifles lined the deck on both sides. Schwieger was still on the jetty with Zentner and O'Dowd.

"Right, then," O'Dowd agreed. "If anyone comes to ask for him today, we don't know anythin'. And tomorrow, I'll report seein' pieces of his bicycle among the rocks. If his body's washed ashore somewheres, it will all be writ down as an unhappy accident. And mine will be the only heart that will still be singin'." He shook hands with both of them, then waved to Seamus, who was high up on the other side of the creek, on a point from which he could make out the open sea. He waved back, meaning there was nothing in sight. "Poor lad," O'Dowd said. "He's brokenhearted he's not goin' with ye." He handed Zentner the brimless seaman's cap which one of the crew had given to Seamus. "And ye'd best take this. If it was found, it would mean the rope for all of us."

Schwieger and Zentner climbed up onto the U-boat's bows. To O'Dowd's surprise, they came to attention and saluted him, while the crew presented arms. He swept off his cap and bowed back formally, then grinned to Lippe, Kurtz and Lammeier, who were by the Maxim gun. "*Gott strafe England!*" he chuckled. "Did I get it right?"

The U 20 backed slowly down the inlet. All the time Seamus was waving, and many of the crew waved in return. Schwieger had taken his position up on the conning tower. He found himself watching Lippe. With a pad over his eye, held in place by a strip of gauze bandage round his head, the torpedoman put him in mind of an old Norse pirate. He was completely still, his one small, blue eye searching the landing space, the path to the cottage and the hillside for any sign of Megeen. He seemed lost and unhappy that she had not come to see them off. Schwieger himself wondered why. Perhaps she had just realized they were really leaving and was too upset.

There was a moment's tension as the U 20 came to the bend in the inlet, but soundings showed she would clear the bar of shingle easily and there was sufficient room for her to maneuver so that her bows pointed toward the open bay. Seamus waved the All Clear before the turn hid him from view. "Secure deck gun. All hands below," Schwieger ordered. In less than three minutes the gun was stabilized, the Maxim unmounted and the deck was empty. Lippe was the last to go below. He looked and looked, until finally he accepted that Megeen was nowhere to be seen. His shoulders slumped and he went heavily down the ladder. "Ahead Half Engine," Schwieger called down the tube.

The U-boat stole forward, steering between the rocks,

while he passed down directions. Gulls rose from the rocks, wheeling and squawking around him. His eyes kept switching from the channel in front to the opening mouth of the inlet. But there was nothing, no enemy lying in wait. To avoid a jagged reef, they had to move nearer to the northern shore. And there he saw her.

Megeen had climbed down a gully in the face of the cliff and stood on a wide stone shelf that projected from it, some fifty feet above the water. Of course, Schwieger thought, she would come to the place where she would be the last to see them. She waved and he raised his hand in reply. Her head moved as she looked eagerly up and down the deck. She was hoping to find Lippe, he knew, and he nearly bent to summon him on deck. But he stopped himself. The incident was over and better for them both that it was so, without more hurt.

As the U 20 came abreast of her, Megeen stretched her arm out and moved it in a wide arc from left to right. From her higher vantage point she had a wider field of vision and was telling him that nothing moved on the sea. He had imagined her as a young queen when he first saw her, and the gesture, the setting, confirmed the image. The wind striking the cliff molded her skirt round her slim body and lifted her hair, like dark wings on either side of her pale face. A barbaric virgin queen. "Secure hatches for diving," he called down. "And let's pray that hydroplane holds together."

They were past her. He turned and saluted, but she made no answering gesture. She stood with her arms lowered, her hands clasped in front of her, motionless. He climbed down the ladder, slammed the hatch shut above him and secured it.

Megeen expected the U 20's prow to point downwards. Instead, the U-boat just settled in the water, slowly at first, then her decks were awash and in a moment only the conning tower could be seen. Then it too had sunk from sight in a swirl of bubbles. Briefly she could make out the sleek, shadowy form until it dropped lower. She thought it had gone, then the water spumed whitely as the head of the main periscope appeared. As she watched its long, feathery wake curve out toward the Atlantic, her hands clenched more tightly together and her eyes grew moist. She watched until long after it had vanished. For a while she imagined she could still hear the throb of the engines; then that, too, faded and all that was left was the desolate cry of the gulls.

Chapter 15

ANGRY AND ACCUSING, WILLIAM JENNINGS BRYAN'S EYES were fixed on President Wilson. "It is intolerable!" the Secretary of State insisted. "This British Order is a direct result of our weakness, I say again, our weakness in not taking sufficiently firm action in the first place, against their deliberate disruption of our overseas trade!"

Wilson himself was troubled. So, he could see, were most of the other members of his cabinet. In reply to the submarine campaign, the British government had issued a new Order in Council proclaiming a complete embargo on all trade with Germany, not only on munitions, but on all other manufactured and raw goods. "We have protested, and continue to protest, with all the firmness at our disposal, Mr. Secretary," Wilson reminded him.

"Lawyers' notes? Mere words," Bryan scoffed. "You and I, Mr. President, have both served our term as lawyers and both know, or should know, what little notice determined evildoers take of written warnings. We cannot submit to an illegal blockade!"

"Well now, Mr. Bryan," Lindley Garrison, another former lawyer, now Secretary of War, said, "whatever else it is, I did understand their latest Order is legal. Based on American precedents. It is the British retaliation for the Germans' unlawful submarine war on neutral shipping."

"Are we to endorse a policy of reprisals?" Bryan demanded.

"Of course not, Mr. Secretary," Wilson said, deciding to end it. "I call on yourself and Mr. Lansing to meet with me at the earliest opportunity. Together, we shall review the facts and legal positions and construct the strongest possible Note of Protest to send to the British government."

"Which they will quibble over and ignore, like all the others," Bryan answered.

Wilson considered Bryan. The only way he could now contain his irritation with his Secretary of State was to ignore three-quarters of everything he said, if he was not to provoke the very split in his cabinet which he fought to avoid. He was more than ever determined to bring the meeting to a close, yet before he could, McAdoo had stepped in. "As the President says, to send a strong Note of Protest to the British is the only option open to us—short of breaking off diplomatic relations."

Bryan had the bit between his teeth and was not to be checked. "May I remind you, sir," he said, "that for a lesser cause, the submarine war which was forced on Germany to save her civilian population from starvation, we have examined the idea of breaking off relations with the German Empire?"

"In an extreme situation," Wilson said, coldly. "And only if American lives are endangered or lost. That is entirely different from what is largely a trade dispute."

"We also have to take into account the illegal activities of German agents in this country," McAdoo added.

Bryan let his breath out sharply in exasperation. He sincerely admired the President, but for all his vaunted neutrality, he allowed himself to be surrounded by Allied partisans, and would not see it.

"Well, I have yet to be shown any definite proof of this so-called German conspiracy against our country. If our federal agents devoted the same amount of time to investigating the affairs of British spies and Intelligence units in New York and here, in Washington, I am convinced we should hear something very revealing."

Wilson had partially switched his mind off while Bryan was speaking. Cabinet meetings to which he had once looked forward as positive and creative political work sessions had of late become like minor college debates, constantly wrangling and raking over the same themes. No matter how hard he tried to keep attention on home needs and problems, the talk always returned to Europe, as though the Atlantic Ocean were no wider than the Potomac. Bryan had stopped and Wilson realized everyone was watching him, waiting for him to comment. "Most interesting," he said. "Perhaps we might

261

ask the Department of Justice for a report on that in the near future. Meanwhile, if there is no further business, I declare this meeting adjourned."

During the short ride back to his own office in the Admiralty Building, von Rintelen could still hear the cold voice of the U.S. Ambassador, James Gerard. "If I mention the name, Major Langhorne, I have reason to believe you'll remember it." The captain had recovered outwardly from his angry disappointment, but his mind was racing. His transfer to what Grand Admiral Tirpitz liked to call "the American Front" had been arranged the previous week in a meeting with the Commander-in-Chief and the heads of the High Command's secret services. Von Rintelen was to leave for New York as quickly as possible. His mission, staggering in its magnitude and potential consequences, was to prevent in any way possible the delivery of American-made arms destined for Russia. And "in any way possible," it was agreed at the meeting, meant purchasing where practical—and sabotage when necessary. Von Rintelen was to have not only vast sums of money, but the entire German intelligence network in the Western Hemisphere at his disposal. The exceptional powers were a proof of the urgency of his mission, to make a maximum impact on the supply of arms within a period of six weeks, when the German army's main eastern offensive was to begin. Gerard's refusal to provide him with a safe conduct to the U.S.A. was unexpected, a serious setback. Some other means would have to be improvised.

He ran through in his mind the schedule he had arranged for the remainder of the day. Later in the afternoon he had meetings set up with his colleague Dr. Helfferich, senior director of the Deutsche Bank, to ensure that funds would be at his disposal in New York, and with Heineken, chairman of North German Lloyd, whose personnel on the ships interned in American ports could be useful. But first he had to conclude his business with Rice, an American entrepreneur who had come to him with an interesting proposition.

When he reached his office, he found Rice waiting for him. The American was anxious to conclude a deal. Time was pressing, he said. The Dupont de Nemours Powder Company which he represented supplied much of the explosives used to fill high-velocity shells. "As you know, Allied purchasing agents have made a bid for the bulk of our stock, Captain," he said. "I would prefer to sell to you, but I cannot delay any longer."

"I understand," von Rintelen told him. He examined the contract. The price was high, yet worth it, if it had an immediate effect on delivery of munitions to the Russians. The six-week deadline he had been given was just about to begin. It all hinged on whether Rice himself was genuine. "I'm more than interested, Mr. Rice," he said. "It is, however, a lot of money to pay sight unseen."

Rice sighed. "Very well, Captain. I tried, but—I can't wait any more. I'm leaving tomorrow." He began to put the papers back in his case. He was a serious man, very sober in his dress and manner. "I thought we could have set something up here. But the essence of all business dealings is trust between the parties involved."

Von Rintelen smiled. "I absolutely agree, Mr. Rice, which is why I shall hang on to this copy of the agreement you propose. We can settle it in New York."

Rice was surprised. "New York?"

"Yes. If you are leaving for home tomorrow, I shall be following in a matter of days. So please decide nothing until I contact you. It will be much easier to finalize matters over there, and to arrange for payment—once I have met your fellow directors."

When Rice had shaken hands and gone, von Rintelen sat in thought. The deal was more or less settled, provided he could still reach the United States in time. Damn that dour-faced little Ambassador! His anger was returning, but it was anger against himself for not having handled the business of the attaché's dispatches more subtly. He remembered his first meeting with the attaché at Baroness Schröder's, the same evening he had met Emilie. Dear Emilie, he had been neglecting her. All at once he sat upright. Even as he began to smile, he was reaching for the telephone.

Matt had borrowed Dan Connally's Model T and gone to fetch the kids from school. Before he left, he had lifted the trunks down from the attic so that Livvy could wipe the outsides over with a damp cloth, take out the mothballs and spare blankets she stored in them and start packing.

They were not leaving for another ten days, but some

cases had to be sent ahead. As soon as she began, she knew that Matt was right. She should have made a list. Packing for such a long holiday was difficult enough without having to work out what she and the children would need now and on the journey. She had no idea what the weather would be like. Anything she sent off now she wouldn't see again until their sailing date. And what would they need in New York? Would it be sunny or cold? She'd better leave their raincoats out, she decided.

Don't be silly, she told herself. You wouldn't pack them anyway. You're getting in a tizzy.

Tizzy. She smiled. That was one of her father's words. Whenever her mother became flustered about anything, he'd look over his glasses at her and say, "Now, don't fuss, old girl. You're getting in a tizzy."

Livvy laughed fondly. The suggestion of the trip had scarcely seemed real at first. England and her parents were so remote, part of another life. Yet now that the arrangements had been made and everything was definite, she could not wait to be there. She kept telling herself it would be only another few weeks before she saw them, but she was still impatient. The children were excited, too, although Peter had been grumpy until he realized they would be back in time for the Calgary Stampede, which was all that was worrying him. Typical.

She couldn't resist it. The letter from home was lying on the dressing table. She had read it at least ten times already, but she picked it up, sat on the bed and read it again. Her parents were thrilled they were coming over and would be able to stay for nearly two months. They would have come on a visit to Canada themselves after his retirement, her father wrote, if it had not been for the war. Younger doctors in the area had volunteered for service in the Army and he was as busy as ever, perhaps busier, working as a locum in their practices. "By the way," he added, "I expect you have considered the possible danger of the trip. Some of the tales one reads of the cowardly and inhuman attacks of those German submarines are quite alarming. We are overjoyed at the thought of seeing you all, but you must only come if Matt thinks it safe." Her mother had added a postscript, too. "These submarines are getting to be quite a nuisance.

Tell the Captain to steer well clear of them. And do remember to wear your life vests at all times." The "all" was underlined twice.

Livvy smiled. Like Matt, she had been able to think of several activities for which the wearing of a life jacket would not be at all convenient. She put down the letter and looked at the piles of clothes she had begun to sort out. It was no use. She was just not in the mood to pack properly.

She went through into the living room and cleared up the litter the children had left, toys and dolls' clothes. She was aware that she was only filling in time, finding things to do, because she was unsettled. She knew what it was. Matt's leave had begun at last and she wanted him with her. The company had been very generous, giving him traveling time as well as the three months. They were going by train across to London, Ontario, to visit his old aunt for two days, before carrying on to New York. Livvy was looking forward to that. She had read so much about it.

She thought she heard the car coming and hurried to the window. But she was mistaken. Wishful thinking. She should have gone with him to pick the children up. She wanted them back, wanted them all round her. She went out to the porch. Bess was lying by the steps and jumped up, hoping they were going for a walk. Old Mrs. Connally was going to take care of her while they were away. Livvy ruffled the hair at the back of Bess's neck as she liked. Poor Bess, she'd wonder where they were.

It was sheltered and warm on the porch. The weather was surprising, a really lovely, early spring. Nearly all the trees were in bud and the flowers were coming. In a week or two the sap would be running in the maple trees and Matt would bore holes in them for her to put spigots in and hang pails on the spouts. When the pails were full, Peter and Diana would help her to carry them to the house and pour them into the big copper pan on the fire, to boil the sap down into maple syrup. If there was enough, she would boil the syrup down even more until it turned into delicious golden-brown sugar. Later she would fill dozens of sealed jars with wild peaches and raspberries, cherries and huckleberries, and make a whole cupboardful of strawberry jam and blueberry and chokeberry jelly. It was the season she really liked best. She would miss it this year and she felt a twinge of disappointment, then smiled at herself for wanting to have her cake and eat it.

Bess whined softly and barked. Then Livvy heard it, too. This time it was the car. It pulled up by the barn and Peter and Diana spilled out of it, arguing at the tops of their voices. Other people have nice, quiet well-behaved children, Livvy thought. Why do mine have to be so rowdy?

"It is, it is, it is!" Diana was shouting.

"It is not!" Peter denied.

Diana thumped him on the chest with her satchel and fled for the porch with him after her. Her knitted hat fell off and Matt picked it up as he followed them, laughing. She hadn't a hope of reaching the porch before Peter caught up with her, but Bess jumped down, barking, and ran to join in the game. She was Peter's dog, really, and she ignored Diana, making straight for Peter and jumping round him so that he stumbled, trying not to fall over her. "Damned dog!" he yelled. "Why do you always trip me up?"

Diana clattered up the steps, cannoned into Livvy and hid behind her as Peter came racing up after her, swinging his satchel. "All right, knock it off! That's enough!" Livvy said, holding him away as he tried to get at Diana, who was clinging to her long skirts and giggling.

"Peter says that New York is bigger than Winchelsea," Diana laughed. "That's just silly!"

"No, it's not!" Peter insisted. "New York's the second biggest city in the whole world."

"Well, Winchelsea's the biggest. So there!" Diana told him. "It's got miles and miles of streets and shops and big churches and schools and everything. Daddy said so."

Peter shook his head in exasperation. "He was only teasing."

Diana looked at her father, who had reached the porch steps. He smiled up to her and shrugged. "Daddy, why are you always teasing?" she protested huffily and marched into the house.

Matt laughed and Peter grinned round at him. Their similarity struck Livvy again. Each year it grew stronger. And the link between them. It was more than just their maleness. There was an understanding, a bond. It did not exclude her, so she could not be jealous, yet it was something she had never felt with Diana. Peter was wearing that thing round his neck, an amulet of dark wood in the shape of a strange bird, with signs burned into it, a tree, the sun, a snake, a spear. An old Indian called Harry something had given it to Matt for good luck when he left the Valley. He said his totem was in it, whatever that meant, and would protect Matt. Peter was fascinated by it and very excited when Matt threaded a leather bootlace through it and hung it round his neck. He hardly ever took it off.

"All right, Big Chief," Livvy smiled, "you go in and make peace with Diana. And tell her you're both to get washed for tea."

"To hear is to obey," Peter said gravely and went inside.

"Where does he get it from?" Matt laughed, coming up onto the porch. "You or me?"

"Wild West comics," Livvy said.

Matt chuckled. "Probably. Finished your packing?"

"I've not even started," Livvy confessed. "I don't know where to begin."

"As long as you leave an empty case," Matt said.

She could not think what he meant. "Empty? What for?"

"For all the clothes and things I'm going to buy you in New York." Livvy's eyes widened. "We're sailing first class and I want my wife to be the most beautiful woman on board."

"Afraid I won't be?" she asked playfully.

"No," Matt smiled. "I just want to make sure."

"You'll spoil me!"

"I want to," Matt said. He raised her hand and kissed it, and she could see that he was quite serious, although he was smiling. "When I brought you over, it was an adventure and it didn't matter how we traveled as long as we were to-gether. I had little enough to offer, but you believed in me—and your folks trusted me. And I made a promise to myself for both of us that when I took you back home, it would be through the front door."

Livvy's eyes were wet. "Matt . . ." she breathed and moved closer to press against him. His arms went round her and, when she looked up, he kissed her gently.

She heard Diana giggling and glanced round. Peter and Diana were kneeling on the window seats in the living room, watching and grinning, with Bess perched between them. They leaned forward, acting stupid and squashing their noses against the panes. Before she could stop herself, Livvy put her tongue out at them.

"Now I know where they get it from," Matt laughed.

"She's missed you," Emilie said. She was sitting on the bed in her white and gold room, sweetly naked, holding the flaxen-haired rag doll, Sophie, between her breasts.

With his index finger, von Rintelen flicked Sophie's pink nose and the pink nipples on either side of her. "I've missed her, too," he answered. "But for the last month I've been on the Russian Front and then . . . in Belgium."

Her hand ran down his chest and scratched under his ribcage, and he tensed. "I think those Americans are awful," she pouted, "refusing to help you."

He slipped his hand over the curve of her hip and squeezed the soft flesh at her waist. "It's their Anglo-Saxon blood. They're hypocrites, really."

"Well, I think you're very brave," Emilie said. She was smiling to see the effect her caresses had on him so soon after they had rolled apart, still trembling and floating back to earth. Her nails scratched across his taut abdominal muscles. "I wish I could see my husband's face when I told him."

"You wouldn't, though, would you?" he warned.

"We wouldn't get Franz'l into danger, would we?" she asked Sophie. "Sophie says no." She laid the doll across his loins and rubbed her slowly backward and forward. "Sophie likes you." She left the doll lying where she was and slid out of the bed.

"Where are you going?" He reached for her, but she was already heading for the dressing table.

She opened the central drawer, rummaged about and came back holding some photographs. "Since Sophie likes you, and since you've been a very good boy," she smiled. She climbed back onto the bed and settled down astride him, with one polished knee on either side of his hips. She held the first of the photographs in front of his face, a two-story Alpine lodge. "Here's our cottage at St. Moritz. That's Aunt Juschka and Uncle Acho on the steps." She moved the rear snapshot to the front. "That's our house in Geneva." She showed him the third snapshot. "And that's our father and mother."

"Can I have them?" he asked.

"They're yours . . . dear big brother," she giggled.

It was Saturday afternoon. By Sunday he had arranged an initial credit of half a million dollars for his personal expenses in New York, through Erzberger's bureau. Helfferich of the Deutsche Bank sent cables advising the bank's branches and subsidiaries that Captain von Rintelen was to be given unlimited credit. By Monday morning Eisendal's expert forgers had produced a perfect reproduction of a Swiss passport, complete with seals and stamps, showing him as Emilie's brother, Emil Victor Gaché, a minor official in the Swiss consular service. He had booked a passage, in the name of Gaché, from the Norwegian capital, Kristiania, to New York and, via the Lisbon consulate, Malvin Rice had been requested to meet the steamer *Kristianiafjord* when she docked.

It was bitterly cold in Berlin. Colonel House had arrived with Loulie in a veritable snowstorm and, after a week, the snow was still lying. However, he preferred cold weather to excessive heat and they were very comfortable with the Gerards. He would rather have chosen a hotel for anonymity, but Ambassador Gerard had insisted, explaining that, since everyone who mattered knew the reason for his visit, he would be less conspicuous at the Embassy. It was undoubtedly convenient, situated in the same square as the Chancellery and main government offices.

He was thinking so again at the end of his first meeting with Bethmann Hollweg in the Chancellor's office. This meeting was, to an extent, a tribute to his perseverance and discretion. "You won't see the Kaiser," Gerard had told him bluntly, "because he refuses to meet any representative of a country that sells munitions to the Allies. And you won't see the Foreign Secretary or Chancellor, either. They're nearly always with the court at Charleville. Besides, the civilian government is shaky. Chancellor Bethmann is comparatively liberal and, I believe, against the war continuing, but he won't risk antagonizing the General Staff by appearing to negotiate peace behind their backs." His most

269

important interview so far had been with Arthur Zimmermann, the Deputy Foreign Minister. Many thought Zimmermann an ambitious and unscrupulous schemer, but he had been disarmingly friendly.

Zimmermann was watching now as the Chancellor rose from his desk. Chancellor Bethmann was an exceptionally tall, thin man with gray hair, the narrowness of his face accentuated by his white pointed beard, and he stooped over House as he walked with him to the door. "We must not expect at this point that anything will move very quickly, Colonel," he said.

"I agree. I do not think one should set any time limits. The great thing is to have established a channel of communication."

"Exactly." They had reached the end of the long office and Bethmann lowered his voice, speaking so softly that House doubted that Zimmermann could hear. "Have you read the story of Frankenstein, Colonel?"

House also kept his voice low. "I do know it, yes."

Bethmann paused. "To an extent we have created a monster in that our people have been led to expect much more from this war than is possible of realization. Enthusiasm, belief in the fruits of victory, had to be created to enable us to conduct our offensives properly. I would welcome peace negotiations, yet if talks were begun now on any terms that would have any chance of acceptance, the people would undoubtedly rise up and overthrow my government—and his Imperial Majesty, the Kaiser."

After House had left, there was a silence in the room. Bethmann looked up. "Does he mean what he says?" he wondered. "Does he understand what he is saying?"

"I am convinced he is perfectly sincere and means it," Zimmermann said. After a moment he laughed quietly. "Whether he understands what it means is another matter."

Colonel House left the Chancellery and headed straight across the square for the von Schwabach Palace, which Gerard had converted into the U.S. Embassy. It was snowing again and he had to place his feet carefully to avoid treacherous patches of ice. How symbolic of this whole trip, he thought to himself, and smiled.

He was highly pleased with Bethmann's response and the

rapport he had felt. Although he was less sure now of Zimmermann, in whose attitude he had detected a trace of hostility. He decided he must be mistaken. Maybe a trick of expression. Certainly, the Deputy Foreign Minister was all on fire for the idea of the Freedom of the Seas. Perhaps when the German people heard of it, it would satisfy them and lay the Chancellor's Frankenstein monster to rest.

House prided himself on having put it rather well. The Germans could see easily what they would gain, the advantage of uninterrupted supplies through their own and neutral ports, while the British lost the Blockade, their main offensive weapon. He would not dream of pointing out that the advantages were weighted on Great Britain's side, since she would have no more to fear from submarines and her defense would be assured.

Jimmy Gerard would be anxious to learn how the meeting had gone and he had a right to know. He was conscientious and courageous, and different from Walter Page in that his point of view was wholly American.

Gerard, a former judge, was short and paunchy, his dark hair receding, his toothbrush mustache turning gray. He was standing at the window of his office, gazing out at the bleakness of the day. "You've seen Bethmann?" he asked.

"I have just this moment left him," House smiled. "We had a most interesting and, I believe, useful discussion."

"Good," Gerard said. "I have to go and see him myself shortly."

House could not resist it. "He wants nothing more than an improvement in the cordial understanding between the States and Germany."

"Let's pray we can at least keep the little we have," Gerard said. He crossed to his desk and picked up what looked like a long cablegram. "This is what I've been afraid of for months. I've just had this dispatch. The *Falaba*, an Elder-Dempster liner on her way from Liverpool to South Africa, has been sunk without warning by the U 28."

"A liner with passengers on board?" House queried, shocked. "Were any lost?"

"A hundred and eleven drowned," Gerard told him flatly. "Survivors say the U-boat crew laughed and jeered at them in the water. But that's not all."

House suddenly realized what Gerard meant. "Any Americans lost?"

"Only one," Gerard said. "But one's enough. The newspapers back home are screaming blue murder and the State Department lawyers are out for blood. As far as relations between the States and Germany are concerned, Colonel, I'm afraid that—in old-fashioned legal terms—the shit has hit the fan."

Walther Schwieger sat at the table in his tiny cabin on the U 20 writing up his log. He was ravenously hungry and, while he wrote, took spoonfuls with his left hand from the bowl of thick pea and potato soup the cook had just brought him, bending sideways to the spoon at each mouthful so as not to drip soup onto the open pages.

They were running partly submerged and only an hour before had completed the dangerous passage of the English Channel on their return to base. The damaged forward hydroplane had performed well after its emergency repair and he had stayed on station for another five days, sinking one more Allied freighter, a trio of fishing smacks and, best of all, a large, armed steam yacht of the British Auxiliary Naval Patrol, off the Devon coast. It had a specially high radio mast to signal submarine sightings to the killer torpedo boats waiting further inshore. It was quartering the approach to Plymouth, sailing in a fast zigzag pattern to avoid attack and to cover a wider area of search, but, observing it through the little eye of the finger stick, Schwieger saw that the zigzag pattern was fixed and therefore predictable. He gambled his second last torpedo on it and his shot struck the yacht squarely amidships by the main magazine, blowing it out of the water in a great gout of flame and steam. When he surfaced to check, for all its size, the yacht had completely disappeared. He had given the others a chance to take to their boats, but this time he had attacked without warning, just as the yacht would have fired at him on sight. She had not had an opportunity to send out a signal, so he had no fear of pursuit. The yacht had simply been sunk without trace. He kept thinking about that and filed it away in his mind.

His orders were to return by the shortest route through

the Channel and, with oil stocks low, he had no option, although the passage was becoming more hazardous each month as the British and French developed their barrage across the Strait of Dover. Returning from the south, U-boats had first to evade a screen of destroyers, then came the main barrage at the narrowest gap between Folkestone and Cap Gris Nez. Apart from the natural obstacles of sandbanks and underwater ridges, there were tiers of deep and surface mines and more of the steel anti-submarine nets, also hung with mines. A twenty-four-hour watch was maintained from both shores and from squat, unsinkable monitor ironclads with huge guns in their revolving turrets. Powerful searchlights were trained across the Strait at night and many of the mines could be detonated electrically from the shore. Beyond the line between Dover and Calais was another barrage of nets, lit by magnesium flares, guarded by destroyer squadrons and covered by reconnaissance aircraft, and then between Flanders and the sandbanks at the mouth of the Thames came the principal minefields, sown with thousands of the deadly overblown pineapples. Not until it was through all these did a U-boat reach the comparative safety of the North Sea.

Following Hersing's tip, he had approached the Strait just before dawn, creeping past directly underneath the destroyer patrols. At first light he surfaced cautiously, judging that the searchlights would then be at their least effective. He was helped by shifting screens of early morning mist and slipped from one to the other as he stole north over the topmost strands of the nets. The sky was clearing when the U 20 reached the second net barrage. From the conning tower Schwieger could even see the black bulbs of the surface mines strung out along them, but his luck held and the U 20 was past them before she was picked up by the field glasses of the shore observers. At just over her own length behind her, a row of mines exploded, spouting fire. The water fountained and the U 20 was rocked sharply, splinters and jagged fragments of metal showering the surface around her and pattering and clanging on her deck plates, but she was unharmed. Schwieger gave the order to crash-dive and was gone before any of the destroyers reached the spot.

With her reduced speed underwater, the problem now

273

was to avoid letting the U 20 be trapped by the special-service trawlers and drifters which would be speeding to seal off the area with their trailing nets. Schwieger steered northwest in a loop that took him much closer to the English shore than they would expect. Zentner and Haupert were examining the charts anxiously and finally turned to him with the warning that they were about to enter the main offshore minefield. "I know," he told them. "But it's low tide now. So just pray the British are still setting their eggs too high in the water."

He surfaced at the last moment and, as he had calculated, the mines were all floating on the surface in the ebb tide. They were everywhere round them, partly hidden by the waves, and the next half hour was a commander's nightmare as the U 20 picked her way through them with Zentner and Boatswain Kurtz keeping watch with him on the open conning tower bridge and relaying instant changes of direction to Haupert and the helmsman, sometimes two or three a minute. At last they won clear and in open sea again set course for home.

Schwieger stayed on watch for another hour, then went below, leaving Zentner and two seamen on the bridge. He did not envy them. The water was choppy and they were constantly drenched with ice-cold spray, but he had not rested for a day and a night and it could no longer be put off.

He was taking a last mouthful of soup when he heard a knock at the bulkhead next to the doorway of his cabin and the green curtain was drawn aside. It was one of the men he had left on watch, the one-piece rubber suit covering him from neck to ankle and the rubber hood fitted tightly round his eyes, nose and mouth slick with sea water. The man saluted. "Mr. Zentner wonders if you could spare a minute, Captain. We've spotted something."

Something big was coming up on the horizon to the west-northwest, masts, a bridge and a tall funnel. Schwieger ordered a change of course to intercept and, a few minutes later, heard Zentner exclaim excitedly, "It's a tanker!"

Rudi was right. The approaching vessel was a large tank steamer, presumably heading for one of the Channel ports on the French side. "You're going to lose your Dutch wife," Schwieger said. He had learned his lesson and kept one torpedo for the return trip, the one lashed to the side of Rudi's bunk.

Zentner grinned and went below as the conning tower hatch was closed and the U 20 sank out of sight. The excitement had spread to the crew. A tanker would boost their score considerably in terms of tonnage and there were almost too many crewmen willing to help, but the forward battery compartment emptied when Weiser relayed the command, "All hands to Action Stations!" The petty officer and torpedo crew unlashed the torpedo, lowered it onto the trolley and wheeled it forward into the torpedo room. Following them, Zentner saw that they had been so far from expecting action at this stage that the folding table and benches still filled the cramped space where they lived. It was fortunate there was no need for haste, since he had to wait while they were collapsed and stowed.

The torpedo was Zentner's and, when the petty officer gave him the chalk, he thought for a moment and printed along its casing *Gott strafe England*, in memory of O'Dowd. Lippe asked shyly if he could add Megeen's name and Zentner offered him the chalk. Seeing the man's embarrassment, Zentner kicked himself for forgetting the torpedoman could neither read nor write, but when he printed *MEGEEN* on the nosecap, Lippe beamed.

The cover of the first tube was unfastened, the torpedo's nose inserted and its length was rammed home. As always, Zentner winced to see how unceremoniously the lethal charge was handled. One man put his boot on the nut projecting behind the propellers, while Lippe turned so that they were back to back, braced his feet and heaved backward. The torpedo slid smoothly in.

Schwieger was bent over the eyepiece of the main periscope and merely grunted when Zentner reported, "First forward tube loaded." The tank steamer was approaching at no more than six or seven knots on a straight track, almost as if inviting attack. She was painted black with a gray superstructure, a considerable size, no guns visible. She was enticing, but Schwieger knew she would not be easy to sink. To seal off their volatile cargo, tankers were fitted with extra transverse bulkheads, forming a number of watertight compartments. Their main engines were toward the stern.

Because of her size and the possibility of hidden guns, Schwieger decided against challenging. "It'll take a tricky shot to stop her," Zentner said, as if reading his mind. Schwieger grunted again. He could not go in too close, either. If her cargo of oil exploded, at anything up to four hundred yards the shock waves could seriously damage the U 20.

There was little chance of the asparagus being seen in the turbulent water. Even so, not to alarm her, Schwieger only showed the eye for seconds at a time as he swung into position. At seven hundred yards, Zentner unscrewed the cover of the firing button on order and stood with his finger hovering over the red key. The tanker was coming into the hairlines of the eyepiece. "Fire One!" Schwieger snapped. Zentner depressed the key and ran the periscope in.

As soon as they heard the explosion, he elevated it again, and Schwieger smiled up at him quickly in satisfaction. "Your ladyfriend didn't let you down," he said. The torpedo had smashed into the tanker near the stern, exactly where her aftermost engine should be. She was yawing and had lost way already, crippled, though not sinking. As he watched, Schwieger saw three boats being lowered toward her bows and men scrambling into them.

Still wary, he took the U 20 in closer at periscope depth and made a circuit of the tank steamer. There was no sign of guns. Her name was blacked out and unreadable from a distance, the naval patent log was hanging over her stern. The flag above it was of the French merchant marine. As he completed the circuit, he saw the boats in the water. As soon as they sighted the periscope, the men in them began to row frantically. Yet Schwieger was puzzled. Where was the rest of her crew? The tanker was still making slight headway. Surely her skipper did not imagine he could escape?

Having used his last torpedo, Schwieger had no alternative but to finish the job with the deck gun. While he maneuvered to keep the lifeboats between him and the tanker, he noticed young Weiser watching him eagerly. "Get your crew up there at the double," he said. "Prepare to surface."

Chapter 16

MALVIN RICE WAS NOT WAITING AS PROMISED AT THE PIER in New York, and von Rintelen had to face the fact that, plausible as he had seemed, the man was probably a confidence trickster.

Now that he was actually on American soil, von Rintelen had no immediate need of his alias, though he preferred to remain inconspicuous. The Emil Gaché identity could prove an embarrassment in a city where he was liable to be recognized and would have to use personal contacts. Under his own name, he booked in at a good, though unpretentious, hotel, the Great Northern on 57th Street. It had steam heat and a telegraph and telephone service, and was in walking distance of the Ritz Carlton and the German Club.

He was eager for up-to-date information on the munitions market and to make his first impact, yet his first priority was to liaise with the attachés, who were technically his colleagues. He went down to the foyer and asked the clerk to call a cab for him. He had heard no real news since he sailed and, while he was waiting, he looked at the headlines of the papers in the bookstall. Most of them dealt with some spectacular murder, the "Thrasher Case" or "Thrasher Affair," but one or two carried the latest war reports in a corner of the first page. With shock he read that the Russians were breaking through in the Carpathians and pushing the Austrians back in Hungary. There were less than four weeks now to Falkenhayn's deadline and he would have to work fast.

He had been a member of the German Club for years and the doorman saluted, remembering him. At the desk, he learned that Captain Boy-Ed was in and took the elevator straight up to his rooms. He had known the attaché socially ever since he entered the navy and, for some time now, they had both worked in Intelligence. Boy-Ed was an interesting personality. Perhaps it came from the mix of his birth, a Turkish father and a German mother, the novelist Ida Boy-Ed, a great favorite in Germany. Like von Rintelen, he had been chosen as one of Tirpitz's Big Six, the cream of the young officers the Grand Admiral was grooming for future high position. Since 1911, he had been in the United States and he liked to pass for an American, but his real interests and activities would have shocked his friends at the Chevy Chase Club and the Army and Navy, as well as the society matrons who dangled their daughters before him as one of the decade's most eligible bachelors. Von Rintelen looked forward to working more closely with him.

However, he was not given the chance. The attaché's manservant showed him into the suite, where Boy-Ed was finishing tea. He had been informed officially of von Rintelen's imminent arrival, so was not surprised to see him. His manner was curt and formal. He was of higher naval rank than von Rintelen and used it to keep him firmly in his place. "Your whole trip was an unnecessary security risk," he said. "If my opinion had been asked, I would have told them that your assistance is not needed here." When von Rintelen began to explain why he had come, Boy-Ed stopped him. "The military attaché is somewhere in the building. You may as well say what you have to say to both of us."

Von Rintelen bowed. He was not ruffled and it suited him better not to have to repeat himself. Boy-Ed was lighting one of his slightly scented cigarettes and, in a delayed action, remembered to offer them. "Thank you, no," von Rintelen smiled. He also refused a belated offer of tea. "May I?" he said, and sat in one of the yielding leather armchairs. He leaned back and crossed his legs, knowing that if he kept his composure he was bound to win. Already Boy-Ed was regretting his lack of welcome and had begun to ask about conditions and mutual friends at home. Von Rintelen replied briefly. There was much he could have told him, but did not see why he should.

When Papen arrived, he rose and bowed again. The military attaché was as distant as Boy-Ed had been, his mouth pursed, his expression faintly accusing. Von Rintelen's attitude to him was delicately different. Their substantive service ranks were equal and there was no reason to defer to him. As with Boy-Ed, he had read his personal file before leaving. Papen came from the First Regiment of Uhlans of the Guard, in Potsdam. He had been given diplomatic and Intelligence training, but, despite his arrogance, did not have von Rintelen's background or experience.

When the greetings were over, Papen demanded, "Well now, what's all this, Captain? Why have you been sent here?"

"In the first instance," von Rintelen answered, "to deliver these." He took two small capsules from his inner pocket and handed one to each of them.

When he explained that they contained miniaturized copies of the new Most Secret Code to be used exclusively from now on, Papen drew himself up. "Are we to assume this is meant as a reflection on the way we run our departments?"

"I cannot imagine how anyone could so interpret it," von Rintelen said smoothly. "Since you gentlemen are not responsible for the entire Embassy, nor for all our activities in the United States. However, if there is a leak somewhere, this new code will plug it—provided it is known only to your most trusted and most essential personnel." The reply was at once calming and a reminder of the limitations of their functions.

"More damned bureaucratic interference!" Boy-Ed muttered.

"Herr Eisendal and Major Nikolai instructed me to tell you that only this code is to be employed until further orders, sir," von Rintelen reported tonelessly. It was of no value to him to antagonize them. "I have also a more pleasant duty, being charged by His Imperial Majesty to inform Captain Boy-Ed that, on his return to Berlin, he is to be invested with the Order of the House of Hohenzollern." Boy-Ed's head lifted and he flushed with pleasure. "I am also to inform you, Captain Papen, that the All Highest has been graciously moved to award you the Iron Cross."

Papen stood totally still. He was struggling, but unable to hide his elation. "Directly from the Kaiser himself?" he asked.

"Directly," von Rintelen smiled. "He takes the keenest interest in all that has been achieved here. He has often mentioned it to me." How odd, he was thinking, that two grown men should be so gratified by baubles . . . And another thought came to him. Had the Kaiser done it deliberately, to ease his path, to remove any resentment at his mission? It was the kind of perceptive move of which the All Highest was capable, and for which he seldom received proper credit.

Boy-Ed was pleased, beyond doubt, and the effect on Papen was almost visible. His whole manner softened. He had been forcibly reminded that von Rintelen was no mere junior captain, he was *hochwohlgeboren*, an intimate of the Imperial family, a protégé of Grand Admiral von Tirpitz and now, presumably, also of the Commander-in-Chief. It would not be wise to offend him unnecessarily. "I am overwhelmed, and grateful to His Imperial Majesty," he said. "And I am sure I speak for Captain Boy-Ed."

"Yes, of course," Boy-Ed put in quickly. He had also been reminded of the newcomer's status.

"Now, however, Captain," Papen went on, "you must tell us why you have been sent and precisely what you expect from us."

Von Rintelen took one of his own cigarettes from his gold case and lit it. "First of all, I must inform you that in the view of the General Staff, for various reasons, the next four weeks are crucial."

"For what reasons?"

"Various," von Rintelen repeated. "In that period, every stop must be pulled out to prevent the flow of munitions to the Entente Powers, particularly to the Russians."

"By purchase and propaganda means?" Papen asked.

"Purchase, propaganda—and others."

"In other words, sabotage?" Boy-Ed asked sharply.

"If absolutely called for," von Rintelen shrugged.

The two attachés glanced at each other, worried. "Open acts of sabotage in U.S. territory could have a disastrous effect on our whole position here," Papen said. "At this moment. In view of the Thrasher affair."

"I have seen headlines, but that's all," von Rintelen told him. "Who or what is Thrasher?"

"Leon Thrasher, an American," Boy-Ed said. "He was drowned when one of our submarines sank a small passenger ship, the *Falaba*, a week ago."

"Without warning?"

"That's not important," Papen declared. "The point is, the public here and the press have gone mad. Forget the thousands killed every day on both Fronts. The death of this one man is the crime of the century, they would have us believe. Massacre—a crime against humanity, and so on."

"Sheer hypocrisy," Boy-Ed agreed. "Nonetheless, until some fresh political scandal or surprising baseball result takes over the headlines, we shall have to be careful. It would not need much to create a demand for America to enter the war against us."

"In the opinion of many of our people, that could harm us little more than they do already," von Rintelen said seriously. "I certainly cannot be influenced by that consideration over the next month."

Papen was becoming touchy again. "Actions here are our responsibility! And will have to be approved."

"My instructions are from the Joint Chiefs of Intelligence and the High Command," von Rintelen stressed.

Again the attachés were disconcerted. "Then what do you require from us?" Papen asked.

"I shall try to involve you as little as possible, Captain," von Rintelen told him. "I shall have to send dispatches through you. I may need some assistants, reliable messengers and the use of your offices until I am established."

"The situation here is complicated," Papen said. "The American security services give very slight trouble and can be discounted. New York, however, is crawling with Allied agents, with nothing better to do than try to follow us. But they can be a nuisance. Seeing you call on us, they may switch their attention to you."

"Then it would be better if I stayed away altogether," von Rintelen smiled. "Might I suggest you each choose one of your best men to liaise between us? Although I shall communicate with you only in an emergency. I am already familiar with all your projects. If you should begin any new ones, please let me know of them, to prevent us stepping on one another's toes."

"For heaven's sake, don't go rushing into anything," Boy-Ed warned.

"I shall be as careful as circumstances allow," von Rintelen

281

assured him. "As far as anyone else is concerned, I am here only on a simple buying expedition."

There was not much more to be said. Before another few days had passed, he intended to have created his own team and be in operation.

The U 20 had surfaced outside the group of lifeboats, to keep them in the line of fire. Her stern was pointed toward the tank steamer's bows and Weiser and his gun crew had raced up through the rear hatch by the cook's galley and were manning the deck gun. Schwieger and Zentner came out onto the conning tower bridge and saw that the tanker was still forging slowly ahead. "Warning shot," Schwieger ordered.

The waves were still choppy and Weiser fired on the upward roll, his shot arching over the French tanker's bows as a signal to heave to. Almost at once she blew off a white, rushing column of steam from her boilers. Evidently the torpedo had damaged her controls and her Master had now decided sensibly to stop her the only way he could.

Schwieger waited for more boats to be lowered. He needed the ship's papers as proof of the sinking, and Zentner shouted through the megaphone for them to be sent over. If they were not, the Master himself would be taken prisoner and brought back to Emden. Yet no more boats were swung out. At the same time, Schwieger noticed the ones in the water pulling strongly to starboard. He called down a correction in course and speed, to hold them between him and the tank steamer. Something was nagging at him, a touch of unease. If he had one more torpedo, he would have submerged and finished it with that.

The U 20's stern swung away to keep pace with the lifeboats. Zentner was hailing them. "Stay where you are! You are in no danger! Stay where—!" There was a flash from the tanker's bows and a shell whistled past over their heads, followed by a roar of a heavy gun.

Herr Gott! Schwieger thought. It's a submarine trap! "Prepare to dive!" he shouted. He slapped the button that sounded the alarm and grabbed Zentner's shoulder, thrusting him toward the conning tower hatch. He suddenly knew what had been nagging him. The tanker's superstructure was too tall! Even as the thought raced through his mind, wooden shutters painted to look like metal were being raised, revealing the muzzles of more guns mounted along her upper deck. They fired a ragged salvo and more shells, six-pounders, screamed past above the U-boat and plummeted into the water beyond her. The tanker's gunners were shooting too high, afraid of hitting their own boats.

Schwieger glanced down. The gun crew had leaped for the galley hatch and were dropping through one after another, but Weiser and the petty officer were still struggling to secure the deck gun. Schwieger swung himself over the conning tower rail and jumped down to the deck. He seized both of them by an arm and pulled them away from the gun. "There's no time for that!" he yelled. A shell smashed into the superstructure behind the conning tower and the U-boat rocked wildly. The petty officer spun out of Schwieger's grip, teetered on the edge and fell backward into the water. Nothing could be done for him. His chest had been ripped apart by flying metal.

Weiser fell down the ladder and lay half dazed at the bottom. Schwieger dropped down after him, slammed the hatch shut and locked it off. Above the blare of the klaxon alarm, he heard Haupert calling to Hirsch that all hatches had been secured. Another shell slammed into the water next to the U 20, shaking her, and Schwieger ran through into central control. "Reverse!" he shouted. "Reverse!"

Hirsch was flooding the tanks to crash-dive. After a second's blankness, he understood. The converted tanker's guns had found the U 20's range and the long seconds it took her to submerge would be fatal. Submerging in reverse, toward the lifeboats, would throw their aim out again, make them anxious. Just as he pressed the switches to obey the order, there was an explosion above them in the conning tower, a yellow flash, and explosive gases swept down through the inner hatch while the U-boat lurched and staggered violently. A shell had pierced her conning tower and burst inside.

Schwieger and the others had been thrown off their feet. He clawed himself upright, choking at the acrid smell of lyddite. "Who was up there?" he gasped.

Haupert had recovered also. "Zentner and the Boatswain. And Siegel, I think."

Schwieger hurried to the ladder and began to climb. He

stopped as a pair of boots swung down toward him. It was Kurtz, who had been badly shocked and was being lowered by Zentner. The electrician, Siegel, had been killed, but miraculously the other two had no major injury, although their leather suits were nicked and torn all over by metal splinters. They were hatless and their hair and the exposed skin of their hands and faces were streaked black and yellow from the explosion.

Another shell slammed into the U 20. At a more oblique angle, it did not penetrate and plowed off along her side with an angry screech. Most of the shells were again falling beyond her.

Schwieger and Haupert caught Boatswain Kurtz and sat him on the floor of central control. Weiser had come through and helped Zentner down.

"Captain!" It was Bibermann, pointing to the conning tower's inner hatch. Water was beginning to lap over the sides and trickle down the ladder. All at once the trickle became a stream. The U 20 was submerging and water flooding the conning tower through the shot hole. With water cascading over his head and shoulders, Weiser, who was nearest, struggled up the ladder, felt for the top of the hinged hatch cover and pulled it down. His boots slipped off the rungs of the ladder and he hung by his fingers, clinging to the bolts. Schwieger stepped in and supported him from below while he pushed the bolts home.

A jet of water spouted across central control from the lower end of the speaking tube. Everyone was too shocked to move. "Close it off!" Schwieger ordered. "Munzer!" The Boatswain's Mate came to and grabbed the stopcock on the pipe. He forced it round, cutting off the jet.

The seawater that had already poured in splashed under their feet, endangering the electrical equipment. They were going down with a flooding conning tower and God knew what other damage. But at least we're alive, Schwieger thought. They were already deep enough not to be affected by the shells that still raked the surface above them, and he blessed the anxiety that had spoiled the enemy gunners' accuracy. One more direct hit and the U 20 would have been done for. "What's our depth?" he asked.

"Sixty-five feet," Hirsch told him.

"Hold her there," Schwieger ordered. "Full Ahead now. Let's get out of here. Haupert, Weiser, and you, Munzer—report on all sections." Zentner had recovered and left for the stern with the Boatswain's Mate. Schwieger had Kurtz carried to his bunk.

In what seemed only moments, Munzer came back. He was stammering. "L-leak, Captain. In the stern t-torpedo room." Schwieger hurried aft with him, along a deck that seemed at an angle.

The last shell to hit them had not penetrated, but must have loosened some plates. Water was spurting into the torpedo room from two places. Afraid of any of it reaching the reserve batteries and the electric and diesel engines behind them, the torpedomen were catching it in buckets. Hanging above them was the tricolor flag taken from the first squarerigger they had sunk. Schwieger ripped it down, wadded it and jammed it into the major leak. "Block the other one!" he snapped. Munzer was already tearing a strip from the nearest blanket. It was too thick and one of the men handed him his spare shirt. When both leaks were plugged, Schwieger said, "Now get your mattresses and blankets up against them—and hold them there!" They did not need to be told what could happen if more water got in.

On the way back, Schwieger met Zentner, who reported another leak in the galley, which the cook had plugged. The rake in the deck was more pronounced and some of the lights had gone out.

More of the lights failed just as they reached central control. Hirsch was working anxiously with the machinists and the remaining electrician at the banks of gauges and dials. "A series of short circuits," he explained. "Half the controls keep breaking down—gyro, main rudder, trimming pumps."

That did not give any reason for the U 20 being down by the stern. Schwieger looked at the depth gauge. It was registering a hundred and ten feet. "I told you to hold her around sixty," he said sharply.

"I can't, Captain!" Hirsch blurted. "It's the conning tower."

Of course! Schwieger realized. As the conning tower filled, the weight of water was forcing them down. In theory, the U-boat could still stay afloat, though no one knew it for certain. Yet he was puzzled. "We're at full speed?"

"Yes, Captain."

Then, being down by the stern, the U 20 should be rising. Instead, the indicator on the depth gauge crept down further, to 120–130 feet. With the gauge reading nearly 140, Munzer came back to report that the leaks were becoming more difficult to control and that more were appearing as the weakened plates were forced apart by increasing pressure outside.

"We'll have to get up, have to get her on an even keel," Schwieger said. "Blow the after and amidships tanks."

Hirsch pressed the switches and they could hear the hiss as the compressed air forced the ballast water from the central and stern compartments. As the U 20 rose slowly, almost reluctantly, he and his team worked on to correct the mechanical failures. She was definitely rising, yet was more down by the stern than ever. He checked the after tank. The water had been expelled, but now he found that the compressed air valves refused to function. He could refill the ballast tank, but not empty it again. And the U-boat was still rising. He cut the electric motors back to reduce speed.

At sixty feet again, Bibermann called to him. Hirsch looked and swore to himself. "It's that damaged forward hydroplane," he told Schwieger. "It's jammed at Hard Down."

They were still creeping up. We've been here before, Schwieger thought. Somewhere above them, the converted tanker was waiting, silent, because he had immobilized its main engine. Its guns would be manned, though, and no boats in the water to restrict its fire. At all costs, the U 20 must not come to the surface. "Flood the tanks," he ordered. "All available men forward."

The use of the crew as living ballast had become routine. When the diving tanks were opened, the crewmen rushed forward on order and the U 20's bows sank at last. She surged ahead for three minutes, then seesawed as her stern dropped. The men were brought back and sent forward again. Again the U-boat moved ahead. Schwieger repeated the maneuver relentlessly, until, after twenty minutes, the men were nearly exhausted and the bow no longer responded. It was impossible to move ahead submerged.

Schwieger looked round the faces of his officers, who were all watching him. Why doesn't one of you say it? he thought.

Somebody else. What would you advise? he wondered, even though he knew he had no choice. They had to go up. But where was the tanker? Had he been able to put enough distance between them to give the U 20 a chance? No, situations did not repeat themselves. This time he did not even have a usable periscope. They would surface blind, to whatever situation was waiting for them. Their only hope would be to get on deck quickly and steer away from the enemy, firing as they fled. If the unsecured deck gun had not been wrenched from its base. "Now listen carefully," he said. "On the command—blow all available tanks. Stand by the galley hatch. We've no gyrocompass, so you, Haupert, will man the stern wheel with Munzer. Weiser—get your gun crew together. As soon as the deck gun is manned, commence rapid fire. Zentner—organize all the men not occupied below. They'll form a chain to bring up ammunition. Hirsch—get the diesel engines ready. Give us top speed as soon as you can. Any questions?"

They were all silent for a moment, knowing the desperateness of their position and the odds against them. Haupert asked the one question that obsessed them all. "Where is the enemy now, sir?"

"If I knew, I'd tell you," Schwieger said. "If anyone else does, I wish he'd tell me."

They were silent.

"Where will you be, Captain?" Hirsch asked.

"I'll be first out."

Weiser had been wondering about something, but was diffident. "Uh—how will we know we've surfaced, Captain?"

"We'll bounce," Schwieger said.

There were no more questions and they split up to alert the crew. Zentner paused. "We could be sitting pretty low in the water," he said. "A lot's going to come in through that hatch."

Schwieger shrugged. "Too bad. Sooner or later, we're probably going to have to swim for it, anyway." Zentner grinned and hurried to make up his ammunition detail from the torpedo crews. Schwieger nodded to Hirsch. "Prepare to surface." His apparent calmness was for the crew. Inside himself, he was raging that this should happen almost within sight of home.

He moved to the rear of central control past the shafts of

the periscope housing and the brass stand of the useless gyrocompass. Looking toward the stern, he saw Haupert and Munzer already in place and, a minute later, the gun crew. Weiser smiled to him, boyish, excited, and he raised a hand in acknowledgment. Well, this is what you joined us for, he told him silently. The thrill of combat. He looked back at Hirsch. "Surface!"

As the U-boat quivered and began to rise, he stepped into the passageway. Haupert and Munzer stood aside for him and he moved to the ladder up to the hatch, taking hold of its vertical supports. The experienced crewmen had warned the others and they were all holding on to something.

The U 20 was shuddering as she rose, gradually at first, then with more speed as the pressure decreased, until they could even feel the ascent. It's like falling upward, Schwieger thought. Faster . . . faster. Then the U 20 broke the surface and leaped into the air bow first, and fell back with a resounding slap that sent water spuming up in white wings all round her.

Schwieger was hurled backward and forward again into the ladder, but he managed to hang on and keep his head from striking the rungs. He was partly winded and gasped as he clambered up and tore at the bolts of the hatch cover. He got them undone. When he swung the cover up, a torrent of seawater rushed in over him and he forced his way through it and out onto the deck. The U-boat was wallowing low in the water and waves poured over her, so that he staggered and slithered and had to grab for the rail to prevent himself being swept overboard.

Haupert had hauled himself out after him and was helping Munzer up. The upper deck section was three or four feet above the surface now, but still wet, drenched with spray from the waves that broke along the sides. Not yet under power, the U 20 lurched and rolled in the swell, and Haupert and Munzer staggered toward the stern wheel, clinging to each other.

Schwieger's eyes were fixed on a point to the southwest. For once, fate had really favored them. While he had forced the U-boat toward the north in stretches of a few hundred yards, the tanker had been carried roughly south by the drift and was now between a mile and a mile and a half distant, although it was impossible for her not to have seen the splash the U 20 made when she surfaced. In confirmation he saw flashes from her deck, and seconds later, shells plunged into the sea a hundred yards short of the U-boat's hull.

Almost at once the deck gun roared behind him and he spun round, to see Lippe sitting on the deck with his legs in the open hatch, hoisting a crate of shells that it took two men to lift up to him. The gun crew was already reloading and the chief gunlayer adjusting the sights while Weiser stood beside him with his field glasses, marking the trajectory of his ranging shot.

"Well done!" Schwieger called. As Weiser smiled to him, the deck gun fired again and, at almost the same moment, shells from the tanker straddled the U 20, showering them with spray.

It's madness, Schwieger thought. How can we hope to fight? How many guns do they have, four, five? Against our one. Range and firepower, that's what will win.

The deck gun crashed out again and, this time, the shot was followed by a cheer from the gun crew. Disbelieving, Schwieger saw a dark ball of smoke balloon from the midsection of the tank steamer's superstructure. A hit! The young gunnery lieutenant was laughing, but it cut off and he crouched as answering shells whistled past, close above their heads.

The M.A.N. motors had started up and the deck vibrated slightly beneath them when Hirsch built up the power. The U 20 began to slew round, no longer broadside on to the enemy. She was responding to the motors and to the stern wheel, where Munzer was steering into the waves under Haupert's direction. They were moving ahead, gaining speed. At last! Schwieger thought. Their only chance was to turn stern on to the tanker, offering the smallest possible target, and becoming smaller as the distance between them increased. Which it must, because the tanker could not chase them. With a thirty-foot hole in her stern, only her chambered construction had prevented her from sinking. And now she had discovered the U 20 could still sting back.

There was a sudden detonation forward and the U-boat shook convulsively. A shot had struck her near the bows. One of the gun crew screamed. He had been knocked down and was dangling over the side, hanging on only by his fingernails to a row of deck bolts. Lammeier, who was in the gun crew, ran forward and pulled him back on board.

Schwieger raced past them and round the narrow ledge that skirted the conning tower. The damage was not great. Two of the deck plates were scorched and buckled and a strip of rail had been blown away. The shell must have struck one of its supports. He turned to go back, and paused. A jet of water was spurting from a hole fairly low on the port curve of the conning tower. It was quite small. As were some of the shells that zipped around them. A two-inch shell, was that what had caused the damage? As he looked, the water jet faltered, then squirted again as the U 20 rolled. Of course . . . The water that had entered was flowing out.

The deck gun had not stopped firing and he heard Weiser call for more ammunition. "Keep it coming!" he was shouting. All at once Schwieger realized what the boy had achieved. He was shooting by eye, laying his shots by instinct. The telescopic sight was still in the conning tower.

Schwieger stepped up onto the tower's forward section and climbed the fixed ladder to the bridge. As he lifted his leg over the rail, there was another loud explosion and the U-boat rocked again, so that he had to cling to the rail to stop himself being thrown back. Dirty brown and yellow smoke rose from a jagged rent in the stern deck near the starboard side. Lippe was bent over with his hands over his ears and Schwieger was anxious until he saw him push himself upright, shaking his head in annoyance.

He made a quick check of the bridge. Both periscopes were canted over, their housing damaged. That was all. The hatch was still watertight, fastened on the inside. He looked at the tank steamer. It was over three miles away now and would soon cease to be a danger, but they were still within range of each other and all it would take to finish the U 20 would be a direct hit from one or two of those bigger shells, the six-pounders.

Down in central control, Hirsch was pleased at having got both the main rudder and the hydroplane to work, yet he was anxious, hearing the explosions above his head and being tossed about. If the pressure hull was ripped open, the men still down below would not have much chance of escaping.

Crossing to check the electrical fuses again, he glanced back, hearing a whistle from the speaking tube to the bridge. "Captain?"

"You're there, Hirsch. Good," Schwieger's voice came. "Get someone up to the inner conning tower hatch. In two or three minutes I'll give the order to open it."

Hirsch grimaced and grabbed the tube. "Open it?" he squawked. "What about all that water, sir?"

"Most of it's drained out by now. There'll still be some, but we'll have to risk it. We must have the telescopic sight."

Zentner had heard and sent Bibermann to fetch a tarpaulin sheet. He called others out of the line passing ammunition. By the time Schwieger's command came, Zentner was standing on the ladder with the bolts of the hatch undone. Below him, a ring of men waited, holding the tarpaulin like a fire rescue blanket. With luck, they could direct most of the remaining water away from the electrical equipment.

Schwieger waited on the bridge, impatient, finding it hard to have to watch and do nothing. They were nearly at top surface speed now, the smoke from the gun streaming away behind them. Even so, the members of the gun crew were blackened by it. Grimy and temporarily deafened, they were working like heroes, loading and reloading nonstop. As grimy as his men, laying alternate shots with the gunner, Weiser had sometimes managed to get two shells in the air at the same time. And he had scored another hit. It might even have knocked out one of the French tanker's larger guns, for their rate of fire had dropped. Of course now the U 20 was a dwindling target to the tanker, while she was still fully visible.

The hatch behind Schwieger was opening and Zentner came out. He was soaked, his hair plastered over his forehead, although he looked more like himself with most of the yellow soot washed off.

"You look wet," Schwieger said.

"I needed a bath," Zentner grinned. He had brought the telescopic sight and Schwieger's spyglass. "I think they're in one piece." He handed over the glass and climbed down with the sight for Weiser. The gunnery lieutenant was so deafened, he only turned when Zentner punched him on the shoulder.

He smiled at Rudi's bedraggled appearance. "This is no time to go swimming," he laughed.

Watching him dry the lenses and slot the sight into place, Schwieger heard a call from the tube. Hirsch's voice came up, tinnily. "Captain, we have about thirty liters of water in a tarpaulin down here. What are we to do with it?"

"For God's sake, think of something yourself," Schwieger told him. "Drink it!"

As he straightened, there was a shout from the deck. "Destroyer! Destroyer to starboard!"

Schwieger turned quickly, tensing again, just when he thought they were almost safe. It was a destroyer, all right, about six miles away, steaming on a parallel course. How the hell had he missed seeing her? "On life belts!" he ordered, and repeated it down the tube.

Weiser fired another round at the tank steamer. "Forget the tanker! Forget the tanker!" Schwieger yelled, and Zentner pulled at Weiser's arm, pointing to the new danger.

The U 20's prow was swinging round. Rightly, Haupert had changed course to head away from the major enemy. But at best it would give them another half an hour, and it was at least three hours till dark. The destroyer would have caught them up long before then. They had twice a U-boat's speed and were armed with four to six guns of 5.9 inches caliber. Already, ranging shots were sending up geysers of water round the U 20's stern. And the tanker was still shooting at her, although now so distant it was more or less at random.

"Hirsch!" he called down. "What's the internal state? Can we submerge?"

The answer was slow in coming, and cautious. "If we have to, sir. I have men repairing the leaks, but we can't risk too much pressure . . . or stay down for more than about twenty minutes."

Useless! Schwieger thumped the rail with his fist, then ducked as a black speck hurtled toward him and whooshed past inches above his head. A moment later, a second shell struck the side of the conning tower. It glanced off without exploding, but the U-boat jerked over and yawed back, like a punching bag. When he stumbled, the eyepiece of the small periscope stabbed him just above the kidneys and he hung over the rail, winded, until he got his breath.

He saw one of the gun crew stretched out on the deck. He had been hit by a ricocheting splinter and was either dead or unconscious. Lippe crawled to him and drew him back toward the hatch. Weiser and the others were still shooting. Their eyes were in and their accuracy was proved by the columns of water that erupted round the destroyer, as high as her funnels. She had begun to zigzag to avoid them. That explained why her own shots were going wild. She was closer, about four miles now, not as close as she could have been. And zigzagging? Schwieger had snapped his spyglass into the clips on the inside of the bridge. He jerked it out, trained it—and his heart leaped.

It was not a destroyer! Through the telescope he could tell it was a smaller craft, a submarine-destroyer of the *Foxglove* class. Twice the size of a U-boat, but armed with the same caliber guns and not much faster. "Keep firing!" he yelled down. "Zentner—tell them it's a Foxglove! She can't risk a hit any more than we can!" When the message was bellowed into his ear, Weiser smiled up to Schwieger on the bridge and saluted. The sound of the deck gun became an almost continuous roar.

Keeping the spyglass trained on her, Schwieger saw the Foxglove veer round, putting on top speed. All her guns, four of them, were belching fire. Her captain was obviously tired of standing off. He meant to catch up and make it as close an engagement as possible. Her shells were pounding and buffeting the waves round the U 20. At the same time, Weiser had found her new range and one or two of his shells were not marked by columns of water. They must have buried themselves in her hull. With her larger bulk, the damage they did was not apparent at this distance, but all at once a cloud of black smoke enveloped her upper deck from the wheelhouse forward, and her stern came round as she lost way. Zentner clapped Weiser on the back and the gun crew began to cheer. Schwieger cheered with them.

Suddenly there was the flash of an explosion and a rending crash that threw them all off balance. Schwieger was hurled forward, landing on one knee in a blaze of pain. For half a minute he could not move and clung to the rail, fighting nausea. The pall of smoke was clearing and through it he saw that the area round the deck gun was a shambles. The shell had burst in the angle of the deck and the after structure of the conning tower. Could have been worse . . . could have been worse, his brain was telling him. If it had landed on the other side, amongst the ammunition, they would all have been blown sky-high.

Wincing, he hauled himself upright, expecting to see the submarine-destroyer racing toward them for the kill. Instead, it had turned away. The smoke pouring from its forward section was thicker and it was escaping from the zone of fire.

Schwieger climbed stiffly over the rail and lowered himself to the after structure, then down to the deck. Lammeier had risen and helped him down. There was surprisingly little injury to the thick metal of the deck and after structure, but many of the gun crew were wounded or worse. The man who had nearly been lost overboard earlier was dead, his skull cracked open and his brains splattered over the ammunition. The gunlayer lay over the breech of the deck gun, moaning. Others were unconscious. Zentner seemed to have been lucky again and was trying to stand. Schwieger helped him up and, together, they turned to where Weiser lay on his back, his legs over the side. His eyes were open and his lips were moving and it was only when they leaned over him that they saw the blood flowing in two bright streams from the stumps where his feet had been.

Schwieger tore open his leather coat and unbuckled his belt. He knelt by Weiser, gritting his teeth at the lance of pain. He slipped his belt under Weiser's left knee and brought the end round, tying it off. Zentner found a length of cord that had been round one of the shell crates and copied him, looping it round under the right knee. With bits of broken wood they twisted the makeshift tourniquets as tightly as they could, until they could not be tightened any further.

The anesthetic of shock was wearing off and Weiser gasped at the bite of the tourniquets. His vision cleared and he tried to sit up. "Help me . . . help—" He was reaching for Schwieger, and Schwieger caught his arm, supporting him with his other arm under his shoulders. "Have to reload," Weiser panted. "Fire the gun . . ."

"There's no need," Schwieger told him gently. "No need. You've won. You've beaten them, Fritz."

Weiser's eyes questioned him; then he seemed to hear the

silence that had fallen over the sea and he smiled. His eyes closed and his head fell slowly back.

Schwieger lowered his face and felt breath on his cheek. The boy was not dead.

Lippe had been blown down the galley hatch and clambered up again angry and frightened. The medical orderly and others had followed him, anxious to find out what had happened. They were taking care of the gun crew, the orderly tending to the gunlayer, who had both arms clasped round his head and was yelping in a series of high, staccato squeaks. Both his eardrums had been perforated.

When Schwieger signaled to him, Lippe stopped muttering and came over. He lifted Weiser and, together, they lowered him through the hatch and carried him into the commander's cabin. The young lieutenant's feet had been blown off at the ankles and Lippe stood staring at him in horror. Schwieger sent him out. He made two pads of cotton wool, smeared them with antiseptic ointment and laid them over the stumps. Quartermaster Wendt brought him a pile of clean cotton towels and he wrapped them round, tying them with bandage. It was all he could think to do. In less than a minute blood was soaking through the pads and towels.

Weiser was becoming conscious again, moaning as he began to be aware of pain. The whimpers grew in intensity until his whole body trembled convulsively and he screamed out in agony.

Schwieger was standing at the doorway with Wendt and saw him turn ashen, touching the bulkhead for support. He glanced along the passageway, where others were watching, transfixed by the gunnery lieutenant's shrieking. He went back into his cabin and searched through the emergency medical chest. He found a green glass vial of morphine and a hypodermic. He had no idea what the dosage should be, but filled the hypodermic to half and stabbed it into Weiser's thigh. In seconds, the trembling and screaming stopped and he lay still, breathing harshly through his open mouth.

When he came back on deck, Schwieger discovered that Zentner had formed a work party and cleaned up the mess. Apart from the buckled plates at the base of the conning tower's after structure, it was hard to believe anything had happened. Hirsch had examined all damage and pronounced it repairable. All electric circuits were functioning. The tanker had vanished. The Foxglove was five or six miles away, on their stern. There was no more smoke rising from her bows and she was still following. Haupert and Boatswain's Mate Munzer were still manning the stern wheel, untouched. Two lookouts stood on watch on the bridge. The sun hung much lower in the sky.

Lammeier was also untouched and had organized what was left of the gun crew. They had restacked the ammunition and now he was overhauling the deck gun. Schwieger promoted him to temporary petty officer, to choose what other men he needed. They would have to stand by.

Zentner was leaning back against the after structure, smoking a cigarette, and Schwieger joined him. "Why is that bastard still following us?" Zentner asked, after a while.

"Hoping we'll break down or founder, I suppose."

"She may be waiting for assistance. She could have signaled our position to a destroyer patrol."

Schwieger shook his head. "They'd have been here by now. We must have hit her radio room."

"May it please Allah," Zentner murmured. He noticed the cook's assistant handing up mugs of tea and fetched two for them. As he settled back, he said, "What if we have to fight again? Who'll fire the gun?"

"We will," Schwieger told him. "You've done some gunnery, haven't you?"

"A bit. But I'm no Wild Bill Hickok," Zentner admitted.

Schwieger smiled. "You said once your mother was American. Is that true?"

"M'mph," Zentner nodded. "From Chicago. If my father had stayed there, I'd be a Yankee Doodle. I'm so glad he didn't stay."

"Why?"

Zentner waved a hand. "I'd have missed all this."

For a moment Schwieger thought he was serious, then caught his grin. "What would you do if we went to war with America?"

"We couldn't be so crazy," Zentner said seriously. "I mean, we have half the world against us as it is. If we had the other half as well, we might as well pack it in."

Schwieger was silent. He did not entirely agree, but he

regretted bringing up the subject if Rudi felt strongly about it. Long minutes passed. He looked to port. The sun was on the horizon and beginning to set, spreading out at its base and sending long, blood-red streamers to either side as though the sea were on fire. The low-lying, trailing clouds were turning from gold to mauve and shading into black on their upper edges. The day was nearly over.

"Captain!" one of the lookouts called down.

He had no need to explain, for already they could hear the rush of the shells. They plummeted into the water in a scattered pattern across the U 20's wake. The Foxglove was coming up and meant to have a last crack at her before the light failed.

"Man the gun!" Schwieger ordered, and limped forward. His knee was seizing up. Zentner followed him, but Lammeier was there first.

"It's loaded, Captain," he reported. "And set for five miles."

"Good man," Schwieger said. He sighted quickly and fired. His shot dropped well short of the submarine-destroyer. His next round was in the air by the time the enemy's second salvo landed just behind the U 20's stern. His shot was also closer. At this range it was bravado on both sides, but with Schwieger aiming, Zentner adjusting for deflection and range and Lammeier handling the reloading, the U boat's rate of fire made the Foxglove start to zigzag again. Schwieger felt a wolfish pleasure in action and heard Rudi laughing beside him. Then one of their shots showed no answering column of water. The enemy ceased firing. In the last brief flare of the sun before its topmost rim disappeared, they saw the Foxglove turn sharply away. The chase was over. They waited, but there was only the sigh of the waves as darkness swept in around them.

Night fell, and the U 20 turned her nose toward home.

Chapter 17

Von Rintelen arrived at the Ritz-Carlton on Madison Avenue exactly two minutes before eleven and took the elevator up to the Ambassador's suite. The hotel was new to him, as was much of the city since his last visit. It had continued its inexorable spread to the north and every available plot in the center was being filled. He had never known a people with such a passion for tearing down and rebuilding. Some of Stanford White's masterpieces of architecture had been demolished already or were threatened, while in contrast some of the major thoroughfares, like Lexington Avenue, were still cobbled.

But he liked what he had seen of the Ritz-Carlton, the latest of the deluxe hotels, the glimpse he had of the lounge with its enormous Persian carpet and mirrored French doors, small, white or black Adam-style chairs, round glass-topped tables, the palm trees on its latticework balcony under a huge glass ceiling giving an open-air Oriental garden effect, the gilded, three-legged torchères with their clusters of electric candles. No wonder the Ambassador preferred it to his stuffy residence in Washington. He was tempted to move here himself.

The last few days had been crowded with meetings, negotiations and reconnaissance trips.

Von Rintelen had made a personal tour of most of the docks, to judge for himself the state of the interned German merchantmen and liners, lying idle, their quays empty, while goods and supplies piled up at Cunard, White Star and all the other Allied docks. The German merchant captains he met were implacably angry at the injustice of it and their own impotence to act. Although one of the oldest and most respected of them, Karl von Kleist, was related to him and spoke for him, they were sullen and suspicious at first, thinking he was part of Papen and Boy-Ed's "Kindergarten," as they called it. On a nod from Kleist, von Rintelen took the captains into his confidence, explaining who he was and why he was here, and their attitude changed completely. It was clear he could count on them for anything. He chose the two toughest and most capable as his lieutenants, Captains Wolpert and Steinberg.

He liaised with Boy-Ed through Paul Koenig, whom he trusted, and with Papen through his able young secretary, Wolf von Igel. He had called on Geheimrat Albert at the Hamburg-Amerika offices and congratulated him on his success in buying essential chemicals and munitions to prevent them from reaching the Allies. Purchases, however, would have to be greatly increased. "Not possible," the Geheimrat told him. "Everything that can be is being done." It was not an answer that von Rintelen could accept.

Yet when he contacted his own sources in Wall Street, he had a sobering shock. The problem was not a shortage of munitions on offer, but that there was so much. Even Erzberger had seriously underestimated the growth of the American armaments industry, with so many producers wanting to share the bonanza and turning their factories over to explosives and weapons. He could not hope to stem the flow, even with the millions of dollars at his disposal.

It all leads to one inevitable conclusion, he was thinking as he left the elevator and walked along the corridor to the Ambassador's rooms. In the short term, only two actions can have the necessary effect, disruption and sabotage. The soft pile of the carpet under his feet was pleasing, and the discreetly elegant decor. Yes, I really must consider moving here, he thought.

The German Ambassador, Count Johann von Bernstorff, was a shortish, dapper man in his early fifties, with wavy graying hair and a thin mustache. His face was highly mobile and his expression charming, seldom without a smile. He was a social favorite and liked to give parties, a man for the ladies, one of the reasons why he preferred the freedom of the big city to the prudent discretion unavoidable in more parochial Washington. He was also a skilled diplomat and his welcome to von Rintelen was warm and cordial. As the meeting was not formal, he wore a dark, single-breasted suit with gray spats over his shoes and a pearl stickpin in his tie. Bernstorff smiled. "I have taken the liberty of ordering coffee for us, Captain. Dr. Dernburg will be here soon and may join us. Please—" He indicated the brocade sofa in his study, while he himself sat in the armchair. "Now, you must tell me just what you are doing here."

Von Rintelen had been prepared for the question. The attachés would have lost no time in informing Bernstorff of his presence and their concern. "I am afraid that if I answer truthfully, it might compromise your diplomatic position, Your Excellency."

Bernstorff drew his chair closer. "Come now, Captain. I am not only your country's Ambassador, but also an old soldier," he chuckled.

It was virtually an order and von Rintelen could not refuse. He did not go into details, but told the Ambassador of the High Command's decision to send him and what he had promised to do. Everything he had seen since his arrival only made him more determined.

Bernstorff listened with growing alarm. This aristocratic and faintly deadly young man meant every word of it. He spread his hands. "But, my dear Captain, Geheimrat Albert already has had enormous success in purchasing supplies and munitions. What more can actually, usefully, be done?"

"I admire Herr Albert," von Rintelen said, "yet he works entirely from his office, not dirtying his shoes in the marketplace. Something might be achieved by someone prepared to venture further afield—and if necessary, to take more drastic steps."

Papen is right, Bernstorff was thinking. He sees himself principally as a saboteur. "You realize that if you—I speak frankly—if you are discovered committing illegal acts in this country, it could have serious repercussions on the relations between the United States and the Reich."

"I discussed that fully with Herr Zimmermann before leaving," von Rintelen told him. "We agreed that, in the unfortunate event of any of my activities being uncovered, the government will disclaim all responsibility for me. I shall confess to having come here entirely without Berlin's knowledge or permission."

"Very self-sacrificing," Bernstorff commented. "However, circumstances change. Since you left home, there has been a move, a definite move, toward an improvement. An American proposal, which we are prepared to accept, which will in effect remove the British Blockade. We have already had the Thrasher incident. Nothing else must be allowed to endanger the success of the proposal."

"In the absence of any countermanding orders," von Rintelen said, "I can only proceed as planned."

Bernstorff's whole function was to represent Germany, protect her interests and nationals, and to preserve United States neutrality at all costs. "I'm afraid you forget to whom you are speaking, Captain," he announced firmly. "I am telling you that you must undertake no rash adventures here. Whatever you plan must be submitted beforehand for the approval of the naval and military attachés."

Von Rintelen's expression did not alter and his voice was even. "And I am afraid that I cannot do that, Your Excellency. In my opinion, it would put my entire mission in jeopardy."

Bernstorff drew himself up at such outright insubordination, his face set. He was about to deliver a withering rebuke when he saw von Rintelen take an envelope from his inside pocket and offer it to him. He accepted it curtly, but, as he opened it, he understood the reason for his visitor's calmness. The paper he unfolded was a *Kaiserpass*, signed *Wilhelm Kaiser und Koenig*. Failure to render all aid and assistance to its holder, without reserve, was answerable directly to the All Highest.

Bernstorff folded the paper again and returned it. "If I had known of this," he said, "I would not have asked so many questions. How may I assist you?" He was impressed by von Rintelen's behavior. Although he had revealed that he held the upper hand, his manner was still polite and respectful.

"I would not risk involving the Embassy in my affairs, Your Excellency," von Rintelen informed him. "I would suggest, however, that your propaganda adviser might concentrate for a time on our willingness to accept the Freedom of the Seas and call for a similar response from England. Whether England agrees to the proposal or not, we shall be remembered as first to respond to America's appeal for peace and our enemies will be branded as the aggressors."

"Very neat," the Ambassador nodded.

"On the same theme, we must continue to protest at the injustice of the authorities here permitting enemy ships to enter and leave American ports freely, while some of our vessels are interned because we armed them for defense. The most glaring example is the *Lusitania*."

"I have not heard she is armed," Bernstorff pointed out.

"We are reasonably certain she is," von Rintelen told him. "Although the naval attaché has as yet provided us with no definite proof. But she is due here again in about a week, and we shall remedy that. We also suspect that she loads considerable quantities of contraband munitions every trip. And cannot be touched, because she also carries American passengers, like a protective shield."

"There's nothing we can do about that," Bernstorff said.

"We could demand her internment as an armed auxiliary. We could challenge the legality of the American authorities allowing her to sail with contraband on board. We could appeal to the morality of her American passengers not to lend her their protection by sailing on her. Her very existence, able to sail unmolested, mocks our national prestige. The Kaiser himself has declared that each time the *Lusitania* crosses the Atlantic, it is a glove thrown in the face of Germany."

The conversation was repeated and tactics agreed to after Dr. Dernburg arrived, a former Colonial Secretary, now head of propaganda. When he left the Ambassador's suite, von Rintelen felt highly satisfied at having secured their wholehearted cooperation, not merely because of the *Kaiserpass*. He had rekindled their fighting spirit. His sense of satisfaction lasted until he reached the offices of the National City Bank.

On his previous visit some years before, von Rintelen had planted agents in several American financial institutions. One of them was a teenage boy, Frederick Schleindl, who had been brought over from Germany and placed for training with a private banking firm. On the outbreak of war, Schleindl transferred to the foreign department of the National City Bank, where he had proved invaluable.

They sat at his desk, apparently a not-too-bright would-be client and an eager investment adviser. Von Rintelen was not studying the papers in his hands, however. He was listening closely and with growing shock. Schleindl had heard a rumor from a reliable source. J.P. Morgan had just returned from a trip to England, he said. "He has arranged to float a loan enabling the British Government to place an order with the Bethlehem Steel Company for shrapnel and lyddite shells, to the value of a hundred million dollars." Von Rintelen had difficulty in preventing the papers he was holding from shaking. "You realize, sir, that this is only the beginning?" Schleindl went on. "The commission the Morgan Bank will earn will make others eager to float loans, too."

Von Rintelen turned over the sheet in front of him. Underneath was a cable from Petrograd, authorizing the bank to allow the Russian attaché, Colonel Golejewski, to draw freely on its deposits to pay for his orders of war materials. He pushed the cable aside quickly, angrily. He had heard more than enough for one day.

Fat Margo's was crowded and smoky, the tables on the upper and lower levels filled with U-boat men, laughing, drinking, singing. The relief of tension after returning from patrol was physical, a lightening of the whole spirit, the sheer, exuberant joy of being still alive, of having survived even for a few more days.

From his table on the upper level, Walther Schwieger watched and felt the sense of release himself, the fiery excitement. The Grand Admiral knew it, he admitted, knew that by taking away the restraints and sending them out as hunting killers, it would bind them closer together, the Wolfpack, making them more and more eager to go for the enemy's jugular. They held themselves with a new pride. Until recently a despised and neglected wing of the Service, they were now the Imperial Navy's principal weapon, its only weapon. Every man of them had heard the latest total. In the past month the boats from here in Emden and the others from Wilhelmshaven and Cuxhaven, only eight or nine on each patrol, had sunk over 140,000 tons of Allied shipping. In a lower corner one group had started up the battle song adopted by the Flotilla. *"Wenn wir fahren gegen*

303

England," they sang. "We are sailing, we are sailing, we are sailing against England."

Schwieger did not often come to Fat Margo's. After a patrol, after seeing to his casualties and accounting for his torpedoes and the number of rounds fired, after reporting to Fregattenkapitän Bauer and going through his log to record his sinkings, confirmed and unconfirmed, to pass on observations and information, after agreeing to the repairs and modifications needed to the U 20, he preferred to be by himself for a time. It was a necessity, after the weeks of cramped conditions, stale air, fumes, and body smells and the strains which never lessened. His fear had been defeated, but other reactions could not be controlled. In the sudden relaxation of tension, there were moments when he could feel his whole body begin to tremble. In public he kept a tight hold of himself to prevent it. In his own quarters he would sit or lie on his bed until the spasm had passed. That was what Weddigen had meant. The shaking had nothing to do with fear. It was the body, the nervous system taking its revenge for the unbearable, constant pressure to which it was subjected.

Ashore, he did not sleep for days like others. He walked, anywhere, in any direction, just to feel space around him and the freedom of movement, and to be surrounded by the open vault of the sky, day or night, it did not matter. If he was granted a few days' leave, he went home to Berlin, to be pampered by his family and remind himself of the life the war was being waged to preserve. He certainly would not choose to spend his first free night in a crowded old inn, eating and drinking too much and reliving the days of his last patrol.

This night, however, was different. Rudi had reminded him of the bet that had been made over the sinking of the Portuguese barque, which Fritz Weiser had lost by taking one too many shots to sink her. He should have paid. So tonight was in memory of him.

It was also in memory of another, older friend, Commander Lepsius, who had been torpedoed off the coast of Norway in the U 6. By tradition, the evening was neither sad nor solemn. Glasses of champagne were drunk for both Weiser and Lepsius and, when they were smashed, all those who heard the sound cheered.

Schwieger and Zentner had been joined by Rosenberg, the dark, intense commander of the U 30. He was incensed when Zentner mentioned reading of the Allied and American storm over the sinking of the *Falaba*. Rosenberg had spoken to the captain of the U 28, which torpedoed her. "He was certain she was carrying contraband!"

"She may have been," Zentner granted. "But she was also carrying about two hundred civilian passengers. Where do we draw the line?"

"Look," Rosenberg told him, "he warned her to stop, but she wouldn't. Because of her passengers, she thought she was safe. So he forced her to stop and asked to see her ship's papers and manifest. Her skipper wouldn't hand them over. So he gave her passengers and crew ten minutes to take to the boats. They were slow about it, so he gave them another ten minutes. Then another extension. By which time he was beginning to think they were going slow on purpose and sending out signals. Sure enough, when he looked round, there was an armed patrol vessel heading for him. So? What would you have done, Walther?"

"Put a torpedo into the *Falaba*," Schwieger said. "And submerged at once."

"Exactly," Rosenberg agreed. "He did everything by the book. So he's not a pirate, not a murderer. If a lot of them didn't make it to their boats, it was their own choice."

Schwieger sat back, letting Rudi and Rosenberg continue the argument. To him, it had become academic. Only the circumstances of the moment decided what was right.

Before coming out, he had done something very difficult, written to Fritz Weiser's parents. At least he could tell them he had died like a hero and was being cited for bravery. He did not tell them of the hours of that last, long night of the voyage home. Of the effects of the morphine continually wearing off and Weiser's screams, which could be heard even on deck. They had stopped just before dawn and he had begun to sing the student *Gaudeamus*: "So let us be merry, while we are young." He was beyond pain. Schwieger hoped that he thought he was back with his student friends and that that was his last memory. They wrapped him in the spare battle flag and slid him over the side into the gray North Sea. *Nos habebit mare.* The sea shall have us all.

His mind came back to the table when he heard Rudi

305

laughing. Rosenberg was telling him about Georg, who was still determined to stick to the Cruiser Rules. He had surfaced at night in the middle of an English fishing fleet, and found himself faced with a dilemma. As soon as he challenged and sank one of them, the others would all scatter.

"So what did he do?" Zentner chuckled.

"Sent a message to the skipper of the nearest one to abandon ship and report to the U-boat before he was torpedoed. It worked like a charm. Within minutes the skipper and his crew came alongside in their lifeboats. So he sent the skipper, his watch officer and two guards over to the next one, and so on round the fleet. It took nearly all night and by dawn he was surrounded by an armada of little boats. What was he to do with them? He saw smoke, an old Belgian steamer. He chased her, caught her, put all the fishermen on board and, for the next hour, sailed backward and forward blowing over twenty trawlers out of the water with his deck gun." They laughed. "Of course," Rosenberg went on, "when they got back to England, they probably told some frightening story of German brutality."

"It's unavoidable, I suppose," Zentner said.

Schwieger signaled the waiter for another bottle. "There is one way to stop lying reports, one sure way."

"How?"

Schwieger paused. "If they had no radio, or if he got their radio masts first, they could all have been sunk without trace."

"Provided there were no survivors," Rosenberg added.

Zentner smiled uncertainly, thinking it was in bad taste. Then he saw that Rosenberg had taken it seriously.

"Yes," Rosenberg nodded. "It wouldn't work with something like a fishing fleet. But a single ship 'sunk without trace' . . . they'd assume it had hit a mine or something."

"Oh, come on!" Zentner protested. "It's not something to joke about."

Schwieger glanced at him, but said nothing.

"I don't think he was joking," Rosenberg said for him. "Not altogether."

For a moment Zentner thought the silence was inside himself. Then that the tables round them had grown quiet because they had been overheard. Everyone had turned toward the door and, gradually, the conversation and singing at all the other tables fell away.

It was Hersing who had come in, lean and taut, his hawk's face even paler than usual. He was not often seen in Emden, but everyone knew him as one of the top three aces, second only to Weddigen. His U 21 had sometimes sunk so many ships in one sortie that her exploits were attributed to a whole pack of U-boats. The enemy was so determined to get him at all costs that he was in constant danger of panic attack or ramming, so, on alternate patrols, he changed his craft's number to "U 51" to confuse them and make them think the flotilla was twice its size. As he stood looking round, the people at the tables began to rise to their feet in respect and admiration.

The waiter had brought another bottle and filled a glass for Schwieger to taste it. Hersing noticed the movement and, as he came toward them, Schwieger realized it was him he was looking for. He did not rise, although Zentner and Rosenberg stood with the others, when Hersing came up the wooden steps to their level.

Something's wrong, Schwieger thought. Something's badly wrong. He could read the signs. Hersing seldom drank, but had been drinking and was holding himself in very tightly. When he spoke, it was so quietly that at first Schwieger could hardly hear him.

"I've just seen the report," Hersing said. "Weddigen's gone. Otto Weddigen. Rammed by a British dreadnought."

Schwieger pushed himself up. He had gone as deathly pale as Hersing. "Where was it?" he muttered.

"North of the Orkneys. He challenged a full squadron of battleships with destroyers following."

Fool, Schwieger thought. Blind, heroic, suicidal fool. He could feel the betraying tremors start in his spine, and tightened his neck muscles and scalp, standing very erect. He could not trust himself to speak. The glass that had been filled for him was on the table. He picked it up, drank it off and smashed it abruptly to the floor.

This time there was no answering cheer.

Chapter 18

WOODROW WILSON SAT AT HIS DESK IN HIS SMALL STUDY. For all that the war was over three thousand miles away, it kept erupting in his backyard. He could only admire Mr. Bryan, but the Secretary did not seem aware that the U.S. was already committed to holding the German government strictly accountable. The torpedoing of the unarmed *Falaba* was a cowardly and brutal deed, and a firm protest must be sent or the administration would be seen to have backed down in the face of aggression. Any weakness would lead to a fatal loss of American prestige.

Wilson knew what the result of the Note to Germany could be, and had lost much sleep over it. Yet it had to be sent. The nation could not submit tamely to injury and, if Germany again deliberately disregarded the warning, any further insult would be clear proof that her objective was war between them. It also meant that, reluctantly, he would have to accept the cries for preparedness, for a vastly increased Army and Navy budget. Roosevelt would be in his tub-thumping element when he heard.

Wilson laid the letter from Bryan aside and glanced at the report which had come with it. It was from the Consul in the port of Falmouth on the southwest coast of England. When he saw that it contained a series of statements taken from survivors of the *Falaba* sinking after they had been brought ashore, Wilson's eyebrows rose. Strange material to be rushed to him by W.J.B. Yet as he began to read, he became motionless. He had been reaching for the handkerchief in his breast pocket to polish his glasses and Tumulty saw him hunch forward, his hand resting against the pocket without moving.

The statements were a straightforward description of what

had happened, of the three periods of grace given to the captain of the *Falaba* by the U 28 to allow him time to get his passengers into the lifeboats and how it was used instead to send signals to the nearest armed British patrol ship, to catch the submarine in a trap. The U 28 had fired her torpedo at the very last minute and the sudden sinking had been caused by the detonation of thirteen tons of contraband high explosives in the *Falaba*'s cargo. It was far from the appalling story of German brutality and callous indifference to the loss of civilian lives which had been invented by the newspapers.

Wilson took the handkerchief from his pocket at last, and used it to dab at the perspiration which gleamed on his temples and upper lip. With no evidence he had been ready to march the United States right to the brink of war—to go against his deepest beliefs and his most cherished policies, merely on the basis of hysterical accusations! It was a frightening, an awesome reminder of how very, very certain he had to be before committing the nation to any action. He thanked his Maker that the Note, which would have amounted to an ultimatum, had not yet been sent.

He saw Joe Tumulty hovering, watching him, puzzled. "I've just had a lesson in not being too hasty, Joe," he said. "A most valuable reminder that there are two sides to every question."

The clearing was shaped like a horseshoe on the edge of the clump of trees and, as Dr. Scheele walked forward into it, he was very conscious of the two men with guns. Guns made him nervous and he jumped, nearly dropping his green canvas bag, when one of them fired only ten yards away. He could hear the lead shot spattering through the leaves and von Rintelen laughing quietly behind him.

"All right, Doctor, this should be far enough."

They had come out to Long Beach, to the shooting ground at Great South Bay. Wolpert and Steinberg carried shotguns like gentlemen sportsmen, hunting wildfowl. Von Rintelen had a large box camera slung round his shoulder and Scheele had the canvas game bag. The fifth man carried nothing. Unlike von Rintelen and the two captains, who had dressed as if they were really going hunting, and Scheele, who wore baggy tweeds, he was in a dark business suit. He had been introduced as Mr. "Freeman," a fairly obvious pseudonym. He was elderly and taciturn, but from his accent and the few remarks he had made, Scheele guessed that he was Irish, a branch official of the Longshoremen's Union.

Dr. Walter T. Scheele, himself, was a German chemist settled in Hoboken, a balding, middle-aged man with a straggly mustache and a mouthful of gold teeth. Von Rintelen had not been too impressed with him when their first meeting had been arranged by Papen, but he soon discovered that the little chemist had a talent for improvisation that amounted to genius. Hearing that one of the most serious shortages in Germany was of lubricating oil, he devised a method of mixing the oil with fertilizer. Von Rintelen arranged to have the resultant "commercial fertilizer" shipped in bulk to Scandinavia, from where it was transshipped to Germany and the oil extracted by a simple chemical process.

Von Rintelen had set up an import and export company in the name of E.V. Gibbons, Inc., using the initials on his false passport, with a small office on Cedar Street, off Broadway in downtown Manhattan. Using a variety of aliases and middlemen, he had begun to buy millions of dollars of raw products and foodstuffs, outbidding Allied purchasing agents who found contracts being snatched away from them. His reckless buying forced market prices up and made American manufacturers eager to do business with his firm, causing the first noticeable domestic inflation of the war. Meanwhile, Captain Steinberg, posing as his partner, F. Hansen, chartered and bought freighters through U.S. subsidiaries, provided false manifests for their cargoes and shipped them off to Denmark. They gambled on them running the British blockade. Some were seized, but enough slipped through to make it worthwhile.

It was a good beginning, but the least urgent part of von Rintelen's mission. In conferences with Steinberg and the others, he had discussed the possibility of direct sabotage of Allied cargo ships. The problem was the difficulty of getting past the tight security at the Allied docks. That was solved by the German Consul's introduction to Mr. "Freeman." Many longshoremen were members of Irish organizations, dedicated to the struggle to win Ireland's independence from England. Employed in loading and unloading ships throughout New York harbor, with access to all docks, they were a ready-made force of saboteurs. Provided, von Rintelen realized, one further problem could be solved.

If Allied or American security became suspicious, the usefulness of the Irish would be over. The trouble was that to destroy thousands of tons of cargo or to sink a ship required a larger amount of explosives than could be smuggled on board undetected. Merely to cause damage was not enough and would lead to dangerous investigations. There was also the difficulty of obtaining a regular and secret supply of detonators and timing mechanisms, and of training the sabotage teams in their use.

Two nights ago, Dr. Scheele had come to the office and made von Rintelen a proposal. He had perfected a device, he claimed, which answered all the problems and which E.V. Gibbons Inc. could acquire for a fee of ten thousand dollars. From his brief description, von Rintelen was sufficiently interested not to haggle over cost, provided it really worked. He agreed with Freeman that there would have to be a demonstration and this Sunday morning the group had traveled separately by train to Long Island City, where they transferred to the southern track, and all met at last at the small resort of Babylon. A mile and a half out of town, in deserted country, von Rintelen spotted the patch of trees with its clearing facing the sea. The occasional shots fired by Wolpert and Steinberg would be heard by any other hunters and make them keep to their own areas.

It was a crisp, clear morning. Scheele knelt on the grass, unpacking his canvas bag. He took out first two lengths of narrow lead tubing about the size of a dollar cigar. Into the middle of each of them, he inserted a thin copper disc. Von Rintelen checked to see that the two captains were on guard, then moved closer, watching as the chemist put on a pair of rubber gloves, then took some bottles from the bag. Pouring very carefully, he filled one half of each tube with sulfuric acid, then plugged the end with wax and an airtight lead cap. The other halves of both he filled with chlorate of potash, and capped the ends. He laid both small cylinders on the ground about fifteen feet apart, parallel to each other. "I think we should stand a little further off," he suggested.

Freeman had been watching skeptically, his hands deep

in his pockets. He jerked his hands out and stepped back quickly. "If those things are going to explode, they'll be heard a mile away," he said.

"They're not exactly meant to explode," Scheele told them, but sounded nervous and retreated further.

Von Rintelen stopped him at the open end of the clearing. "I think it's time you explained, Doctor," he said. "What kind of bombs are these?"

Scheele glanced back at the cylinders. "Well—strictly speaking, they are not bombs at all. Or to be more precise, they are fire bombs. The mingling of the two ingredients will cause intense heat."

"How do ye make them go off?" Freeman asked.

"Nothing can stop them going off. As soon as the acid eats through the copper and the ingredients connect, combustion will occur."

Von Rintelen nodded. "How long will it take?"

"This is all experimental, you understand?" Scheele said. "I put a very thin copper disc in the first one, which I calculate will take about an hour to dissolve. The second disc was very slightly thicker and should take an extra twenty minutes or so." He saw von Rintelen look at his watch, and began to edge away. "I'll just pop down to—"

"We'll all stay here," von Rintelen said.

There were roughly fifty minutes to wait before anything would happen. For the first ten or so they all watched the lead cylinders, but gradually their attention wandered. Conversation faded out. At intervals the captains fired into the air. Once another pair of hunters passed lower down and waved. When their waves were not returned, they moved on.

Half a mile below them, the sun glinted on the waters of the huge bay. In the distance was Fire Island. Perhaps we should have staged the experiment there, von Rintelen thought to himself, and smiled. He could see that Freeman was becoming more and more distrustful of the whole enterprise. The German officers sent to liaise with revolutionary groups in Ireland had reported back that they were too unstable and too divided among themselves to justify the risk of setting up joint military operations. The most that could be done for them was to smuggle in supplies of small arms. Perhaps if they had spoken to more people in the movement like Freeman, their recommendations would have been different.

Freeman had taken his old fashioned watch from his vest pocket. Von Rintelen checked his own. The hour was up. He turned to look at the clearing. At that moment, he heard the faintest hiss and, suddenly, a searing white flame about ten or twelve inches long leaped from either end of the nearest cylinder. Its brightness was blinding, and he clapped both hands over his eyes. With them shut, he could still see that bar of pure white flame burning across his eyelids. He could feel the heat from where he stood, and heard both Freeman and Wolpert cry out in pain.

It lasted for almost a minute. When he was sure it had stopped, he risked another look, blinking, his eyeballs hurting. Smoke was rising from a shallow trough in the ground, where the grass had vaporized and the sandy earth had been baked black. Small flames flickered round the trough where the grass around it had caught fire, and von Rintelen ran to stamp them out.

"Careful, Captain!" Steinberg shouted and hurried to help him.

Von Rintelen kicked at the blackened earth, searching for the lead tube, but it had completely disappeared, melted by the intense heat. When he moved toward the second cylinder, Steinberg caught his arm and pulled him away.

Scheele was leaning against a tree at the edge of the clearing, still shaken by the success of his device. Wolpert had dropped his shotgun and was wiping his streaming eyes with his handkerchief. Freeman's head was bent and he flicked at his eyes with his fingers. "Holy Mother, did ye see that?" he muttered. "Did ye ever see anything the like of that?"

"It worked," von Rintelen said.

"It did, didn't it?" Scheele agreed, beginning to smile.

"And the next one's due to go off in twenty minutes?"

"Fourteen minutes from now."

Von Rintelen's mind was racing ahead. "How can you be so accurate?"

The chemist shrugged. "It depends entirely on the surface area and thickness of the copper. I chose an hour as the shortest possible safety margin."

"But it could be longer?"

313

"Almost anything you like," Scheele said. A disc could be inserted which it would take the acid days to eat through.

Von Rintelen, however, had not asked for himself, but for Freeman, who had to be convinced that it was safe to handle or he would warn his longshoremen against it. "So there's no danger until the ingredients mix," von Rintelen said. He walked forward, picked up the second cylinder and turned, holding it in front of him.

Steinberg had moved back to his lookout post. "For God's sake, drop it, Captain!" he shouted urgently.

Von Rintelen made himself relax, although the hairs prickled on the back of his neck. He held the cylinder lightly, knowing that his life depended on the fractional thickness of a strip of copper. "There's no feeling of warmth," he reported. "It is silent, undetectable." He slipped the cylinder into his inside pocket and smoothed his coat over it. He heard Wolpert gasp. Scheele stood upright and moved to stand beside Freeman, whose eyes had opened wide. "One man could smuggle three or four of these on board a ship quite easily," von Rintelen went on. "If they were stowed in different holds next to inflammables, like oil or sugar, or explosive materials, they would start a series of fires that would be impossible to put out. Even if by some miracle they were, no one could ever tell how they had begun." He did not want to push his luck and pulled the cylinder from his pocket. He laid it on the grass, stepped over it and walked back to the others.

"By the Holy, ye're a cool one," Freeman murmured admiringly.

"Dr. Scheele assured us that the timing system was perfect," von Rintelen shrugged. He took out his cigarette case. As he lit his cigarette, he heard the faint hiss behind him and shielded his eyes.

The second cylinder behaved exactly like the first, shooting out the same ravening white flames, whose searing heat consumed the grass on either side within seconds and fused the soil beneath. This time they all helped to stamp out the burning grass before it caused a more widespread fire. Of the cigar-sized tube, all they could find was a tiny, shapeless lump of lead.

Freeman clapped his hands and rubbed them together.

"The boys'll deliver these babies for ye with the greatest tender care and pleasure, Captain," he chuckled.

Von Rintelen smiled to Dr. Scheele. "I think you've just earned yourself ten thousand dollars," he said.

It was risky for them all to be seen together, so Freeman and the doctor caught the first train back, sitting well apart. While Steinberg and Wolpert walked down to Babylon's small harbor, von Rintelen bought himself a double Scotch at the Sherman House Hotel. He felt he needed it. His mind was filled with pictures of ships burning, of sailors tumbling out of their bunks at the cry of "Fire!" flames licking through cargo hatches and lifeboats blazing as they fell into the water. The images sickened him, although he knew that the greedy little chemist with his gold teeth and nervous manner had given him just the weapon for which he had been searching. But after this is all over, he promised himself, I shall bathe in carbolic acid to get myself clean again.

From Bushwick Station in Brooklyn he telephoned his lawyer to meet him later at the office. Steinberg, who had been tagging him, gave him the sign that they had not been followed. He took a trolley to the far side of the bridge and a hack straight to his hotel.

He strolled into the Great Northern, as relaxed as if he had spent the day sightseeing. There was one message for him at the desk, an International Cable signed *Your Loving, Marie-Luise.* It read, "Weather improving. Uncle Waldo's birthday in three weeks. Can you send present?" and was from Eisendal to remind him that the date of Falkenhayn's offensive was coming closer, that the ice was breaking and Russian munition ships would now be able to reach Archangel. Von Rintelen had sent details of those which had already sailed, for the attention of the U-boat Flotilla. After today, he could do something about those that were still loading. Uncle Waldo would have his present. With luck, many of them.

While he waited for the elevator, he noticed a young woman coming from the restaurant. Her ankle-length suit dress was quietly fashionable, coffee-colored, high-collared and fitted at the waist, with a cream lace jabot at the throat. Her figure was slim but full-breasted, a combination he admired. The line of her neck and chin was very fine. When she

315

glanced at him, he saw that she was really lovely, with a flawless complexion and wide dark eyes, the oval of her face framed in rich chestnut hair, which she wore tied back in a plain knot on the nape of her neck. She paused near him, but when he smiled to her, she looked away.

There was a pretty little girl with her, with long dark hair, and a tousle-headed boy, slightly older, very square-jawed and manly, wearing a gray knickerbocker suit. "Press the button, Peter," his mother said.

When the boy stretched for the call button, von Rintelen saw that he had a wooden amulet hanging round his neck on a leather cord. It was shaped like some strange bird and had magic signs burned into it. "Is that an Indian charm?" von Rintelen asked.

"Yes, sir," the boy named Peter answered.

"It looks like very powerful medicine."

"Harry Hightree gave it to Daddy," the little girl announced.

"Oh, well, then," von Rintelen said, as though that explained everything. The young woman smiled to him quickly. The children's accent was distinctly Canadian, but he had been unable to place hers. The elevator arrived and they all went in together.

"Twelve, please," she told the attendant.

Von Rintelen was conscious of the woman watching him. He did not make the mistake again of smiling. "I'm sorry," she said, "but are you English, by any chance?"

He had the accent now, pure English Home Counties, shortened and flattened by years in Canada. It warned him to be careful. "Of the colonial variety," he replied. "From South Africa."

"Please forgive my asking," she said.

"Not at all," he smiled. "By the sound of it, I'd guess you were quite a long way from home yourself."

"Yes." Livvy was not accustomed to speaking to strange men, and wished she had not begun the conversation.

"We're going to England in a week or two," Peter said.

"In a big boat, with Daddy," Diana added. "We're going to Winchelsea."

"Are you, now?" von Rintelen smiled. "How very nice."

"Do you know it?" Livvy asked, surprised.

316

Von Rintelen had once spent an entertaining weekend at the old Mermaid Inn in the nearby resort of Rye, with the freethinking daughter of a Liberal Peer. "Indeed, yes," he nodded. "I remember the church and the wonderful seafood from Rye Bay."

"It's a small world," Livvy laughed.

"It is indeed," von Rintelen agreed. The elevator had stopped at the twelfth floor and the doors opened. "What ship are you sailing on?"

"The *Cameronia*," Peter told him. "To Glasgow."

"Well, I hope you have a . . . . a comfortable crossing," von Rintelen said. He raised his hat and Livvy inclined her head, ushering the children out. He watched the slight sway of her hips as they walked off down the corridor, until the doors closed.

In his own room, he burned the cable from Eisendal before he showered and shaved. It was still early, but he would not have time to change again after his meeting, so he laid out his evening clothes. Before he left Berlin, Erzberger's Bureau had prepared a list for him of Congressmen and labor leaders known to be approachable, provided the money was tempting enough. They were not, however, likely to respond to a direct offer from a German agent, even one with impeccable manners and millions in the bank. Von Rintelen needed an intermediary, preferably American, with some reputation in the financial world.

One man had exactly the right qualifications. He was a stock manipulator named David Lamar, charming, ingenious and totally unscrupulous, whose dubious deals involving political figures had earned him the label of "The Wolf of Wall Street." He was rumored to be currently short of ready cash to maintain his style of life, a situation which von Rintelen proposed to remedy. He had arranged to meet Lamar at Pabst's restaurant at nine o'clock for dinner.

When he reached his office on the eighth floor of the Trans-Atlantic Trust Company's building, he found his secretary, Max, at the desk in the outer room, processing a pile of invoices. "They're all here," Max told him.

"Boniface?"

"He's with them."

Mr. Boniface was the E.V. Gibbons Company's legal adviser. A small-time lawyer, working out of a hotel room down by the docks, his clients until these last weeks had been petty criminals and waterfront racketeers. What had interested von Rintelen was that he had a reputation for getting them off, due to his unrivaled knowledge of the by-ways and loopholes of the legal system. Working for von Rintelen, his system was simple. For each piece of advice or information, he charged fifty dollars, totting them up and presenting his bill at the end of each meeting. There was nothing on paper, but von Rintelen settled promptly and without question and so, according to Mr. Boniface's peculiar ethics, had his complete loyalty.

He was sitting slightly apart from the others in the inner office, a tall, thin, elderly man in a shabby old-fashioned suit, with pince-nez perched on his beaky nose. Steinberg and Wolpert had already told him the purpose of the meeting and he looked uncomfortable, von Rintelen noticed. With him, in addition to the captains, were Dr. Scheele, Karl von Kleist and Dr. Bünz of Hamburg-Amerika. Paul Koenig, head of security at Hamburg-Amerika, sat at the side of the desk, and next to him was a man sent by Freeman. He was Mike Foley, an Irish stevedore, with a round, red face, blunt nose and blue eyes. He had shoulders like a packing case and arms so thick they made the sleeves of his coat seem unnaturally tight. His roughness masked a highly political intelligence and considerable organizing ability.

"Good evening, gentlemen," von Rintelen said. There were murmurs from the others at the sight of his immaculate evening dress, starched white shirt front with gold studs and white tie.

"Do we start with the soup or the fish?" Foley murmured.

Von Rintelen smiled and sat at his desk. "We start with the business on hand."

Foley nodded. "I'm all for that. Let's get down to brass tacks. Where do we pick up these fire bombs?"

Mr. Boniface blinked and looked away, as if not seeing meant he could also not hear.

"Unfortunately it's not quite so simple, Mr. Foley. Doctor?"

Scheele moved his shoulders apologetically. "I only have a small laboratory. It takes time to produce them. I could let you have four or five tomorrow, perhaps."

"Four or five?" Foley protested. "We want dozens of them. And we want them now!"

"There's a lot of prime targets loading, Captain," Koenig warned. He had brought a list of ships loading, or waiting to load, with cargoes of war supplies for Archangel. He passed it over.

Von Rintelen read down the list quickly and grimaced when he saw the nearness of the sailing dates, some within days. It was further confirmation of what the High Command suspected, that the Russians intended to step up their own spring offensive as soon as their supply position improved. At present, thanks to the Turkish resistance to the British attacks in the Dardanelles and to the pack ice in the north, munitions could only reach them via the single-track railroad from Siberia. But the ice had broken. "Yes," he said. "These cargoes must be destroyed at all costs."

Boniface coughed. "I'm sorry, Captain Rintelen. I think maybe I should wait in the other room." He was rising.

"You'll stay here, Mr. Boniface," von Rintelen said firmly. He had taken out his billfold. He peeled off some notes and handed them over. "We need advice, and we need it quickly."

Boniface counted the money, three hundred dollars. "For a start," he muttered, "you can forget about trying to blow up the docks. The U.S. Penal Code, Paragraph—"

"To hell with the Penal Code!" Bünz told him.

Boniface sucked in his cheeks and blew them out again. He took off his pince-nez and rubbed them against the side of his nose, then looked up. "It occurs to me, from what I was told earlier, that those, uh, devices will be harmless at the moment they are installed. If they are timed to, uh, function after ten or twelve days, then any destruction they cause will take place in mid Atlantic and therefore will not have been committed within U.S. territorial limits."

"Exactly," von Kleist agreed. "But of what use is that?"

"A mitigating factor, sir," Boniface said. "If the devices themselves were also constructed outside U.S. territorial limits—on German or neutral territory shall we say?—that would be another mitigating factor."

"I see your point, Mr. Boniface," von Rintelen said. "However, transporting them would be risky and take too long."

"I'm afraid that is the best I can do for you, Captain," Boniface said. His brown derby lay on his knees. Turning

319

it over, he folded the notes lengthways and slipped them into the lining. He rose and moved to the door, where he paused. "I really cannot be a party to the rest of this discussion," he apologized. "Of course, it could be argued that those interned liners and merchantmen of yours constitute German territory." He put on his hat and went out.

"Sodding ould fake!" Foley muttered. "What was all that about?"

Von Kleist and Koenig had understood almost as swiftly as von Rintelen and were leaning forward in excitement. "Is it possible?" Koenig asked.

"Why not?" von Rintelen answered. "They all have engine room workshops."

The others had now also understood. "Turn your ships into bomb factories, you mean?" Foley said.

"Not all of them. Just one. Secrecy is essential, and that's the only way we'll maintain it."

Dr. Scheele's shoulders were hunched and he bit nervously at his lower lip. "There is one thing," he blurted. "I—I don't want attention drawn to me. I can't spend every day on some ship."

"Don't worry, Doctor," von Rintelen told him. "If you give us the specifications, we'll cut the tubes to the right length and weld in the copper discs. They'll be delivered to you and collected. All you have to do is fill them." He checked his watch. He had just under an hour to get to Pabst's and should do it comfortably. If his meeting with the financier, Lamar, was successful, this would be a memorable day. Even without Lamar.

He thought of the next few weeks, of the Allied freighters that would sail, blacked out, preserving radio silence, on constant lookout for U-boats and surface raiders, while the acid would be eating away at those little copper discs hidden deep in their bellies. Soon he would have his own sinkings, his own tonnage to total up. Inside the deadline he had been set.

The feeling was good. If Lamar proved congenial, perhaps he could even relax, just for a few hours. It would be even better if he were dining with an attractive woman. He thought of the dark-haired young woman he had spoken to in the hotel, someone like her would do very nicely. Or she herself.

A pity she had a husband with her. Her children were very natural, charming, the boy about the same age as Marie-Louise. What ship were they sailing on? The *Cameronia*, bound for the port of Glasgow, Scotland. The thought of their crossing troubled him, so soon after linking them in his mind with his daughter. His was not work one could do if one thought of the people, the lives involved. He grunted in annoyance at his own sentimentality, but he knew he would have to give orders, very strict orders, that the *Cameronia* was not to be touched. At any rate, not on her next sailing.

"A league of nations," Sir Edward Grey said. "I have advocated such a development for some time—but that's quite another matter from what we are discussing, surely?" He looked inquiringly at his visitor, Ambassador Page.

"One could lead to the other," Page argued. "It could be the first real step toward peace." Dr. Dernburg, the German propaganda spokesman, had announced in Washington that Germany refused to give up Belgium, but would consider doing so if Great Britain accepted Colonel House's Freedom of the Seas. "What you're telling me," Page said seriously, "is that England will not agree to our proposal?"

"We cannot," Grey answered. "The fact that our people first heard of it from Dernburg's statement, with its threat to Belgium if we do not accept, means that it is seen as just another German attempt to beat the blockade. In short, I'm afraid there is little point in us even discussing it, for the British public would throw us out of office, if we did not reject it."

So that's that, Walter Page thought, as he sat in the cab taking him back to his Embassy. The Freedom of the Seas is a dead duck—thanks to the Germans jumping the gun. In his report to Washington he would put it in more diplomatic language, but that was the gist of it.

Page had done his duty. He had put forward the proposal and expanded the President's and Colonel House's statements, explained their reasoning, as fluently as he knew how. Now it was over, and he was profoundly grateful. The Freedom of the Seas was one of the most half-baked, impractical pieces of downright nonsense he had ever heard, the product of some kind of juvenile idealism that had no place in the real world. It was an aberration in House, whom he respected. That Wilson, whom he reverenced, should also champion it was incomprehensible.

A large number of Americans supported it because it would boost the profits to be made out of the war. Surely the President saw this crisis in the history of the world in higher terms than profit and loss? Above all, it was madness to expect the British to give up their one real strength, the Royal Navy which kept the Kaiser's fleet immobilized, and leave the Germans with their large army as military masters of Europe. No wonder that Bernstorff and the Wilhelmstrasse were delighted with Colonel House. Stopping the blockade would remove the only real fear that Germany had about the outcome of the war. And that Wilson should lend himself to it . . .

No one knew where America stood. The only certainty was that she desperately did not want to become involved, and refused to acknowledge that she already was, whether she liked it or not. Page would listen to no criticism of the President. "We only see one side of it here," he always said. "The President sees all sides, and from a higher viewpoint." But as each day went by and the Administration's position became harder to defend, he began to lose his own once-unconquerable confidence in the future.

Count von Bernstorff had hurried up from his Embassy in Washington after reading a secret report on von Rintelen's activities. They were staggering. Von Rintelen had already bought up an immense quantity of arms and ammunition to prevent it being available to the Allies, so much that he could never hope to export a tenth of it to Germany. He did not intend that it should all be wasted. Through Papen and his own contacts with Irish-American organizations, he had established communication with James Connolly of the Sinn Fein and Patrick Pearse of the Irish Republican Brotherhood and sent shipments of arms for them to South America, where they were transferred to neutral freighters and delivered as farm machinery to ports in Ireland. He had diverted all suspicion from E.V. Gibbons by taking orders from Russian purchasing agents to deliver huge supplies of tinned food and rifle ammunition. It was a daring double bluff, protecting his company from investigation by Allied and American Intelligence and swindling the Russians, who would wait and wait for supplies which would never arrive.

With the enthusiastic help of David Lamar, he had been put in touch with a number of union leaders who were ideologically in favor of an arms embargo, and with others who could be induced to campaign for one. They were in the process of forming an association to be known as Labor's National Peace Council, funded by von Rintelen. It was already beginning to attract thousands of members, from factory workers to dockers and farmers, and was potentially a powerful new propaganda weapon. Thanks to Lamar, it had an air of respectability by having at its head Frank Buchanan, Representative in Congress, and ex-Congressman H. Robert Fowler.

The fire bombs were now being manufactured, fashioned by the engineers of the *Friedrich der Grösse* at the North German Lloyd pier and finished by Dr. Scheele at his Hoboken laboratory. A further spectacular demonstration had proved they worked. Set with short-term copper fuses, a number had been smuggled by Austrian and German-American workers into selected factories and warehouses from Aenta, Indiana, to Seattle. The resulting fires had halted production and created considerable damage, and in no case had the cause been discovered. Bernstorff knew that the first batch had already been planted on munition ships and cargo boats, some of which had now sailed. "You realize there are passengers on some of those ships," he had said.

"I am only too aware of it, Your Excellency," von Rintelen had replied. "I can only repeat the words of Secretary of State Bryan, that those neutrals who travel on the ships of the fighting nations during a war do so at their own risk."

After von Rintelen had gone, Bernstorff sent for Albert, Dernburg and other heads of Embassy departments. "The situation is now one of extreme danger," he told them. "The war on merchant shipping is growing in intensity. If we win it soon, then victory will be ours. Yet precautions must be taken. We have already seen the unfortunate effect of one incident, the sinking of the *Falaba*. There are bound to be others, possibly with greater loss of life. At all costs we must prevent the United States from taking up arms against Germany, but neither the American government nor the American people have understood that our warnings are meant in good faith. They cannot ship goods or travel through a zone of war and expect total immunity simply because they are neutral. Accidents will happen. They must be warned and warned again, so that no blame can be attached to the Reich."

George Sylvester Viereck, a writer and German agent, currently editor of the propaganda newspaper *The Fatherland*, saw his cue. "The naval attaché has been urging us to increase our efforts in that direction," he said.

"We should publish our own warning as soon as possible," Geheimrat Albert agreed. Albert was privy councillor to the German Embassy and the Imperial government's fiscal agent in the U.S. "Do not forget that the *Lusitania* will be docking here in about three days."

Bernstorff ran his hand over his thinning, crinkly hair. "*Lieber Herr Gott*," he muttered.

Viereck was looking at the shipping advertisements in the back pages of the evening newspapers. "She's due to leave again at the end of next week, Saturday, May first. The *Cameronia* sails on the same date. And the *New York*, an American ship."

"Then we must act quickly!" Bernstorff urged. "What form should our warning take? You're the newspaperman."

"A straightforward notice to passengers intending to travel to Europe. In the form of an advertisement."

"How soon could it be arranged?"

"Well, for maximum coverage, it would have to be inserted in forty to fifty major papers," Viereck explained. "That might take two days, three at the most. Certainly by this weekend."

"Good," Bernstorff approved. "Then people will have a clear week to think about it, before that sailing date."

In the murmurs of agreement, Dernburg said, "If it's printed on the ocean travel page, it might be near Cunard's *Lusitania* advertisement and so make its point more strongly."

Walther Schwieger was having lunch in the Adlon in Berlin with Otto Hersing. They had meant it to be a quick meal before Hersing returned to Wilhelmshaven and Schwieger to Emden, but the conversation proved so interesting to both of them that hours slipped by. They had run into each other purely by chance near the Admiralty Building.

Schwieger had managed two days at home while the U 20 was being refitted after her recent mauling. Hersing's U 21 was also being completely refitted, he explained. They were not close friends, but both had been feeling that strange sensation of having become aliens in normal surroundings.

"You were damned lucky on that last trip, Walther," Hersing said.

"I was," Schwieger admitted. "One shell at a slightly different angle or one of the bigger ones finding our range sooner and that would have been it." He studied the bubbles in his narrow fluted glass. "In my report to Bauer, I told him we should consider the Straits of Dover to be permanently closed from now on, and that no one should be ordered to attempt the passage again."

"Thank the Lord for that," Hersing chuckled.

"Why?"

"I said exactly the same thing myself in my report," Hersing confided. "And that I refused to risk the passage again unnecessarily. I was afraid I was the only one and that they'd send me back to minesweeping or something."

Schwieger smiled. "About as much chance of that as of them asking Hindenburg to take over running the railroads." Hersing toasted him, acknowledging the compliment. Schwieger drank off his glass in return. "Anyway, I'll soon be trying out the passage round the north of Scotland. My patrol's been ordered out again in three days."

Hersing hesitated. "So—yes, so has mine," he said.

Schwieger noticed the momentary hesitation, but attached no importance to it. If Hersing preferred to put it out of his mind, that was his affair. He took the bottle from the ice bucket before the waiter could move in. "I think there's just about two glasses left." He filled Hersing's and his own, and stood the bottle upside down in the ice. "To Otto," he said.

"Otto," Hersing repeated, and they touched their glasses together.

They set down their empty glasses and there was a pause. "Well, I suppose," Schwieger said.

"I suppose," Hersing shrugged. Neither wished to be the first to break it up. "It's been very enjoyable, Walther," Hersing said. "Really, most enjoyable."

"I agree," Schwieger smiled. "We must do it again. Perhaps not in such an elegant setting. Somewhere in Emden or Wilhelmshaven."

"I wonder when," Hersing murmured.

"Oh, no hurry. Sometime when we have a little longer between patrols than they're giving us these days."

Hersing seemed uncomfortable. "I didn't mean that." He glanced round and back. "I'll tell you something, but, mind you, it's as secret as the color of the Empress of Russia's drawers." Schwieger grinned. The phrase had been a favorite of an old instructor, years ago when they had been at submarine school. Hersing smiled briefly, too, then was serious again. "I've been ordered to take the U 21 to Constantinople."

"The Dardanelles?" Schwieger had spoken more loudly than he meant to, in his surprise. He lowered his voice. "To help the Turks?"

"Apparently, we've promised them support," Hersing said. "No one will be on the lookout for a U-boat in the Eastern Mediterranean. With luck I should get some of those British battleships."

"Before they know what's hit them," Schwieger added, excited. He felt a rush of envy. What an opportunity! "But no U-boat can sail that far. How will you get there?"

"That's the problem," Hersing admitted. "There's no safe harbor between Wilhelmshaven and the Austrian port of Cattaro, on the Adriatic."

"That's still thousands of miles."

"Four thousand," Hersing nodded. "I've arranged to rendezvous with a Hamburg-Amerika steamer off the coast of Spain, to pick up oil. If she turns up and we get past Gibraltar, we should just have enough fuel to reach Cattaro. A quick overhaul in dock, and on to the east."

"I'd give anything to be coming with you," Schwieger breathed.

Hersing smiled. "I wish you were. The pair of us. Think what we could do, if we were hunting together."

It was not such a fanciful idea. As he thought about it on his way home to pick up his bag, Schwieger told the driver to take him, instead, to the Admiralty. He had an old acquaintance in Strategic Planning, Hans Feldt, tubby, self-important, an incurable gossip.

"So you know about Hersing?" Feldt said. "That's supposed to be under strict security. Oh, well, I suppose you underwater fellows all chatter among yourselves." He chuckled. "I'd give a lot to see the faces of the Tommies and the Frogs when he bobs up in the Sea of Marmara. Eh? And they start to bob down. Touch wood!" He tapped his desk. "Yes. I've no doubt that he'll make it. Largely because nobody will be watching for him. Of course it's tough to be the first."

"The first?" Schwieger queried.

Feldt's voice dropped nearly to a whisper. "This is strictly between us. But I know you're as safe as the Deutsche Bank, Walther. The fact is, the one thing the Allied bombardment of the Dardanelles has proved is that you can't take a series of strong forts purely with naval guns. You have to have troops to back it up. There's a whole fleet of transports off Alexandria. If Hersing makes good time, he'll have first crack at them. If he sinks the battleships, the transports will have no big guns to support them. The others will go for supply ships and so on."

Schwieger had tensed. "Others?"

"Well, of course," Feldt said. "He'll need other U-boats to back him up. As you know, we can't spare many. But they'll have to be the best. They have one hell of a job to do."

As soon as Schwieger arrived at the base, he went straight to the operations room, but there were no new orders for him. In the morning, he reported to Fregattenkapitän Bauer, who merely repeated that the next patrol would leave on the twenty-fifth of April. All day he kept checking with the signals officer, but no orders detaching him for special duties were received. By evening, he had begun to realize that they would not come.

He had been passed over. The U 20 had been passed over for the most challenging mission of the undersea war. He sat alone in his quarters and the injustice of it angered him, not for himself, but for his men and the U 20. What was it Feldt had said, without knowing how bitterly it would be remembered? "We can't spare many. They'll have to be the best." And Schwieger had been passed over.

Chapter 19

Livvy Fletcher had fallen in love with New York. She had not expected that she would. She had not known *what* to expect, since she was not used to cities.

The bustle, the jostling crowds in the streets and the ceaseless traffic, carriages and hacks, trolleys, motor buses, automobiles, trucks and pushbikes and handcarts, rattling, hooting and blaring, the screech of brakes, the clanging of bells, tires rumbling over cobbles and the intermittent roaring rush of the Elevated Railroads, all combined to bewilder her senses. She caught herself gaping like a real country cousin at the electric signs in Broadway, at the staggering variety of stores and display windows, the styles, the street vendors and restaurants, cigar stores, bars, hatters, jewelers and dry goods stores, which had puzzled her until she found out they sold drapery and dress materials. It wasn't the size of the buildings, she told Matt, the skyscrapers, she had been prepared for that, it was the sheer number of people, all hurrying and milling, as if each one of them was on some vital journey that could not be interrupted for one second.

On the third day, Matt had to attend the first of several meetings which had been arranged by his company and, with the children becoming restive at having to stay indoors, Livvy knew she would have to take her courage in both hands. Studying the map, she saw that if she could get them onto the Third Avenue El heading downtown, they could just sit tight until it reached the terminus at South Ferry. They did not have to change anywhere and nothing could go wrong. Everything, in fact, went very smoothly, but they stopped at so many stations that she became anxious and asked the old lady seated next to her if indeed the train did only go to South Ferry and no further. "I'm a stranger, you see," she explained.

"No, you are not," the old lady said. "Nobody's a stranger in New York. Or rather, everybody is a stranger. So you don't got to worry."

"I'm sorry?" Livvy asked.

"What's New York?" the old lady said. "A lotta bricks and glass and concrete? That's nothing. It's people, that's New York. And if there's ten million people, there's ten million New Yorks. It's one city that's for everybody, what you make it. A home, a playground, an office, a cemetery. What you make it. So you don't know your way around, that's a different thing. You'll learn. But don't ever feel a stranger. It's your city. Enjoy it. As for the question—if this car goes further than South Ferry, you'd better be able to swim."

Mrs. Rabinowitz lived in the Borough of the Bronx and was going to visit her son, who owned a hat and gown retail house on Division Street. She gave Peter and Diana some of the brightly striped candies she was taking to her grandchildren and warned them to brush their teeth as soon as they arrived back at the hotel. She herself was a widow, whose husband had died ten years ago of a heart attack, after hearing of the death of two of their granddaughters in the burning of the steamer *Slocum* in the East River. Neither she nor her married sister in Jersey City would cross water from that day and had not seen each other for years, until the opening of the River Tunnels. As she left at her stop, she patted Livvy's cheek. "Remember. It's your city. Enjoy it." She paused and shook her head. "You're very pretty. But you don't mind a little advice? You need to put on some weight."

Livvy and the children had a marvelous morning. They walked through Battery Park and visited the Aquarium to see the sea lions and giant turtles. Livvy remembered what Mrs. Rabinowitz had said, and on the way home chose another route by a series of streetcars, turning it into a game for the children and stopping at the soda fountain in a midtown drugstore, where they all had cream doughnuts and chocolate ice cream sodas. Matt was waiting when they arrived back at the hotel. "I've just discovered I'm a New Yorker," she said. "And I enjoy it."

He had booked a table for lunch and could not understand why Diana insisted on going up to her room and brushing her teeth first. "Because Mrs. Rabinowitz said we had to," Diana explained.

"Who on earth is Mrs. Rabinowitz?" Matt asked.

Livvy smiled. "My guardian angel. Do you think I ought to put on some weight?"

"Not an ounce." Matt was puzzled. "What's been going on?"

"It's a long story. I'll tell you at lunch," Livvy said.

The next six days had been magical. Matt took her shopping for clothes to Lord and Taylor's, Macy's, and Wanamaker's. They went boating on Central Park Lake and twice to the Bronx Zoo, so that Peter could see the herds of elks and bisons. They took the ferry to the Statue of Liberty and spent one whole day at Coney Island, where Diana was sick with excitement, but refused to be taken back home. In the evenings the hotel provided a babysitting service and Matt and Livvy dined out and went to the theater and, once, to a public rehearsal of a New York Symphony Concert at Carnegie Hall, conducted by Walter Damrosch. Matt was as attentive and loving as though they had only been married for six months. He had threatened to spoil her and he did, with flowers and new dresses and hats and shoes. She felt cherished and pampered, but best of all was just having him with her night and day, to explore the canyons of the city with him and the children and laugh with them when he pointed out funny things and made up his stories, to drive home from the restaurant or theater leaning against his solid shoulder and wake in the morning with his arm round her and watch him as he lay sleeping.

That second Saturday morning he had a surprise for her, something she had not done for years. Early, before even the children were awake, he took her to Central Park where he had arranged to hire two horses. She was surprised to see how many people were on the bridle paths already. "The Liver Brigade," Matt said, and she laughed as they trotted between the lakes and on toward the reservoir.

"Well, well," Matt murmured, slowing down. "There's your mash."

Livvy did not understand him at first, then looked ahead and recognized the tall man she had met in the elevator at the hotel. She had noticed him three or four times after that and had pointed him out to Matt. He always smiled and bowed when he saw her, and once when the children were waiting for her by the kiosk in the lobby, she found them sucking sticks of almond rock which he had bought for them. "He says it's his little girl's favorite," Diana explained.

He was riding a superb roan mare and looked very elegant in faultless clothes that showed off his strong shoulders and narrow waist. He had stopped to talk to an older man and an attractive young woman in an open barouche. When he glanced up and saw her, Livvy could not mistake the admiration in his greenish-gray eyes. He smiled and raised his hat.

Matt touched the brim of his cap and Livvy inclined her head with a faint answering smile as they trotted by. She felt ridiculously pleased that Matt also looked very neat in his needlecord pants and brown-check tweed coat over a black high-necked sweater and that she had worn her new rust-colored traveling dress with its matching fitted jacket that would pass anywhere as a riding habit. She could hear Matt chuckling softly and knew what he was thinking. "I don't encourage him," she protested, embarrassed and half laughing, too.

"Oh no, not a bit," he mocked.

"Anyway, I think he's charming."

"Too smooth by half," Matt said.

Von Rintelen watched them ride away.

"Who was that?" Bernstorff asked.

"Oh, just an acquaintance."

"I admire your taste," Bernstorff murmured, and the young woman with him rapped his hand teasingly.

Matt and Livvy were exhilarated by their ride and had a race along the gallops. He almost, but not quite, let her win and admitted it was a very close thing at the end. "You arrogant brute!" she laughed, and he nearly pulled her out of the saddle as he kissed her.

When they arrived back at their room, Livvy was glowing. "I wish there was time for a shower," she told him.

"Why don't you have one?" he suggested. "The kids'll wait another quarter of an hour." The door through to Peter and Diana's room was still closed.

Livvy flung off her clothes and hurried into the bathroom adjoining their bedroom. The hotwater shower with a temperature you could regulate yourself was a luxury that would have made the trip for her on its own. She pulled on the frilled waterproof bonnet which Matt said made her look like old Mother Hubbard and stepped into the cabinet. She always turned the dial right up to the red mark at first, as hot as she could bear it, then gradually lowered the temperature until the sting of the cold water made her relaxed body tauten and tingle.

She did not have time for the full ritual now, so only gave herself a few seconds of the biting heat before bringing it down to a more temperate level where she could soap and rinse herself comfortably. She was just allowing herself two minutes to relax when she heard the door of the cabinet snick open. In a startled reflex she dropped the bar of soap and clutched her full breasts with both hands, swiveling her hips away from the opening door. She glanced round over her shoulder and saw that it was Matt, as naked as she was. "What are you doing?" she gasped.

He was looking at the line of her back sweeping down to the swell of her haunches, the long, sleek thighs. A tendril of dark hair had slipped from the elastic at the nape of her neck. He lifted it with one finger and tucked it up inside the bonnet. "I'd say that was a pretty superfluous question."

He stepped inside and fitted himself against her wet back, his hands slipping round to support the soft weight of her breasts. "But Matt," she whispered, "the children. They'll be in here any minute."

"Not with the door locked," he grinned.

Diana was grumpy at having to wait so long for breakfast. "Why didn't you take us riding, too?" she complained. "And why didn't you open the door?"

"Something came up," Matt said, and Livvy giggled.

She was lighthearted over breakfast and soon cheered Diana up, but Matt grew serious. He had picked up a morning paper and was reading the first brief account of the Canadians at Ypres. Alone at first, then with detachments of English and Indians, they had blocked the German breakthrough. Thousands were dead and wounded.

"Poison gas?" Livvy queried, horrified.

"What does it do to you?" Peter asked.

"It sort of chokes you, so you can't breathe," Matt told him, "And—"

"No, Matt, it's too horrible. Please!" Livvy begged. "Not now, anyway."

Matt looked at Peter and Diana, who was sitting with her head sunk between her shoulders, scared. "All right. All right," he agreed. "It's a long way away, and we can't do anything about it." He swung his head back for a moment and breathed out, then he folded the paper and laid it aside. "So fine, now, troops," he smiled, "what are we going to do today?"

"Let's go up to Bronx Park," Peter said.

"No, not again," Matt decided. "It's Diana's turn. What would you like to do, Princess?"

Diana's mouth rounded at the thrill of having to choose. "Anything I like, Daddy? I want to see the big ship we're going to sail on."

Peter smiled in surprise. "That's a very good idea!"

"Of course it is," Matt approved, and winked to Diana.

"Will it be in dock?" Livvy asked.

"It should be," Matt said. "We can have a look at the street market in Bleecker Street and a couple of other things and walk right through to the North River. We should come out just by the *Cameronia*'s pier."

They took a taxicab the length of Fifth Avenue to Washington Square and Livvy discovered yet another New York. The whole city was rushing ahead, tearing down, developing, desperate to get to tomorrow. This was the first place where she felt any real sense of the past. Many of the old houses had been demolished, but the stately broad-fronted mansions with white marble steps leading up to their doors, set back from the sidewalk behind trim box hedges, still remained on the north side. Their warm old brick fronts, partly clad in climbing wisterias whose purple, butterfly-shaped flowers were just unfolding in the sun, gave a sense of mellower, more tranquil times and the square's character was set by them. Everywhere were trees. There seemed to be more birds than anywhere else in the city and Diana cried out, pointing to the flash of scarlet tanagers in the branches of a sycamore.

Matt and Peter looked at the vista of Fifth Avenue through the Centennial Memorial Arch, and Peter craned his neck to try to make out above the frieze of garlands and the projecting marble cornice the words carved across the very top. "It's something that George Washington said," Matt told him. " 'Let us raise a standard to which the wise and the honest can repair. The event is in the hands of God.' " He paused. "Well, that's what he said, anyway."

South of the square, they were suddenly in the Italian Quarter and after two blocks came to Bleecker Street. It was much more exotic than Livvy had expected, the painted barrows and handcarts of the vendors piled high with fruits and vegetables, great mounds of all sorts of pasta, white, green and yellow, the scent of spices and coffee stalls and others selling fresh-made doughnuts and apple fritters, the racks of secondhand clothes, trestles covered with cakes and pies and more types of bread loaves than she had ever seen. The people in the street were fascinating, the young women in bright flounced skirts and shawls, the older ones in black with black headscarves and the men with colorful waistcoats and bandanas round their necks, full mustaches and some with rings in their ears, and the noise of them all shouting, bargaining, flirting, arguing, singing, laughing. Matt bought Peter a wooden Indian puppet with a tin tomahawk and a headdress of real feathers and, for Diana, a Florentine doll in a peasant dress with legs and arms of twisted string. They all had big cornets of striped ice cream and shared a bag of salted pistachio nuts.

It was further to walk than they had thought and the children were lagging by the time Matt whistled up a hack, which carried them through to West Street and dropped them on the broad space by the Cunard and White Star line docks on the North River. The *Cameronia* was at her pier, a medium-sized passenger and cargo ship, and Diana was very impressed with her and with the stacks of crates and packing cases waiting to be hoisted on board. "Is she going to carry all these?" she asked. "Can you see our trunks?"

Matt smiled. "I think they'll still be stored in the sheds somewhere, pet."

"Look! Look, Daddy . . ." Peter breathed.

Even as they turned to look where he was pointing, they

heard a strange noise. All the ferries and tugs and barges, all the ships in midstream and on the east side of the river, had begun to sound their horns and hooters and bells, the wail of sirens mingling with the whoop-whoop of tugs and the blare of steam whistles. Over on the west side, from the Hoboken docks, there was silence. Into view, in the center of the channel, came a ship like no other they had ever seen, vast, yet incomparably graceful, her white superstructure over her black-painted body towering above everything in sight and four huge black funnels soaring high above all. Many-colored signal flags ran in lines up to her mastheads fore and aft. A pilot's flag waved above her signal bridge, and the Stars and Stripes on her control bridge. At her stern fluttered a giant Union Jack. As she advanced, her massive bulk blotted out the prospect of the Jersey shore.

Knots of people were hurrying to the Cunard piers and they cheered as the great ship's horn boomed out in answer to the welcome of her lesser sisters. The Fletchers caught the excitement and moved with the others, watching as the giant liner swung her nose toward the east shore.

"What is it, Daddy?" Peter asked eagerly. Beside him, Diana was hopping up and down, waving.

"Only one ship it can be, son," Matt said. "That's the *Lusitania*." Livvy slipped her arm through his and hugged it, as thrilled as the children.

The dark water of the Hudson churned white as the *Lusitania*'s powerful reversing propellers began to revolve, arresting her momentum and slowly drawing her back in a curve to the west shore. They could see people lining the deck rails, all waving and cheering, and above the din they could make out the sound of an orchestra somewhere on her promenade deck.

On the *Lusitania*'s bridge, Will Turner had taken over from the American harbor pilot for these last moments. He paced out onto the starboard observation wing to check his angle and passed back a fractional course correction through Third Officer Lewis to First Officer Arthur Jones and the helmsman. That done, he took his pipe from his pocket, lit it and watched the approach without another word until he judged the exact second to stop the reversing propellers. There were several minutes of silence on the bridge, then on his order the turbines roared for a few seconds while the main propellers halted the reverse momentum. The *Lusitania* slid forward and her starboard side kissed the fenders protecting her from the concrete wall of Cunard's Pier 54. Her seamen were lowering outsize hawsers for the dockworkers to attach to bollards on the pier and First Officer Jones rang down to stop all engines.

Quartermaster Johnston was on duty on the bridge and murmured to himself admiringly, "And that, my boy, is how you get to be a commodore of the line."

Turner gave a small grunt of satisfaction. It had been nothing like his own record docking time of nineteen minutes, but it had been smooth enough. He could hear the cheering of the crowd that always assembled to watch the *Lusy* come in. Some of the passengers had spotted him up on the wing and were waving their congratulations. He saluted them back, gravely. The uniformed ship's orchestra had finished "God Save the King" and were playing a token chorus of "The Star-Spangled Banner." He stood to attention, hearing the rumble as the stevedores rolled the heavy shore-to-ship gangplanks into place; then he walked back into the bridge house. "Welcome again to America, gentlemen," he said.

Already the passengers were lining up at the main and steerage gangplanks, although they would have to wait until their baggage was unloaded before they could go ashore and clear Customs. All that side was organized by Staff Captain Anderson and Purser McCubbin. Anderson was also responsible for loading and unloading cargo, as well as his more social duties during the voyage. Before joining him to bid farewell to the most influential passengers, Turner had half an hour to complete his formalities with the pilot and have a cup of tea in peace. It would be early afternoon before he could go ashore himself, although he was impatient to see Cunard's representative, Charles Sumner, to make certain that full coaling would take place as usual and, more importantly, that Sumner was doing all he could to find extra crewmen. Serious, and becoming more so as more transferred to the navy, was the shortage of able seamen. It had been calculated that a minimum of seventy-seven were needed for the efficient running of the ship, and he had completed this crossing with only forty-one, out of a crew of nearly seven hundred. Something would have to be done.

At last he was free. He had a snack lunch and a glass of beer with Archie Bryce, who had already finished his engine room report. The Chief Engineer's heavy body slumped in his chair with tiredness. "Oh, everything's in working order and bearing up, Will," he explained, "but this weekly turn-around leaves us no time for a proper overhaul. I have to do what I can, as we go along. And with not enough fully trained engineers for normal maintenance."

"I know you do your best, Archie. None better," Turner said. "I appreciate it."

"It just means longer hours," Bryce said. "The real worry is, with one whole boiler room out of action, the strain on the other three, if we have to maintain maximum speed for any length of time."

"I don't see how that should arise," Turner told him. "The Germans have only one surface raider left afloat, the *Karls-ruhe*, and she operates in the Caribbean. And we're nearly twice as fast as any submarine." He smiled. "We'll try to keep her cruising nice and smoothly. The passengers will appreciate it, and we won't tell them it's all for you."

Turner changed into his civilian suit, took his bowler hat and headed down to the service gangway. The passengers had all landed and the crowd dispersed. The small amount of cargo the *Lusitania* carried on her outward voyage was being unloaded. As he stopped for a word with the Purser, James McCubbin, a friendly little man, he saw some of the temporary crew already going ashore. One of them caught his eye. He knew all his crewmen, even those who only signed on for one crossing, but this was someone he had just not noticed, heavy-faced, in his late thirties or early forties, his short dark hair worn flat to the skull with a cowlick over his forehead. He was fairly ordinary except for a trick of walking with his chin tucked down and his right shoulder slightly raised, and it was odd, because Turner was sure he recognized him from somewhere else. "Who's that man, the third one?" he asked.

"Temporary Steward, Second Class, Captain," McCubbin said. "Name of Thorne, Charles Thorne."

Turner snapped his fingers. "That's it! I was certain I

knew him. He's sailed with me before, steward on the *Transylvania*, that trip I was chased into Queenstown by U-boats. I wonder why I haven't spotted him before this?"

"He kept himself very much to himself, Captain," McCubbin said. "Quite a good worker, but not one to push himself forward."

Turner was sorry that Thorne and the others were leaving. All trained men were valuable nowadays, and stewards were a special problem. Many of them only signed on to get a free passage to the United States. Once they landed, they often disappeared.

Charles Thorne had his grip examined by the customs officer and was passed through the gate. He nodded goodbye to the others and walked leisurely down 14th Street to the Ninth Avenue El, which he rode uptown to 104th Street, where he transferred to the subway, which he rode all the way back downtown to Bowling Green. After leaving the subway, he watched the exit for twenty minutes before crossing to the Ninth Avenue El again, which he took as far as West Houston Street, then walked under its track to Leroy Street, leading to the river and the docks from which he had started. After checking again that he had not been shadowed, he went down to 20 Leroy Street, a nondescript brownstone boardinghouse, where he let himself in with his own key.

He went silently up the linoleum-covered stairs to the second floor and he unlocked another door to a back room. He stopped, tensing when he saw a man sitting in a chair by the table, watching him. His right hand was out of sight below the level of the tabletop. "Any trouble?" he asked.

"None."

The man at the table was Paul Koenig. He rose, bringing up his hand, which held a Luger. He clicked the safety catch back on, put the pistol in his inside breast pocket and smiled. "It's good to see you, Curt. The Captain is waiting. He is anxious to hear your report."

Charles Thorne's real name was Curt Thummel, one of German Intelligence's most trusted agents. His apparently slow, reticent manner concealed a sharp and active mind and a strong streak of violence. Boy-Ed had devised a near perfect cover for him. With an American passport and serving as a steward on Transatlantic liners, he was able to slip in and out of English ports unsuspected. For months now, he had been traveling between London and Liverpool, supposedly seeking for employment and actually gathering information on arms supplies, troop movements and naval dispositions.

With Koenig he crossed in the ferry to Hoboken and the Hamburg-Amerika docks. They were heading for the stateroom on the *Vaterland*, the naval attaché's secret office.

Boy-Ed rose and shook hands when Koenig showed Thummel in. "Welcome back," he said. "Your reports have been invaluable."

Thummel stood to attention. "Thank you, sir."

Boy-Ed smiled. "Now, I'm sure you have more for me, but first I want you to give us an exact description of the guns the *Lusitania* carries."

Thummel hesitated. "I'm afraid I cannot, sir. I did not see any."

Boy-Ed frowned. "Not?"

"I saw mountings for naval guns, twelve concealed mounts on the shelter deck, others on the forecastle and after deck. There is a forward section where the guns themselves may be stored, but it is permanently locked and under guard. I could not penetrate it."

Boy-Ed was rocked back. He took one of his Turkish cigarettes from his case, tapped both ends and lit it. "Well, at least you have seen the concealed mountings. But Berlin most particularly and urgently wants a description of her guns as confirmation of their existence."

"Well, sir, I was careful to have my discharge papers signed by the Staff Captain on board," Thummel said. "I'm sure he would take me on again and, somehow, on either crossing I would get into that forward section."

Boy-Ed was tempted, but shook his head. "No," he decided. "I honor you for volunteering, but you have already been lucky to survive so long without being caught. We must not overstretch your luck." Besides, he told himself, it would take too long. It had seemed the perfect solution, to pull one of his best agents out of England before he was detected and to bring him back on the *Lusitania*, killing two birds with one stone, and it was damnably annoying that it had been only partially successful. "No. You now know the layout of the *Lusitania* very well and that is a great advantage. Among the three of us, we must work out some way to get the information we need. We have seven days."

Seven days, Charles Frohman thought. In seven days he would be sailing for England. The trip was overdue. He had business affairs to attend to, new London productions to mount. His closest friend and dearest companion, Jamie Barrie, was writing a new play for him. They had done many together over the years, from *Quality Street* to the worldwide triumph of *Peter Pan*, which no one else had believed in. Because of the war, there was a noticeable slump in the English theater and his presence there cost money, his rooms at the Savoy Hotel, his suite of offices in Waterloo Place, the manager and secretaries, and his nineteen-year lease on the Duke of York's Theater in St. Martin's Lane. Friends advised him to cut his losses and pull out, but he was convinced that business would improve. "Besides, they're going through hell over there," he said. "They deserve distraction and the best entertainment the theaters can provide."

He panted and shifted his position to ease the pain in his knee. The friends were right on one account. He certainly had more than enough to keep him busy here in the States for the moment.

He was seated at his desk in his office on the third floor of Broadway's Empire Theater, which he owned. The theater . . . it was his life, his love, his fortune and fulfillment. Over the years he had staged nearly seven hundred productions and almost single-handedly raised the American drama to the status of art. Considered for so long to be disreputable and socially unacceptable, actors and producers were now seen as members of an honored profession, because of him. And they revered him for it, knowing there was no one kinder, more tactful and understanding, or with a surer and more constructive artistic judgment.

It had not been easy, the struggle since the days when he used to serve with his brother Daniel behind the counter of his father's small cigar store in Lower Broadway after school, and the days when he worked as treasurer and publicity man for a traveling minstrel show, prancing in a silk hat in the gaudy parade through each new town and living on fifteen-cent meals. And the struggle had continued through his first productions, which revolutionized scenic effects and created theatrical stars, but made no money.

Now he had touring companies filled with stars all over America, an interest in many theaters, and the Empire, which was his pride. His production of *A Celebrated Case*, the fruit of his reconciliation with Belasco, had just opened there and was a hit. *The Shadow*, in which Ethel Barrymore's performance had confirmed her position as the leading young dramatic actress, had now moved to Boston, where it was repeating its success. He had other plans for her for later in the year, and new plays commissioned for his stable of leading players, from William Gillette to Nazimova. All his present ventures were flourishing except one, and that was the one he had most wanted to succeed.

Still, it had been worth it.

He shifted again. Three years ago, he had fallen on the porch of his converted farmhouse at White Plains, in Westchester County, damaging his right knee. He returned to his apartment in the Hotel Knickerbocker and thought that a day or two in bed would cure him, but he developed articular rheumatism, which became acute. He was bedridden for over six months, feverish and helpless, the excruciating pain spreading to all his joints and muscles, his temperature falling, then rising again alarmingly as his lungs and heart became affected. His friends were frightened, the few who were allowed to see him reporting how wasted and weak he was. Then one morning, using almost the last of his strength, he reached for the telephone beside his bed and assumed control of his empire again. He desperately needed something to help him to forget the pain and began to plan productions, holding rehearsals in his drawing room. The casts never realized the torture he was in as he advised and applauded and encouraged them. His devoted valet, however, and his most intimate friends who took turns sitting with him at night always knew when it was becoming unbearable, for he would get them to play the latest hit tune, "Alexander's Rag-Time Band," over and over again on the phonograph, often as many as twenty times.

In his slow convalescence, the grinding pain gradually

faded, except in his right leg, which ached constantly. He refused to become a permanent invalid and forced himself to walk with a stick, shuffling and crying out on his own, until he could control himself sufficiently to appear in public. The two blocks down Broadway from the Knickerbocker to the Empire were almost his limit, but it meant he could attend rehearsals and performances and again be a part of his special world.

The door of the office had been left open a crack and beyond it he could hear the murmur of voices, which meant that his visitor had arrived. He did not want the coming meeting to be formal, so he pushed himself to his feet. He tried to keep his weight off his right leg, but the movement sent a lance of pain through his ankle and knee. As he grunted and paused, he saw the painting of Maude on the shelf behind his desk, Maude Adams in her Napoleonic costume for *L'Aiglon*. She had been his Peter Pan, his Joan of Arc. He had made her into a star. Like all the others who worked for him, there was no written contract between them. With Maude, a contract would in any case never have been needed. She had his heart, instead. The painter had captured the delicacy of her features, the slight downward turn at the outer corners of her eyes, which made her expression so serious, so wistful. He wished she were not on tour so far away, yet the knowledge that she would always come to him if he needed her was comforting. He would not admit it, not even to himself, especially not to himself, yet the greatest wrench at leaving New York in a week's time was the thought that it separated him even farther from Maude.

He had just sat himself on the couch when his secretary opened the door. His visitor was a serious young man, trying to look composed, although Frohman could tell that he was troubled and nervous. Frohman smiled and waved a hand. "Good morning!" he called. "How nice of you to drop by!"

Justus Miles Forman was a novelist, a writer of popular romances, who had sent his first play to Frohman a few weeks ago. Frohman read it in the morning and had its author tracked down and brought to this very room in the afternoon. The office was spacious and fairly austere, high-ceilinged, with an imposing stone fireplace on which stood a marble bust of Napoleon. In one corner there was a grand piano, and in the middle was Frohman's plain mahogany desk. Busts and pictures of his favorite stars were ranged on the chest-high bookcases and the shelves were filled with bound volumes, which gave the office the air of a study, except that the volumes were all copies of plays Frohman had presented. And there on the couch as he was now, with his left leg tucked underneath him, sat the Czar of the Theater himself, plump, squat-bodied, his hair thinning and receding over his full-lipped, moon-shaped face.

It was all very daunting and Forman had prepared himself for a disappointment, a condescending lecture on the art of Drama. Without preamble, Frohman had shaken him by saying, "I am going to produce your play. There's nothing to discuss. A manager often discusses at great length the play that he does not intend to produce. Therefore all I have to tell you is that your play is accepted. I have already engaged the chief actors, and the scenery was ordered two hours ago. I am glad to present a play on this timely subject, but I am especially glad that it is an American who wrote it."

The play was called *The Hyphen* and had opened this past Monday, having set a new record for speed in mounting a first-class Broadway production. With the Empire not available, it had been booked into the Knickerbocker Theater and the First Night was crammed. Unfortunately, despite Frohman's belief in it and Forman's hope, it was a resounding failure.

This Saturday morning, Forman had walked slowly past the front-of-house billboards and pictures for the last time and up to the corner to the Knickerbocker Grill, where he had a couple of solitary drinks. He sat at the bar, looking at Maxfield Parrish's new mural of Old King Cole, which was supposed to cheer everyone up. It depressed him. Frohman was the King and he was one of the Fiddlers who had struck a wrong note. After his third drink, he asked for the telephone and rang the office.

"Why don't you grab a seat, Justus?" Frohman suggested.

"I guess you know why I'm here, Mr. Frohman," Forman said. "I want to apologize for landing you with such a turkey."

"Turkeys are something I reserve for Thanksgiving," Frohman said.

He was smiling, and Forman felt a twinge of bitterness. It was all right for him, with hundreds of productions all over the country. One more or less didn't matter. But he had to say his piece. "I want to thank you for your faith in my play and assure you that I don't need more than one lesson in failure. I won't trouble you again."

Frohman frowned. "Do you think it was a failure? I don't. I think the audiences weren't up to it. And that there were certain people determined not to give it a chance."

The Hyphen had its setting in Pennsylvania. It was a play about war and the conflict of loyalties in a German-American community contacted by secret agents, a serious attempt to examine a theme which Frohman understood very clearly. It was not only topical and well-written, he felt it was his patriotic duty to present it. There was trouble from the first day of rehearsals, threatening phone calls and letters warning him that any theater in which it appeared would be burned down. He was friendly with many members of the diplomatic world, and one evening the German military and naval attachés cornered him. "Why are you lending yourself to Allied propaganda, Charles?" Papen asked. The first night was packed, but whole blocks of seats had been bought by the Embassy for German sympathizers, who jeered and cat-called, drowning out the play's arguments and making it hard for the rest of the audience to follow. The new Broadway subway was under construction and the periodic sound of blasting outside added to the tension, being mistaken for bombs. Next morning's confused or unfavorable notices kept audiences away.

"It is a fine play and you have nothing to reproach yourself with," Frohman said. "I only pray that people who have ignored it or condemned it are not forced to look back one day and see that it was prophetic."

"Yet you are going to take it off," Forman said.

Frohman raised both palms in admission. "It would be economic madness not to." He smiled. "But I'm still convinced it's worthwhile. I shall let it run here for one more week, then transfer it to Boston. It may get a better reception there."

Forman winced, becoming uncomfortably aware of his egotistical lack of gratitude. "I don't—don't know how to thank you."

345

"You don't have to," Frohman told him. "I enjoy it. I go every night. Well, what are you planning to do now?"

"Write something else, I suppose. Only not a play."

"Why not?" Frohman asked. "You have talent." He paused. It would be tragic if the play's rejection made the younger man lose his confidence. "I'll tell you what. I'm sailing to England at the end of next week. Why don't you come with me? I'll make the arrangements."

Forman blinked in astonishment. "To England? You're inviting me? What for?"

Frohman smiled. "I want some more plays out of you. As I said, I believe you have talent—but it needs to be developed. I know you're an established novelist. You understand character and have a gift for dialogue, but to be a playwright takes more than being born with a flair. Like most other things, there's a craft to be mastered."

"Yes, I get that," Forman said. "But why England?"

"Well, I have business to take care of there," Frohman explained, "and I want to catch up on the British theater scene. We could talk over any ideas you may have. And I'd like you to meet one or two friends of mine, Jamie Barrie, Granville Barker, Bernard Shaw. You could learn from them. So will you come?"

It was the opportunity of a lifetime. "I—I'd be honored to," Forman stammered. "Again, I—I can't think what to say, Mr. Frohman."

"My friends call me Charles." Frohman clapped his hands together. "And how about some lunch? What would you fancy?"

Forman's mind was blank. "Whatever you're having."

The secretary came to the door and Frohman said, "Send out for two double portions of pumpkin pie, will you? And two bottles of, let me see, ginger ale? No, sarsaparilla." The secretary left.

Forman was even more thrown. It was hardly what he had expected. He doubted that anyone would expect to sit with the world's leading theatrical magnate, eating pumpkin pie and drinking sarsaparilla.

"If you feel the need of anything stronger," Frohman said, "it's in the cabinet over there."

Forman grinned. "Thank you very much." He crossed to

the walnut drinks cabinet and looked at the array of bottles and glasses. He hesitated. "There were moments this week," he confessed, "when all I wanted was to get drunk and stay drunk. I'll never forget that awful first night." There was silence and he looked round.

Frohman had taken a small paper bag from his side pocket and out of it had poured himself a handful of peanuts. "No, no," he said, shaking his head. "A failure, a loss—forget it! It's over. Don't ever revive the past. What we must do is get busy and pulverize the future." He smiled and stuffed the peanuts into his mouth.

"Seven days," Elizabeth Duckworth said to her friend Myra Grodin. "In seven days, I'll see the back of all this."

"Sooner you than me," Myra replied. They were in the line for clocking out after the early morning shift at the mill, where they were employed as cotton weavers. Elizabeth was in her early fifties, a widow. Myra was also in her fifties. A short, wiry woman, she worked to support her husband, crippled in an accident at a power loom in this same textile mill fifteen years ago. She took her card and waited while Elizabeth pressed hers into the slot under the clock to be stamped, then placed it in the rack on the other side.

Elizabeth moved out into the yard and stood still for a moment, breathing deeply, enjoying the fresh afternoon air and the sense of space after the ceaseless chatter and dust and the close monotony of the weaving rooms. She was a much heavier woman, capable and solid. Her first husband used to claim in fun that she should have been a man and wrestled with her to prove it. Sometimes she won. They had emigrated to the United States in search of a better life. He died, and she married again. And was widowed again.

Myra came out to join her. "Are you sure you know what you're doing, Lizzie?" she asked.

"I know," Elizabeth told her, "I've thought about it enough." Outside the mill gates, a small group was handing out pamphlets. Elizabeth looked at the one she was given. "What is it?"

"Socialist Picnic tomorrow, against the Arms Trade. Emma Goldman's going to speak. Will you be there?"

347

"Not if you paid me," Elizabeth said and dropped the pamphlet on the sidewalk.

Myra was worried as they walked up the hill. "You shouldn't speak to them like that, Lizzie," she warned. "They'll remember, and after the next election, you'll be in trouble."

"If Eugene Debs becomes President," Elizabeth said, "pigs will fly. And so will I. Anyway, I won't be here to worry about it." She left Myra at her door, refusing the offer of a cup of tea. Myra was a good sort, but she did not have much time for her husband, a self-pitying man who always smelled unwashed.

"You think what you'd be giving up, Lizzie," Myra said. "There's grand days coming, now we're getting more money with the extra overtime."

Elizabeth thought about it as she went on another two streets to her own little clapboard house. It was true. She could soon be making four dollars a day, even four-fifty, now that the mill was taking War orders. That was good money, but it was too late. She had been alone too long, with her daughter married and living away, and she had started to think back.

She had been born in Blackburn, a grimy, crowded city of mills in Lancashire, the center of England's cotton-weaving trade. Her whole family had worked in mills, as she had ever since she was a young girl, a relentlessly hard life. After one especially severe winter, with short hours working, she had come out on an immigrant ship and settled finally at Taftville, Connecticut. She and the man she married had not made their fortune, but America had been good to her. She liked living in a small town out in the country, away from smoke and factory dirt. Although there had been difficult years, as a skilled and willing worker she had never starved. She had a house with three rooms in which she could bring up children decently, where she had her own privacy.

Yet this last year, the death of her second husband and her loneliness made her remember the sights and sounds of Blackburn, her brothers and sisters and childhood friends. She began to miss them and the war made her worry about them. She could not afford to stop working, but she became restless at being here in safety and comparative comfort, while her people were struggling, some dying. She wanted to help, to do her bit, however small. And all her life, when Elizabeth thought of something, it was as good as done.

She opened the screen door of her neat house and went through into the kitchen to put on the kettle. While it boiled, she sat at the table and let herself relax. She did not feel like eating. There was a tin of Blue Label tomato soup and some boiled ham if she felt hungry later. After she had had her cup of tea, she thought, she would take out the two old suitcases. She had always known they would come in handy again one day. She would have to start thinking what to pack, for she had no idea how long she would be away. Tomorrow she would go to church, then walk over to her daughter and son-in-law's to spend the afternoon with them and her grandchildren. It would be the last Sunday she would be able to do that for some time.

She glanced across at the mantelpiece. In the middle were two prints almost side by side. One was of President Wilson's birthplace in Virginia, with a photograph of the President himself inset in one corner. The other was a tinted portrait of King George and Queen Mary. Propped up between them was what had arrived in the post yesterday, on which she had spent half her savings, a third-class ticket on the *Lusitania*, sailing in exactly one week.

Fregattenkapitän Bauer was feeling uncomfortable and did not enjoy it. In a plain cardboard box, as ordered, he had taken the logbook of the U 20, Kapitänleutnant Schwieger's War Diary, to Wilhelmshaven, marked "For the Eyes of the Minister of Marine ONLY." He did not know why it had been asked for, nor why he had to keep it secret. He liked all his dealings with the officers of his Half Flotilla to be straightforward, to give unambiguous instructions and receive honest reports. He left deviousness to politicians, who had leisure for it.

On delivering the box to the flagship, he was told to wait for ten minutes, which stretched to nearly two hours before he was summoned to the Commander-in-Chief's stateroom. Admiral Pohl seemed to have recovered from whatever was wrong with him, he was glad to see. Admiral Scheer was with him, as flag officer with responsibility for the Sub-

349

marine Flotilla. What was surprising was to see Tirpitz sitting behind the desk. Everyone assumed the Grand Admiral to have moved to the temporary G.H.Q. at Pless, in preparation for the Eastern Offensive.

Bauer stood at attention while they congratulated him on his part in the spectacular success to date of the U-boat campaign. "I thank you on behalf of the commanders and crews," he answered. The logbook was lying on the desk. "Forgive me. I trust there is no dissatisfaction or doubt over Kapitänleutnant Schwieger. He is one of the finest and most capable commanders in the Service."

"We entirely agree," Tirpitz assured him. "And what we have just read confirms our opinion." He smiled.

Bauer was relieved, although still puzzled as to why he was here. For the next half hour, they questioned him about morale and efficiency in the crews, returning frequently to the records of the U 20's junior officers and asking Bauer to compare her performance with those of the other boats under his command. Tirpitz seemed particularly interested in the fact that Leutnant Zentner's mother was American and that he had formed a comradely friendship with his commander. He frowned when Bauer mentioned in passing that Schwieger had been disappointed not to be one of those chosen to extend the campaign to the Dardanelles.

"That is supposed to be secret!" Tirpitz rapped. "However . . . I would have expected Schwieger to realize we cannot send all our best commanders to the Mediterranean." He paused. "No doubt you are wondering why we have concentrated to an extent on those few officers. As you know, thanks to our program of construction, the Flotilla will double or treble its strength in the next six months. We must decide in advance those who are to become commanders."

"Of course, sir," Bauer said, relieved.

"Naturally," Tirpitz went on, "you will not mention this conversation to anyone, nor allude to any questions you have been asked. Now or henceforth."

Bauer returned to Emden, bringing back the logbook. He had thought he understood, but the orders he was given before he left perplexed him again. He was only just in time to carry them out, as the next patrol was due to set out in the early hours of the following morning.

The orders had scarcely been issued when Schwieger came to his office. "I understand the U 20 is not to leave with the rest of the patrol tomorrow."

"That is correct." Bauer was conscious of the cardboard box and its contents, which he had not yet removed.

"Why is that?"

Bauer coughed. "They are not satisfied with the repair to the periscope housing. It was badly knocked about on your last trip. They want to have another go at it, test it out properly."

"How long will it take?" Schwieger asked.

"Oh—four or five days. It'll mean you'll be a little later setting off, that's all." Bauer had been fiddling with papers on his desk while he spoke. Now his head rose. He could see that Schwieger had accepted the explanation. "Why don't you have two or three days off, Walther?" he suggested. "No point hanging around."

"I may do that, sir," Schwieger said. He saluted and turned to the door.

"You're not still brooding about the Dardanelles business, are you?" Bauer queried. "Just remember, we can't send all our best men to the Mediterranean."

Schwieger returned to his quarters. He had been surprised by Bauer, who seldom if ever said anything that could be thought of as praise. To him, something was either well done or not well done. The remark about the Med was uncharacteristic, although heartening.

Still, Schwieger felt restless. He had prepared himself for the patrol mentally. He would have spent the later part of the evening going over the U 20 himself. Now Rosenberg and the others would collect their logbooks and be given their final briefing at dawn, without him. Those of his crew who had been on leave and came back today would grumble. Naturally he could not take the U 20 out if she was not completely seaworthy, and if her periscopes were malfunctioning, she would be blind. Yet it was annoying. He did not want extra leave himself. It was too soon to go back to Berlin. And tomorrow, instead of concentrating on the start of a new patrol, he would have nothing to do but think of Hersing, sailing off that day for the Dardanelles.

A knock at the door roused him and he was pleased when Rudi came in. "You've heard?"

"Just now," Zentner nodded. "Bit of a surprise."

"One of those things," Schwieger said. He had a sudden idea, which appealed to him. "Our beloved Fregattenkapitän suggested I take two or three days leave. Why don't we both do it—go back to Wilhelmshaven?"

"I can't," Zentner said. "Don't you know? I've been sent on a course."

It was news to Schwieger. "What course?"

"Wireless Telegraphy."

The U 20 had just been fitted out with radio apparatus and a receiving mast, not before time. "But we'll be carrying a radio operator," Schwieger said. "What's this course?"

"Apparently it's some new idea that one officer in each crew has to understand the technicalities of the air waves," Zentner shrugged, and smiled. "And apparently I'm one of the lucky ones to be selected. I wouldn't mind, but it means I'm going to miss this next patrol altogether. I've had orders to travel tonight and report at the Wireless Telegraphy School first thing tomorrow."

Rudi could not even spare half an hour for a drink in the mess bar if he was to catch his train. Schwieger went with him to his room and waited while he packed his case. "I'm sorry about this," Zentner said. "It means you'll have a new gunnery lieutenant and no first officer."

"We'll manage," Schwieger told him.

"Thanks," Zentner chuckled. "It's nice to feel indispensable."

They walked down together to the front hall of the officers' quarters. "Well, enjoy yourself," Schwieger said as they shook hands. "And good luck."

"The most that can happen to me is an electric shock." Zentner was serious for a moment. "It's for me to wish *you* luck. Break a leg." He looked back from the door with his familiar grin. "On second thought—I hope you break both legs."

Schwieger's smile faded after Rudi had gone. He felt more on his own than ever. Some mine-laying officers were playing a noisy game of Skat in the bar and scarcely glanced at him. He ordered a glass of hock. It was no use inviting Rosenberg or any of the others to join him. No one drank much or went out on the town, the night before a patrol. If

Rudi had been here—damn that snap course! He had a mind to find Bauer and ask why he had not been consulted or even told about it.

Schwieger touched his glass, but pushed it away without drinking. The feeling of restlessness had increased. He had been gearing himself up again for action, and suddenly his energies were left with no outlet. There was something at the back of his mind, something that had been there ever since he thought of going to Wilhelmshaven with Rudi. Trying to hide it from himself was futile. He had thought of Wilhelmshaven because of Anneliese and to go there on his own would be disastrous. He would spend his time remembering what he had consciously made himself forget. Until this evening, he had succeeded.

Now that she was in his mind, she would not leave it. All his assuring himself that she was only an interlude, all his reasoning had gone for nothing. The memory of her was as clear as ever, as though it had not been months since he had been with her. Where was she now? He had a brief sensation of panic when he could not remember what she had said. She had been going from Wilhelmshaven to Dresden for two weeks. Then? Bremen? No, that was later. Dresden, Münster, Oldenburg, then Bremen. She could be in any of these towns, and how many theaters were in each of them?

Erhlich, senior signals officer, had come in and crossed to him, smiling. "On your own, Walther? May I join you?"

"I'm sorry," Schwieger heard himself say. "I have a call to make."

It was almost as if something had taken possession of him, as if he were watching himself as he hurried through to the telephone cubicle in the hall, searching his memory for the number of the stage door in Wilhelmshaven. The Doorkeeper there grumbled, but looked up the list of companies currently on tour. Hers was just finishing its first week in Bremen. After more grumbling, he gave the number of the theater.

As his call to Bremen was put through, Schwieger realized he did not know her second name. He had never known it. "Anneliese," he told the man who answered. "She's in the chorus."

While he waited, he checked the map on the side wall of

353

the cubicle. To reach Bremen, he would only have to change trains once, at Leer.

Someone else took up the receiver at the other end. "Yes? Who is this?" It was a female voice, but not Anneliese.

"My name is Walther Schwieger," he started to explain. He heard laughter. "Walther? It's me, Dora! Hang on."

There were whispers, then Anneliese's voice at last, deeper, breathless in surprise. "Walther? Is that really you?"

"Yes, it's me."

"I don't believe it!" she laughed. "How did you find—? I only have a second. The curtain's going up."

"I have some leave," he told her. "Can we meet?"

"Just like that?" She laughed again when he did not answer. "Where?"

"I can be there in two to three hours. In Bremen."

There was a slight pause. "I'm sharing a room with Dora and another girl. It would be difficult." She broke off. "Yes, yes, I'm coming," she said to someone.

Schwieger did not know Bremen and wanted to see Anneliese alone, not with her friends. On the line to Bremen, the nearest place of any size was a small market town. It was bound to have at least one decent hotel. "Delmenhorst, between Bremen and Oldenburg," he said. "You must have passed through it. I'll meet you there, as soon as you can, after the show."

"Delmenhorst? Tonight?" She sounded flustered. "But I'll have to collect some things and— Walther, are you sure?"

"I'll be waiting on the platform," he said.

His hand was unsteady as he hung up the receiver. The note of doubt in her voice had revived his own uncertainty. He had been mad to call her, to expect her to come running. Well, he was committed now. He would have to hurry himself if he was to get to this unknown town and find a hotel. Madness. He had behaved like a romantic fool. Most likely, she would not even turn up. He could think of a dozen reasons why she wouldn't. But he was committed, and would be waiting.

Chapter 20

ANNELIESE WAS GONE.

Schwieger knew it as soon as he woke. He called her name, in case she was in the bathroom attached to the room, but there was no answer. Her dress and underthings were no longer draped over the chair where she had left them. Her coat and hat were gone from behind the door, her small wickerwork overnight case from the dressing table. She must have got up quickly, dressed and slipped out while he was still sleeping.

He pushed himself higher in the bed and leaned back, shivering when his shoulders touched the cold mahogany of the headboard. She had drawn one of the curtains and there was enough light to see his watch on the bedside locker. It was nearly ten o'clock in the morning. The latest he had slept for months.

He moved his leg to the side. The space where she had lain still had a trace of warmth, so it could not be long since she had risen. Perhaps it was the closing of the door even that had wakened him. If he hurried, he might be able to catch her. Perhaps waiting for a train, at the station where he had waited for nearly an hour last night. He stopped himself. If she wanted to leave, it was her right. He could only make it worse by trying to talk her into staying longer, although he would have liked to apologize, to tell her it was all his fault.

He had reached Delmenhorst shortly after nine in the evening and quickly found the only hotel of any pretensions, the Viktoria, on the corner of a square near the station. It was a solid gray stone building, dark and formal on the inside, frozen in respectability. On the train he had planned everything in detail, deciding to book under the name of

355

Hirsch, but as he walked up to the desk he suddenly realized that, arriving late and in civilian clothes, he was bound to be asked for identification. No doubt Rudi would have carried it off with charm and assurance, but he had no experience of this situation. He glanced round the reception area, making the clerk wait, while he collected his thoughts. A double room with bath was available and he booked it for two nights. "For myself and my wife," he said. It sounded forced even to him. He saw the clerk look beyond him and added, "She'll be here later. She's visiting someone." Careful! You're explaining too much, he warned himself.

As expected, the clerk asked to see his papers, becoming immediately more deferential when he noticed Schwieger's rank and service. "It is an honor to welcome you, Herr Kapitänleutnant," he said, bowing. "Are you visiting relations in the town, perhaps?"

"My wife's," Schwieger said. "In the neighborhood."

The bellboy took his bag and showed him up to the room on the third floor. It was a reasonable size, but its high ceiling made it cold, an impression emphasized by the drab wallpaper and heavy, mahogany furniture. The bellboy checked that the curtains were tightly closed because of the new blackout regulations and inquired if there was anything else he could do for the Herr Kapitänleutnant. Schwieger ordered champagne. While it was being fetched, he laid out his pajamas on the left-hand side of the bed, for the sake of appearances, then took his toothbrush and razor into the white-tiled bathroom. He had not shaved since early morning, so he soaped his face and shaved again quickly.

He was just finishing when the bellboy returned with glasses and the champagne in an ice bucket. Schwieger was drying his face and the bellboy's half-concealed understanding smirk irritated him and made him overtip. You're doing everything wrong, he told himself. Already he was put out by having had to use his own name after he had decided on anonymity. This was not the kind of hotel where one could brazen things out. One had to be careful, and the weekend, which had seemed like an adventure on the train, was becoming slightly sordid.

He went down to the desk again to ask about dinner. It was over and the chef had gone home, he was informed.

However, a cold supper could be laid for two in the dining room, if he wished. There was nowhere else in the town at which it was possible to eat at this late hour, nowhere respectable.

The night air was chill and Schwieger turned up the collar of his overcoat when he went out. There was at least an hour before Anneliese could arrive. He walked up the unlit cobbled street at the side of the hotel, away from the station. The houses were small, with high, pointed gables, only the barest glimmer showing behind the blinds at some windows, and after a few minutes, the sensation of being in an unknown town with no streetlamps or landmarks to guide him became fairly disturbing. There was a strange smell in the air, cloying and unpleasant like bad drains. Yet unlike drains, it was not an occasional smell, it was everywhere. He had noticed it first on his way to the hotel. He took the next side street to the left, then turned right again, but the smell pursued him.

After another few minutes, the narrow lane he was following came to an end in a broader cross street, as dark and deserted as the others. It led him back to the station. Alone on the platform, he became increasingly aware of the cold. The buffet was shut and there was no shelter from the night wind. His pacing slowed. He remembered the final note of uncertainty in her voice on the telephone and his own doubts returned. They had had a few days together, a passing affair. He had no claims on her, nor she on him, yet this weekend might change their relationship into something more serious. He shied away from the idea, refusing to think about it coherently.

As he waited, he was more and more convinced that she would not come. He had offered her very little, no fun or bright lights, just a weekend with him away from everyone. She could not even show him off. That was what had attracted her, the glamour of his uniform and the Flotilla. Apart from that, what was there? Their backgrounds, their worlds, were totally different, and neither fitted into the other's. However much he wanted to see her, if she did not come, it was probably for the best. At least it would settle the matter, get her out of his mind.

The shaded lights in the center of the platform winked on

to announce the last train. When it steamed in, he was waiting by the exit, ready to go back to the hotel and straight
to bed as soon as he had made sure she was not on board.
A number of people got off, workers returning from late
shift, soldiers on leave, couples who had spent the day in
Bremen. They headed for the barrier and surged round and
past him. That was it. The train jerked and moved on, last
stop Oldenburg.

In spite of himself, he had been keyed up and felt a sense
of disappointment. More than that, he admitted. Then as he
turned away, he saw her. She came from the darkness at
the end of the platform into the glow of the lamps and looked
round uncertainly. "Anneliese!" he called, and she hurried
toward him, smiling, taller than he remembered, elegant in
a high-collared, dyed musquash coat and a black velour hat
tilted forward on her upswept hair. She paused when she
reached him and he took her wicker overnight case, leaning
forward to kiss her. She had not realized that he meant to
kiss her cheek and turned her face at the last moment, so
that their lips grazed awkwardly.

She laughed and wiped lipstick from the corner of his
mouth with the tips of her fingers. Even in the dim light,
she seemed deeply flushed. "This is crazy, you know," she
said.

"I know," he smiled. He took her arm and they walked
through the yard and out into the street.

"I had a terrible scramble to catch the train," she told
him. "I didn't have a chance to go home or anything. That's
my make-up case, really. I borrowed the hat from Dora and
this coat is one of Trudi's, the leading lady. They were all
marvelous."

"It looks very smart," he told her. He had a vision of all
her friends backstage rallying round, helping her, joking
about the weekend. It was oddly inhibiting.

"Did you find a hotel?" she asked.

"Yes. It's quite near."

"Separate rooms?" He glanced at her quickly and saw that
she was teasing. "What name did you use?"

"Schwieger."

"Oh." Her voice was very soft. She hugged his arm lightly.
"I thought of writing to you," she said. "But I wasn't sure
you'd want me to." He smiled instead of answering. "At

least since you called me, it means you've been thinking about me."

"Often," he told her. "I've thought about you a lot."

They were at the Viktoria and he held the door for her, ushering her in. The receptionist popped out of the office, his eyes flicking pointedly to the wall clock behind the desk, which showed it was after eleven. "Ah—Kapitänleutnant. They wondered if you had changed your mind about dinner." He smiled and bowed. "But your gracious lady has arrived." As he rose from the bow, his smile faltered.

Schwieger could now also see Anneliese clearly. What he had taken to be a flush was make-up, heavy and blatant. Her whole face was a pink and white mask, thick black lines circling her eyes and elongating the corners, their lids coated with green eyeshadow, her cheekbones highlit with white and shaded underneath with rouge, garish in the electric light of the lobby. Her lip salve was smudged where they had kissed. She looked like a street whore, covering the pallor of disease with paint.

The reception clerk's expression was at the same time arch and disapproving, and Schwieger could tell exactly what he was thinking. "We can go up right away if you'd prefer," he suggested to Anneliese.

"Did someone mention food?" she laughed. "I'd love something to eat. I'm starving."

They went through into the dining room, a large, echoing room split into sections by square pillars stained to imitate marble. A table in the central area had been laid for two, while the meal to be served was on the table next to it, covered by a cloth. In one corner, an old wine waiter had nodded asleep. He woke up and shuffled forward, yawning, when they came in. As Schwieger helped Anneliese off with her borrowed fur coat and held her chair, another, younger waiter bustled out of the swing doors to the kitchen. Anneliese was wearing a tight-fitting dress in blue silk with a ruched wrapover skirt which accentuated her narrow waist and the swell of her hips. The wrapover effect continued above the waist, the neckline daringly low, held together across the breasts by a pearl brooch. The younger waiter's eyebrows rose at the sight of her and his mouth quirked in a knowing smile.

Schwieger sat in silence while the wine was poured and

they were served with cold consommé. Anneliese thanked the waiters charmingly for having stayed on and the younger one preened himself, as though she were flirting with him. His glance across the table was one of conspiratorial envy and Schwieger was rigid with anger at his insolence. Yet the man could partly be excused. Anneliese, with her painted face and the inner crescents of her breasts exposed, looked like a tart.

"You're not eating," she said.

"I—I had something earlier," he muttered. The two waiters had retreated to stand by one of the pillars and he was conscious of them watching and listening. Anything that was spoken above a whisper boomed through the empty room. He took a spoonful of soup just to appear relaxed.

"You're only eating to keep me company?" Anneliese smiled. "That's very noble. You're going to think I'm a pig." She laughed. Her laughter echoed round the dining room, sounding unnaturally raucous, and she bit her lip in amusement.

Doesn't she realize the impression she's making? Schwieger wondered. Evidently not. He was embarrassed, and felt his embarrassment as a betrayal of her, but could not overcome it.

"I'm so hungry, because I usually eat directly after the show," she whispered. "But tonight I just rushed for the train. I didn't even have time to take off my stage make-up. I hope I don't look a fright."

"No, no," he lied.

"But . . . ?"

"Well, it is a little startling." He smiled at last.

Her laughter echoed round the room again. "This place is like a mausoleum," she whispered.

"I'm sorry," Schwieger apologized, and signed to the waiters.

They refilled the glasses and served the cold chicken and salad, the younger one hovering over Anneliese to peer down her neckline, only moving away when Schwieger glared at him. Schwieger had grown tense again. The thought of these people leering and sniggering sickened him. He had hoped to spend the weekend in a happy, romantic mood, with their affair taking up where it had left off. But the whole atmosphere was wrong. It had been cheapened. By circumstances, not by Anneliese, she could not be blamed. It was his fault for having forced her to come.

She was eating hungrily, concentrating on her food. Even in her lurid make-up she was attractive, highly attractive. She looked up and smiled. "I'm trying to get through it, but if I eat any more quickly, I'll choke."

"Please. There's no hurry," he told her.

She considered him for a moment and said quietly, "You look worried."

"Tired, that's all. I've been on some long patrols recently." It was partly true. No amount of rest between patrols could relieve the tiredness that had seeped into him.

She laid down her knife and fork and stretched a hand out across the table. He took it and held it briefly, conscious of the waiters smiling to each other and pretending not to watch.

"Fancy you remembering the dates I was playing," she smiled.

"It was lucky," he agreed.

"I couldn't believe it was you!" she laughed. "And just think, if you'd left it another week— We finish next Saturday. The company splits up. How would you have got in touch with me then?"

He shook his head. "I don't know."

"It was Fate," she breathed, making it sound dramatic, and smiled.

He smiled back, although he was thinking that if his patrol had not been delayed, he would not be sitting here. If he had waited until after one more trip, it would have been too late. Fate, as she said, and perhaps unkind to both of them. He refilled their glasses before the old waiter could move. "Where are you going next? What happens after Bremen?" he asked her.

"I have two or three weeks off," she told him. "Then Dora and I are joining a new company in Wiesbaden."

"I know it, a very pretty town," he said. He asked about her tour and how the performances were going, and made himself seem interested as she brought him up to date. He was fighting a growing sense of detachment. He felt no nearness to her, only awkwardness, as with a stranger. The purpose of the weekend was slipping away, and the more

361

he tried to save it, the more awkward he became. Fortunately Anneliese did not appear to notice, filling in any gaps in the conversation brightly and amusingly. He was glad, for he did not want to make her uncomfortable or hurt her.

She decided against dessert or coffee. "It would keep me awake," she said. "I'm tired, too, now."

Schwieger tipped the waiters, although it felt like bribery and he did not say good night. He could hear the young one laughing as they went out. The clerk had left their key on the desk. It was after midnight.

In the room when she had set her case on the dressing table, she turned and pressed against him. "Hold me," she said, and he put his arms round her. They stood together for a long minute; then she eased back from him and shivered. "You might have lit the fire," she smiled.

"I'm sorry," he said. "I didn't think to."

Her coat was round her shoulders and she held it closed, watching him as he knelt and lit the gas fire with a match. It had taken her longer than she expected to become used to him again. In his narrow-lapeled civilian suit, formal waistcoat and tie, he seemed younger and less distinguished. As handsome and charming as ever, yet more intense, much less at ease with her. She was grateful to him for his obvious efforts to relax, and remembering the dangers he had lived through, wanted to do everything she could to help him. When he had adjusted the flame in the burners, he rose and moved to the table. She took off her coat and hung it beside his behind the door.

Schwieger kept his back to her. It was the moment of truth. Here they were, and he should be excited, but he had seldom felt more uninvolved. Nothing that was happening seemed real. He had created a situation that could be painfully embarrassing for them both. His puritan conscience had been unable to accept the animal desire he had felt in Wilhelmshaven for what it was, and he had salved it by imagining a romantic attachment which did not exist. Why had he not listened to all the arguments he had worked out himself for not seeing her again? He did not resent her, only his own weakness for dragging her into this squalid charade. He owed it to her to go through with it as though nothing were wrong. She liked him and trusted him, and he was

362

more determined than ever not to hurt her, however much of a mistake he had made. As he brought himself under control, he covered it by opening the champagne with meticulous care, stripping off the foil and the wire, twisting out the cork, instead of popping it with his thumbs. It came away with only a gentle hiss. He took the bottle from the ice, dried it on the napkin and made himself smile as he turned to her. He stood still.

Anneliese was standing watching him, her arms by her sides. Her dress, petticoat and chemise lay on the chair behind her. She was wearing only her pink satin knickers, flared and scalloped with lace at the sides, dove gray silk stockings gartered above the knees and her buckled shoes. He had not let himself think of her body and had almost forgotten its erotic fullness, the sleek shoulders and plump, tight-skinned, pointed breasts, the coral tips of her nipples always erect, the slender hollow of her waist and the soft pout of her belly under the pink satin, her full, incurving thighs. When he did not move to her, she clasped her arms lightly across her breasts, but not from modesty. "I'm cold," she said.

He recovered his voice. "I'll pour the champagne."

"It's not champagne I want," she told him shyly. When he still did not move, she held herself more closely, her hands slipping up to her shoulders. "Walther . . . ?" she pleaded uncertainly.

He put the bottle down and, as he stepped toward her, she came to meet him, smiling in relief, her arms going round him under his coat to press herself against him. When they kissed, her mouth was avid under his and he felt his body respond. Thank God, he thought, and let himself surrender to his instincts, pressing his loins against her yielding belly.

"You've too many clothes on," she whispered.

She undid the buttons of his waistcoat while he shrugged out of his coat and unfastened his tie. She was smiling, helping him to undress, keeping up the contact by caressing his chest and stomach, her fingers sliding over his skin until she cupped the surge of his loins with both hands, kissing him again, open-mouthed.

They moved to the bed. The coverlet had been turned down, and while she folded back the thick goosedown quilt, he switched off the main light, leaving only the fringed lamp on the locker. When he came back, she was lying on the bed, her legs raised by the folded quilt, holding herself again and shivering at the touch of the cold undersheet.

She looked up at him standing over her and whispered, "Now I'm the one who's overdressed."

He undid the straps of her shoes and took them off. When he sat beside her, she moved her thigh and he felt the rasp of her stocking and frilled garter on his hip. She was holding her breasts, squeezing their turgid nipples, and she trembled and arched her hips as he peeled down her knickers. She reached for him, pulling him to her, as his hands slid between her knees to unclip the garters.

It was cold in the room and their legs squirmed, wriggling under the quilt. He grabbed it and drew it up over them as she kissed his neck and shoulders, her breath warm on his chest. He had partly lost his erection, but the mixture of cold and heat and her nearness roused him fully again. He touched her gently, finding her open and ready. "Harder," she gasped, "harder!" and trembled against him as his fingers flexed and probed. "I can't wait. I don't want to wait," she muttered. "Please—please, Walther!"

He moved over her and penetrated easily, tensing as she clamped around him. He bore down more strongly, entering her more deeply, and she climaxed almost at once, sobbing, clutching him, her knees rising until the soles of her feet were against the mattress and she could thrust back. When her sobbing stilled and her head fell to the side, he began his movements, regular, pistoning slowly, and her eyes opened, her mouth working and smiling. Her hands came alive on his back, her nails scratching at his shoulders, and her feet lifted as her legs scissored round his hips and locked, her heels drumming on the backs of his thighs.

In a few minutes she climaxed again, her body tautening and quivering like a bow, before collapsing as the tremors coursed through her and she caught at his hair, dragging his face down to hers to kiss and pant into his mouth to stop herself squealing. Her legs slowly uncrossed and fell apart. Her arms dropped from him and lay by her sides. Her body was limp.

But still he continued. He had become an automaton. If

364

he felt pleasure in making love to her, he was not aware of it. He had gone beyond conscious thought, his only wish to satisfy her. He was an instrument. He leaned on his elbows, gazing down at the smeared mask of her face, working himself backward and forward, fast and slow, fast and slow.

Her mouth was open, her breathing ragged, her head turning from side to side. Her arms were heavy. She arched her breasts to brush his chest with their tips. Her legs trembled and jerked. Her eyes opened and she bit at her full lower lip, smiling up at him. She was past the point of desire herself, and, seeing his concentration, tried to help him. In his strange detachment, he had preferred it when she lay still, and the bucking and writhing of her loins under him only made him more nauseated with the whole exercise.

As the mechanical movements went on and on, Anneliese's smile faded. Her eyes became troubled. Her body felt used and pummeled. She was willing to suffer for his sake, but his expression was fixed and she saw no sign of pleasure or tenderness in it. "What is it? What's wrong?" she whispered. He did not seem to hear and she caught at his arms under the shoulders, digging her fingers in until he grunted and stopped moving. He looked down at her, as if just beginning to realize she was there. "Walther, what's wrong?" she repeated.

He did not answer. After a moment he levered himself up and reached out to snap off the bedside lamp, the action making him withdraw from her painfully. She could feel that he was still stiff and erect. He rolled over on his back away from her. In the sudden darkness, she could hear his shuddering, panted breathing.

"I love you," she whispered. "I love you so much." He did not answer or respond in any way and she closed her eyes tightly, feeling the sting of tears.

Schwieger lay unmoving. He knew he had failed her. Her confession of love cut into him. It was gentleness and togetherness he had wanted from her, not the make-believe passion he had pretended. Real desire could only come from them, and he had forfeited any chance of that. He could not steal her love, as he had stolen the use of her body. His mind was confused. He no longer knew what he really felt or wanted. He had been shut in for too long, the prisoner

365

of his own scruples and inhibitions. He wanted to comfort her and be comforted, but as the silent seconds drifted by, the moment passed when he could respond convincingly to what she had said. He had to do something and moved his hand toward her.

"Please, no," she said quietly. "Don't touch me." It was too late.

She turned over on her side and he heard a stifled sound, as though she were sobbing, covering her mouth with her hand. It was a forlorn sound and his heart was torn by it. In his exhaustion, he did not know what to do. Something . . . he must do. As he tried to think what to say, how to make it up to her, he fell asleep.

When he woke, she was gone. He could not blame her, but he felt empty. He had failed her and himself, and he knew he wanted her. It was not mere perversity. His damned stupid bourgeois restraint had prevented him from admitting the truth to himself. He wanted and needed her; instead he had driven her away by his coldness. The evening, what there was of it, and the night had been a disaster. His embarrassment at her appearance had been the first of a series of insults and she would not risk a repetition. He could not try to see her again.

His matches and cigarettes were on the locker. He lit one, grimacing at the acrid taste. She would not have said anything at the desk. She would just have gone. It was up to him to explain that she had promised to visit her relations and that he too was checking out. He did not care any more whether the mousy little clerk believed him or not.

The taste in his mouth was sour. He stabbed out the cigarette and got out of bed. The gas fire had been left on all night and the room was warm. His pajamas lay crumpled on the floor. He pulled on the trousers and knotted the cord as he moved to the table to pour himself a glass of the untouched champagne. He drew back the other curtains at the two small windows. The day outside was fine, sunlight slanting into the broad street outside the front of the hotel, the few people he could see not wearing coats. The champagne was flat and sickly.

As he padded toward the bathroom to brush his teeth, he was startled to hear the door to the corridor open. He did not want to be caught half dressed by a maid and looked round to call a warning.

It was Anneliese who came in. She was wearing her coat. Her dark copper hair had been combed into loose waves like a young girl's and fell to her shoulders and down her back; her face had been cleaned and washed free of make-up. She was very lovely. "You look as if you'd seen a ghost," she smiled.

Schwieger was thrown. "I—I didn't know where you had gone."

"I wanted to make a phone call," she told him. "A private one, without those characters downstairs listening."

"I see."

She was taking off her coat. Under it she wore a simple cotton print dress, buttoned high to the neck, full sleeved. The bathroom door was open. Her blue dress was hanging inside and her overnight case lay on the washstand. All Schwieger had had to do was look in. "What was the call?" he asked.

She picked up her hat from where it had fallen behind the chair. "To Schani, our company manager. I told him I wouldn't be on tomorrow night. He didn't like it, but I didn't give him any choice."

Schwieger's hands were unsteady and he folded them together round the champagne glass. "You're staying here tomorrow?"

"With you, anyway," Anneliese said. "That is, if you want me to."

"Very much."

She smiled, then became serious. She smoothed the brim of her hat. "I wasn't sure," she said quietly. "I hoped you'd want me to. I know it's hard for you to say things. Not like me." She laid the hat on top of her coat on the chair and looked at him. "When you rang me yesterday, out of the blue, I was so excited. But I was worried, I admit it. It had been nine or ten weeks, and I wasn't sure how I'd react to you again. Then, when I saw you waiting at the station, I knew everything was all right." She hesitated. "But it wasn't, was it? Something went wrong. Perhaps we were both trying too hard. And you were angry with that waiter who kept peering down my dress. I felt I had disappointed you, that

I was behaving badly or something. Then I thought—I thought, maybe you just couldn't wait to make love to me. But it wasn't that, either. Was it?" She was silent, giving him a chance to speak. When he said nothing, she smiled briefly. "I don't suppose you could tell me what it was, if you knew. I lay and watched you sleeping this morning, and I nearly said goodbye, nearly ran away. Then I remembered how tired you were and what you've been through, and how desperate you looked last night before you put the light out. And I remembered how wonderful it had been in Wilhelms-haven. I don't know if there is really anything between us, if there could be anything. If there is something worth saving, then one of us has to try. Anyway," she shrugged, "that's why I rang Schani."

"You'll never—never know how glad I am, Anneliese," he said.

There was a knock at the door. "That's breakfast. I ordered it on the way in. So if you don't want to be caught with your pajama pants falling down, you'd better make yourself scarce."

She came to him, kissed his cheek and took the glass. He went into the bathroom and showered and shaved quickly. The bathroom was scented by Anneliese's perfume and the cream with which she had taken off her make-up. He was almost lightheaded with relief and happiness. His bag was by the washstand and he put on his country clothes, worsted trousers, a soft brown sweater and belted Norfolk jacket with patch pockets.

When she saw him, Anneliese smiled admiringly. "Well, aren't we the country gentleman," she said. The champagne had been removed and the table laid. Coffee and toast were keeping warm by the fire. As they ate, they heard a church bell tolling to summon the congregation. Full carillons had been forbidden until peacetime. "Do you feel like going to church?" she asked him. He shook his head. "Well, let's go for a walk."

As soon as they had finished, they went out. Anneliese did not wear her hat and slung her coat over her shoulders. Schwieger left his behind. They walked up the street down which he had run the night before. In daylight the houses seemed even smaller, more old world. Anneliese's nose wrinkled at the smell and she was amused when he explained. Delmenhorst was a little market town, only recently industrialized. "But didn't these poor people know what it would mean to have a linoleum factory?" she laughed.

"I doubt it," he smiled. "I expect you get used to it."

They reached the old market square with the town hall beyond it and walked on along a tiny canal-like river. After a few turns, they came to a promenade by the winding moat round the ruins of the stronghold that once stood in the center of the town. The ruined walls were stark and moss-covered, the moat half filled with waterlilies, its still surface rippled only by the passage of two pairs of swans. The promenade was quiet and secluded. In front of them a young soldier strolled with his arm round a girl. They disappeared behind the long, trailing branches of a willow that drooped its narrow leaves down to the water. Schwieger and Anneliese stopped and breathed in the peace of the scene, moat and swans and ruins blending in an image that neither would ever forget. When Anneliese leaned closer, he swung her gently to him and kissed her. She gazed up at him, her delicately slanted hazel eyes questioning, and when he kissed her again, she laughed softly, happily, taking his arm and laying her head against his shoulder as they turned and walked back.

They followed a series of signs to the Tiergarten and, after twenty minutes, arrived at a broad road leading out of the town. There was a bar on the opposite side and they crossed over to ask if the Tiergarten was anywhere near or if they had gone completely wrong. "No, it's just along there," the barman told them. "Hot work, walking."

"That it is," Schwieger agreed. He bought beer for Anneliese and himself and they sat with the locals for half an hour, couples and families with children who had come to the bar to gossip the Sunday morning away. There were a number of young women among them, but few young men, as most of them had been taken for the forces. They were friendly and hospitable, insisting on Schwieger and Anneliese joining them, including them in their orders of drinks, telling them of places to visit just outside town, country inns and farmhouses where strangers were welcome. They were the same kind of people Schwieger had thought so suspicious

369

and distant the previous night, and now he could not understand why. They left with handshakes and good wishes all round. "It must be you," he assured Anneliese. "They never welcome me like that."

She smiled. "Did you see those girls? They all looked as if they could eat you."

"What a way to die," he laughed.

She pretended to be disapproving, but could not sustain it. "I think you'd take a lot of them with you," she giggled. "But if anyone's going to eat you up this weekend, it'll be me. So be warned."

They carried on down the wide road, with occasional prosperous villas set back from it, and at last came to another sign, pointing across a patch of heath to a line of trees. The trees marked the outer fringe of a woodland area, all that remained of an old forest of beech and ash and pines. If it had once been a Tiergarten, there was no longer any trace of the animals, but it was green and peaceful and the carpet of ancient leaves rustled springily under their feet.

Anneliese paused and caught Schwieger's hand, her head tilted, listening to a strange staccato sound, a high-pitched tok-tok-tok that stopped and started arrhythmically, surprising her each time and making her smile. "What is it?" she whispered.

"A woodpecker," he told her.

When she glanced at him in disbelief, he showed her the beech tree ahead where the small bird perched high on the trunk, a bright green with a yellow belly and rump. It pecked dementedly at the crevices in the bark with its long beak and the sound rang out again. She tried to creep closer, but at the rustle of the leaves the woodpecker darted away in a flash of olive green.

The woodland sloped down and they took a slanting path which led them to a stream, tinkling and gurgling under its high banks. The trees were even denser on the far side, shading them from the sun which was almost at its height. It was like a summer's day. Anneliese still held Schwieger's hand and they followed the path along the bank, smiling to each other now and then, not talking, right to the edge of the wood.

Where the trees ended, the bank dipped to a wide shelf

of mud by the water. The opposite bank dipped down, too, and beyond it they could make out the beginning of a rutted track. "Is this a ford?" she asked.

"It must be."

"But you can't cross here."

He grinned boyishly. "Is that a challenge?" To her surprise, he pulled off his shoes and socks.

"What are you doing?" she laughed, watching as he tied his shoelaces together and slung his shoes round his neck. He rolled the legs of his trousers up to his knees. "You're crazy!"

He took one step into the stream and yelped, turning back, his mouth open in agony. "I don't know where this water's from, but it's freezing," he said. "Come on!"

"Oh, no," she told him. "You're not getting me across there." Before she could jump away, he grabbed her and swung her up into his arms. "Walther! No—put me down!" she protested, laughing, clutching at her fur coat to prevent it falling in the mud. "No! Please, put me down!"

"Don't struggle or you'll have us both over," he warned her, and began to ford the stream. When he pretended to lose his balance, she squeaked, clinging to him and laughing. With her weight added to his, his feet sank into the stony mud and it really was an effort to walk. He had also misjudged the depth of the water and, halfway over, it was above his knees, soaking his rolled trouser legs. He stopped. "My feet are going numb. I'll have to put you down."

"Don't you dare . . . Don't you dare!" she threatened.

He laughed and carried on over, setting her safely on the opposite bank. She threw her coat up onto the grass and rounded on him, beating his chest with her fists. When he seized her hands, their fingers twined and she stretched up to be kissed.

They broke apart and at once they both started giggling like children at the sight of his feet, coated thickly to above the ankles with oozy, brown mud. He sat on the grass of the bank, dangling his feet down into the water again to wash them clean.

"How are you going to dry them?" she asked when he swung his legs up.

He shrugged. "Try blowing on them."

She smiled and knelt in front of him, lifting his feet and placing them on her lap. Her hands smoothed the drops of water from his skin and she leaned down, blowing softly, warmly, between his toes. He caught his breath. The long waves of her hair had tumbled forward and she gathered them together, rubbing them gently over his ankles and the soles of his feet. The gesture was ritual, somehow submissive, and he put out a hand to stop her, but could not. When she finished drying his feet with her hair, she looked up and smiled. "Today I am Mary Magdalene," she whispered.

He frowned. "No. That's sacrilege."

She kissed her fingers, touched them briefly to his lips and shook her head.

They walked on up the rutted track and soon had nearly forgotten the town existed. On either side of the hedgerows were only fields and meadows, with some scattered copses, a few sheep and cattle. Away in the distance a dog yelped. There was no sign of another human being, apart from one or two far-off farmsteads. Swifts and swallows circled above the plowed fields. The air was filled with bird song. It reminded Schwieger of early morning in O'Dowd's valley in Ireland, but he thrust the memory away. Today he wanted only the sights and sounds he shared with Anneliese.

After some time the track divided, and they chose the lefthand fork because there were more trees. It wound on and on, passing another farm and a woodman's hut, now bordered by thickets of hawthorn and blackberry, with hedge mustard, convolvulus and dogroses in bud, now by open fields or a screen of trees. Anneliese stopped to pick some tiny blue star-shaped flowers. She wore the pearl brooch pinned above her left breast, and as she tucked them through it, she saw that he had paused ahead of her and was looking at something.

"What is it?"

"A milestone."

She rose and joined him. "How far have we come?"

"Ten kilometers."

She gasped. "Ten? I haven't walked so far since I was a little girl."

He smiled. "Do you want to turn back?"

She glanced round, then ahead. "No," she decided. "Now

that we're here, we might as well go on. Wherever we're going."

There was no change in the road. It meandered on, as peaceful and deserted as ever. It had lost none of its charm, but knowing the distance they had covered brought them back slightly to reality. "I don't know about you," he said, "but I'm beginning to feel hungry."

She hugged his arm. "I didn't like to say, but so am I." They laughed.

After some minutes they glimpsed a farm off to the side and, when the road began to curve nearer to it, they stepped out briskly. The farm, however, was gloomy and unwelcoming, with a high fence round it. Two Dobermans were chained to the gate at the end of the short drive and they barked savagely, straining at the extent of their leashes. Anneliese held Schwieger's arm and walked him past.

Beyond the farm the road led through another belt of trees. They went on more slowly and Schwieger was wondering if it might not have been wiser to turn back after all when the trees thinned out and gave way to open country again. About half a mile ahead of them was a squat dark building set back from the road. As they drew nearer, they could see two open carriages and a gig parked in the yard beside it.

"What do you think?" Anneliese asked.

"I think it's an inn," he said.

It was broad across the base, with low side walls and a steeply pitched, thatched roof. The end wall was criss-crossed by wooden beams, and on a board above the main door was the word *Gasthof*. A pole with a painted inn sign stood by the road, but the paint was faded and showed only the outline of what had once been a golden rooster. The door opened into a large hall with exposed rafters and a wooden gallery running across the far end. Doors on the right led to the kitchen and private rooms. There were other closed doors on either side of the paneled end wall and a row of high windows. The door nearest them on the left opened into a taproom with booths round the sides and a counter with a beer barrel lying on it.

About a dozen people sat at the tables, farmers and their wives. They nodded back when Schwieger bade good day to the room. The man behind the bar was the innkeeper, heavy-faced and fat, his hair cropped close to his round skull, wearing a collarless shirt and an apron tied over the massive bulge of his stomach, slow-moving and slow-speaking like many countrymen. Schwieger ordered beer for himself and wine for Anneliese and asked if there was any possibility of food. The innkeeper scratched his chin doubtfully, but melted when Anneliese looked at him appealingly. "There's nowhere to eat in Delmenhorst," she said. "We walked all the way here."

"Walked? Oh, well. Well then," the innkeeper rumbled. "I'll have to ask my wife." He disappeared through a door in the corner, and after a minute they saw him beckoning.

The parlor behind the bar was neat and plain, and a neat plain stout woman with gray hair and apple cheeks was smiling to them, drying her hands on her apron. She was Frau Dansker. She bobbed to Anneliese. "We don't have many folks these days," she explained. "So there's only what we had. But if soup and beef with dumplings would be all right—?"

"It sounds perfect," Anneliese assured her. "Just what I'd make myself."

The innkeeper's wife beamed. "Well . . . You can eat in here, if you like. Or we could set a table in the hall?"

"In here's fine," Schwieger said. "We don't want to put you to any trouble."

While they waited, they wandered across the hall and through a rear door to a pretty garden where a boy of about seven and a girl of ten were playing with iron hoops, keeping them rolling round and round the cinder paths with taps of their sticks. "I haven't done that, since—well, not this century," Anneliese laughed. She could not resist joining in.

Schwieger sat on a bench in the sun and finished his beer, watching as she ran with the boy and girl, laughing, taking turns with the hoops. Frau Dansker came to tell them their meal was ready and stood beside him, smiling. "She has a knack with children, your good lady," she said. "Do you have any of your own?"

"No," Schwieger said. "Not yet."

The lunch was delicious and substantial, and afterwards the innkeeper brought them a great wedge of soft cheese. As he sat with them over a glass of Korn, it became obvious that under his slow manner he was really fairly shrewd and perceptive. He even seemed pleased to hear that Schwieger was in the navy, having an uncle and some cousins of his own in the Merchant Marine. His two eldest boys were in one of the East Saxon regiments and had just been sent to the east. "Anything rather than that west front," he said. "That must be terrible."

When Frau Dansker cleared the table, she was delighted to see they had finished everything. "There's no shortages here, not yet," she told them. "So it's best to eat up while you can. It's all a bit rough and ready, but you're very welcome."

"I haven't felt so at home for ages," Anneliese smiled. "I only wish we could stay here."

"Well . . ." Frau Dansker said, hesitantly. "We do have a room." Anneliese's head turned to Schwieger quickly, her eyes alight. "It's not much. Maybe it wouldn't do."

"Could we see it?" he asked.

Frau Dansker led them down the hall and up a flight of steep wooden stairs to the gallery, then up more stairs to the attic room. It was warm and snug under the thatch and rafters. Its leaded windows faced south and the bed was a wooden box frame with a high, fluffy duvet covered by a check counterpane. The floor slanted and an old carved chest served as a dressing table under the window. There was a large bowl and jug for washing. "Like I said, it's not much," Frau Dansker apologized.

"It's lovely," Anneliese breathed. "Walther? Would there be any problem?"

He smiled. "No. I booked the hotel for two nights, but I paid in advance, so they can't object. The only trouble is, we've left our things there."

"If you're really sure," Frau Dansker said. "Andreas is going into town this afternoon. He could pick them up."

The innkeeper chuckled when he heard. "My niece works at the hotel," he said. "I'll get her to pack your cases, so it's done properly. Leave it to me." A few minutes later he rattled off in the gig.

"Are we mad?" Anneliese asked.

Schwieger put his arm round her. "Not if we want to make a new beginning."

There was not much of the afternoon remaining and they

both felt they had walked far enough, but they were intrigued by a hill about a quarter of a mile from the inn, a low cone topped by a cluster of trees. Andreas, the innkeeper, had told them it was the main reason for people visiting the area on weekends, an ancient burial place of Teutonic heroes, The Graves of the Huns. "If that's what those old stones really are," he chuckled.

They took their familiar road and turned off on a path to the hill, realizing as they approached that it was almost perfectly conical. The angle of its sides was steep and the soil crumbled under their feet like shale, so that Schwieger had to climb sideways, digging in his heels and pulling Anneliese up after him. The top was broader and more flat than they had suspected, the stunted elms that ringed its summit warped into weird shapes by the wind.

They crossed the uneven, rocky surface to the inner circle of trees. Up here all sounds were hushed and distances exaggerated, so that even the inn seemed much further away than it was. There was no other sign of habitation in any direction, only rolling countryside. At the very center were the stones, tumbled and fallen together, the core of a burial mound thousands of years old. They were blue-gray, pitted with age, and Schwieger and Anneliese moved slowly round them, trying to imagine how they had once been arranged.

There was a triangular gap between two of them at ground level, with a third massive boulder balanced above. "What was it he told us?" Anneliese whispered. "That if you crawl through there, your wish comes true?"

"I don't need to wish," Schwieger said. "I have everything I want."

She closed her eyes as he kissed her; then he caught her by the waist, hoisting her up to sit on one of the stones, and she drew him to her, cradling his head against her breasts. In a little while they moved to sit under one of the twisted elms on the cushion of dry leaves and turf between two of its thick, spreading roots. They sat with his arm round her and her head against his shoulder, watching the land and the distant haze of earth and sky, half dreaming, until the cawing of rooks nesting in the lower trees roused them. The sun was sinking into the horizon and, although their sheltered spot was still warm, the night air would be cold. They slithered down the steep slope, laughing like children, and walked back hand in hand, across the fields tinged rose-red by the last glow of day.

That evening they drank and gossiped with the locals and Andreas. Neither was hungry, to Frau Dansker's disappointment, and they picked with the others at the platter of cold ham, sausages and slices of smoked meat which Andreas brought for everyone. They excused themselves early and went up to their room.

Their bags were by the door. For the first time they were self-conscious with each other. When she had undressed to her chemise, Anneliese said, "I don't have a nightgown," as though it were important. He gave her the coat of his striped pajamas and she moved round to the opposite side of the bed. She put on the pajama coat, slipped the chemise off and climbed into bed.

Schwieger blew out the lamp and got in beside her. He could hear her steady breathing and after a moment made out her profile, pale in the moonlight. He turned toward her. "Hold me," she said softly. "Please, just hold me." She shifted to let his arm go round her and turned her head, drawing back her hair and laying her cheek on his bare chest. And like that, they fell asleep.

Schwieger woke when the sun crept across the bed. She had rolled over on her side during the night. He rose quietly, took his shaving things and clothes and went down to the bathroom on the floor below. When he was ready, he carried on down and out into the yard. He could hear the scratching of a hoe and found Andreas at work at his vegetable plot. "I didn't think you'd be up for an hour or so yet," the innkeeper chuckled. Frau Dansker called from the kitchen window that she would start breakfast.

Anneliese was up and dressed when he got back to the room. She was so rested, she felt as though she had been on holiday for weeks, she told him. She was sitting combing out her dark copper hair and, as she began to braid it, he stopped her, combing it again with his fingers. "Leave it like that," he said.

They took their coffee out into the garden and saw the boy holding logs for Andreas to split. Schwieger pushed up the sleeves of his sweater and went to join them. The girl, Brigitta, came out with a basin of feed for the chickens and Anneliese helped her to gather the eggs from the orchard behind the garden, where the hens tried to hide them. Afterwards Schwieger borrowed the gig. The old horse seemed glad of the exercise and they spanked along, exploring the roads beyond the inn. Anneliese was not used to the country and was fascinated by everything, a fox watching them from a gap in the hedge, its bright red tongue lolling, storks nesting on the roof of a barn, new lambs. The sun was shining for them again and the drive back, with the horse clopping at its own ambling pace, seemed timeless.

Lunch was roast chicken and a huge apple strudel and cream. As she cleared up, Frau Dansker said shyly, "We've made up our minds, Andreas and I, we've made up our minds only to charge you for the food—if that's agreeable."

When they protested, Andreas spoke up from the door of the parlor. "No, it wouldn't be right to make you pay twice for a room. Anyway, it's an honor to have you here." He paused. "You see, we know who you are, Commander." One of the farmers collected pictures of U-boat aces from the illustrated magazines, and had recognized him. "In fact," Andreas apologized, "I'm sorry, but there's some folk through here who'd be privileged to buy you a drink. Of course they'll understand if you'd rather be left alone." Frau Dansker scolded her husband for bothering them; yet because of their kindness, Schwieger could not refuse and they went through into the taproom.

Some of their friends from last night were there, but the conversation was not so easy, now that Schwieger had been identified as a celebrity. After toasts had been drunk to the Flotilla and to him and the U 20, he answered one or two questions tersely on life in a submarine. Andreas and the others obviously felt that he resented their intrusion and an uncomfortable pause followed. The moment was saved by Anneliese. She knew how much he disliked to talk about his experiences, so it proved how at home he felt here, she said. "This is the first time I've heard him say anything at all about my rival, that blessed U 20." They laughed and the atmosphere lightened. She even managed to turn the affair into a kind of party, and Schwieger surprised himself by telling them about the fight with the disguised tanker. It was enough to excite and satisfy them.

It was midafternoon before they got away. He had not accepted most of the drinks he had been offered, but even so his head was heavy. "Why don't you lie down for a little?" she suggested.

"I don't want to spoil the day."

"I'd rather you had a siesta now than fall asleep this evening," she laughed. She went up with him to the room, helped him off with his shoes and tucked the counterpane round him.

It was two hours later when he woke. He felt refreshed, but was angry with himself for wasting so much of their last day. Tomorrow he would have to be back at the base in Emden. He rinsed his face in the bowl, swilled out his mouth and hurried downstairs. Anneliese was not in the parlor, nor in the garden. "She went for a walk, your good lady," Frau Dansker told him, worried. "I'm sorry, I didn't see in what direction."

"It's all right," he smiled. "I know where she'll be."

He cut straight across the fields. The afternoon had stayed fair and the sun was low in the sky; the undersides of the far, high clouds blushed pink and gold. When he reached the hill, he heard her singing. He had never heard her voice before, soft and liquid. She was singing "The Little Hedge Rose" by Schubert and stopped when his foot scraped on the slope.

She was lying between the twisted roots of the elm, her back against its bole. "Why did you stop singing?" he asked her. She smiled and he sat beside her. The air was hushed. In all the expanse round them, not even a bird broke the silence.

"I love you, Anneliese," he said.

She caught her breath and raised her hands, touching the sides of his face.

"I want . . . I would like—"

"No, Walther," she whispered. "You don't have to say anything else." She touched his mouth, smoothing the tip of her finger across his lips. "I don't expect you to marry me. Maybe . . . afterwards. When it's over. We'll see. I know it's difficult for you. As long as we can be together now and then."

"I do love you," he told her. She drew his head down and kissed him.

She had undone the top buttons of her dress. He undid the others, folded the two halves aside and kissed the deep, warm valley of her breasts. This time their lovemaking was gentle and perfect.

Chapter 21

THE TRAIN SPED THROUGH THE NIGHT, THE LONG PLUME OF smoke stretching almost flat along its back, its blinds drawn and sealed. Warnings had flashed from Berlin and all other rail traffic was shunted into sidings until it had passed. By early morning it would be at Pless in Silesia.

In the salon of his private coach, Grand Admiral Tirpitz sat alone. He wore his old wine-colored dressing gown and sat with his hands gripping the leather arms of his chair, his head lowered, brooding, motionless. The bed had been turned down for him in his sleeping compartment, but he knew that he would only toss and turn, kept awake by his anger.

Great General Headquarters had moved to the castle of Pless in preparation for the Eastern Offensive, and he would be in time for the morning meeting. No one would ask where he had been, except perhaps Kaiser Wilhelm, who might demand the reason for the Grand Admiral's absence without his leave. Tirpitz would answer with perfect honesty. He had been at the headquarters of the High Seas Fleet, to check personally on morale of the Fleet. He had found that morale was slipping, as was only to be expected in a Fleet which was not permitted to venture beyond the inner ring of mine defenses round its base. That would shut the All Highest up. He would glower and change the subject.

Tirpitz stirred in his chair and his head rose as he breathed in slowly to control the surge of anger that welled through him at the thought of the idiot Duke of Württemberg. For months the Army had begged, with the Grand Admiral's support, for permission to use its most deadly secret weapon, poison gas. In a large-scale surprise attack, clouds of it released from canisters and bursting shells would drive the enemy back in panic. As the German army advanced behind its wall of chlorine and mustard gas, organized resistance would be impossible. Before any form of defense could be improvised, the army and the gas would be at Paris.

Instead . . . Duke Albrecht had chosen a day on which the prevailing winds blew in the wrong direction and had only been able to release the gas shortly before nightfall. Even so, it had opened up five miles of the Allied trenches, surprising Duke Albrecht as much as the enemy. Instead of rolling back the whole Allied front, he had only succeeded in making a dent in the Salient. Tirpitz brought his fist down hard on the arm of his chair. When he had gone storming to the High Command, he had been told blandly that the attack had only been in the nature of an experiment and that they were *gratified* by the result. They seemed incapable of seeing that the whole impact and surprise of gas warfare had been thrown away.

Tirpitz grunted and shifted again, flicking apart the spikes of his beard. His mind had turned to the United States. Falkenhayn always called it his obsession. As well it might be. England was the enemy, but only because she was backed by American raw materials and munitions. So who then was the ultimate enemy? The man who keeps trying to burn down your house, or the one who keeps giving him the matches with which to do it? Tirpitz was in no doubt of the answer. The problem existed, and he had taken steps of his own to deal with it. Only when the Yankees had been humbled would the world accept the Reich's supremacy. Delicate negotiations had been taking place to arrange for the landing, after victory in Europe, of six hundred thousand German troops in Mexico and South America. Transport and dreadnought versions of the latest oceangoing U-boats would police all vessels leaving and entering American ports. Japan would certainly see the folly of continuing to resist alone, and in return for being given a free hand in the Pacific would join in the blockade of the American West Coast.

Yet all depended on the next few months. The U-boat campaign was the success he had promised, but was still short of final triumph. If only he had concentrated on building more submarines sooner! At least Kaiser Wilhelm had completely surrendered on their use, his only fear being that some action of theirs might provoke the U.S. into entering the war on the side of the Allies. The Kaiser was correct in believing that all hinged on the U.S., but as blind as the rest in not seeing that she herself at present was no threat to Germany.

If she did declare war, she would have to divert her money and materials into building up her own forces and defenses, and have less to spare for her allies. German-American reservists would cause disruption. Von Rintelen would launch a devastating campaign of sabotage and stir up violent unrest in Mexico. America would have more than enough to occupy her within her own borders and it would be a long time before she was ready to make any physical intervention in Europe. By then, starved by the U-boats, France and England would have collapsed. With them crushed, America would soon make peace.

On the other hand, victory would also be achieved if she could be forced into declaring an embargo on the sale of arms. Either way, now was the time, before she had built up a military force and while Germany was still dominatingly strong.

The train jolted over a set of points and Tirpitz rocked in his chair. He became aware of tiredness, too many hours spent chasing the paper bogeyman, the empty threat of America. He pushed himself to his feet, yawning, deciding to lie on his bed for a while.

As he walked down the corridor, he told himself that at least he had done what he could. The train lurched again, passing over a series of tracks at some main junction. He held the corridor wall to steady himself, and it helped him to calm down. Damn Wilson and his interfering little Colonel! At the very start of the war, their attempts at intervention seemed to make the Kaiser waver. Now they were interfering again, at the wrong moment, before the U-boats had brought England to her knees.

Only a nightlight burned in the sleeping compartment and Tirpitz was suddenly overcome by tiredness as he eased himself onto his bed. The Freedom of the Seas . . . America must be provoked into jumping one way or the other, in the immediate future. A sharp shock would need to be administered, a taste of terror and danger, to show her what she risked by meddling in a total war. He yawned deeply. The choice was limited, but he could not have asked for better. Nor for a more dependable instrument to carry it out.

Karl Boy-Ed could see that it was up to him to keep the peace. Instead of working smoothly together, von Rintelen and Papen were like cat and dog. "Surely this is a matter which can wait?" he suggested. "The subject of this meeting is more urgent."

They were in the captain's cabin of the interned liner *Vaterland*. He was seated at the circular table with Papen opposite him. As usual, von Rintelen had not sat down. Nor was he standing in an attitude of respect. He was leaning against the bureau, his ankles crossed, taking a cigarette from his gold case. Boy-Ed had grown to accept his non-chalance, but it clearly still irritated Papen.

"I wish to know why he has not delivered, as instructed, a full report of all his activities!" the military attaché snapped.

Von Rintelen tapped the end of his cigarette on the case. "I am sorry, Captain. I have reported to you as much as I am permitted. Any other activities in which I may or may not be engaged are to be communicated only to Herr Eisendal and the joint chiefs of Intelligence." He lit his cigarette and shrugged.

You have to admire his coolness, Boy-Ed thought.

Papen's narrow face was set hard with baffled anger. "As coordinator of Intelligence in this hemisphere, I should be informed of every single action that is taken," he said tightly.

"There is no question about that, naturally," Boy-Ed agreed. "But one must obey orders."

Papen snorted. "And now there is this." He touched the decoded message in front of him. It was fairly lengthy, a series of demands for an intensified propaganda effort to induce the U.S. to impose an embargo on the sale of arms to the Allies, for more stringent checks by Port Authorities to prevent the sailing of Allied cargo vessels and liners loaded with contraband, with particular reference to the *Lusitania*, and for the immediate internment of all armed Allied vessels, again with reference to the *Lusitania*. Boy-Ed was specifically asked why he had not yet provided information on the location and number of the *Lusitania*'s naval guns. The Embassy was asked why it had not issued the warning to American travelers and was ordered to do so, forthwith.

"It's all very important, of course," von Rintelen said. "But my plans are laid. There's nothing here that urgently concerns me."

"What about your National Peace Council?" Boy-Ed asked.

"Members are flocking in, thousands of them," von Rintelen told him. "Labor leaders, churchmen, professors. We're holding our first convention in Washington next month, with Congressmen Fowler and Buchanan on the platform, and Monnett, the former Attorney General, and Hannis Taylor, former U.S. Ambassador to Spain. After the meeting we'll arrange for thousands of telegrams to be sent to the President, calling for the nationalization of all munitions factories and the banning of all exports of armaments."

Papen was as impressed as Boy-Ed. "You'll have to be careful," he said.

"I'll be there only as an observer," von Rintelen smiled. "And to guide things along. But this kind of affair has to gather its own momentum. The bulk of the members are genuine peace lovers, and we dare not let them suspect they are being led."

"I can see that," Boy-Ed nodded.

"You have handled it most expertly," Papen said, grudgingly. He rose. "Well, I must find out what has happened to that advertisement."

"As a priority," Boy-Ed agreed. "And I shall make another attempt to locate the *Lusitania*'s guns."

"Why is it so difficult?" von Rintelen asked. "If she's armed, surely any passenger could tell you?"

"Not if the guns are cleverly concealed," Boy-Ed explained. The argument sounded thin even to him, and he seemed uncomfortable.

Papen left shortly afterwards. Von Rintelen lingered, stubbing out his cigarette. "Why all this concentration on the *Lusitania*?" he asked.

"She's sailing for Liverpool on Saturday," Boy-Ed told him.

"Is that the only reason?"

Boy-Ed was silent for some time. "She is a symbol of England's mastery of the seas, and if we could have her

385

interned or banned from entering American ports, it would be a victory."

"And is that all?" von Rintelen insisted.

Again Boy-Ed paused. "I hope so."

Papen had arranged to meet George Viereck by the statue of Garibaldi in Washington Square, where they could walk and talk without being overheard. The editor was apologetic. He had given the warning to an advertising agent to insert. "We had decided on forty newspapers," he explained. "But Schaffer could not contact them all in time for it to appear last Saturday. He thought that for maximum impact it would be better to wait until it could be published in all of them simultaneously."

"This Saturday?" Papen asked.

"Without fail," Viereck assured him.

The young Englishman was fairly drunk already, Koenig saw. The girls kept filling his glass with bourbon and he could not stop looking at the gleam of Trude's knees in their black silk stockings through the parting in her wrapover skirt. An experienced girl, she made the display seem accidental, and the young idiot was obviously unaware that, like the impromptu party, it was all for his benefit. The drink was loosening him up. Another two or three and he would be at his most receptive.

His name was Leach, Neil Leach, Stahl had reported. His family in the West Indies had sent him to Cambridge in England to study modern languages, and during the previous summer he had found vacation work in Germany as a tutor. He had been interned when the war started, and had only recently been permitted to return home, on giving his promise not to join the British forces. On the voyage home via New York, on a Holland-America line steamer from Rotterdam, he had met a friendly steward, Gustave Stahl, who was most sympathetic to learn that he was nearly penniless. While Leach was waiting for a passage to the West Indies, Stahl took pity on him and brought him to the boardinghouse at 20 Leroy Street, where they could share a room. Stahl had also reported that he was immature and suggestible, and he should know, as one of Boy-Ed's most reliable agents.

Leach was overwhelmed by the kindness of his new friend, a happy-go-lucky older man who insisted on their sharing the little money he had. "What the hell!" Stahl laughed. "We owe ourselves a good time. You ought to enjoy yourself while you're young." Drink, pretty girls, it was paradise after internment, and Leach began to wonder how he could delay his return to the stuffy respectability of his parents' home a little longer.

The other people in the boardinghouse were just as nice and as welcoming. He had met Curt Thummel, who was introduced as Chester Williams, an American personnel officer, who thought he might be able to get him a temporary job. The party had developed out of a lunchtime drink in Thummel's room. Other friends had dropped in, and the two girls from upstairs. Trude was the one Leach admired, a bright-eyed honey blond with a teasingly demure smile. She was a stenographer for a shipping company, she told him as they sat together on the bed. It was exciting to be close to her at last and he was grateful to Gus, who had arranged it quite cleverly, calling the other girl over and winking to him to take her place.

"It's nice to have someone young in the house," Trude smiled. "I hope you're going to be around for a while."

"So do I," Leach told her. He was sure he wasn't mistaken about the promise in her eyes. He was sitting on the edge of the bed and she was sprawled beside him, supporting herself by her elbow on the pillows. "I'm hoping to get a job. Chester's promised to help."

"Chester?" Trude laughed. "Oh, yes—Mr. Williams." She sat up and lifted the bottle from beside the bed. "We're lucky," she whispered. "No one else seems to have noticed this one." He chuckled as she half filled his glass. It brought her closer and he seemed wrapped in the patchouli perfume that she wore. "What if you don't get a job?" she asked.

"Well, in that case," he said reluctantly, "I suppose I'll have to go home."

Trude pouted in disappointment and set down the bottle. As she lay back on her elbow, she stretched and her skirt parted even more, showing a triangular strip of white thigh above the rolled top of her stocking. He was certain she did not notice his eyes drop to it, but she caught the fold of her skirt and twitched it closed, shutting off his view of her legs altogether.

Good girl, Koenig nodded approvingly.

Leach took a swallow of his whiskey, not like real Scotch, yet not unpleasant. He could tell that Trude was upset and it added to his excitement. It was difficult with other people here, but he tried to make it sound intimate. "I mean—you don't think I should go home?"

She pouted again and shrugged, then looked up at him through her lashes. "I just thought it would be nice if we got to know each other."

"I'd like that," he said softly.

Trude sat up and smiled. "Would you, really?" she whispered. Her lips were red and soft, and her teeth caught briefly at her lower one. The promise was definite now.

"Well, hi, Phil! I hadn't seen you there," Thummel said loudly beside them.

Leach glanced up and saw a tall, dark-haired man with a heavy jaw and long arms ambling toward them. He looked like a bruiser.

"Thought I'd just call in," Paul Koenig smiled.

"Neil, let me introduce a friend of mine," Thummel said. "This is Phil Kelly. And careful what you say. He's a newspaperman."

They laughed, and Koenig was politely interested when he was told about Leach's experience, interned in the Kaiser's Germany. "Might be a story in that."

"Oh, not really," Leach told him. "I had a pretty easy time. And they did let me go. I'm sort of on parole."

"How about a drink?" Stahl suggested.

"Maybe just a little one," Koenig chuckled.

Thummel gave him a glass and refilled Leach's. "Well, how's business, Phil?"

"Oh, pretty good," Koenig nodded, then grimaced. "As a matter of fact, no. I've got my editor on my back."

"What about?"

"He's got this crazy idea—keeps on and on about it. Well, you know it's the *Lusitania*'s two hundred and first Atlantic crossing. He keeps after me to do a feature on it, what it's like to sail on the Queen of the Seas in wartime, eyewitness, personal experience stuff."

"Sounds fascinating," Trude said.

"It could be, I guess," Koenig admitted. "Only they don't allow newspapermen on board, wartime regulations. But you try explaining that to my editor."

"Get one of the passengers to tell you what it's like," Thummel said.

Koenig shook his head. "I've tried that. They never notice the right things. I'd have to find someone, brief him what to look for. But it's an idea. I'd pay—oh, two hundred dollars to the right person."

"Two hundred!" Trude exclaimed.

"That's a fortune," Thummel said. "Hey, what about Gus? He's a steward. He could do it."

"That so?" Koenig queried, and looked at Stahl. "You interested?"

Stahl's face twisted. "For two hundred dollars? Of course I'm interested. Trouble is, Cunard's only signing on British subjects. And anyway, I've signed up with Holland-America." He paused. "Hey, wait a minute, though! Neil—what about Neil?"

Leach was puzzled when they all turned to him. "I didn't know your young friend was a steward, too," Koenig said.

"I'm not," Leach laughed.

"That's no problem," Stahl said enthusiastically. "Cunard's so short-staffed, they're taking on anyone presentable. You'd only have to show your passport."

"So how about it, young fellow?" Koenig smiled. "Do you fancy a round trip on a luxury liner, with two hundred clear, over and above your pay?"

Leach was tempted. The round trip would take only a few weeks, then with all that money he could stay on in New York for at least six months, and be with Trude. He glanced at her. Her eyes were shining, urging him. He had been drinking, he knew, but he was still cautious. "I mean—what paper are you with?" he asked Koenig. "And what would I have to do?"

"The *Mail and Express*," Koenig said. It was all planned. The New York *Mail and Express* was secretly German-owned and, if Leach decided to check up, the features desk would vouch for "Phil Kelly." "I'd want real eyewitness material. Any change in standards because of wartime, how the passengers react to the blackout, entering the war zone. Stuff like that. I believe she usually carries a number of Canadian volunteers going to fight for the homeland, British reservists, uniforms on the promenade deck, that kind of thing too. You could take a camera. For photographs we always pay extra." Koenig smiled. "And there's her guns. The secret cannons we all know she carries. How the Greyhound of the Seas protects herself against marauders—that would be a scoop! What do you say?"

Leach was not quite sure, not able to think clearly. He had no doubt that he could do it, but Kelly had not told the whole story. There was a risk, too, of submarines. Not that they would ever touch the *Lusitania*. He looked at Trude again. She had sat up and leaned toward him. He felt her hand on his thigh. "Two hundred dollars," she breathed.

The U 20 was moving down the two-mile canal from her Emden base to the deepwater channel of the Ems estuary. During her overhaul she had been fitted with radio apparatus and now sported a retractable wireless mast. It was just after seven in the morning and the few people on the canal banks waved and cheered, noticing the garlands of flowers and wreaths of laurel which hung on her masts and conning tower to wish her luck on her patrol. To the workers in the yards and factories and the people living along the canal, the U 20 was a dashing, almost festive sight, and their hearts went out to the sailors on the deck and her commander up on the conning tower platform.

It was a chill morning and Schwieger was glad he had put on his leathers. The sporadic cheers and waving were infectious and he smiled as he raised his hand to the visor of his cap in reply. Even the solemn Haupert, who stood beside him, smiled and nodded. Behind them, the smaller, older man in the dark uniform and cap of the Merchant Marine seemed to be taking all the greetings and good wishes as meant for him and was beaming, shaking his arms above his head. "Do you always get this kind of send-off?" he chuckled.

"Usually," Schwieger said curtly. The civilian made him uncomfortable and he realized he had sounded impolite. "In the summer, when the boats go out," he added, "sometimes it's like the Battle of the Flowers." Below him, on the very front of the conning tower, hung a large horseshoe wreath of purple violets from Rudolph Zentner. He was missing Rudi already. It felt odd without him.

He had returned to base and found the U 20 in first-class condition, her periscope housing repaired, but there had been an irritating delay of another two days while the casualties in his crew were replaced. He had a new gunnery lieutenant, Scherb, who seemed keen and efficient, and he had been given Mate of the Reserve Lanz, one of the many master mariners cooped up in port by the blockade.

"I know what it's like having civilians on board," Bauer told him. "But it's somebody's bright idea. And it's a good one. Old salts like Lanz can identify the vessels of any nationality at once by their outline, their speed and rigging. He can help you to avoid genuine neutrals and decoys. And you'll have a built-in witness, an independent confirmation of all sinkings."

It was official, so Schwieger could not argue. On the face of it, it *was* a good idea, although he had misgivings. Leaving so long after the rest of the patrol, he would be on his own. He did not want a civilian standing at his elbow, telling him what to attack. That had to be his judgment as commander, to engage or break off an attack without having to explain why to anyone. His orders were to proceed round the north of Scotland, to circle Ireland on the west and come up into the Irish Sea, taking a position off the Mersey River bar, outside Liverpool. At last he had been given an ideal hunting ground. Hersing's favorite. But now Hersing would be well on his way to the Mediterranean, and it was time to show what the U 20 could do.

Yet the position was also highly dangerous, patrolled in depth. He would need to keep his wits about him, against destroyers, torpedo boats, mines and nets, enemy submarines. He saw a knot of workmen grinning and waving. To them the thought of the U-boat was daring, romantic. They saw the garlands and fresh paint, the red and black Imperial ensign at the stern, not the men on duty below, oiling and polishing the torpedoes, double-checking the batteries and engines, Hirsch and his crew testing the instruments and gauges on which their lives depended. The smallest malfunction or accident, apart from enemy action, might turn the U 20 at any moment into an airless floating coffin. Each time she returned safely from patrol was a dispensation, a postponement of an end that was statistically inevitable.

An old woman lifted her arms to them from the bank. "God bless you, brave boys!" she called.

Schwieger raised his hand, while the crewmen on deck watch cheered her. *Morituri te salutant,* Schwieger thought, and surprised himself. He was becoming depressed. He knew the reason. He was uneasy without Zentner and with changes in his command personnel, and he was still affected by saying goodbye to Anneliese. It was unfortunate that his train had left first. He would have preferred to see her off. She had been composed and smiling until the very last moment. But he could not forget how suddenly the facade had crumbled when his train began to pull out. She had been holding his hand at the corridor window. She had snatched it back and turned away, her shoulders bent, not wanting him to see her sobbing. How long would it be until they met again?

He heard laughter, girlish. A group of young women in smocks and headscarves had come out from their workshop to the low wall by the canal. They had thrown a bunch of yellow tulips to the U 20 and one of the crewmen had caught it. It was Lippe. He bowed and thrust his great, bearded face into the flowers, kissing them extravagantly, then held out his arms to the girls to show them the tulips were only a substitute for what he really wanted. The girls giggled and walked along behind the wall, blowing kisses back. The crewmen were laughing.

In spite of himself, Schwieger began to smile, too. Lippe . . . It was incredible, but just that morning he had received a letter from another young woman asking for compassionate leave for the torpedoman, who had been unable to marry her because he was always on patrol. And she was pregnant. Schwieger shook his head. Every time Lippe went on leave, he must pop another one or two in the oven. By the end of the war, he would have created a one-man population explosion in East Prussia.

They came out into the estuary, past the boom into the deep channel between Germany and Holland, steering for the heavily defended island of Borkum at its mouth. Looking back, Schwieger could see the low-lying coast, the spires of the country churches standing up clear and distinct above the flat marshes of East Friesland. It was the last picture he always took with him of home.

At ten, passing the buoy of Westeren, he ordered a trial submergence for thirty minutes before picking his way cautiously through the new minefield reported in Sector 081. He spent the afternoon testing his wireless telegraphy sets, exchanging messages with the naval advice boat *Arcona*. By eight in the evening he was at the Dogger Bank and set his course across the North Sea for the northern tip of Scotland.

Will Turner was disappointed. He had been looking forward to seeing Ethel Barrymore in her play at the Empire, but the production had transferred to Boston. I should have gone on my last trip, he told himself. Instead, on that last night in New York, he treated himself to dinner at his favorite downtown restaurant, Lüchow's.

He felt no twinge of guilt at patronizing a German restaurant. Cooking, like music, was international. German cuisine might have gone out of fashion in England, but here he could order Bismarck herring or Wienerschnitzel without a qualm. As he studied the menu, he noticed someone he recognized across the room. It took him a moment to place him because he was dressed so differently, in a smart blue suit, but it was the heavy-faced steward who had been with him on the *Transylvania* and then the *Lucy*. He had just sat down with a bigger man, sharp-eyed and craggy, like a pugilist. Turner nodded across to them, just as the waiter came. When he had given his order, he looked over again, and they had gone. Odd, he thought, and smiled. Hope it wasn't my ugly mug that chased them away.

The meal was delicious and he allowed himself a bottle of Rhine wine with it. It was one of the perks of his position to be able to spend occasional evenings in port like this. And he liked his own company. To be decent, he ought to go back to the pier and see how Staff Captain Anderson was getting along. The loading and other preparations had been going on all day. A stream of cargo and provisions was being loaded, the largest amount of both for months. It was the traditional time for many to take European vacations, and people apparently saw no reason to alter their plans or habits because of the war. They knew the *Lusitania* was the safest ship afloat and her passenger list was fuller than it had ever been since the start of the war. The shortage of seamen and cabin staff was a headache and those who had signed on were working all hours, with the loading, making cabins ready, cleaning and painting and polishing.

They grumbled, but they were proud of her, Turner knew. He ought to go and show himself, though first he had a visit to make. The doorman whistled him up a taxi and he took it uptown to the New Amsterdam Theatre, to say goodbye to his niece, Mercedes. She had told him he was a miracle man, for C.F. had been to see her play and had sent round a black cross. He was going to interest himself in her career when he returned from his trip to London.

In the corner of his taxi, Turner sucked on his pipe and smiled. They were heading up Broadway and had slowed down because of the traffic. The sidewalks were crowded. Carriages, hacks and taxicabs were dropping people in evening dress off outside the theaters. Over twelve hundred passengers were booked to sail with him and it was a racing certainty that in this excited, bustling crowd were quite a few whom he would be welcoming on board in the morning.

He was passing the front of the Knickerbocker Theatre and in the swirl of people about its doors were Matt and Livvy Fletcher. They both wore evening clothes, Livvy in a dark emerald gown and a short cape of black ruffled satin which brought out her perfect coloring. The play, *The Hyphen*, had been recommended to Matt and she hugged his arm with anticipation, although she had heard that it was very serious and controversial.

It was the final performance and Justus Miles Forman stood at the side of the main door, watching the audience come in. There were not very many, and he was grateful to each and every one of them. He had seen Charles Frohman in the afternoon and the producer had told him that he still had no regrets.

A block further up the street Frohman was standing with David Belasco in his Empire Theatre. He was leaning on his stick, also watching the audience come in, greeting his friends. "I can imagine no better way to go than with the knowledge that I leave behind a full house every night," he said.

Belasco smiled, yet was troubled. "Are you sure you have to go, Charley? Couldn't your London manager take care of things?"

Frohman winced. "Not you too, David?" he sighed. "I

have had everyone at me all week. I went to say goodbye to old Abe Hayman today. He begged me not to go, practically on his knees."

"What did you say to him?"

Frohman's eyes twinkled. "I told him if he wanted to write to me to send it care of the German U-boat Fleet."

Belasco laughed. He had no great friendships, no special connections, in England, so had no compulsion to brave the dangers of a crossing. And he knew better than to argue with Charley when his mind was made up.

There was a stir of recognition round them. Tall and handsome, Alfred Gwynne Vanderbilt was coming in with his beautiful wife, Margaret, and some friends, whom he paused to introduce. "I believe we're to be fellow passengers tomorrow," he said.

"I believe so," Frohman smiled. They had crossed on the *Lusitania* together before and met socially in London.

"Well, I think you're both mad," Margaret told them. "Mr. Frohman may have essential business in England. But to risk your life for a stable of silly horses . . ."

In recent years, Vanderbilt's sporting interest had switched from racing cars to thoroughbreds. Amongst other honorary posts, he was a director of the International Horse Show Association. The previous year the autumn show had been canceled, but he agreed with his fellow directors that this year, in view of the improvement in the war situation, it might be held. Discussions were to take place in London.

"If we give up everything because of this war," he said, "afterwards there will be no civilized life left." He smiled. "I hear this play is excellent, Mr. Frohman. I'll tell you tomorrow what I think of it."

Frohman only watched from the back for a few minutes after the curtain rose. He had one or two notes to write, last instructions to leave, and went up to his office.

His right knee was very painful and he stretched his leg as he sat at his desk. He really had to go to London. He had the next season's plans to prepare. Besides, his second home was there and he missed his friends, especially Jamie Barrie. It was hard to explain to his friends in New York. Marie Doro had been sitting in that very chair yesterday, sobbing her beautiful eyes out. And this afternoon Ethel

Barrymore had arrived unexpectedly from Boston. He knew what she was going to say the moment he saw her. "Ethel, my dear," he told her, "you are a sensible young lady and I've had to sit through too much overacting about this trip already."

"Because we care about you, C.F.," she said. "Everyone's afraid that something will happen to the *Lusitania*. Ellen Terry's going home to England tomorrow as well, but she's sailing on the *New York*."

"I shall send her some flowers from London, to await her arrival."

Ethel laughed in spite of her exasperation. "What are we going to do with you?" she said fondly. She was more subtle than the others. She did not plead or harangue. Instead, she talked to him about the old days, when she first met him and he gave her her start, and all the others he had helped. All the hundreds of people who depended on him.

"You're very dangerous, my dear," he told her. She kissed him and, when she left, there were tears in his eyes.

Thinking about her, he reached for the phone and put through a telegram to her in Boston. "Nice talk, Ethel. Goodbye. C. F."

He wrote some other notes, as always on a yellow pad with a blue pencil. His friends would get them on Monday and recognize them and think of him. He had taken care of almost everything at this end. One person he hadn't seen, but that was not possible. He would write to her from London, as lightly and amusingly as he could, and until then try not to think about her.

His valet would be packing now, and probably his friend and associate Paul Potter would be looking for him to discuss last-minute business. He was just rising to make his slow way back to his rooms at the Knickerbocker when the telephone on his desk rang. As soon as he heard her voice say, "Charles? Charles, is that you?" his hand shook and he sat back in the chair. He shut his eyes.

"Why, yes, Maude," he said. "How nice to hear from you! Is something wrong? Why aren't you on stage?"

"It isn't time yet out here," she told him. "This is Kansas City."

Of course . . . With his eyes closed, listening to her soft

voice, he could see her, conjure her up, until her presence was with him. Maude Adams, his leading lady, her delicate, elfin face and gentle spirit. He had loved her from their first meeting. He did not tell her. The thought of his froglike ugliness next to her delicate beauty was grotesque, and he did not want her to pity him. He treated her, instead, with devoted care and tenderness.

"Charles? Are you still there?" she asked.

"Yes, my dear," he said. "How lovely to talk to you! You must have known I was thinking about you."

"Why not? I always think of you." Her voice sounded strained, far away. "Are you still sailing tomorrow?"

"Yes," he smiled. "Jamie is impatient for me to be there, to have news of you."

"Please, Charles, be serious!" she begged. "Everyone's saying it's not safe! That you'd be throwing your life away."

Frohman's knee stabbed with pain and he gripped his thigh above it. "Oh, that's all exaggerated, Maude," he laughed. "Really, there's no danger, not on a huge liner, with half the United States on board. I have to go over there. But I'll be back in a month or six weeks, and I'll come and see your tour "

"I want you now," she said quietly. "I want you to stay."

He hesitated, finding it difficult to deny her anything. "I really can't, my dear. I'm needed there. It's all arranged."

"I need you too," she said, so quietly now that he could scarcely hear her. Yet he could tell that her voice was breaking.

"Believe me, my dear," he said gently, "if anything could make me travel west tomorrow, instead of east, it would be the thought of being with you."

"No, Charles, please . . ." she faltered. "Why won't you understand? Don't you love me?"

The signals from the British Admiralty to the Dover Patrol and other Patrol Areas were intercepted by German listening stations. Deciphered, they were rushed to Naval Intelligence in Berlin. The signals warned patrols of the serious likelihood of attacks on all large troop transports off the West Coast and in the Channel.

The missing piece had been found, the justification that

Tirpitz needed to lay before the politicians. Instructions were relayed to Fregattenkapitän Bauer, the only flotilla commander with a patrol in the western area, and signals were sent to any U-boat with radio apparatus still within receiving distance. The U 30 was directed to Dartmouth in the English Channel, the U 27 to the Bristol Channel and the U 20 to the Irish Sea. "Expect large English troop transports. Attack transports merchant ships warships."

Chapter 22

LIVVY HAD ENJOYED HER LAST DAY IN NEW YORK. THERE had been no rush, since she had packed the night before. The morning was fair and they took the children to the carousel in Central Park, then boating on the lake. After lunch Matt went with Peter for a farewell visit to the American Indian ethnic collection at the Metropolitan Museum while the women of the family did some final shopping.

As they set off, Livvy and Diana ran into the tall, good-looking man with greenish eyes in the lobby. It would have been impolite to walk past. "You're sailing tomorrow, aren't you?" he said.

"Tomorrow morning," Diana told him.

"Well, I shan't be able to watch your mother from afar any more," he smiled. "In any case I'm leaving myself."

If he was flirting, it was very discreet, and Livvy smiled back. "Are you going home, too?"

"Unfortunately, no," he laughed. "Just changing my hotel." He looked down at Diana and hesitated before putting out his hand and touching her long, dark hair. "Have a good and a safe trip," he said. And somehow Livvy knew that he was thinking of the daughter he had told them about.

They met Matt and Peter again at four, and as a treat, Matt took them all to the Nickelodeon. Livvy had considered them not quite respectable, but it was really very sumptuous inside. They saw a news film of Henry Ford at a peace rally with the suffragette Rosika Schwimmer, of ex-President Teddy Roosevelt reviewing a march past of General Wood's volunteers, and actual battle scenes from Flanders with bombs exploding and men dying, which were horrible. Then there was a silly but very funny short film about a fat man who kept having to dress up as a woman, and a longer one about the Pony Express, with an attack on a stagecoach by Apaches that had Peter jumping up and down in his seat with excitement.

In the evening Matt and she had gone to *The Hyphen*, which they both found absorbing in spite of the fairly thin audience and some who booed at the end. "Could it really happen?" she asked.

"Well, people have to decide where they stand, what they believe in," Matt said seriously. "And if necessary, fight for their country."

Afterwards, they were both thoughtful and silent, but Matt had a surprise for her. He had booked a corner table at Delmonico's, a wicked extravagance. Quite a few heads turned to watch Livvy, dark and striking in her emerald gown with its high waist, long narrow skirt and deep neckline, and made her feel very special. The wine and the music, the whole atmosphere was sparkling and romantic. Matt told her she had never looked lovelier. He even danced with her twice.

In the morning they were up just after six and were all bathed, dressed and breakfasted before eight. "We're not sailing till eleven!" Livvy protested.

"We have to check in at the *Cameronia* before ten, and I think we ought to get there in good time," Matt said.

At the last minute Diana did not want to leave. She burst into tears and kissed the black roommaid, who hugged her and began sobbing herself. Peter's mouth curved down. "England's going to be moldy," he muttered, but he refused to cry.

Like the children, Livvy was sorry to be leaving New York, where they had been so happy. The day was overcast, with a drizzle of rain, which helped to lower her spirits. She hugged Matt's arm in the taxi and tried to remind herself that she was going home and would soon see her parents, and that in ten or eleven days the kids would probably be just as sad to leave the *Cameronia*.

When the taxi reached the riverfront at West Street, they were held up by the tangle of hacks round Pier 54. There was a crowd of sightseers and newsmen outside the gates and there seemed to be some confusion. Apparently the giant *Lusitania* had not finished loading, although her passengers were already going on board. They moved on and discovered a similar, though smaller, confusion at the *Cameronia*'s pier. Her cargo derricks were swung out and a group of early passengers like themselves appeared to be arguing by the Customs Shed.

Matt signaled to the porters, who were standing watching, but they only pointed to the gate. "Better wait here," he told Livvy.

She waited with the children by their bags. When Peter asked why they could not go in, she shook her head. "I don't know, dear. I think maybe we're too early." She was glad the rain had stopped.

She could see Matt with the people at the gate. He went inside, to the Customs Shed, and after a minute or two came out with a gray-haired man in a purser's uniform. He beckoned her over and she could tell that something was wrong. "They can't take us," he said.

Livvy jolted with surprise. "Can't? What do you mean, they can't? We booked weeks ago!"

"I very much regret the inconvenience, Mrs. Fletcher," the purser said in a soft Scots voice. "But you see, the *Cameronia* is not sailing for the United Kingdom today."

Livvy looked from him to Matt. "Just like that?" After all their preparations? It was outrageous.

"She's been commandeered," Matt explained.

"Requisitioned," the purser corrected. "By the British Admiralty. I'm sorry. We were notified only a few hours ago."

"I can't believe this!" Livvy exclaimed. "The Admiralty decides to take over a ship, and throws all the passengers off without any warning? I mean, what do they expect us to do? All our trunks and things are in there somewhere. You talk about inconvenience. Are we just to be left standing here?"

"Now, hold on, Livvy," Matt said. "They have made other arrangements. We've been offered alternative accommodation on the *Lusitania*." He smiled as her frown of annoyance changed to surprise.

The children walked along beside the man pushing their suitcases, asking him a battery of questions, as they crossed to the other pier. Matt and Livvy were following. "It seems that quite a few ships have been requisitioned lately," he told her. "The *Cameronia*'s only the latest." He lowered his voice. "She's sailing for Halifax to pick up a load of Canadian troops and supplies."

"Of course I understand that things like this are bound to happen," Livvy said. "I'm sorry I lost my temper back there. It was such a shock."

"Don't worry," Matt grinned. "I was a little sharp myself. But really, it's no inconvenience at all. And we'll be in England sooner. The *Lusitania* only takes six days on the crossing."

"Yes." Livvy looked ahead to the huge liner, towering above the pier, making everything else seem puny by comparison. "There was no trouble getting a cabin?"

"No. Apparently, second class is quite full, but there's room in first."

"Matt!" Livvy gasped. "We can't—we can't afford first class on the *Lusitania*."

"I promised you first," he said, smiling. "I told them. I booked first, and that's what I intend my wife and family to travel. Any difference in fare can be made up by the British Admiralty." She laughed.

They were passed through the gates of Pier 54 by the guards, on producing their *Cameronia* tickets. Security was strict. In the Customs Shed, passengers had to identify their bags individually and open them to be examined by Cunard personnel. Turner and the Line were taking no chances with saboteurs. As she climbed the steep main gangplank with Diana holding her hand, Livvy looked up and was almost dizzied by the view of the liner's side, stretching above her like a vast black wall. There was only a glimpse of the white superstructure and the lifeboat davits from this angle, but above them the four enormous black funnels filled the sky, each one as wide as a street. It was like climbing a ladder to enter the Waldorf-Astoria by a window on the third floor, she thought, except that the black side of the *Lusitania* was so much longer.

At the top of the gangplank a dozen stewards in white tunics were waiting with some ship's officers and Purser McCubbin, who saluted as Matt showed him the transfer note from the *Cameronia*. "Ah, yes, Mr. and Mrs. Fletcher and two minors," McCubbin murmured, ticking them off on his list.

"Is he the Captain?" Diana whispered.

"No, silly, that's the Captain," Peter told her.

Staff Captain Anderson was easily identifiable by the four gold rings on the cuffs of his uniform and the gold braid on the visor of his cap. He was standing to the side, looking at a telegram which a thickset, crop-haired passenger had just shown him. "I'm sorry, Mr. Lehmann," he said. "I'm at a loss to explain it. It seems like the work of some crank."

Lehmann, a New York stockbroker, took back the telegram and showed the Staff Captain the morning newspaper he was carrying. "I don't expect you can explain this either?" he rasped.

Anderson barely glanced at the folded page. "It's been brought to our attention already, sir," he said politely. "I can only point out that it is a propaganda statement. Apart from that, I have no useful comment to make." He saluted and came forward, smiling, to welcome the Fletchers on board.

"I can offer you a very nice stateroom on D Deck," McCubbin was saying. "On the port side, with a smaller cabin adjoining."

"That sounds fine," Matt nodded. "If we could see them?"

"Certainly, sir." McCubbin clicked his fingers and one of the D Deck stewards came to take their hand luggage. "This is Biggs. He will show you your cabins."

"I'm sorry about the inconvenience you've had," Anderson said. "But we'll try to make you as comfortable as possible."

"I'm sure you will," Livvy smiled. It was her first real smile of the day, radiant and spontaneous, and all the men watching felt warmed by it. McCubbin beamed and Staff Captain Anderson, whose usual attitude to passengers was respectfully correct, found himself smiling back. He converted it into another salute to cover his embarrassment.

Peter returned the salute and Diana copied him. She was wearing a straw sailor hat with her navy blue coat and sailor's collar. "My apologies, miss," Anderson said, bowing. "I mistook you for one of the crew."

Diana laughed delightedly. "Silly man," she remarked,

and walked off with Peter and the steward carrying their bags.

Livvy could see the Purser and stewards stifling their grins and was glad that Anderson chuckled, taking it in good part. She held Matt's arm as they followed the children and the steward, Biggs, to the nearest elevator. He was a stocky bustling middle-aged Cockney with thinning hair he wore carefully brushed across his forehead and the balding crown of his head. "This 'ere's the main deck," he was explaining. "The lifts go up and down to all six decks above the 'old. That saves a deal of climbin' stairs, you'll find."

The elevator purred upward and opened onto an even more elegant corridor, gleaming white, with wall lights in fluted amber shades and other lights colored blue, white or red to show the position of exits, washrooms and fire extinguishers. There was a broader carpeted area off to their left, and Livvy gripped Matt's arm tighter as they caught a glimpse of the white and gold Corinthian columns supporting the balcony of the first-class dining saloon through the etched glass of its swing doors. Their feet were almost soundless on the cushioned linoleum flooring.

" 'Ere we are, D Deck," Biggs told them. "Otherwise known as the upper deck. There's another three above us, C, the shelter deck—B, the promenade deck—an' A, the boat deck. Above that there's only the navigatin' bridge an' the officers' 'ouse. This way, if you please." He led them across amidships, past another wide corridor and into a narrower, door-lined passage leading to the port side. He opened the second door from the end on the right. "This 'ere would be your cabin, young sir and miss," he told Peter and Diana. As they peeped excitedly inside, he opened the door at the end. "An' this would be yours, sir and madam."

The stateroom was more spacious than Livvy would have thought possible on board ship, the inner bulkheads paneled in natural walnut, while the twin bedheads, tallboy and built-in wardrobe were in the same wood polished to a lacquer finish. The carpet was a soft sage, with the brocade bed covers and heavy drapes above the padded window seat a slightly darker shade. Only the large round porthole with its brass bolts reminded her that she was on a liner and not in a luxury hotel.

"You'll want a minute or two to think about it," Biggs said. "I'll just see the nippers are all right." He put their hand luggage down on two folding stands and went out.

"I think Mr. Biggs knows he's on a winner," Matt laughed.

Livvy was examining the tallboy and the wardrobe, checking the hanging space and the drawers. There was a door by the wardrobe, opening into a small dressing room and a private bathroom with a washstand and a miniature green tub like a hipbath. "It's so perfect I'm afraid I'm going to wake up," she breathed. "Thank you, Matt." He came to her and kissed her, very gently.

There was a knock at the narrow door in the inner bulkhead. Matt unbolted it and they saw Peter and Diana grinning through at them. "Come and see our cabin," Diana insisted. "It's beautiful!"

The second cabin was slightly smaller, without the dressing room and bathroom, its colors pink and cream, and Peter bounced on the beds to show how springy they were until Livvy stopped him. Biggs was smiling at them from the doorway to the passage.

"There's no window or porthole. Won't it get stuffy in here?" Matt asked.

Biggs pointed to two louvered openings near the ceiling. "Thermo-tank ventilation, sir, electrically controlled. For heating and air circulation. It's one of the features of the *Lusy*."

Matt chuckled. "There's no arguing with that, Mr. Biggs."

Biggs touched his forehead with the tip of his index finger. "I'll let the Purser know. 'E'll be most gratified."

"Our trunks will be coming over from the *Cameronia*," Livvy reminded him.

"Leave that to me, ma'am. The cabin maid'll be along to 'elp you unpack. Anything you want, just press that button there—only, we're a bit short'anded, so we'd appreciate it if it could be just for essentials like, till sailin' time."

When the steward had gone, Livvy had another look at the dressing room. When she came back into the cabin, her heart turned over. Matt was in the children's cabin, checking the controls for heating and ventilation. Peter had undone the bolts of the porthole and swung it open and both he and Diana had wriggled their heads and shoulders out through

405

it. Diana seemed to be hanging right out, her legs dangling in the air, Livvy stopped herself from calling to them, hurried across and caught them both round the waist. "Come on, you two," she said. "It's too early to go for a swim." She had a glimpse of a sheer drop and water beyond them between the liner and the next pier. They were struggling as she pulled them in. "You must never do that again," Livvy warned them. "It's very dangerous."

Matt was coming in. "You listen to your mother," he agreed. "No opening portholes or leaning over the rail. You don't want to be watched all the time and treated like babies, do you?"

"No, Daddy," Peter said.

"Well, then, it's up to you. Any nonsense and I'll put reins on you." The children smiled, but they knew he meant it.

"We'll be really good," Peter promised. "Redskin's honor."

"Cross our hearts," Diana added solemnly.

"Right." Matt nodded, accepting their promise. "Now, you keep out of mischief till I get back. I'm just going for a word with the Purser."

"Can't I come with you?" Peter asked.

"Me, too?" Diana pleaded.

"They might as well," Livvy said. "It would be a chance for me to unpack their bags without them under my feet."

To her surprise, Matt hesitated and seemed about to refuse. Then he shrugged. "Why not? Come on, you two." He smiled. "Stay close, now. I don't want you getting lost before we've even sailed."

In his day room on the boat deck directly under the wheelhouse, Will Turner sucked at his unlit pipe as he considered the sheaf of New York morning papers spread out on the table in front of him, the *Tribune*, the *World*, the *Herald*, the *Sun* and the *Times*. It was a certain bet that at least 90 percent of his passengers would have read one or another of them before coming on board. Whether they had turned to the advertisements and travel pages was another matter, but some must have, if only to confirm their departure time, and they would tell the rest. He frowned as he reached a decision. He laid his pipe down, rose and went out, taking his bowler hat.

He walked along the starboard promenade and paused in the slight shadow between the third and fourth lifeboats to look down over the rail. There were streams of passengers coming up the gangplanks, now that they and the friends and relations who had come to see them off had been cleared by the assistant pursers and Cunard officials. The pier was much more crowded and he saw the flash of newsmen's cameras as some notable stepped through the gate. The start of the summer season and the announcement that Turner was in command had brought a rush of bookings, and the passenger list was more full than for any crossing since the war began, including a fair number of well-known names. The *Lusitania* was doing her bit. Providing there was no panic, no mass cancellation. Then the whole operation could boomerang.

The elevators were in constant use and he went down the main companionway, raising his bowler to groups of passengers and their guests hurrying up to experience the view from the boat deck. Turner was aware of the familiar excitement of approaching departure in the people he passed. They were in for a disappointment, since there was no hope of casting off at the scheduled hour of ten o'clock. His first priority was to find out how long the delay was likely to be and why he had still not received his official sailing orders.

Coming up toward him was a good-looking, slim young man in a brand-new uniform. The *Lusitania* had sailed from Liverpool without a Junior Third Officer and this one had been signed on only two days ago. Turner had liked the look of him, not least because the uniform he had worn at the interview, in spite of being sponged and pressed, had obviously seen some use. Which suggested that he was not afraid of hard work. Now the boy had spent his savings on a new one, more suitable for a top-class liner, and that showed conscientiousness. Turner grunted in approval.

The junior officer paused on a lower step and saluted. He was carrying a copy of the *Tribune* folded open at the travel page, which he held out. "Mr. Lewis's compliments, sir," he said. "And he wonders if you have seen this?"

"Of course I've seen it," Turner growled. "Stop waving the bloody thing about!" More passengers came hurrying up the wide companionway past them and he grabbed the newspaper, folded it again and stuck it under his arm. "Where is Mr. Lewis?"

"By the main entrance, sir. Welcoming passengers."

"And you were with him? What's your name again?"

"Bestwick, sir. Albert Bestwick." The Junior Third Officer pronounced it without the *w*, Bestick.

"Very well, Bisset, I think you'd be better employed helping to get the rest of the cargo loaded."

"Aye aye, sir." Bestwick hesitated. "Bestick, sir."

"Right you are, Bisset. Cut along and report to the second officer."

Bestwick stood to attention as the Captain stepped round him and carried on down. He swiveled, watching the oval black crown of Turner's bowler, and let himself grin. He had thought it was just one of those stories. But the Old Man really did wear one. He had also heard that Turner was intimidating and unfriendly. He was gruff enough, but Bestwick didn't feel intimidated. Disconcerted was the word, maybe. Turner wasn't a man to take liberties with, but there was a twinkle behind his eyes that stopped him from being frightening. It was odd. They had only met twice, yet already Bestwick knew he'd go through fire for him.

As Matt came along the passage with the children, he saw another passenger being shown to his stateroom. It was the man, Lehmann, whom he had overheard talking to the captain. Lehmann was still carrying his newspaper, but dropped it in the metal bin in the passage before going into his cabin. As he passed, Matt fished it out, wondering what it was that had been such a cause for concern. The children were so agog, gazing all round, that they did not even notice.

He took them up the companionway to the shelter deck, which was enclosed for almost half its length, but open toward the stern in a series of observation bays. Peter and Diana were fascinated to be able to look down at the activity on the pier from this height. Matt had something urgent to attend to in which he could not involve the children. They were perfectly safe, yet he was reluctant to leave them alone. He noticed a young pantry steward at the door of the shelter deck bar and moved along to him. "Are you going to be here for a while?" he asked.

"At least until sailing time, sir," the steward told him.

Matt smiled in relief. "I have some business to take care of. Would you mind keeping an eye on those two?"

"A pleasure, sir," the steward said, and seemed embarrassed when Matt gave him a dollar bill. "That's not necessary, sir."

"Maybe not," Matt told him. "But it would make me feel better. They can be quite a handful." He went back to the children. "Now listen, you two, I have to go below for a little."

"I want to come with you," Diana said.

Matt shook his head. "Not this time, pet. I'll be quicker if I'm by myself. You see the steward there? He's going to look after you. If you want anything, you ask him. And don't start wandering off."

"No, Daddy," Peter promised.

"Okay then." Matt nodded and left them, hurrying back to the arrowed sign he had spotted, pointing the way to "Lifts."

The steward saw the children looking at him and moved toward them. He had been feeling nervous and conspicuous, having nothing to do. Watching over the children would at least help to take his mind off the other thing.

Diana smiled to him as he came to stand beside them. He smiled back to her, a nice smile. He had fair curly hair and a white tunic with a high collar and shiny buttons. "My name's Diana," she said. "What's yours?"

"Neil," he told her. "Neil Loach."

Matt walked quickly along the cross corridor and found the elevators. They were occupied, and while he waited, he opened the paper. It was folded at the travel page. The most striking thing was an advertisement for Cunard's sailings to Europe via Liverpool. Under a drawing of the *Lusitania*'s prow was the announcement "LUSITANIA. Fastest and largest Steamer now in Atlantic Service Sails SATURDAY, May 1, 10 A.M." The rest were advertisements for rival lines, steamboat trips, river cruises, the maiden voyage of the new S.S. *Czaritza* of the Russian American Line. There was nothing that would—Matt suddenly saw it. To the left of the Cunard quarter column, under the same heading, Ocean Travel, a statement in a black border like an obituary. It read, "NOTICE! TRAVELERS intending to embark on the

Atlantic voyage are reminded that a state of war exists between Germany and her allies and Great Britain and her allies; that the zone of war includes the waters adjacent to the British Isles; that, in accordance with formal notice given by the Imperial German Government, vessels flying the flag of Great Britain, or of any of her allies, are liable to destruction in those waters and that travelers sailing in the war zone on ships of Great Britain or her allies do so at their own risk." It was signed, "IMPERIAL GERMAN EMBASSY, Washington, D.C., April 22, 1915."

"How many of them have read it?" Turner asked.

"I'd estimate just under half, sir," Senior Third Officer Lewis told him. Lewis, a capable, quiet man with a noticeable Welsh lilt in his voice, was standing with Turner and Staff Captain Anderson a short distance from the main entrance, where Purser McCubbin still welcomed arriving passengers. "That's about the percentage who've mentioned it."

"Did they seem anxious?" Turner asked. "Any of them want to change their bookings?"

"No, no, nothing like that. No cancellations," Anderson said.

"Although," Lewis added hesitantly, "the stewards have reported that some don't want their bags unpacked. Not until they've heard something official."

"That's what we're all waiting for," Turner muttered. "Still no word from the Senior Naval Officer?"

Anderson shook his head. "Nothing. And it makes it difficult. Those damned reporters keep asking for a statement."

"The pier's crawling with them," Lewis said. "If I might make a suggestion, sir, perhaps it's time someone had a word with them."

"You could be right," Turner agreed. "Get on to the Cunard office. I want Sumner, the manager, over here on the double. It's all hands to the pump. The Germans are trying to start a panic and we have to squash it. I'll deal with the press who're already on board."

"Aye aye, sir." Lewis saluted and left.

Anderson coughed. "It's not merely the press. There's been a series of anonymous messages and telegrams directed at the better-known passengers. The Sparks very sensibly referred them to me."

Turner glanced at him in surprise. "You're holding back passengers' telegrams?"

"Only the more obviously bogus," Anderson explained apologetically.

Turner chuckled. "Good for you! Lost in transit—the best thing that could happen to them."

There was a commotion at the head of the gangplank. As if from nowhere, photographers and newsmen with press cards in their hatbands began to converge on it. Charles Frohman was limping up it, leaning on the arm of his friend, the playwright Paul Potter, followed by his valet, William. Even the impresario seemed surprised by his noisy reception, the flare of the cameramen's flashtrays and the shouted questions. Turner and Anderson came forward to welcome him. After Anderson had saluted and Turner raised his hat, he smiled and shook hands. "I must admit I am flattered," he said. "And a little mystified at the tumultuous interest the Fourth Estate appears to be taking in an ageing producer's business trip."

"Why'd you choose the *Lusitania*, Mr. Frohman?" one pressman asked.

"I always sail on her," Frohman told him. "I reckon I've had more dinners with Captain Turner than with my bank manager."

They laughed and another asked, "Did you read the German notice this morning?"

"I must have missed it," Frohman murmured. "The only notices I read are the ones of my plays. Now if you'll excuse me?"

A jabber of protests began to rise around them. Turner cut it off by holding up his hand. "Gentlemen, I'm sure you'll appreciate that Mr. Frohman wishes to see his cabin and to settle in."

"What's the stall, Captain?" someone shouted.

Turner seemed surprised. "No stall, gentlemen. I was about to say that I shall be available to answer any questions you may have in about twenty minutes on the boat deck. Perhaps Mr. Frohman may care to join me?"

"I'd be delighted to," Frohman smiled. "Until then, gentlemen." His glance to Turner was grateful for rescuing him and giving him time to recover from the long, painful walk along the pier and up the gangway.

411

A young seaman, Leslie Morton, was passing the third-class entrance as Elizabeth Duckworth reached it. He had been a cadet on a round-the-world training cruise on a naval tall ship, the *Naiad*. When they sailed into New York, the cruise had already lasted over two months and it would be a full year before they got back to England again and home. With his elder brother, Cliff, and some of their friends, he had applied to Staff Captain Anderson for permission to work their passage on the *Lusitania* to Liverpool, where they would join the regular navy. Anderson was only too happy. Even half trained, a dozen keen and active cadets were a valuable addition to his crew.

The shortage of stewards was more noticeable in steerage and Elizabeth rested her two heavy suitcases, panting, while the assistant purser examined her ticket. Her arms were aching from carrying the cases through the rush hour and the hour-long wait at customs, then up the steep gangplank.

Les Morton saw her loosen the collar of her thick serge overcoat and tuck some stray hairs back into the bun in which she wore her hair under her black straw hat. When she bent to lift the suitcases again, he stepped forward. "Allow me, madam."

"There's no need," Elizabeth told him. "I can manage, thank you."

"I've no doubt, madam," he smiled. "However, it's against company policy to let passengers carry their own baggage." He checked her ticket. "Just along here. If you please."

Elizabeth was on a strict budget and had made up her mind to do without luxuries like porters, but she was grateful. Les led her by the shortest route through the narrower third-class corridors and down a short companionway. He saw her note a sign pointing to the third-class dining saloon. "Closed, I'm afraid, madam," he told her.

Elizabeth was worried. "I thought we got fed," she frowned.

"Yes, of course," Les smiled. "It's only been taken over for extra storage space. Steerage passengers share the second-class dining saloon now. Here we are." He knocked on a door and showed Elizabeth into her cabin. "Have a good trip, madam." He was gone before she could give him the fifteen cents she had decided on.

The cabin was small, cleverly designed to hold two bunks on either side and two divided lockers, with not much room for anything else except a washbasin, two chairs and a folding table. It was a four-berth cabin and two of her traveling companions had already arrived, a slight, rather pale, pretty woman and a little boy.

"Hello," Elizabeth nodded. "I'm Mrs. Duckworth."

"Oh, I'm sorry," the younger woman apologized. "I'm Mrs. Scott, Alice Scott. And this is my son, Arthur." Arthur was perched on the edge of the bunk beside her. He jumped down and hid his face behind his mother's skirts.

"I thought you'd be too big to be shy," Elizabeth said. He peeped round at her and she smiled. She was unbuttoning her coat and looked at the two unoccupied bunks. "Is one of these mine?"

"It must be," Alice Scott said. "Either one, I suppose."

That's a bit of luck, Elizabeth thought, deciding on the lower one. "The other person hasn't turned up yet?"

"There's not going to be anyone else, I believe," Alice told her. "Just the three of us."

Elizabeth had shrugged off her coat and paused. Better and better

Third Officer Lewis reported back to Staff Captain Anderson. "Mr. Sumner's at the pier gates now, sir. Captain Turner was right. The newspapers all want to know when—and if— we'll be sailing."

"Of course we'll be sailing!" Anderson muttered irritably. In spite of his urbane exterior, he was much more easily ruffled than Turner. It's all right for him, he thought, but I have the responsibility for loading and unloading, and if there are any delays, I'm the one who'll have to explain them to the Board. He pulled out his watch. Less than twenty minutes to departure time, and not a hope of meeting it.

"The Chief Engineer was wondering if you could give him an idea of how long before we'll be leaving, sir," Lewis said.

"No, I cannot!" Anderson snapped. "Mr. Bryce will just have to possess himself in patience like the rest of us." As he turned away, he was startled to see the tall Canadian transfer passenger near them. He had undoubtedly over-

413

heard. And he was holding a paper with a copy of that damned German announcement.

"I hope I'm not interrupting," Matt said. "But I wondered if I could have a word with you, Captain?"

Anderson controlled himself. "That is purely an enemy contrivance, Mr. Fletcher," he assured him. "It is a matter of chance that it has been printed next to Cunard's advertisement in some newspapers, and cannot be taken as a direct threat to the *Lusitania*."

"I realize that, sir," Matt said. "What I really wanted to ask was if you could tell me where the *Cameronia*'s other passengers have been accommodated?"

Anderson had to stifle his irritation again. Why did even the most sensible-seeming landsmen ask these inane questions? "The purser on duty will have precise information. Now if you'll pardon me, Mr. Fletcher, I'm sure you understand that we have no time to spare. It is not merely the transfer of some forty passengers and their baggage, but also several hundred tons of stores."

"That's the other thing I wanted to speak to you about," Matt said, stopping him as he began to move away. "I think I can help you—with the baggage at least. If I can talk to the *Cameronia*'s passengers. I could get some of them to join me in shifting it for you."

Startled, Anderson glanced at Lewis and back. "Well, it's certainly an idea, Mr. Fletcher," he conceded. "And I'm grateful. But transshipping portmanteaux and steamer trunks is hard and tiring work, and I doubt that you'll find any passengers willing to assist you."

Matt smiled. "Oh, I'm pretty sure I will. In fact I guarantee it."

Charles Frohman's suite on B deck was comfortably luxurious, with its dayroom, bedroom, bathroom and valet's room. William was already unpacking, and Paul Potter watched Frohman as he limped across to the large basket of flowers in the shape of a ship which stood on the sideboard. "That's beautiful, Charley," he said.

"It certainly is," Frohman agreed, running his fingers over the line of the basket. It was from Ann Murdock, a fresh, delicately lovely New York girl with Titian hair whom he had spotted and turned almost overnight into a star, the latest in a long line.

"A lot of people care an awful lot about you," Potter said.

Frohman sighed and nodded. He limped to the swivel chair by the writing table and sat carefully, leaning back and lifting his right leg to drape it over the arm. He could tell that Paul was worried and hoped he was not building up to some scene that would embarrass both of them.

"I've tried not to talk about this trip, Charley," Potter said.

"I trust you'll persevere in your good intentions," Frohman murmured.

Potter smiled. He was an open-faced, gray-haired man, most famous for his dramatization of *Trilby*, like Frohman dedicated to his profession. "I still don't see why you're so set on making the trip at this moment."

"Sheer vanity, Paul," Frohman assured him. "I have led the first successful invasion of that tight little island since William the Conqueror—the American Invasion of the London Theater. And I don't want to surrender all my bridge-heads."

"That I can understand," Potter nodded. "But aren't we in danger of falling between bridges? Things are getting tougher here too. Quite a few of our productions aren't making any money. How long can you go on subsidizing the whole American Theater?"

Frohman shrugged. "What's money? All I ask is sufficient food, some decent clothes, somewhere to sleep—and enough credit to put on any play I want whenever I want to." He was relieved to hear Potter laugh. He took out a thick black cigar and lit it. "Talking of the drama, I hope you'll have finished your latest piece before I come back."

"I expect to," Potter said, and paused. "What about yours? Will it be finished?"

Frohman chuckled. It was an old joke between them, ever since he had confessed once that his dream was to leave one memorable play behind him, one he had written himself. "It's coming along, coming along," he smiled. The funny thing was that it really existed, a secret drama which he had been working on for years. The unfinished manuscript, a hundred yellow quarto pages, lay in the document case on the writing table beside him. Not even Paul had ever seen it.

"What are you aiming to call it?" Potter joked.

Frohman flicked his cigar. "Ambition. A comedy in four acts."

Neil Leach enjoyed looking after the children. They were lively and amusing, and although the little girl, Diana, had a tendency to wander off, Peter kept fetching her back, having given, as he said, his sacred word of honor on Harry Hightree's amulet. He showed the carved wooden charm to the young steward, who was fascinated by it. "I wish I had something like that," Leach muttered. "To bring me a bit of luck." He sounded so odd that Peter asked him what he meant. "Nothing, really," Leach told him. "Somebody walked over my grave, that's all. That's what my black nanny used to say when she felt down in the mouth." Peter laughed, but Diana shivered and said it was scary.

It had been a strange week for Leach. He had woken up the morning after the party with only a muzzy recollection of having promised the newspaperman something. After he had splashed his face with water, his memory was clearer. He laughed. He had no intention of going within a thousand miles of the war zone. As soon as possible he would have to get in touch with that reporter, the big man, Kelly, and tell him he had had one drink too many and now had changed his mind.

But then Gus had breezed in with another bottle of bourbon, followed after a few minutes by Trudie, all excited about the fine time they'd have with the two hundred dollars after he returned from Liverpool in three weeks. He hadn't the courage to tell them he wasn't going, and almost before he knew it, he was applying to the Staff Captain on the *Lusitania* for a job as a temporary steward. He more than half hoped that he would not be accepted because of his inexperience, but he was signed on at once.

He had one more meeting with the reporter, Phil Kelly, in Chester Williams's room, where he had been briefed again on the kind of information he was expected to bring back. Only this time the emphasis was more on the naval guns the *Lusitania* was supposed to carry, "Huge, copper-colored cannons," Kelly said. The meeting had developed into another party when the girls had come in with Gus Stahl and one or two others.

"It's your farewell party," Trude had whispered to him. He felt her plump thigh squirm against his, where they sat on the bed. "Ooh, I can't wait to have you back."

He had reported for duty on Thursday morning and been set to work cleaning cabins and polishing the first-class corridors. He had slept at home in Leroy Street that night, hoping again unsuccessfully to spend it with Trude. There had been constant loading of cargo at Pier 54 and Gus had asked him about it, but he had seen very little of it. The next morning he was assigned to pantry duty on the shelter deck. He could not have wished for anything better, as he had not been relishing the thought of fetching and carrying as a cabin steward, "It's your posh accent," the older man who showed him the ropes confided. "Go down well with the nobs in first, that will. It's a good skive, up 'ere. Plenty of fresh air, no 'eavy work, time to yourself." He pitied the seamen who were loading and shifting cargo nonstop all day. One annoying thing. He had lost his Cunard security pass and had to apply for another.

In the evening he went back to the boardinghouse to collect the things he would need for the crossing. He was deeply disappointed, for Trude had not been expecting him and was not at home. Gustave Stahl, however, insisted on accompanying him and carrying one of his bags. By chance he had found Leach's missing pass, so they had a spare.

When they reached the pier, they were allowed through the gate on showing their passes to the guards. They stood watching the loading for a while, the great nets swinging up crates and bales, the smaller cases manhandled by seamen and Cunard dockworkers up the gangplanks into the holds. Although it had been going on for a day and a half, the loading was by no means finished, and now was being completed under arc lights. Leach was puzzled by how fascinated Stahl seemed. He must have seen cargoes being taken on hundreds of times. It was fairly late when they went on board at last. All Gus wanted, he said, was to have a look at the pantry where Leach was to work. One or two other members of the crew had friends seeing them off, but they stood chatting in groups while Gus seemed anxious to avoid everyone, and it made Leach nervous.

They climbed to the shelter deck without any trouble. Leach's official station on the voyage was to be the portside pantry, which was in darkness. He switched on the light and Stahl nodded approvingly. "Oh yes, you'll be comfortable here. She's quite a ship." He was unbuckling the grip he had been carrying and, to his surprise, Leach saw him pull out a pint bottle of bourbon.

"Where did that come from?" he asked.

Stahl grinned. "I slipped it in when you were saying goodbye to Chester. Can't have you sailing off without one for luck."

Leach laughed. Everything was all right, and Gus was the best of fellows. Yet he was puzzled again when they had had a drink and Stahl took something else from the grip, a squat leather box. "What's that?"

Stahl opened the case and showed him. It was a camera. "The latest Kodak, foolproof. All you have to do is point it and press the button. It's already loaded." He handed it over.

Leach held the compact camera gingerly. "What do I need it for?"

"You remember what Phil Kelly promised," Stahl said. "He'll pay a special bonus for pictures. And you're in the best place—the shelter deck. That's where the guns are mounted."

"That's crazy, Gus!" Leach laughed. "You saw for yourself. There aren't any guns."

"Not in port," Stahl agreed. "But who knows when they might be run out for some reason. And you'll be here to get a shot of them." He took a square, nearly flat electric torch from his inside pocket. "Come on," he said. "We might as well have a look around now. Bring the camera."

The whole forward section of the shelter deck was blocked off by a solid gate, secured by thick bolts and padlocks. Beyond were the former third-class ladies' room and second-class smoke room, the lower windlass and capstan room and the store in the prow, making an enclosed space of about a hundred and twenty feet. Stahl shone his torch over the gate and the padlocks. "You'd need a crowbar and a sledge-hammer to break these open," he said.

"For God's sake, Gus!" Leach pleaded.

Stahl glanced at him and smiled. "Don't worry. It would make too much noise. But you're ideally placed to keep an eye on this gate. It has to be opened sometime, and that's when you have a look. Just one sight of what's inside could be worth an extra grand."

"Who from?" Leach asked.

"Certain parties. I'm sure Kelly will put you in touch when you report to him."

To Leach's relief, they moved away from the closed sections, heading back down the port side toward the pantry. However, about two yards from the door, Stahl stopped again, shining his torch down on the deck. "Let's get inside," Leach urged.

"Hang on a minute," Stahl said. "Here." He gave Leach the torch and knelt on the deck.

In the torchlight, Leach could see a groove in the teak planking. Gus was following it with his fingers, tracing out a large square panel like a hatch cover. "What is it?" he asked.

"A gun mounting," Stahl grunted. He was feeling the outer edge with his fingertips, trying to lever it up. "If we can raise this, we can tell what caliber gun it's meant for. Help me."

Leach was frozen, staring down at him. Again he heard a sound that terrified him, a quiet footfall as someone came toward them from the stern. He snapped off the torch. For a second he saw a figure in the brighter light from one of the bays; then whoever it was stepped aside into shadow. Stahl was rising. He fumbled for the heavy torch and took it back, holding it flat in his hand, as if he meant to use it as a weapon. "Who's there?" Leach called.

The answer came back from the darkness. "Who are you?"

"Leach. Pantry steward."

They heard a chuckle and the man came toward them, pausing just inside the zone of light from the lamp above the pantry door. He was of medium height, wiry, wearing a stained boiler suit and peaked denim cap, a sweat rag knotted round his neck, as swarthy as an Arab with grease spots and ingrained dirt. He grinned to them. "Frank Tower, oiler. I nearly pissed meself back there. I thought you was one of the officers."

"What are you doing?" Stahl asked.

419

"Havin' a walkabout," Tower told him. "I always come up top as much as I can when we're docked. Get some exercise, fill the old lungs, keep in trim. All right for you, but down in the boiler rooms it's like breathing hot pea soup." He glanced up. "'Ere—anyone up on the promenade deck?"

"I don't know," Leach told him.

Tower blew out his cheeks and sucked them in again. "Think I'll chance it, anyway. If you 'ear a yell an' a splash, you'll know old Bowler Bill's chucked me overboard." He winked and started back for the companionway. At the foot of it, he paused and they heard his hoarse whisper. "Twice round, that's a fair stroll. Each breath a guinea in the bank of 'ealth, eh?" He went up the companionway quickly. He was so silent, they could not catch his footsteps.

Leach moved nearer to the pantry door. "Whatever you're up to, it's got to stop, Gus," he insisted. "It's not safe here. What would anyone think?"

"Up to? What am I up to?" Stahl said reproachfully. "I'm only trying to help you, so you'll have something interesting to tell Kelly." He followed Leach to the door. "But you're right. It's not safe, Neil. One more drink and I'll be off."

They had gone back into the pantry, and as they killed the bourbon, Gus became his usual, cheerful self. Leach saw him down to the service gangplank. They shook hands and he joined some other visitors going ashore and walked off quite unconcerned. But afterwards, when Leach was stowing his gear in his locker and saw the camera again, he had an attack of the shivers. What in hell had he got himself into?

He was distracted by a loud squeal from Diana. She had climbed onto the base of the rail and was leaning over it. Leach caught the belt of her coat at the back. "Steady on there, young lady," he warned.

"Look!" she said excitedly. "It's Daddy!"

"Where?" Peter asked. He looked where she was pointing and saw their father down on the pier. He was pushing a cart. There were fourteen or fifteen other men with him and they were all pushing a series of flat carts, piled high with hampers, boxes and cabin trunks. A young ship's officer met Matt and saluted him, directing him to the nearest gangplank, where a party of seamen were waiting to assist in hoisting the *Cameronia*'s baggage on board.

"And there's Uncle Dan," Diana said.

"Don't be silly," Peter told her.

"But it is!" Diana protested. "See? There he is, behind Daddy."

Peter looked and, sure enough, there was Dan Connally at the rear of their father's cart, pushing with another man whom Peter thought he recognized. It was very puzzling. Uncle Dan had driven them in his Model T to the railroad station in Calgary a month ago and stood on the platform until they were out of sight, waving goodbye.

Chapter 23

CHARLES FROHMAN CLIMBED SLOWLY UP TO THE BOAT DECK.
He wanted nothing more than to sit quietly in his dayroom
and rest his leg, but he had given his word to Captain Turner.

He saw the ship's masters-àt-arms holding back a crowd
of waiting newsmen and photographers and raised his Hom-
burg to them. Turner was standing in the open space beyond
the last lifeboat with a slim, handsome man wearing a tweed
cap and three-piece suit, gray with a faint stripe, and a polka-
dot bow tie, Alfred Gwynne Vanderbilt. He limped toward
them, leaning on his cane.

"I'm glad you've brought your wife," Turner said. Frohman and he laughed.

Vanderbilt's smile was more reserved. Few things really
amused him any more, or excited him, for that matter. Some
of the savor had gone out of life these last years, and he
hoped this voyage would revive his spirits. "So here we are,"
he said.

"You promised to tell me what you thought of the play
last night," Frohman reminded him.

"I enjoyed it, but perhaps we should talk about it later."
He unfolded a telegram, which he held out. "I received this
ten minutes ago."

The shore-to-ship telegram was addressed to A.G. Vanderbilt. "Have it on definite authority the *Lusitania* is to
be torpedoed. You had better cancel passage immediately."
It was unsigned. Frohman's eyebrows rose. "Any idea who
it's from?"

"No." Vanderbilt put the telegram in his pocket.

"Have you had anything like this, Mr. Frohman?" Turner
asked.

"In point of fact, yes," Frohman said. "Telegrams, letters,

anonymous phone calls. And Captain Papen from the German Embassy rang me to suggest that it might be unwise to make this voyage."

"Did he say why?"

"Merely that because of the submarine campaign the waters round the British Isles have become extremely dangerous." Frohman paused. "I thanked him for his courtesy in calling me and told him I was sure that the officers of the German navy would display the same courtesy by not attacking passenger ships."

"Aren't you afraid of the U-boats?" Vanderbilt asked Frohman.

"No," Frohman murmured. "I am only afraid of the IOU's."

Turner could tell that he need have no fears about the press conference. "If you're ready, gentlemen," he suggested, and signed to the masters-at-arms.

The newsmen and photographers surged forward and in a moment had formed a clamorous half circle round Turner and his two most distinguished passengers, shouting questions, demanding to know why Frohman and Vanderbilt were risking the crossing, cutting in on one another. "Wait a minute, wait a minute!" Turner said strongly. "One at a time, please! Let's have some order."

The noise subsided and, as the jostling stopped, the photographers eased to the front to snatch their shots.

"Did you read the German warning in the paper this morning, Mr. Vanderbilt?" a man from the *Times* asked. "Do you think it's to be taken seriously?"

"We have no quarrel with Germany and therefore have nothing to be afraid of. I think the warning was meant kindly. That's how I see it."

"Why not sail on an American ship?" a *Tribune* reporter asked.

"I am a busy man," Vanderbilt told him. "I wish to get to England quickly, and the *Lusitania* is the fastest vessel afloat."

"Then you discount the danger of a submarine attack?"

"That is the last thing I am afraid of, sir."

The man from the *World* said, "Three years ago, you canceled your passage on the *Titanic* at the last minute. Do you think you'll be lucky this time?"

Vanderbilt smiled to Turner, who chuckled and laid his hands lightly on Vanderbilt's and Frohman's shoulders. "Now do you imagine these gentlemen would be booking on the *Lusitania* if they thought she could be caught by a German submarine? It's the best joke I've heard in many a day."

"Why is that, Captain?" the reporter asked.

"If you look at it objectively," Turner said. "The Germans could concentrate their entire submarine fleet on our track, and we'd still give them the slip. We can make up to twenty-seven knots. That's nearly twice as fast as any U-boat—as we're willing to show them if the need ever arises."

The reporters were smiling now too. "What about you, Mr. Frohman?" one of them called. "You haven't said anything."

Frohman's expression was mild. "I have made it a rule never to answer when I haven't been asked a question."

There was more laughter. "Then what is your attitude to the warning?"

"I think it is in very poor taste," Frohman said. "Here we are on a ship with some two thousand noncombatant passengers. How can there be any suggestion of threat or danger?"

"Do you know that Miss Ellen Terry, the actress, is sailing for England today on an American vessel?"

"Do you know, sir," Frohman countered, "that Miss Rita Jolivet, the actress, is sailing for England today on this one?"

"So you have no fears for the voyage?" the *Times* man asked.

"None whatever," Frohman answered, and frowned. "Provided that the pantry has a plentiful supply of orange juice, soda water, ginger ale, sarsaparilla and buttermilk."

Livvy couldn't believe she had finished already. The drawer units and hanging spaces were so well-designed that she had unpacked her own and Matt's things in record time, and the children's. She laid the Italian string doll on Diana's bed and the painted Indian on Peter's, and there was nothing left to do.

She went back into her own stateroom and, being alone, couldn't resist it. She hurried to the window seat, knelt on it and opened the porthole. She leaned her head out and caught her breath at the suddenness of the drop down the black side of the *Lusitania* to the waterline. The harbor smell of tar and brine, oil and decaying matter made her wrinkle her nose. A harbor lighter was stationed alongside near the bows, and cargo was being piled onto what seemed to be a giant, flat net. She saw that was exactly what it was when the corners were drawn up over a huge hook hanging from a steel hawser.

The net tautened and jerked, taking the weight of its load. It lifted, spinning slowly as it rose higher and higher as the cargo derrick hoisted it on board. It must be stuff from the *Cameronia*, she thought, and all at once she wanted to be with Matt and the children. These final moments before departure were so exciting, they ought to be together. He had said they were going up to the shelter deck.

Neil Leach was still looking after Peter and Diana. For the past twenty minutes they had been watching their father and the team of transfer passengers he had somehow managed to collect all working busily, unloading the baggage carts. The last of the cabin trunks was just going up the service gangplank. Leach smiled. It was fairly amusing to stand idly with the children while their father and other paying passengers strained and sweated down below.

"Steward!" someone called.

He glanced round disbelieving at the voice. Gus Stahl was coming toward him with two other men, one of whom carried a box camera. They had press cards in their hatbands and Stahl wore a card reading *Mail and Express* pinned to his lapel. "Watch the birdie," Stahl said, grinning at Leach's open-mouthed surprise.

"What are you doing here?" Leach gasped.

"Just picking up a few bucks," Stahl shrugged. "Phil Kelly asked me to show these two gentlemen around, since I'd already been here."

"Why didn't he come himself?"

"He's on another job," Stahl said. Koenig had wanted to come, but could not risk being recognized by the private detectives guarding the gangplanks and mingling with the passengers.

Leach saw Stahl nod to the photographer. By a trick of the slanting light, the trapdoor of the gun emplacement in the deck near them was revealed as a definite shadowed rectangle, and the photographer began to line up a shot of it. There were more people on the shelter deck now and Leach looked round anxiously. Suppose one of them noticed, suppose there were detectives among them . . . "For God's sake, Gus!" he protested. "Stop him!"

Stahl grabbed Leach's arm. "Keep your voice down! Don't be stupid," he snapped. When Leach gazed at him, tensing, he forced himself to smile. "Come on, Neil, it's only a photograph," he soothed. He released Leach's arm. "Let's get out of here. Take us round to your pantry."

All Leach's fears and suspicions were reawakened. "I—I have to stay with the children," he faltered.

Stahl became aware of the boy and the little girl beside them. They were intent on something down on the quay. "They're fine," he said. The photographer and the other bogus reporter were closing in on Leach and he had no choice but to go with them.

Livvy was coming along the side of the shelter deck and, as the men moved off, she caught sight of the children. She had expected to find Matt with them, but he was nowhere to be seen. The rain which had been threatening all morning had not developed and the sky was clearer. The crowd of sightseers outside the gates had doubled at least. There was even a newsreel camera on a tripod, with a man cranking the handle to take pictures of the new arrivals. Another moving picture camera was covering the people mounting the gangplanks.

Diana was pointing to it and squeaked in surprise when Livvy tapped her on the back. "What are you doing here alone?" Livvy asked them.

"We're not," Diana said. "The steward's with us." She turned round, but the nice young man in the white coat had gone.

"Where's Daddy?" Livvy asked.

"Down there."

"With Uncle Dan," Peter added. "And Mr. Olsen."

"Dan?" Livvy repeated, puzzled. "Dan Connally?"

"Down there by the gangplank," Diana told her. "With Daddy."

Livvy spotted Matt at the foot of the main gangplank with

a young ship's officer. Dan Connally was next to Matt, and several other men, including Larry Olsen, were beyond them. They were all relaxed and chatting. She could not understand what they were doing here, and her first thought was that they had come to see them off. That was absurd. She had a moment's surge of fear that something dreadful had happened at home. Then abruptly she realized.

Blood pounded in her ears. She felt hot and breathless, stifled, and her head swam as though she were going to faint. She gripped the rail to steady herself and shut her eyes. She should have known. There had been so many hints and indications, things Matt and others had said. She had been blind and, more than that, deliberately deceived. She heard Diana calling, "Uncle Dan! Uncle Dan!" and opened her eyes to see the group on the quay beginning to look up. As well as Dan and Larry Olsen, there were two others who had been at the dance in the schoolhouse, Barney Ferguson and the youngest Nyquist boy, and amongst the others were men she recognized who had worked with Matt in the Valley oil field.

Matt was hurrying up the gangplank and she spun away from the rail, forgetting the children, forgetting everything in her horror at his betrayal.

Neil Leach was in a panic. His only thought was to get out, to get away from here, off the ship, but the bigger of the two men with Gus was blocking the door of the pantry and the "photographer" had picked up a bottle by the neck. They both stood between him and his only hope of escape.

Stahl caught Leach by the arm and pulled him round to face him. All at once he was no longer happy, friendly Gus. "You've taken money," he said. "You're committed."

"But I didn't know then!" Leach protested. "I didn't know what I was doing—who I was really working for!"

"Who are you working for?" Stahl's voice was dangerously quiet.

"Oh, for God's sake!" Leach glanced round at the other two men.

"You are in no danger," Stahl said. "If you behave sensibly."

"No danger?" Leach whimpered.

427

"You have a contract. You'll fulfill it."

Leach was staring at Stahl. They were so sure of him, so sure they had him by the balls. He felt sick with loathing for them, and for himself, for his gullibility. They must all have been laughing at him, Gus and Chester and the man who called himself Kelly. Even Trude. That was what hurt most. "You think I'm going through with that now?" he whispered. "You think I'm going to work against my own country?"

"You're not a fool," Stahl said. "You must have known all along that the information you were asked to collect could be useful to . . . other parties. And not merely to the newspapers."

"I trusted you," Leach said bitterly. "But not any more." He drew himself up. "So you can just clear off, all three of you. Or I'll go straight to the Captain and tell him everything I know."

"What do you know?" Stahl asked calmly. "And what could you prove?"

"He's the sort of little bastard who just might do it," the big man at the door warned.

Stahl shook his head. "I don't think so. Shall I tell you why? Because he couldn't accuse us without condemning himself."

"I'm not a spy!" Leach protested.

"No, but you're a traitor—and that's worse," Stahl said. "We might be sent to jail, but you would most probably be shot. We would have to tell them how you had been allowed to leave Germany to gather information for us." He smiled. "So you see, it is far better to go ahead exactly as we arranged. Far better for everyone." Leach had begun to tremble again. His head jerked when Stahl reached out and patted his cheek. "There, there," Stahl murmured. "Just do the work you're being paid to do. You'll still get your money. And who knows? Trudelein may even keep her part of the bargain." He paused. "She's very skillful in bed. You can believe me. I recommend her."

The man with the camera laughed softly as Leach put his hands over his eyes.

Matt came quickly along the corridor. He had run up from the pier, but Livvy was no longer with the children. "One minute she was there, and the next she was gone," Peter told him.

Matt paused outside the stateroom and swore at himself for his clumsiness. Not like this, he told himself, I didn't want her to find out like this. He saw her as soon as he opened the door. She was standing between the tallboy and the wardrobe, pressed against the bulkhead as if to get as far away from him as possible. "Is it true?" she demanded. "Tell me it's not true!"

He closed the door behind him and took a step toward her.

"Don't come any closer!" she said. Her arms were wrapped round her tightly to stop herself shaking. "Is it true? You've volunteered?"

"I didn't have any choice."

She caught her breath in a long sob which stabbed through him. "You didn't have any choice? What do you mean?"

He was trying to find the words. "Livvy, it's not just your people, it's mine as well. I couldn't just sit at home while they're fighting and dying for us."

"You want to die?"

"I want to help, to do what I can. Surely I don't have to explain?"

"Yes, you have to," she insisted. She tensed as he moved a few steps nearer. "You've been through a war. You were wounded. You don't have to do it again."

"They need everyone. Everyone who's trained."

"And what about me—what about the children? Don't you care about us?"

"It's because I care about you so much that I have to do this," he told her. "Not enough people understand this war. It's not just a struggle for land or for who gets the biggest share of trade. It's not because the flag's been insulted or any rubbish like that. It's about the whole world and the future, how people are going to live—free or always in fear. It's a war to prevent the possibility of war ever again. It's about Peter and Diana, and their children, and their children's children."

"You've been thinking this for months," she breathed.

"I knew I'd have to do something."

She shook her head. "And you never said anything? How

were you going to keep it from me?" She pushed herself away from the wall. "When did you think I'd find out?"

"On the *Cameronia*," he said. "It was too small. You were bound to run into the others right away. That's why I wanted to get there early this morning, so we'd be there first and I could tell you before the others came on board."

"The others," she repeated tonelessly.

"Dan and Barney and the rest. It was all worked out months ago. They wanted to volunteer, to get into the war as soon as possible, and that meant paying their own fare to England so they could enlist. They asked me to make the arrangements and lead the party."

"You talked about it and set it up. All the time you were telling me how generous the Company had been in giving you leave and we were planning what to do with it? When you came up with the idea of taking the kids and me home to visit my parents, our first real holiday?"

Matt was silent.

"All that time you were lying to me, Matt."

"I'm sorry, Livvy," he apologized. "I just didn't want you to worry. I wanted everything to go on as normal and for us to enjoy ourselves as long as we could."

"What were you going to do—leave us at my father's while you went off to the army?"

"More or less. I have to report in a couple of weeks."

She moved nearer to him. "And you knew about this, all the time, but you didn't trust me . . . All the time we were laughing and having fun, when you were making love to me or playing with the children, you were thinking about it. You were saying goodbye."

"No, honey! It's not goodbye."

"Well, what else is it?" Her voice was breaking. "You talk about the children's future. Well, what do you think it will be like for them without you? And for me? You're just throwing your life away!"

She had been so controlled, he had not realized how shocked and close to hysteria she was. He stretched up his hand to touch her cheek and she knocked it away.

"Don't touch me!"

"Livvy—" He reached for her to take her in his arms and she slapped him. The slap was like the crack of a stick and his head rocked back.

"All the time!" she sobbed. "You must have thought me such a fool! And all those things you got for me—flowers, dresses, rings—you thought they would make up for everything! I thought it was because you loved me, but you were just buying me!" She was becoming irrational in her distress. "My God . . . I'm getting off," she muttered. "I'm taking the children and I'm getting off!"

He had been standing motionless, but when she tried to push past him, he caught her arm. She hit him again across the face, and again. He still did not move. He stood with his arms by his sides, watching her as she struck at him. At that moment she hated him, yet hated herself more. Her head dropped and she began to weep. When he attempted to hold her to comfort her, with the last of her strength she tore herself away and fell across the nearer bed, face down, sobbing.

Matt had never seen her like this. She had taken it even more badly than he had feared and he did not know what to say or do. His instincts warned him it was probably best to do nothing. He was suddenly worried that Peter and Diana might come looking for them and he did not want them to see her while she was still overwrought. He wondered if he was being cowardly, using them as an excuse to get away, but the thought became more urgent. And Livvy would not accept comfort from him, anyway.

When she heard the click of the door shutting, Livvy rolled over. She could scarcely make out the door through her tears, but she sensed he had gone. She lay sobbing quietly, her tears flowing unchecked, knowing that their happiness was over.

"I've stopped all shore-to-ship telegrams now," Anderson said. "Well, I noticed that most of them were sent from the same post office. There's no question that they're all part of some campaign."

"I'll buy that," Turner agreed. Vanderbilt had gone to his suite, but Frohman was still standing by the rail of the boat deck. His shoulders were slumped and he looked to Turner like a man who was deeply worried. All it would take was someone as well-known as Frohman to decide not to sail and the rush to get off would start.

Turner grunted. He did not show his concern as openly

431

as his Staff Captain, yet he too was disturbed that he had still not received his official sailing orders, although it was nearly an hour past departure time. "No one could have foreseen this amount of delay," he said. "We're only taking on another two hundred tons."

Anderson bridled. "Plus another forty passengers and their baggage," he said sharply. "It's meant a deal of shifting and redistribution of load so that the trim won't be affected."

"Yes, yes, of course," Turner soothed. He might have expected Anderson to be touchy, he thought. He had had to revise his stowage plan once already to accommodate the cargo of the freighter *Queen Margaret*, which had been commandeered and diverted to Halifax two days before. "No reflection on you," Turner added. "But when do you estimate completion now?"

"Within half an hour."

"Very good," Turner nodded. "If I haven't heard from the Senior Naval Officer by then, I'm going ashore."

Although the number of sightseers outside the gates had swelled, the crowd on the quay itself was thinning. Most passengers had arrived around check-in time at nine o'clock, had their hand luggage and packages examined and come aboard, but there were still holdups as reporters and cameramen converged on celebrities for their comments and impressions: Commander J. Foster Stackhouse, the explorer; the young, free-speaking suffragette Lady Mackworth and her father, the Welsh coal baron and former Liberal M.P.; D.A. Thomas; Rita Jolivet, the actress and protegée of Frohman's; Charles Klein, the playwright; Sir Hugh Lane, the art expert; George Kessler, millionaire wine importer; Lady Allan and her two beautiful teenage daughters. Purser McCubbin was one of the busiest men on board, and one of the happiest. "This is more like it, a bit like the old days," he chuckled in an aside to his senior steward. McCubbin was retiring after this trip and it would have been depressing to go out on an anticlimax, with the passenger list only half full and no distinguished travelers to whom he could give that extra touch of care which made him so popular.

Justus Forman had arrived at Pier 54 in a panic. He had been later than he meant in setting off and his cab had been caught in traffic. As the minutes ticked by, he had begun to imagine himself reaching the Cunard pier to find the *Lusitania* gone or, worse still, just maneuvering out into the channel with people still waving and the band playing and no hope of getting out to her. Frohman would think that he had decided against coming, that he had rejected his offer of help and all ambition for a theatrical career. He was sweating by the time he jumped out of the cab at the gates, and it took him several minutes to realize that there were still a good third of his fellow passengers waiting to go on board.

After half an hour he had recovered enough to be irritated by the slowness of Customs and ticket inspection and was able to smile at the paradox. Ahead of him he could see Charlie Klein answering reporters' questions at the top of the gangplank and pretty, dark-haired Rita Jolivet posing for photographs. That was his world now, the theater. When it was his turn to run the press gauntlet, a casual remark that he was traveling with Frohman for talks with J.M. Barrie could hardly fail to rate a mention in half a dozen columns and would make some of his critics sit up.

He reached the little Purser at last and smiled as the reporters heard him give his name and moved in. Instead of asking why he was making the trip, their only interest seemed to be in U-boats. Had he seen the German warning, what did he think of the submarine threat? "I've no time to worry about trifles," he told them, and the next moment he was alone while they jostled round the latest arrival, a short, Bohemian-looking man of about sixty with twinkling eyes and long hair bunched over his ears under a wide-brimmed hat, wearing his dark overcoat open to show the flourish of his flowing black cravat. The hat and cravat identified him at once, Fra Elbertus, the sage of East Aurora, and Forman almost snorted in derision. Yet he was very quickly given a lesson in how to attract and generate publicity.

Elbert Hubbard, self-styled philosopher and moral pundit, was a joke to the literary set, although many of his fellow countrymen thought of him as something between a prophet and a saint. Whatever the reviewers said, there was no denying his success as an essayist on political, ethical and historical subjects. "A Message to Garcia," which he had written during the Spanish-American War, had sold a staggering forty million copies, and his monthly magazine, the *Philistine*, had a steady print run of quarter of a million. The Roycrofters community of which he was the leader lived in deliberate rustic simplicity at East Aurora, New York, devoted to rural arts and crafts and the dissemination of Hubbard's humanist ideals.

A light rain was falling again and Hubbard took his wife's arm and drew her into shelter beside him at the head of the gangplank. "Now, now, boys, let me just get Mrs. Hubbard in out of the wet," he told the reporters in his quirky Midwest accent, which he used like an actor. "Then you can fire away." A deft touch, it put his questioners immediately on his side and set them an example of politeness. A former journalist himself, he knew that what was most wanted from him was an angle and, by the time he had thanked the Purser and turned to them again, he had one.

"Are you going to Europe, Mr. Hubbard?" someone asked.

"If not, I'm on the wrong ship." There was laughter and the *Herald* man cut in with a question about the danger. What was sufficiently important in Europe to make Hubbard risk his life and his wife's? "Well, sir," Hubbard said quietly, "it may have escaped your notice that the greatest cataclysm in the world's history is raging over there. Or perhaps not, since you are a metropolitan dweller. Yet I assure you, out in the wider regions of our fair country the majority of our fellow citizens are unaware of it or indifferent to it."

"You're going as a war correspondent?"

"With a difference, sir. We are a young nation, which I have seen in my lifetime almost torn apart by the stresses and aftermath of a Civil War. Yet that war, in terms of numbers and bloodshed, was but an introductory overture, albeit devastating, to the full-scale symphony of death and destruction that is reverberating in Europe. I wish to judge the moral effect of that carnage on older and more stable societies. May the Supreme Being forbid that we should ever become involved, but if we do, our people have a right to be forewarned of the possible impact on our national psyche."

In other words, Forman thought wryly, he wants human interest stories for his magazine.

"Will you be dropping in on the Kaiser, Mr. Hubbard?" the man from the *Times* put in with exaggerated casualness.

It was a slanting reference to the sage's latest sensational essay, "Who Lifted the Lid off Hell?" with its strong censure of the German Emperor, and Hubbard's look in reply was droll. "I shall certainly make every effort to interview him," he said. "But of course he may be too busy, or huffed, to grant me an audience at this moment."

In the laughter, the *Herald* reporter returned to the basic subject. "And what about the submarine danger? There seems to be a direct threat against this vessel. Does that worry you?"

Hubbard paused. "From a strictly personal point of view, I wouldn't mind if they did sink the ship." His expression had become impish and the reporters were alert at once, their pencils poised. This was what they had been waiting for. "It might be a good thing for me," Hubbard went on. "I would drown with her and that's about the only way I could succeed in my ambition to get into the Hall of Fame. I'd be a regular hero and go right to the bottom." They were all chuckling, writing busily. He glanced back at the line forming up the gangplank. A small child was calling loudly for its potty. "We seem to be holding up the traffic here, boys—and about to cause a nasty accident. If you'd care to chat some more, my cabin's on the promenade deck, port side. There might even be some refreshments." He took Alice's arm again and headed for the elevators. Two reporters decided to follow him and all the others suddenly surged after them, anxious not to miss anything.

And that's how it's done, I guess, Forman thought, with a trace of envy. He had to admire Hubbard. His twaddle sounded sincere, even impressive until you analyzed it. But seers needed personality more than Euclidean logic. One other thing, he noted. Hubbard might preach simplicity, the work ethos and self-denial, yet he was traveling in one of the most luxurious staterooms in the whole floating palace.

Will Turner watched the knot of reporters dissolve from around the top of the gangplank and trail off in the wake of the man of the moment in his slouch hat. However, the group of passengers which had also gathered there did not move and he was conscious of many of them watching him. He checked the time on the Customs shed clock. The half hour was up and the loading virtually complete, as Anderson had

435

promised. Turner had called the engine room and knew that Archie Bryce and his team were ready, had been ready for nearly two hours. Bryce was complaining at the waste of maintaining steam pressure that did not seem likely to be used. The cargo manifest, or at least its shorter, diplomatic version showing no munitions or other contraband, had been passed by the Collector of Customs and the *Lusitania* given clearance to leave. There were only ten or twelve last passengers to come on board. Yet the sailing instructions had still not arrived.

To Turner, it meant only two things, either that departure was to be delayed until another day or that this sailing was to be canceled altogether. For the sake of his passengers, he had to know. Arrangements would have to be made for those who wished to transfer or cancel their passage. He would have preferred to go ashore unobtrusively and was troubled by the people watching him, but he had no choice. "Put a call through to the S.N.O.'s office and say I'll be there in quarter of an hour," he told Lewis, and nodded to his personal steward who was standing by with his overcoat. There was a stir among the watching passengers and some moved forward to ask him what was happening. Just then, however, the party which had been struggling up the gangplank made its appearance, Mr. and Mrs. Paul Crompton and their six children, ages ranging from fifteen years to eight months, with the children's nurse. As a director of the Booth Steamship Company and a personal friend of Alfred Booth, Cunard's Chairman, Crompton rated special attention, and Staff Captain Anderson hurried to welcome him and his wife on board. McCubbin saluted and stewards closed in to collect their hand luggage. Two of the younger girls, Catherine and Alberta, had been arguing all morning over a one-eared Teddy bear and had begun to scuffle on the gangplank. The fight now broke out in earnest. Nine-year-old Paul tried to separate them and was punched unkindly for his pains. He was crying while they screamed and flailed around him and infant John kept up his wail for the potty. Turner passed them in the confusion and went quickly down the gangplank.

Matt had been lucky again. Left alone, Peter and Diana had attached themselves to the pretty little Allan sisters from

Montreal and their maid, Annie, who was happy to keep an eye on them all. Matt thanked her and told Diana, who was asking for her mother, that Livvy was lying down and not to be disturbed. He only hoped that, later, when he had to face Livvy again, she would be able to control herself in front of the children. He went up the gangway with them to the promenade deck and, as they moved forward to see the view from the bows, he turned and found his way to the second-class smoke room at the stern.

Dan Connally and Barney Ferguson had made use of the wartime concession rates, paid the small extra fare and transferred to second class. They had brought the others up here, where they had all arranged to meet. Young Piet Nyquist, whose family still lived in two log cabins in the hills behind Calgary, gawked at the elegance of the stained-glass windows, Tiffany-inspired lamps, inlaid tables and the leather-covered upholstery of the chairs and sofas. The deep Axminster carpet felt as springy as turf under his feet. "If this is only second, what in hell is first class like?" he whispered.

Matt saw between twenty or thirty men gathered at the far end of the smoke room with Dan and Barney, more than twice the number who had engaged to travel with him. He was embarrassed when they all rose and stood to attention as he approached.

Dan and Barney came to meet him. "These other fellows are from Ontario," Dan explained. "They want to link up with us."

"There's another group from Quebec," Barney said. "And another, even bigger, from Winnipeg."

"So how many of us are there, d'you reckon, all told?" Matt asked.

"Well, I make it about fifty," Dan said. "But Barney's estimate is nearer eighty."

"At least," Barney confirmed. "A lot of them spotted us shifting baggage this morning and they want to join up with us."

As Matt glanced at the strangers among his party from Calgary, one young man stepped forward, introducing himself as a Temporary Lieutenant in charge of the Toronto group. "Since you seem to be the senior officer on board, sir," he said, "we are placing ourselves under your orders."

Matt realized that since he had been given the rank of Acting Captain for the trip, it was probably true and he could not refuse. His embarrassment increased. It was over twelve years since he had had any contact with the army and all these young men were looking at him as if he were Kitchener, at least. After his hideous row with Livvy, only a sense of duty had made him keep this appointment. Now he was suddenly at the head of a much larger contingent and that would bring its own problems. They were all looking at him, waiting for him to say something. He was also conscious of five or six other passengers who had come to relax in the smoke room, watching in surprise.

"Well, I'm not going to make the speech," he began, and hesitated. His impulse was to tell them just to carry on as they were. He could see himself having enough troubles in the next few weeks without adding to his responsibilities. But he could not leave it there. It would not be fair on these men who had left their homes and jobs and traveled many hundreds of miles, with many more ahead of them, to fight for their country. Rightly or wrongly, they respected him as their first real contact with the army in which they had come to serve, and he could not let them down.

"We all know why we're here," he began again, speaking more firmly, yet just loud enough for those in front of him to hear. "We've had to hide the reason to get here. But now we're on a British liner, on British territory, and we don't have to hide it any more." The men smiled to one another and some who had seemed uncertain stood straighter, more soldierly. Matt made himself forget about the other passengers and his voice could be heard more clearly. "I want to tell each of you that where we are going, you will be made welcome—for we are going where every one of us is desperately needed. But don't expect to be treated like heroes when you get to England. We are only doing what many others have done there already, and many do every day. And don't expect to be sent straight to France. First, there will be weeks of selection and basic training and arms drill, much of it frustrating and much more of it backbreaking, until you never want to march another mile or see another rifle. It's the only way to build an army out of farmers and clerks and storekeepers. The enemy has been preparing for years, and we have to catch up fast. Remember that when it gets tough, as I can promise you it will be." He paused. The men listening were serious now. The journey so far had been exciting, even lighthearted, but now they had been brought up short, facing reality. "Some of you may have depots to report to," Matt went on. "Those who don't are welcome to travel with our party when we reach Liverpool. The first volunteers were directed into British units, whichever were understrength or just being formed. But now, after how it's handling itself at Ypres, I think you can be guaranteed posting to the Canadian Division." The effect on his listeners was stirring and Matt smiled for the first time. "What more can I say? We have seven days sailing ahead of us. Take some exercise, it'll help with the training. Get as much rest as possible, it could be the last you'll have for the foreseeable future. Those of you who already have uniforms may be tempted to wear them. I see nothing wrong in that. But as a courtesy to our American fellow passengers, I suggest you don't put them on until we are outside U.S. limits." He paused again. "One more thing. I'm proud to be sailing with you."

For a moment it seemed as if the men facing him would cheer; then they remembered where they were and just looked at Matt until he turned away.

Dan Connally stepped closer to him and said quietly, "I thought you weren't going to make a speech." Matt smiled, but it cut off when Dan asked, "How did Livvy take it?"

"I don't want to talk about it," Matt said. "Not here, anyway."

Dan sucked air in through his teeth. "Bad? Would it help if I had a word with her?"

Matt shook his head. "No. Thanks, Dan, but I think she's best left to herself. She'll see things differently in a while."

"I hope so, for both your sakes," Dan said, concerned. He had no chance to add any more. Matt was kept busy for the next twenty minutes meeting the new men and some others of the Winnipeg group who arrived to join them.

It was shortly after twelve when Will Turner walked back to Pier 54. He had stopped for a minute to watch the *New York*, the old steamer of the American Line, set sail in a flurry of confetti and paper streamers. It was a tribute to the *Lusy* and himself, he supposed, that none of his passengers had transferred to her or to any of the other neutral liners.

His visit to the senior naval officer, Sir Courtenay Bennett, had been inconclusive, oddly disconcerting. No Admiralty sailing instructions had been sent, Sir Courtenay explained, because none had been received. Apparently no one in London considered the latest German threat to be any added cause for alarm.

In the circumstances, it was hardly surprising to find Captain Gaunt, the naval attaché, with the S.N.O. Turner told him about the warning telegrams. "It's obviously another of their propaganda moves," Gaunt concluded.

"That's all very well," Turner pointed out, "but what am I to do, officially?"

All Sir Courtenay could suggest was that he follow the same instructions as for his previous trip, keep to the same course and use the same call signs and merchant code for messages. "Avoid headlands, stick to mid channel and be ready to zigzag when threatened. After all, even at reduced speed, there's no real danger. No vessel making over fourteen and a half knots has ever been struck by a torpedo." He warned Turner unnecessarily to maintain a sharp lookout and wished him good luck.

The crowd outside the gate was now dense, its excitement subdued and hushed, and Turner passed through it unnoticed in his overcoat and bowler. Nearer the gates, vendors sold popcorn and small British, French and American flags. One selling photographs of the giant liner against the New York skyline raised a nervous laugh by hawking them loudly as "Last voyage! *Lusitania*'s last voyage!" Turner nearly rounded on the man and the people who were laughing, but stopped himself. His face was set as he shouldered through the gates and made for the main gangplank.

The atmosphere on the pier was as subdued as the crowd outside. The Cunard dockworkers, Customs men and detectives stood looking up at the higher decks, which were now almost entirely lined with passengers, but there was none of the waving, the cheers and laughter of a normal sailing. The unprecedented two-hour delay had added to the uncertainty and apprehension which now affected everyone. One last late passenger, surrounded by well-wishers, was being passed through Customs. She was an attractive woman in her thirties, Marie Depage, wife of the heroic Dr. Antoine Depage, director of the hospital at La Panne in Belgium. For the past eight weeks she had been on a tour of American cities, appealing for medical supplies and support for Hoover's Relief Commission, which struggled to help her occupied country. Her voice with its charming accent carried clearly as she thanked her sponsors who were seeing her off. Her tour had succeeded beyond all expectation. Booked to sail on the steamer *Lapland* the previous day, she had transferred to the *Lusitania* in order to fit in one final appeal.

Turner had paused briefly for a word with Sumner and the Pier Superintendent at the foot of the gangplank. Anderson and Third Officer Lewis saw him coming up and could judge by his expression that all was not well, but that a decision had been reached. "Prepare to cast off," he told them as soon as he touched the deck. His head swung toward McCubbin. "What's happened to the band? Why isn't the band playing?"

McCubbin was startled and realized that the ship's orchestra, affected by the tension like everyone else, had fallen silent for some time. The only sound was from a Welsh male voice choir, returning from a concert tour, which was singing the beautiful, plaintive "David of the White Rock." He started to apologize and assure the captain that he would see to it, but Turner was already making for the elevators.

Within minutes of his coming on board, the ship and pier were galvanized. Dockworkers converged on the gangplanks and bollards. The ship's orchestra, its bandsmen colorful in red and blue uniforms frogged with gold, struck up a spirited medley of Stephen Foster songs, "Camptown Races" and "The Old Folks at Home," while the Welsh choir further forward, responding to the change of atmosphere, stimulated their audience with the martial "Men of Harlech." For the people waiting and wondering in their cabins and in the restrooms, the indication that something was happening at last came more slowly, yet unmistakably.

Livvy still lay across her bed, limp and drained of feeling.

She had cried herself out and to her open, unfocused eyes the unfamiliar cabin with its muted colors seemed like a cell, silent and isolated. No whisper of sound or sensation of movement reached her, yet she gradually became aware of a vibration under her, the faintest tremor at first, increasing rapidly as the *Lusitania*'s giant boiler rooms built up to full pressure. She closed her eyes tightly, then opened them again and the room leaped into focus. She was lying facing the door, which had closed half an hour ago behind Matt. In all that time, her only coherent thought had been that she must find the children and take them ashore, to make him follow them. If she did not rise now, this moment, it would be too late.

Down in the cavernous engine room, Archie Bryce paced past his team of engineers, checking dials and pressures. He felt a genuine sense of relief, for he had been about to take it on himself to damp down the boilers and lower pressure to a more economic level if this waiting was to continue. He was profoundly grateful he had not given the order, because once reduced the pressure would have required several hours to build up again, and he could imagine Will Turner's reaction. The boilers had been fired shortly after seven and now, in spite of the electrically controlled ventilation, the temperature in the engine room was sweltering. He picked up a reasonably clean wad of cotton swabbing and wiped the beads of perspiration from his mustache, then dabbed at the sides of his thick neck where he had developed an almost permanent rash from the combination of sweat and close shaving. He had started to climb to another level when he remembered and went back down to the low-pressure turbines. His Senior Second Engineer, Andrew Cockburn, was checking them with the oiler, Frank Tower. "Ah, good, Andy," Bryce said. "Keep a sharp eye on those valves." These were the turbines used for maneuvering in the confined space of docks and harbors. Until he could get them replaced, Bryce nursed them carefully, afraid that the valves might blow under the sudden pressure of Full Astern.

Alfred Vanderbilt had taken refuge from the persistence of the reporters in his dayroom. He had read through the morning papers and looked at the pictures in the current edition of the *National Geographic*. He felt unsettled, and more so when he gave in at last and read the German warning. It was even more blunt than he had expected and he wondered briefly if, having read it earlier, it would have altered his intention to make this trip. It would not, so he put it out of his mind. His valet, Denyer, brought him a whiskey and soda, which meant it was some minutes after midday. As he raised the glass, he heard the sound of gongs on the deck outside and the voices of stewards calling, "All visitors ashore!" At last, he thought, and tilted his glass in a toast of farewell to America. Being honest with himself for once, he was not entirely certain that he intended ever to return.

Outside, on the boat deck, Charles Frohman still stood alone by the rail, leaning on his cane. He was not sure how long he had stood there. He never carried a watch. Too long, the dull ache in his right leg told him. He had been sunk in thoughts of the past, which was unlike him, memories of his first theater job, highstepping in the parade of Haverly's Mastodon Minstrels in a grotesque silk hat, frock coat and lavender pants, of Maude, elfin and magnetic as Peter Pan, begging the children of the world still to believe in fairies. The play itself, and Barrie, its author and his most intimate friend, almost his twin. The thought of not surviving this trip was unbearable because it would mean never seeing either of them again. He was becoming morbid, and he forced his mind back to the present, to now. It was like waking from a dream. Where the boat deck had been virtually deserted, it was filling rapidly, and the people who had been low-spirited were smiling and animated. Many were waving down to the pier and he could see visitors streaming down the gangplanks and looking up to wave back. He recognized the gongs warning all visitors that only a few more minutes remained for them to get ashore.

Many in the watching crowd outside the gates cheered when the *Lusitania*'s ensign was run out at her stern and when the Line's flag rose at her foremast. They were followed by strings of brightly colored signal pennons fore and aft and the pilot's H flag on the signal-bridge, and all at once her somber black and white was transformed.

Turner had removed his overcoat and changed into his uniform cap. When he stepped onto the bridge, Chief Officer

443

Piper saluted and reported. "All ready for departure, sir. Crew of seven hundred and two, one thousand two hundred and fifty-seven passengers booked and accounted for. No cancellations." Piper could not prevent a slight smile of relief.

Turner was expressionless, although he knew he had won a major propaganda victory. All the officers on the bridge, the helmsman and Quartermaster Johnston were looking at him. " Well, let's give them a smooth crossing, gentlemen," he said.

Elizabeth Duckworth came up one of the rear companionways with Arthur, who stopped abruptly, his eyes widening in delight. Ahead of them was the ship's orchestra, which had just begun to play "It's a Long Way to Tipperary" in march rhythm. Around them, people were waving and cheering, shouting down messages and farewells to others on the pier which from that height could not be heard.

Further forward on the promenade deck, Matt found Peter and Diana still with the Allan girls and their maid. The girls assured him politely that it had been no trouble, then made him feel guilty by hurrying off at once to hunt for their mother.

"I want *my* mummy," Diana insisted, her lips drawn together. "Why didn't you bring her with you?"

"Well, she's still resting, pet," Matt told her. "She won't be coming."

"She's missing everything," Peter said. "Look!"

They looked over the rail and saw the dockworkers heave on the looped ropes attached to the massive gangplanks, dragging them away from the *Lusitania*'s side inch by inch. The gap was increasing. "Now you couldn't step across," Peter said. "Now you couldn't jump it!" The gangplanks were rolling back faster and were swung away. At hand signals from Lewis at the bows and Bestwick at the stern, the hawsers were cast off and came snaking up the liner's side. The newsreel cameramen cranked their handles, recording as many details as possible, gangplanks, dockers, the flags, sightseers flourishing their hats, passengers waving back.

The deck under Matt's feet seemed to vibrate as the mighty engines five levels below came to life. The watching crowd had doubled again in the last twenty minutes. There was applause from it and the loudest cheer yet when the reversing screws started to revolve, churning the scummy harbor water to white foam. Two and a half hours late, when many had become convinced she had been immobilized by the danger which threatened her, she was slipping gracefully away. Matt was as excited as the children, waving like them and the people on either side in response to the cheers, until he remembered Livvy and lowered his hand. This is it, he thought. Goodbye to the New World. Goodbye to a lot of things.

All at once he was startled and winced as the liner's horn blared out deafeningly. The children shrieked and covered their ears. Three times the bass horn blared out, leaving everyone laughing and protesting. Peter grinned, but Diana was frightened and Matt smiled to her. "They must have heard that in Calgary," he said.

He glanced back and saw that already there was space between the bows and the end of the pier. There was no feeling of motion, yet the people on shore had grown smaller. The cheers were fading and the waving faltered as the momentary elation died away. The liner's stern was at mid channel and the three attendant tugs bumbled in, nudging her prow which loomed over them like a cliff, coaxing it round to face toward the mouth of the Hudson. Behind him, Matt heard Diana squeak, "Mummy!" and his head turned quickly.

Livvy had come to stand on the other side of the children. Diana hugged her round the waist, rubbing her cheek against her hip. Peter smiled to her briefly. She was pale, her eyes hollow, and Matt reproached himself for having hurt her. He was grateful to her for joining them and, to ask her forgiveness, stretched out his hand to her across the children. She did not take it. She would not even look at him.

Once again the other ships, tugs and ferries whooped out their salute to their matchless sister as her main propellers now began to drive her forward. On the Hoboken docks, the officers and crews of the interned German liners watched in silence, hating her, hating her grace and power. As she slowly passed, her length and bulk, added to by the black pillars of smoke from her four colossal funnels, blotted out the skyline.

Outside Pier 54, the crowd was dispersing, the taxis and

445

hacks drawing away. The cameramen were packing up their equipment and lines of dockers converged on the gates to be passed out. No one spoke much. A handful of confetti spun in a shallow puddle of rainwater, flicked by a gust of wind.

Chapter 24

THE LUSITANIA STEAMED OUT INTO THE UPPER BAY OF NEW York Harbor, gathering speed. Many of her passengers were still at the rails, while others had gone below to unpack or explore the public rooms.

Charles Frohman swiveled on his left foot and walked very stiffly away from the rail, heading back to his suite. He was absolved from the need to make any further decisions. He felt an easing of tension and, as if to emphasize it, the sun had broken through the dark cloud cover at last, sparkling on the water, warming him. He had not noticed before that his thick double-breasted suit was damp still from the brief spell of rain. He would have to change. But first he must write a note of thanks to Ann Murdock for the basket of flowers shaped like a ship. If he did it now, the harbor pilot could take it when he went ashore. He was so intent that he passed Alfred Vanderbilt without seeing him.

Vanderbilt had grown tired of inactivity and was finishing a stroll round the boat deck promenade before lunch. He let Frohman go by without intruding on his thoughts. Apart from him, he could not claim any acquaintances on board, but he was not seeking company. He paused and looked round. People certainly appeared happier, or less anxious, now that the sun was out and they were under way.

There was the usual mixed collection of family groups and strangers. In the nature of things, unless he kept to his suite, as Frohman usually did, he was bound to get to know some of them in the next week, although from long experience he had learned to accept shipboard friendships for what they were, to expect nothing lasting. The same with love affairs. A liner was an ideal place for romance, a self-enclosed, timeless world suspended between two realities, where all normal ties and obligations seemed less binding. In earlier years he had looked forward to each trip as a new adventure. Lately, however, he had become . . . not more moral, exactly. More cautious. It had to be something very special for the game to be worth the candle. He had been through the final moments once too often, the embarrassment of the return to reality at the close of the voyage. Yet affairs on land were much more difficult to conduct, to conceal and to end. As witness his divorce seven years ago from Elsie, when he was thirty. That had been a bad business.

He looked round casually and stopped in surprise as his eye caught a woman's profile, finely modeled, perfect, a clear brow and straight nose, the mouth slightly full, but delicately etched, her chin rounded and firm above a high, proud neck. She was really lovely. She wore no hat and the sunlight gleamed in the dark tendrils of her hair, stirred by the wind. Her head turned and Vanderbilt tensed, in case she had sensed him gazing at her. But she was unaware of him. She was looking down at a boy and girl beside her. Vanderbilt knew he should move on, but he was held by her expression. There was sadness and love, something of despair in it. Full face, she was still beautiful, the high cheekbones emphasized by her wide, grave eyes.

It was a moment before Vanderbilt was conscious that there was a man with her of his own age, taller, darker. He was also looking at the woman and was clearly troubled by how she avoided his eyes, speaking only to the children, a little girl in a sailor dress and hat and a boy who was the image of the man. Vanderbilt glanced away as the family moved from the rail and made for the nearest companionway. He felt that he had trespassed on a private drama, yet his curiosity was roused. The woman's expression had been sad, as if in mourning, but the man's had been—guilty? Remorseful? Intriguing. Perhaps it was no more than the old story, and he had been caught out, poor devil. Vanderbilt smiled to himself, for he could sympathize.

He stepped forward and took their place at the rail. Liberty Island was falling behind, and as he nodded to the Lady, he wondered how long it would be until he saw her again. Ahead, to starboard, was the tree-clad bulk of Staten Island, where the farm had been in the days of the van der Bilts, where the Commodore, his great-grandfather and founder of the family fortune, had been born, and where in death each generation joined the Commodore in the family mausoleum in the Moravian Cemetery. Neither death nor the family were subjects he cared to think about just now, and he let himself be distracted by the sound of laughter from his left. It came from half a dozen girls in their early twenties, fresh and pretty in their summer suits and dresses, pink and white and pale blue. They all wore their hair up in thick waves over the ears and looped back in rolls and knots, their picture hats gay with artificial flowers, swathed with lace or muslin to match their dresses. And each of them held a small Stars and Stripes, bought from the vendors at the pier. They were obviously traveling as a group, but he could not work out what they were. Students? Chorus girls? Another puzzle.

Their lightheartedness was infectious and, as he moved on, he could not resist pausing to smile and wish them a good trip. They wished him the same, smiling back, not at all shy, although he could tell that one or two of them were nervous. They were definitely American. Were they going to England, he asked, to study perhaps? They laughed, and one who was slightly older than the others said no, they were going to Belgium. They were volunteer nurses on their way to work with Dr. Depage in his hospital for the wounded at La Panne. He honored them silently. You're so brave, braver than I am, he wanted to tell them. One of the nervous ones said that now their secret was out, they had no right to be up here at all, in first class. They only wanted to see the view.

"If you have any trouble from the stewards, if anyone objects," he told them, "just say you are guests of Mr. Vanderbilt."

They laughed and the older one protested, "But we don't even know him!"

"He won't mind," he assured them. "You can order refreshments, whatever you'd like, on his tab. And you can come up here whenever you want."

The nurses were surprised and delighted, and thanked him as he touched the brim of his cap and moved on. "Who was that?" one of them whispered. "Is he kidding us?"

449

"We could soon find out," the older one said. They laughed again, but none of them accepted the dare. It made them oddly self-conscious, and a few minutes later they had just made up their minds to leave when they saw a uniformed steward coming toward them. They were apprehensive until they realized he was carrying a tray with six glasses of champagne.

On the third top step of the companionway to the deck below, a young woman had seen Vanderbilt smile, tipping his cap, and turn. She had recognized him at once and caught her breath. He came toward her, passing within a few feet, and stopped for a word with a steward before rounding a corner and going out of sight. Her eyes had never left him.

She was another nurse, Alice Middleton. She had come farther than most, right across the continent from the fast-developing harbor city of Seattle. Even in her short lifetime it had doubled and redoubled its size and now had fine buildings, a cathedral and university, but Alice still longed to see more of the wide world. The trip across the whole of the States had been exciting, then her first glimpse of New York and coming on board the great liner that was to take her to Europe. She had seen Rita Jolivet and envied her dark, slender poise, and wondered what other celebrities might be traveling. Stewards were moving along the promenades and through the passages, announcing the first call for lunch and politely shepherding people down to the levels on which they had booked, now that the turmoil of leave-taking and departure was over. Alice had slipped past them just to have one peep at the boat deck, and in the very first minute . . .

She felt like pinching herself. There was no mistaking him. She had seen his photograph in newspapers and pictorials hundreds of times, in one of his racing cars on the Florida beaches or at his Oakland Farm stables, at yacht clubs and social events, handsome in evening dress. She had read about his dash home from the Far East when his father lay dying and how he had heard that his elder brother had been disinherited and all the fortune left to him. As well as being a Prince Charming, he was now worth millions and millions. She had been reading about him since her teens and knew all about the family feud, of his marriage and divorce, and the suicide of the beautiful woman who had been involved, the wife of the Cuban attaché in Washington. Like thousands of other girls, she had daydreamed of meeting him and being swept off her feet. Then he had married again and there were pictures of him and his new wife, and the Vanderbilt Hotel which he built on Park Avenue, and of his little son and the second baby boy born last year. And he had passed so close to her, smiling, that she could almost have touched him, so close she could see the warm blue of his eyes. Now she really did have something to write home.

Will Turner strolled out of the wheelhouse onto the portside wing of the bridge, his hands in the side pockets of his uniform jacket, thumbs hooked forward. He sniffed the air appreciatively. Clean and fresh, it was a good omen for the crossing.

This was the hour he enjoyed most, when the pilot was still in charge and he could relax. From then on, from the moment they dropped the pilot, he seldom left the bridge. Today, he was more glad than ever of the short breathing space. It had been an anxious morning, with the strong possibility that he would not sail. That would have been a moral defeat, he knew, yet he was not as sure as the Cunard manager and the Admiralty that the German threat was all bluff. He reckoned the Huns capable of anything at all, no matter how barbaric, if they thought it had the slightest chance of helping them to win. And there was no point in starting if you didn't plan to win.

What was he saying? That the Germans were right and anything was justified, provided you won? No, he bloody well was not! What, then? It was a damned hard question to answer. Yet he knew that the end did not always justify the means, and the fact that so many nations as well as individuals were beginning to think and act as if it did was a sickness that could destroy the world, the old, pleasant ways of the world.

He turned to look at the view he never tired of, the skyline of Lower Manhattan, its planes and surfaces merging and shifting almost imperceptibly, yet constantly, with the motion of the ship, a three-dimensional kaleidoscope. They can keep Naples and Rio, he told himself. I'll settle for this any time. With the ability he had to block out unwelcome thoughts and distractions, his mind began to concentrate on the present. The *Lusy* helped. He did not have to wait for his officers' summaries or the engine room report. Archie had nursed those faulty turbines through the demands made on them and they would not be used again until she was docking at Liverpool, perhaps not even then, if he brought her in himself instead of leaving it to Anderson. She was in fine trim, responding as sweetly to the helm as a two-masted yawl, not a flutter in the throb of her mighty heart to which he could match his pulse and the rhythm of his breathing. He closed his eyes and the sense of fusion was complete.

Von Rintelen was in his office listening to Captain Steinberg, who had just begun his report, when his secretary, Max, came in quickly. "A telephone call, sir."

"I'm busy," von Rintelen said.

"It's Koenig."

Von Rintelen tapped his pen on the desk, laid it down and picked up the outside receiver. "Gibbons speaking," he said.

"P.K.," Koenig answered, identifying himself.

At von Rintelen's nod, Max went back to the outer office to monitor the call on the extension. The message was short, that Boy-Ed's team had discovered nothing. Von Rintelen already knew that no attempt had been made to mount guns on the *Lusitania* from the reports of the men he had stationed with powerful binoculars at the Narrows and on the terrace of the Atlantic Yacht Club at Norton's Point on Coney Island. At last he could forget Berlin's obsession with information about the guns.

"You might suggest to your principals that now they should concentrate on what is possible," he told Koenig. He hung up. It was then that he noticed that Steinberg was smiling, something he had never seen before.

"It's like you told us, Captain," Steinberg said. "Patience is always rewarded in the end."

"Yes indeed," von Rintelen agreed. He had comforted the men who kept watch at the docks with that banality. "But how?"

"Four things," Steinberg said. "First, as you know, the *Cameronia* was diverted to a Canadian port this morning and her cargo transshipped to the *Lusitania*." He paused.

"Ryan's men unloaded her and are prepared to swear that among the cargo were between five and six hundred cases of ammunition. And another hundred of shrapnel shells."

"Ah . . ." Von Rintelen breathed out audibly. Because of the vigilance of the Cunard pier superintendent and detectives, no precise evidence had ever been available before that the *Lusitania* carried contraband. Now they had it.

"Second," Steinberg continued. "A few days ago, the S.S. *Queen Margaret*'s cargo was also transferred to the *Lusitania*. I got Mike Foley to check for us. Her manifest showed, among other military items, two thousand cases of .303 rifle ammunition."

Von Rintelen's eyes were alight and his fingertips drummed briefly on the edge of the desk. But he waited, because Steinberg had not finished.

"Third, and perhaps most useful to us," Steinberg said. He had stopped smiling. "On both those vessels, there were bookings for groups of male passengers from Canada, volunteers for the British army. They are now on board the *Lusitania*."

Von Rintelen had also become more serious. "You don't need me to tell you how important this is," he said. "If it can be confirmed."

"It is definite, absolutely definite," Steinberg assured him.

"Then whether she carries guns or not is of no significance," von Rintelen murmured. Due to the chances of war and the patient observation of his men, he now had the vital information which Tirpitz, the High Command and the chiefs of Intelligence most wanted. He had no doubt left how they would use it. He looked at Steinberg. "I am very grateful. Please thank the others for me." He remembered. "You said there were four things."

Steinberg hesitated. "Well, that's really Wolpert's pigeon. I thought he'd have been here by now. I ought to let him tell you about it—if it's worked out." Before he could go on, they heard voices in the outer office, the door opened and Otto Wolpert came in. "Here he is," Steinberg said. "He can tell you himself."

Wolpert was now serving as pier superintendent for the Atlas Line, which gave him access to many offices. It was proving most useful. "I got it!" he declared triumphantly.

Steinberg gave a grunt of excitement and the two merchant captains smiled to each other, leaving von Rintelen mystified. They saw him look from one to the other of them blankly.

"He doesn't know," Steinberg chuckled. "He doesn't know yet."

Wolpert took some typewritten sheets of paper from his inside pocket and handed them to von Rintelen in silence. He unfolded them. They were smudged carbon copies of lists of items, and when he finally realized what they represented, he felt his heart begin to pound suddenly in his chest. He was holding a copy of the *Lusitania*'s manifest for this sailing, not the short loading manifest, but the much more detailed supplementary, which was filed confidentially in the Collector's office after departure. He glanced up at Wolpert, speechless for the moment, and the older man nodded, acknowledging with pride what he had not been able to say.

Von Rintelen began to skim through the manifest quickly. Consignments to Liverpool: 260,000 pounds of sheet brass—111,762 pounds of copper—58,465 pounds of copper wire. 342,165 pounds of beef. 189 packages of military goods. What were they? They were valued at over sixty-six thousand dollars. He stopped and forced himself to go back to the top of the first page, reading more carefully. On the second page, he found it. To Liverpool, 1,271 cases of ammunition. There must be more. He read on. To Bristol, Dublin and Glasgow. To London, and there was the second consignment. 4,200 cases of cartridges.

The supplementary manifest was still not complete. There was no mention of the shells and shrapnel she must be carrying. Nor of weapons and explosives. The shells would be left off deliberately, the explosives could be concealed in those huge consignments of butter, cheese and bacon, or those fifty-one cases of bronze powder, whatever that was. Any last doubts he had about the legitimacy of the liner as a target were swept away. With the items from the two freighters, whatever else was concealed by the manifest, the *Lusitania* was carrying well over seven thousand cases of contraband ammunition. He had no hesitation in— He stopped and looked up at Steinberg. "That first ship you mentioned?"

"The *Cameronia*," Steinberg nodded. "Anchor Line, diverted to Halifax, Nova Scotia." He could not understand and broke off when he saw von Rintelen shake his head slightly, as if refusing to believe him.

The *Cameronia*, von Rintelen repeated to himself. All at once he remembered Livvy Fletcher's smile and her boy and the little girl, Diana, so like a younger version of his own Marie-Luise. And the father. Yes, he could be a soldier, was the type to volunteer. And now they were on board the *Lusitania* . . . Because of them, he was reminded that there were not only them, but hundreds and hundreds of others like them. On a ship he might be sending to her death. His eyes closed tightly. Dear God in heaven . . . Yet the final decision would not be his. He had no option. His duty was clear and the information must be sent.

Chapter 25

"NOW THAT," ELBERT HUBBARD MURMURED, "IS WHAT I call a truly beautiful creature." His wife smiled and agreed. "Natural, dignified, with none of the arts of the coquette. A rare creature," Hubbard added. The other four people sharing their table in the dining saloon looked round, intrigued.

A man and a woman had just come in and were being shown to their places, the man tall and dark, wearing evening dress as casually as he would hunting or work clothes, the woman wearing a gown of dark red velvet, the fashionably low neck revealing the slope of her shoulders, the skirt subtly draped across the hips and overlaid like the bust with delicate black lace. Her elbow-length gloves were also of black lace, her only ornament a narrow black velvet band round her throat, set with a single drop pearl. Her rich chestnut hair was scooped back and drawn to one side in a style distinctly old-fashioned, yet perfectly complementing her pale, finely molded features. Her look was grave and withdrawn.

"Very dramatic," Oliver Bernard agreed. Principal designer for London's Covent Garden and the Boston Opera House, he was one of Hubbard's table companions. "You have an eye for such things, Mr. Hubbard."

"Why not, sir?" Hubbard answered. "A beautiful woman is the most admirable of Nature's creations." He placed his hand over his wife's and smiled.

Alfred Vanderbilt had also noticed the couple come in. He was at the main table with Staff Captain Anderson and other prominent fellow guests. "Who's that?" he asked.

A moment later he realized he had cut into a conversation between Anderson and Commander Stackhouse about the expedition the Commander was preparing to explore the Antarctic in the following year. Anderson blinked. "I'm sorry, sir?"

"Your pardon, gentlemen," Vanderbilt apologized. "I was wondering who that—uh—" He paused, conscious of the ladies listening. "That tall man who's just come in. Do you know him?"

Anderson recognized the transfer passenger who had been so helpful that morning. "Oh, yes," he said. "That's Mr. Fletcher, with Mrs. Fletcher. From Canada."

"Canadians?" Lady Allan smiled. "Where from, Captain?"

"Alberta, I believe, Your Ladyship."

Vanderbilt was watching Livvy, admiring the grace with which she moved, unstudied, fluid. "What does he do, do you know?" he asked. "Fletcher?"

"I'm not entirely sure," Anderson told him, and lowered his voice. "I believe he's leading a party of volunteers for the Allied army."

"Good man!" David Thomas exclaimed. He had been in America on business for the Ministry of Munitions.

"I'd like to meet him sometime, shake him by the hand," Stackhouse remarked to Father Basil Maturin, the Catholic theologian from Oxford.

"Yes, indeed," Maturin agreed.

Well, that's that, Vanderbilt was thinking. The most ravishing woman on board, with her superb figure and sad eyes, was married to a hero. Hail and farewell.

"His wife's quite pretty," Lady Allan decided.

"Oh, more than that, surely?" Marie Depage laughed. "*Elle est exquise.* Don't you think so, M'sieur Vanderbilt?"

Vanderbilt saw the Belgian woman smile to him across the table. Her smile was slightly teasing, not flirtatious, but perceptive. You're a pretty shrewd lady, he thought, as well as being a shrewdly pretty one yourself. "I'd guess that was an example of Anglo Saxon understatement," he said, and they laughed. "The lady seems very charming."

"Charming?" young Lady Mackworth, D. A. Thomas's daughter, challenged. "Is that what's important in a woman? Couldn't you have said she seems intelligent or unaffected?"

Vanderbilt had no wish to become involved in a suffragette argument. "I thought that went without saying, since those qualities so often go together," he answered, and raised his glass to her. "As witness the fair company at this table."

Margaret Mackworth blushed and could not think for a moment of a retort. Her father chuckled to himself. If his daughter was going into politics as she threatened, she would have to learn not to be disarmed by gallantry. And these second- or-third generation Yankee millionaires could be as polished as the old aristocracy.

Matt and Livvy had been shown to their table. Matt would have preferred for them to be alone, but that was not the custom. Their companions were a young couple, Lee and Beatrice Arnstein, from Philadelphia, Alexander Campbell, the general manager for Dewars Whisky distilleries, and the wine merchant George Kessler, a forceful man with a thick black beard. The two men were deep in a conversation on the effect of the war on the wine and liquor trade and returned to it as soon as the social niceties had been observed.

The two couples sat in silence. The younger pair seemed shy, even nervous, and only spoke to each other occasionally, too quietly to be overheard. Matt and Livvy had not reached any kind of understanding. He had hoped that the children's excitement and spending the afternoon together, seeing the sights of the liner, the games room, the British warships at the three-mile limit, trying on their life jackets, all the things to which they had been looking forward, would bring them together again. She had been quite normal with the kids, who had noticed nothing wrong, but she had avoided him as much as possible, hardly talking to or looking at him. Peter and Diana had their supper in the children's dining saloon on C Deck, another excitement, then had their baths and went to bed.

It was fairly late by the time he had finished telling them a story and went through into the larger cabin and closed the door. Livvy was sitting at the dressing table. "They're both dog tired," he said. "I think they'll drop off soon." She did not speak. "Well, I suppose we should get ready for dinner." She still did not answer and sat half turned from him, motionless and silent. He moved round so that he could see her face. "Livvy," he said quietly, "it can't go on like this. I've told you I'm sorry, as humbly as I know how. The last thing I wanted was to hurt you. I wanted to—to keep it fun and carefree for us all as long as possible. That's all."

"Carefree," she repeated tonelessly.

"Oh, Livvy, please," he begged. "I wish it had worked out differently. But surely you understand? I can't go back on what I've done. And the only thing I regret is the way you found out."

"Yes," she said at last. "I see that."

"Well, how about it? Shall we bury the hatchet?" He tried to smile. "We've never had a real fight before."

"We've never had a reason for one." She glanced at him briefly, then turned to see herself in the mirror. She had not realized her hair was so untidy. She unpinned it and began to brush the long, heavy waves falling beyond her shoulders. It's so thick, the salt in the air will make it difficult to manage, she thought. But all the time she knew he was watching her, waiting. In the glance she had seen the hurt in his eyes, and her reaction surprised her. Once, a few hours ago even, she would have run to him, to hold him and ask forgiveness. But now she could not. She had had a premonition as soon as she learned what he was doing, a hideous certainty that he would not come back from this war. That he had planned it all secretly, counting on her trust and belief in him, only made it worse. He had not given her a chance to protest or even to share in the decision. There was no easy forgiveness for such a betrayal.

He was still waiting for her to speak.

"You're right, of course, Matt," she said. "It can't go on like this. I'm sorry I was so emotional and stupid. Naturally you did what you believed you had to do. And we have the children to think of. I won't spoil it all." She paused. "I'd better change now."

When she rose, he was standing behind her, relieved, with that special smile of his and his hands raised to go round her, but she moved directly to the wardrobe to fetch her red gown and take it into the little dressing room.

The dining saloon was even more elegant than she had imagined, in the style of Louis XVI, the predominant color vieux rose, ringed by the Corinthian columns supporting a circular balcony, where there were more tables and the orchestra. High above, the saloon and balcony were spanned

459

by a breathtaking glass dome with painted panels in the warm, sensuous manner of Boucher. The orchestra was playing the "Kashmiri Song," which had always been one of her favorites. "Pale hands I loved beside the Shalimar. . ."

Their waiter was removing the Sole Walewska, which she had barely touched. "Aren't you hungry?" Matt asked.

"Not really." The men beside her were talking about champagne production. Beyond them something caught Livvy's eye, a huge and stately mahogany sideboard with gilded fittings. She turned to comment on it to Matt, but stopped herself.

Mrs. Arnstein, seated on his other side, had noticed her look and smiled. "It's amazing, isn't it? I was just wondering what size of house you'd need, to have something like that in it. It would fill our dining room at home, and not leave any room for the table."

Livvy smiled. In spite of her name, Beatrice Arnstein had a distinct Scottish accent, expressive and appealing. She was a quietly attractive young woman, little more than a girl, with a girlish figure and soft light brown hair. "I was just thinking that if we had it," Livvy confessed, "it would be a constant dare to my two terrors. They'd be unable to resist using it as a climbing frame."

Beatrice Arnstein laughed, and her husband, a large, heavily built young man, smiled at her amusement. "I'd be tempted to climb it myself," she admitted.

"She would, too," her husband said. He was as clearly American as she was Scots.

Livvy smiled more openly, and Matt began to breathe a little easier. After half an hour of sitting in awkward semi-silence, the ice was breaking. "Do you have any children yourself?" Livvy asked.

The young woman was startled. She bit her lower lip, glanced at her husband and lowered her head, all in the same second. He seemed just as confused. "No. Uh—no, we—we don't," he answered for her, lamely.

Matt and Livvy had both understood. "I take it you haven't been married long enough," Matt smiled.

"No. That is—no, we haven't, as a matter of fact," Arnstein said. His wife frowned at him and attempted to look composed, but could not keep it up. She smiled again nervously, and he confided, "Well, as a matter of fact, we—uh—we were only married yesterday afternoon."

"Why that's—" Livvy paused. She had been about to say "wonderful" when she remembered her own hurt, the dependence on Matt which would make being without him so terrible. "That's very exciting," she went on.

"Congratulations," Matt said.

Livvy looked at the younger couple. They were holding hands under the tablecloth, so vulnerable and very much in love. "I hope you'll both be very happy, Mrs. Arnstein."

"Thank you so much," the girl said, shyly. "Beattie—my name's Beatrice, but everybody calls me Beattie. And he's Lee."

The two men at the table excused themselves and left to finish their conversation over coffee and brandy in the smoke room. The two couples relaxed still more. Lee Arnstein turned out to be an accountant, working for his uncle's firm. Beattie had come out to the States for a year as an exchange teacher, after completing her training course. They were going to live in Philadelphia, but first were paying a surprise visit to her family in St. Andrews in Scotland. "The home of golf," Matt said. Beattie laughed, because her father ran a small, prosperous business dealing mainly in golf clubs. "Well, there's only that in St. Andrews," she explained. "Golf and fishing and the university."

Another surprise was that Lee and Beattie had also been booked on the *Cameronia* and had chosen the *Lusitania* out of all the other liners to which they could have transferred. "Well, we—we couldn't imagine any better place to spend a honeymoon," Lee said.

Matt did the right thing. He signaled the wine waiter and ordered a bottle of champagne in spite of their embarrassment and Beattie's protests that the tiniest sip went to her head. "Just take half a sip, then," Matt advised her, smiling. "You can't have a honeymoon without champagne."

Listening and watching, Livvy felt more and more detached. The more she thought of the other couple's happiness, the more she contrasted it with her own emptiness, all her expectations for this trip, and all so altered. She used the first opportunity after the toasts had been drunk to suggest that it was getting late and that she for one ought

461

to call it a day. Lee appeared reluctant to let them go and offered to repay their hospitality in the main lounge, but Matt reminded them that Peter and Diana would be up and demanding attention as soon as it was light.

Matt was cheerful when they got back to their cabin, more at ease than he had been all day. The evening which had begun so uncomfortably had been unexpectedly enjoyable. "A really nice couple," he said when Livvy came back in from checking that the children were asleep.

"Yes, they are," she agreed.

"I hope they're not so bashful when they're alone together," he smiled. She had rolled up her gloves and put them in a drawer in the tallboy. He came to help her, but she had already unhooked her dress and passed him, going into the dressing room. He told himself he was lucky Livvy was not the type to bear resentment. He put out the top light, leaving only the two bedside lamps, and began to undress. "Did you hear that guy at the table," he called, "the bearded one? He said he's brought two million dollars worth of securities to pay for what he buys from the French vineyards. How much champagne do you think he'll get for two million bucks?"

He paused admiringly when Livvy reappeared. She had changed into a coffee-colored satin nightdress which clung to the rounded lines of her body as she moved. "You look quite something," he breathed.

Both beds had been turned down. She sat on the nearer one, shook off her mules and slipped under the covers. She had not looked at him. "It's been a long day," she said quietly. "I'm very tired. Good night." She switched off her bedside lamp and moved over on her side, facing away.

Matt stood motionless for a long moment. It was possible that she was tired, only tired. A day ago he might have finished undressing and got into bed with her, fitting himself against the yielding warmth of her back. Instead, he undressed to his shorts and lay down on the other bed. "Livvy?" he asked softly. She did not move or reply. He switched off his own lamp. He could hear her steady, unhurried breathing and assumed that it was true, and she was asleep.

Livvy, however, lay gazing into the dark, feeling the wet prickle of her eyelids as the silent tears came.

* * *

Lee Arnstein studied his cigarette with distaste. It was the third he had lit in the twenty minutes he had been walking on the shelter deck. He flicked it over the side and it curved away toward the stern, vanishing in the darkness. He had come out to give Beattie time to do whatever she had to do when she got ready for bed.

For a young man of twenty-four, he was fairly inexperienced. Not innocent, for who could live in these days of one-piece bathing suits and art galleries and shows where the chorus girls wore abbreviated skirts and flesh-colored tights and not know something about the female form? And he had seen some photographs and read a couple of books that astonished him. He could not imagine Beattie ever looking or behaving like that. He had to admit that he did not know exactly how one did behave or how precisely one set about things of an intimate nature. He had kissed one or two girls at parties and after dances, and he understood the whole theory of what one was supposed to do, but he had never actually done it. In a way he felt guilty even thinking about Beattie like that, in a male and female sense, but he couldn't help it.

He stopped himself from reaching for another cigarette.

The evening had been fun and the couple at the table good sports, nice people. Someone like Matt was the kind of person he would like to be able to ask things. He was sure Matt would understand and not make him feel embarrassed.

There were seven days to go until they reached England. Seven days and seven nights. Then he supposed they'd have to go straight up to Scotland, since he'd only been able to arrange three weeks holiday. He wasn't looking forward to Scotland. In fact he had to confess he was plenty scared. The trouble was, his family was reasonably orthodox Jewish and Beattie's was Scots Presbyterian. And neither family knew about the wedding yet.

He could imagine his own folks' reaction. There would be a bit of shouting and sniffing and weeping behind closed doors. A lot of sitting with nothing being said, and his father just shaking his head slowly once in a while. There'd be no trouble with the firm. With the others it would be different, though. Even his parents might not speak to him for a month or two. But it would all come right eventually. Once they met and got to know Beattie. They wouldn't be able to resist her. Not even his grandmother.

The real problem was her father. He sounded hell's own strict, a respected elder of the Kirk. Beattie said he was very fair and kind, although a little forbidding when you first met him maybe. That was what Lee dreaded, that meeting. How he would take to his only beloved Protestant daughter marrying an unknown American Jew was anybody's guess. All Lee could do, he'd decided, was tell him the truth, that they couldn't live without each other. That next year he was to be made a junior partner and, although it would be a struggle until then, he could support a wife. And that no one loved anyone in the whole world as much as he loved Beattie.

Twenty-five minutes. Surely that was long enough? He started back for their cabin.

They had been married at three in the afternoon yesterday at City Hall, and then had taken a walk in the park. In the evening they had dinner at Fleischmann's. He had booked a room for the night at the St. Regis. At least he had known what not to do. He had read a book on etiquette and was grateful for it. Most men, he had learned, were ignorant of how distressing marriage was for a woman. Irreparable damage could be caused by the husband not showing self-restraint and consideration, by not allowing the lady time to become used to the wedded state and all its implications before forcing his attentions on her. On the sensitive subject of the marriage bed, the book recommended that on no account on the first night should the husband attempt more than to kiss his wife gently, assure her of his devotion and assuage her fears. The process, requiring self-sacrifice on the part of the male, should even be continued for several days if the female appeared unduly apprehensive. He had already failed in one respect. Last night he had waited in the lounge for nearly an hour after Beattie had gone up to prepare for bed, and he had been unable to kiss and reassure her. After the excitements of the day, she had fallen asleep by the time he got to their room.

She was not asleep tonight. She was sitting up in bed, waiting for him, wearing a white nightdress with puffed sleeves and lace ruffles down the front. She smiled, hesitantly and looked so tiny and fragile and adorable that his breath caught in his throat at the sight of her. Her eyes had dropped to her hands which lay folded on top of the coverlet on her lap. When she glanced up again, he asked quickly, "Are you all right? I mean . . . all right?"

"Yes," she nodded. "But you were gone so long, I wondered what had happened."

"Well, I didn't want to—you know."

"Yes," Beattie said, although she was not entirely sure what he meant. She hesitated and, when he neither moved nor spoke, asked shyly, "Aren't you coming to bed?"

That was another thing, and also his fault for not being specific. Their cabin had a double bed, not twin divans. They would be under the same covers. He could only admire Beattie, that she had accepted it so well, had even urged him not to make a fuss about it.

"Yes," he answered her. "Yes, of course." His night clothes were laid out in the dressing recess and he went to it hurriedly. As he undressed, he thought of her only a few feet away and turned automatically to face the wall, although she could not possibly see him. Excitement gripped him again and the shameful reaction which he had to fight to control. He was physically almost overendowed, he knew. His friends and teammates used to laugh about it.

Stripped, he appeared even bulkier, having put on some weight in the last three years since giving up football, but he was still strongly muscled. His apparent slowness of movement was deceptive. As a halfback for his college team he had been almost unstoppable running with the ball, smashing through the opponents' line, and just as lethal in defense. His strength was something else that worried him. He was almost afraid to hold Beattie, who was so fragile in comparison he was afraid he might crush her.

Beattie was still sitting waiting and smiled to him when he emerged, with his dressing gown over his striped sleeping suit. She was as inexperienced as he was, although not naïve. Conversations with more advanced girlfriends had given her a more vivid idea of what to expect than he realized. She felt very warm and loving as she smiled to him, for she could see how hard he was trying to appear relaxed and self-possessed. It was his shyness, in spite of his halfback's physique, which had first drawn her to him. They were well matched at least in that, but she knew that one of them was going to have to make the move. She had had a glass and a half of the champagne and it helped. She felt strangely daring and folded back the coverlet even more on his side.

He draped his dressing gown over a chair and climbed into bed beside her, sitting up like her with his back against the headboard. Any other feelings were almost immediately wiped out by the realization that he had forgotten to switch out the main lights. He kicked himself mentally.

Beattie noticed him glance at them and at the switch by the door. "Never mind," she told him gently. "It doesn't matter." She slipped a little further down into the bed, so that her back rested on the pillows. He was looking down at the fair curls that crowned her head and wanted to caress them with his cheek. Instead, he moved down too so that their shoulders were more nearly level. "Here we are," she said, very softly.

He would have smiled, but she seemed quite serious. Her eyes searched his, a clear blue. He could smell the very faint perfume like honeysuckle that seemed to come from her skin, her hair. "You haven't kissed me all evening, Lee," she whispered.

He turned slightly, bent and kissed her very tenderly. It was perfect. Everything the book had said it would be. He had never in his life dreamed of being so close to anyone, so protective.

As he eased away, Beattie's right arm shifted and crept up round his neck to draw him down again. At the same time her head fell further back, so that he had to stretch partly over her. Her lips were just open and the difference in the kiss was dizzying. All his senses swirled at her perfume and nearness and the giving warmth of her mouth, so that at first he was not conscious of her taking his hand and bringing it up until she laid it on her bosom.

The soft shapes under her nightdress felt so tiny that he could cover both with his one hand. The sudden knowledge of what he was touching and the force with which he had begun to kiss her shocked him. He raised his head and pulled back, taking his hand away. He was panting, and he could tell that so was she. Her eyes were closed, and when she

466

opened them, they looked almost drugged. "I'm—I'm sorry, honey," he faltered. "I didn't mean to—I didn't want to hurt you."

"You couldn't hurt me," she whispered. "Not even if you tried." She wetted her lips, as though they were dry and crushed. His own were still tingling. "Hold me," she said. "Please?" She lifted herself to make room for his arm to slide under her shoulders. With her head raised, it was natural for him to kiss her again. Her hand was urgent on his neck, her fingers crisping in the short hairs behind his ear.

The kiss prolonged itself until they were both breathless. When they broke apart at last, he found that he had grasped her round the side, his thumb lying over her left breast. He took his hand away again quickly. The warmth had increased because she was tighter against him, lying in the crook of his arm with her lower body swiveled so that he could feel the pressure of her knees against his thighs. Their faces were still so close that their breath mingled. Her eyes were shining, and her heart-shaped face was flushed into a new prettiness. More than prettiness, she was lovely.

Her shoulders moved and he glanced down to see her left hand busy among the lace ruffles of her nightdress. Her hand paused, then pushed one, then the other side apart, baring her almost to the waist.

Her torso was fine, rising to the swell of her ribs whose outline could just be seen. In spite of her slimness, she was not thin. Her breasts were small and delicately shaped, the nipples tiny and softly pink against the cream of her skin. He had never seen anything so beautiful.

She had acted on impulse, not knowing what to expect. He lay so long, motionless, gazing down at her, that she became embarrassed. She could feel her nipples puckering and turned quickly, hiding them against him, burying her face against his chest. His hands were on her back, stroking, and he kissed her hair, his lips moving on her scalp. She could feel her whole body responding, tensing and thrilling and opening. He was murmuring, "Oh, my darling . . . my own darling . . ."

His sleeping suit came to a vee at his throat and she felt him shudder when she kissed him there. "Lee," she gasped, "Lee . . . ?" She kissed him under his chin and the line of his jaw; then his lips closed down again on hers. She moved her mouth to his cheek and whispered, "Lee . . . I want to be your wife. Really your wife."

His head swung back and he looked at her, troubled, questioning, but the eagerness and need he read in her eyes could not be misunderstood. Her lips were working, and when he saw that she was smiling, his own smile in answer brought a brief sob from her. They kissed open-mouthed, both her arms round his neck as she pressed closer.

She felt something hard touch her lower down at the division of her thighs. His hips pulled back, but she followed him, urging her body against his until he stopped. She felt it again, a stiffness against the slight pout of her belly. She took her left hand from his shoulder and moved it slowly down. Their kiss broke off and they looked at each other, almost without expression, frozen in suspense as her hand crept between them and reached lower.

Her eyes widened suddenly in astonishment at what she found. For a second he thought she was afraid, then she squirmed against him. Her teeth caught her lower lip and she twisted slowly on to her back, bringing him with her.

Charles Frohman had dined alone in the stateroom of his suite. He was far from unsociable, but he always considered these days on the *Lusitania* as precious and personal, a rare gift of time to think and to work without any meetings, telephone calls or other interruptions. It was when he came to many major decisions, had some of his best ideas.

Tonight, however, he had been unable to concentrate. It was not only the pain in his inflamed knee, which was suddenly as bad as ever it had been. He was unsettled and could not school his mind to any one thing. Manuscripts, a pad for the telegrams he had meant to send, his own unfinished play, lay on the desk beside him untouched and unread.

He had taken off his suit coat and unbuttoned his vest. He sat as he so often did with his painful leg hooked over the arm of his chair, his mind drifting in the same directionless stream as it had all day. Through the half open window, he could just make out the sound of the ship's orchestra as it played the wistful "In a Monastery Garden." That would be exactly right for me, he thought, where I should be. What did they call it—on retreat? Watch it, Charley, he warned himself, you're getting sorry for yourself. The least pleasant form of self-indulgence.

He shifted in his chair. The remedy was simple, as he had prescribed for himself over and again, stop thinking about Maude. Just that.

It was ridiculous to be so obsessive. Why should he single her out from all the beautiful young actresses he had discovered, who were devoted to him by gratitude? Marie, Ann, Rita, Ethel, many others, genuine, warm friendships. And if he wanted something more, there was a legion of other young actresses, some even more desirable, offering themselves, willing to give anything for him to manage their careers. He could— He would end up disgusting himself if he wasn't careful. He had never taken advantage in that way of his position. He had not been a saint, but artistic ability and what was best for the theater had always come first.

He almost began to resent Maude for the effect of her hold on him. But it was not her, it was himself. Her influence, her sovereignty, was unconscious. He made a deliberate effort to distract himself from her and thought ahead to London, to being with Barrie again. They would laugh and reminisce and make more plans for the future. And when the need for talk ran out and the shadows lengthened, they would sit silent in Barrie's flat in Adelphi Terrace off the Strand, him with his cigar and Jamie puffing reflectively on his little black pipe. The silences were longer now that Jamie's wife had left him. When they felt the urge for extra company, they would open the window and hurl things across the narrow street, cigar butts, erasers, bread crusts and rolls, at the window opposite, until it rattled up and Bernard Shaw, bearded and puckish, would stick his head out, yelling, "Cease fire!" The Irish playwright hated to be disturbed, but not by them, "Are you inviting me to a feast, Barrie?" he would shout. "Are you casting bread upon the waters—or is it just Frohman?" Frohman chuckled.

His valet, William, who had been hovering for some time, reluctant to break into his thoughts, came forward. "Was there something, sir?" he asked.

"No, thank you, William," Frohman told him, still smiling.

"Oh, yes, if there's any of that soda water left, you can get me a glass. And some more peanuts."

Frohman was as at home in that flat in Adelphi Terrace as he was in his own rooms in the nearby Savoy. Those were memorable evenings with magical words dancing in the air with the tobacco smoke. In no time at all there would be a party, for Granville Barker lived in the flat above, and downstairs was Galsworthy. He wanted to introduce Charles Klein to that circle, and young Forman. It would be a testing ground for the younger writer, to see how he stood up to the impact of those minds, penetrating and scintillating, the wit so deft and light you often did not understand the profundity of what had been said until long after. It would be a baptism of fire for young Forman, who tended to take himself too seriously. How he handled himself, how he joined in and at what level and, more importantly, what he absorbed from it all would help to show if he really had something to offer, something more than mere promise.

The orchestra was still playing the same dismal tune. It seemed interminable. William brought a dish of peanuts and the soda water. "Thank you," Frohman said. "And would you mind closing the window?"

William clicked the window shut and drew the curtain. He was a good fellow, Frohman thought, and it was unfair to keep him up or away, perhaps, from one of the bars. "I shan't need you any more tonight," he said.

"Very good, sir." William bowed. "Are you sure there's nothing else?"

"Nothing." As soon as he said it, Frohman sensed a return of the unsettled, despondent mood. All the result of that damned tune to which he'd been listening without meaning to. William was almost at the door. "Oh, yes," Frohman called. "Would you set up the phonograph?"

William carried the box of the phonograph to the writing table by Frohman, opened it, inserted and cranked the handle. He did not need to ask which record to put on.

When he had gone, Frohman reached out, pushed the little starting lever over and lowered the pickup arm. Sound erupted into the cabin and he sat back, letting the music enfold him, his fingers beginning to dance on the arms of his chair. Strident, catchy, its rhythm tricky and extrovert, "Alexander's Rag-time Band" chased the blue devils away, as he had known it would.

Will Turner had also dined alone, in his dayroom. Now he was in the wheelhouse, standing in his favored position at the portside forward windows, looking out into the night. The lights were shaded to give maximum observation and, as always when he was on the bridge, the atmosphere was quiet and calm.

Junior Third Officer Bestwick was still not used to it after the bustle and continual banter of other bridges, although he had been warned what to expect and to make no unnecessary noise. Speech was kept to a murmur. The others with him, First Officer Jones, Second Officer Hefford, the quartermaster and helmsman, were so still, attending exclusively to their duties, that he could hear the tick of the wheelhouse clock. Gradually on the journey eastward it would be advanced to match the time in Europe, and that promised to be the major sign of activity on this bridge.

Yet Bestwick was impressed. He would not care to have Turner's responsibility for two thousand souls and millions of pounds of ship and cargo heading into dangerous waters, and he wondered what kind of thoughts must go through his mind.

Turner was thinking about the clematis on the south wall of his house in Great Crosby. It had just been coming out and lasted such a short while. Would it be past its best, or would he still be able to catch it?

The *Lusitania's* horn blared out and he grunted with it, peering ahead. There was no visible improvement in the patchy fog through which she was moving at restricted speed.

"What's the glass doing, Mr. Jones?" he asked.

"Rising, sir."

Turner hunched his shoulders, peering forward into the dark. From the decreasing roll under his feet he could tell that the wind was dying away. At the same time a rising barometer meant the likelihood of more fog, and he swore softly to himself, as he had been hoping to make up the hours lost by the delayed departure. Instead he had to resign himself to losing even more. There was always danger of collision in fog and it was on that which he had to concentrate. He had no fears for the *Lusy*, virtually unsinkable because of her double bottom and watertight compartments. He was more concerned about smaller, lower vessels which she might run down, unseen in the fog banks.

Unsinkable? A dangerous boast, he knew, especially since her rival, the White Star's *Titanic*, had gone down on her maiden voyage three years ago after an iceberg ripped a three-hundred-foot gash in her side. She also had been "unsinkable," but she lacked the enormous longitudinal bulkheads, the second skin inside the *Lusitania*'s hull which ensured her special buoyancy and safety. He thought briefly of the oiler, Frank Tower. Tower had served on the *Titanic* and many of the crew considered him a sort of mascot. Turner had a particular soft spot for Tower, as he too had survived a shipwreck, when the squarerigger on which he had made his very first voyage as a cabin boy had smashed into a reef off the Irish coast during a gale.

Steady, Will, he told himself, your mind's wandering.

All that mattered was the situation at this moment. He had to think of his crew and passengers and get them safely through the night. And his cargo. As he ate his supper, he had studied the true manifest. On one hand he wished he had not, since it made disturbing reading. The thousands of pounds of butter and lard, the barrels of lubricating oil, a thousand-odd cases of shrapnel shells and the mass of .303 ammunition, not to mention the unspecified goods being shipped to the Naval Experimental Establishment, all sounded like a highly combustible mixture. On the other hand, he thought of his two sons, one at the front line and the other menaced by submarines in the merchant navy. Both saw the *Lusitania* as an expensive luxury in these days of war, yet for the first time her cargo was even more important than her passengers. If only for one item. The guns and rifles of the Allies were silent for long hours through lack of ammunition, and Turner could not help feeling a reluctant pride at what she was bringing on this one trip. With her own original load plus those from the *Cameronia* and *Queen Margaret*, there were over seven thousand cases of cartridges stowed in the decks under his feet. At a thousand rounds per case, the *Lusitania* was carrying upward of seven million bullets for the rifles and machine guns of the Western Front.

* * *

Walther Schwieger had an unquiet feeling about this trip. Now, in the fourth day out, he could no longer ignore it. It had nothing to do with the U 20. There was no trace of the damage she had suffered. Tests had been run by each department and, technically, she seemed in perfect condition. Yet there was an odd feel about her. As he strode from central control to his cabin, Schwieger tried to put his finger on what it was. The crew had returned from leave refreshed. The new members were slotting in well and all functioning efficiently. Karl Scherb, the new gunnery lieutenant, was a more than acceptable substitute for poor Weiser. Aggressive, even a little pushy, Scherb had proven today how eager he was to see action. No, the problem lay elsewhere. Reluctantly, Schwieger had to admit to himself that the source of his uneasiness was Mate of the Reserve Lanz.

Everywhere he went, in every section of the U-boat, he could smell the faintly rancid aroma of the small black cigars that Lanz smoked. Whenever he entered central control or the officers' quarters, he was conscious of Lanz's shrewd, half veiled eyes watching him, assessing him. If he went up to the conning tower, within three minutes Lanz would follow him, asking questions, proffering advice. All the other men who had ever sailed with him understood that the commander's position was solitary, deliberately isolated. No one must intrude or query orders, for nothing must distract or inhibit the commander's ability to make instant decisions in the certainty that they would be instantly obeyed.

Lanz, however, made full use of his civilian status to question and give his opinions, always with deference, but with the air of a man convinced that he was always right. He seemed to interpret his appointment as involving something more than merely indentifying merchant shipping, or perhaps someone had given him the impression that it would be. He had a habit when orders were issued of either nodding his approval or else swaying his head and sucking his teeth doubtfully, which was highly irritating. To ease the irritation, Schwieger had pointed out that he would ask for his advice when it was needed. The hint had not been taken.

Schwieger paused briefly when he passed the U 20's tiny officers' quarters and spotted Karl Scherb sitting with Haupert and Lanz, the three of them glum and silent. He knew at once that the sour mood had to do with today's disappointment.

"Don't take it personally," Schwieger said to the young gunnery lieutenant. "It was a mechanical failure."

Scherb looked up and nodded gratefully. He still felt keenly the failure of the first attack of the sortie, after the excitement it had promised.

They had sailed all the fourth day and seen nothing except a few fishing smacks until just before sunset, when Scherb's straining eyes had at last caught the smoke of a steamer on the horizon. Submerged to thirty feet, racing to intercept, they had found her to be a fair-sized cargo ship, probably carrying supplies to the naval base at Scapa Flow. It was Scherb's victim, his very first, and he sweated as the U 20 closed for the attack. He had set and primed the torpedo himself and waited with his thumb poised over the red button, until Schwieger had given the order to fire. At the short range of three hundred yards, it was impossible to miss. But nothing had happened. The torpedo misfired, remaining wedged in the forward No. 1 tube, and the enemy steamer churned past to the north in safety.

"These things happen," Schwieger said and moved on to his own cabin.

"That's the truth," Lanz agreed quietly once he had gone. "They do happen. But more often in some commands than others."

"What do you mean?" Haupert asked.

"It seems to me that our Kapitänleutnant is very cautious."

"He's also ranked as sixth in the list of aces," Haupert reminded him tautly. "And we're all still alive—probably just because he's cautious." Haupert went out, leaving Scherb and Lanz alone.

Schwieger had taken the logbook from his locker and sat at the table to bring it up to date, skimming first through the main items of the previous day, May 2. For most of her journey to the North of Scotland the U 20 had to travel underwater because of thick fog which blanketed the entire area. One attempt to make better speed on the surface had almost ended in disaster when they had all but run into an armed enemy trawler; then when the fog began to clear and

474

he had surfaced to circle round above the scattered Orkney Islands for the mine free channel between Ronaldsay and Fair Isle, he had found himself facing a reception committee of the same six destroyers which had nearly rammed him earlier. Forced to dive again, the temptation to accept the challenge was strong, yet he knew they would all be on full alert, guns manned and loaded. He might get one, but at periscope depth the U 20 would be too vulnerable to the guns of the other five. He stole on far below them and, when he came up again twenty minutes later, sighted through the asparagus the other two farther-ranging destroyers of the patrol forward to starboard. He still could not surface. The hounds were waiting to pounce.

"That's it, though," Lanz had said. "All accounted for."

Schwieger's sixth sense, however, warned him not to take risks. He knew they must be almost at the very spot where Weddigen went down, but it was not only that, not superstition. Pure instinct. He navigated the channel underwater in spite of Lanz's insistence that they were now safe and Hirsch's concern that power was being used up. They had not risen even to periscope height for four hours and then had returned to seventy feet after ten minutes on seeing another patrol ship. They had continued on course submerged until dark, when he had at last given in to Hirsch's pleas that they must surface to recharge the batteries.

For the first time the U 20 had been given a really prime hunting ground and he wanted to reach it intact and in top fighting condition. That the campaign had begun to bite was obvious from the increased vigilance of the enemy patrols. He had no doubt they were trying to sew up the northern route as tightly as they had the English Channel. He took up his pen and wrote under the day's entries, "P.S. If the surveillance of the line Fair Isle–Ronaldsay is not accidental but set up by the enemy command, the passage by daylight in good visibility is now dangerous. The U 20, forced to submerge before dawn and to travel 50 nautical miles underwater, would have found herself in a critical situation if one more destroyer had been on patrol to the north of the line, for the accumulators were running down and the power supply beginning to give out." He felt restless and closed the log. It was time to check the watch.

They were on the surface south of the desolate Shiant Isles in the wide channel between the west coast of mainland Scotland and the Outer Hebrides, and before long would be passing Skye to port. The sun had set, although the air still held that strange luminescence, the prolonged twilight of northern latitudes. Even the sea had its own special sheen, like dark, burnished pewter. The U-boat's wake was a dull, swirling silver. His scarf hung loose and he folded it over, tucking it inside his leather coat against the chill. No reason to feel uneasy, he told himself. There was no need for extra precautions until they were south of Barra Head and entering the approaches to the Firth of Clyde and the Irish Sea, always heavily defended by seagoing patrols. The hunt was on, but could not be for him. He relaxed as he had taught himself, breathing slow and measured.

"Dead ahead, sir." It was Lammeier who was on watch beside him. His promotion to petty officer of the gun crew had been confirmed after the last voyage. "A little to starboard."

Bibermann was with them and was pointing, and now Schwieger could see it too, a black speck virtually at the limit of sight. Lammeier handed him the telescope and he trained it, adjusting to the slight pitch of the U 20's bows. The speck became clearer. It was a steamer, all right, totally blacked out. It was difficult to judge the distance to her in this light, or even how far above the horizon she was. But she would make up for the earlier disappointment with the misfiring torpedo. He snapped the telescope shut. "Action Stations."

Action was the surest cure for restlessness, and Schwieger concentrated on nothing except the approaching target as the U 20 slid forward at just under periscope depth to intercept. The Number 1 tube was reloaded and again Scherb stood with one hand on the periscope's elevating lever and the other hovering over the firing button. Schwieger saw him grin past him to Lanz, who was on his left. The young lieutenant's eagerness was infectious and, even as he responded to it, Schwieger wondered if what had affected him was Scherb's frustration at the escape of the earlier target. He could remember the days when he had resented anything that got away from him. Now he had grown more philo-

sophical and more selective. Yet everything was right about
the approaching target, particularly the timing. With nearly
four full days of the sortie gone already, the crew needed a
kill to bring their keenness and efficiency to peak before the
U 20 arrived at her official operating area.

She crept up in the water and Scherb reacted instantly
to Schwieger's signal, stopping the stick so that only the
hooded eye appeared over the waves.

Schwieger had trouble locating the blacked-out steamer
at first, then frowned in surprise. She was much closer than
he had expected, than she had any right to be, unless she
was traveling at phenomenal speed. All at once he understood. His eyes had been deceived by the light. What had
appeared to all the watch to be a large steamer at a considerable distance was in fact a small one much nearer. In a
minute or two she would be broadside on. "It's a washout,"
he said flatly, straightening. Scherb almost gaped at him,
his hopes dashed again.

"Why's that?" Lanz asked.

Schwieger gestured and stood back to let the older man
take his place at the eyepiece. "Not worth attacking," he
said.

Lanz swiveled the stick and grunted as the steamer came
into vision. She was really tiny. "Not much more than a
thousand tons," he confirmed.

"One and a half at most," Schwieger agreed. "Besides, in
this light, it's impossible to tell what nationality she is."

Lanz glanced up at him. "She's blacked out and she's a
freighter. You could still sink her."

Schwieger was not used to having to explain himself, but
he did so for Scherb's sake. "And waste a torpedo we might
need for a battleship?" He shook his head. "We'd only ad
vertise our presence and put bigger ships on the alert without achieving anything."

The crew was stood down and the U 20 surfaced again,
continuing her journey south. Schwieger went back to his
cabin to write up the second abandoned attack. Even in his
log he did not put the real reason, the psychological effect
on his crew of beginning the patrol by sinking such an insignificant victim. After a few major kills he would have had
no compunction about blowing her out of the water, but not

477

now. He was just as disappointed as Scherb, and with more cause, for it had occurred to him that only one thing could have stirred up the British coastal defenses to such an extent. The U-boats which had left before him must have scored some spectacular successes in the past week. The U 20 and he would have to pull out all the stops if they were to catch up.

There was a knock on the bulkhead outside his door. The green curtain twitched aside and Lippe looked in, forgetting to salute in his excitement. "Please, Captain!" he blurted.

"What is it?"

"Please!"

Lippe had gone again and Schwieger rose and stepped to the door, to see the big torpedoman hurrying off through central control. Schwieger followed him, pausing to ask Hirsch what was going on. Hirsch was just as mystified, having only seen Lippe rush through control and back. Schwieger signed to Kurtz and, as they moved on, Lanz and Scherb went with them.

Through the opening ahead, Schwieger heard raised voices as Lippe pushed the other torpedomen and technicians out of the forward torpedo room. Above the voices he could hear the little wirehaired dachshund, Hansel, barking agitatedly. What in hell's going on? he wondered, as the crewmen made way for him. He came to the door of the torpedo room and stopped.

Lippe was kneeling on the deck, hunched over, peering under the lower torpedo secured against the side, ahead of the collapsible bunks. "What's this all about?" Schwieger asked, and Kurtz growled beside him when Lippe did not answer or look round, but merely waved at them to be quiet.

Schwieger tensed as Lippe started to reach in under the torpedo, only to draw back quickly. Lippe glanced up, his blue pebble eyes wide with anxiety, and reached under again. He touched something and began to draw it out, with infinite care. *"Herr Gott . . ."* Kurtz breathed. "What is it?"

To his surprise, Schwieger saw that Lippe was holding between the thumb and index finger of each hand the corners of a folded blanket. He could not make out what it contained, for Lippe shuffled round on his knees blocking his view. Hansel was barking again, sharp and anxious, but stopped when Schwieger moved forward. Lippe's head rose, his cheeks wet with tears, but he was smiling. On the crumpled blanket in front of his knees, Hansel's mate Maria was lying with four newborn puppies, their coats beginning to dry to a dark fluff, nuzzling blindly for her teats.

Schwieger crouched and Hansel's head tilted, inquiringly. As he stretched out a hand, Lippe whispered, "Careful, Captain," but Schwieger had not touched the pups. He patted Hansel's head. "Congratulations, *Vati*," he said, then moved his hand carefully to stroke behind Maria's damp ears and murmur, "You too, little mother. Well done." He lowered his hand to her muzzle and she licked his fingers tiredly. She only whined softly, asking him to be gentle, when he lifted two of the pups.

Lippe copied what he had done and lifted the other two from the blanket gingerly, one in each huge hand. He was as proud as Hansel, sniffing back his tears. "This one's a boy," he decided. "But this little one, I think she's a girl. Could we call her Megeen, Captain?"

"Why not?" Schwieger agreed, and Lippe beamed.

The men with Kurtz were laughing at how Hansel's tail drummed proudly against the side of the torpedo, and some applauded when Schwieger and Lippe turned, displaying the four latest members of the crew. All were smiling. Except two. Scherb was puzzled, watching, and Lanz was bland, but the expression which Schwieger glimpsed for a moment on his face as he turned was of contempt.

Chapter 26

THE SHOE ON THE STAND BEGAN TO WIGGLE. THE HEEL tapped, then the toe in a series of happy little beats. The shoeblack stopped in surprise and looked up, but all he could see was the open newspaper held by the elegant gent in the chair.

Franz von Rintelen had strolled down Cedar Street from his E.V. Gibbons office to the corner of Broadway, where he had bought a midday paper and paused to have his toe caps polished before calling a cab for his appointment with David Lamar in the lunch bar at Sherry's. He had been feeling the strain of the last few days. For many, May 1 had been the sailing date of the *Lusitania*, but for him it was also the deadline he had been given before he left Berlin and, in spite of all his efforts, he was conscious of a lack of achievement. To an extent he had done wonders, but his prime objective had been the disruption of the flow of munitions to Russia, the whole reason for the business with Dr. Scheele, the firebomb factory and the secret meetings with Foley and his Irish longshoremen. Days and now weeks had gone by with nothing to show for it. The enthusiasm of his own men as well as of the more volatile Irish was cooling fast, and he could not blame them.

He had taken his place on the shoeshine stand and his eyes flicked from heading to heading on the paper's front page. Expecting nothing, he missed it at first, the half column down on the right, but when he saw it the blood rushed to his head. The report was that a German-Austrian army under the commander-in-chief, Falkenhayn, was advancing in Galicia after defeating the Russians in battles at Tarnow and Gorlice. Another army under General von Bülow was reputed to be advancing in the north. Obviously the editor

480

had not realized fully what it meant. Exactly on schedule, the Eastern Offensive had begun! Not only that. The Czar's army must now be in retreat, leaving open the way to Ivangorod and Warsaw.

He could remember Falkenhayn's quiet, determined voice. "In four months, there will not be a single Russian alive or in arms between the Carpathians and the Baltic . . ." He would do it, von Rintelen knew, but only if the Russians were unable to mount an all-out counterattack. And the ports of northern Russia were now free of ice, so that munition ships could reach them. Von Rintelen's boast had been that he would stop those supplies. How stupid even to imagine it could be done.

He leafed through the rest of the paper, but there was no editorial, no other comment on the offensive. As routine, he looked at the shipping news, the reports from Lloyds of London. "*Accidents*. S.S. *Phoebus* from New York—destined Archangel—caught fire at sea. Brought into port of Liverpool by H.M.S. *Ajax*."

Von Rintelen stared at it. It was so perfect, he needed a moment to take it in. The *Phoebus*, an American freighter. His men had been under strictest orders to place their firebombs only in the holds containing nonexplosive cargo, to run less risk of destroying a neutral vessel. But the captain's immediate action would be to flood the munition hold to save his ship, and the ammunition he had carried would be no more use to anyone.

Von Rintelen felt like singing. His toes were tapping and he looked down, to see the shoeblack grinning up at him. "Yoh hoss come in fust, suh?" the man asked.

"Something like that," von Rintelen chuckled, "Yes, very like that." He folded the paper, rose and hurried back up Cedar Street.

The shoeblack was left speechless, gazing at his hand. For a ten cent shine, he had been given a fifty-dollar tip.

The *Lusitania* steamed eastwards across the Atlantic at a steady twenty knots. That was pushing it with six of her boilers shut down, but Turner wanted to make up as much time as possible. The fog had thinned south of Nova Scotia and she sailed into calm, mild weather with a pleasant warmth in the sun. Even the most experienced passengers could not remember more perfect conditions or a smoother crossing.

Elizabeth Duckworth was finishing the lunch sitting for steerage passengers in the second-class dining saloon. The meal had been plain but satisfying, just as she liked it. With the added luxury of coffee. She had grown used to the slight roll of the ship, slept soundly and felt more rested than she had for months. It was all most enjoyable, although she was becoming impatient now to see sooty old Blackburn again and get into some kind of war work.

She closed her ears to the yammering of a family of small children at the next table. They were not nearly so well-behaved as little Arthur, although she could hardly blame their mother, Mrs. Williams, who had a hard time taking care of all six of them on her own. On her other side, the man who was always complaining was at it again, haranguing one of the waiters about the lack of proper blackout precautions at night. "Last night this whole ship was lit up as if we were on a holiday cruise!"

"Lot of folks are," the waiter said. When the man bridled, he explained patiently, "Y'see sir, there ain't no point in dousin' all the lights yet when the Jerries are still a couple of thousand miles away. We'll start blackin' out tomorrow night, when we're past 'alf way. But even then it won't be a complete blackout, like."

"Why not?" the man demanded.

"Well, sir, if we was to blackout completely, a Jerry submarine might think we was a ruddy great battleship or something, an' 'ave a go at us. So we leave just a few lights on to let them see it's the *Lusy*. Not even them bleeders is goin' to attack a passenger ship."

Alice Scott was sitting beside Arthur and looked relieved. Elizabeth winked to her. It was just what she had told her last night, to reassure her.

Dan Connally stood with Matt, watching the daily boat drill. Six able seamen stood by one of the lifeboats on the port side. At a whistle from a junior officer, they leaped in and scrambled to their places. They pulled on life jackets and sat with folded arms for a minute, then at another whistle they took off the life jackets, climbed out and dispersed. The boat drill was over.

"That's a fairly pathetic exhibition," Dan said, unimpressed by the sailors' casualness. He eyed with misgiving the sixty or seventy feet the boat would have to be lowered to touch the water after it had been swung out on its davits. "I hope they know what they're doing," he muttered. The lifeboat, like the others, was massively heavy, built to carry about sixty people.

"These things are very carefully designed," Matt said. "There's no danger." He paused. "You'll be missing your lunch."

"I'll grab a sandwich later," Dan shrugged. "Do me good to miss it. I'm putting on weight."

"You could have a run round the deck," Matt said. They laughed. As part of a fitness campaign, Barney Ferguson had announced that he planned to run ten times round the promenade deck every morning before breakfast. He had given in on the first morning, after discovering that one single lap was a quarter of a mile.

Matt and Dan walked on. They met at least once a day, Dan acting as liaison with the other volunteers. Matt refused to consider himself as a kind of honorary commanding officer, but they insisted on bringing all their problems and queries to him, instead of to one of the several English regular officers on board. At least it helped to keep his mind off Livvy and their future, and the nagging ache in his left shoulder where the muscles had still not completely mended after crashing the Overland that night in the Valley.

Ahead of them he saw Lee Arnstein strolling with his arm round his pretty little wife, Beattie. He had become very friendly with them, almost a father confessor to Lee, and he smiled. "What?" Dan asked.

Matt thought about it. "I don't think I can tell you."

"Oh, come on," Dan urged, intrigued. "What's the joke?"

"Just some people I know. Newlyweds," Matt said. "It's sort of—" He chuckled, and realized he would have to tell Dan. "Well, he's Jewish, you see, and his wife's not. After the wedding he thought he ought to point out to her, explain that of course he was circumcised." Dan nodded. That morning Matt had run into Lee in the smoke room. The younger man was embarrassed, but so tickled he couldn't keep it to himself. "The wife took it very well, said naturally she understood, it was all right. Then last night, they were talking in bed and she asked him to tell her how it had happened, if it wasn't too painful. He said it had all happened when he was a little boy and he couldn't remember if it was painful or not. That it was a sort of religious ritual, and so on." Matt began to laugh, and stopped himself. "He could see that his wife was puzzled, and more and more as he went on. Well, eventually he discovered the reason. Like many young ladies she was almost totally ignorant of the male anatomy and wasn't thinking about that at all. She'd been expecting him to confess to her about an affair he'd once had with a woman." Matt laughed again. "When he first mentioned it, she'd thought it meant the same as saying he'd been compromised."

Dan laughed with him. From the direction Matt was looking, it was evident that the husky young man and the girl he had his arm round were the couple they had been talking about. They were patently very much in love. Newlyweds, Matt had said. He was anxious, seeing how Matt watched them, affectionately but with a suggestion of envy. "Where's Livvy?" he asked casually.

"With the children, I expect," Matt said, and corrected himself. "No, they're having lunch with the other kids, then going to the playroom. She's around somewhere, at some ladies' meeting."

He was just as casual as Dan, but it did not hide the hurt. "I know it's none of my business," Dan said quietly, "but I'm making it mine. How are things between you and Livvy?"

Matt swung away to stand looking out over the rail. He was almost exactly at the spot where they had waited with the kids to wave to the Statue of Liberty. "She's quite friendly, Dan," he said. "Friendly—but that's all. It's like it's all over."

Livvy was sitting with Lady Allan and Margaret Mackworth in the first-class ladies room, listening to a talk by Marie Depage. The doctor's wife was speaking mainly to the groups of nurses, the medical personnel and Red Cross volunteers about the conditions they were likely to find in the military hospitals in France and Belgium. Some of her unemotional descriptions were sickening and Livvy tried to blank out her hearing, thinking of other things.

Lady Allan had introduced herself on the second day,

saying she believed their children had already met. She was charming and her girls were delightful, although too old for Peter and Diana, who had made other friends among a large family, the Cromptons. They would be playing with them now. There were so many children on board. Well over a hundred, Lady Allan had told her, as well as pregnant women and mothers with young babies. They were all so well looked after, with trained staff, nurseries and special diets.

Lady Mackworth she had met yesterday evening. She had made up her mind not to bother with supper, but the purser had brought an invitation for Matt and her to dine at the Captain's table. It was an honor they could not refuse and she had found herself seated between Alfred Vanderbilt and Justus Forman. Forman had seemed highly pleased to hear that she had been to his play, *The Hyphen*. So had Vanderbilt and they had discussed it animatedly. Vanderbilt was a very good-looking, cultivated man and she was flattered to discover that both he and the writer were exerting themselves for her benefit. But more than either of them she had liked the sweet old man Elbert Hubbard, who had teased them both by pretending that she had agreed to join his community.

Matt had spent most of the evening talking to Lady Mackworth and her Welsh father, to Captain Anderson and Señor Padila, Consul General for Mexico in Liverpool. Apparently, some danger was threatening his country from the former dictator Huerta. They had been warned both by the British and American Secret Services.

Afterwards Matt told her he had been quite jealous of how attentive all the men had been to her, particularly Forman and Vanderbilt. It was true that both Matt and she had been made much of by all these important people. But Livvy knew that she was not the reason.

"Isn't it appalling?" Margaret Mackworth observed. "The only role they seem able to approve of for women in this war is that of nurses and comforters. If they used some of us to help in the strategic planning, instead, perhaps the whole thing would not have developed into such a filthy muddle."

"I'm not certain I can accept that," Lady Allan objected gently. "Ladies like Madame Depage and this Nurse Cavell she's been telling us about seem to me to be doing the noblest work a woman can. I know you have been sent to prison on behalf of women's suffrage, my dear, and I am sure that it will benefit us all greatly in time. But a war reduces us all to our basic selves. It is for women to preserve and heal. For men to plan and fight, to destroy and to conquer. I'm sure Mrs. Fletcher agrees." She smiled.

Livvy could not prevent herself from smiling back automatically. It was the response expected of her, married to a hero, whom everyone admired.

The U 20 had sailed on the surface all day, in poor visibility which helped to ensure her safety, but also cut down the chances of spotting targets. She had dived only once in the afternoon, to inspect a fast steamer heading toward her, but Schwieger broke off the attack when he became aware of the advancing steamer's erratic course. It was an armed sloop, as Lanz confirmed, probably searching for the U 20 or one of the other submarines of the patrol which she had come to relieve. Because of the sloop's speed and irregular changes of direction, she would be next to impossible to hit with a torpedo, and it would be madness to challenge her on the surface without knowing how heavily she was armed. Reluctantly, Schwieger stole on southwards, surfacing again when the enemy had vanished behind him.

In the evening he was on watch on the conning tower platform with Lanz and Haupert when he saw what he had been waiting for, the dark smudge of land rising to port. "There it is, gentlemen," he said. "Ireland." It was ridiculous to feel so elated. Certainly it was not over the simple fact of making a landfall. Analyzing his reaction, Schwieger realized it was because sighting the Irish coast was a guarantee that he was nearly at his hunting ground. These past weeks of inaction, the short leave with Anneliese, the delay until the U 20's repairs were completed had relaxed him physically, but his inner tension had grown, mounting with the frustrations of the last five days, five days without a single kill. He had been forced into the role of quarry, while his whole instinct was to be the hunter.

In the few minutes since he had spoken, the shape of the land ahead had become more distinct. "The question is," Lanz murmured, "just exactly where are we?"

Lights twinkled on what appeared to be a projecting headland. "That should be Farland Point, I think," Haupert said.

Lanz sucked air in through his teeth, in the irritating habit he had when he was doubtful. "No offense, Lieutenant," he said, "but I fancy it's more likely to be Malin Head and the entrance to Lough Swilly."

His dismissal of Haupert's estimate was bland but total, and Haupert stiffened. As Navigation Lieutenant he had had to suffer more of the former pilot's implied criticism than anyone. However, if he lost his temper, he would have to be disciplined. Before Haupert could reply, Schwieger said quietly, "Well, whichever it is, they are both too far east for comfort. We want to be well to the west of Donegal. Hard to starboard." Haupert saluted and relayed the order. The U 20 turned and sailed parallel to the land in the gathering darkness.

After twenty minutes Lanz slapped the rail and snorted with satisfaction. A light had begun flashing regularly to port. "There you are! See?" he exclaimed. "I was right. That's the lighthouse on Tory Island."

Schwieger nodded, expressionless. As he had suspected, the pilot's guess was correct. He did not doubt Lanz's skill, only wished the man was not so insufferably pleased with himself.

Haupert had not commented and was deliberately looking out to the open sea. Lanz eyed his back and chuckled, shaking his head, "An old dog always remembers the paths he's sniffed."

"You've sailed this way before, Herr Lanz?" Schwieger asked.

"Many times, many times," Lanz confirmed.

"Do you know the Kerry coast, south of Ballydavid?"

Lanz thought for a moment. "All rocks and shoals. Yes. Best to give it a wide berth."

"There's a small creek to the east of Ballydavid Head," Schwieger said. "We have a contact there. If this hunt for us persists, we might hole up there one night. Could you take us in?"

Lanz grunted. "You can forget it, Captain. These are tidal creeks filled with rocks. Nothing can get in or out, not even a submarine. Especially at night."

"No?" Schwieger queried, innocently. "Haupert got us in

and out on the tide three weeks ago." Not to overstress the point, he turned away, facing the beam from the lighthouse, which grew brighter almost by the second as the darkness deepened. He hoped that Lanz would understand and stop needling Haupert, who was prevented both by regulations and courtesy from hitting back.

Lanz scowled, however. How very clever, he thought. He resented being under the command of someone half his age. He used to think Schwieger was a cut above the rest, polite at least. But these young naval officers were all the same. Prima donnas, flaunting themselves, considering themselves superior to any mere civilian, even one who'd had thirty more years of experience at sea. He had been warned what to expect in so many words, at Flotilla Headquarters. "Our commanders are fighting a different kind of war from the one for which they were trained, Herr Lanz," he was told. "A war not against capital ships, but against commerce. It is repugnant to them. Yet victory depends on it, on the volume of tonnage they sink, to break the spirit of the Allied merchant fleets. Your function will be to help the commander to whom you are assigned to identify and evaluate targets and to make certain, wherever possible, that they are those whose loss would cause the greatest despondency to the enemy." At first, he had been delighted to be assigned to the U 20, but the more he observed Schwieger's caution and skill in evasion, the more he doubted his fighting ability and will to destroy. Lanz had hoped to return to the Fatherland as a member of a victorious crew. Instead, this patrol was turning into a practice voyage, with a captain whose first thought was always the safety of his craft and his own skin.

Schwieger had gradually become aware of a second light under the beam of the lighthouse, not a reflection as he had thought at first. It continued to move out, becoming more separate, and he realized what it was at the same moment as the bow lookout.

Once again, the order for Action Stations was given and the U 20 dived, curving in to make a closer examination of the large steamer that was sailing toward her. Lanz watched her for a full three minutes before giving up the eyepiece to Schwieger. "A cargo ship for sure," he said. "I'd wager she's French built, or Scandinavian."

There was an immediate heightening of excitement among those listening. Schwieger felt it too as he bent again to the periscope, yet the fact that the freighter was so brightly lit with no attempt at blackout nagged at him. He heard Scherb ask, "What size is she?" "About eight thousand tons," Lanz answered. Someone whistled softly.

As the steamer came on, Schwieger slipped the U 20 in closer, so that he could read her markings. He winced in disappointment. She was the *Hibernia*, registered in Sweden. When he told the others, there were grunts and quiet mutters of frustration. "She's probably carrying contraband," Lanz said.

"Possibly," Schwieger agreed. He swiveled slowly, keeping the cargo ship in view. She was at his mercy and he knew the terrible temptation of the hunter with a target in his sights, legitimate or not. He made himself straighten and gave the order for the crew to stand down.

"You could challenge her," Lanz suggested. When Schwieger did not reply, he asked more loudly, "Why not?"

Schwieger nearly told the man to go to hell and take his damned insolence with him, but he was aware of Haupert, Kurtz and Scherb watching tautly. He controlled himself. "One, she is neutral and we are not pirates," he said tonelessly. "Two, to stop her at night we would have to surface and fire a shot across her bows. It would be heard by every guard boat within twenty miles. It would take a minimum of half an hour to board her, read through her manifest and check the holds. By that time we would have become a sitting target ourself. Three, it is not a sinking I could justify to the Flotilla Commander."

Lanz was silenced and shrugged, putting his hands in his pockets to fumble for a cigar.

"Well, I don't— I don't understand how we can ever attack anything, sir, in that case," Scherb said, hesitantly.

"With luck you'll soon find out," Schwieger told him, and moved to the helmsman to correct their course.

"That's all we need, a little luck," Haupert explained to Scherb. "Even in perfect conditions we can sail for a day and spot nothing in the whole twenty-four hours. But our luck's bound to change soon."

Lanz had recovered his cockiness. "Tomorrow," he predicted. "That's when we'll be crossing the lanes used by the biggest steamers, the cargo and passenger ships."

"Passenger ships?" Scherb repeated, puzzled.

"Like the *Falaba*. Eh, Commander?" Lanz winked to Schwieger. "Stuffed to the gunwales with contraband, ten passengers and one or two regulation Americans to protect them." He chuckled and the others laughed with him.

Schwieger did not respond. He left orders to surface in ten minutes with Haupert as officer of the watch and went to his cabin. As he threw his cap onto his bunk, he made up his mind. Lanz had become more than an irritation. His lack of personal discipline was affecting the crew. Next time the man raised his voice or questioned one of his decisions, he would have him confined to his quarters for the rest of the voyage.

Laughing and shrieking with excitement, children were running and jumping, careering across the stern section of the *Lusitania*'s promenade deck. Matt smiled, watching Diana's intense concentration as ten-year-old Katie Crompton taught her how to do a hop, skip and jump. Beside him, Dan Connally was watching Peter, who was tearing round the outer limit of the deck so fast he almost skidded on the corners, with Paul Crompton trailing yards behind him. As Peter raced past him, Dan stepped out and caught him with both arms, spinning round with the momentum. "Hey, hey, hey!" he laughed. "Steady on, Chief. What are you doing?"

"Have to train for the race, Uncle Dan," Peter panted.

"Well, not like that, Chief," Dan cautioned. "You'll wear yourself out before the sports have even started." The Crompton boy came skittering to a halt beside them. He leaned forward with his hands on his knees, gasping for breath. "Look at the two of you," Dan chuckled.

"But we have to train," Peter insisted.

"You listen to your Uncle Dan," Matt said. "He knows what he's talking about. You never see Indians wasting their strength like that." He tapped the amulet on Peter's chest. "Old Harry Hightree, now. He'll lope along nice and easy for miles and keep the speed for the end, when it's needed. You sit down and get your breath back and think about that."

Peter nodded, and drew himself up. "The advice is good,

O Sachem," he said gravely. He pivoted and loped away slowly to where the rest of the Cromptons sat, watching. Paul plodded along behind him.

"I think he'll do well," Matt said.

"Truly, O Sachem," Dan agreed, "O Father of Wisdom."

"Shuddup," Matt said. As they smiled, they heard a wail from Diana. Between a skip and a jump, she had tripped and fallen on the deck. Matt went to her quickly and crouched, helping her up. She clung to him, sniffing. "Does it hurt, pet?" Matt asked.

"Yes," she told him. "It really hurts." She had landed on her knees and she lifted her short dress. Her legs were bare above her short socks and the skin of her right knee was roughened where it had scuffed on the deck planking.

"Oh, yes. We'd better do something about that," Matt said. He pretended to spit on the palm of his hand and rubbed it carefully over her kneecap. He snatched his hand away and shook it, as though the pain had passed into his palm, then repeated the process with her left knee. It was a baby ritual, but it still worked. "That any better?" he asked.

"Lots, Daddy," Diana assured him. "How's your hand?"

"Oh," he shrugged. "Be fine in a minute."

Lady Allan had come to them and smoothed Diana's hair back from her forehead. "You're a very brave girl," she said.

"As brave as Peter?" Diana asked.

"I'm sure of it," Lady Allan said. Her daughters, Anna and Gwen, were with her and smiled when Diana stood up proudly. They took a hand each and led her over to the Cromptons and her brother. "I haven't seen Mrs. Fletcher anywhere," Lady Allan said.

Matt was rising. "No. Unfortunately she has a slight headache. But I expect she'll be along a little later."

Dan looked round. More people were arriving, filling up the chairs to watch the children's sports which would start any minute now. Staff Captain Anderson was going over final arrangements with Purser McCubbin, Junior Third Officer Bestwick and the Chief Steward. Other stewards were setting up a table with small prizes. Behind the table, the members of the ship's orchestra had taken their seats and struck up a lively version of "On Moonlight Bay." There was no sign of Livvy.

Dan was worried about Matt and Livvy. He had not seen

her so far on the voyage and Matt avoided talking about her, but could not conceal the pain their estrangement caused him. Dan would never have believed, knowing them, that it could have gone on so long, five days now. He remembered how much Livvy had been looking forward to the trip, like a young bride almost. He thought that at least the children would have brought them together again. Since she was not here, even when it meant so much to the kids, he realized the split was not healing. It could only grow worse, the longer it lasted.

Livvy was alone in the cabin, sitting on the window seat by the open porthole. It had not been entirely an excuse that she had a headache; the light current of air was cool on her forehead. She felt guilty at letting Peter and Diana down. They had been so excited by the thought of the sports and wanted her there to see them compete, but she could not have borne being with other families, pretending to be carefree and happy. She had played her part in public, and in private with the children. No one could have suspected the depth of her distress, but she did not know how much longer she could keep it up.

Matt had also played his part. They had dined twice at the Captain's table, had been to parties given by Elbert Hubbard, by Kessler, the champagne millionaire, by the Cromptons, and to an exclusive lunch in Vanderbilt's sumptuous suite. Although Matt was as charming and attentive as ever, they were reserved with each other. He had stuck to his decision and had not apologized again or even mentioned the cause of the rift between them. He made no demands on her, for which Livvy was grateful. On the second night, after dining with Captain Anderson for the first time, she had felt exhilarated, slightly heady with wine. Normally, the evening would have ended in only one way, and she had been aware of her attitude softening toward Matt at her body's urging. It confused her and, if he had touched her, she was not sure how she would react. But as she sat at the dressing table in her nightdress, brushing her hair, she had caught sight of him in the mirror. He was seated on his bed, his face shadowed, motionless, thinking. And a terrible conviction came to her that in his mind he was already dead. If he put his arms round her, it would be like making love with a corpse. She shivered. The thought was horrible and she tried to push it away, but could not. She laid down the brush and got into bed without Matt even seeming to notice. It was long minutes before he rose and put out the lights. "Good night," he said, in the darkness. Livvy had to control her voice to keep it steady. "Good night, Matt," she said. She heard him get into his own bed and then there was silence. She could remember drawing the sheet up to her chin and shivering again with cold, in spite of the warmth of the cabin.

Since then, the thought of Matt lying dead had come to her often. Pallid, his arms flung out, eyes staring. There was no blood. She had never seen him wounded or bleeding. She knew it was morbid and made herself concentrate on other things, but the hideous image was there and could not be exorcised.

They had spent quite a lot of time with the Arnsteins, but for the last two days Livvy had been avoiding them as much as possible. She could not listen to their asides, the little coded remarks which lovers imagine are so secret, hinting at hidden intimacies. The honeymoon couple's delight in each other, their smiles and need to touch each other, reminded her too acutely of all she had lost. Whenever possible, she escaped to the cabin to be alone when Matt was in the smoke room or attending to the business of the other volunteers. She did not need to worry about the children. They were safe with the Allan girls or the younger Cromptons and their nursemaid, Dorothy.

In two days they would be docking at Liverpool. Matt would take them to London and on to Winchelsea. They would be in a crowded train, then at her parents' home, with all the commotion and her mother and father's joy at meeting their grandchildren. There would be no real opportunity for Matt and her to be alone, not really alone with time to think and talk. Then he would be gone. Their life together would be over, effectively, the moment the *Lusitania* tied up at the pier. Part of Livvy wanted the voyage to go on forever, yet she could never bear it. She did not know how she could survive even the next two days. Matt would not speak of what kept them apart and neither could she, and the barrier between them became more impenetrable every day.

She was leaning back and had closed her eyes, but opened them again, hearing a knock at the door. It would be the cabin maid, she thought. She should have hung the "Do not disturb" notice outside. "It's not locked," she called, intending to send the girl away again. To her surprise, it was not the maid who came in, but Dan Connally.

Dan had wanted very much to see her. To be on the same ship as she and not to have even a glimpse of her was torture. He would never, could never, come between her and Matt, but no one could ever conceive how much she meant to him. He was taken aback at how much thinner her face had become in such a short time, shaded with strain under the eyes.

She was sitting up. "Dan . . . ? I'm sorry. Matt's not here."

"It's you I wanted to see," he told her.

"Yes, it's funny how we've missed each other," Livvy said. "Of course I've been so busy and—"

"I want to talk to you, Livvy," he cut in.

Once Livvy would have welcomed him. He was close to her. She was fonder of him than she had ever been of any man, except Matt and her father, and had confided in him more than many women would have believed possible. She had trusted him completely, yet he was part of the conspiracy. He had helped to plan it and keep it from her. "It's lovely to see you and we must get together," she said. "But I'm not feeling too grand, so if you wouldn't mind—"

"It's important, Livvy," he said. "We have to talk."

All at once she knew why he had come. "If Matt sent you—"

"He doesn't know I'm here. If he did, he'd probably never speak to me again." He closed the door behind him. "Have you any idea how much you've hurt him?"

Instead of the sympathy she might have expected, he was severe. She had never heard him so serious. "Hurt him? Hurt Matt?" she said. "You seem to have got it the wrong way round."

"How could you do this to him, Livvy?"

He was putting her on the defensive and it made her angry. "Me? I'm supposed to have done something?" she exclaimed. "It doesn't occur to you to wonder how I feel! I'm the one who was lied to, the one you all lied to!" Even as she said it, she realized she sounded petty. She could not explain how deeply she had been hurt, how empty her life had become, in ordinary words. "Not that it's anything to do with you!"

"It has to do with me," Dan said levelly. "And you know why." Her eyes were on his and what she saw in them made her ashamed. She did not have to tell him. He took a step nearer. "There's no one in the world I—I care about more than you and Matt. I can't stand by and watch you break apart."

She lowered her head. "Don't be unfair, Dan," she whispered. "It's not just some silly quarrel. What he did, what you all did, is not something I can just forgive and forget. I can understand him wanting to do something. But he should do what he's best at. Going back into the army, he's throwing his life away—and our whole life together and the children's. He says it's for them, for me—but there's no future for me without him." She paused and added gently, "I'm sorry. I have to say it, because it's the truth."

"Have you told Matt this?"

"I tried. There's no point, though. The time for talking was over before I was given the chance." She caught her breath as her voice broke. "He treated me like one of the children, Dan. But it's not even that." She raised her head and brushed her eyes, although she was not crying. "He's going away. If he goes, he'll never come back. I know it. I could wave him goodbye and go on waiting and hoping. And dying a little more inside every day. I thought, if anything happens to him, I'll kill myself. I won't be able to stand being alone. But I couldn't because of the children. The only way I can bear it is to know that it's already over, that he's really gone already."

"While he's still here, you can adjust to the thought that one day maybe he won't be. Yes, I can see that," Dan said quietly.

Livvy was grateful to him. "Maybe I'm a coward. Maybe it won't even be like that and he will come back. But I can't let myself hope, or even think about it."

Dan nodded. "It's how to survive. But there's someone else in all this. As well as the kids and you, there's Matt."

Livvy looked up, hurt. "I thought you understood."

"Oh, I do," Dan told her. "How you found out, it must have been a hell of a shock. They don't come much worse. And I'm sorry now I didn't make him tell you earlier. Or tell you myself."

"He was afraid to tell me."

"Afraid? He's the bravest man I know," Dan said. "Not just because he's going off to fight. There's a lot of us doing that. We could all be killed, I guess. But none of us has much to lose. Matt, now, he had no need to volunteer at all. He'd done his bit once. He could have stayed home and worked hard, like you say, and finished up head of the company, safe and respected and rich. Instead . . ." Dan paused. "And he knows what he's giving up. Not the money and position—you and the kids. You especially. The most valuable, the most perfect thing in the world. And to risk losing you, loving you how he does, I've never heard of any bravery to match that." Dan shrugged. He was talking about Matt, but it was the nearest he had ever come to telling her how much he loved her himself. "People say, why did we volunteer, why did we get involved? We're not English. No, but we're British. And maybe from our side of the world we can see more clearly what would happen if France and England were destroyed. We could survive without them, but a light would go out in the world. A lot of our ideas about life, about how to make it worth living, come from that little corner of the earth. I mean, that's not me talking. I was never much of a one for politics and things. That's Matt. And every word of it is true. No one wants to take a knife or a gun and start killing. But if it's the only way, then none of us, specially Matt, would feel like a man if we didn't go out there to fight for what we believe in—and the people we love." Dan stopped. Livvy's head was turned away and lowered so that he could not see her expression. She was so silent, he was afraid he had only made the situation worse. "I don't even know if I'm making sense, Livvy," he said. "I only know I have to do it. I have to stand up and fight for my folks—and for you. And I don't even have you to lose. Matt does. And to go ahead and take that risk, that's a hundred times braver than I could ever be. And by God, he deserves more than to be told he's throwing his life away! Any woman who was half a real woman would try to match his courage! She'd try to make what might be the last few days they ever have together something that was worth a lifetime." He stopped again. He had tried to put it clearly, what he felt, what he knew was the truth, but he could not go on if she would not answer. He was looking at her hands folded in her lap and all at once saw how they glistened. They were pressed together so tightly left over right that the knuckles shone, and they glistened because of the tears which fell on them. She could not restrain them. She was past control or speech, and could not answer.

Lee Arnstein was cheering and shouting as the boys tore round the stern deck in the four-hundred-yard race. He had told Matt he was crazy letting Peter go in for it. Some of the other competitors were half as old again and he had finished nowhere in the hundred-yard dash. However, Peter was more than holding his own. When the larger boys had sprinted off at the start and were already dropping back, he was still up there and still running inside his strength.

Beattie was almost embarrassed at the noise Lee was making. He had been sitting with her and Matt, but had leaped to his feet. A moment later, Matt sprang up too, unable to sit still. Yet it was all right, for so many people were cheering and urging on their favorites now. "Look at him!" Lee exclaimed admiringly. "Look at the position he's got himself into!"

Coming up to the final bend, Peter was at the shoulder of the second leader, a taller, heavier boy. The actual leader was more wiry, flushed and running flat out. They swept round the last corner with only sixty yards to the white tape held by Biggs and one of the other stewards. "Come on, Peter! Come on!" Matt shouted.

And Lee was shouting, "Look at that! Look at it—he's moving out!"

As they turned into the straight, Peter cut round in front of the taller boy, who tried to elbow him aside, but missed and stumbled. It was enough to give Peter an advantage of two or three yards. Either by accident or instinct, he had made his move just when the leader was tiring and, when the boy glanced desperately over his right shoulder to see who was behind him, Peter passed him on his left. "Look

497

at him go!" Lee yelled, flinging his arms in the air. And Peter was past them racing straight for the tape, which he hit a full two seconds before the wiry boy, with the taller one a bad third and the rest of the runners nowhere.

Lee thumped Matt on the shoulder and Matt thumped him back. Beattie had risen with all the other spectators, applauding, and Lee threw an arm round her, hugging her in excitement. Last night he had told her he wanted them to have four boys, just like Matt's Peter. She had smiled and said she was promising nothing, but now she understood what he meant.

Matt was laughing with pride and applauding as he watched Peter being congratulated by Bestwick and Purser McCubbin, who pinned a winner's rosette on him. He stopped applauding and his smile faded when he saw Livvy just beyond the group at the tape.

Peter saw her at almost the same moment. He was getting his breath back and beginning to realize that he had really won. Everyone was clapping and telling him it was the best race of the day. He was proud and happy and just starting to look for his father and Diana when he saw his mother coming toward him. He ran to her. "Did you see it, Mummy?" he asked anxiously.

"Yes," Livvy smiled. "I saw it. I saw all of it. You were splendid." Peter hugged her delightedly, and she held him to her as they crossed in front of the rows of spectators, with many of them congratulating him.

People moved up and made room for Livvy to sit beside Beattie. Lee patted Peter on the back and Matt ruffled his hair and smoothed it again. "Knew you could do it, Chief," he said. Then Diana and the four younger Cromptons were clustering round them to examine Peter's red winner's rosette.

"Are you feeling a bit better?" Beattie asked Livvy.

"Much, thank you," Livvy said, and laughed. Beattie had always thought her very attractive, if a little too pale and reserved. Animated, the glow of color in her cheeks, her eyes sparkling, she was irresistible. The children were all over her, laughing, perching on her knees, squatting at her feet, as though she had been away for a long time and they had missed her. It was Matt who seemed reserved now, but

Beattie had noticed that the presence of his wife had that effect on him.

Somehow, with Livvy there, the rest of the sports were even more fun. It was very much their day, for Peter came in first again in the obstacle race and Katie Crompton in the hop, skip and jump, with Diana a close second, although she was the youngest competitor. Just before the end, a mothers and daughters three-legged race was announced. Some of the more straitlaced ladies would not enter and one or two in first class sent their governesses or nursemaids in their places. Livvy, however, agreed as soon as Diana asked her, and Beattie could tell that Matt was surprised. At the line, Livvy slipped off her heeled shoes and laughed as her right ankle was tied to Diana's left. "Set off on your right foot," she whispered, and Diana nodded.

"No carrying now, ladies," McCubbin warned. "Ready? Steady—go!"

Many of the couples were out of the race almost as soon as it began, hopping and stumbling and tripping each other up, but three or four of them took it seriously, running determinedly round the hundred-and-fifty-yard track. To Livvy it was only fun until she heard Matt and Lee yelling and saw there were only three couples ahead of them. "Come on, Diana!" she called and put on more speed, remembering to match her stride to Diana's shorter one. As they gained ground, the whole crowd started to egg them on and they sped past the field to break the tape with yards to spare. "We won, we won, we won!" Diana squeaked, jumping up and down, so that Livvy had to hold her still for McCubbin to pin the red rosette beside her blue one. Livvy could see Matt smiling to them through the shifting heads round them, a smile that held a hint of relief. She turned to the Purser to accept her rosette and pin it on.

Afterwards everyone gathered round the table, where Staff Captain Anderson announced the winners' names and Lady Allan handed out the prizes. Everyone who had taken part was given a *Lusitania* badge. For his two red rosettes, Peter received a scale model of the great liner herself, the one thing he had wanted most, and had his choice of a row of books. He chose an illustrated history of the Pony Express. For her blue rosette, Diana was given a miniature telescope. When she went up again with Livvy, both wearing their red rosettes, there was particularly loud applause and Lady Allan smiled and gave her a sailor doll. Livvy was presented with a huge box of chocolates and both Anderson and Lady Allan congratulated her on being mother of such a talented family. She was flushed with the applause, feeling ridiculously pleased with herself and as excited as the kids, and turned to where Matt stood at the side with his arm round Peter's shoulders. As she walked toward them with Diana, Matt smiled to her and she answered his smile for the first time since they left New York.

The restaurant of Washington's Shoreham Hotel on 15th Street was still faintly Edwardian in atmosphere, the service unobtrusive but excellent, the tables widely spaced to give a comfortable privacy. It was one of Guy Gaunt's favorite spots for lunch and he usually booked a corner table, partially screened from more than half the room by a flourish of potted palms, as some of his guests preferred to be not too conspicuous.

Today, while waiting for the other two, he shared a bottle of 1902 Médoc with the first to arrive. "Ordinarily I'm not a wine drinker," his guest admitted, "but I'd say this was pretty good. Of course you Europeans know more about it than we do."

"Strictly speaking, I'm not European," Gaunt told him. "I'm Australian." It had the effect he had often noticed in the States.

His companion relaxed a little more and smiled. "I didn't know that," he said. He glanced round the visible section of the restaurant, his movement casual, but his eyes sharp, missing nothing.

"It's a theory of mine," Gaunt said, "that for a meeting to be really discreet, it is best to hold it in public."

His guest was Bruce Bielaski, Chief Agent of the Department of Justice. "You read my mind," Bielaski said. "All that closed sedan and back of the Cenotaph at midnight stuff, that's just to impress the peasants. And I'd say you were a professional, Captain Gaunt."

"It takes one to know one," Gaunt smiled.

Bielaski nodded. "It occurred to me that, if they knew we

were here together, certain people might wonder what the hell we were up to."

"They might well," Gaunt agreed, and refilled their glasses.

It was an odd situation in which Bielaski found himself. A large part of his job was to hunt out foreign Intelligence agents in the States. Since all British Intelligence overseas was run by the navy and Gaunt was British naval attaché, that placed him near the top of the suspect list. He was, however, protected by diplomatic immunity. Also suspect and diplomatically protected were the German attachés, Papen and Boy-Ed. Yet it suited Gaunt to respect the law and cooperate with the American agencies, while the Germans were forced into criminal acts.

So many German and Austrian agents had been identified that only a percentage could be kept under surveillance owing to the Department's limited resources. Bielaski had discussed the problem with William J. Flynn, head of the Secret Service. "Whatever the politicians preach, we're being forced to take sides," he explained. "That's how it goes, Bruce," Flynn had agreed regretfully. "We have to deal with the ones who endanger American lives and property. If the British stepped out of line, we would deal with them too, but they're boxing clever. In the meantime, if they have any information that might be useful to us . . ." He had let the thought hang in the air and Bielaski lowered his voice. "You mean we ought to cooperate with British Intelligence?"

"You never heard me suggest that," Flynn told him, and swung away to gaze blandly out of his office window and scratch his chin. "As you pointed out, we are entirely neutral in this conflict and all that concerns us is the security of the nation. But any information which relates to that must be followed up, even if it comes from a private, non-American source."

Bielaski's first approach to Gaunt had been cautious and wholly unofficial, but it was as if the attaché had been expecting it. Yes, he was in a position to pass on certain information which might be of interest to the American authorities, information which he had happened to come by accidentally in the course of his duties. Their first meeting led to the arrest of several officials of the Hamburg-Amerika Line on criminal charges. Since then, the relationship had developed very profitably for both of them. Before long the meetings had become more frequent, although still undercover and unofficial, and mutual problems were gone into with a frankness that would have outraged Capitol Hill, and Bielaski himself a few months ago.

"You know that Papen paid a visit to the German Consul in El Paso last week?" Gaunt asked.

"Did he, now?" Bielaski had given up being surprised by the accuracy of Gaunt's information. Federal agents had boarded a train for Chicago behind Papen, only to lose him at the terminus. "That figures. He would want to check up on his arms deliveries."

"He's only a front man in all this," Gaunt said. "The real organizing is handled by the other one, von Rintelen."

Bielaski rubbed his index finger under his nose. "I know you have a bee in your bonnet about him, Captain," he objected, "but I'm sorry. I've had Rinty tailed uptown and downtown. I can even tell you the brand of champagne he prefers and where he gets his hair cut. But he's too busy socializing to organize anything. He's just a playboy who dabbles in trying to buy supplies for Germany. He's only glad to be out of the war and somewhere he can still get three squares and a broad every day."

Gaunt smiled, but shook his head. It was a long-distance tail on von Rintelen by one of his men which had stumbled on the original meeting with Huerta. "He likes Dom Perignon '98 and has his hair cut in the St. Regis," he said. "As for the rest, let's agree to differ."

They were silent as a waiter came to the edge of the cluster of ornamental palms, saw they were still waiting for the others of their party and retreated.

"There is something else," Bielaski said, "nearer to home. We've been working more closely lately with the New York Detective Bureau, and Captain Tunney of the Bomb Squad has reported that some of his men are picking up stories of explosive devices being smuggled onto cargo ships, something entirely new. And the rudders were blown off two freighters in New York Harbor by some kind of floating bombs last week. That makes it our business."

Gaunt was serious. "I think we can expect an increase in those incidents you spoke of."

"Why?"

Gaunt paused. "Well, it's no secret that the U-boat campaign is having an effect, but this is strictly off the record. Our factories are not geared for wartime yet and we're running out of ammunition. At the present moment, England has only just over two weeks' stock of food and raw materials. Our enemies will be trying everything they can, here and at sea, to prevent supplies reaching us or our allies. And if they succeed . . . The next few weeks are critical."

Bielaski was uncomfortable. "I—uh—I'd like to say I sympathize. Hell, of course I understand what it means! If American supplies don't get to you in time, you'll go under. But—well, you have to understand my position, too."

"Yes, naturally," Gaunt said shortly. "You stand resolutely on neither side of the fence."

"It's not me, personally," Bielaski explained. "The Bureau and the Secret Service are under the orders of the State Department and, frankly, we're bending the rules already. We can only—"

He broke off as the other two guests came to the table. As he glanced up, he was glad that his training had schooled him to control his expression.

"Mr. Bielaski I believe you know," Gaunt said.

"Yes, indeed," Counselor Lansing nodded, and smiled. "Sorry we were delayed, Guy."

Bielaski picked up his glass and swallowed what was left of his wine. As he looked round the table, he wondered again just what the hell he had got himself into. The third guest was Lindley M. Garrison, Secretary of State for War.

On the bridge of the U 20, Schwieger stood watching as the ship's boat pulled toward them. The fog had completely lifted and the air and sea were so calm that the splash of the oars sounded unnaturally loud. Below him, he heard Scherb laughing with the gun crew. Only a novice could be excited in circumstances like these.

Another day had gone by without a kill. During the night, in the breaks in the fog, the only craft sighted had been armed patrol boats searching in pairs, which warned him that at some point he had been spotted. Since dawn, although the fog had unexpectedly cleared and the U 20 was now in the lanes used by the largest steamers to follow the coastline round the southwest of Ireland, not a single ship had been reported. In the late afternoon Scherb had eagerly reported a vessel heading south, confirmed by Lanz as a large sailing ship.

Approaching, curving in underwater to intercept, Schwieger had felt his expectation growing that at last they were to shake off the bad luck which had dogged them, but as they swept nearer, he had found the sailing vessel to his disappointment to be only a small three-master. It was too late to break off the engagement without putting his crew once again through the dispiriting anticlimax of standing down after Action Stations. *Kriegspiel interruptus*, Rudi used to call it, the ultimate in frustration.

Schwieger surfaced within hailing distance, keeping the three-master between him and a fishing boat about half a mile to port. The moment the U 20 rose dripping water alongside her, the three-master swung away to port in panic, but lost the wind and her master prudently and promptly dropped his mainsail and wallowed to a halt. Schwieger had been working on his English and shouted to him through the megaphone to abandon ship and hand over his ship's papers and flag; then he eased the U 20 away aft to give her stern gun its best field of fire. At least he would see how Scherb conducted himself.

The barque's dinghy came alongside with five men in it, the master and his crew of four, and the papers were passed up to Schwieger. She was the *Earl of Latham*, bound from Liverpool to Limerick with a cargo of building stones. Stones . . . Schwieger felt the depression drive its claws deeper into him.

The master, a grizzled middle-aged fellow, was taking a lively interest in the U 20, his eyes jumping from her number to her narrow prow to the gun crew on the stern deck. "Been here long?" he asked Lammeier, who gazed back uncomprehendingly. "Any more of you about?"

"It is better you do not ask questions," Schwieger said. "Now get well away, out of the line of fire."

The men in the boat suddenly woke up to their possible danger, pushed off from the U-boat and began to row frantically in the direction of the shore, as though they expected the gun to be turned on them and although the fishing boat was closing in foolishly to see what was going on.

Schwieger's eyes were on the fishing boat as he gave the order to Scherb, "Rapid fire!" As soon as the first shots crashed out and the shells exploded along the waterline of the *Earl of Latham*, the fishing boat veered away hastily, ignoring the men in the dinghy.

Poor little ship, Schwieger was thinking. A cargo of stones. It was a struggle to prevent his depression from showing and affecting his crew's morale. It was caused by nothing more than the persistent fog and this run of poor luck, he knew, but there was also the growing conviction that the area had been swept clean, that Rosenberg and the others had created such a panic in the enemy that all ships of any size were confined to port for the time being and he was patrolling an empty sea.

He had set out with such high hopes. With Weddigen gone and Hersing en route for the Mediterranean, he had been given the chance at last to take the U 20 to her rightful place at the forefront of the Flotilla, with himself as leading ace. It was not an unworthy ambition. It was not even solely for himself. The Flotilla still had to face stupid prejudice and envy from the rest of the Service. He could fight for it at his level, as Tirpitz and Admiral Scheer fought for it at theirs. It meant promotion, status and widening opportunities to serve the Fatherland and the All Highest.

Yet time was passing. Patrols were shorter now and already the boats which left before the U 20 would have turned home. They'd had the best of the weather and could be sailing back in triumph while he floundered on in the grip of the fog with his torpedoes unused and his only catch a cargo of stones.

Subconsciously he had been counting the number of shots fired. Twelve. He heard a ragged cheer and looked up to see the *Earl of Latham* sinking rapidly by the stern. Twelve shells to send a little tub like that to the bottom. Weiser would have been ashamed of himself.

Scherb was pointing to the fleeing fishingboat. "Shall I let them have a couple for good measure?" he called.

"Let them be," Schwieger said. The sinking barque's

mainmast cracked as she went under and he started, hearing a chuckle beside him. It was Lanz.

The Mate of the Reserve was watching the swirl of debris where the *Earl of Latham* had been. "Well, at last I'll have something to put in my report," he said.

Schwieger frowned. "Report?"

"Naturally, Commander," Lanz smiled. "I'm not here merely for the joyride. I have to make a report on what appears to be the state of enemy merchant shipping, any unusual sightings or occurrences." He paused. "And of course on the results and effectiveness of our sortie."

Schwieger nodded curtly. He could have anticipated it himself, knowing the bureaucracy of the Admiralty and its obsession with summaries and statistics, but it numbed him to think that his official records would contain a report on his conduct of this patrol by Lanz. If anything was needed to spur him on, that was it. No wonder Lanz was so intrusive, so sure of himself. By chance or deliberately, someone had placed the future of Schwieger's career in his hands.

Two hours later, Schwieger was conscious of him as he stood gazing into the eyepiece of the periscope. The hairline of the lens was centered on a British freighter of at least 3,000 tons. Although his instinct was to ignore Lanz and reject any offered advice, he played it by the book and agreed with him on the target's nationality, tonnage and estimated speed, thirteen knots. He swung the U 20 into position, having judged the bearing and timing of the torpedo with his usual precision. "Fire number one!"

The torpedo whooshed from the forward starboard tube and Hirsch compensated immediately for the loss of weight. The U-boat barely shuddered.

"Forward One fired," Scherb confirmed.

Schwieger did not submerge. It was too important to him and he kept the eye of the asparagus trained on the torpedo, watching the bubbles of its wake streak toward the target. The angle was pefect. It would be a clean kill.

At the last moment, however, something happened inside the torpedo. Something had gone wrong with its mechanism and it lost speed until only its momentum carried it forward. Its wake had evidently been spotted and the freighter swerved wildly. The torpedo grazed its bows without exploding and the freighter fled away on its altered course at full steam. There was no hope of catching it and, as it did not stop zigzagging, a second torpedo would only have been wasted.

The officers and crewmen in central control were completely silent. Schwieger was icy and did not look at Lanz as he demanded an explanation of the torpedo's failure. Neither Scherb nor the technicians could explain it. Some unknown malfunction was all that could be said, except that it was one of the early bronze type, the same as the one which had misfired three days earlier. Of the U 20's remaining five torpedoes, four were of the newer G type. Schwieger gave orders that the last of the bronze models was to be used only in an emergency, and went to his cabin.

As he took the logbook from his locker and sat at the table, a spasm of anger shook him and he gripped the edge of the table until it had passed. The entries in the log were a mockery. No one was to blame, not even himself. Not even Lanz. But this patrol, despite all his hopes, was unmistakably doomed to failure.

Chapter 27

ALFRED VANDERBILT TOWELED HIMSELF CAREFULLY AFter his bath. Normally, this was when he felt at his best, relaxed and confident. But this evening he had a sense of depression, a dissatisfaction with life, the cause of which he could not pin down.

He had stripped off and gone through his exercises, working up a glow before his tub. The water was exactly the temperature he liked, thanks to his impeccable manservant, Denyer. Now, as he dried himself, he did not need the full-length mirror or the weighing scales to tell him he was in pretty perfect physical condition. The problem was not physical. He had always kept himself in shape, had a good appetite and never any trouble sleeping.

No, that was not strictly true. Of late, he had had some disturbed nights. Only last night he had tossed and turned for what seemed like hours, although usually he could just switch off like a light. It was odd. The dissatisfaction had obviously been developing in him for some time without his realizing it. To be more accurate, perhaps, without his admitting it.

He wrapped a towel round his narrow waist and padded through into the bedroom of his suite, where Denyer was finishing laying out his evening clothes. "Pleasant bath, sir?" Denyer inquired.

"Fine, thank you," Vanderbilt nodded. He had twenty minutes or so to dress for the pre-dinner party in Frohman's suite, but just at the moment he shied away from the prospect of dressing up and meeting people. On the side table he noticed the two Marconi cables he had received that afternoon. One was from London, from May Barwell: "Look forward very much to seeing you soon." That might have lifted his spirits, given him something pleasurable to look forward to, if it had not been for the second cable from New York, informing him that one of his dearest friends, Fred Davies, had died. They had been in the same class at Yale and it did not seem possible that someone as vital, as successful as Fred could just die like that, without warning. It was unsettling, but so unexpected that it was clearly not the cause of his malaise.

"Shall I fix you a drink, sir?" Denyer asked.

Would that help? "No, thank you," Vanderbilt decided. He wanted nothing so much as to be alone. "I shan't need you, not for half an hour, anyway."

Denyer's eyebrows rose imperceptibly at the break in routine, and he inclined his head. "Very good, sir."

Left on his own, Vanderbilt stopped prowling and looked at the bed where his things were laid out with precision, socks, suspenders, underpants, starched white shirt, black pants. Faced with a problem, he usually found it helped to concentrate on a single thought or some definite task. He sat on the end of the bed, put on his black socks and attached the suspenders. Beginning to dress induced an illusion of normalcy, but his mind kept drifting, and finally he gave in and sat unmoving, still wearing the towel, puzzling at the chaos of memories which filled his head.

Fred, May, Margaret and the children, the family tomb, his office at Grand Central, his stables outside Newport, being bounced as a small boy on President Ulysses S. Grant's knee, Agnes naked and eager in the bedroom of his private railroad car, Livvy Fletcher at the rail of the Lusitania's boat deck, his brother Neily white with shock at being cut out of their father's will, horses flying down the straight at Royal Ascot, Fred serious and telling him to take care on this trip. "Do you really have to go? I mean, is it essential, life or death?"

The one thing Vanderbilt was certain of was that the trip was essential. And it was not merely a matter of arranging the horse show. Why it was not was a long story, the story of his life.

If he had not been richer than most people could dream, what would he have done? he wondered. Been a farmer, a horse trainer? Become a railroad engineer like Neily had done when he found himself broke and rejected by most of the family? Cornelius, Neily, had married against his father's wishes, had even struck the old man during their argument and caused his paralysis, or so the story in the family went. Since then his life had been a struggle because Alfred, the younger brother, had been left nearly everything. Since then, even though he worked hard and proved himself, even though Alfred had given him six million dollars, Neily had never been content. His marriage, after such a dramatic beginning, wasn't even happy. Which proved there was no special virtue in hard work.

Vanderbilt caught himself up. He was scarcely in a position to judge. He had never done any work, hard or otherwise, in his whole life. Not even at Yale. Not even in the family's railroad empire, although it was his duty and his right. He had an office at Grand Central, but had been there exactly once. He had so much money that money made more money automatically, so it was self-defeating to waste the most active years of his life in work.

What had he done? Lived like a merchant prince on a fortune he'd inherited, with no need to hoard it or enlarge it. He had made the mistakes many men made, his first marriage and the affair with Agnes which broke it up. It was not the end of the world. But then after her Cuban husband had divorced her, too, Agnes had killed herself in a hotel in London. He could not take all the blame for that. He had never promised to marry her. Yet guilt had robbed life of its flavor for years after.

Then he had married Margaret. She was more clever than Agnes. She had talked her first husband out of suing for a divorce. When she was free, they had married. It was a good marriage, dynastic, and he was fond of their two boys, and of Billy, his son by his first wife.

And his friend had died, not yet forty. At least Fred had achieved something personal with his construction business in New York.

Was that it? Vanderbilt wondered. A combination of feeling his age and knowing that, as he approached forty, he had achieved nothing, produced or created nothing positive, had no aim in life? His father, who had been reared under the eye of the old Commodore and had worked without cease

510

from his earliest years, first in a bank, then at New York Central, to increase and pass on the increase of the Vanderbilt fortune, his father would certainly have thought so. Yet it was still not the whole story, although partly it. There was also the war.

God, we're a funny lot. In the family there was everything from cranks to geniuses, from sportsmen to ladies who preferred other ladies instead of their husbands. "I could a tale unfold," he thought, or whatever the quotation was. But where did he fit in? Nowhere.

The whole trouble was the war. So many of his English friends were in it. Many of them lay in unmarked graves, the best of a generation. And every week the post brought news of others commanding companies and regiments, or crippled, or missing, presumed killed. The truth of it was, he felt guilty for not being with them. He had always stood by his friends, and to do nothing was like running out on them. It was not America's quarrel, many people had reminded him, but that was too easy an out.

It was madness, of course. As a Vanderbilt, technically head of the family, he was not a free agent. If he volunteered for the British forces, the repercussions at home and abroad, national and diplomatic, would be enormous. It would be an act of total irresponsibility, however much he personally supported the Allied cause.

He knew what had brought everything to a head. In spite of his troubled night, he had fallen asleep, but had been wakened again just before dawn by a disturbing sound. All the lifeboats were being swung out. It was not a drill. He quickly realized that no alarm had been given, so it was purely a precautionary measure, yet it was eerie to lie and listen to the crumps and rasping sounds as the heavy boats were raised from their wooden supports and the screech of ropes in the pulleys as one by one all twenty-two boats were swung out on their davits, each one tethered to the deck by a length of canvas-wrapped chain. It was an abrupt notification that the *Lusitania* was now approaching the war zone.

Vanderbilt had not got back to sleep. The dissatisfaction with himself had started then and gone on all day. Like most of the other passengers he had been lulled into forgetfulness by the smoothness of their crossing and the spell of the liner herself. Cocooned in every comfort, with the whole Atlantic between them and their destination, most had happily put all thought of possible danger out of their minds. Those who had not were politely but firmly taken aside and requested to keep their scaremongering to themselves, for fear of frightening the women and children. That morning, however, the carefree atmosphere had vanished at the sight of the lifeboats hanging out, eleven to a side, their swaying restrained by their chain tethers, the constant creaking of their rope falls ominous and unnerving.

Groups of anxious passengers stood talking quietly, made nervous by rumors and the memory of the German warning, while stewards and deck officers went from one to the other answering questions and reassuring them that the boats had only been made ready as a routine precaution, since they were now within five hundred miles of the Irish coast, and that there was no present danger. Cabin staff reported more cases of seasickness than there had been in the entire voyage so far.

On board, Vanderbilt had been surprised and pleased to meet an old acquaintance, Allen Loney from New York. They had often ridden together. He noticed Loney forward on the boat deck with his wife and their fifteen-year-old-daughter, Virginia, who was developing into a beauty. They were talking to Jay Brooks, an auto chain salesman from Bridgeport, Connecticut, a likeable, bustling man of about forty. As he came up to them, Brooks was saying, "Nothing to be scared of. That German threat was only a bluff. It stands to reason they'd never attack the *Lusitania* with maybe a couple of hundred Americans aboard."

"I only hope that's true," Mrs. Loney said, worried. Vanderbilt saw that both she and Virginia were carrying their bulky life belts. "What do you think, Mr. Vanderbilt?" she asked him.

"I agree with Mr. Brooks," he told her. "They might try to scare us, but they'd never dare to attack. And even if they were crazy enough to, they wouldn't succeed."

"That's what I've been trying to explain to her," Loney said. "For one thing, we're too fast. And for another, all those watertight compartments can be closed off just like that by one electrical switch, so the *Lusitania* can be damaged, have a hole blown in her by a stray mine or even a torpedo, and still not sink."

"Exactly," Brooks nodded. "That's why I chose her. How she's constructed, she'll take a minimum of two to three hours to go down. She could be hit several times and still be able to reach the nearest port without sinking."

The girl, Virginia, laughed and held up her life belt. "Mummy's made me carry this around with me since before breakfast."

Mrs. Loney smiled with some embarrassment. "Well . . . I suppose we can leave them in the cabin, really. As long as we know where to find them, if we need them."

Vanderbilt was wondering if he had a life jacket. Presumably there was one in his suite somewhere, although he had never bothered to look for it.

"I feel such a baby carrying it about," Virginia said.

"The best thing," Brooks advised, "is to make sure you know how to put it on properly, then stow it away and forget about it."

By afternoon everything had returned to normal, at least on the surface. People were ashamed of having shown their anxiety. The crossing continued smooth and the sun shone. Nursemaids wheeled babies in their prams on the sheltered side. Children played hide-and-seek round the collapsible boats, tethered to the deck under the hanging lifeboats. The adults resumed their conversations and books and card games, and the orchestra entertained those taking tea in the verandah restaurant over the first-class dining saloon.

But Vanderbilt had become more and more restless. After lunch he had had a drink with Commander Stackhouse and two young Englishmen, both soldiers, one a lieutenant, the other, Captain Scott, paying his own way back from British India to join an active regiment. Now they were almost in sight of home, they were both wearing a uniform. A fair number of uniforms had suddenly appeared that morning throughout the ship, volunteers, reservists, officers returning from assignments in South America, the States and Canada.

"It seems crazy," Vanderbilt said, "to lose twenty or thirty thousand men defending a patch of ground you're just going to give up."

The conversation went on, but more guarded and restrained, which Vanderbilt realized was due to him. The two officers were treating him politely as someone sympathetic but uninvolved, and he tried to correct the impression by saying, "I care very much what happens out there. This is our quarrel too, you know."

"We tend to think so," Stackhouse said with a smile. "Unfortunately, the majority of your countrymen don't appear to agree."

"They will," Vanderbilt promised. "Sooner or later America will enter the war."

"I hope not," Captain Scott muttered.

"Why not?" Vanderbilt asked in surprise.

Scott seemed embarrassed. "Well, sir, with all respect, the American army is hardly large enough to be of any assistance to us, and we don't need any additional navy."

"Again with respect, sir," the lieutenant said. "If the United States should by some chance get dragged into this, it would take at least a year to train sufficient men, and the bulk of her supplies would be needed to equip and maintain them. So really, from our point of view, it's best for America to remain neutral and keep selling us the tools to get on with the job."

Vanderbilt had thought about that conversation off and on for the rest of the afternoon. The officers had talked to him as one might to a stranger who was a guest in one's club or to an elderly relative who was out of touch with the realities of modern life. It had irritated him. All at once, however, he realized that it was the natural attitude of fighting men to someone who says he is with them in spirit, yet does nothing to prove it. Sympathy was not enough.

Even Allen Loney was doing something. He and his family had moved to England and led a prosperous, civilized life. When the war started, he had no need to become involved, yet he had sent his wife and daughter home to safety and exchanged his peaceful existence for the dangers of driving a Red Cross ambulance in France. Because his wife missed him so much, she had begged him to come for her and bring her back to England where she would be nearer him.

Vanderbilt admired and honored Loney as he admired Matt Fletcher. In Fletcher's case there was more than a touch of envy. The more he saw of her, the more he came to appreciate Olivia Fletcher's qualities. There was a vitality about her, a warmth of personality that made anyone with her feel more alive. Her beauty was natural, not used as a weapon or a defense. She scarcely seemed aware of it. As one of the richest men in the world, he was accustomed to a certain amount of deference, to being run after. Neither Fletcher nor his wife showed any sign of doing that. Instead, he had to cultivate them. It put him on his mettle. It was hard to know how to impress her, yet he recognized that he wanted to—like one of the beaux surrounding a Savannah belle in some tale of the old South.

He could not dismiss it with a laugh. He envied Fletcher, envied his certainty, his ability to make decisions, his freedom to make them. He was so used to being envied himself, it was a strange sensation to find someone with whom he would gladly change places. To go off to fight in the knowledge that it was the right thing to do. To be married to Olivia and have her care deeply what happened to him. To share the tenderness of those final days before the decision came irrevocably into effect and he left for the war. To feel a genuine passion, lifting one out of oneself. At least . . . he assumed those days were poignant for them. He had made the mistake at first of assuming they were indifferent to each other. Only closer observation revealed how devoted they were, although always polite to each other and unde monstrative in public. Unless there was something wrong that no one could guess at. He hoped not. Although it opened possibilities.

He was disgusted with himself and broke off the whole train of thought. There were other kinds of profiteering than making money out of the necessities of war. There were those who preyed on the wives and sweethearts of the men who had left for the Front. Of all, perhaps the most despicable.

He threw his towel away and carried on dressing. But his depression remained. He could not volunteer to fight like Matt, or to drive an ambulance right up at the lines like Allen Loney. He had money, but he was not a financier like Morgan, who could use his know-how to set up deals in favor of the Allies. As he fastened his pants, he paused at a thought. Though he could not act himself, what was to stop him letting his money act for him? He had dined twice with pretty Marie Depage and heard at first hand about the atrocities in Belgium, which so many accounted too hideous to believe. They and the unending hardship were confirmed by Lindon Bates. As soon as he landed he could contact—what was his name?— Herbert Hoover, and see what an injection of a hundred thousand dollars would do for the Relief Fund. He could shame his fellow millionaires into following his lead. He could forget the rabidly anti-Allied Hearst, and Henry Ford, who bleated about arbitration and supported pacifists and international socialists. There were others he could rally.

All right, Teddy Roosevelt complained at America's lack of readiness and that, if called in, she could only send a humiliating contingent of around a thousand men to Europe. There were other things that could be done. As a kick-off, although he would not be allowed to drive one of them, he could provide a whole fleet of ambulances for the Red Cross.

He was fitting the gold studs into his shirt front when Denyer knocked and showed in the steward who had come to check the blackout. "I'll have that drink now," Vanderbilt sang out, and patted the tautness of his stomach, smiling. He could face himself in the mirror again.

On the bridge of the 6,000-ton steamer *Candidate*, her captain alternately cursed and blessed the weather. The intermittent heavy fog they had sailed through since before dawn had been a pure curse as he had picked his way through the St. George's Channel and past the dangerous shoals off the southeast coast of Ireland. The worst of them lay some ten miles east of Waterford Harbor and were marked by the Coningbeg Lightship. The light had been damned difficult to make out. Now, however, it lay behind him, which placed his position at fifteen to twenty miles south of Waterford.

The *Candidate* was en route from Liverpool to Jamaica and had another hundred miles to sail along the Irish coast before reaching Fastnet Rock and turning into the Atlantic sea lanes. Although he could do it by dead reckoning, he would have preferred the sight of a landmark to give him his exact position, but the breaks in the fog were too local to let him see the coast as anything but an indistinct blur. So it continued to be a curse. At the same time, with all the

U-boat sinkings reported in the last couple of weeks, he could look on the fog as a mixed blessing, wrapping the *Candidate* in a cloak of invisibility. Yet he still had to worry about the usual possibility of collision. He had lookouts in the crow's nest and up at the bows. Every man on duty was keeping his eyes peeled. Bloody war, he thought. As if there weren't enough problems already for any ship's captain.

He was peering forward and gave an "Uh-huh" of satisfaction as the murk ahead began to clear. In a few minutes, the *Candidate* had emerged from the fog bank, although to his disappointment he could still not make out the coast. They were in a pocket of clearer visibility with soup all round them. They were making eight knots. "Might as well hold it steady," he said.

Almost at the same moment there was a whistle from the voice tube and the crow's nest lookout reported a vessel approaching from port. It was veiled by wisps of fog and difficult to spot at first, but the captain saw no cause for alarm. It was a good two miles off, so there was no danger of ramming. It did not change course, however, and he went on watching it, becoming puzzled. It seemed fairly small and narrow. It sat very low in the water and had some kind of construction at midships. His first mate came to stand beside him and they watched it together. Now it was turning. And he realized abruptly that the construction was a conning tower. There was a deck gun behind it with a uniformed gun crew manning it. "Holy Jesus . . ." the mate gasped. "It's a bloody U-boat!"

"Hard to starboard!" the captain roared. As the helmsman spun the wheel, loose charts slithered off the chart table and a tin mug balanced on the shelf beside it fell to the deck. The second mate stooped quickly to catch it, but was off balance and gashed his forehead on the corner of the table. The mug bounced and clattered across the deck of the bridge.

The first mate was hurrying to the engine room telegraph. "Full Speed Ahead!" the captain called.

On the conning tower of the U 20, Lanz smacked the rail with his open palm. "They're on to us!" he exclaimed. "Running for it."

"Better than coming at us," Schwieger said, and nodded down to Scherb. "Commence firing!"

The deck gun crashed out and the shell plumed into the water short of the steamer's stern. The second shot was also well short. The U 20 was broadside on to the waves and rolling with the swell. That and the limited visibility hampered the gun layer's aim, but Schwieger saw that in his eagerness Scherb was firing when they were at maximum height. In the fraction of a second it took to react to his order, the U-boat was already on her downward roll. "Fire on the upswing!" he shouted. "On the upward swing!"

The third shot was another miss, but the next smashed into the steamer's broad stern. There was a cheer from the watching crewmen, and a louder cheer when the following shot plowed into the fleeing enemy's after section. In the next second, the steamer vanished into the fog.

"*Scheisse* . . ." Lanz hissed through his teeth. Typical! To come on a prime target in a break in the fog like this was a chance in a million, and Schwieger had muffed it. As was only to be expected.

The deck gun sounded again as Scherb loosed off a blind shot in frustration. "Cease firing!" Schwieger ordered. At the same time he signed to the helmsman to bring the wheel round. Lanz had judged the target to be British, of the Harrison Line. "What sort of speed can a steamer like that make?" Schwieger asked.

Lanz shrugged. "A good few more than us. Eighteen knots."

Schwieger was bending to the voice tube. "Hirsch, you hear me? All engines Ahead Full."

The U 20 raced through the fog at her maximum surface speed of 14 1/2 knots. It was weird, feeling her plunge, hearing her prow slice through the waves, with the rush of damp fog against the face, its acrid taste in the throat, and seeing nothing beyond a few feet all round but a yellow brown wall. Lanz had drawn instinctively closer to Schwieger for protection. "She can't keep this up for long," he muttered.

"Long enough," Schwieger said, hoping it was true. At this speed the risk of engine failure heightened by the minute. But he had scented blood. Somewhere ahead his prey was running from him, already wounded. To flush out a steamer of that size, just when he was on the point of giving up and returning home, was a gift from the God of Battles.

He could feel his whole crew and the U 20 herself urging him on.

He could see how Lanz's hands clutched the rail in the merchant mariner's instilled horror of collision. He could never catch the steamer at her full speed, but he was gambling on her captain having the same reaction as Lanz and throttling back, gambling on him maintaining a fixed course. If he did so, the risks of ramming him were minimized and the chance of catching him up at least doubled.

Lanz muttered something, then asked nervously, "How long are you going on with this?"

"If necessary, right up to the range of the patrol ships' guns." It would do no harm to let the Mate of the Reserve sweat for a bit. Privately Schwieger had decided on a time limit of twenty minutes. But the twenty minutes came and went. Twenty-five, he told himself. Then thirty, counted off on the luminous dial of his watch. Another one, another two. The nervous tension of the sightless race was coiling tighter inside him. He would not give up!

Then he heard a faint call from Lippe, who had taken the most dangerous lookout post, forward in the bows. "Clearing ahead! Clearing ahead! . . ."

"Stand by!" Schwieger rapped, alerting the gun crew.

The next moment the U 20 swept out of the fog into daylight that was almost dazzling by contrast. As Schwieger shaded his eyes, there was a whoop from Lippe and the rest of the deck crew. Lanz was pointing excitedly to where, on a virtually parallel course not fifty yards to starboard, was the enemy steamer.

"Warning shot!" Schwieger called. He could see clearly the men working at the steamer's stern and the startled faces of the officers looking down at him from the bridge. When the gun roared and the shell whistled over its bows, the men scrambled for cover, but their captain did not accept the warning. Idiot! He was veering away again.

The *Candidate*'s captain had no fear of the U-boat's small-caliber gun, only of her torpedoes. If he could keep his stern to her, he had a slight chance of outrunning her to the haze of the coastal fog bank about six miles distant.

"Commence rapid fire!" Schwieger ordered. It was distasteful to him, a waste of time, ammunition and possibly lives. At this range Scherb could not miss, not with Lammeier aiming. The gun belched smoke, and again, even as the first shell exploded in the steamer's superstructure. The second ripped away a section of its portside rail. No one could fault the captain's determination. He managed to bring his helm round and the narrower target of the stern was more difficult to hit, while the gap between them was widening. But then Scherb increased his elevation and his next shot landed full on the bridge. The steamer yawed to port, out of control.

"Cease firing!" Schwieger called. Scherb was enjoying himself and looked up, disappointed, but Lammeier pointed out to him that the steamer's propellers had stopped. She was heaving to.

More of the U 20's crew had come up through the hatches and there was another cheer, then silence as they watched the steamer's four lifeboats being swung out. There was a murmur of appreciation at the efficiency with which the wounded were put on board and the crew took their places. To his astonishment, Lanz saw Schwieger stand to attention and salute as the captain was lifted into the last boat on their side. When the boats were lowered to the water, one of them foundered as soon as its ropes were released. Schwieger had no facilities for prisoners and merely waited to see that all the survivors had been picked up from the water.

When the three remaining boats left for the shore, heavily overloaded, he moved in closer. Boatswain Kurtz had rigged the collapsible boat and Schwieger called to him, "Take Lammeier and a boarding party. See what you can find." The boarding party left and Schwieger cruised slowly round, gazing up at the bulk of the steamer's stern. The name *Candidate* and the port, Liverpool, were easily read, although covered by a layer of paint.

Lanz laughed and rubbed his hands together. "I told you! Harrison Line—six thousand tons."

Schwieger nodded. He could see Lippe gesticulating as he began to shout. He could make them out now, also, two dark shapes emerging from the faraway coastal haze. Even before he had trained the telescope on them, Schwieger had guessed what they were, armed trawlers of the British auxiliary patrol. He snapped the telescope shut, picked up the megaphone and ordered his boarding party back to the U 20 on the double.

With Kurtz and his men safely on board and the boat restowed, he withdrew to six hundred yards from the immobilized steamer. There was little time for finesse, for planting explosive charges on the *Candidate*'s keel which he had intended, but he did not want to waste one of his new-type torpedoes. He had one of the older bronze models fitted into the portside forward tube, positioned himself and fired. The torpedo sped true and exploded at the steamer's engine room depth. Although he waited, there was little effect, however. The *Candidate* settled slightly toward the stern, but did not sink. He swore softly, knowing the crew was watching him, their jubilation turning to concern again. The patrol boats were stopping to pick up the survivors from the lifeboats and would not try to engage him until that was over. He refused to be robbed of the kill at this stage, nor would he squander another torpedo. "We're going in," he said. "Keep a lookout for enemy submarines."

The order had the result he wanted, taking the crew's attention off the patrol boats. He swung the U 20 round and ran her in reverse to within two hundred yards of the steamer. "Now, she's yours" he told Scherb. "Aim for the waterline. Rapid fire!"

Shells poured into the *Candidate*'s side, gouging holes in her, which gradually turned into one massive gap. She was burning internally and rocking on the water, but still would not sink. Schwieger was swearing in unison with Lanz at every explosion which left her afloat, when all at once the seesawing became more violent and she dipped lower in the water. Her stern bucked skittishly, as if in farewell, and she was gone. Over where she sank, a large bubble of air bloomed and burst and the waves rushed in, swirling and eddying, with debris spinning round and spreading out. The U-boat felt the tug of the down current and was spattered with oily water from the air spout. The sound from the crew was more like a growl of satisfaction than a cheer.

The whole operation had lasted for all of twenty-five minutes. The three lifeboats had been picked up and the trawlers were coming on cautiously, edging out to catch the U 20 in their crossfire. Except that she would not wait for them. The main belt of fog was less than a mile away. "Ahead full!" Schwieger ordered, and the U-boat raced away, surprising the trawlers by her surface speed. Schwieger steered her into the fog at a slant, as though making for Fastnet and the open sea. Once certain that she was out of sight, he brought her round nearly 180°, doubling back toward Coningbeg Light to confuse any unlikely pursuit.

Shrouded again in fog, he could hear the men's voices as Kurtz shepherded everyone except lookouts and the gun crew back down below. They sounded stimulated and excited, more like themselves. Even the U 20 seemed more vibrant under him. He had made up for the miserable hundred-ton *Earl of Latham*. At least he would not be returning empty-handed. The spell was broken and there was a warmth in his belly he had not felt for days. He would like to share the moment with someone, even Lanz, but the Mate of the Reserve had been relieved on watch by Quartermaster Wendt, who stood stolidly silent, staring at the impenetrable wall of fog. The cook's assistant brought them up scalding mugs of coffee. A moment later, Lammeier came up, saluted and presented Schwieger shyly with a carton of English cigarettes from the bar of the *Candidate*'s saloon.

Schwieger accepted them with thanks, took one and handed them back. "Everybody deserves them," he said. "Pass them round."

Frohman's party was a huge success, one of the best he had ever given on shipboard. Usually they could be quite sticky affairs, since he could not choose and balance his guests as he did at home, but everyone fitted in and circulated freely. Even those who looked in only for one drink found themselves staying on, enjoying themselves too much to leave.

He knew it was not due entirely to his talents as a host. There was a special sense of camaraderie about this voyage. The underlying tension had broken through the barriers and, whether admitted or not, a feeling of excitement, of shared danger now they were nearly in the War Zone, was in back of the animation and lightheartedness. He could appreciate it himself. Few if any of his guests could imagine that the urbane, smiling figure who greeted them and had set the whole carefree tone of the party had been in such agony an hour ago that he had almost sent for the Purser to ask him to present his apologies to those he had invited and prevent their coming.

Frohman rarely undersold himself, yet he was more important to the party's success than he realized. It was largely because he had been so rarely seen on the voyage. He had held small dinner parties for Charlie Klein and Forman, Rita Jolivet, his own people. Yet to most of his fellow passengers he had become a man of mystery, with the additional glamour of his theater connections and celebrity. With only one more full day and night before the *Lusitania* reached Liverpool, it was the perfect time for him to open his doors and show himself. He had scored an extra coup, for Captain Turner had come to his party, another mystery man barely glimpsed by most of the passengers, except for those who had attended the Sunday morning service he had conducted on the second day out.

Both men were surrounded by a sizable crowd, laughing as they sparred verbally with Jimmy McCubbin, the Purser, a droll and appealing man when he was off duty. "I vow, Mr. McCubbin," Frohman told him, "I should like to put you on the stage. Perhaps a Yankee version of *Our American Cousin*. We could call it *Our English Cousin*. You would knock them dead in the States."

"I'm much too fond of your countrymen to wish their general demise," McCubbin assured him, and their listeners laughed again. "Besides, I'm really too old to consider embarking on a new career."

"Yes, we're all very sad," Turner said. "Our Jimmy is retiring at the end of this trip."

"I didn't know," Frohman said. "The *Lusitania* won't seem the same without you. Can you bear to give her up?"

"It'll be a wrench," McCubbin admitted. "But I've been saving up and I've bought a little farm in the country, outside Golders Green, and I'm looking forward to getting back my land legs, after all this time."

"Well, we'll all miss you," Frohman assured him.

Isaac Lehmann, the stockbroker, had been waiting for a chance to talk to Turner and moved in with a question about the War Zone. People's attention immediately switched to them.

"Now, tell me," Frohman said quietly to McCubbin, "is that *the* Mrs. Fletcher?"

"That's her indeed," McCubbin nodded.

Off and on Frohman had been watching the dark-haired young woman with the fine cheekbones and perfect natural carriage. She was remarkably beautiful in a full-skirted dark emerald evening dress with a daringly low neck to which only someone with her splendid shoulders and bust could do justice. He had guessed who she must be from Forman's enthusiastic descriptions, and Vanderbilt's. They were both with her now.

Livvy was amused and flattered. She was not accustomed to being paid court to openly by men, good-looking, intelligent and famous men, moreover. She knew she was lucky she did not take it seriously, or it might have turned her head. It was only a social game and she found she played it surprisingly well. She was not embarrassed by compliments. She caught shades of meaning and often replied to them rather than the words used. That was a legacy from her father. She had quickly understood that she was not required to lead conversations, but to follow and react to them, which she could do with hardly any difficulty. That was also inherited from her father, who had filled in her education and liberated her mind in the hope that she would go to university, which she would have done if she had not met Matt.

She glanced across the room to where he was in conversation with Lindon Bates and Madame Depage. People had taken to him too, seeking him out, although he tried to remain in the background. She had seen more clearly than ever how unavoidable it was for him to be a leader, even in spite of himself. It was his personality, confident and resourceful, that drew people to him.

With only this evening and one more day, they had still not had the talk they must have before landing. It was hard for either of them to begin it, but time was growing short. It should have been this evening, but Purser McCubbin had told them that Mr. Frohman insisted on them attending his party. They had arrived with the Arnsteins, who were among the few who had already left. Beattie had been enjoying herself and looked like staying on until Lee reminded her that they wanted to start their packing. She had actually blushed, realizing what he meant. They really spent an amazing amount of time in their cabin. Who could blame them? "You run along," Livvy said. "We'll see you at dinner."

Beattie bit her lip. "Maybe not at dinner," she whispered. "But at the concert after."

Justus Forman was aware that he had lost Livvy's attention. "So I jumped overboard and got eaten by a shark—or was it a mackerel?"

Vanderbilt laughed. Livvy pulled her mind back to him and smiled, apologizing. "Oh, I'm sorry. You've both given me so much to think about, I was trying to catch up."

"I hate to contradict a lady, but I'm sure Olivia is way ahead of us both," Vanderbilt said.

Forman had been delighted to find that she had thought constructively about his play, which she had seen in New York. "Of course, I'm only speaking as a member of the public," she told him.

"Well, it's the public that's important in the long run," Forman said, and added ruefully, "or in my case, unfortunately, in the short run."

Rita Jolivet swept up, took his arm and, with a bright "Excuse me!" to Livvy, led him over to Charlie Klein. At Frohman's request, Klein had promised to help to introduce the younger writer to the London theater. He was a sensitive, highly successful man, handicapped by a club foot, which had been the saving of him, he maintained. But for that, he might have been an actor. Instead he was forced to become a dramatist. "We were wondering where you would be staying in London," he said.

"I'm not quite sure," Forman confessed. "Charles has arranged it. I think it's the Savoy."

"Where else?" Rita laughed.

She was still holding his arm and Forman smiled to her. She and Livvy were easily the two most attractive women on board. It was almost impossible to choose between. Rita was maybe a little more forthcoming. Perhaps because she was an actress and, as a playwright, he might be of value to her.

"We'll be neighbors," Klein said. "We must see something of each other."

Forman was flattered. He admired Klein, who was the

kind of dramatic writer he wanted to become. At the moment, though, he was more interested in Rita. "Yes, we must," he agreed. He smiled to Rita. "I hope I'll see more of you, too, in London."

Vanderbilt was smiling, watching. "Our Mr. Forman is a *boulevardier manqué*."

Livvy smiled back. "Whereas you are a *boulevardier realisé*?"

Vanderbilt inclined his head penitently. "I deserved that. One should not blame others for one's own faults."

Livvy laughed. She liked him. He was extremely handsome, of course, and there was the attraction of all that money, but it was more than that. There was something unsettled about him, something lost. He could be very dangerous to women.

"Your people live in the country, don't they?" he asked.

"Yes. Near Winchelsea, in Sussex."

"Will you and your husband be able to have some time there before he . . . has to go off?"

Livvy paused slightly before she answered. "No, unfortunately. He has to report almost straight away."

"That's a shame," Vanderbilt said. "But if you're at loose ends . . . The Astors have a summer place at Sandwich, I think. That's not too far from you. If I come to visit them, perhaps we might motor over and call on you?" Livvy nearly giggled, but stopped herself. She could imagine her mother's face if Vanderbilt and the Astors arrived at their modest brick and timber house off the Hastings Road. "If you've no objection," Vanderbilt added when she did not reply.

"None at all," Livvy assured him. "It's only that . . . my parents' house is not very grand." She glanced over at Matt, who was now with Captain Turner, Stackhouse and some others. "But you'd be very welcome."

Vanderbilt understood. She had hesitated in case her parents might be embarrassed, which was the last thing he would want. He had also noticed her almost involuntary look toward her husband. He had an absurd wish to tell her about the Red Cross ambulances he was providing, to impress her, like a small boy showing off. Instead he touched her hand and smiled. "Perhaps it might be better if you contacted me some time your husband is home on leave. And let me take you both to dinner."

526

"I'd like that very much," Livvy said sincerely.

Will Turner was becoming irritated by Lehmann and another passenger who were attempting to cross-examine him. It was spoiling a good party. "Now, now, gentlemen," he said reasonably, "I've already told you. I shall be speaking to you tonight at the end of the concert after dinner. I'll answer all your questions then." He saw a messenger boy hovering beyond them with a signal envelope from the Marconi Room. "Excuse me, gentlemen," he said. He took the envelope and half turned away, opening it. Inside was a signal decoded by Leith. It was very brief. "Submarines active off south coast of Ireland." Turner frowned. What the hell was it supposed to mean? A general alarm, a specific warning, or what? He took out his pen and wrote on the signal, "Is that all there was? Request confirmation and further information." He put it in the envelope and handed it to the boy. "Take this up to the Marconi operator right away."

"Trouble?" Stackhouse asked.

"No, no. Routine," Turner smiled. "There's no peace for the wicked." Frohman was near them, talking to Elbert Hubbard and Fletcher's pretty wife. He crossed to them. "I'm afraid you'll have to forgive me, Mr. Frohman," he said.

"Surely you're not leaving so soon, Captain?" Frohman protested. It was by way of a private joke, since McCubbin had pointed out to them that the party had already lasted half an hour longer than scheduled and that both dinner and the concert would be delayed. Turner chuckled, said his farewells and left.

"I'm sorry, but I'll have to be going, too," Livvy said.

"Oh, no, Mrs. Fletcher!" Frohman objected, this time genuinely. "I've been looking forward all week to meeting you."

"Now then," Hubbard cut in. "Remember, I saw her first."

"With a beautiful woman," Frohman said, "it is not who sees her first, but who is seen with her last that counts."

Livvy laughed with them, yet persisted. "I'm afraid I still have to go."

Frohman sighed. "Very well. Only on condition, however, that you and your husband dine with me tomorrow evening, our last opportunity."

Livvy felt the strange, ugly-attractive man's magnetism. His smile was puckish, his eyes warm. "We've promised to have dinner with two young friends of ours."

"Bring them along," Frohman said. "I guarantee all your intimates, even Mr. Hubbard, will be here. It will be your evening."

"She's weakening," Hubbard chuckled.

Livvy gave in. She knew now why Forman had sworn that Charles Frohman was irresistible. Heaven help his business rivals. "Very well. What can I say? That would be charming," she told him. She could hear Matt's voice behind her.

Commander Stackhouse was describing some of the aims of the international oceanographic expedition he was organizing for the following year. "You're just the sort I'd like to have along," he said. "We might be able to arrange a leave of absence for you if you'd care to join me."

"Well, thank you, Commander," Matt smiled. "But I didn't come all the way to Europe to leave almost at once for the Antarctic."

Livvy turned. "I'm going down, Matt. I want to look in on the children before dinner."

"I'll come with you," Matt said.

"I don't want to drag you away."

"It's all right." He nodded to Stackhouse. "It's been fascinating, sir. I hope we can talk again later."

They said their thank-yous and took the elevator down to D deck. Livvy had told Matt about accepting Frohman's invitation for the last evening. He was silent and waited in their cabin while she went in to see the children.

Diana had kicked her covers off and she tucked them up round her again. Peter was sleeping on his back, his arms thrown up above his head like a baby. Livvy stood looking at them, her children, hers and Matt's. She had wanted a little time by herself, a few minutes to think.

She was perfectly aware of what had been happening this week. She had become an independent woman. Men had responded more and more to her, the further she had grown away from Matt. She was no longer the provincial housewife she had been. All it had taken was the snapping of the emotional ties. The men had sensed that somehow, by instinct. They still circled, unsure, because of how she played them off, one against the other. If she chose one, she knew it would be Vanderbilt. If not now, then later. If not him, then someone else who could give her all the things a woman dreamed of.

She thought of all the hard times she had been through, the subzero camps, the miserable quarters, the long separations when Matt was away on drilling or construction projects and she was left with only the children. She had accepted it uncomplainingly as part of being a wife, part of being in love. But that was not how most people lived. She need never go through it again. All it needed was for her to take the last step and admit that Matt was replaceable.

It was not just the flattery she had been receiving, the admiration. Through the long days of this week, she had thought back over her whole life, and her life with Matt. What relationship could survive such an examination?

All the thoughts were jumbled in her mind. And Dan Connally's voice. She remembered everything he had said, every faltering word of it. Out of it all, one thing had become clear. But she had not been able to tell Matt. She had not been able to bring herself to tell him.

She went back into their cabin. She made no sound on the thick carpet and he was not aware of her. He stood in profile to her, his head lowered, with that same expression that had so horrified her before, bleak and remote. He was still unaware of her as she watched him.

"Matt," she said quietly. He looked round, hearing the catch in her voice. She was trembling. "Oh, Matt . . . I've been such a fool."

For a moment neither moved; then as he took a step toward her, she ran to him and his arms went round her. He scooped her up and, as he held her against him, tighter and tighter, shaking like she was, all the foolish wasteful hideous days of that week were forgotten.

Schwieger's eyes were still smarting from the long hours of keeping watch in fog. He had to restrain himself from rubbing them.

He had had two near misses and could feel the sweat still drying on his body. He had filled in his log, but it told only the barest story. To anyone except him, it would read as only one incident.

The U 20 had doubled back toward the Coningbeg Light. While he was still smoking Lammeier's cigarette, still feeling the warmth of having broken the bad luck of this patrol, a miracle had happened. With the fog banks continually shifting, they had run out into better visibility again and there, near the fog's horizon, he had sighted another large steamer in exactly the same circumstances as the first. It was a million-to-one chance and he raced at full speed on the surface to intercept.

The steamer, like the first, ran for the fog bank and vanished. He kept after her, urging the control room for more speed. Lanz had scrambled up to the conning tower platform again, eager for more action. They both knew that, if they caught up, there would be no warning given this time. The boarding party had reported the six-pounder mounted on the *Candidate*'s stern and a machine gun emplacement on either side. Schwieger admitted his own recklessness. It had been sheer bloodlust, madness. With a kill behind him, he was in full command of himself again. He owed it to his crew. Even one half-trained but determined gunner at that six-pounder could have blown the U 20 to Kingdom Come.

He was smiling faintly, watching Lanz nerve himself for another blind dash into the fog, when the steamer suddenly reappeared to starboard. It was big, even bigger than he had thought. And it was slicing through the water straight for them.

Unlike the *Candidate*'s skipper, its captain had obviously taken to heart his Admiralty's instruction to ram on sight. It was fortunate that most of the gun crew was still below and the gun was locked off. The crash dive was a near run thing. As the U 20 submerged steeply, the turbulence of the large steamer passing above her shook lockers open, broke light bulbs and burst a steampipe in the rear engine room. What's happening to me? Schwieger thought. That was twice he had failed to anticipate the enemy's possible moves. It was as if his whole judgment had been affected. "Bastard, bastard," he kept repeating tightly, although he could not have said whether he meant Lanz or the steamer whose engines they could hear swelling in sound and fading as it circled.

He was in the conning tower with Lanz, Scherb, Kurtz and the helmsman. "He's waiting for us," Kurtz said, listening.

"A sensible captain would be far away by now," Lanz murmured. "It would be really something if we sank him for his presumption."

Schwieger saw everyone looking at him. His mind was working quickly. The dive would have carried them under the edge of the fog, where a periscope was hardly likely to be spotted. "All right," he said. "Since he's waiting for us, let's call on him. Take her up—nice and smooth." When the order was relayed, he moved in to the eyepiece of the asparagus, with Scherb handling the lever. At periscope depth, he watched the steamer approach and swing away as it circled. "It's big," he said. "Very big."

"More than twice the size of the *Candidate*," Lanz confirmed. Scherb gasped in excitement.

Schwieger had to agree that the estimate was probably correct. The fact that the steamer was still circling meant that its captain was in a fighting mood. It also argued that it was strongly armed, and so must be approached with caution. He slipped the U 20 out of the fog, stealing in gradually for a shot with one of the newer G-type torpedoes in his forward tubes. The steamer was weaving so erratic a pattern, however, that it was never possible to fix a satisfactory angle of incidence. All at once, it veered away as it abandoned the search and was soon dwindling toward the St. George's Channel. He rose from the eyepiece and shook his head. "What a pity," he heard Lanz say flatly. Now he had something else to put in his report.

"Are you sure it was so big?" Scherb asked disappointedly.

"Of course," Lanz told him. "Fourteen thousand tons."

"Fourteen thousand?" Kurtz queried in disbelief.

"How can you be so positive?" Schwieger asked.

Lanz smiled. "Because I recognized it. It was from the White Star Line. One of their big passenger ships."

"A passenger ship . . . ?" Schwieger repeated. There was dead silence in the conning tower. Schwieger found he was staring at Lanz and turned abruptly to the periscope until he could control himself.

Lanz had known all the time that it was a passenger ship, all the time he had been urging Schwieger to sink it. Of the

531

other commanders in the patrol, Rosenberg would attack nothing without warning. Von Forstner would have demanded identification and refused to attack altogether. Schwieger did not agree with them. Warnings should only be given when there was no risk to one's own craft. But he would have been the first U-boat commander to torpedo a noncombatant liner. It would have been no excuse that it had tried to ram him or that it might have been armed. He felt a mixture of nausea and relief at his escape. Cargo vessels which carried only a few passengers, like the *Falaba*, were a different matter. He could imagine the reaction he would have received from Fregattenkapitän Bauer.

That had been his second near miss. He rose and went through to central control.

Dense fog had closed in almost as soon as the liner had sailed away, and he had brought the U 20 down to eighty feet. An hour had gone by, and although the crew had been kept busy checking all sections, it was obvious they were restless. Having tasted action at last, they were keen for more. "Take her up," he told Hirsch.

Through the lens, he could see that the weather had brightened again. It would not last, but visibility was temporarily around three miles. The sea was calm. He swiveled slowly, not expecting anything, and again his luck was with him. Action Stations sounded when he picked up another steamer heading for the St. George's Channel.

As he ran in submerged to intercept, he acted strictly according to the rules, stepping back and asking Lanz to identify the target. "It's a cargo steamer," Lanz said.

"Are you sure?"

"Positive. About six thousand tons, Harrison Line. I'd say a sister ship to the one you sank earlier. Traveling at ten to eleven knots."

"Thank you," Schwieger said shortly.

"It'll most probably be armed."

"I realize that. Stand aside, please." Schwieger resumed his station at the periscope. There was no case here for a warning. He ordered the G torpedo set for a depth of ten feet. Scherb was ready at the firing button.

"Fire Number One!"

The U-boat lurched slightly. "Number One Forward Tube fired," Scherb reported.

Since the *Candidate* had not sunk when struck by the engine room, Schwieger had aimed for a different point. He watched the whole path of the torpedo and saw it explode exactly where he had intended, slightly more forward. The cargo steamer rocked and smoke belched up through the forward hatches. It went down a little by the bows, but did not sink, although it had been a perfect shot. The U 20's crew cheered, having heard the explosion, and Schwieger waved his hand for quiet. He could make out figures rushing about on the steamer, but it looked in no danger of sinking. It was those damned watertight bulkheads.

He scanned the horizon carefully for patrol ships. There were none. When he turned back to the steamer, he grunted in satisfaction. "They've swung their boats out!" As he watched, the steamer's crew piled in and lowered the lifeboats to the water. When they had pulled clear, Schwieger moved in and circuited the stricken steamer at periscope depth. It was the *Centurion* of Liverpool, Harrison Line, exactly as Lanz had predicted.

So far everything had been clean and efficient, unlike the hectic chase of its sister ship or the messy farce with the liner, but over an hour had passed and the *Centurion* had still not gone down. Apart from the danger of patrol ships, the fog was rolling back in. There was not enough time for cannon fire or grenades, if Schwieger was to have confirmation of the kill. He had no choice and rose to the surface. He had one of his last two bronze torpedoes loaded into the tube, eased in carefully to minimum safety range and fired it directly into the steamer's stern. It was not a moment too soon. He had only just seen the water round the breached stern begin to seethe and foam when it was blotted out by impenetrable fog. He waited another five minutes, listening to the fearsome wallowing and rumbling as the *Centurion* struggled against sinking like some wounded sea beast. It was almost unbearable, then there came a final groan of tortured metal and the clash of waters closing and he knew it was over.

The crew was celebrating, but he could not join in. He submerged again to eighty feet and set a course for the open sea.

* * *

Livvy felt terribly conspicuous as Matt and she crept quietly into the first-class smoke room. It was filled with chairs and passengers, although the concert was already over. The Arnsteins had kept two seats for them near the back and they slipped into them quickly.

"I don't believe it . . ." Lee grinned.

"Talk about us!" Beattie whispered. "And you've missed both dinner *and* the concert."

"Well, it was worth it," Livvy said.

Lee nodded. "I'll bet!"

"How would you know?" Matt asked, frowning. They laughed, then lowered their heads when people near them looked round in annoyance.

Captain Turner was on the small rostrum at the end of the room, answering a barrage of questions. "Yes, I assure you, we do have adequate lifeboat accommodation," he was saying. "In fact we can accommodate a thousand more passengers than there are on this present voyage. I can also assure you that the boats have never yet been needed in over two hundred crossings."

"Yes, but there's a war on now!" someone shouted.

Turner was indicating another questioner. It was Charles Lauriat, a prominent bookseller from Boston. "Why have we slowed down, Captain?" he asked.

Turner had been expecting that, and he had promised to tell them the truth. "It is because, sir, we have had a warning of submarine activity off the Irish coast." Even he was not prepared for the jabber of alarm, with everyone trying to talk at once. There was little he could tell them. His request for more information on the first message had been answered by an identical signal. Later Leith had decoded another signal to all British ships. It contained routine instructions for all vessels bound for Liverpool, but ended with the words "Submarines off Fastnet." He was holding up his hand and at last won a measure of attention. "We have lowered our speed in order to pass Fastnet Rock during the night—at least, well before dawn. That is a possible danger area. Yes?"

Lauriat smiled and sat down again, but Lehmann was standing. "And what about the blackout? The stewards have

534

asked us not to light cigars outside on the deck. If you're worried about that, why not just switch off all the lights?" There was a murmur of agreement.

"We do not black out all lights, sir," Turner said, "only bright lights. We wish it to be seen that we are a noncombatant liner. At the same time we do not want to draw undue attention to ourselves."

Turner sympathized with his passengers, particularly the non-Europeans who were not used to the proximity of war. His straightforward manner and lack of any personal agitation gave people confidence. His forthright manner of answering questions had a calming effect, but he could tell that something more was needed. "Believe me, ladies and gentlemen," he said, "if I thought you were in any real danger, even at this stage, I would turn about and sail back to New York. But I can promise you the best guarantee of your security—from noon tomorrow, you will be safely in the hands of the Royal Navy."

Chapter 28

CHARLES FROHMAN STRETCHED OUT HIS HAND TO THE BED-side table as he read. His fingers fumbled inside the dish, but it was empty and he looked at it in surprise. He had already eaten all the peanuts.

He was sitting propped up by pillows and cushions in bed, wearing his sleeping suit, rereading the manuscript of *Our Mrs. McChesney*, the play he had chosen as the next vehicle for Ethel Barrymore. He knew it must be late, somewhere between two and three in the morning, yet he still felt stimulated and was unable to sleep. After the party and dinner, he had gone to the ship's concert and had enjoyed the evening so much, he regretted having kept to himself for almost the whole voyage. He had even forgotten the pain in his leg for a time.

He had been standing near the back of the smoke room and had seen Olivia Fletcher and her husband come in just at the start of Turner's question-and-answer session and had joined them and their young friends. They all agreed that the only thing to do was to trust Captain Turner and follow his recommendations and instructions. A striking couple. Matt Fletcher was the finest kind of man and Frohman did not find the admiration professed for his wife by such different witnesses as Vanderbilt and Elbert Hubbard so difficult to understand now that he had met her.

As their small group walked slowly back along the boat deck, they had paused, held by the shimmer of the moon's track on the dark, sleeping sea. It was a warm, still night and the *Lusitania*, shrouded in nearly total blackout, forged majestically ahead with practically no sense of motion. It was easy to think of the ocean as limitless space and the great liner as some wandering inhabited planet. All of them felt it in one form or another and were silent, looking at the sea and the immense vault of the night sky. Frohman glanced at Livvy, whose face was just catching the light of one of the shaded lamps. She was watching her husband, and he had seldom seen an expression of such tenderness. If she had been younger and unattached, he would have been unable to resist suggesting that she become an actress. In a year or so she would probably be another in his private galaxy of stars.

Did he really want any more? he thought. He already managed so many, to have to keep them all busy and brightly shining was a certain recipe for dyspepsia. For this year alone, he had another sixteen productions planned, including a revival of *Sherlock Holmes* with Gillette and the annual Christmas run of *Peter Pan* with Maude.

Maude . . .

He tossed the manuscript on to the bedside table and grimaced at the empty dish. It had been filled with peanuts and he could not even recall eating them. What he really needed, he decided, was a cigar. His promise to Maude to cut down was the one promise he had never been able to fulfill. To preserve himself from temptation he had left his cigar box in the day room, but it was no use. He pushed himself out of bed, put on his dressing gown and padded through.

The cigars he preferred were not expensive Dutch or Havanas, but short, thick black ones like his father used to make, real cigars. As he puffed one alight, he smiled, remembering how Purser McCubbin had suggested he start one up to clear the room when the party was continuing well past its scheduled time. There was no point in going back to bed and he sat in the chair by his writing table, settling his right leg comfortably over the armrest.

In the silence he could almost hear her voice as she had spoken to him on the telephone the night before he left. She would still be in Kansas City, at the Grand, and might even now be just going on stage in Barrie's *Quality Street*, which she was touring. He could never forget how she blossomed in that last act, changing from spinsterhood to exquisite youthful beauty almost magically. It was just after her first appearance in that part that she had given him a bad fright, disappearing for months into a convent near Tours, in France. He had thought he had lost her and treated her with great care when she came back, more serene but more reserved than ever.

He shifted his leg down from the arm of the chair as he tried to remember what she had said that night on the telephone. He had been surprised by her call, he had told her, because he was thinking of her. "Why not?" she had said. "I always think of you." She had been worried about him making the trip, and he had assured her there was no danger and he would be back in six weeks or so and would come to see her. "I want you now," she said quietly. "I want you to stay."

There was something about her voice as he remembered it, a strain, an urgency. It suddenly seemed vitally important to remember exactly what she had said and how she had said it.

He had told her that he could not postpone his trip, that he was needed in London. She had said, "I need you too." Her voice had sounded as if it were breaking.

He could hear himself attempting to answer lightly. "Believe me, if anything could make me travel west tomorrow instead of east, it would be the thought of being with you."

"No, Charles, please . . ." Her voice had faltered. And then, after a pause, "Why won't you understand? Don't you love me?"

He sat utterly still. The conversation had been unbearable, nearly breaking his resolve to go, and he had ended it fairly abruptly by telling her he had people waiting. He had been a coward, afraid of revealing his own feelings by some unguarded words which she could not mistake.

Why won't you understand? Don't you love me?

He had been thinking so hard about himself, concentrating on his own thoughts and on controlling himself, that he had not really taken in what Maude was saying. Not until now. If only he had let her go on . . . He dropped the stub of his cigar in the ashtray and laid his hands flat on the writing table to stop their trembling.

That would be the greatest irony of all, if Maude had been trying to tell him that she loved him, really loved him. If all those years, when he had been afraid to confess his feelings, so had she, each afraid of being rejected. It was too impossible. Yet the memory of her voice and of what she had said stabbed into him. How could she love an ugly squat monkey like himself? All those years, those squandered, lonely years.

He could not believe it, yet his whole being told him it was true. He was almost lightheaded. "Why won't you understand? Don't you love me?" All at once he could not wait to finish his business in England as quickly as possible and return to the States, to Maude, and a future that might be different from anything he had ever dared to imagine.

Will Turner was wakened by his steward with another Marconi message. He had got to bed late and been wakened five times already during the night to receive signals. They had all been the same warning repeated and this was no different, the identical, unspecific but disturbing message, *Submarines off Fastnet.*

Turner squinted at his watch. There was no point in trying to sleep any more and he sent his steward for some tea. He lay in bed a few minutes longer, breathing deeply to clear his head, then rose and crossed to the side window. It was half an hour to dawn by his watch, but any sign of it was obscured by the fog which had settled in again round the *Lusitania*, the first he had seen for five days. Welcome to bloody Ireland, he thought. He shaved and dressed, and swallowed two cups of the scalding tea his steward brought before going up to the bridge.

The Chief Officer was on duty with Second Officer Hefford and Junior Third Officer Bestwick. The *Lusitania* had sailed steadily throughout the night at just under 21 knots and had made good progress, but Fastnet Rock was still some distance ahead. It was west of there that he had made rendezvous on his last crossing with the cruiser *Juno*, under the command of Admiral Hood. *Juno* would be waiting for him, he expected, but with visibility now down to a scant thirty yards the risk of collision was added to the dangers of the Rock itself, and any lurking submarines. He rechecked their course, seeing that it would carry them past Fastnet with a safe margin. Because of the fog, he reduced their speed to 18 knots, which would still take them through the danger area before it was fully light, and he doubled the watch, with two men in the crow's nest, two in the bows and a quartermaster on either wing of the bridge. "What's the hour, Mr. Bisset?" he asked.

Bestwick glanced at the wheelhouse clock. "Just on eight, sir."

"No, it's not. It's just on seven. We're now on Greenwich Time."

Bestwick flushed and moved to the clock. Rotating the brass knob underneath, he turned the hands back an hour. When he looked round, he was surprised to catch the suggestion of a smile on the Captain's face. Following his eyes, he saw Hefford and the very correct First Officer both surreptitiously adjusting their wristwatches. He looked back at Turner and was even more surprised to see his left eye close in a wink. A second later, the Captain was as impassive as ever, and Bestwick could hardly believe it had happened.

Turner regretted having to disturb his passengers so early, but there was one thing left to do before he went down to breakfast, and he gave orders for the foghorn to be sounded at regular intervals. Not only would it warn other ships of the *Lusitania*'s presence, it might serve to contact the *Juno*, which she was otherwise almost bound to miss under these conditions.

Back in his quarters, he read quickly through the Admiralty advices and instructions previously issued to him. They were not much help in this situation, yet he would soon have to come to several decisions. The latest positive instructions from the Admiralty had been the signal to all homeward-bound British ships repeated during the night. As well as the Fastnet warning, it read, "Take Liverpool pilot at bar and avoid headlands. Pass harbors at full speed. Steer mid-channel course." It was a reminder of the earlier general advice, "The danger is greatest in the vicinity of ports and off prominent headlands on the coast." That went on to say, "Important landfalls in this area should be made after dark whenever possible. So far as is consistent with particular trades and state of tides, vessels should make their ports at dawn." That seemed to Turner the most sensible suggestion in all the reams of red tape and impractical nonsense put out by the Admiralty.

He was just starting on his kippers when he was interrupted by a knock at the door. His annoyance vanished when he saw that his caller was Archie Bryce, the Chief Engineer. "Official or unofficial?" he asked.

"Bit of both," Bryce said.

"Come in, then. Fancy a spot of tea? There's a spare cup over there."

Bryce took off his narrow-brimmed cap, lowered his bulk into the chair opposite Turner at the table and poured himself a cupful, adding a quarter of a spoon of sugar as if he were measuring gold dust. Turner watched in amusement as he brushed his bushy mustache to either side and sipped at the tea with formal delicacy, sighed in appreciation and set the cup down carefully, all with the little finger of his massive right hand crooked like a society matron's. "Hope this fog lifts, Will," Bryce said.

"I don't," Turner told him. "The fewer folks who see us till we're safely tied up at the Landing Stage, the happier I'll be."

Bryce frowned. "Things a touch more serious than we thought, are they?" In answer, Turner nodded to the sheaf of signals at the side of the table and, with a glance for permission, Bryce read the top two. His eyebrows rose. "Their Lordships seem to be getting steamed up about something."

"There's nothing that refers specifically to the *Lusitania*," Turner said. "But it doesn't pay to take unnecessary chances."

Bryce nodded. "You're right there." That explained the order during the night to close all watertight doors except those necessary for the operation of the engine room. "But if there's submarines about, why reduce speed?"

"We're still four knots faster than any U-boat," Turner said. "Besides, I don't want to have to hang about off the Mersey Bar in daylight. The ideal time is just after four A.M. tomorrow morning, at high water. Continuing at our present speed, we'll reach St. George's Channel in darkness and be at the bar before four-thirty. I'm cleared to proceed without a pilot, so we can head straight in."

Bryce grunted admiringly. It was typical Turner, efficient and seamanlike, no fuss or panic. "You think those perishers might try to lob a torpedo into us?"

"I doubt it personally," Turner told him. "But there's no saying for sure." He had finished his kippers. He helped himself to a wheaten scone and spread it thickly with marmalade. He chuckled when Bryce frowned again, pursing his mouth, which disappeared under his mustache.

"It's not up to me of course," Bryce said slowly, "but if there's real danger, why don't you put into Queenstown? Or we could sail up the west of Ireland and round through the North Channel."

Turner shook his head. "I wish I could, Archie, but I can't without definite orders. And they're not permitted to send them by wireless in case they're intercepted. That's one of the reasons I'd hoped to make contact with the *Juno*. She might have orders for us, but it looks as though we'll miss her."

Bryce picked up his cup very carefully. "What if the fog clears by midday?"

Turner picked up his own cup and toasted him. "Well then, as our musical friends say, we'll have to play it by ear."

It was nearly eight o'clock when Turner finished breakfast and returned to the bridge. He could see passengers on the boat deck, grouped by the rail. They were watching for the first glimpse of Ireland, but the fog had closed in even more thickly. He made a slight course alteration to 87 degrees east and cut back the speed by another three knots. He trusted his instruments, but after thousands of miles of emptiness it paid to be cautious with land only twenty or so miles ahead.

Walther Schwieger jerked awake. His hands were raised in front of him for protection and, under his leathers, his woolen underclothes were stuck to him with sweat. He knew he had cried out.

As he swung round in his bunk and set his feet on the deck, the green curtain at the door was drawn back and the Cook's Assistant asked, "Did you call, sir?"

"Yes, damn you," Schwieger muttered. "Get me some tea or coffee or something." It required the most intense effort to hold himself steady and, the moment the curtain closed, his whole body was shaken violently by a convulsive spasm.

It was the first time for weeks he had had the dream and

it left him numbed. He had thought he had driven it away or that it was buried so deep it could never return. He shivered and passed his hand over his face, wiping off the film of sweat. When it had been at its worst, he had never betrayed himself like this on patrol. If it had been Hirsch or Kurtz, or Lanz, God forbid, who had heard, any of them would have recognized the symptoms of fear at once.

Schwieger breathed out in short, panted breaths, relaxing the tension in all his muscles. No, he would not call it fear any longer. He knew the cause was strain, cumulative strain, added to by the stress of this frustrating patrol. The U 20 was scavenging for scraps in the wake of the other boats of the Half Flotilla which were now on their way home, having scoured the area and frightened all enemy shipping and coastal defenses into a state of constant readiness. And had the best of the weather. Schwieger's expectations, his high hopes, had been completely thwarted by circumstances over which he had no control. As a ranking ace, Fregattenkapitän Bauer had given him the prime station from St. George's Channel to the Liverpool Bar as his hunting ground, the one he had always wanted for the U 20, but it had been a washout, saved from being a total failure by those two freighters yesterday. Because of the weather and his delayed arrival on station, he had had to rely almost exclusively on luck, and he had never known such a run of ill fortune. That it had to happen with Lanz on board, whose report he could not expect to be remotely favorable, made it a doubly un- fortunate omen for the future and increased the strain.

He looked at his watch. It was just after eight. He had had less than three hours sleep, but he could not hope for more. Nor risk slipping back into the dream. If only he could be certain the involuntary spasms of his muscles would not attack him again and betray him in front of his men.

They had spent all night recharging their batteries and were still on the surface. He could feel the U 20 rocking gently under his stockinged foot. He pulled his boots toward him. As he drew them on, the Cook's Mate scratched on the panel outside the door and came in with a steaming mug, which he set down on the table. He did not leave and hovered anxiously.

Schwieger wondered why he was waiting, then smelled

something and took up the mug. It was filled with strong black tea flavored with powdered cloves and two or three spoonfuls of sugar, the cook's special brew. From somewhere he had even found a slice of lemon. Schwieger sipped the tea, wincing as it seared the roof of his mouth and his throat. "That goes right where it's needed," he said. "Just what I wanted."

The man could not hide his pleasure. "Whatever we can do for you always, Captain," he said. He came to attention and left.

Schwieger put down the mug and stamped his feet more firmly into his boots. There was still some water in the bowl. He dipped the cloth in it and held it to the back of his neck, then wiped it over his face. He could feel the drag of stubble. It was not the custom to shave until they were on the last leg of the journey home. He hesitated, opened his razor and in a few sure strokes shaved off the worst of the stubble. He felt fresher and more awake when it was done. The tea was not quite so scalding and he drank it off, panting as the heat traced its way down through his chest. He took his scarf and cap and went out.

With the hatches open, the air below decks was fresh, but there was a lingering smell of the crew's breakfast. Apart from the machinists and electricians, everyone was resting or at routine tasks. From forward, he heard Hansel barking shrilly. The little dachshund had placed himself in front of the space where Maria nursed her pups and barked warningly when anyone passed too near. Maria had begun to show herself occasionally, trotting the full length of the corridor and back while he stood guard. At each appearance she was thoroughly spoiled.

From behind him in the crew's mess room, he could hear laughter and someone singing. Since the two sinkings on the previous day, the entire atmosphere on board had altered. Pride had been satisfied and everything was again like a normal sortie. He made for the after hatch, pausing to help himself to some bread and a piece of sausage from the galley before going up the ladder.

Although it was lighter outside, the fog was still all round them and visibility no more than sixty or seventy feet. There was no indication that it might lift. He had taken the

U-boat further out to sea during the night, away from the normal lanes of traffic to lessen the risk of accidental collision and let more of his crew rest. He himself had stayed on duty with a skeleton watch, seeing and hearing nothing. Seeing nothing? That of course was what had brought back the terror. A submarine usually spent most of a patrol on the surface, slipping underwater only for concealment in defense or attack. On this sortie, because of the increased activity of enemy patrols and then the weather, the U 20 had been submerged for much longer periods, hour after hour. Even on the surface, she had been wrapped in clammy fog in which one could not trust one's eyes or ears. Senses became disoriented, stretching the nerves beyond endurance. Schwieger had limited spells of lookout to two hours, but he himself had stood watch for most of the night. He had had not one glimpse of the sky or the stars. It had been foolish, he now realized, a kind of bravado to expose himself to such strain. That and the memory he could not forget of the second freighter going down in the fog, the hideous wallowings and groaning as she sank, the thought of what was happening to her crew in that nightmare, torpedoed without warning, had freed the dream from his subconscious. As Rudi would say. Yet to know the cause was little comfort.

He had finished his improvised breakfast and made himself smile as he went round the lookouts, with a word or two for each of them. Coming round the conning tower, he paused and frowned, seeing Lippe at the bows. He had been stationed there when Schwieger went below. He called up to Lammeier, who was petty officer of the watch. "Why hasn't Lippe been relieved?"

"He doesn't want to be, sir," Lammeier told him. "He asked for a double spell."

The big torpedoman was crouching as far forward as it was possible to be, supporting himself with one hand on the sawtoothed beak which had been mounted at the prow as a protection against nets. He had brought his fishing line, but it lay beside him, unused. He was gazing off into the fog, in the direction of Ireland. He was aware of none of his surroundings, only of the memory of one small cottage with its smell of burning turf, the cry of gulls outside and a girl with a green shawl wrapped over her shoulders smiling to him. There was a memory of tenderness and rage, and the remembered vision of her body, white and slim, glimmering in the shadows. Had he really seen that? He cursed his stupid mind. He could remember details, scents, the feel of things. He snatched at moments, but the more he tried to piece them together, the less clear they became, the more confused. And without them, without even that, he felt empty and lonely in a way he could not explain.

He heard a step and looked up to see the commander beside him, watching him. "Good morning, Lippe," Schwieger said.

"Good morning, sir," Lippe answered. "Nothing to report."

Schwieger smiled. "No. You'd better get below. I'll stay here until your relief comes."

Lippe felt a surge of panic. In the torpedo room with the others, cramped and with no privacy, he could remember nothing. His mind could only cope with one situation at a time. "I'm fine, Captain," he explained. "I'd rather complete my watch."

"I understand," Schwieger told him quietly. "But it won't do you any good. And in the meantime a whole British cruiser squadron could come past and you wouldn't even hear it. I want you fit and rested. Get below."

Lippe reluctantly saw the truth of it. He rose to his feet and saluted. "At your orders, Captain." He moved slowly past Schwieger toward the open hatch, but stopped. He half turned, his head lowered, his embarrassment almost grotesque in someone so bulky. "Do you remember? Please? What color were her eyes?"

"They were black, very black."

Lippe straightened in relief that his undependable memory was confirmed. He smiled, nodding happily, and went down through the hatch.

Ten minutes later, Schwieger crossed through central control. He paused to check the barometer and said to Hirsch, "Let me have a report on our fuel position." He went back to his cabin and, while he waited, read through the appraisal of the situation he had written in his log the previous evening. His conclusions then were still valid.

Hirsch came to him, but not alone. Behind him was Lanz,

who had sensed some decision was to be reached. "We are in no immediate danger," Hirsch reported, "but fuel consumption was high on the outward journey. We have used approximately two-fifths of our supply to date."

"What if we advance to the Liverpool Bar and then double back round the south of Ireland?"

Hirsch was troubled. "Considering the detours we may be forced to make on our return journey, I doubt if that would be feasible, sir. And still leave us with sufficient fuel for an emergency."

"That's what I was afraid of," Schwieger said. He thought for a moment. "Very well. Tell Haupert to prepare a course for the voyage home."

As Hirsch turned to the door, Lanz broke in. "Wait a minute! Isn't this something we should discuss?"

Schwieger and Hirsch looked at him. Hirsch was plainly shocked that anyone should query the commander's decision, but Schwieger could see that Lanz was serious, and also anxious, for some reason. He nodded to Hirsch, who went out, bristling with disapproval.

Schwieger leaned back in his chair. "What is there to discuss, Herr Lanz?"

He seemed so sure of himself that Lanz hesitated. "You've made up your mind to go home?"

Schwieger had been half expecting a reaction from Lanz and had thought out his position very carefully during the night. If there had not been the two freighters, which gave the U 20 a score of over twelve thousand tons of enemy shipping on this sortie, he would have been reluctant to order a return yet. Now, however, he could do so with no loss of face. "I don't believe I have any option, Herr Lanz."

"And simply abort this patrol?" Lanz queried. "You cannot!"

"Cannot?" Schwieger's voice was deadly calm.

Lanz bit back what he had been about to say. His lips pursed and he wetted the lower one with the tip of his tongue. "You are in command, Herr Kapitänleutnant," he acknowledged. "But have you fully examined the circumstances and alternatives?"

"There is absolutely no point in staying on," Schwieger said. "The fog shows no sign of lifting. It makes any plan of campaign futile. Our only successful attacks so far were given to us by a near miracle, and we cannot logically expect that to be repeated. And you heard Hirsch."

"Hirsch only said it would be impossible to double back round Ireland. You could proceed to the Irish Sea, to the Mersey Bar to intercept those enemy transports, in accordance with your orders. Weather conditions may be much better than here. You could complete your patrol and return through the North Channel."

They were arguments which Schwieger had already put to himself. "The barometer reading does not permit us to predict any improvement in the near future in this entire area," Schwieger told him. "I have considered that alternative, but the Irish Sea is scoured constantly by enemy surveillance ships, trawlers and destroyers, which in fog are impossible to identify quickly enough. We would have the continuous danger of being surprised and having to navigate submerged all the time."

"You could concentrate on night attacks. That's when most of those large transports enter and leave the Mersey."

Schwieger was growing irritated by the man's insistence. "Herr Lanz, I have a responsibility to preserve my command. It would be madness to wait in poor visibility outside Liverpool to attack large enemy ships, not knowing whether or not they have a destroyer escort. In any case, in my experience, they are always escorted, particularly at night."

"Is it not even worth the attempt?" Lanz asked, then tried another tack. "Apart from anything else, the North Channel is the shortest route home from our present position."

"I do not think you have traveled it by submarine," Schwieger said.

"No," Lanz admitted.

"Then let me assure you that at all costs I want to avoid a return journey through the North Channel. The area is a maze of shifting minefields for which we have no maps. The inshore lanes are continuously patrolled death traps. Surveillance is at its height in the Firth of Clyde, and the North Channel itself is only twelve miles wide between Tor Point and the Mull of Kintyre. To attempt it when there is an available alternative would be criminally irresponsible." He stood up, ending the discussion.

"If you leave this hunting ground, the entire southwest will be open to enemy shipping!" Lanz protested. "The other boats of this patrol have already turned home. You know that!"

"I know that, Herr Lanz," Schwieger said quietly. "But how do you?"

Lanz hesitated again. "The situation was fully explained to me when I was briefed at Naval Headquarters," he said. "The distinction conferred on the U 20 was also impressed on me, that she would be the only one of our U-boats left on station in this sector."

"Exactly," Schwieger agreed. "Then you will also have realized how vital it is not to throw away any of the limited number of boats at our disposal on an unnecessary gamble."

"So you still intend to bring this patrol to an end?"

Schwieger nodded. "I do." Yet, while Lanz spoke, he had been thinking, prompted by the older man's unconcealed disappointment. During the night, they had cruised to the open water south of the Bristol Channel and were now heading back for the Coningbeg Light. He had not forgotten the report which the Mate of the Reserve would eventually submit. "We are in no hurry, however," he said. "We shall scout the approaches to major harbors and coastal landmarks on our route. I still have three torpedoes in hand, and shall try to make the best use of them."

Neil Leach came out of his pantry on the shelter deck. It was midmorning. The fog had faded away unexpectedly and it had suddenly turned into a beautiful day. The sea was calm and sparkling in the bright sunshine. Some passengers were below, beginning their packing, but many more were on deck, crowding the portside rails for a sight of land. The *Lusitania* was sailing parallel to the shore. Spirits which had been dampened by the fog were revived and there was laughter and a new excitement, although some grumbled that the Captain was staying so far out that the Irish coast was only a dark blur.

Leach felt the lightening of spirit himself, adding to his own excitement. He had had a fairly lonely crossing, finding it more or less impossible to fit in with the other stewards and crew members. Their interests and preoccupations were just not his, and he disliked waiting on passengers who were his own sort but treated him like a menial. He looked forward to the whole business being over. It would be three miserable weeks out of his life, a distasteful lesson with nothing to show for it.

In his resentment he had begun to feel alien from everyone else on the ship. At first he had cursed Gus and Trude and Kelly, or whatever his real name was, every time he remembered how they had manipulated him, yet as the days went by and he felt more and more estranged from everyone, he began to miss the good fellowship of those weeks in New York. What, after all, was so bad about what Gus and Kelly were doing, what they wanted him to do? It was only information about morale and the different types of passenger. He had overreacted because of war hysteria. The Germans had treated him quite decently when he had been interned, had even let him go. Even in the matter of the photographs, what was so wrong in confirming the existence of guns which everyone knew were there?

He had begun to think of his return to New York also. He was only slightly disturbed that Kelly might cut up rough. He thought more of Trude. He would have to go back to the lodgings for his trunk, and she would not want to see him. How much more pleasant it would be if she were waiting. If he claimed his reward, she could not refuse him now. If he brought photographs, he would even collect his bonus from Kelly. They would not need to be anything specific. He could take a shot of the locked doors of the forward section to prove they had remained closed. Not his fault. The more he thought about it, the more he realized he could end up having the last laugh on all of them. He had no more illusions about Trude. He just wanted her to yield to him, to use her and get her out of his system, a sweet revenge.

He was standing by the pantry door, his right arm down by his side unobtrusively holding the Kodak camera. Further along from him among the people in the open bay were a number of army reservists in a variety of uniforms. Almost without thinking, he raised the camera, focused and clicked the shutter. He had committed himself.

One of the reservists noticed him and waved, grinning. Leach swallowed, lifted his hand and waved back. In a moment, the whole group had turned and was posing for him, among them the tall Canadian passenger, Fletcher, very spruce in the uniform of a British army captain with a Sam Browne belt and medal ribbons. Kelly would be interested in that. It was a gift, and Leach took the photograph, smiling. He moved off toward the enclosed forward section. Light was slanting in and picked out the gun mounting concealed in the deck which had interested Gus. No one was paying him any attention and he snapped that, too.

It was all so amazingly easy. The doors to the forward section were locked as usual, but unguarded. The masters-at-arms, like many others of the crew, were busy at one or another of the many routine tasks which had to be completed before the liner docked. Standing near the doors, finishing a surreptitious cigarette, was the older steward, Albert Biggs, and Leach suddenly had a brilliant idea. He would rouse no suspicion whatever if he appeared to be photographing Biggs while actually framing on the doors. "Stand still a minute, Albert!" he called.

Biggs tucked the hand with the cigarette behind his back and smiled, posing until the shot was taken. "What's this for?" he chuckled

"Oh, just for my scrapbook," Leach told him. "Souvenir." He moved closer and looked past Biggs through the bars of the door. "This is where the guns are kept, isn't it?" Biggs grinned. "Well, isn't this where they store the guns?"

"Guns?" a voice echoed behind him

Leach's heart missed a beat and he glanced round to see Billy Williams, the senior master-at-arms, coming toward them.

"What about the guns?" Williams asked.

"Neil was inquirin' if this is where they're kept," Biggs chuckled.

"The passengers are always asking about them," Leach said.

"Load of rubbish!" Biggs snorted. "There's nothin' there, stands to reason."

Leach could not stop himself asking, "Why not?"

"They'd need a trained crew to man them," Biggs shrugged. "There's nobody on board like that. Besides, they'd never waste big guns where they're no use."

"That's a fact," Williams agreed. "They might be in there. Who knows? But we'd need tackle to shift them. If we were challenged, it would take at least twenty minutes to get just one of them mounted, and by then it would be too late. So we might as well not have any."

"I see," Leach said. It was something that had never occurred to him. He nodded to them and turned away.

"I'll have that," Williams said. He reached out and tugged the camera from Leach's hand. Leach's mind went blank and he stared at the master-at-arms, who waited a long moment, then asked, "Aren't you going to object?"

Leach realized he had made a bad mistake. His silence was almost an admission of guilt, that he had something to hide. "Well, of course!" he protested. "That's my personal property!"

"Taking photographs, were you?"

"Well—well, yes," Leach stumbled. "No harm in that, is there? It's a hobby of mine."

"M'hm." Williams considered him. He had not forgotten the strange incident at the start of the voyage when three "journalists" for the pro-German press had been found in Leach's pantry in New York Harbor. Since then he'd been in no other trouble. He was not too popular, evidently thinking himself a cut above the people he worked with, but he'd kept his nose clean. Still, he was a marked man. "You'd better come with me."

Leach's throat was dry. "Where to?"

"We'll have a word with Captain Anderson. You come too, Albert."

"What's this about?" Leach demanded. Williams only jerked his head and moved off.

Biggs had a last puff at his cigarette and buried it in the sand of the fire bucket beside him. "You're makin' a lot of fuss about nothin', Billy," he complained, but sighed and followed them.

Leach was fighting panic, telling himself it would be all right as long as he stayed calm. He had a long experience in pleading innocence in minor misdemeanors and could be very convincing. He had done nothing overtly criminal, nothing that could be proved. All he had to say was "I don't understand what this is all about." He couldn't have asked

552

for anyone better than Anderson, who was his own sort and would give him the benefit of the doubt.

Staff Captain Anderson, however, was very busy. His desk was littered with paperwork, the hundred and one details which had to be dealt with before docking. Turner, as usual, was happy to leave all that to him. As well as passenger and port formalities, there were the more perishable items of cargo to be checked and the cargo to be shifted, to allow the most urgent sections to be unloaded first. Chief among these were three thousand sacks of mail which had to be brought up from the mail hold this afternoon. He was in the middle of arranging that when Williams reported and handed him the Kodak. "Leach?" he queried. "Him again, is it?" Williams explained the circumstances, the oddness of the temporary steward taking photographs and asking about the guns. "I don't much like the sound of it," Anderson admitted. "It may be nothing of course. Still, I'm far too busy to go into it now. The port detectives can question him after we dock."

"What am I to do with him, sir?" Williams asked.

"Oh—shove him in the brig," Anderson said exasperatedly, and put the camera in a drawer in his desk.

Leach was bemused at being led down and locked into one of the *Lusitania*'s cells, a converted lower deck cabin. "This is ridiculous!" he complained. "I haven't done anything wrong!"

"Only till tomorrow," Williams told him. "If there's nothing to it like you say, then it'll be all over and no hard feelings."

Leach sat on the bed. How stupid to get himself into this, but it could be much worse. They had nothing on him, really, only a vague suspicion. He would protest his innocence, tell them about being interned. He had no cause to love Germany. He was only a young Britisher, eager for a glimpse of his homeland. The photographs of passengers and fellow crewmen were to remind him of his trip, harmless, no one could imagine he was a spy. He had cheered himself up. He had always managed to charm himself out of unpleasant situations.

Yet something was nagging at him, and all at once he remembered the shot of the concealed gun mounting. He had been proud of its clarity. When the film was developed, no one could mistake it for anything but what it was and there was no way he could explain it . . . He had started to tremble. He was facing prison or a firing squad! It was Trude's fault. She had betrayed him again, the thought of her waiting for him. Dirty lying cheating bitch . . . He was leaning forward with his elbows on his knees. He lowered his face to his hands and began to whimper.

Livvy walked slowly by herself on the promenade deck. Peter was with the Crompton boys and she had left Diana in the playroom with Lady Allan's daughters, who would take care of her till lunch. Matt had gone off for half an hour to talk to the group of reservists he was leading and had promised to meet her back here. The relief of being close to him again, since she had accepted the inevitable, was indescribable.

She had been talking to Marie Depage and seized the opportunity to ask her advice. As a girl she had helped her father in his dispensary and learned to be useful in other ways, applying dressings and bandaging minor injuries. She might have gone into medicine herself but for Matt. She had been thinking she ought to volunteer for nursing or Red Cross work, something like that. Madame Depage had surprised her, however, by telling her she would possibly be more useful for the moment by helping her father again and looking after her children. There were many local organizations she could join, which were often short-staffed. Later, if the war dragged on, she might wish to think again.

Livvy was not sure she agreed with the advice. If more people were one day to be needed, it was better they were trained now rather than later. That much she had learned from Matt. She felt someone take her arm familiarly and looked round. It was Elbert Hubbard.

He was wearing his long overcoat in spite of the warmth of the day, but had changed his floppy hat for a checked cap. It made his thick hair stand out like bushy wings over his ears. Livvy smiled, yet was puzzled to see that he seemed agitated. He drew her closer to his side. "Livvy, please be my protectress!" he whispered. "Save me from that intolerable woman."

Advancing toward them was the tall, angular but attractive figure of Theodate Pope. She was in her late forties and unmarried, a rather remarkable woman from Connecticut, a leading progressive, an architect and a noted expert in psychical research. She wore a severe suit with a buttoned hip-length jacket and a plain straw hat. Livvy had attended a talk she had given on board on spiritualism and the investigation of hauntings which had disturbed her but left her unconvinced.

"Because I once met Madame Blavatsky, she thinks I'm a secret Theosophist and ripe for conversion," Hubbard whispered. "She wants me to spend the afternoon with her talking about clairvoyance and spooks."

Theodate Pope swept up to them. "Ah—there you are, Mr. Hubbard," she declared in a tone which meant he would not escape again.

"You're just in time, Miss Pope," Livvy said brightly.

"Indeed, Mrs. Fletcher?"

"Mr. Hubbard and I are locked in disagreement," Livvy pouted. "It's too bad of him. Especially since he's helping to design my wardrobe."

Theodate Pope frowned. "Your wardrobe?"

"Why, yes," Livvy smiled "That dear man, Mr. Frohman, has offered to introduce me to all his theatrical friends. Naturally one must dress suitably. To be in the correct fashion is so important, don't you think?"

"I do not give it too much thought," Theodate Pope said.

"Oh, but you're right! One mustn't be too frivolous in wartime. Although it is up to us women to provide a little pleasure and distraction, don't you think? But Mr. Hubbard is being so naughty. He has perfect taste in clothes and I was depending on him."

Hubbard's eyes were twinkling. "I still think osprey plumes are a more fetching trimming for an afternoon hat than peacock feathers," he stated firmly. "Even white ones."

"I can't abide feathers at all," Livvy retorted with a shiver. "Except on toques. You can't have a toque without a feather. But you can only wear them with these new Turkish trousers, which are simply too daring, don't you think?"

"I really have no opinion on the matter," Theodate Pope told her stiffly. "If you will excuse me." She nodded curtly and marched away toward the verandah café.

"I don't believe she wanted to talk to us," Livvy said.

"No, siree," Hubbard agreed. He hugged Livvy's arm to him. "My name'll be mud in certain quarters after this—but it was worth it." His impish smile became a chuckle and their laughter startled some of the people near them. Matt heard it as he came up the companionway. Hubbard saw him and sighed. "Here's the only man to whom I would willingly surrender you." He swept off his cap and bowed over Livvy's hand.

"Will we see you at lunch?" Livvy asked him.

"I'll ask the steward if we can be at your table," Hubbard said. "My dear wife will enjoy that." He waved a hand to Matt and bustled off.

Livvy watched him fondly as he searched for his wife among the older people in the lounging chairs spaced out along the deck. "If he was twenty years younger, I think I might have a rival," Matt murmured.

"I think you might," Livvy smiled.

Matt kissed her cheek. "Give me a couple of more minutes," he said. "I want to run down to the cabin and change out of this uniform."

"Don't do it on my account," Livvy told him. "You look very dashing."

He grinned. "That's just it. I feel like a tin soldier. I'll put it on again when I have to. Won't be long."

"I'll come with you," Livvy said.

In the cabin, Matt tossed his peaked cap onto the window seat. Livvy was taking off her brimless hat of blue gathered velvet and laid it on top of the tallboy. Matt unbuckled his belt and Sam Browne shoulder strap and shrugged out of them. Livvy released the silk sash at her waist. Matt turned to face her and, as he jerked out his tie and unknotted it, he saw her untie the chiffon scarf at her throat. She left it hanging loose, as he had left his tie. She was wearing a casual thigh-length tunic of pale blue shantung silk over a cross-over blouse and an apple-green pegtop skirt, the deep, pleated tiers over the hips narrowing to a hobble style at the hem, caught up in front to reveal her black patent shoes and the openwork clocks of her black silk stockings. She was watching him, smiling very faintly.

Matt pulled off his tie and Livvy flicked away the little

scarf which had filled in her low neckline, veiling the shadowed cleft of her bosom. He unbuttoned his tunic, dropping it on the window seat behind him, and she unbuttoned hers, draping it across the bed. Very slowly he unfastened his shirt to the waist and she unclipped her wrapover blouse at the sides, slipped it off and laid it by her tunic. Above the flounced tiers of her skirt, all she wore was a chemise with slender straps supporting its lace bodice, whose cups molded her high, full breasts.

He stood perfectly still, watching her as she waited. Slowly he drew off his shirt and let it fall to the floor beside him. He was bare from the waist up. Livvy crossed to the door and pushed home the brass bolt to lock it. She turned and, just as slowly, smiling, lowered the straps of her chemise.

On the portside wing of the bridge, Will Turner scowled at the bright sky which his passengers had greeted with such pleasure. The fog had simply dissolved and visibility was clear to the far horizon. The sound of laughter drifted up to him from the boat deck as he stumped back into the wheelhouse. The barometer was still rising, which meant the likelihood of continuing fine weather. He glanced at the spirit level on the binnacle. The sea was so calm, the level showed scarcely a tremor of roll, which the deck had already told him.

Everything should have combined to make it an ideal homecoming, yet he had a sense of uneasiness, almost the same feeling as on that night months before when he had raced the *Transylvania* into Queenstown under threat of attack. He had no orders to do that now and could not do so without permission. Besides, he could not set a course for it, as he was not precisely sure where he was. He had a fair idea of his position, but could not get an exact fix until he could identify a definite landmark. And that was impossible unless he steered nearer to land, against which both his instructions and his common sense cautioned him. Admiralty instructions, for fear of U-boats, and his common sense, since the fog might blind him again, leaving him too close to a notoriously rocky and irregular coast.

At least he should by now be past Fastnet and the submarines reported west of it, although the uncertainty disturbed him. There was one thing he could do. "Increase speed to eighteen knots," he told First Officer Jones.

He felt more confident as the *Lusitania* responded, easing up to her faster cruising speed. It was more than enough to shake off any U-boat which might be on her track and, in spite of the time lost in the early morning and always provided she met with no more adverse weather, she should still arrive at the bar at high water and slip straight over into the safety of the Mersey.

Chapter 29

THE U 20 SAILED NORTH AT GOOD SPEED UNDER THE POWER of her diesels. The weather was brightening and, as she left the open sea behind, the fog receded, with only a few scattered wisps and spirals remaining. Ironic, Schwieger thought. It had begun to clear almost as soon as he decided to return home.

He was in central control checking their course with Haupert. His intention was to scout the areas of the main Irish south coast ports, Waterford and Cork Harbour, leading to the naval base at Queenstown, before swinging further out to avoid coastal patrols, and to slip through the dangerous stretch west of the North Channel at night. He was aware of Lanz watching him, leaning against the ladder to the conning tower, and could imagine what he was thinking. *Since the weather's improving, why not continue the patrol?* The answer was that fuel was now the deciding factor. They had little to spare for side trips.

He heard a whistle from the voice tube. Scherb was officer of the watch and reported something approaching from the direction of the Coningbeg light. Lanz was already halfway up the ladder as Schwieger started for it.

A fresh wind was blowing away the last shreds of fog and creating a gentle swell which the submarine cut through like a thoroughbred. The approaching craft was still a considerable distance away. Scherb handed the telescope to Schwieger, who refocused it and after a minute gave it to Lanz. "What do you think?"

"A steamer," Lanz said. "She's rigged like a trawler."

"Patrol boat?"

"Could be."

The U 20 submerged unhurriedly and gracefully to periscope depth. As if to mock him now that the patrol was as good as over, Schwieger saw that visibility was suddenly better than at any time since leaving Emden. Each detail of the approaching steamer stood out sharp and clear, although diminutive through distance and the effect of the lens. The hump at the bows could only be a gun emplacement, matching another at the stern, undoubtedly a patrol boat. It could not have failed to spot the U 20, yet had neither changed course to challenge nor increased its speed.

Schwieger glanced round and saw that Lanz and Scherb were puzzled. "He's boxing clever," he explained. "His gunsights are on us at this very moment and he's enticing us to come a little nearer, a little nearer, and as soon as we're in range . . ." He turned back to the eyepiece. "In the meantime, he's signaling every other antisubmarine boat within twenty miles to come and help him bottle us up." As he spoke, he swiveled the stick through 180 degrees, searching for any telltale break in the surface of the water. "Of course there's always the possibility that he's a decoy for a British submarine and that it's closing on us." Scherb's startled intake of breath was audible.

"Starboard full rudder!" Schwieger ordered abruptly. "Ahead Full." As the helmsman spun the wheel and the order was relayed to Hirsch, Schwieger swung the stick to keep the patrol boat in view. Two plumes of smoke belched from it and, seconds later, two high-velocity shells fountained into the water on the U 20's port beam, well over a hundred yards short. His maneuver had triggered the enemy into firing prematurely. "Take her down now!" he called. "Dive!" He straightened and Scherb ran the periscope in.

The U-boat's nose dipped as her forward ballast tanks flooded, and she glided down. At fifty feet they heard the twin slap and whoosh as two more shells plowed into the water closer to where she had been, but not close enough at that depth even to rock her. "Trim her off at seventy-five feet," Schwieger said.

He was smiling, having answered the patrol boat's captain with a double bluff, the first that he had turned starboard to intercept, and the second that he was making for St. George's Channel and the Irish Sea. For the next two or three hours the armed trawler would stay on the alert, waiting for an attack that never came, while directing the attention of the rest of the auxiliary patrol to the area further east. Whereas, as soon as he was steady at his chosen depth, Schwieger intended to bear away slightly west of his original course and travel submerged for the next two hours. Anyone hunting him would hopefully be steaming in the opposite direction. It would mean he would miss Waterford. However, given luck and the clear spell continuing, he could surface and take a long, leisurely look at the approaches to Cork Harbour and Queenstown.

Although only slightly above medium height, King George had a commanding presence, which came partly from his bearing and partly from the direct look of his bright blue eyes, inherited from both parents and from his grandmother, Queen Victoria.

He had a habit of frowning as he spoke, which perhaps made what he said seem more significant than it was. His voice, as Grey had warned, was gruff and forceful, yet House detected an underlying warmth which helped to put him more at ease. It was welcome after his fairly intimidating arrival past the guards of the Household Brigade, the ushers and flunkeys in the two-hundred-foot-long Marble Hall, hung with full-length royal portraits, the divided Grand Staircase with its intricate gilded balustrade leading to the state rooms and endless vistas of ever more imposing corridors, galleries, drawing rooms and reception rooms. The King had received them in the 1844 Room, commemorating a visit by Czar Nicholas I of Russia. Again House was grateful, for it was of more human proportions than many others, a pleasing apartment in white and gold, with a crimson carpet and amber pillars. It was here that ambassadors presented their letters of credence to the Court of St. James's, and King George had chosen it as a gesture to the President's confidential adviser.

The ritual greetings and messages of goodwill had been passed, although House's audience was unofficial and informal. Afterwards the King acknowledged the difficulty for neutral nations at a time when war engulfed almost the whole of Europe. In contrast to Kaiser Wilhelm he was neither boastful nor aggressive, and seemed to appreciate both House and Grey joining frankly in the conversation. He went on to speak gratefully of the tacit help given to the Allies by many people in America, in particular of the multi-million-dollar loan floated by the Morgan Bank for the purchase of arms. House was in a dilemma, since it was not a topic on which he could comment, even unofficially. He stepped round it gracefully by saying how much many of his countrymen appreciated their British heritage, the sights and sounds of England, as he had rediscovered for himself that morning at Kew Gardens.

"Ah, yes," the King said. "Very beautiful. They were laid out for the palace of a predecessor of mine, George the Third. You'll have heard of him, no doubt." House and Grey smiled, and the King chuckled. "Well, he may not have known how to deal with a revolution, but he certainly knew a lot about gardens. The Queen, my wife, is very fond of them." He paused, frowning. "Quite a few of your fellow Americans seem devoted to nature. Ambassador Page, Astor. And of course, President Roosevelt. He's almost as keen a bird fancier as Sir Edward here. A fine man, very fine man." As House had spent much of his political life fighting the Republican Roosevelt and all his policies, he confined himself to a restrained inclination of the head. "He attended my father's funeral in person," King George went on. "The gesture was much appreciated. It's not generally known, but they were very close friends. Never met, but corresponded over the years on all sorts of matters."

"I remember his late Majesty, King Edward, telling me that Theodore Roosevelt was his one and only pen friend," Grey said.

"Pen friend. Exactly." The King smiled briefly, then frowned. "I wonder what he's making of this bloody business?" Sir Edward coughed discreetly and the King waved his hand. "Oh, I realize we're not supposed to talk about it, but how can one avoid it?"

"How indeed, Your Majesty?" House agreed.

"Yes," King George said, "Mr. Roosevelt sends us a copy of each of his books, as soon as it comes out. Your President Wilson writes books too, doesn't he?"

"He does, sir," House confirmed. "Though of quite a different character."

Grey smiled, but the King did not recognize the humor

behind it. "I can imagine that," he muttered. "I pray that America is not drawn into this mincing machine—for that is all it is." He shook his head. As a youth he had envied and admired his dashing Cousin Willy. "How Germany, which was once the most civilized of nations, could stoop to the acts of barbarism of which it stands condemned, I cannot comprehend. Atrocities, and now this asphyxiating gas. And the worst of it is, the only answer is to reply in kind."

"As you say, Your Majesty, it is appalling in a civilized world," House agreed. "Yet we may hope that the President's efforts and the good faith of both sides may serve to bring it to a speedier conclusion."

The King glanced at Grey, who waited expressionlessly. "It's not for me to comment, I suppose," the King said. "However, I don't think we can depend on much good faith from my cousin the Kaiser and his High Command. Even at sea, they have shown themselves ready to break all rules if it gives them an inch of advantage. And Lord knows their submarine campaign has given them more than that." Grey coughed again and King George growled, "Dammit, Sir Edward, it's true! They have spread their policy of Frightfulness to the oceans in an attempt to cut this island off! They are like cornered rats biting at anything that comes within reach."

"There have been some unfortunate occurrences, sir," House conceded.

King George was brought up short, reminded that he was talking to the representative of a strictly neutral country. "There certainly have been, Colonel," he said. "Each day I wait for news of some fresh atrocity, especially since that disgraceful warning was published. They're excusing themselves in advance for sinking passenger ships. And we all know which one they'd like to get."

"That is naturally only an assumption, sir," Grey put in.

"Look at your morning papers. They're full of it. All speculation, you say, but the Kaiser has always hated the *Lusitania*, ever since she snatched the Atlantic Ribbon from the *Kaiser Wilhelm II*." He turned to House. "Your President's attitude is all very correct and proper, Colonel, as it should be. But suppose they should sink the *Lusitania* with American passengers on board?"

Colonel House was disconcerted with the King's blue eyes

fixed on him. He could not in the circumstances answer as forthrightly as he had when Grey had asked him virtually the same question earlier. "I'm afraid it is too hypothetical, sir. We are all agreed that no civilized Power could permit the carrying out of such an act."

King George was conscious that the Colonel was again hedging. "Possibly," he said. "We can only pray that she is well-protected."

Turner took the cup and saucer without looking. It was only when he tried to drink and nearly overbalanced that he discovered he had been leaning forward, gazing out through the window. He eased back and made himself appear more relaxed, as an example to his junior officers.

But where was the *Juno*? He would give a year's seniority for one glimpse of her at this moment. Or of any one vessel of the auxiliary patrol; a bloody converted fishing boat would do. Anything, just as long as it was a sign the navy had thrown out some defenses along their route. U-boats seldom if ever attacked when there were patrol boats about. But there was nothing, not a single solitary hull to be seen in any direction. He could not ever remember being so close to land and seeing so little evidence of traffic. With ports and small harbors all along the coast, it was almost uncanny.

You're getting too old for this sort of thing, Will, he told himself. You're getting anxious. It was over fifty years since, to escape being made into a preacher, he had run away to sea and that first voyage, which ended in shipwreck. Not even that had put him off and since then he had been in every imaginable situation. Except this one. But this was a new kind of nightmare for everyone. No wonder Paddy Dow had a breakdown.

Last night one of the passengers had the effrontery to ask if he intended to fly the Stars and Stripes. Turner reckoned he'd managed to keep his temper fairly well. As if the *Lusitania* were some tramp steamer that could be disguised by flying a false neutral flag. She was unique, nothing like her at present throughout the Seven Seas. She could not be mistaken for anything other than herself, and therein lay her major defense.

Pointless to worry. As he had told inquirers this morning,

the U-boat reported off Fastnet was certainly far behind now, even if it was dogging them. He kept to himself the nagging thought that, given the time it was first reported and the dense fog, it could by now be anywhere.

Where the hell was that escort they'd promised would always be waiting?

He finished his midmorning tea and, as he laid the cup and saucer on the window shelf, heard a knock at the wheelhouse door. It was the assistant Marconi operator, McCormick, who came in and saluted. A carroty-haired young man, he had brought a signal just received. Turner took it with a nod of thanks. This surely was what he had been waiting for, the order to divert through the North Channel or into Queenstown. He opened it, read it and passed it without comment to First Officer Jones.

It was from the Admiralty. "Submarine active in southern part of Irish Channel, last heard of twenty miles south of Coningbeg Light Vessel. Make certain *Lusitania* gets this."

Jones swallowed and looked up, dismayed. "So where is it, then, sir? Behind us—or in front of us?"

"You pays your money, Mr. Jones," Turner said, "and you takes your choice." He nodded again to the assistant Marconi man. "Acknowledge."

The signal was passed round the other officers on the bridge. When it was handed to Bestwick, he heard the Captain speaking to him. "Cut round the watch, Bisset. Tell them to keep an extra sharp lookout."

"Aye, aye, sir." As Bestwick left, he saw the First Officer bend to the voice tube to call the two most important men up in the crow's nest.

Turner had swung back to the window. His officers, he knew, were waiting for his decision on what action was to be taken, if any. The curse was, those Admiralty instructions which had to be obeyed robbed a man of initiative. But for that, from here he might have put on all speed and made a wide sweep out into the Atlantic, to come up through the Bristol Channel at night from the south. He could still have timed it to reach the bar during high water. He could not even run for Queenstown, the obvious refuge, without instructions. The only danger there was the short period of waiting outside until someone arrived to guide him in through the mine-free channel. He could not even send for advice or permission to divert, since he was under the strictest orders not to use the radio for outgoing signals. He was completely boxed in.

Manifestly he could not depend on any help from the Admiralty. He was on his own. The most sensible thing was probably to do nothing, certainly not to flap, but to stick to the original plan. Yet the Coningbeg light was directly ahead, some ninety-odd miles away, and to enter St. George's Channel he must sail south of it, exactly where the U-boat was reported. At most, at present speed, that would take another five and a half hours. It would just be growing dark, but not dark enough. He certainly did not want to arrive there any earlier. One of the pieces of official advice recommended irregular changes of course to confuse a submarine's aim. It was difficult to swing a vessel the size and height of the *Lusitania* about too sharply, without causing discomfort to passengers and possible damage, yet it would give the illusion of something positive being done and delay their progress slightly.

"Maintain present speed," he ordered, "but warn the engine room to stay at full pressure in case we have to get a move on."

Matt and Livvy rose from his bed. She felt sleek and contented, like a pampered cat. During the night, their love-making had been hungry, at times fierce, but this morning they had been at ease with each other again, more tender, matching each other's quieter rhythm. Livvy purred in her throat and pressed against him, her arms going round him under his. "We're not greedy, are we?" she whispered.

Matt smiled. "No. Just making up for lost hours."

As he kissed her, the cabin lurched suddenly. They stumbled and fell back across the bed. Outside, something toppled over with a crash, perhaps one of the red fire buckets.

Matt had landed on top of Livvy and she looked up at him, startled. "What is it? What's happened?"

He pushed himself up and ran to the closed porthole, kneeling on the window seat to look out. He had been so absorbed in Livvy, he had totally forgotten where they were and the possibility of danger. There was nothing to be seen, he told her. From outside in the corridor, they heard agitated voices, then recognized the steward Biggs' voice, calm and pacifying. "There can't be anything wrong," Matt said. "Just a change of course." He waited, but they heard nothing more, and beyond the porthole the sunlit sea was as empty and peaceful as before.

Livvy lay watching him as he knelt looking out. His body was as strong and straight as when she had first met him. Now she really knew its strength, which could be so demanding and passionate, then so gentle. She knew she was lucky, much more than lucky, that they had found each other again. She still hated what he was doing, but had accepted his need to do it. And she realized it was a paradox, that she was also proud of him. Dan had been more right than even he understood. She had been positive she loved Matt so much, it could never alter. Yet it had. Somehow, in this last week, her feelings for him had become even deeper. He was part of her, she could never lose him.

The cabin lurched again, although not so violently. He saw the horizon veer away and looked round. "That's it, of course," he said. "The Captain's zigzagging." His eyes stayed on Livvy. She was lying on her back, her hair disheveled. her legs sprawling, naked except for the black silk stockings rolled over garters above her knees. "Mrs. Fletcher," he said, "you look like a French postcard." Livvy smiled and squirmed slowly, relaxed and wanton. He rose and crossed to the bed. "It's nearly lunchtime. We'd better get dressed."

She shifted on to her hip and eased herself back to make room. "Not yet."

Matt lay down on his left side, facing her, their bodies just touching. Livvy laid her head back, arching her neck. As he kissed the hollow of her throat, his hand ran softly down the slope of her breast, down her side to the in curve of her waist, up over her polished hip and along the smooth taper of her thigh. His fingers dipped under the tightness of her garter and slid round to the back.

Livvy wriggled. "Eek!"

"Translation?"

"Tickles."

Matt chuckled, but winced when he felt a stab of pain in his left shoulder, where he had been wounded and where the muscles had been torn again so recently.

"What's wrong?" Livvy asked.

"Nothing, really." He rolled on his back. "I'm just a bit stiff."

She glanced down and smiled. "So I notice."

Matt grinned. "One of the things I love most about you is your schoolgirl sense of humor."

"Mr. Fletcher," Livvy said, "you must know some very strange schoolgirls." As he laughed, she slid over to lie on top of him, fitting her body exactly to his. Her mouth came down on his and her hair tumbled round them, dark and perfumed, masking their faces.

The sound of the engines was loud as they approached. Schwieger could hear heavy propellers churning and the U 20 rocked perceptibly when the vessel, whatever it was, passed over her a little to port. He waited five minutes before giving Hirsch the order to rise slowly to periscope depth and hurried to the stick.

It was almost precisely the time he had chosen to come up in any case. By now, Haupert had confirmed, they must be in the approaches to Queenstown. Schwieger tapped the handles of the eyepiece impatiently and had the asparagus run up the moment the opacity of the water through the forward port lessened.

Visibility was still very good, although here there were lingering wisps of fog. He had no difficulty in locating the vessel which had crossed above them. He zeroed on it, an English naval cruiser, medium-sized, of the old style, with two masts and two funnels. It was traveling fast, but was too tempting a target to ignore, certainly worth the expense of one of his three remaining torpedoes.

"Action Stations!" he called. "Ready forward tubes!"

The red lights flashed and the bell began to shrill, alerting the crew. Scherb was standing by to race to the forward torpedo room with the settings. With her speed building up to underwater maximum, Schwieger brought the U 20 round a few points to keep the enemy in sight.

Lanz had been eager to see the target until the Commander described it. It irritated him to be asked so often only for confirmation. Schwieger surrendered the eyepiece at last and they changed places. Lanz could not help smiling, however. It was the first warship which might be a real possible on the whole patrol. "Beautiful . . . beautiful," he breathed. "It's a cruiser, all right. A good size, too. Quite heavily armed." He stood back. "It's making something over eighteen knots. Can't say what class it is, though."

"Pelorous, I think," Schwieger said, and added casually, "If I'm not mistaken, it could be the flagship of the coastal patrol." As he bent to the eyepiece, he heard exclamations of excitement around him. Scherb's mouth gaped open like a child's.

Schwieger's guess was correct. The warship was the old cruiser *Juno*, under Rear-Admiral Hood. In the last few weeks he had been dismissed from command of the Dover Patrol and sent here to take over the Irish Coast Patrol in War Area 21, from Dingle Bay to St. George's Channel. The senior officer commanding Area 21 was Vice-Admiral Coke, stationed at Queenstown. Hood was nursing a strong grievance over his demotion, which had been ordered by the First Sea Lord, Admiral Fisher, on the assumption that, since enemy submarines were operating off the south and west coasts of the British Isles, they must be getting past the ships, nets and mines of the Dover Patrol. Further evidence of Jacky Fisher's galloping senility, Hood fumed. If those last weeks had shown anything, it was that U-boats had developed the necessary techniques and endurance to reach the Western Approaches by sailing round the north of Scotland.

At the same time Hood had become increasingly concerned about the security of the area for which Coke and he were responsible. Until he arrived here, he had not really considered the fact that nearly all the main ocean routes converged on this area, using Fastnet as a landfall and passing through St. George's Channel for Dublin and the country's chief port at Liverpool, passenger, transport and cargo ships, by far the greatest percentage of Britain's overseas trade. Neither had the Admiralty realized it. The bulk of coastal defense was concentrated on protecting the supply lines to France in the English Channel and the bases of the Grand Fleet. To guard an immense and crucial area, Hood was left with a few elderly cruisers like the twenty-year-old *Juno* and with Coke's auxiliary patrol, a handful of converted yachts and small fishing trawlers, of which there were seldom more than a dozen fit to be at sea, some of them unarmed except for rifles and many not even equipped with radio. It was pitiful and would have been ludicrous if it had not been so fraught with danger for the whole future of the war.

The Admiralty refused to accept that priorities would have to be adjusted to meet the unexpected menace of large-scale submarine warfare. In spite of Coke's pleading, the War Staff would not send suitable reinforcements, nor detach warships from other areas. Any that might have been available were being swallowed up in the shambles of the Dardanelles. Even the four torpedo boats at Queenstown base were expressly ordered only to protect the approaches to the harbor and were not permitted to be employed outside. The navy had not had to fight a major war since the days of Nelson, and many on the War Staff, apparently, thought that nothing had changed since then.

After two spells of patrol in his new area, Hood was a worried man. From his flagship down, he had nothing that was equipped to hunt and destroy submarines. Like the three cruisers sunk by the U 9, the *Juno* and her elderly sisters had been constructed with longitudinal bunkers, unarmored below the waterline, making them desperately vulnerable to underwater attack. For four days Hood had maintained his latest patrol out in the Atlantic off Fastnet light, in drifting fog and with continuous reports of U-boat sightings. He knew of the disastrous total of sinkings in the previous two weeks, twenty-three ships sunk in the last week alone. *Juno* was a sitting duck and he only hoped someone in the Admiralty would realize it. When orders finally came for him to break off his patrol, he had set course for Queenstown at once. He thought briefly of the *Lusitania*, with which he had been supposed to make rendezvous, but had no sense of guilt. She was much faster than the *Juno* and was amply shielded by her civilian status. It was out of the question for him to escort her, as *Juno* should never have been sent into these waters without an escort herself.

From the lipped shelf behind him, Scherb had taken the two books issued to U-boats as a means of identifying enemy warships. Both were originally printed in England. He was leafing through one, *The Naval Annual, 1914*, while Lanz searched in the other, *Jane's Fighting Ships*. Scherb found it first. From the outline and specifications, there was no more doubt that they were chasing the cruiser *Juno*.

Schwieger knew he had no chance of catching up. What he was waiting for was for it to alter course, giving him the possibility of a flank shot. Twice he thought he had it, but the enemy captain was too experienced in evasive tactics and perhaps the feathery wake of the periscope had been spotted, for the cruiser did not stop zigzagging at irregular intervals and with frequent changes of speed. It passed out of sight, heading in the direction of Queenstown.

It would have boosted the U 20's score by another five or six thousand tons, with the bonus of being a warship. The odds against getting a decent shot had been long, but it was still a disappointment. "We have no luck, it seems. Such a pity," Lanz murmured. The crew was stood down and returned to normal duties.

At 12:30, fifteen minutes after the cruiser had disappeared, Schwieger brought the U 20 to the surface. In the very fine weather with the sea almost as placid as a lake, the last traces of fog had finally dispersed. Schwieger stood first watch on the conning tower platform with Scherb, and Lanz clambered up to join them. The shape of the land to starboard was quite distinct and, to sea, visibility was clear to the horizon. On any normal day in this sector they would have expected to see a variety of craft, but the U-boat was completely alone.

Scherb grinned. "We've scared them all away."

Schwieger nodded. Just like a stretch of prairie when the game has scented a hunting predator, the expanse of sea was empty.

"They can't all be hiding in port," Lanz pointed out carefully. "Some, maybe some of the biggest, could be making for shelter here at this moment."

"If they are, they'll come like that cruiser," Schwieger said, "going hell for leather and zigzagging. It's useless hanging about here."

"It's the seventh, Friday," Lanz said.

"What does that matter?"

Lanz hesitated. "Many voyages are timed to end on a

Saturday. It would do no harm to wait here another day, surely?"

Schwieger thought about it, but shook his head. "Don't forget this is a patrol area. It's an exposed position, where we have to rely on surprise. To stay here when we may have been spotted is asking for trouble." Lanz was uneasy and glanced at the crewmen below on the deck, on lookout for enemy submarines. He made no more objection and Schwieger bent to the voice tube. "Empty water ballasts. Tell Haupert to reset our course for Fastnet."

Zigzagging herself, at a comfortable ten knots, the U 20 continued her voyage to the west.

In the *Lusitania*'s seamen's mess, Les Morton was with his brother Cliff, other cadets and one of the friends he had made on board, Joe Parry, a young seaman. They were laughing at Cliff who was nodding asleep over his plate. He had been on night watch and had stayed awake to see Ireland.

"You might as well turn in," Les said. "If the Captain keeps as far out as this, we won't see anything till we're in the Mersey."

"Yes. You get your head down," Parry advised. "We'll all be on duty tonight and unloading most of tomorrow." He turned to the others. "Take a tip. Stay out of sight for the next couple of hours in case one of the officers is looking for extra hands to shift the mail. That's a hell of a job."

"I'm all right," Les grinned. "I'm on extra lookout at the fo'c'sle head."

Some of the U 20's crew were grumbling. It was the custom on the way home to wash shirts and underwear and hang them along the deck rail to dry. The commander, however, had forbidden it. Even fishing was not permitted. Boatswain Kurtz was short with those who complained. "Idiots! We're still in the war zone!" he told them. "The commander hasn't forgotten it, even if you have."

It was always a tricky period, as Schwieger knew. The subconscious relief of turning home could lead the men to relax too far and become slack. It was his job to hold them on a tight rein. Every moment she was in enemy waters, the U 20 was at risk, and she had a voyage of well over a thousand nautical miles ahead of her before she docked again at Emden. He had told the petty officers to impress on every man in their sections that everyone was still on partial standby.

He had remained on watch himself on the conning tower platform with Lanz and Scherb, and they had eaten their midday meal there, thick stew with beans. Lanz was slumped against the rail watching the horizon. He did not even mutter his thanks when the cook's mate brought mugs of coffee and collected their mess tins. He had lapsed into a moody silence, which Schwieger preferred to his usual intrusive chatter. Scherb had been affected by the Mate of the Reserve's sullenness and was also silent. They drank their coffee without a word being said.

The sun was high and warm for early May. Schwieger untied his scarf and let it hang loose. He saw that the men on watch below him had unbuttoned their tunics. Some had even taken them off. He had no objection, provided they did not start to lose their concentration. There was already a distraction. Hansel and Maria, the two dachshunds, were scampering about on the forward deck, chasing each other and barking. Someone had lifted them up, Lippe or Bibermann. As he thought of them, he heard the sound of Lippe's concertina coming up through the hatch. For once it was not one of his bawdy ballads, but a simplified version of "Tales from the Vienna Woods." Schwieger caught himself whistling it under his breath. With only three torpedoes left, and already loaded, two in the forward tubes and one in the stern, there would be little for the torpedomen to do for the rest of this patrol.

There was a sudden hiss of warning from Lanz. At the same time the man in the bows flung out his arm and shouted, "Captain! Dead ahead!"

Schwieger looked quickly and saw a smudge of smoke on the rim of the horizon. Seconds later, black funnels began to appear, three, no, four, in a straight line. Lanz was standing erect now. Scherb had seen them, too, and asked, "What is it, Captain? Destroyers?"

"Could be," Schwieger said, and called to the watch, "All hands below! Don't forget those dogs. Close all hatches!" His eyes went back to the distant smokestacks. They were still rising, climbing above the skyline. They rose so uniformly that it was puzzling. As he unclipped the telescope, he had a glimpse of Lanz's face, alight with anticipation.

Schwieger focused on the funnels and realized at once why they were so regular. Instead of being several vessels, they belonged to just one . . . What size were they, for God's sake? The ship was so far away it was impossible to make out any details, but it had to be big, very big. "What is it?" he murmured. "A passenger ship?"

"A transport," Lanz said quietly, and repeated it. "A troop transport."

Schwieger glanced at him. Not even Lanz could be so certain at this distance. Yet if he was not mistaken— He watched the steamer for another full minute. It was so large that Scherb and Lanz could see it plainly with the naked eye now that all of it was over the horizon. It was traveling fast, directly across their bows. The U 20 sat so low in the water, there was little chance of her being spotted and Schwieger kept his telescope trained on the steamer, feeling the stirring of excitement. It must be fifteen thousand tons at least. Maybe nearer twenty. "Get below," he said at last and moved to the voice tube. "Prepare to dive."

Scherb went down the ladder at once, but Lanz lingered, still gazing intently. "Two masts, four funnels, it's a transport. I promise you."

"If we're seen," Schwieger said, "it won't matter what it is. Get below."

In the first-class dining saloon, Matt and Livvy were at one of the largest tables. It was a very enjoyable lunch party, with the Hubbards, Lee and Beattie Arnstein, the Loneys and their daughter Virginia, Charles Lauriat, the bookseller, Marie Depage and Father Basil Maturin. The group at the table next to them was almost as large and noisier, the Cromptons and all their children, except the baby. As a special treat, they had asked Peter and Diana to join them, and Livvy was relieved to see that they were behaving themselves and minding their manners.

Matt had wanted to invite Dan for this last lunch on board, but all seats were booked. It seemed that nearly everyone had decided to lunch early today and the saloon was crowded.

Vanderbilt was with the Allans and Lady Mackworth and her industrialist father. Even Frohman had shown up with his writers and Rita Jolivet and her brother-in-law. The orchestra played selections from Gilbert and Sullivan and the atmosphere was lighthearted.

"It's nice to have so many children today," Father Maturin said.

Marie Depage smiled. "I've just come from the nursery. They lunch at noon there and rest afterwards. It's so sweet to see all the little ones lying asleep."

There was a burst of laughter from the neighboring table. The second youngest Crompton boy had stuck two French beans up his nostrils. "John, for Heaven's sake!" Mrs. Crompton exclaimed. His brothers and sisters started imitating him and there was hubbub for a minute. Peter and Diana were on their best behavior and did not join in the game, but Diana pretended she was going to and giggled when she saw Livvy's worried look. Matt winked to her.

"I hope to visit your country," Elbert Hubbard said to Madame Depage, "to find out for myself what conditions are like there."

She sighed. "To enter, I'm afraid you will have to have permission from the German occupying authorities."

Hubbard scratched his chin. "That might not be so easy. After my latest little pamphlet on the Kaiser, I may not be precisely welcome in Germany."

"I shouldn't think so," Lee smiled. "I've read it."

"Oh, let's not talk about the war," Mrs. Loney suggested. "There are so many more pleasant things."

"Hear, hear," Beattie said. "Every time we mention it, we ought to put ten cents in some kind of swearbox."

"We'd end up bankrupt," Hubbard drawled.

In the laughter Matt told them, "We have a friend in second class. He says there's a passenger there who has spent every waking minute of the voyage in the smoke room. He settled at the bar this morning and intends to remain quietly intoxicated until he steps ashore at Liverpool."

The others smiled, but he had reminded them of the underlying strain, the hidden anxiety they all shared.

"Well, I agree with the ladies," Livvy said. "It should be

a forbidden subject at mealtimes. And we don't have to get drunk."

Mrs. Hubbard smiled to her. "It's certainly not so hard to forget about it on a day like today."

The U 20 was racing ahead with only the tips of her periscope showing above water. Schwieger was trying to cut off the steamer en route, to identify it and to challenge or attack. It was still so many miles away, he calculated that the periscope's narrow wake could not possibly be seen.

His gaze was fixed on the eyepiece and he held the lens centered on the steamer. He had constantly to keep revising his estimate of its size. Certainly his second on the surface had been more accurate. It was more like 20,000 tons, perhaps over that. His mouth was dry and he was chewing unconsciously at the inside corner of his lip until it stung rawly. Don't think of the size, he told himself, it's the speed that matters. Even as he thought it, he knew it was another one to write off. The U 20 was up to her top underwater speed, but at the rate the steamer was moving, it would pass across her bows in less than twenty minutes, hopelessly out of range. There was nothing he could do about it. There was no conceivable reason for it to change course, which might have given him a chance, and he had used up what little store of luck he had been granted on this patrol.

The others were waiting. He dabbed with his tongue at the raw place inside his mouth. "It's as big as we thought," he reported, "traveling at maybe twenty knots. And it's definitely a passenger ship. It has several decks." As he counted them, he could hear his own astonishment. "Four, five, no, six, above the waterline."

"*Six* decks?" Scherb questioned, voicing the disbelief of the others.

"Six," Schwieger repeated. "Black hull and funnels, white superstructure."

"The Commander is correct," Boatswain Kurtz said. "It must be a passenger liner."

"Not any more," Lanz disagreed. "It's a troop transport."

Again there was the note of certainty in his voice and Schwieger glanced up. "How can you be so sure? Take a look."

"I don't need to," Lanz told him. "From your description, there's only one ship it can be." He paused, adding almost casually. "The *Lusitania*."

Schwieger straightened. In his own shock he scarcely heard the exclamations around him. "It can't be!"

"On this route today, Friday. That's what it must be," Lanz said. "It is due to dock at Liverpool tomorrow morning. Or was."

"How can we challenge something that size?" Scherb wondered.

"There would be no point," Schwieger said. "It's a passenger ship."

Lanz grunted with exasperation. "I keep telling you, Captain. It was a liner, but has been converted into an armed cruiser, used to convey troops and contraband cargo."

"To stop and search it would take a full day," Schwieger said.

"It is a warship and may be sunk without warning," Lanz countered. He handed Schwieger the manual, *Jane's Fighting Ships*, already open. "See for yourself. It is armed with twelve six-inch naval guns."

On the page in front of him, Schwieger saw the silhouette of the ship he had been watching. The *Lusitania*. It was listed as "Auxiliary Cruiser. Tonnage, 31,000 (Gross)." He registered it. Fully laden, it would be something like 45,000 tons.

Over the book he could see Lanz's face, set and eager, and glanced from him to Scherb, who was excited but anxious, and to Kurtz, who was patently worried, watching him. He looked again at the silhouette to give himself time to think. His mind was churning, and he felt a tightness in his throat. Something was nagging at him. Lanz had known exactly to which page to turn.

He thought back, realizing that it fitted into a pattern, Lanz's keenness to reach their station and insistence on remaining on it, his sullenness earlier. He had come on watch at every opportunity. "On this route today, Friday . . ." Lanz had been expecting it, waiting for the *Lusitania* for days, the most famous civilian ship afloat. Does he really imagine I would torpedo it without concern for its passengers . . . ? Hersing would not, nor Max, nor Rosenberg or

Forstner, or any of the others. But the other boats of the patrol were already well on their way home.

He had been detained and sent out later. So that he would be left alone on station? For the *Lusitania*?

"Well, Commander?" Lanz asked.

Schwieger closed the book and turned it over in his hands. His movements appeared deliberate, but his mind seethed with questions and possible answers. He wanted to pin Lanz against the bulkhead and force the truth out of him. What instructions did they really give him? "We want the *Lusitania* sunk, but we cannot issue a specific order?" No, that would be too direct. Any child would realize the storm an attack on such a liner would cause. Whatever else it carried, it also carried hundreds of passengers. It was not naval strategy, but international politics. Lanz would have been primed, though, and they had chosen their man well—for his advice and his report.

So I was chosen too, specially chosen, Schwieger thought. He remembered his meetings with Tirpitz and the Grand Admiral's eyes on him, assessing, while he spoke of the need for commanders to be given the right to sink without challenge, without warning. And he remembered Bauer's orders, which only seemed strange now, thinking back. "Await large English troop transports." He had been given the most coveted hunting ground for once. Were they so sure of me?

"Well?" Lanz asked again impatiently.

Do I have a choice? Schwieger thought bitterly. If he refused, it would go down in Lanz's report that, presented with a prime target officially classed as a naval cruiser, he made no effort to attack. He could write an end to his career. He would certainly lose the favor of the Grand Admiral, perhaps incur his enmity. What have I become that they were so sure of me?

He knew the answer already, for behind all his chaotic thoughts, he had been conscious of one thing which he could not suppress. 45,000 tons.

"We shall continue our attempt to intercept," he said. Lanz smiled abruptly, a tight, triumphant grin. Scherb smiled too, but nervously. Kurtz appeared more troubled than ever.

Schwieger turned back to the eyepiece. He swung the stick carefully, 90 degrees to either side, searching for an escort vessel or patrol boats, anything which might neces-sitate breaking off an attack. There was nothing. He gazed again on the liner. Now that he knew what it was, the ex-citement leaped in him. With one kill, he could leapfrog everyone's total except Hersing's. 45,000 tons . . . But his effort to intercept was merely a gesture. The *Lusitania* pounded steadily on, not deviating from its course. The de-cision was out of his hands.

On the upper bridge, Will Turner strained his eyes to make out the land in the distance, about two points abaft the beam. Five minutes ago, he had thought he could recognize the twin spikes of Galley Head, but he could not be certain. There were so many jagged capes and promontories on this coast, a whole series of them. If it was Galley Head, he was further along than he had reckoned and that could be tricky. He could well arrive before dark south of the Coningbeg light, where that U-boat was reported to be in wait.

He felt the cold lump of his pipe in his pocket. He pulled it out and sucked on it, even though it was unlit. On a peacetime voyage, as soon as the fog lifted this morning, he would have moved closer inshore to pinpoint his position precisely. It was damnable, this uncertainty.

A messenger boy, very spruce in his short tunic, was coming across the upper bridge to him and saluted smartly. "Mr. McCormick's compliments, sir," he piped, and handed Turner a signal envelope.

Turner nodded affably to the boy. He put the pipe back in his pocket and as he opened the envelope thought, what next? "Mr. Jones!" he called.

Bestwick had accompanied the boy up from the lower bridge and reacted with interest to the captain's sudden alertness. Jones read the signal and passed it to Second Officer Hefford. He also seemed relieved and Bestwick was very intrigued by the time the latest signal reached him. It read, "Submarine five miles south of Cape Clear, proceeding west when sighted at 10 A.M."

"Well, what do you make of that, Bisset?" Turner asked.

Bestwick could not understand why the others appeared to be so pleased. "There's a third submarine, sir?"

Turner chuckled. "No, lad. It means our friend at Fastnet

Rock has given up his vigil. We've escaped Scylla. Now we only have to avoid Charybdis."

"Sorry, sir?" Hefford asked, puzzled.

Bestwick smiled broadly but stopped when Hefford and First Officer Jones glanced at him.

"A classical allusion, Mr. Hefford," Turner said. "My apologies." In his relief he had lost the sense of uneasiness which had been lowering his spirits. Cape Clear lay approximately thirty miles astern and, assuming the U-boat had continued west after being sighted at ten o'clock, the last three hours would have widened the gap between them to at least ninety miles, roughly the same distance as the second submarine lurking ahead. The *Lusitania* for the moment was safely in the middle. There was no earthly reason why she should not swing nearer to land. A short divergence would be doubly useful, using up the extra hour he needed to arrive at St. George's Channel after dark, as well as letting him fix his exact position on the chart. It was heaven sent.

"Change of course, Mr. Jones," he said. "Bring her round twenty degrees to north. Maintain present speed."

Schwieger closed his eyes briefly. When he opened them again, he saw that it was not an illusion. The *Lusitania* was curving to port, standing in toward the coast.

His first thought was that even at this distance his periscopes had been spotted, but it was not feasible. Obviously the liner had started to zigzag. Yet it was not that, either. Its course remained steady. By reflex, he swiveled the stick quickly to check if there was anything on his starboard beam, a vessel with which the liner intended to rendezvous. The surface of the sea was as empty as ever, and he swung back. The *Lusitania*'s course was unaltered. For some inconceivable reason, it was heading on a slanted course to bring it nearer to land.

In these few seconds, subconsciously, Schwieger had begun to make calculations of relative speeds and angles of incidence. At the same moment, all other considerations, personal, political and humanitarian, were swept aside as if they had never existed. He stepped back and snapped his fingers to Lanz, who was hovering anxiously nearby. "What's it making?"

Lanz stooped to the eyepiece. His observation lasted for maddeningly long minutes of silence. When he straightened, his expression was almost smug with self-gratification, although subdued by recognition of the difficulties. "I'd estimate around twenty knots," he said.

Or a little less, Schwieger thought. "What's its top speed?"

"Twenty-six and a half knots."

"God in heaven," Scherb muttered.

Schwieger took a last look through the lens and told the helmsman to come round hard to starboard. He shouted to Hirsch. "I need every ounce of speed you can give me!"

"How long for, Captain?" Hirsch asked.

"Until I tell you to stop." Schwieger signed to Scherb to lower the periscope. He could not risk its betraying wake any longer. From now on, it was a race, and he would be racing blind. There was no time for circling or maneuvering. He had to reach a position directly ahead of the *Lusitania* on its new course to give himself one brief chance of attacking as it swept past. It was an all-or-nothing gamble, for if the liner increased its speed or changed direction again, the U 20 would be left so far behind, she could never catch up.

Elizabeth Duckworth was having lunch with Alice Scott and Arthur in the second-class dining saloon. Alice was looking quite pretty, she decided. It was the new touch of color in her cheeks, after all the sea air. "Can I come and visit you in Blackpool, Aunt Lizzie?" Arthur asked.

Elizabeth smiled. "Blackburn. It's quite different, all soot and chimneys. Blackpool's all fairy lights and candy."

"You see, you wouldn't like Blackburn," Alice said, misunderstanding.

"I didn't mean you wouldn't be welcome," Elizabeth said when she saw his face fall. "Don't worry. We'll work something out."

"But remember Mrs. Duckworth's going to be very busy," Alice said.

"What doing, Aunt Lizzie?" Arthur asked.

"Oh—weaving stuff for uniforms, most like. Or working in a munitions factory, wherever there's hands wanted."

The party in the first-class saloon was over. Matt and

Livvy had expected to spend part of the afternoon with Lee and Beattie Arnstein, but the younger couple had excused themselves to return to their unfinished packing. "You know, I think they do even more packing than us," Livvy said, and Matt laughed quietly.

They were waiting in the hall outside the saloon for Peter and Diana and were caught in the cross flow of people leaving it and others, like First Officer Jones, coming down for a late lunch. It was a continuous murmur of greetings, with smiles and nods. "I feel like the King at a reception," Matt told Livvy.

When the throng had passed, they were joined by Lady Allan and her daughters, who hoped that Livvy would visit them in London and bring Diana, to whom Gwen and Anna had become very attached. Just then, the Cromptons erupted from the dining saloon with their parents vainly trying to keep them under control. Diana saw Matt and Livvy and came flying over. "Daddy! Mummy!" she squeaked, and leaped into Matt's arms in a flurry of ringlets. The Allan girls had spent half the morning dressing her hair.

"Steady on, pet!" Matt said, laughing, and set her down.

"Did you see John with the beans up his nose?" she giggled. "He was pretending to be a walrus."

"We wondered about that," Livvy told her, laughing with the others.

Peter had come to them and said, "Can I go down to the games room with Paul and Steven? They're teaching me how to do real handstands."

Matt thought about it. "Okay, chief. Why not? We'll be down to collect you in about an hour." Peter grinned and left with the two older Crompton boys.

"What about me?" Diana pouted.

"You can come with us," Gwen suggested. "We're going to help bathe the babies."

"Oh, no," Livvy said. "You took care of her all morning."

"She's no bother," Lady Allan assured her. "The girls enjoy having her. And you probably have things you want to do."

"Oh, please, Mummy, please!" Diana begged. "Can I go with Gwen and Anna?"

She looked so wistful that Livvy consented at once. She was grateful to the Allans for being so sweet with Diana.

582

They had done her hair very prettily, although a tomboy in ringlets would need getting used to. Livvy kissed her.

"I have an idea," Matt said. "Why don't we all meet at four-thirty for tea in the verandah café?"

"That would be very nice, Mr. Fletcher," Lady Allan said, accepting.

Matt and Livvy went with them to the elevator and, when they turned back, found themselves suddenly alone. "Deserted by all," Matt said. He smiled and offered Livvy his arm, and they walked up the central companionway together.

A few minutes later, they reached the top of the companionway and the Main Hall, and strolled out onto the starboard side of the boat deck. Jay Brooks, the auto chain salesman, who was a fitness enthusiast, ran past them at a trot on a circuit of the deck and they waved to him. "Why don't you join me?" he called.

"I will!" Matt called back. "When you start to fall apart."

Livvy was standing still, gazing. "Oh, look, Matt . . ." she breathed.

The liner's curve had brought her much closer to shore in the last three-quarters of an hour. Now the land could be seen quite clearly, the green of grass and tiny white houses perched on the cliffs. Ahead to the right was a massive promontory with a white-painted lighthouse at the point, picked out by the early afternoon sun. "Now you can believe you're nearly home," Matt said. "Happy?" As soon as he had spoken, he wished he had not, seeing her swiftly covered expression of distress.

"In some ways," she answered quietly, and moved in to stand touching him. He put his arm round her shoulders and they were silent, watching the land.

At the same moment, they both became aware that Dan Connally had come to the rail beside them. "Enjoy your lunch?" he asked.

"I'm sorry about that, Dan," Matt said. "I tried everything."

"Hey, listen, it's okay," Dan told them. "I was only kidding." He had not seen Livvy since their conversation in the cabin two days ago, and was relieved when she smiled to him. "Some view, huh?"

"Beautiful," Livvy said. "It's like a painting."

"Yeah," Dan nodded. He seemed embarrassed as he glanced at Matt. "I hate to interrupt, but there's a bunch of guys waiting in the smoke room for you to talk to them."

"Oh, my God! I clean forgot," Matt confessed. He turned to Livvy.

She smiled. "It's all right. You go with Dan."

"I can't get out of it, honey," he explained.

"I know," she said. "It's really all right. I'll wait here. I'll be somewhere along this side."

He squeezed her arm. "Be as quick as I can."

Dan shrugged to her apologetically and Matt and he went off. Livvy watched them go down the outside companion ladder, hurrying down to the second-class smoke room. She would have to become used to Matt having other demands made on him.

She swung back to look at the land, which had grown even more distinct. She was at the rail, in the space between two canvas-covered collapsible boats with lifeboats hanging above them. Like everyone else she had come to accept them and scarcely noticed them, but she gradually grew conscious of the faint creak, creak, of the boats dangling from their davits, an oddly sinister sound. She shivered and wrapped her arms round herself as she gazed at the friendly land which was still so far off.

On the wing of the bridge, Captain Turner was also watching the large promontory to starboard. He was easier in his mind now that he knew where he was. The three-mile peninsula with its lighthouse could only be the Old Head of Kinsale, with the small fishing harbor of Kinsale tucked round out of sight on its other side. He wished he had a guinea for every landfall he had made at the Old Head. From here it was less than thirty miles to Queenstown and safety, if it was needed.

He had done what he had planned to do, used up some time and found out his position. Yet they were still some eighteen miles off shore and it was one thing to be satisfied himself, and another to be exact enough to satisfy the ship's log and the records. Besides, the deep-water lane in St. George's Channel, at its narrowest between Wexford in Ireland and St. David's in Wales, was not much more than twenty miles wide, bordered by shoals and rocky shores. He had no intention of running the *Lusitania* through it in the dark by dead reckoning, without a definite starting position. He went back inside.

Bestwick was stifling a yawn. It was almost the end of his spell of duty and he was looking forward to a couple of hours with his feet up. He came to attention as Turner made for him.

"Ah—Bisset," Turner said. "You know how to take a four-point bearing?"

"Yes, sir," Bestwick told him.

"Good lad," Turner approved. "Then kindly take one on that lighthouse there."

Bestwick nearly opened his mouth to protest. To take a four-point bearing required a minimum of half an hour, with the ship kept to a fixed course and speed. The Captain was waiting. "Aye, aye, sir," Bestwick said.

Turner smiled slightly and moved away. He knew just what Bestwick was thinking, but scrupulous attention to tasks like that could one day change a junior officer into a master. He gave the order for the *Lusitania* to be brought round to starboard onto her earlier course, south 87 degrees east. "Eighteen knots," he said. "And hold her steady."

Copying the slow rise of Schwieger's right hand, Scherb slid the U 20's main periscope up very cautiously. He stopped abruptly when the hand cut to the side.

The hooded eye was just breasting the low waves and Schwieger rotated it very gently to cause as little disturbance of the surface as possible. The U-boat was crawling now, after almost an hour's blind dash underwater. Schwieger could not prevent himself from holding his breath as he searched. Nothing . . . nothing . . . then he had it!

He swore softly to himself. It was big, bigger than anything he had ever seen through the lens. But it was still over four miles away to port. And still heading for the shore.

He felt a bitter disappointment after the mounting excitement of the race. The *Lusitania* was still too far away, out of range of anything but the most desperate and rash shot. Yet in spite of his frustration, he could not help but admire her grace. He had leisure to appreciate her now and saw that she was beautiful, a masterpiece of construction and design. He had to remind himself of Lanz's description of her armament and of the stories he had read in newspapers at home of the deadly cargo of contraband she carried, with the connivance of the Americans, the same arrogant and selfish race whose presence on board had always protected her.

As he watched her, he noticed the long wave curling back from her bows leap higher. Surely she was not putting on more speed so close to land? Slowly he became aware of a shift in the perspective of her giant funnels. Almost imperceptibly the gap between them was growing narrower. She was not increasing speed, she was turning! Turning toward him . . . In a few minutes, her bow waves had equalized and the funnels had merged into one. She was coming straight for him.

He glanced up and saw the others intent on him, trying to work out the reason for his silence, prepared for the cruelest disappointment. "She's ours," he said quietly.

Junior Third Officer Bestwick had taken the second of his four bearings and was preparing for the third. He put his tongue out at the lighthouse as Third Officer Lewis came toward him. "Yes, I know," Lewis smiled. "You should be off duty. All right, I'll relieve you. You get along and I'll finish off for you." Bestwick could hardly believe what he had heard. "Beat it," Lewis said. "Before I change my mind." Bestwick handed over gratefully and hurried for his cabin.

Jay Brooks, stripped to his shirt and flannel pants, had trotted up the ladder to the Marconi deck and began his run round it, which would be the end of his exercise. Bestwick smiled and saluted him as he went by.

Livvy was moving forward along the boat deck. She had promised to wait for Matt on this side, but with the *Lusitania* sailing parallel to the shore, she could no longer see the land from starboard.

Alice Scott and Arthur had finished their lunch. He was impatient to see the Irish coast and could not sit still while they waited for Elizabeth Duckworth to get through her ice cream. "I don't like to hurry it," Elizabeth said. "Just you go on up, Mrs. Scott. I'll find you on the shelter deck."

In their cabin, Beattie drew the coverlet up over her as she lay on the bed. She was breathless, and felt as though she were floating. "It will never, ever be so good again," she whispered. Lying beside her, Lee smiled and pulled her gently to him to prove her wrong.

The weather was so charming that Charles Frohman had decided against returning to his suite after lunch. As he strolled on the promenade deck with Rita Jolivet and George Vernon, her brother-in-law, he was not listening to them, but composing a cable he would send to Maude the minute they docked. They passed Alfred Vanderbilt, who was smoking a cigar and reading the ship's newssheet. "Justus—Mr. Forman—said something very interesting this morning," Rita was saying. "He's seen most of the things I've been in. And he thinks it was in *Kismet* that I first showed my true potential."

"You certainly did, my dear," Frohman murmured. "That costume was very revealing."

Will Turner had come down to his day room, where his steward had laid out a light lunch. Turner did not want to eat, for it would keep him away from the bridge too long, but he was glad to be able to light up his pipe at last. Just a minute or two, he told himself. You've certainly earned your money this trip, Will. As Commodore, he had a salary of two thousand pounds a year now. That was something he would never have thought possible when he was Bestwick's age. He stretched his back. Something odder than that. Only two hours ago, he had never thought it possible for him to relax again.

In the second-class smoke room near the stern on the promenade deck, Matt was facing a muster of nearly all the Canadian volunteers. A group of civilians at one of the tables had stopped their poker game to listen. "Those of you who have units to go to," Matt was saying, "report to the military authorities in Liverpool and you'll be provided with travel warrants and instructions. Those of you for the Canadian Division, get on the London train with me. I'll telephone ahead and have someone meet us at the London terminal." He paused. "I want to wish each of you good luck, and say I'm happy we're all going to be serving together. Tomorrow's when it all begins."

"Three cheers for Captain Fletcher!" the temporary lieutenant from Toronto called. To the astonishment of the poker players, the volunteers crowded round Matt, cheering and shaking his hand.

Scherb came hurrying back through central control. He was proud, though self-conscious, knowing that everyone was looking at him as he hurried to rejoin Commander Schwieger. There had never been such a silence in the U 20. The only sound was the faint hum of the motors. The whole crew from Hirsch to the cook's mate was motionless, waiting.

"Forward torpedoes adjusted for depth of nine feet," Scherb reported. "Forward tubes ready."

"Thank you," Schwieger acknowledged. He watched as Scherb unscrewed the caps protecting the red firing buttons from accidental discharge. Haupert had taken over the periscope elevating lever. Lanz was standing at the side, next to Kurtz. He was sweating profusely.

Schwieger stepped to his place at the eyepiece and signed to Haupert. As the periscope rose, Schwieger tried to blot everything from his mind except the image in the lens. He had run the U 20 as far forward as he dared, considering the *Lusitania*'s powerful guns. He had maneuvered carefully and her bows were now pointing as straight as the helmsman could hold her at the line of the *Lusitania*'s path. For the next four or five minutes Schwieger needed total concentration.

The identity of the ship he was preparing to attack had ceased to have any relevance, like her size and gracefulness and passengers. To him she had become simply another target. He had angled the U-boat's position to give himself the chance of an ideal bowshot, calculated on the relative speeds of the target and of the torpedo, at a range of seven hundred yards. His only concern was the liner's construction, the watertight compartments and the cavernous coal bunkers along her side which could absorb shellfire without harm. With only three torpedoes left, two G-type in the two forward tubes and one older bronze model in the stern, he wondered if he had enough for the job. He had had them set with delayed fuses to explode after maximum penetration. It would be highly dangerous after the first shot. When the U 20 showed her asparagus again, it could be met by a full broadside.

The *Lusitania* was approaching on her straight course, still parallel to the shore, her speed unchanged. Her stark funnels stood out against the egg-shell-blue sky. He could see her masts and radio antennae clearly now. And every detail of her white superstructure, even the tiny figures of people moving on her decks. He could not spot the guns, but she was so huge they might be easily concealed.

"Steady!" he called to the helmsman. "Stand by forward tubes!"

The target's prow was about to enter the hair-thin calibrations on the lens. *Lieber Herr Gott* . . . It was enormous! A towering black cliff. The closer the target came, the more Schwieger was staggered by its sheer size. Its side, a vast black wall studded with portholes. How could he even hope to make a pinprick in such a leviathan? Until now he had had no real conception of its bulk and was almost unnerved. He fought to control himself, readjusting the angles in his mind. In a moment it would be too late. He counted slowly to himself. Now! "Fire Number One!"

Chapter 30

LIVVY HAD MOVED FORWARD ON THE BOAT DECK UNTIL SHE was under the overhang of the starboard wing of the bridge. Ahead of her, she saw Marie Depage walking with the American doctor and two of the young volunteer nurses traveling out to work in her husband's hospital. They were talking earnestly and Livvy stopped, not wishing to intrude.

Beyond was the Irish coast. They were just opposite the point of the rocky promontory with its lighthouse and the smaller buildings, which Matt had reckoned might be a signal station, but already it was drawing away. Somehow the thought that they were leaving the land behind again was depressing, and Livvy felt the need of company. Passing the outside companionway ladder, she had heard Elbert Hubbard's chuckle and had glanced down to see him strolling toward the rear of the promenade deck with his wife Alice and Charles Lauriat, the bookseller. If she hurried, she could catch them up, but it might mean missing Matt. It was better to stay on this deck. She turned and began to walk slowly back.

There were just over two hours until the time they had arranged to meet the Allans for tea, and she hoped that Matt would really not be too long. They had still not had their serious talk. This afternoon they had a chance to go into everything calmly, where he expected to be billeted, whether she and the children were to remain in England and so on, to settle the practical details, so that their last evening on board would not be wasted in discussing them.

Two girls and a young man came chasing toward her, tossing a medicine ball from one to the other. The man threw the ball to Livvy, who smiled and bounced it back to the slim redheaded girl beside him. The girl missed it and scrambled for it, laughing, before following the other two who had started back toward the stern. Livvy had paused by the gap between the first and second starboard lifeboats. Something through the gap caught her eye, a frothy white line running across the surface of the sea. It ran so straight that it puzzled her.

Forward, in the very bows of the ship, Les Morton was stationed as starboard fo'c'sle lookout. He had come on duty ten minutes earlier, one minute after the older seaman with him, who had chosen the port side for their two-hour watch. The sea seemed as motionless as a pond. Although there was little wind, the *Lusitania* at her cruising speed of eighteen knots created her own and Les blinked against it. As his friends had predicted, the last week of constant hard slog had been very tiring and, because of the warmth of the day, he welcomed the breeze to prevent his nodding off to sleep.

At the same moment as Livvy he caught sight of the line in the water, a frothy, bubbling white streak heading at an angle for a point ahead of the *Lusitania*'s prow. It had not been there a few seconds before and, although he knew instinctively what caused it, it was another second or two before his eyes traced quickly back along the line to a V-shaped disturbance in the water and the periscope which projected about three feet at its apex.

He leaped up and leaned out dangerously over the bulwark, gazing at the approaching white streak. Ahead of it, he could just make out the long dark cigar shape driven at high speed by whirling propellers which threw back its foaming wake. He had thought it would shoot past some distance in front of the bows, but all at once he realized that the *Lusitania*'s own speed was carrying her inevitably into the torpedo's path. It could not fail to strike somewhere along her 785-foot length.

He dropped to the deck and snatched up the megaphone, shouting to the bridge, "Torpedo coming! Starboard side—torpedo coming!"

Second Officer Hefford was on duty on the upper bridge and heard Les's shout. He could not believe it, yet even as he turned to Chief Officer Piper, it was confirmed by a frantic message from one of the able seamen on lookout in the crow's nest halfway up the towering foremast.

Will Turner was watching the Old Head, about eighteen

591

miles away. To be in charge of a lighthouse would be an almost ideal life for a retired skipper, he was thinking, to be snug on land in fair or foul weather, and watch the ships go by. He thought of his money in the safe in his day cabin. He had never greatly trusted banks and always carried his savings with him, not much to show for a lifetime of work, yet over the three or four years remaining he could add to it out of his commodore's pay and, with his pension, have enough to live out the rest of his days quite comfortably. He was not sure, however, that after this trip it mightn't be wiser to lodge his savings somewhere ashore. He agreed with Archie Bryce. For all who went down to the sea in ships in these uncertain times, things were going to get worse before they got better.

He was roused from his reverie by Hefford calling for him urgently. "A torpedo coming on the starboard side!" the second officer shouted down. Turner's mind reeled, but he recovered instantly and whirled round, beginning to hurry across the lower bridge. There was no dismissing the report as a false alarm. Over the far bulwark he could make out the torpedo's white trajectory. It seemed to be rushing straight toward him. In the next split second, the tip was out of sight below the bulwark and he braced himself instinctively.

The eighteen-foot-long torpedo slammed into the *Lusitania*'s starboard side at a speed of over forty knots, ten feet below the waterline and slightly behind the bridge, smashing through her steel plating into the cavernous coal bunker behind. The great liner quivered all along her length and Turner staggered, then was thrown to his knees as her bows bucked violently and water spouted up her side when the torpedo's delayed fuse detonated its warhead packed with 290 pounds of TNT.

The sound of the explosion was oddly muffled, but Turner knew a gaping hole must have been blown in her hull. Already she was heeling over, slewing to starboard as tons of water poured in. He pushed himself to his feet and made for the ladder to the navigating bridge. He sprinted up it and had just reached the door when a second, even more savage explosion shook her convulsively with a tremendous roar. He had grabbed the doorjamb and the force of the eruption spun him round, hurling him into the wheel-house.

Livvy had stepped back quickly the moment she recognized the wake of the torpedo for what it was. She had wanted to run, but her legs seemed leaden. She was directly above the point of impact and the first explosion flung her against the bulkhead of the cabin behind her, drenching her with water. The second lifted her up and sent her toppling and rolling across the deck to fetch up against one of the collapsible boats. She lay crumpled and dazed, her arms clasped round her head to shut out the ear-splitting, screeching thunder of the blast.

The deck steadied under her and she looked up, wide-eyed with shock. Just then, a hideous cloud of coal dust, debris and steam, forced up by the detonation, spewed from the giant ventilators by the forward funnels and fountained twice as high as the masts before dropping back. The entire bridge was enveloped in smoke and steam lit by random flashes of fire as the vapors from the coal bunkers ignited. Livvy choked in the thick suffocating air as she cowered for protection against the side of the collapsible boat with wooden debris and jagged pieces of metal falling and ricocheting from the deck and bulkheads around her. With a jarring crash, something landed on the wildly swinging lifeboat beyond her, smashing it to pieces.

In the U 20, Walther Schwieger watched through the periscope incredulously. It had been a perfect bow shot from a range of 700 yards, angle of incidence 90 degrees. Technically it could not be faulted, although he now suspected the liner had been traveling at three or four knots less than the twenty-two which Lanz had estimated. For moments it had even seemed likely that the torpedo would shoot past ahead of its target. What held him so silent, intent on the eyepiece, was its devastating effect. He had hoped at the most to slow the liner down and prevent it taking evasive action, but the first explosion had been much more extensive than he anticipated. While the crew was still cheering, thirty seconds later had come the second detonation, so strong that, until the cloud of smoke dispersed, he half thought the entire forward section had been blown away. As it was, the superstructure by the bridge was badly damaged, and whatever had caused the second explosion—bursting boilers, coal or gunpowder—the huge liner was already settling noticeably by the bows.

Of the five people on the *Lusitania*'s bridge, Will Turner was the first to recover. From the angle of the deck he knew the situation was serious and he hurried to the binnacle to check the spirit level. The indicator oscillated sharply between 15 and 18 points of list. Already the surface of the water was much closer to the forecastle deck.

Quartermaster Johnston had taken over the helm and Turner called to him, "Bring her round to port! Steer for the lighthouse!" Johnston fought the helm round against the starboard drag of the bows. He had realized at once that, however unthinkable, the liner was in danger of foundering and that the captain had decided to try to beach her in the shallower water off Kinsale. It all depended on her maintaining sufficient speed to cover the distance, and already it had been reduced by several knots.

Turner had snatched up the telephone linking him to the engine room, but the wires must have been severed and the line was dead. He stepped quickly to the voice tubes. "Engine room, this is the Captain! Report. Engine room?"

After a pause, they heard the hesitant voice of the Senior Second Engineer. "Cockburn, sir. I don't know what's become of Mr. Bryce. He was up forward in Number One boiler room. What was it, sir?"

"Torpedo," Turner told him tersely. He could not let himself think of Archie. If he had been working in one of the forward boiler rooms . . . "Report. How are things down there?"

In the vast engine room the explosions had been magnified. After the first, the lights had gone out, plunging them into darkness, and Cockburn had clung to the high grating on which he stood while it bounced like a trampoline at the second mammoth thunderclap. In the pitch blackness, there was the hiss of steam and the smell of coal dust. He had known moments of sheer terror, then some of the lights began to flicker back on. Coal dust was billowing in through the door to No. 4 boiler room, the one that was shut down.

He suspected that the engineers, firemen and Chief Engineer who were further forward were done for, and he shouted to the men on the lowest level to close the watertight door while he started down the suddenly inclined ladder for the level with the pressure gauges. "We—we're all right here, sir, for the time being," he reported. "But the pressure's falling. We've lost a lot of steam."

It was a hard thing to order men to remain in a metal prison below the waterline. "Stay with it," Turner said. "We need as much as you can give us for as long as you can." He called to Chief Officer Piper to check on the telltale board that all watertight doors were closed. Speed, buoyancy . . . He bent to the end voice tube. "Crow's nest? Are you all right up there?"

The massive foremast, soaring to 170 feet above the water, had quivered like a wand at the convulsion of the bows, and in the open-topped crow's nest the two able seamen on watch, Quinn and Hennessy, had been whipped backward and forward, then enveloped by the choking cloud of steam and coal dust. It had taken them until now to recover and the backs of their hands, with which they had protected their faces, were beginning to blister. "Shaken about a bit, Captain," Quinn coughed, "but we're all right."

"Any sign of that submarine?"

". . . Still there, sir. Keeping pace with us."

"Very well," Turner said. "You'd better get down."

Now that she could breathe again, Livvy pulled herself up to her knees. Her throat felt raw and her ears were ringing. Her clothes were wet through and her arms and suit spattered with oily coal dust, but she knew she was lucky the steam had cooled before it reached her. All she could think of was Matt. Matt and the children, where were they?

As she began to stumble forward, she saw the pretty redheaded girl who had been playing with the ball. She was lying on her face on the deck beside some broken pieces of timber from the shattered lifeboat. The girl was unconscious and her hair had come loose. Livvy hurried to her, but as she crouched to help her up, she became aware that the girl's hair was still neatly waved, matching in color the pool of bright blood spreading round her head. Livvy started to turn her over gently and recoiled in horror. One of the heavy timber spars had crushed the girl's face beyond recognition. Splintered bone and teeth protruded through the pulped skin and one eye dangled obscenely on her cheek. Her neck was broken.

In the second-class dining saloon, toward the stern on D deck, the noise of the explosions had been much fainter, scarcely audible, although everyone had felt the jolt, which sent bottles and glasses spinning. There were many passengers for the late lunch sitting and, when the glasses smashed on the deck, an excited babble broke out. Robert Leith, the Marconi operator, was the first to react. The moment the jolt came, he dropped his coffee cup, pushed the table aside and ran for the door.

Elizabeth Duckworth had been on her way out. She was thrown off balance and fell sideways, catching at a large-mustached foreign man in a chair and nearly bringing him down with her. He managed to hold her. As she stammered her apologies and thanks, the lights went out.

In the darkness there was a surge of movement as everyone rose. Women were screaming and voices began shouting that the boat was sinking. The man was still holding Elizabeth and jabbering to her in Russian and she felt bodies blunder past them, seeking for the exit. The lights came on again and immediately there was a panic rush for the door, which was soon jammed with people pushing and falling on the strangely tilted deck.

Everyone was hurrying up the gangways to the shelter deck and Elizabeth was nearly carried with them. She drew aside, however, thinking of Alice Scott and Arthur. Alice had decided to return to their cabin for a coat before going up on deck. She would be there now with Arthur, two levels below and further forward, much nearer where the explosion must have come from. Unlike the others, Elizabeth turned and went down. The long passageways were sloping forward and to the side and made walking difficult. She heard voices, children crying, and had to lean against the bulkhead when three stewardesses helped a frightened group of elderly passengers toward a companionway beyond her.

When she reached her own corridor at last, it was strangely dark and she stopped in horror. Normally it was lit by two small portholes at either end, nine or ten feet above the water. The ones on the starboard side were completely obscured, the sea pressing against them outside like a dark green curtain.

As she inched herself up the sloping deck, she thought what a fool she would be if the Scotts had already gone. But when she opened the door, there was Alice sitting on the lower bunk with her folded coat over her knees and her arm round Arthur. "What are you doing?" Elizabeth asked.

"I tried to find a steward," Alice said, wide-eyed. "We heard a terrible noise and everything shook. I didn't know what to do."

"We get out of here, for a start," Elizabeth told her. "And bloody quick about it."

Leith had raced up a series of companionways to the boat deck. Here the list was more evident. The huge funnels seemed to hang over him and it was an effort to climb the outward-slanting ladder to the Marconi deck. There was a man clinging to a stayrope, breathing raggedly as though he had nearly drowned. He was plastered with greasy soot and Leith had difficulty recognizing him as Mr. Brooks, the passenger who often used this deck for exercise. "Are you all right, sir?" he asked.

Brooks could only nod. He had almost suffocated. He let go of the rope and stumbled off toward the opposite side of the deck.

Leith hurried into the radio shack. His assistant operator, McCormick, was at the transmitter, just waiting. "There's been no orders," he explained.

From what he had seen, Leith knew there was no need for orders and, if anyone had survived on the bridge, they would be too busy. He shoved McCormick away and, as he took over the chair, was already tapping out the *Lusitania*'s call sign and the beginning of the message. "Come at once, big list, ten miles south Old Head Kinsale."

Above deck in the second-class smoke room, the sound of the explosions had been unmistakable and there was a shocked silence when the liner shuddered and a pyramid of glasses cascaded from the bar. Someone shouted, "They've got us! Torpedo!" The men at the tables and standing at the bar scrambled for the door.

"She's going over!" Dan Connally gasped.

The angle of the deck was shifting under their feet and the party of volunteers round Matt nearly scattered, but when he did not move, they stood firm. His hand was half raised and, after long seconds, when he lowered it, they realized the angle was steady.

"Was it torpedoes?" Barney asked.

"Most likely," Matt said. "But you know this ship. It's unsinkable unless the hull's breached in a number of places. We'll have to trust the captain to take us out of range."

"What do we do?" Dan asked.

"First, get your life belts," Matt said. He was thinking, Livvy's alone up there! Where are the kids? They could hear from outside the sound of confused shouting. "There may be some panic. Do what you can to keep it down—and to assist the ship's officers." He turned and led the way to the door, forcing himself not to run until he was outside.

Will Turner had no doubt in his mind about what had happened. His first thought had been that the second blast had been caused by part of his lethal cargo of ammunition, but it was all stowed over a hundred feet further forward than the site of the explosion. The explanation was much simpler, if he read the belching cloud of steam and dust and the instant loss of power rightly. Archie Bryce had maintained the nineteen enormous boilers in the three forward boiler rooms at full steam. The *Lusitania* had used up nearly half of the coal stored in the compartments of her longitudinal shell. The torpedo, detonating inside one of those immense half-filled compartments and aided by the combustion of its gases, must have fractured the inner bulkhead of one of the two most forward boiler rooms. Water flooding in had collapsed the furnaces and cracked two or more of the boilers, or jammed them together. All along he had worried needlessly about the ammunition, although he had been assured it could not be set off by impact. The colossal boilers, maintained at a pressure of 195 pounds to the square inch, had exploded and jack-knifed upward, a more destructive force than any bomb yet invented.

It was only four minutes since the torpedo had struck. All on the bridge were watching him, waiting for orders. He was silent, calculating rapidly. The list was acute but steady at just over 15 degrees, which meant most of the watertight bulkheads were holding. She was settling slowly by the bows, but should have several hours before it became fatal—if the U-boat left her alone. With reduced speed and difficulty in steering, he could not escape or even attempt to ram it. Cork Harbour was thirty miles to the east, too far to reach. His order to turn toward land had been instinct, yet it was right. Already the Old Head was nearer and in less than an hour he would run aground in shallower water. His passengers and cargo would be safe. Provided the *Lusitania*'s remaining power kept up. And that damned U-boat did not blow more holes in her. He tensed, hearing a popping rattle like irregular gunfire.

Hefford was helping First Officer Piper to lift the quartermaster who had been on starboard watch and been knocked unconscious. "It's—it's the ammunition!" he stammered. "I knew it! That's shells going off."

"No, Mr. Hefford," Turner said. "It's the high-pressure pipes."

Now the others could also make out that the noises were coming from the ventilators. Far below, the banks of steam pipes were bursting. In confirmation, the *Lusitania* all at once lost more headway and Quartermaster Johnston had to fight to control the steering.

Third Officer Lewis, gray-faced, had come in from the port side of the wing. "My compliments to Captain Anderson, Mr. Lewis," Turner said. "And would he kindly lower the boats in preparation to abandon ship." It was an order which Turner had never expected to hear himself issue. The others stared at him, still unable to face the terrible reality. "Jump to it!" Turner barked.

The keepers of the lighthouse on the Old Head of Kinsale had watched the attack and were still stunned. Below them, by the low wall of the lighthouse enclosure, the observer from the signal station had also been watching with a small crowd of boys and elderly fishermen who gathered every second Friday to cheer the Greyhound of the Seas as she passed. Sighting conditions were ideal and they had laughed and waved to see her head toward them and turn, giving them a perfect all-round view. The crump of the explosion and the fountaining smoke that enwrapped her bridge and bows shocked them.

"They've been laying for her for days," an old fisherman muttered. Two days earlier, he had watched a U-boat sink the little three-masted *Earl of Latham* with continuous fire from its deck gun at exactly the same spot.

"She'll never make it to shore," another one said.

The observer hurried for the wireless transmitter inside the station to alert the boats of the navy's coastal patrol.

Leith's distress calls had already been picked up by many receivers. Admiral Coke at Queenstown base had been worried by the submarine reports and had asked for a decision on diverting the *Lusitania* into Cork Harbour. True to its policy of leaving merchant vessels to fend for themselves, the Admiralty ignored the request, and while Coke waited for orders, he had done nothing. He realized suddenly that by summoning the antiquated cruiser squadron into port for its protection and by concentrating all available vessels of the auxiliary patrol on St. George's Channel and the approaches to Queenstown, he had left the great liner defenseless. The truth was that any suggestion she might be attacked was unthinkable. Yet it had happened, and apparently without warning. No such outrage had ever been perpetrated in all the annals of naval warfare.

The more he thought about it, the more obvious it became that she had been the prime target for all the increased U-boat activity in this area around the estimated time of her arrival. If only he had done something . . . He was strictly forbidden to send his torpedo boats outside the harbor, but he put on standby every yacht and trawler of the auxiliary patrol which could be made seaworthy. And he ordered Admiral Hood to investigate and possibly escort the stricken liner.

Hood's first thought was that it could easily have been his flagship the *Juno* that had been torpedoed. He was immediately ashamed of himself, remembering the thousand and more civilians on the *Lusitania*. Then he swore loudly, to the surprise of the *Juno*'s captain.

Sacked unjustly from command of the Dover Patrol and now skulking in harbor, while the most important vessel afloat was attacked under his nose, how would it appear?

Not good for him nor for the Admiralty to let it be so clearly demonstrated that they preferred to look after their own rather than the civilians they were pledged to protect. Dammit, couldn't they see that the U-boat campaign was as much a part of the real war as any fleet engagement? While they waited for the unlikely event of German battleships emerging, they should concentrate on defeating the enemy submarines, on organizing regular convoys and weapons for underwater attack, on bringing the war right up to the mouths of the U-boat pens.

The *Juno* had been tied up at her quay for nearly two hours and in that time her furnaces had been gradually damped down. Hood fumed as he waited for the engine room to report that she was operational. "Get that steam pressure up!" he roared. "I don't care how you do it, but get it up! For God's sake, don't let us arrive too late!"

Civilian vessels, tugs and fishing boats, were beginning to move out as the news spread, and others who were already at sea heard the distress calls, the freighter *City of Exeter* some forty miles south of the *Lusitania*'s position, the fishing smack *Bluebell*, the merchantman *Etonian* and the Greek tramp steamer *Katerina*. Largest of them was the Anglo-American Company's tanker *Narragansett*. Nearest, and most unable to help, was the Glasgow trawler *Peel 12*. Becalmed under the cliffs of the Old Head of Kinsale itself, her master could only watch and try to use any passing gust of wind to bring his sailboat closer. All came as fast as their circumstances allowed, knowing that every minute was precious.

In the *Lusitania*'s radio room, Robert Leith kept tapping out the new distress signal, SOS, and the message "Come at once, big list, 10 miles south Old Head Kinsale." He was heartened by the acknowledgments and promises of assistance which he had begun to receive, but he had to jam his foot against the table to prevent his chair sliding toward the open door and he could read on the dials that the strength of his signals was growing rapidly weaker.

McCormick was hovering nervously by the door. "They're launching the boats," he said.

"You'd better go to your station," Leith told him. "I'll stay here." His assistant left quickly and Leith carried on tapping out the signal, his eyes on the ammeter scale.

First Officer Arthur Jones had been sitting alone, enjoying a late lunch in the first-class dining saloon, when the torpedo struck. As he helped to usher the few passengers out, the list of the deck became more pronounced. The orchestra had been playing a medley of Strauss waltzes, but scattered when a lifesize portrait of King George and Queen Mary fell off the wall behind and crashed among them. Plates and cutlery slithered to the carpet and potted plants started to tumble over the rail from the fixed tables up in the verandah café, their glazed pots bursting on the dining saloon's floor. He ordered the waiters to close any portholes that were left open and ran up the main companionway to the boat deck.

People were flowing out of every corridor, crowding up to the main hall and promenades, and he had to push through. A few of the women were weeping and frightened, yet there was no atmosphere of panic. The knowledge that they were on the safest ship afloat gave the passengers confidence. However, Jones saw at once that there was a problem. Because of the list, the lifeboats on the starboard side had swung outwards to the limit of the restraining chain. The gap between the rail and the boats was too wide to step across, and was even wider when the pins that fastened the chains were knocked out, while the sheer drop down to the water was still over forty feet. The height was least toward the bows, since they had settled lower.

With Third Officer Lewis and some of the male passengers, Jones managed to organize groups of women and children to fill the first boats, but the women refused point-blank to try to cross the gap, which seemed more dangerous than staying on board. No.1 boat nearest the bows was lowered by its rope falls to the water. Another rope was tied to the rail and two young seamen volunteered to climb down it. They made it fast to the boat, but the women refused to risk sliding down. Meanwhile, the boat next to it had also been lowered to the water. To free it if the list increased, the falls of No.1 boat were cut. The single rope holding it parted and it slid swiftly along the side of the liner, crunching against the other lifeboat. The two seamen leaped over into the one that was still attached to its davit, and Jones and the passengers watched in dismay as No.1 boat floated away, safe but empty. The sight started a scramble to get into the remaining boats, however risky or difficult it was. They were hauled back and held as close to the rail as possible while the women and children were helped into them, now more frightened.

The situation on the liner's port side was more chaotic.

Bestwick had gone to his cabin to put his feet up and was disgusted when an order came from Staff Captain Anderson for him to supervise the transfer of the sacks from the mail hold. From experience, he knew it was one of the dirtiest and sweatiest jobs anyone could be landed with, and he paused to change into his old uniform so as not to spoil the one he had bought last week in New York. He had not finished changing when his cabin rocked with the explosions.

He hurried immediately to the port side of the boat deck, where he shared command of the boat stations with Staff Captain Anderson. Half the stokers and engine room staff who made up the crews did not appear, and he was shocked to realize that many of them must have been killed or injured in the boiler rooms.

More people had rushed to the port side, which was higher because of the list and further from the water. Many had not waited for instructions but clambered into the boats, in some cases without a single crewman to handle them. Women were weeping at being separated from their husbands and searching for lost children. Men were shouting, insisting on the boats being cast off, clutching at Bestwick and demanding to be told what was happening. He kept repeating the formula that there was no danger while he grabbed anyone in uniform, sending them to take the place of missing crewmen. All the time he was conscious of something which no one else seemed to have realized. Because of the list, the *Lusitania*'s port side now sloped back from the water and the lifeboats had swung inward. Somehow, they would have to be pushed out beyond the slope of the side before they could be safely lowered.

He threaded through the crowd and up the steeply inclined deck to report. Anderson was agitated, trying to establish some kind of orderliness out of the tumult. He was

603

obviously relieved to see Bestwick and exclaimed, "Thank God! I thought you'd gone to your death." Bestwick did not understand. "All the men working down in the mail hold and the baggage room—they were wiped out in the explosion."

Bestwick could not grasp it fully. It was too horrifying. The cargo elevator had crashed, mangling the detail bringing up the first load of mail sacks. If he had not stopped to change his uniform, he would have been down there with them.

"Bloody Huns," Anderson muttered. "But there's no time to lose! We must get these boats launched."

"It won't be easy with this list, sir," Bestwick warned.

"It will only become worse, the longer we wait," Anderson said. "Start at the end nearest the bows. Hurry, man!"

Elbert and Alice Hubbard were standing against the bulkhead behind them. Hubbard had his arm round his wife to protect her from the surge of the crowd. Charles Lauriat, the bookseller, pushed through to them. He had been hunting for life belts. "No luck, I'm afraid," he told them. "There's no spare ones left up here."

"Well, thank you for trying," Hubbard said, smiling. "We appreciate it."

"Come with me," Lauriat suggested. "We'll pick some up somewhere."

"Thank you, Mr. Lauriat, you've been most kind," Hubbard said. "But we have decided, if we can find space in a boat, we shall take it. Otherwise, we shall not struggle against the inevitable."

Hubbard's serenity was incomprehensible to Lauriat.

"Neither of us could survive prolonged immersion in the water," Hubbard explained. "So it is best if the end comes quickly."

"You must have a life belt!" Lauriat insisted. "Yours are in your cabin. That's only one deck down. I'll come with you."

"Please, no, Mr. Lauriat," Alice Hubbard said gently. "By all means get one for yourself, but forget about us."

"You have many years ahead of you. We should regret it deeply if you suffered any harm because of us," Hubbard said. He chuckled wryly. "As it is, I have only one regret— that Kaiser Bill appears to have taken the last trick."

Bestwick had won through to the end boat, where the distance to the water was least, but it was still over sixty feet down the *Lusitania*'s side, whose slope even in the last minute had become more pronounced. Holding on to the rail with one hand and to a davit with the other, he leaned out. The electrically operated mechanism controlling the davits was not working. If they could be turned and the lifeboat swung outwards, there was just a chance that it could be lowered to the water without scraping the side. What worried him was the considerable weight of the clinker-built boats.

"What are we waiting for?" someone shouted.

"All right," Bestwick said, turning. "You can all see this is going to be difficult. We'll have to push the boat outwards as far as we can. I'll need some of you gentlemen to assist."

Led by some of the Canadian volunteers, a large number of men swarmed forward, eager to do whatever they could. They helped one another up onto the collapsible and spread out, bracing themselves with their hands against the curved side of the lifeboat. Crewmen were already at their places in the boat, which was filled with women and children, two able seamen poised to pay the ropes out through the thick wooden blocks. Bestwick leaned out again to check the angle of descent. "All together now!" he called. There was comparative silence round them as the men gritted their teeth when they felt the weight and began to thrust. In the silence, Bestwick heard a metallic click and a rattle. Someone to be helpful had hammered out the pin securing the restraining chain.

"No!" he yelled, but it was too late.

Freed from the chain which held it, and with the added weight of over sixty people, the ponderous boat swept suddenly inwards, mashing through the men who had been trying to push it out. It crashed over the collapsible onto its side, throwing out most of its passengers and tearing loose from the davits, before slithering erratically down the angled deck to wedge itself in the passage under the port wing of the bridge. Bestwick clung to the splintered davit which had stopped him from being pitched overboard, gazing in disbelief at the tangle of bodies and screaming, blood-spattered children and women. With a terrible sense of powerlessness, he saw that what they had tried to do was being copied by the men in charge of the next boat. He yelled to them, stumbling over the broken bodies on the collapsible to get to them, but before he could, the second boat had also smashed inwards and toppled over. Even as he shouted, it came slewing down the deck faster than the other, crunching over the dead and the living who were trying to rise and carrying the first boat's collapsible with it until they fetched up against the first and the whole lower end of the deck was jammed with damaged lifeboats and dead and injured. Bestwick found he was sobbing uncontrollably.

Matt had raced up to the stern end of the boat deck. The starboard side where he had left Livvy was already crowded. Many were pointing to a lifeboat, which he saw swirling past in the water with no one in it. He realized he was lucky he had come from the stern. All the companionways further forward were packed with people attempting to force their way up from the promenade deck below, desperate with the need to get higher. They were quiet, ominously quiet, but although a ship's officer kept calling, "Please stay where you are! Let us clear this deck!" no one paid any attention.

All the time Matt was moving forward, looking for Livvy. He passed young Lady Mackworth and her father, Rita Jolivet, Justus Forman and Theodate Pope, and asked all of them if they had seen his wife, but no one had. He hoped she had teamed up with someone, Lee and Beattie maybe, or Vanderbilt and some of the others. He saw Biggs, the steward, tying a life belt on someone, a woman in clinging wet clothes caked with coal dust. He almost did not recognize her.

First Officer Jones had discovered Livvy near the girl's body and the wrecked boat. She was dazed and he asked Biggs to assist her into the next boat to be launched. Supporting her, Biggs got her as far as the rail before she realized where she was and what he was doing. She pulled back in alarm. "Better climb on board, ma'am," he advised her.

"Not without my husband," she told him, backing away. "Not without my husband and children."

"They'll be fine, ma'am," Biggs soothed. "But take your place."

"I'm not going!" Livvy insisted. "Not without them."

Biggs was afraid of her becoming hysterical. "You don't even 'ave a life belt, ma'am," he said. He called to the senior steward in command of the boat, " 'Ere! Chuck us a vest, will you?" The steward threw one of the spare life belts to him.

"I don't want it," Livvy said.

"Now, you wouldn't like me to get cross, would you?" Biggs asked her severely. "You be a good girl, and stand still. It's no use if it's not put on proper."

While he was fastening it, Livvy saw Matt coming toward her. She held him, sobbing in relief. He brushed a smear of damp soot from her forehead. "What on earth's happened to you?" he asked, worried.

Biggs had followed her and was fastening the tapes of the life belt. "Got caught near the blast, sir," he explained. "Now she won't get in the boat."

Matt turned with her, his arm round her. "Come on, Livvy."

"No!" she said. "We have to find the children!"

"I'll find them. Come on."

"Not without you! You can't make me!"

She was fighting away from him, but he caught her wrists. "All right! All right, honey. Don't worry. We'll find them."

"For God's sake, Fletcher! Give me a hand!" someone called. It was James Brooks.

The list had increased and the surface of the water was only twenty feet below the boat deck. Brooks had been helping Purser McCubbin to fill the lifeboat, which had now swung out to the end of its restraining chain, leaving a gap of over six feet between it and the rail. Brooks was standing on the rail with his left arm hooked round the lefthand davit end lifting the women who stood on the collapsible over the gap one by one with his right arm. There were thirty or so still waiting, scared. Matt left Livvy with Biggs and jumped onto the rail by the righthand davit. Anchoring himself with his right arm, he matched Brooks, letting the women clasp his left arm and swinging them across the gap to the crewmen in the swaying boat.

Elizabeth Duckworth had insisted on Alice and Arthur putting on their life jackets before leaving the cabin, but it took longer than she expected. When she led them out, she nearly fell sideways. The floor of the transverse passageway was slanting so much that they had to put one hand on it, holding the rail on the wall with the other to pull themselves up. Alice crawled into one of the longer passages leading to the stern. "Not that way!" Elizabeth told her sharply. "It's too far. We might not make it."

Drawing Arthur behind her, Elizabeth turned in the other direction, toward a narrow companionway connecting with others which led up through four deck levels to the bows. Now she had to hold on tightly with her free hand to stop herself from sliding downwards. Following them, Alice was moaning softly, unable to stifle it. She could hear something more terrifying than anything she had ever known, the sound of water rushing into the ship.

Will Turner was gazing at the Old Head of Kinsale. It was closer by two or three miles, but still a damnable way off, and the water was creeping inexorably up the bows toward the forecastle deck. 2:19. It was not even ten minutes since the torpedo struck.

Quartermaster Johnston had been ordered to report every variation of the list indicator and Turner heard him call out, "Eighteen points to starboard!" Still not fatal. The designers and marine engineers had calculated that the *Lusy* could be sailed in safety with a list of up to twenty-two points. Beyond that . . . He had a disturbing vision of the sea pouring over the bow gunwales and flooding the well of the fo'c'sle deck.

"Mr. Hefford," he said, "kindly check the hatch covers in the fo'c'sle deck, and make sure all doors are closed."

He watched Hefford hurry out and go down the outside of the ladder, lowering himself down the slanted upright. A good man, Hefford. A bit prickly, but a good man. They were all good men, and how many would be here tomorrow? His eyes switched back to the Old Head and the small fishing boat becalmed under it, the only other craft in sight in all the wide sea. Were any others heading toward them? If he managed to beach, they could ferry the passengers ashore. If that damned U-boat let them. What were they doing on it now? he wondered. Laughing and congratulating themselves, no doubt. Pirates. Damned inhuman pirates!

Containing his rage, he stepped carefully to the door and out onto the sloping starboard wing. He searched the sea,

which was so unruffled he had no trouble locating the ar-
rowhead wake. It was much nearer now and he could make
the periscope out more clearly, a shaft not more than four
inches wide with an arched lens at the top. It was following
them. Why? Just to enjoy the *Lusitania*'s death struggle—
or to hurl another torpedo into her? The sun glinted on the
lens of the unwinking eye. What manner of man was watching them? he wondered. What kind of devil, watching and
gloating?

"You'll have to put another torpedo into her," Lanz advised.
Schwieger was intent on the eyepiece and did not answer.
The liner's loss of speed had allowed him to creep closer,
cautiously because only one shot from the *Lusitania*'s powerful guns could tear the U 20's conning tower apart.
"She's not going to sink!" Lanz insisted. "Her hull's honey-
combed with watertight compartments. With only one hole
in her, she can stay afloat for hours and still reach port!"
He could scarcely keep the rage of frustration at Schwieger's
hesitance out of his voice.
Schwieger was hardly aware of him. The elation had drained
from him as he watched, unable to take his eyes from what
was happening, although it was almost unbearable. From
his position slightly astern, he could see the difficulty in
lowering the boats. There was wreckage in the sea and
bodies, people leaping from the rails of the shelter deck that
was angling down toward the water. He could see the flutter
of women's dresses, but no uniforms. No soldiers. A surge
of passengers toward the uprearing stern.
As the U 20 came more abreast, he swiveled the lens very
slowly, raking the liner from stem to stern. The list was so
great that he could examine the whole sweep of the upper
decks on the starboard side. *Where were the naval guns?*
There was nothing amidships except a thousand frightened
people. Nothing at the stern except more people. The projection at the bows which he had supposed to be a gun
emplacement was only a small derrick. No guns? Unarmed,
defenseless, after all . . . ? His mouth was dry and he reminded himself desperately of the second explosion. The
Lusitania's cargo of weapons and ammunition, explosive
materials, gunpowder, that must have been what caused it.

He looked up. At what could be read in his expression, Kurtz closed his eyes.

After a nod from Lanz, Scherb reported, "Number Two forward tube ready, Captain."

Schwieger saw that the gunnery lieutenant had uncovered the No. 2 firing button, and that his hand was cupped over it.

"Patrol boats may arrive at any moment," Lanz stressed. "Will you give the order to fire?"

"If I have to," Schwieger said, and bent again to the eyepiece.

Elizabeth's scramble up the series of inclined companionways to the bows, wearing a bulky life jacket and half carrying Arthur, was exhausting. She was panting and could feel her underclothes sticking to her unpleasantly. She knew where she was now, the bottom of the last flight of steps, leading to the rear of the forecastle deck where third-class passengers had been permitted to take exercise.

She heard Alice Scott's ragged breathing behind her and called encouragingly, "Come on, Mrs. Scott! Only one more to go!" Up here the light was brighter, from larger, uncovered portholes, and she saw Arthur gazing up at her anxiously. She made herself smile and chucked him under the chin, and started up with him the moment Alice joined them. Although it cramped her feet, it was easiest to walk in the angle made by the steps and the wall.

At the top Elizabeth lifted the bar to open the door. It did not move. She pushed harder, but still the iron door would not open.

"What's wrong?" Alice asked nervously.

"Stuck," Elizabeth said. She set her shoulder to the door, and shoved with all her strength, again and again, with no effect. Oh dear God, she thought. Someone's locked it from outside! She knocked on the door, then again harder, although the metal hurt her knuckles. "Open up!" she shouted. "Open the door!" But it was useless. There was no one outside, no one answered.

Elizabeth was nearly weeping. She glanced back down the companionway and Alice whimpered, knowing what she was thinking. All the way back down there? Stumbling about in that maze of small passages. In the semi-darkness, with the knowledge of the water rising below them, Alice's nerve broke and she screamed, a piercing scream of sheer terror, reverberating in the narrow space. She flung herself past Elizabeth and began to beat on the door with the flat of her hands, sobbing and howling. "Open the door! Someone— please! Open the door! Let us out! Let us out!"

Elizabeth had drawn Arthur to her and covered his ears, but in spite of herself, she felt her own nerve going. In the next second she was also beating and kicking at the door and begging someone to save them.

It was almost an anticlimax when the door gave and she saw a young sailor looking at them in astonishment. It was Joe Parry. He caught Alice as she fell forward. "You're lucky anyone 'eard you, missus," he told Elizabeth. "Wouldn't 'ave in another minute. Step lively, now."

Elizabeth grabbed Arthur and pulled him out onto the forecastle deck with its hatches and capstans and the derrick forward at the bows. Alice was faint, still sobbing. "Anyone else in there?" Parry asked. Elizabeth shook her head and he dogged down the companionway door again. "Best not 'ang about 'ere," he warned. "Not unless you want to swim for it."

"Look, Aunt Lizzie!" Arthur gasped.

Elizabeth looked and bit her lip. Beyond the rail beside them the sea was foaming past, only a few feet away.

Elizabeth shook herself and breathed in deeply. She had been behaving like a silly Sunday school girl. Time she pulled herself together. She nodded to Parry and somehow between them they hoisted Alice and Arthur up to the boat deck. Once they were there, Elizabeth thanked him and said, "You do whatever you have to. We can manage now."

Joe Parry was relieved. It was a hell of a thing to have been made responsible for them and lessened his own chances of getting out of this in one piece. "If you're sure," he said. "Good luck, missus." He left quickly before she changed her mind.

The tilted deck was difficult to walk on because of the film of greasy coal dust and they kept slipping. Elizabeth had to support Alice round the waist. With Arthur gripping her other hand, she shuffled along the deck as fast as she dared to a group of men round the nearest boat. They parted as they heard her calling, "Please . . . please . . ." She saw a lifeboat slung on its davits. It seemed very full. Two men were standing on the rail, and two women on the collapsible boat under it. One after the other, the men swung the women out to the dangling lifeboat. Elizabeth lifted Arthur onto the collapsible and nudged Alice to follow him.

The senior steward in charge of the boat protested, "There's no more room! We can't take any more!"

"You can take the boy," Matt said and held out his hand to Arthur. Arthur's face crumpled and he looked up at his mother.

"Go along now," Alice said. "Don't keep them waiting, dear."

Arthur looked at Elizabeth. "Do as your mother says," she told him.

Matt reached down and put his arm round Arthur's chest. "Grab a hold!" he warned and swung him up, almost throwing him across the gap to the seamen in the boat. Matt looked again at Livvy, who was watching, taut. She stepped back. "Lower away!" he shouted.

The crewmen at the stern and the bows paid out the rope falls carefully and the lifeboat creaked down until its keel touched the water. When they cast off, the boat laden mainly with women scrunched down heavily, sending a spouting wave up all round it, but it steadied and was steered safely away through the turbulence of the *Lusitania*'s passage.

Alice was crying and trembling and Elizabeth supported her again. "Arthur's safe, that's all that matters," she said. "Now we'll get you on a boat."

Matt and Brooks jumped down from the rail. They were both stiff. Matt's left arm was aching and the lancing pain in his shoulder was as if the muscles had been torn again. Everyone round them had rushed toward the next lifeboat. Brooks ran back and slithered down a rope to one already in the water to help to free the rope falls which could not be released. Matt held out his hand to Livvy and she took it quickly, her eyes wide, anxious. "I'm sorry, honey," he said. "I had to help."

"I know," she muttered.

"Are you all right now?" She nodded. "Let's go and find the kids."

Will Turner had been watching the launching of boats on the starboard side. The problems of boarding and lowering them in an emergency with the *Lusitania* listing heavily had never been sufficiently taken into account, he realized. Most serious was the overbalancing effect of her tremendous height and the distance from the boat deck to the water. He himself had questioned her designer, Leonard Peskett, about it, to be told that the situation was hardly likely to arise and, if it did, any list could easily be corrected by flooding the trimming tanks on the opposite side until her balance was restored. Simple, all electrically controlled. However, Peskett had not allowed for war damage. The trimming tanks did not respond and the chief electrician reported that the linkages must have been broken. Access to the tanks had been blocked by the second explosion, and the men who could have operated them manually had been wiped out.

Turner did not blame the designer. With only the hole blown out of her by the torpedo, the *Lusitania* could have crossed the Atlantic. But no ship could survive the explosion that followed. Turner had known then that his beautiful ship, his pride, was doomed. It was only a question of how much time he and she together could give their passengers to make their escape.

He still had to check how launchings were proceeding on the port side, which should be easier. As he moved, he heard Johnston report nineteen points of list. Chief Officer Piper came to him and saluted. "Hefford's by himself on the fo'c'sle deck," he said. "I'd better go and help him."

"Very well, Mr. Piper," Turner agreed. It was a brave gesture by the Chief Officer and for once Turner returned the salute. Piper ran to the ladder and Turner hurried for the upper bridge from which he could observe everything that was happening. He crossed quickly to the port side. What he saw there appalled him.

More of the port lifeboats, each laden with seventy or eighty people, had crashed inwards irresistibly and, with the liner's stern heaving up higher, had slalomed down the deck between the bulkheads and the collapsibles, throwing out most of their passengers on the way and ramming into the hideous wreckage heaped up under the bridge. The last boat had mounted the wreckage like a ramp and lay on its beam on top, pressing down on the mound of smashed boats and bodies. The ship's doctor, stewards and some of the Canadian volunteers were trying frantically to free the living injured from the carnage.

At midship, he could see all that was left of one boat hanging halfway down the *Lusitania*'s vast side, the bow section and a few shreds of splintered wood dangling from one of its rope falls. With the added list, an attempt had been made to slide the boat down the slope of the ocean queen's side. It looked smooth, but her steel plates, the size of billiard tables, were ringed with roundheaded rivets projecting two inches above the surface. The overlapped planks of the lifeboat snagged on the rivets as it came down sideways, tipping the boat over sharply and flinging half of its occupants out. The rest clung to it, screaming, while the ropes ran too swiftly through the blocks and it scraped raspingly down the slope until the rivets ripped the bottom out of it.

Fear and panic were building as the *Lusitania*'s passengers saw the precious boats being destroyed one after the other. Turner was shouting to Staff Captain Anderson, but could not make himself heard above the uproar of voices. He had spotted Anderson directing the men who were loading another batch of women and children into a boat, which sensibly he had had winched over to the outside of the rail before permitting anyone to enter.

"No! No! No!" Turner yelled, beating the balustrade of the upper bridge at his impotence to stop it.

On the Staff Captain's orders, some of the crewmen were holding their bulky oars between the lifeboat and the side of the ship as buffers against the rivets, while others pushed it away from the side. They steered it safely down from the level of the boat deck, but its keel wedged itself behind the rail of the promenade deck. The crewmen were reluctant to thrust their oars into the mass of people on the promenade and called up for the boat to be raised. Men and women were reaching for the rope looped along the lifeboat's gunwale and trying to clamber into it. The boat was rocking and all at once tipped over as the stern ropes gave way, tossing everyone out to pour down the black glacis of the *Lusitania*'s side, shrieking and cartwheeling like a human avalanche. The boat broke loose from its davits and plunged down on top of them.

Turner was hoarse, his mind hazed with shock. How many boats had now been wrecked or lost? Nine or ten. Enough for over seven hundred people! He'd always said the *Lusitania* had twice as many boats as the *Titanic*, but hers had got away safely. She had a full crew who'd had two hours to launch them. Someone was shouting to him desperately, and he looked down.

Bestwick was standing on the wreckage, calling up that Staff Captain Anderson wanted the portside stabilizing tanks flooded. "It's no use! They're not working!" Turner yelled back. "Tell him—tell him what he's doing is too dangerous! Tell him not to lower any more boats until the way is off the ship!"

Land was less than fourteen miles off now, but he knew they would never make it. Rather than try, it was better to stop the *Lusitania*. Once her speed had dropped, the starboard boats could be lowered safely at least, however far her stern was from the surface, and pads and rollers could be improvised to get the rest of the portside boats to the water in one piece. He was hurrying for the engine room telegraph. He wrenched it up and slammed it back down again to Full Speed Astern.

Cockburn and the junior engineers had been nursing the engines, maintaining as much pressure as possible. The immense wheels and pistons were still churning and pounding without a falter. But when he switched to the low-pressure turbine for full astern, the valves which needed repair, as Archie Bryce had kept insisting, seized up. The blocked pressure blew out the pipes and vicious jets of steam scalded the men near them. In seconds, the central low-pressure engine room was a blinding white hell, with engineers, oilers and stokers clawing for the ladders to the exits.

At the same moment Turner heard Quartermaster Johnston call out, "She's not responding!" The wheel had gone dead.

In the radio room, Robert Leith felt the resistance in his transmitter key give out in the middle of a word. He pressed the key sharply, but there was no spark. His earphones were silent. The needle of the ammeter had swung back to zero. The main generators had stopped and cut off the ship's electricity supply.

To his left through the door, he had an uninterrupted view

615

of the sea, closer than ever. His radio shack was heeling over toward it and he could see flotsam in the water that could only have come from the *Lusitania*. The urge to save himself was strong and he stood up, staggering slightly on the angled floor. But instead of making for the door, he turned to the emergency dynamo and flicked the switch. The dynamo hummed into life. Its batteries, he knew, would give him power for several hours. He took a deep breath and sat at the table again, beginning to tap out the message he had repeated over and over again, "SOS. *Lusitania*. Come at once. Big list."

All over the liner, fans and air extractors, bells, telephones, control switches, ovens, hoists and signal mechanisms had stopped working. There were many people still in their cabins in the lower decks, collecting their belongings together or waiting for instructions on what to do. Stewards and stewardesses were handing out and checking life belts, nursery maids helping parents to carry their children up to the higher levels, nurses assisting the elderly, passengers from steerage who did not know the route to the boat deck. When all the lights flickered and went out, there was a terror-stricken stampede, people running in every direction in a panic fear to escape. In third class, the man who always complained about the blackout had gone back to fetch his life vest and the woman with six children had paused to change the baby. Stumbling in the dark, they discovered the watertight doors at the end of their passageway shut fast, with no means of opening them.

Hugh Johnston had been winning his fight with the wheel, but now without power for the steering, he could only watch the *Lusitania*'s prow drift away from the land. Dragged round by the list, she would drift in a long, continuous curve.

Will Turner had felt the last throb of her engines. Although they no longer drove her, her speed had not noticeably dropped. She would plough on under her own momentum for some time.

Even as he thought it, he felt her dragging and her head yawed from side to side. He was on the upper bridge and ran to the forward rail. His heart hammered in his chest. Water was flowing over the gunwales of the fo'c'sle deck. It was only fifteen minutes since the explosion and her bows were going under . . . There was no trace anywhere of the

Chief Officer, nor of Hefford, not on the swamped deck or in the water. They had simply vanished.

Frank Tower, the oiler, had recovered consciousness. He could not understand it. He was lying near where he had been working and he was covered with water. Only his head, propped up by a grating, was above it.

He sat up and, as he looked around, remembered the explosions and being hurled off his feet. What the hell was it? Where the hell was everybody? He had been working in number two boiler room. The Chief, old Archie, and his team had just completed their daily inspection and moved forward into number one. The doors were closed—and boom! He'd been thrown off his perch and, as he picked himself up, there'd been another bloody boom, even bigger. The whole boiler room had seemed to dance and—water?

His head was clearing and he shivered uncontrollably. The water he was sitting in had risen to his waist and was ice cold. Oh, fuck, no . . . Oh, shit. Jesus, not again! He stood up and, swaying, grabbed a bracket to steady himself. He noticed a burn across his hand and up his arm, where the sleeve of his denim tunic was charred away. There'd been a bloody great flash from up forward. Firemen screaming they'd been scalded.

It was hard to see in the cavernous boiler room, for most of the lights were out, except the red warning lamps. Now he was standing, the water was up to his knees, and rising. It was coming through the deck-level hatches in the starboard bunkers. The coal which had sealed them for a while had been swept away by the force of the water pouring in. By this time, the stokehold and number one boiler room must be completely flooded, and if the doors gave way . . .

As he turned, he caught sight of one of the firemen crouching on the deck, leaning over against the base of one of the iron ladders. They had only two or three minutes at most and he couldn't just leave him. "Hey, mate!" he called. "On your feet!" Tower splashed over to him and shook his shoulder. "Come on—wake up!" The man slumped sideways and Tower saw that the top of his head had been sliced off in the blast, scooped out like a softboiled egg. He backed away, retching, nearly falling with the tilt of the deck. He ran, splashing through the water, for the watertight doors aft. They were locked off and he pounded and beat on them,

617

until he realized he was wasting vital seconds. His seared arm had been numbed by the coldness and now was beginning to sting. The water had reached midthigh. The *Lusy* was filling and sinking, beyond doubt, the bloody *Titanic* all over again.

It was then that the last lights went out.

Tower yelled for help in his fright, but there was no one to answer. He was in pitch blackness and all he could hear was a metallic creaking and the rush of water. He knew there were other ways out if only he could get to them. He started forward, his hands reaching out blindly. He had to get higher, find a ladder. Something bobbed against his legs. He lost his balance and fell into the water. He had opened his mouth and was choking as he went under, rolling over and over submerged. When he came up, spluttering, he had no more sense of direction. The level was above his waist and the inrush pushing him backward.

One thing he could go by, the tilt of the deck, and he floundered up it until his outflung hands touched the portside bulkhead. He felt his way along it and at last grasped what he'd been searching for, one of the inspection ladders. The water seemed to be sucking him back as he hauled himself out of it and clambered up hand over hand, until he came to a perch. The ladder went no further. The small open perch was slippery and tilted downwards. He could not stand on it. On his hands and knees, he felt cautiously round it in the darkness until he touched a catwalk. Holding the rail, he inched along it until he located another iron ladder, narrower, leading up. Below him, there was a menacing hiss of steam.

Carefully but quickly he climbed higher. In the darkness his head struck something, dizzying him. It was a metal grille, and he tugged and clawed at it with one hand until the catches snicked back and it fell open. He pulled himself up.

He was in the shaft of one of the giant ventilators. The climb up the height of six decks was agonizing, with the ladder inclined so that he was hanging backward, but at least he could see daylight and finally crawled out onto the lip of the opening of the ventilator, so large that a man could stand in it with another on his shoulders. As he gulped in air, he chuckled to himself lightheadedly. It was the highest he had ever been. At long last he had made it to the Marconi deck.

Below him was the wreckage on the port boat deck and the steep black slope of the *Lusitania*'s side. The bows were underwater and, to his left, her stern rose like a bloody mountain, crowded with hundreds of people. They were not his concern. He lowered himself to the Marconi deck, ran across it and came to a halt in shock. He had to see it to believe it. To starboard, the sea was nearly up to the forward promenade deck. There were hundreds more passengers clustered aft round the last few boats. He could see other people struggling in the water and three or four lifeboats drawing away. With no more pause for thought, he let himself over the edge of the Marconi deck, dropped to the empty section of boat deck, ran across it to the rail and dived.

He came up shaking his head, and saw what looked like an upturned boat off to his left. He swam strongly toward it. You dozy bastard, he scolded himself as he kicked out. Why didn't you stop to take off your bloody boots?

A second burst of smoke and steam spewed from the ventilators round the *Lusitania*'s two central funnels. Matt and Livvy, hunting anxiously for the children, felt the vibrations as more of her furnaces collapsed. There was no sign of Peter and Diana in the crowd, nor of the Allan girls or any of the Cromptons. Livvy saw Alfred Vanderbilt helping to load one of the boats. People on the starboard side were still being polite, offering places to others first, and readily stood back to let him and a middle-aged woman lift a younger woman over the side. It was the pretty mother of the boy Matt had swung over into the last boat. She was lucky, knowing her child was safe, Livvy thought. She herself was really alarmed, and only Matt's hand gripping her arm prevented her from becoming frantic. Whatever we do, we mustn't lose our heads, he'd told her. They had met Dan and Barney, who had joined in the search. "What's Diana wearing?" Dan had asked, and Livvy couldn't remember. She couldn't remember! She had paid so little attention to the children, these past few days, only too glad to have them taken off her hands. She could not stop blaming herself. Where were they?

Matt's hand jerked her arm. "Livvy!" he said. Then she heard a piercing cry of "Mummy, Mummy! Daddy!"

Lady Allan was coming out of the main entrance hall. With her were Gwen and Anna, and between them was Diana. She did not seem at all frightened. She was smiling and waving. Livvy pushed through to her. "Isn't it exciting, Mummy?" Diana said. She had on her sailor dress and straw hat with a blue ribbon. Mercifully, over the dress, she was wearing a child's padded life vest.

"Yes, it is," Livvy agreed. "Very exciting, darling." She crouched and drew Diana to her, holding her very tightly.

"Isn't it fun, Daddy!" Diana laughed.

Matt nodded. "It sure is, pet." He pushed her chin playfully with his fist. "We wondered where you'd got to."

"I'm sorry. We had some trouble locating the right kind of life jacket for her," Lady Allan told him. "Annie found one." Matt smiled his thanks to the girls' maid, who was behind them.

First Officer Jones had become more worried after the second cloud of steam and cinders. "This way, ladies!" he called. "Quickly, please!"

They moved toward the boat which was almost full. Beside it, Virginia Loney was arguing with her parents. She gave in, kissed them both, and Vanderbilt helped her over the side. He seemed very cheerful, debonair in a sports suit and checked cap with a pink flower in his buttonhole, and kissed her cheek as he set her down. "That's to remember me by," he said, and she blushed. He lifted Gwen Allan in and kissed her, too. He was so evidently enjoying himself that some of the people watching smiled.

Jones had lifted Gwen's sister in and their maid. Lady Allan was hanging back. "Please, Mother," Gwen begged.

"It's time to leave now, my lady," Jones advised.

"They're all so damned polite. Why don't they get on with it?" Matt muttered, and was relieved when Lady Allan let Jones take her hand and assist her over the rail into the lifeboat.

The quartermaster in charge of it was counting the number of passengers he had. "The little one next, sir," he said, "and that's it."

"Off you go, darling," Livvy told Diana and urged her forward.

"Aren't you coming?" Diana asked, looking from Livvy to Matt.

"In a minute," he said. "We have to find Peter first."

Her face fell. "You'd rather have fun with him."

"Of course not, darling," Livvy assured her, and stroked her hair. "We just don't want him to get lost. Now off you go. We'll all tell one another our adventures later."

Diana brightened up. Vanderbilt took her under the arms and lifted her. "You're the prettiest of the lot," he whispered.

She squealed when he kissed her on the nose and passed her over to the quartermaster. She remembered something and called, "Goodbye, Mr. Ferguson! 'Bye, Uncle Dan!" They waved to her.

Dan said, "We'll be looking for Peter," and he and Barney left quickly.

"Stand by to lower away!" the quartermaster shouted to the men at the rope falls.

The launching crew was having trouble releasing the pin of the restraining chain. Some of the pins had been painted over so often, they were almost cemented in. Elizabeth was watching, seated next to Alice in the lifeboat. She felt uncomfortable at taking up a place in it when others even older and not so fit as herself were still waiting. She saw a young woman hurrying toward the boat station, pale and agitated, carrying a baby in a Moses basket. She had been turned away from the boat beyond them and was crying as she pleaded with the ship's officer in French. "We could maybe take the baby," Jones was trying to explain, "but—"

"She can have my place," Elizabeth said loudly, louder than she had meant. She patted Alice Scott's hand, reached for the rail and climbed out. Vanderbilt helped her over and bowed to her, embarrassing her. The young Frenchwoman took her seat without a word of gratitude, she was so frightened for herself and her baby.

The pin was knocked out and Jones ordered, "Lower away!"

Livvy could tell that Diana was more excited than ever when the boat began to bump slowly downwards. She was waving and blowing kisses to Matt and her. She stood up to watch and giggled when Lady Allan pulled her back onto the seat. She doesn't know what's happening, really, Livvy thought. Thank God she doesn't know. Along from them, a

621

small group of the volunteer nurses was singing, "Abide with me, fast falls the eventide." It made Livvy shiver.

"Isn't that one of the Crompton boys?" Matt said suddenly. "What's his name—John? Peter's friend." Livvy looked. She could see a few children, but not John. "He was heading into the main hall," Matt said. "Come on!" He started off, but Livvy did not follow. She was torn. They had to find Peter, yet she did not want Diana to see them leave and perhaps become afraid. "Come on!" Matt repeated.

"I can't," Livvy told him. "In a minute. Only a minute."

He understood and they moved closer to the rail, next to Vanderbilt and Allan Loney and his wife. Mrs. Loney was crying and smiling at the same time, waving to her daughter Virginia, who was gazing up at them, biting her lip. Diana sat behind her, between the Allan twins, with Lady Allan and their maid on either side. She was upset that she was not staying on board with her parents, but the excitement made up for it and she waved up to them. "She's a brave kid," Matt murmured. "I'm not sure about the ringlets, though." Livvy smiled and he put his arm round her. It was reassuring. Yet she knew he was as worried about Peter as she was and could think of nothing until he was also safe.

The *Lusitania*'s stern swung higher and the lifeboat rocked. "Steady there!" the quartermaster shouted up to the men at the davits.

As he shouted, the liner lurched wildly. Matt's arm tightened round Livvy and they heard people cry out as they were thrown off balance and rolled down the slanting deck.

Elizabeth Duckworth was watching Alice, whose head was turning from side to side in alarm as the lifeboat shuddered and jolted at the end of its ropes. The young Frenchwoman was bent over her baby. There were many male passengers in the boat, too. Surely that wasn't right when there were still women and children left?

Livvy's mouth was opening. What she saw seemed to be happening in slow motion, yet it was over in seconds. Either the lifeboat's bow ropes parted or they were wrenched out of the hands of the men at the davit, but they suddenly raced through the block. The bow plunged instantly and all the seventy people on board were hurled out. There was a split second when Diana seemed to reach up both arms imploringly, her eyes wide and terrified; then she was gone, swallowed up in the sea.

Livvy's gasp rose to a scream. Bodies were thrashing and tumbling over in the water. For a moment she thought she glimpsed Diana again, her long hair streaming behind her. She lunged forward to dive over the rail to save her, but Matt caught her fiercely round the waist and held her. The foaming rush of water along the *Lusitania*'s side, as fast as a millrace, swept the capsized passengers away toward the stern, where many of them were caught remorselessly in the suction currents of the vast propeller blades, still revolving with her momentum.

It was all over in seconds. There was nothing anyone could do.

Chapter 31

CHARLES FROHMAN WAS BRACING HIMSELF WITH HIS CANE, his back against the outside of the smoke room high on the port boat deck. His left arm was held closely by Rita Jolivet and beyond her stood Justus Forman and Charlie Klein. She was smiling and poised, yet from the hardness of her grip he could tell she was as scared as hell, poor kid. As well she might be.

They had all agreed there was no possibility of the ship sinking and had refused to join in the undignified and needless scramble for the boats. How right they had been! They had seen sights that no one would have believed, lifeboats splintering to matchsticks and drowning their human cargoes, others mutilating the very people they were intended to save, men begging for places on them, even if it meant leaving children behind. Here on the port side, the confusion was indescribable. All attempt at order was abandoned, and the only way one could cope with it was to pretend it was not real, to withdraw oneself and pretend these last ten minutes had never happened.

Himself with his crippled leg and Charlie with his club foot, they both knew they would have little chance in the sea. Young Forman was putting a brave face on it like Rita, but it would not take much more to crack the facades of her brittleness and his manly detachment.

Charlie Klein had taken his cue from Frohman and was treating everything with nonchalant humor to help the younger pair keep their nerve. "At least we have a nice day for it," he was saying, and Rita laughed.

"Yes, I don't fancy swimming in an overcoat," Frohman agreed. "Especially not from here to Ireland."

"Very true," Charlie nodded. "I can't help wishing the mountains of Mourne swept a little farther out to sea."

Justus Forman smiled as Rita laughed and Frohman chuckled appreciatively. But Forman was thinking, what are we doing, standing here? These theater people are crazy! We could be minutes from death and they're chatting and joking as if they were in some tinselly bar on Broadway.

"Did I ever tell you about my father's overcoat?" Frohman asked.

"I don't think so," Rita said.

Frohman smiled fondly. "He was a great character, very independent. No one could have been prouder of me or my brothers, though he was convinced he was the only businessman in the family. Even after I was doing pretty well, he would never take money. 'You keep it. You're gonna need it one day,' he'd say. What he really liked were free passes for shows, which he could hand out to his old customers. He always paid for them, mind. He'd turn up with his pockets filled with homemade cigars and give them to the doorman, ushers, all the theater staff." Frohman chuckled. "Well, one day he looked in. It was a raw spring day and the overcoat he was wearing was too thin, so I asked him please to go to my tailor and get a new overcoat. 'Not much,' he said. 'Your tailor's too expensive. He robs you. He wouldn't make one under seventy-five dollars, and I never pay more than twenty.' I told him, 'Look, I'll prove you wrong, Poppa. My tailor will make you a coat for twenty dollars. Go down and get one.' He doubted it."

"But he went?" Rita asked.

"That he did," Frohman said. "And the moment he left for Fifth Avenue, I called up my tailor and told him to make a coat for my father at whatever price he wants and charge the difference to me. An hour later, Poppa came back all excitement, very pleased. 'You were right,' he said. 'I persuaded him to make me a fine coat.' So I gave him the twenty dollars and sent ninety-five to the tailor. That was the difference. Then I forgot about it."

"That was sweet!" Rita exclaimed.

"No, listen," Frohman chuckled. "A few days later, Poppa came back. He was in high glee. 'You don't accept I've the real head for business in this family,' he told me. 'Well, learn a lesson. Last night, Sam Wiseman—you remember my old friend? Talks big, knows everything about cloths and stuff.

Well, he admired my new coat so much, I sold it to him for thirty-five bucks. Whaddya think of that?'"

The others were laughing. "What did you say?" Charlie Klein asked.

"Nothing," Frohman shrugged. "I didn't want to spoil it for him. But I had to buy him another hundred-and-fifteen-dollar overcoat. So one coat for my father cost me two hundred and thirty. That's good business."

As Frohman laughed quietly, remembering, he became aware that the bulkhead against which he had been leaning was now tilted so far that he was virtually lying back on it, at an angle of about forty degrees. It was startling and he pushed himself upright, bringing Rita with him. He had to jab his cane against the bulkhead to steady himself.

Klein and Forman followed them to their feet and were astonished at how much higher the liner's stern had risen. It was difficult to stand without slipping. There was still chaos round the remaining boats, which were empty for some reason. People were milling round them, but the sailors seemed to be pushing them back. Forman suddenly noticed that the sea was washing over the bows. "What are we doing?" he muttered. "This is sheer damned—" He stopped himself and looked at Frohman. "I mean—we don't even have life jackets. I thought your valet was fetching some?"

"He was," Frohman said. "But William hasn't been with me very long. I expect he has other preoccupations at the moment."

"Well, it's madness to wait here without life jackets!" Forman said, and started off down the steepness of the deck. He glanced back, almost apologetically. "Aren't you coming?"

"Maybe we should, C.F.," Rita suggested quickly. "I haven't seen George anywhere, my brother-in-law."

"Very well," Frohman smiled. "I don't have much of a head for heights, anyway." Linking arms with Charles Klein, they slid and stumbled down the deck.

Livvy was breaking out of shock into hysteria. She was shaking and Matt held her tight, pressing her cheek against his chest. He was desperate with the need to calm her, saying anything that might help. "No, Livvy! No. It's not your fault. Not mine. Not anybody's. It just happened."

"She was so little . . ." Livvy wept. "So little. And she didn't know what was going on. She was so excited. She didn't know!"

"That's the only thing," Matt told her. "The best thing. She wasn't frightened. She didn't have time to be frightened. It was all over so quickly." As he spoke, he had a sickening memory of Diana's eyes, for the fraction of a moment when her face turned up, pleading with them to save her. A little girl.

"To see it!" Livvy sobbed. "To see it—and not do anything! Not be able to do anything!"

"That's why we have to find Peter," Matt said. He was stroking Livvy's head. His fingers caught in her hair and he pulled her head back, forcing her to look at him. "That's why it's all the more important to find Peter! We'll think about it later. But now you have to help me!" She was gazing up at him. "Please, Livvy. We have to find him. I need you! Please."

She was fighting against the hysteria, against the urge to give up hope. She turned with him and they made for the main hall, where he had thought he had seen the Crompton boy.

Vanderbilt was helping Loncy to support his wife. She had collapsed when the boat tore loose. He could see it below them, hanging by its stern ropes, its bows just skimming the surface and sending up a thin spray. All those people . . . The Fletchers' little, pretty daughter. The girls he had kissed, and their bright futures. He had actually believed he was saving them. He could make out bodies in the water, floating, very few of them even moving. Lower down the deck, people were kneeling with Father Maturin, who was praying, giving them absolution. It was all so irrelevant.

He heard a strange sound beside him, a half cut-off moan. It was Allan Loney. "No . . . No . . ." he was muttering, his voice growing louder. "No . . . No, look. Look! There—who is that?"

Vanderbilt looked where he was pointing. Some distance off, someone was swimming, a girl, swimming neatly and effortlessly. She was turning over, resting on her back now, buoyed up by her life vest.

Mrs. Loney's head had risen. "It's her . . ." she breathed. "It's Ginny!"

627

Loney was laughing excitedly and waving. The girl in the water raised an arm and waved back. "Virginia . . . Virginia . . ." he was saying over and over. His wife hugged him and they kissed and turned again to wave.

Vanderbilt stepped back. It was a moment for them alone. Their daughter had been reborn. Had been lost, and was born again. It had not been for nothing. Not entirely for nothing. To a very slight extent, he had contributed.

Staff Captain Anderson had nearly become distraught. The unconsidered problems caused by the list, the appalling suddenness of everything. Because of the manning shortage, he had had all too few AB's to handle the lifeboats and half of them were missing. Others of the crew were willing, but inexperienced. Who could have imagined the trimming tanks being put out of commission? He had taken Turner's point instantly, that it was hopeless to attempt to launch any more boats with the *Lusitania* still forging on.

Purser McCubbin, young Bestwick and Commander Stackhouse had been invaluable, pacifying people, explaining the situation, but even so there was great confusion. Turner's orders and his had become garbled as they were passed on. No more women and children to be permitted to use the lifeboats—the ship was perfectly safe and all passengers were to go below—no more boats to be launched—all launching to be from the promenade deck and everyone to hurry down there. Women were told to leave the boats in which they were seated. No sooner had they climbed out than others struggled to take their places. Another boat had just overbalanced, toppling its occupants down the precipitous side. That had sobered the crowd, but only for a few moments.

Anderson was in his shirtsleeves and sweating profusely. Commander Stackhouse watched him with pity. The man had done the work of ten, but all his efforts had ended in disaster. He was only just managing to keep his head. "No response from the pumps?" Stackhouse asked quietly.

"Nothing," Anderson told him. "Turner's tried them, but without power they're useless. And we can't reach them."

"That's it, then."

"Looks like it," Anderson muttered, and added confidentially, "If you make your way to starboard, sir, you'll probably have a better chance of getting on a boat."

"I have no intention of doing so," Stackhouse said firmly. "I will not enter a boat while there is one woman left on board."

The main entrance hall round the top of the main companionway at midships was emptying, although there were still people being shepherded up by stewards from below. A scramble for life vests had begun, since many passengers had left theirs in their cabins and it was now too difficult and dangerous to return for them. Stewards and stewardesses brought spares up from the emergency lockers in the passageways.

Taking a side each, Matt and Livvy searched the hall. In a corner, Livvy saw Marie Depage and the American doctor bandaging injured passengers and crewmen, with Lindon Bates of the Relief Committee and some of the young nurses applying splints and tourniquets, wiping away blood. Beyond them on a brocade sofa, paying no attention, two very composed ladies with immaculately upswept hair and plumed hats, wearing silk afternoon dresses, pearls and long fur stoles, sat chatting casually as though they were at a tea party. Their maids stood respectfully beside them holding their life jackets, which they would not put on until the last possible minute. Nursery attendants were bringing up the last of the babies. Others were trying to gather together all the children separated from their parents. There were children everywhere in the hall, bewildered, clutching dolls and toys, but neither Peter nor any of the Cromptons were among them.

"No sign of him?" Matt asked when they met at the port entrance. Livvy shook her head, not trusting herself to speak. They hurried outside.

The anarchy of the port deck shocked them. On starboard where everything had been urgent, but reasonably disciplined, with most people behaving rationally, they had been completely unaware of the confusion and destruction here. Matt had been eager to get Livvy to this side, where he had thought she would be safer, but the deck was crammed all along its length with hundreds of jostling, demoralized people. There was no time for second thoughts. "You go left, up toward the stern," he said. "I'll go right."

She caught his arm. "No! Please, Matt. Don't leave me!" she begged.

He looked back. She was not frightened for herself, he realized, only by the dread of them becoming separated again. "Livvy—" he began. He pulled her to him and for a moment they stood pressed together. "Come on, then. We'll have to hurry."

When they turned, they saw Isaac Lehmann, the stockbroker, standing near them, watching with contempt the failure of Anderson's effort to organize the boat crews.

A decisive man, Lehmann had raced from the first-class smoking room to the nearest boat on the port side. Before any of the crew had arrived, he had called for volunteers, packed the boat and given the command to lower. The four gentlemen at each rope were unskilled and the ropes themselves stiff with paint and lack of use. One rope rode freely through its block and the other became stuck, tipping the overloaded boat nose down. While the gentlemen debated what to do, the jammed rope, now bearing most of the weight, broke. The other was torn out of its block, and boat and passengers plummeted eighty feet to the sea, bursting on impact like a human shrapnel bomb.

Even before Lehmann had recovered from his surprise, Staff Captain Anderson had appeared and ordered no further attempts by passengers to launch the boats. Resenting the implied criticism, Lehmann decided it was time to think of himself, turned on his heel and hurried below to his cabin to fetch his life vest, only to discover that someone had been there already and taken it. He quickly collected his papers and money and opened his dress suit case to get his jeweled stickpin and shirt studs. In the case was also his revolver and, without knowing why, only that it might somehow be needed, he grabbed it and put it in his pocket.

Returning to the upper decks, he met his cabin steward and told him to find him a life vest. He waited until the man came back and put it on for him, then walked back up to the boat deck, where the situation was even worse than he had expected.

Matt asked him urgently, "Have you seen my son anywhere?"

"I regret, sir, I have not," Lehmann said. "Have you ever witnessed such a disgraceful exhibition? Why are those boats not being launched? Why has the Captain not stopped the ship?"

"I guess he's trying to," Matt said, moving on with Livvy.

"Sheer incompetence!" Lehmann snorted. "I intend to take the matter up with the directors of Cunard. If necessary, I shall sue!" He called after them. "I advise you to do the same, sir!"

Dan Connally and Barney elbowed through the crush of people retreating from the bows. They were nauseated. "He's not this end, for sure," Dan said. He glanced at Livvy. "And you don't want to go down there."

As they turned to climb up to the stern, they were thrust aside by a stampede of third-class passengers erupting from the forward companionway. Livvy was knocked down and Matt seized her, crouching over her and holding her, while hundreds of panic-stricken steerage passengers shouldered and pushed and clawed past them, shouting in a Babel of languages, making for the empty boats higher up the deck. At the same time a gang of temporary stokers and boiler-men, sweat-stained, some scalded and burned, rushed from the aft companionway. McCubbin tried to bring them to order and was punched and kicked. They ran on and the two streams, stokers and steerage passengers, clashed by the boats, fighting and scuffling, while the crowd around them eddied and seethed. The stokers smashed through to the front into the space maintained round the last three empty lifeboats and came to a stop, irresolute, facing Anderson and Bestwick. They were not quelled by the officers' authority, but by the sight of the able seamen standing on the col-lapsibles behind them, holding long handled firemen's axes, which they were ready to use. The third-class passengers, having been halted, realizing there was no further to go and they were no nearer safety, lost the cohesion their impetus had given them and began to split up into frightened groups and individuals, merging with the crowd.

Elbert Hubbard was still sheltering his wife, Alice, in the gap between a small ventilator and the bulkhead. In these minutes he had been saddened and profoundly disturbed. He had always considered humanity to be capable of infinite courage. He saw all history as a refining process from which Man would emerge as the noblest and most selfless of spe-cies. Although he watched with compassion, his beliefs had received a cruel blow.

He would have liked Alice to survive, but he knew that

neither of them was strong enough to battle through the mob, nor to remain afloat for long in the icy water. As he looked at Alice, he saw that, attuned as they were, she had read his thoughts and understood. Linking arms, they moved carefully down the deck through the entrance hall and down the crazily angled companionway to their stateroom situated just at its foot on the promenade deck.

In the stateroom, the furniture was bolted to the floor, but everything else had toppled off surfaces and slithered down to pile up against the fixed beds and lower wall. His watchstand and the pages of the article he had begun had fallen from the writing table, Mrs. Hubbard's vanity set, mirror and brushes from the dressing table. They no longer mattered, he knew. He helped his wife off with her coat, then removed his own and his cap while she took off her hat. He righted two comfortable chairs, placed them securely against the paneled wall, and they sat next to each other companionably.

The sounds from outside were muted in here, but they still could hear occasional clattering of feet and indistinct voices calling. He noticed that Alice's hands were folded together very tightly in her lap. "It is going to be a lovely summer, I believe," he said. "And in the fall the trees along the Allegheny will be a glorious flame and russet and golden umber, beyond the power of any pen to capture." He paused. His eyes twinkled and his face creased up in its puckish smile. "Even mine."

Alice relaxed and she echoed him tenderly, "Even yours, perhaps."

There were many, many more things that could be said, yet only one was important. "I have always loved you," he said. "And I shall always love you very deeply, my dear."

Alice smiled and held out her hand. He took it and they sat quietly with each other, waiting, side by side.

As soon as he had warned the bridge that the torpedo was coming, Les Morton had run for the companionway down to the crew's quarters to wake his brother Cliff. The explosion threw him halfway down the steps, and, when he reached the long seamen's cabin with its rows of bunks, Cliff was already scrambling into his clothes. Les explained quickly what had happened and hurried back up to his starboard station at No. 13 lifeboat. Filling it with passengers, he was too busy to think of being afraid and he gave up his own seat to a lady's maid before helping to winch the boat down safely to the water.

He knelt by the collapsible that had been underneath and began to cut away its canvas cover. It was as hard as dried hide. His brother and two of their friends came to his assistance. When they finally ripped the cover off, they found that the flat-bottomed collapsible life raft, designed to float away in an emergency, had been painted so often it was glued to the deck. Cliff had to give up and left to report to his own boat station.

There had been so many accidents with the lifeboats that, on Turner's orders, the remaining ones on the starboard side had been filled but were not to be released until the water was practically level with the davits. The order made sense, although it was a difficult one to obey, and the crews waited tensely while First Officer Jones moved from one to the other keeping control. At least the delay had enabled him to arrange places for all passengers in the midships section who wanted them. Incredibly, there were some who preferred to risk staying on board.

While he tugged and sweated uselessly at the life raft, Les noticed Elizabeth Duckworth. She was climbing hesitantly up the steeply sloping deck, reluctant to ask for a seat, since there were people who appeared to be waiting. She had tried to pray, but could not think sensibly. She was stretching out for a handhold on a painted sign when her feet went from under her and she fell heavily, rolling down the deck toward the rail. Les thought she was going straight through between the lower rungs, but she was too broad. He ran to her and helped her up.

Elizabeth was winded and embarrassed. "You're a stupid woman," she scolded herself. "Really stupid!"

"Lean on me," Les told her. "I'll get you to a boat."

"No, I'm all right," she protested. "I'm a strong swimmer."

"You may need to be," Les said. He saw the First Officer watching them. "Could we find a seat for this lady, sir?" he asked.

Jones recognized Elizabeth as the woman who had given

up her place in the boat which was wrecked. "I think so," he said. "Quick now! Let me have her."

The petty officer in charge of the next to highest boat was cursing his davitmen nervously for not holding their ropes steady. "I'm sorry, sir," he objected. "There's just no more room."

"Yes, there is," Jones told him. "You'll make room for this lady." Elizabeth wanted to assure them that she would be perfectly all right, but before she could, they had lifted her and dumped her over into the lifeboat.

Livvy's head was spinning from the double shock of the explosion and seeing Diana swept away. When the crush had passed, she seemed barely conscious as Matt raised her to her feet, and he was worried about her. Behind them, he could hear the moaning and screaming of the people knocked down and trampled on the companionway stairs. Dan was helping Barney up. He had been sent sprawling by the stampede and had wrenched his knee.

"Look at that!" Dan said. The crowd was retreating further up toward the stern, packing together more closely. "It's hopeless. We'll never find him in that mob."

Matt had been thinking. At the very start of the voyage, he had warned the children there might be danger. He had not wished to alarm them, but made them promise that, if there was any trouble, they would go directly to the cabin and wait for him or Livvy. He had forgotten himself, but Peter would not have. It was a promise, Redskin's honor. "I think I know where he is," he said. "I'll go and get him."

Dan stood up. "I'll come with you."

"No, I want you to keep an eye on Livvy," Matt told him. "If I don't make it back for any reason—take care of her, will you?" Dan nodded.

"We'll get her into one of the boats," Barney promised.

"They're not going anywhere," Matt said flatly. "If you want to do something, round up some of our fellows and make sure those life rafts aren't fastened to the deck. Everybody seems to have forgotten about them, but they're going to be more use than anything else."

Before he had finished, Barney was limping toward the collapsibles which had been under the smashed lifeboats. Dan glanced from Matt to Livvy, troubled, then followed him.

By the entrance to the main hall, young Lady Mackworth was waiting. She had been to her cabin to fetch life jackets for herself and her father, but now could not see him anywhere. A stewardess had fastened her own life jacket for her and she had the other over her arm. A man sprang toward her, demanding in broken English, "Where you get that? Where? Where?"

"It's—it's for my father," Margaret said.

"I, father!" the man exclaimed. "I, father!" He grabbed the life jacket and Margaret Mackworth was going to tussle with him for it when she saw that he was crying. She let go and he ran off, not taking it to some child as she had supposed, but pulling it on over his head.

Matt came to her, supporting Livvy. "Lady Mackworth," he asked quickly, "I wonder—could I leave my wife with you?" He saw her hesitate. "I have to go below."

Margaret Mackworth was anxious about her father and wanted to look for him, yet Livvy, her clothes torn and discolored, had evidently been through some dreadful experience and was scarcely able to stand. "Certainly, Mr. Fletcher," she agreed. "Is she hurt?"

Matt had no time to explain. "I'm sorry. I have to go," he said. He laid Livvy against the sloping bulkhead and turned to leave, but she was grasping his sleeve and would not release it.

Livvy was trying desperately to make her body obey. Although it seemed to be at a distance, she heard and saw everything around her. It was the greatest physical effort for her to hold on to his sleeve, and to form words. "With you . . . take me with you," she whispered.

It was a relief to hear her speak, and her need to be with him tore at his heart, but Matt could not weaken. He caught her wrist and drew her hand away, breaking her grip. "I can't, Livvy! You know I can't," he told her.

"Please . . ."

"There may be very little time," he said. "It's a gamble. If there's to be any chance, I have to go alone." He kissed her hand. "I'll be as quick as I can."

Livvy felt him go. She had used up her strength. Her head fell back and tears welled through her closed eyelids. It was as if they had said goodbye.

Matt ran into the entrance hall and skidded to a stop by

the main companionway. Without electricity, the elevators were not working, and the companionway was the fastest route down. The list and the liner's erratic jerking made the going difficult as he started for the cabin four decks below, swinging himself with both hands from the higher, tilted balustrade at first, then sliding along one step to the lower balustrade, and walking in the angle of the stairs and side railings. At least here there was daylight. There was no guessing what to expect further down.

In the *Lusitania*'s brig, Neil Leach was crouching by the locked door, his head lowered, sobbing. In here, the explosions had sounded very loud and fairly near, and the whole cabin had rocked. Almost at once, he had felt himself slipping off the cot on which he was lying and discovered that the floor was sloping down toward the door. "What's going on?" he shouted. He knocked loudly. "Somebody!" When the liner did not roll back to an even keel, putting together the explosions and the list, he realized that she had been torpedoed. Like everyone else, he knew that she could not be sunk and, as he knocked, the thought came to him, what a pity! If she went down, the only evidence against him, the camera, would be lost and they would have to set him free.

As the list continued to increase, another thought came, that everyone had been wrong and the *Lusitania* was vulnerable after all. His impression that she was going down became a certainty and he began to laugh. His luck had held good again. Throughout his life, he had come out of any scrape he had got into without a scratch, and had usually been able to turn it to his advantage. This would get him out of trouble perfectly, both in England and New York. Injured innocence was what was called for, leading to apologies all round, perhaps even compensation. He laughed again and blessed the submarine, the unknown ally of Kelly and Gus and Trude. He had stopped knocking and became conscious of something odd. He could not place what at first, then realized he could no longer hear the faint perpetual murmur of the forced air ventilator. He moved to it and reached up. There was no movement of air through the grille. As he thought about that, the light went out.

When it did not come on again, he was uneasy. The cell cabin was in impenetrable darkness. He moved back cautiously toward the door, but tripped over something and threw his hands out to the wall to steady himself. He had forgotten it was no longer upright and pitched forward, splitting his lip against the doorjamb. It hurt, but he was more frightened by the angle at which he was lying and he began to knock again. "Hurry up! Open the door!" he yelled. "It's dark in here! Let me out!" There was no answer.

Automatically he was feeling over the door's surface, although he knew there was no handle and it was bolted and padlocked on the outside. The office of the masters-at-arms was just along the short passageway and one of them was bound to hear him. He banged on the door again. The darkness worried him and the lack of noise. He could make out nothing from outside. He knew it was sheer imagination, but already it seemed to be becoming harder to breathe. He had a terror of suffocation. "Come on—let me out!" he shouted. "There's no air in here!"

His voice died away as he had just realized something else. Not only was there no light in the cabin, there was none coming through the small transom above the door. The lights were out in the passageway, too! He knocked more loudly and kicked at the door. As it became more obvious that no one was going to answer, he grew more frantic, beating and pounding on the door until his knuckles split and he was hoarse with shouting.

He slumped to the floor, crouching over exhausted, sobbing for breath. What was he going to do? How long was he going to be left here before someone remembered him? His hands throbbed with pain and he could barely call out any more.

There was a different sound in the cabin and he listened, trying to identify it. It was the trickle of water coming through the ventilator grille. Trembling, he shuffled quickly backward until he was close against the opposite wall. His left ear was against the bulkhead and he began to scream, a low mewling sob that rose in intensity and faded away to a ragged whimper. Outside he had heard the splashing whisper of water as it flooded the passageway. The trickling sound from the ventilator became louder. Water was collecting in the angle of the floor and bulkhead in which he was squatting. A shallow tongue of it licked out and touched his knees. His luck had finally run out.

Matt came down the narrower, sideways sloping companionway to D deck and swore at himself. On the shelter deck, he had doubled back through the deserted nursery as a shortcut, but the doors beyond it were locked. Instead of the companionway, which led to his own corridor, he had been forced to use this one, which brought him too far to starboard. The corridor he was in sloped to his left and even more steeply upward toward the stern. It was lit only dimly by daylight filtering from a cross passage ahead and from a wider space beyond it, which he knew must be the entrance hall of the first-class dining saloon. His cabin was up there, to the right across the hall and off the corridor parallel to this.

His feet could find no purchase on the highly polished linoleum. There was only one way to get up there and he let himself slide across to the lower side of the corridor. Bent over, his feet slipping, he hauled himself up by the handrail. He did not know how long he had, only that it might be a matter of minutes and that his progress seemed painfully slow. All at once, as he reached out, he could not feel the rail ahead. He had come to a passageway leading down to the liner's starboard side. It was too dark to see along it and he realized the portholes at its end must already be deep under water. He poised himself, his feet balanced on the corner, and leaped for the far side. His fingers just managed to hook themselves over the opposite rail, but on landing, his leathersoled shoes skated sideways, swinging his body round to slam against the wall of the passageway. He allowed himself a second or two to regain his breath before pulling himself up.

A few yards farther on, he had to negotiate another side passage. As he poised himself again to leap across, he could hear water pouring into its lower end through a porthole which had fallen in or been left open. The sound spurred him on and, as he climbed, he began to calculate. He could see a transverse passage to the right. It ran through midships to the corridor on the port side, off which was the passageway with his cabin, but its floor was covered with the damned linoleum and there was no handrail. Ahead was the hall of the dining saloon. It was farther, but carpeted, and he hauled himself on faster.

After crossing another side passage, he came to where the corridor opened out. There was more light, slanting down from the port side. The hall was twenty-five feet deep by forty wide, and suddenly seemed vast. Looking up the slope, it appeared untouched, but overturned chairs, plant stands and potted palms, fire buckets and lacquered cane tables were piled up against the cabin doors of its starboard wall. On the side facing him was the long cloakroom between the two entrance doors to the dining saloon. On all fours, he used the pile of debris to take him higher and lunged for the paneling round the base of the cloakroom counter. Beside him, the lower door of the dining saloon hung open and he saw that the once supremely elegant room was a shambles. Railings and furniture had showered down into it from the upper gallery. The grand piano had fallen from the bandstand and smashed a lane of destruction through the tables. There was broken glass and crockery everywhere. Even as he glanced in, there came a thunderous crash and the deck on which he was kneeling quivered. The towering mahogany sideboard had torn loose from the wall and toppled over. Worst of all, although light still showed through some of the shut starboard portholes, through two which were open the sea gushed fitfully when the bow wave passed them.

Matt pulled himself along the edge of the counter, then went crabwise on his hands and knees again over the expanse of carpet to the elevators. For the first time in that hectic journey from the boat deck, which in all had lasted less than three minutes, he paused. His stomach was heaving and he nearly cried out in despair. He could hear voices calling and pleading, a woman screaming, voices coming from the elevator shafts of people trapped in the cages. He could not even begin to help them.

He pulled himself up past the elevator doors and was in the portside corridor at last, where there was light and he could hobble along in the angle of the deck and the bulkhead until he was opposite his own passageway. Please, God, let him be here, he was praying. Let him be here. He knelt again and lay across the corridor, stretching out and pushing off with his toes until he could catch a radiator pipe and draw himself up. He pulled himself round into the passageway and swung from door to door until he was at the children's cabin. He flung the door open and for a moment stared. It was empty.

He moved past it to his own door, opened it and went in.

All his and Livvy's things were scattered. The clothes she had been laying out were on the floor. Drawers had spilled from the tallboy. He came in further and gasped in relief.

Peter was sitting crosslegged like an Indian in the lower corner, the model of the *Lusitania* over his knees. His eyes were very wide. "I knew you'd come, Daddy," he said.

"I knew you'd be here, Chief," Matt said.

Alfred Vanderbilt had left the Loneys at the rail and crossed the sloping deck at an angle to reach the main entrance hall. There were three or four other people to whom he wished to say goodbye, if there was an opportunity.

He was intensely interested in his own reactions. He could tell himself truly, in spite of the imminence of the mighty liner plunging to the bottom, that he was not afraid. In the circumstances he could not congratulate himself, yet he had always been afraid of being afraid if he ever found himself in a perilous situation, and he felt a certain amount of pride. It was mixed with a genuine curiosity to observe how others behaved. He had glimpsed Captain Turner alone on the high bridge and that was where he would really like to be, up there with him, with the master of this foundering leviathan, yet he knew that it would be unpardonable in these moments to intrude on that lonely figure.

It was becoming difficult to stand upright in the main hall. Most of the crowd had fled from it to the port deck. He could hear screams and cries from there and saw people surging restlessly outside the wide entrance. There was no one he knew in the main hall and he moved toward the far entrance, but stopped as he noticed a bundle of children's life vests, next to some Moses baskets. As he looked at them, he did not see Matt run past and go down the main companionway. Vanderbilt was frowning. There were still children about. Some were clustered by the entrance. There were even some babies lying on the floor by the door to the music room, wrapped in their cot blankets. One anxious young nurse was the only one who seemed to be doing anything for them.

Vanderbilt's valet, Denyer, came hurrying to him, carrying two life vests. "Here you are, Mr. Vanderbilt!" he panted. "I managed to locate these."

"Good man. Thank you," Vanderbilt nodded. Denyer moved to help him on with one of the life vests, but Vanderbilt stopped him. "No, that's all right, Denyer. First, let's get yours on. Then you must try to get yourself a place on a boat."

Denyer blinked, reproachfully. "Oh, no, I—I couldn't, sir," he stammered. "Not without you."

Vanderbilt looked at him. It was beyond doubt the greatest compliment he had ever been paid. "Thank you, Denyer," he said, and allowed his valet to put the life vest over his shoulders. Before it was fastened, however, he stepped away. "That's fine," he said. "Now, if you want to make yourself useful, why don't you gather up all the kiddies you can find?" He scooped up the Moses baskets and crossed to the nurse, who was kneeling, rocking a fretful baby. Her head rose anxiously when Vanderbilt dropped the baskets in front of her. "Let's get to work," he smiled.

Charles Frohman had come in through the port entrance, glad to escape from the noise and bustle. Justus Forman had vanished and Rita had gone with Charlie to hunt for her brother-in-law. His hands were beginning to shake. The worst of having nothing to do, he told himself. As he lit a cigar to steady his nerves, he saw Vanderbilt and the nurse tying some babies into Moses baskets. Near them, Vanderbilt's valet was with a group of children. He was trying to persuade a five-or-six-year-old girl to let him fasten a life vest round her, but she was rigid with fear, infecting the others.

Frohman limped over to them. "Hello, honey," he beamed. The little girl looked up at him. "You know what? I have some chocolate candies in this pocket and a bag of peanuts in this one. If you lift your arms and let the man slip the life jacket on, you can have whichever you want." All the children's arms went up.

While he waited, Peter had tried to think what his father would expect him to do. Inside his shirt he had their passports and his mother's jewelry, he told Matt. He had put on his life vest and collected the other three. He was picking them up.

"I don't think we can manage these," Matt said.

"But Mr. Biggs showed us how to wear them," Peter protested. "And Diana'd be upset if I have one and she doesn't."

Matt winced. He took Peter's face between his hands and

641

held him for a moment. "You're right. She would be," he agreed. He slung the life vests over one arm and turned. Because of the list, he could see only sky through the porthole. "We'd better be moving, Chief." Peter was laying the model *Lusitania* on the end of Livvy's bed. "You can bring that with you if you like."

"I don't think so," Peter said quietly.

As Matt pulled him up to the doorway, the model fell from the bed to the floor, breaking off one of its funnels.

"It's a bit slippy," Matt warned. "Hang on to my belt." They edged quickly down the passageway from door to door. Matt could still make out faintly the screaming of the people trapped in the elevator cage and hoped that Peter could not hear it. To cover it, he asked, "What became of the Cromptons?"

"Their maid came for them," Peter said. "To take them up to the boats. I wouldn't go with them."

"Probably just as well."

"Why?"

"The boats haven't been too lucky, Chief," Matt said.

"Are we really sinking, Daddy?"

"We're not going up, that's for sure."

Peter grinned. It was all an adventure and, now that he was with his father, he was no longer worried. "Were they real torpedoes, from a U-boat?"

"That's what they were. One or two, I didn't see them. But they were real enough." Matt stopped. They had come to the last door in the passageway. From here it would be easier, a straight slide to the far side of the wide corridor, along it to the stairs to the deck above, then up two flights of the main companionway. If there was time. At least the slope was with them most of the way, and its angle had not shifted for several minutes.

Matt was holding on to the edge of the doorway. He tossed the life vests down to make a cushion against the opposite wall of the corridor and brought Peter round in front of him. "All right, Chief? Not scared?" he asked. Peter shook his head. "That's the boy. Now just sit yourself and slide down to those life vests."

Peter squatted and, with his hands on the floor, began to inch downwards. The deck was rocking slightly. "Keep moving, Chief!" Matt said. Peter lifted his hands and slid down faster, bumping into the life vests. He looked round and grinned. But even as he turned, his mouth opened in surprise. His impact had dislodged the life vests and, with them under him like a toboggan, he was beginning to slither away down the corridor.

Matt pushed off from the doorway and crossed the corridor in a skater's crouch, slamming into the lower wall with his knees and hands. He grunted and swiveled to go after Peter, but for a moment he could not move. He was paralyzed by a vicious pain in his left shoulder, where the unrepaired muscles had been wrenched again.

"Are you all right, Daddy?" Peter asked anxiously. Trying to slow himself with his fingers and toes, he had slid down until his foot rammed against a small projection in the bulkhead at the start of the larger cabins.

Matt breathed out and could straighten. "Fine . . . just fine," he said. Easy, there. Easy does it, he told himself. It was not the time to panic, although he was aware of something new, the smell of smoke. To add to her troubles, the *Lusitania* was on fire somewhere below. He began to move toward Peter, planting his feet cautiously. "Turn around and keep moving, Chief," he said. "But careful!"

Peter picked up the life vest for Diana and imitated his father, squatting and shuffling down with one hand on the sloping bulkhead acting as a brake. Without conscious thought, Matt took up the other two as he followed him.

Will Turner had come down to the wheelhouse, where there was no one left but Quartermaster Johnston. They stood side by side, supporting themselves by the binnacle, gazing at the brass oil level and the bubble in it which constantly quivered. "Still twenty points, sir," Johnston muttered.

Turner was silent. Worst of all was the feeling of powerlessness. There was nothing he could do, no action he could take. There was not a skill or instrument in the world that could reverse the damage as the *Lusitania* swung in her long curve away from the land, sinking by the head. In the waiting, it had become clearer to him that the very factors which had created her grace and boasted safety were speeding her destruction, her height in relation to her narrow beam, with seven of its nine decks above water, and the huge sealed bulkheads along her sides. With one or two breached as they had been, and the mechanism to flood the opposing bulkheads and correct her balance not functioning, it was inevitable that she would keel over. Except for his passengers, he would have welcomed the fact that the list seemed to be stabilized. To get them away, he had to pray for something to give. Break through! he was repeating to himself over and over. Break through, damn you!

He tapped the glass plate of the binnacle and said, "Sing out if there's any change, Mr. Johnston." Hobbling sideways up the deck, he went out onto the port wing and up the ladder by the chartroom to the upper bridge. The distant trawler was still becalmed and there was not a trace of a hull or even smoke on the horizon. He could not see the U-boat, but knew that it would be watching. Other eyes would be watching, too, from the lighthouse and the white cottages which stood out so distinctly against the green and brown cliffs. Are they saying a prayer for us now? Turner wondered. He hoped that some would be running for the quay at Kinsale and setting out in whatever boats they possessed.

He heard feet hurrying and stumbling and saw one of the electricians making for him. "There's fire, sir!" the man gasped.

"How bad?"

"Can't tell, sir," the man said. "It's in the engine room and between the after hatches above."

Fire was to be expected. If it was confined to the engine room and lower deck and had not yet reached the main deck, it might not be too serious, provided it did not work forward to the ammunition. In any case, there was no means of combating it now. As he calculated, Turner heard what he had been waiting for, a rending crash, and the *Lusitania* shuddered beneath him as more of her forward bulkheads collapsed under the pressure of thousands of tons of water.

He grabbed the rail and hung on, still waiting. The change came quite quickly. He could judge by the horizon, which had been tilted and was leveling out. The *Lusitania* was righting herself. Johnston's voice came up to him, loud and excited, "Eighteen—fifteen—ten points!"

Turner held his breath, his lips drawn back in tension.

"Come on! Come on, my beauty!" he muttered. Already he could stand upright without difficulty. A moment later he let go of the rail. She was still slanting steeply toward the bows, but her decks were practically on a plane with the horizon. He patted the rail and stepped away, smiling.

Just then, the *Lusitania* lurched. It was not the main fore and aft bulkhead which had collapsed, but smaller sections further forward. The inrush of water had caused her to swing. She trembled along her length as though striving to retain her balance, then plunged over again to starboard, as if she were capsizing.

Turner was sent sprawling across the upper bridge. The electrician was thrown across the Marconi deck and somersaulted over the rail, breaking his back on the wreckage of No. 5 boat. There were screams of terror as people were hurled off the decks and the stern, and the hanging boats danced on their ropes. From below came the snapping and crashing sounds of destruction, as pillars cracked and mirrors shattered and heavy furniture and machinery were ripped loose.

Badly shaken, Turner pulled himself up by the forward rail and up along it. He had been convinced the *Lusitania* was going to turn turtle and could not believe the angle at which she was now hanging. From the port rail, he looked down along her black flank obliquely, almost to her lowest deck. He heard Johnston's voice call, falteringly. "Twen-twenty-five points . . . to starboard!" Miraculously, the liner's phenomenal buoyancy was still keeping her afloat. She was virtually lying on her side.

Down on D deck, Matt and Peter had heard the caving in of the bulkheads as a kind of rumbling thunder. "Don't move!" Matt said sharply as the deck shivered beneath them. He was astonished when it gradually began to level off. The angle at which it sloped down increased slightly, but it meant they would have less trouble making the stairs which they could now see a short distance ahead. "Come on," he said, and took an experimental step across the corridor. Peter laughed and coasted across on a slant to catch the handrail on the other side. He was halfway when the floor rocked, and he fell on his back.

Matt was thrown forward and just managed to hook one arm over the handrail. Peter was sliding away again. Matt snatched at him and missed. His stomach heaved and his feet shot away from him as the liner rolled over on its starboard beam. He saw Peter spinning back across the corridor, hit the lower wall and start to slither toward the bows, then disappear. Peter had dropped into the transverse passage and cried out as he slid headlong down the precipitous incline to the unlit depths of the starboard side.

Matt was almost hanging on the rail. No! . . . Oh, no . . . ! he was screaming inside. "Peter . . . !" he shouted. But the corridor was empty.

Matt did not hesitate. Even as he shouted, he dropped to the opposite side of the corridor, landing in the space between its handrail and the deck. He was crouching on what had been the wall, nearly deafened by the splintering, crashing noises from the cabins all round him and the smash of overturned machinery somewhere below. An avalanche of small objects came skittering down the corridor toward him, pots and chairs, books, clothing, rugs and flower vases. Much of it fell through doorways, where cabins had been wrenched open. Some passed him, cascading down into the steep shaft of the transverse passage.

He squatted and let himself go with it, controlling his speed by the handrail. His impulse had been to launch himself after Peter, but he knew that would have been madness, ending with him unconscious or with broken arms or legs. For there to be any hope at all, he had to get to the starboard corridor in one piece.

Kneeling, holding on to the rail, he looked over the drop which had been the corner of the transverse passage. The passage was the length of three double staterooms, and he could dimly make out the far wall of the corridor beyond. Striking it, the falling debris slid out of sight again downwards. Peter was not to be seen. He must already have gone on that long slide all the way down to the closed-off third-class dining saloon at the bows, if he had not tumbled into one of the many side passages.

The wall of the transverse passage facing Matt was angled away from him. He leaped across. His hands caught on the lip of the corner and he swung until his toes touched the projecting side post of the door of the first stateroom. Releasing his hands and searching below him with one foot, he managed to find a toehold on the lower side of the doorway, then twisted his hips to bring his other foot down. It was like climbing down a cliff face only slightly off vertical without a rope, using the doorjambs less than an inch wide as ledges. For much of the descent he had no handhold and he pressed his body against the wall, his left palm flat on what had been the deck to preserve his balance at each hazardous step down.

He was conscious of the seconds racing by, waiting for the liner to complete her final roll. He did not have time to be too careful and, when he could grasp the jamb of the third door, lowered himself and jumped the last fifteen feet to the wall of the starboard corridor. He grunted, forcing himself to ignore the jarring pain in his left shoulder when he landed. He had come down straddling the handrail and he gripped it, stopping himself as he started to slide.

He was back in semidarkness, with light behind him and a faint patch fifty or sixty feet down the slope ahead, marking the small companionway. He had swiveled round and was already shuffling downwards, his legs out in front of him, his right hand on the rail. He was peering ahead, searching the corridor, when he suddenly saw Peter.

His son had plummeted down to the lower corridor and had been thrown sideways. His momentum had carried him right across the mouth of the first side passageway and he lay bent over the corner at the waist, his arms flung out, his legs dangling. He lay limply, without moving.

The *Lusitania* was beginning to shudder again and Matt saw Peter's body shift. In a moment, he would slip backward into the passage which was filling with water like a well. Matt leaped again desperately. He had two chances, to catch a wall lamp on the other side of the passage or the fixed reel of a firehose, lower and beyond it, otherwise his leap would send him shooting down toward the bows. His hands snatched at the lamp, but the glass shattered and the bracket snapped off. The impact twisted his body, however, and he hit the hose reel with his legs, scrabbled for it and hung on.

He swung round to kneel on the frame of the reel. As he looked back, he saw Peter start to slip and he lunged forward, his hands fastening on his son's wrists, holding him.

For a moment he could do nothing more except lie still

and recover his breath. He was gazing up at Peter, trying to work out where and how badly he had been hurt, when Peter's eyes flickered open. He was dazed and unfocused. "Peter?" Matt said. "Can you hear me? Can you hear me, Chief?"

Peter's eyes cleared and his head jerked abruptly. "Daddy?" he whispered.

"I'm going to pull you out of the passage and down to me," Matt said. "But first you have to tell me, can you move your legs? Do you hurt anywhere?"

"All over," Peter said. "It's hard to breathe."

Matt had to risk it. He drew Peter up and rose to his knees as the boy came sliding down to lie against him. Matt cradled him in his arms. He saw blood on Peter's life vest and was worried until he realized it was from his own hands, cut by the glass of the lamp bracket. Peter was largely unharmed. He had been relaxed when he fell, and the child's life vest he was carrying and the one he wore protected him. When he hit the corner, all the breath had been knocked out of him and he had lost consciousness for a minute. That was all.

"Thank God . . ." Matt muttered. He held Peter tighter for a second, then glanced round. "This isn't going to be easy, Chief. We don't have much time. We have to slide down here from door to door until we get to that light. It's some stairs. I'll lift you up to them. Think we can do it?" Peter nodded. "Right. Hold on to my hand."

As Matt turned carefully to lower him, Peter said, "Listen, Daddy." Matt listened, but could hear nothing. "Listen!" Peter insisted.

Matt could hear it now. Behind them, in the flooding side passage, a woman was calling. He saw Peter's eyes fixed on him. It was a terrible decision Matt had to make and one a child could not understand. "There isn't time," he said. "There just isn't time."

"It's Mrs. Arnstein," Peter said.

Matt's head flicked round. The voice was faint and muffled, but there was no mistaking it now. It was Beattie. Matt glanced back at the light from the companionway, and at Peter. What the hell was he to do? Yet he knew he had no choice.

Chapter 32

WHEN THE LUSITANIA HAD BEGUN TO REGAIN HER BALANCE
Livvy swayed *and would have fallen*, if Margaret Mackworth had not caught her. The area around them emptied
as the crowd surged toward the rail. A man who had been
working to free one of the life rafts ran up from the submerged bows and threw his arm round Livvy's waist. "I've
got her," he said.

He was quite tall and good-looking, with fair hair. Not
knowing him, Margaret was uncertain. "Thank you, sir,"
she faltered, "but I—I promised her husband I would take
care of her."

"My name's Connally. I'm a friend of the family," Dan
told her. "You can leave her with me."

Margaret hesitated only for a second. "Well . . . I have
to find my father," she explained. She was already turning
and climbing up toward the stern.

Dan was left alone with Livvy. Because of her bulky life
jacket, he had to put both arms round her and hold her
closely. It was the first time he had ever done so. Her eyes
opened. She was trying to speak. "Matt . . ." she whispered.
"Help Matt . . ."

"He's all right," Dan said. "Matt and Peter are fine." He
knew what he had to do. In Livvy's condition, she would
only survive if she got away in one of the lifeboats. He did
not trust any of those on the port side and too many were
trying to board them. With the liner coming practically to
an even keel, although still pointing sharply down, it was
easier to move and he hurried her through the main hall to
starboard.

The three higher boats already seemed overfilled, but the
one nearer the flooded bows looked as if it might have room.

Livvy was trying to struggle away from him, but he held her firmly, snatching at the rail with one hand every few steps to stop them falling, while he half carried her down.

No. 3 boat swung back in to the rail as the list corrected itself. On the collapsible underneath it, a young seaman was standing with a hammer to knock out the pin of the restraining chain. It was Les Morton. He laid the hammer on the collapsible and helped Dan to lift Livvy up to James Brooks, who hoisted her into the boat. "If you're coming, too," Brooks told Dan, "you'd better get in quick."

Dan was watching Livvy. After her brief flurry of protest, she had lapsed again into semi-consciousness. He wanted to stay with her, but he could not desert Barney and Larry and the others. At least she was safe now. "No, I have things to do," he said, backing away before he could change his mind.

In the main entrance hall, three more young nurses had come to help Vanderbilt, Frohman and Denyer as they fastened life belts round the children. The babies had all been strapped into their Moses baskets. "What now?" Frohman asked.

"Get them to a boat," Vanderbilt said, and nodded to the nurses. "Bring the little ones, will you? And all you kids, join hands." With Denyer at one end of the line of children and himself at the other, he led them out.

Bestwick had been having some success in keeping one boat, commanded by the ship's barber, from being overloaded. It was just about to be lowered, now that the *Lusitania*'s port side was nearly vertical. He spotted Vanderbilt's signal and shouted to the men at the ropefalls to wait. The crowd's panic had subsided and the seven or eight children were willingly passed overhead to the rail. As soon as they were on board, the boat was swung away.

Vanderbilt turned to lead the nurses with the babies up to the next higher boat. He felt the deck heave underneath him, and all at once the liner began its ponderous roll to starboard. One of the nurses fell. The others were sliding away, grabbing at anything that might stop them and trying not to drop the baskets. Vanderbilt seized the side of the entrance doorway with one hand and the arm of one of the nurses with the other.

Dan Connally was halfway up the starboard deck and was thrown off his feet, sliding straight across for the gap in the rail where a lifeboat had been. Unable to slow himself, he shot right over the side and fell thirty feet into the water.

The people in No. 3 boat screamed in terror when it swung sharply outwards again, dancing and rocking as it was brought up short by its restraining chain. The hammer on the collapsible, then the collapsible itself, slipped off the deck into the sea and Les just managed to save himself by leaping for the nearest davit and clinging to it. When the liner's sideways roll halted, the lifeboat was only six feet above the surface and he was staring down into it. "Jump!" Brooks called to him. "For Christ's sake, boy, jump!" Les braced himself and leaped again. He missed, striking the gunwale, but Brooks and Charles Lauriat grasped his arms and dragged him on board.

Dan rose to the surface coughing and spluttering, although he had enough of his wits about him to keep moving his arms to prevent himself sinking again. He recovered his breath and looked up, his eyes opening wide in shock. He was still near the *Lusitania*'s side and, as she keeled over, debris showered down into the water around him, but he was only conscious of her four vast black funnels looming slowly over him, each as big as a house. When her roll halted, they were slanted above him at an angle he would not have believed possible. For some reason he had not been swirled off into the foaming wake. It was only when he tried to turn and swim away that he discovered that his legs were snarled by a tangle of the ropes and hawsers which had dropped from her decks and uncoiled, forming a kind of spider's web along her side. He nearly panicked, but knew that if he did so, he was lost. Paddling with one hand, he used the other to try to release his legs.

The lifeboat commanded by the ship's barber had been winched down to below midpoint when the liner rolled. It crunched in against her side, tipping over and hurling half its occupants out. The rest hung on and scrambled back in. When the roll stopped, the barber gave the order to continue lowering, using the oars as buffers for protection against the lethal rivets. It grated down the side, until it suddenly jolted over the hump of the rising keel and hit the water with a bouncing splash. Immediately, the ropes tautened as it was swept backward, but the barber and an AB cut them free and it spun toward the *Lusitania*'s stern. Thrusting desperately with their oars against the bulge of the keel, the crewmen pushed the bows out just enough to clear the still revolving giant screws and the bulk of the enormous rudder which was rearing up from the water. Seconds later, the lifeboat was shuddering in the turbulence of the liner's wake, still afloat, although it had lost many of its passengers. It was the first from the port side to reach the water in one piece and, as he watched from the rail of the boat deck, Bestwick felt like cheering.

Charles Frohman had been near the top of the main companionway and clung to the carved scroll at the end of the mahogany banister, when the roll started. He found himself lying on the branched and gilded railings of the balustrade. One of the Moses baskets was near him and he caught it instinctively, when he heard the baby inside it cry. The nurse who had been carrying it had disappeared, probably sliding away through the starboard door. He had lost his cane, his "wife," and struggled to his knees, cradling the baby in his arms. He knew he could never climb the sharp incline which the polished floor had become, and to step off the balustrade was to slither straight down to the water he could see through the starboard entrance, incredibly near the deck. He looked back along the line of the banister. By a quirk of the downwards and sideways tilt of the liner, the balustrade on which he was kneeling was more or less horizontal. It was infinitely disturbing to his sense of balance and, for the first time, he felt a genuine sensation of fear. The world was turning upside down.

He heard a scraping sound and glanced up to see Vanderbilt by the higher banister lowering a nurse toward him. She was clutching another of the baskets and Frohman rose to his feet to help her down. A second nurse followed, also holding a baby, then Vanderbilt handed down another two baskets, before joining them himself. Three of the five babies were crying, but to Frohman's amazement the other two were asleep.

"We can't get them to a boat," Vanderbilt said. "They'll have to take their chances in the water."

Frohman was horrified. "We can't just throw them in!"

"Whatever we do, it'll need to be quick," Vanderbilt said. The balustrade on which they were standing shook constantly and was already tilting perceptibly as the *Lusitania*'s bows sank deeper. He picked up two of the babies and set off along the balustrade. The others followed, each carrying a basket, keeping their footing with difficulty on the jerking ornamental railings.

From what had been the lower end of the flight of stairs, Vanderbilt saw what he had been counting on, water washing over the starboard side of the promenade deck. The others understood at once. Frohman gave the baby he was holding to one of the nurses and knelt, taking a grip on the carved boss of the banister. Vanderbilt had laid down one of his two baskets. He grasped Frohman's free hand and slid toward the opening of the lower exit, as far as the reach of their arms allowed. The water was lapping the deck five or six feet below and he pushed the Moses basket down gently. The water licked under it. It shifted, spun slowly and floated away.

"May the Lord go with you," Vanderbilt murmured.

The other four baskets were passed to him and mercifully were all launched safely, although in the last the baby was fretful and kicking and there was some danger it might capsize. Frohman hauled Vanderbilt back up and they stood listening to the baby's cries, which they could still hear, although it had curved out of sight. The nurses were weeping. The wailing stopped abruptly and one of them gasped. She started forward and Vanderbilt caught her arm.

"I have to," she told him simply. "I just have to."

He saw that at least she was wearing a life vest and let her go. She sat and took off her shoes, placing them neatly by the inside of the balustrade, then slipped down the deck into the water. She gasped at the coldness of it, glanced round at them and the current whirled her away. She was trying to reach the Moses baskets. The second nurse sobbed and jumped after her, vanishing just as swiftly.

Vanderbilt and Frohman were left alone. After a moment Vanderbilt said, "Well, I guess we should try to get back up top."

Frohman looked along the balustrade. It was quaking and

shimmying like one of the carnival cakewalks he remembered from when he was a boy. After his exertions, the pain in his leg was excruciating and he could make no more effort. "My mountaineering days are over," he smiled. "I think I'll just stay here."

"As you please," Vanderbilt said. "It's been a pleasure knowing you, Mr. Frohman." They shook hands. Vanderbilt touched the brim of his cap and went off along the balustrade.

Watching him leave, Frohman felt very alone. He was tempted to follow him, but realized it would be futile. He patted his pockets and remembered he had given the last of his sweets to the children. He had lost the cigar he had begun a few minutes before and took out another one. Not even Maude could blame him for lighting up again so soon, he told himself, and chuckled. It was bravado, he knew, a gesture to prevent himself screaming for help and making an exhibition of himself. An empty gesture, as it turned out. Even as he put his hand in his pocket, he remembered that he had used his last match.

He was beginning to tremble when he heard his name called. He looked up and saw Rita above him, hugging the side of the port entrance. She had found her brother-in-law with the English officer, Captain Scott, on the promenade deck. They were holding her as she called down anxiously, "Charles! It's dangerous there. Come up here!"

He controlled his trembling and shrugged. "Not being a fly, it's a trifle beyond me, my dear. But if either of your friends has a box of matches, I'd be most obliged."

At the other end of the balustrade, Vanderbilt flexed his knees and sprang for the banister above him. It was like working out on the wall bars of his sports club, and he made it easily, swinging up and round. The angle of the floor of the main hall did not seem as steep as it had been and he was sure he could get to a sofa that was bolted to the floor, and from there to the entrance. While he tensed himself for the jump, a young woman came slithering down and landed beside him.

It was Alice Middleton, the nurse from Seattle. Having left her life vest in her cabin, not knowing where to go or what to do, she was frantic. Vanderbilt had never seen her before, but she had watched him often on the voyage, relaxed and handsome, always in the distance. Seeing him now had given her hope. As long as she was with him, she would be safe.

She was shaking and Vanderbilt held her. "Steady," he said. "Steady now." His voice was deep and warm as she had known it would be. "Here, you'd better have this." He was taking off his life vest and she protested. "Come on, now. Don't be silly," he said. "You're going to need it pretty soon." He helped her to put it on and tied the tapes for her.

Alice was gazing up at him. "I don't—don't know . . . how to thank you," she stammered.

He smiled and ran the knuckle of his index finger down her cheek. "Too bad there's not time to think of something."

When he moved her round him, she understood what he was going to do and clutched at his arms. "No! Let me stay with you!" she pleaded.

"Wouldn't do you any good, my dear," he told her. "Try to get to the starboard boats. If you can't—at least it won't be so far to jump." He pressed her down until she was sitting

"Please, no . . . please!" she begged. She could see the green water just beyond the rail of the deck outside and it terrified her. Vanderbilt kissed her on the forehead and gave her a push. She wanted to scream, but her throat seemed to clamp shut. She clawed at the floor, but her nails found no purchase and she slid down toward the starboard entrance. She managed to grab its marble side pillar and pulled herself up.

The nearest boat, the only one she might have reached, was just being lowered. It was not his fault, not Vanderbilt's, she knew. He had done his best for her, given her his own life vest, and more than anything she did not want him to think badly of her. She looked round and saw him still watching her, with the strangest expression on his face. "Jump!" he called down. "Now, while you have the chance!" She tried to smile to show that she was grateful. He waved back, turned away and was gone behind the side panels of the companionway. She whimpered. Lying along the side pillar, it was as if she were hanging over the sea.

In the second-class smoke room, Martin Mannion, who

had determined to spend the last day of the crossing in carefree oblivion, recovered consciousness to find himself lying on a pile of broken glass. After a moment he worked out that he was behind the bar counter.

He had stumbled over to the bar after the bang, but the steward had most ungraciously refused to serve him, had even run out, leaving him completely alone. There was nothing else for it and Mannion had climbed over and served himself, meticulously noting down each tot of whiskey on the steward's notepad. The last thing he could remember was sitting on the stool behind the bar and wishing he had stayed home in St. Louis.

He sat up cautiously. There were some bottles of beer lying beside him and he opened one, taking a long drink, while he considered the situation. Something would have to be done. The notepad with its attached pencil was near the bottles. He picked it up, tore out a page and finished the beer while he thought some more. It was not easy to concentrate. "*Lusitania*, May 7, 1915," he wrote, and underlined it. "Have been torpedoed. Send help." He rolled up the message and popped it into the bottle, which he managed to recork after several attempts.

So far, so good. Yet somehow he had to get his vital message into the water. He shuffled up the bar on all fours and crawled through the little gate in it, with the bottle under his arm. He had a fleeting impression of the smoke room's carpet falling away from him before he passed out again and rolled all the way down through the open door and into the hall beyond.

As soon as Matt decided he must try to save Beattie, he had thought of how he might just do it. The Arnsteins' cabin was the first in the side passage. The water was rising, but was still a few feet below it. He made sure that Peter was gripping the corridor's handrail, then knelt astride the frame of the hose reel. He pulled out the bottom of the hose, slammed it into its ring and turned it until the metal threads locked. Holding the brass nozzle, he squirmed up to the corner. As he payed the hose down into the passageway, he told Peter, "Go very carefully along that rail until you're opposite the light from the companionway—and wait for me there." Peter nodded, and Matt let himself down over the edge, using the hose like a climbing rope.

Below him, the water level in the passage suddenly ebbed as one of the lower cabin doors collapsed and the water rushed in. It would give him another minute, two at the most. The door of the Arnsteins' cabin was still shut and nothing happened when he shouted to Beattie to open it. He kicked at it, but it did not give. He had to gamble that the flexible hose would not break and swung himself out, thudding back against the door with both feet. It burst open and he dropped into the cabin. It was so dark, he could see nothing at first.

Beattie was crouching inside the dressing recess in the lower wall beside Lee, who was unable to stand. They had been making love when the torpedo struck. Lee rose at once from the bed and stood on a stool to fish their life vests down from the shelf above the recess. When the cabin rocked at the second explosion, he had overbalanced and hit his head. He was unconscious, but instead of calling for help or dragging him out straight away, Beattie had dressed herself hurriedly, buttoned his shirt and got his pants and shoes on him. By then it was too late. The liner rolled over and she was not strong enough to lift him to the door, now almost directly overhead.

"Thank God . . . Oh, thank God," she sobbed when Matt came sliding down to land on the wall beside her. He drew her to her feet and thrust the hose pipe into her hand. She tried to make him take Lee first, but there was no time to argue. With his hands round her waist, he hoisted her until she could kneel on the upturned end of the bed. "Get moving! Go on!" he said. She began to wriggle up the hose, catching the edge of the door frame to pull herself over into the passage.

Matt heaved Lee up to sit. He weighed nearly fifteen stone. With him only half conscious, it felt more like a ton. His head was lolling, his eyes unfocused, and Matt slapped him. He slapped him again hard, and Lee grunted, his arms rising to protect himself. Matt grabbed them and shook him. "Lee!" he urged. "Snap out of it! I have to get you up. If you don't help, we won't make it!"

"Up . . . ?" Lee muttered.

"Come on! On your feet!" Matt said. With his arm under Lee's shoulders, he hauled him erect. Matt looked up and saw that Beattie was gone from the doorway. Water was beginning to drip over the edge.

Just then the cabin lurched, as though the liner were rolling back to an even keel again. But the roll stopped. With the motion, more water splashed over the lower door-jamb.

"Climb onto the end of the bed!" Matt ordered. "Come on!" He pushed Lee's arms up, got behind him and levered with his shoulder. Lee was like an automaton, his movements clumsy and unsure, but he had taken in what was expected of him and clambered onto the bed's inlaid footboard. Matt climbed up after him, supporting him "Beattie?" he shouted. "Are you all right? Can you make it?"

There was a pause and Beattie's voice came back, breathless. "I'm . . . at the top. I'm—I'm over!"

"We're coming after you!" Matt shouted. "Follow the handrail down till you find Peter. Wait there!" As Matt leaned out to take it, the hose went slack and slipped to the lower corner of the doorway, too far for him to retrieve it.

Water was trickling into the cabin steadily now. In a few moments it would become a deluge. "Can you reach the door, Lee?" Matt asked. Lee was swaying like a drunken man and Matt jabbed him with his elbow. "Try it! Try!" But even Lee was not tall enough. His fingers groped in the air two feet below the side of the door frame.

"Right," Matt said. "I'm going to lift you. Understand? For God's sake, don't fall back!" He bent and clasped Lee round the thighs, heaving him up. The strain of holding him was agony to the wrenched muscles of his left shoulder. Squinting past Lee's body, he saw that his hands were over the edge. "Hang on, man!" he yelled. "Hang on!" Lee's fingers tightened on the jamb just as Matt had to let go.

Lee hung on as he had been told. Water was running down his arms. It acted like a goad and he dragged himself up, with Matt thrusting at his feet, until he was wedged in the doorway. Below him he could make out the glint of more water and he reared away from it, his back against the wall of the passage.

Matt sprang for the doorjamb and gripped it, but when

he tried to draw himself up, the pain in his shoulder was too intense and he could only dangle helplessly, knowing that he was going to fall. He kicked backward, trying to find the hose and hook it toward him. His heel touched the brass handle of the open door and he jabbed down on it. Just resting his weight for that second gave him the impulse he needed and he hurled himself up, getting his elbows over the jamb and wriggling round until he was astride it. His right leg was in freezing water, his left hanging down into the cabin. He could grab the hose now, and he used it to pull himself up to lie on his face against the wall of the passage beside Lee, shuddering, gulping in air.

He was aware of two things, that the slope of the passage wall was less acute and that Lee appeared to be passing out again. Somehow he had to get him up fourteen feet to the corner of the corridor. The less steep angle was in their favor, but if Lee became a dead weight it would be impossible.

Just to rouse him was dangerous. Water was flowing now over the side post of the door on which they were standing precariously. Matt gritted his teeth and seized the hose pipe with his left hand. He put his other arm round Lee, supporting him and jostling him awake at the same time. "Lee! We have to move again!" he said. "Come on, there. Only a little farther!" Lee's head turned and his feet shifted. If Matt's arm had not been round him, he would have plunged downwards. "Stand still!" Matt shouted. "Stand still!"

Lee clutched Matt's arm. His eyes were open, staring around at the walls of the dimly lit, tilted passageway in shock. He had only the haziest memory of the last fifteen minutes. He recognized Matt, who was bracing him up. There was a hole under their feet. It didn't make sense.

"Easy now," Matt said. "Just do what I tell you. Take it easy." Lee nodded. "You'll have to turn round, face the wall. But be careful. Don't lose your foothold." With Matt steadying him, Lee shuffled round. "Hold this," Matt told him and moved the hose to between them. "Lift one foot. When you're sure you've found the other side of the door, pull yourself up." Lee raised his foot. It was a much higher step than he expected, but he could feel the lip of the other doorjamb under his toes. "Now the other foot," Matt said.

The second step was harder to take and Lee was scared, but he had to trust Matt. He drew himself up and was standing on the tiny ledge at the upper side of the door. Above him, there was a little more light and he could see the corner he had to get to. His limbs seemed leaden and, although he was aware of what he had to do, it was difficult to force them to obey him.

"Keep going!" Matt insisted. "It's only a few more feet!" He was still standing below Lee, propping him up. His chief fear was that the laminated hose might come apart under the younger man's weight and, as Lee began to inch upward, he got his arm, then his shoulder, under Lee's bent knees and shoved with all his strength.

With Matt taking much of the strain, Lee hauled himself up until he could touch the corner. He felt along it with one hand, but his fingers kept slipping off the rounded edge. He sensed that Matt's arm was giving way. He was beginning to slide back and he reached frantically over the corner, trying to catch hold of the hose pipe, but it was stretched flat and his fingertips only scraped along its surface.

Hands closed round his wrist. His head jerked and he saw Beattie kneeling at the corner, holding him. Peter was beside her, pulling with her. They held him just long enough to let his other hand move along the pipe until he could heave his chest up to the edge. His ribs took his weight and, with a last push from Matt, he was over.

Matt lay flat against the wall, exhausted. He could do no more. The water which had been eddying past his ankles had risen to his knees, which meant the cabin had been flooded. He lay panting, waiting for the liner to make her final sideways roll. He heard Peter calling and looked up. His son was lying over the corner, trying to reach down to him. "Don't move!" Matt shouted. "I'm coming up!" Fear for Peter made him forget the pain in his shoulder and he went up the hose hand over hand. Then Lee and Beattie grabbed his arms and in a moment they were all kneeling together on the side wall of the corridor. Peter was hugging him tightly.

"Matt . . . Oh, Matt," Beattie was sobbing in gratitude.

"It's not over," Lee said. "We still have three decks to climb."

To his relief, Matt saw that Lee had almost completely recovered. The younger man went first down the handrail. There was no need any more to tell anyone to hurry or be careful. Seawater was creeping up the corridor toward them from the bows. They could hear it lapping below them. It was already welling up from the lower side passages.

When they came to the light, Beattie held Lee's legs while he and Matt turned themselves into a human ladder up to the small companionway. The wall by the stairs was nearly horizontal and they hurried along it. At its end, gripping Peter's hand, Matt eased himself down to the right to lead them to the forward companionway, but stopped in horror. Water was already gushing down it, filling the starboard corridors of the shelter deck.

As they clawed their way back up to port, Matt was trying to remember the nearest exit. He had already found the doors of the children's dining saloon locked and those farther forward were under water. The door to the stewards' room by the dining saloon was hanging open. "There's stairs up through there," Peter said. "Mr. Biggs showed me."

The narrow service companionway to the promenade deck ran toward the stern and Beattie gasped when she saw it. It had become perpendicular, while tilting crazily to the left. It looked impossible, but Peter grinned. In the woods behind the house in Alberta was a big old hollow tree and Matt had shown him how to climb it with his feet on one side of the shaft, his back braced against the other. This was easier. There was even a wooden rail to grip and, when Matt lifted him, he swarmed up it like a squirrel. Matt followed him, leaning back at the top to pull Beattie and Lee up after him.

They came out at last into daylight, well below midway on the promenade deck, and Matt was shaken by the number of people still clinging to the rail and clustered in the angle of the deck and bulkheads. He had assumed that most of them by now would have got away in the boats. He was suddenly very worried about Livvy, whom he had left one deck above, and took Peter's hand, making for the nearest ladder. Lee and Beattie scrambled after them.

On the boat deck, Isaac Lehmann had worked cautiously round behind the smoke room to starboard just in time to see the three higher boats being lowered away. The one nearest the bows was already in the water. He turned back, cursing the instinct that had driven him and so many others to the port side. The shambles there, he was convinced, was entirely due to the incompetence of Staff Captain Anderson and the crew. Even now that one of the port boats had reached the water intact, proving that it could be done, no attempt was being made to lower the remaining two. Anderson himself had vanished, leaving only one younger officer who appeared to be solely concerned with the life rafts. No one seemed capable of taking the kind of decisive action that was required. A rabble of frightened crewmen, stokers and white-dressed cooks and kitchen staff brushed past him. Without hesitation, the ones behind driving the others forward, they vaulted over the rail, shrieking in terror as they plunged eighty feet to the sea. Lehmann had been pushed against the bulkhead and felt the hard lump in his side pocket pressing into him. As he fingered his revolver, he realized that Providence had put it there.

Matt and Peter clambered up to the boat deck, with Lee and Beattie behind them. They came up just above the carnage of the smashed boats and bodies, where Anderson and Marie Depage and others were working deperately to free the injured before the water from the bows washed over them. Matt led Peter quickly away and up toward the stern, where hundreds more passengers were crowding round the last two boats, although they were already full. Livvy was not where he had left her. He could not see her anywhere, nor Lady Mackworth, nor Dan, nor anyone he knew.

People milled around them, staggering and stumbling on the raked deck, many like him hunting for friends and relatives, others still seeking frantically for life vests. Yet the whole demoralized mob was strangely quiet apart from isolated weeping and shouted questions. Grasping Peter's hand, Matt forced a way through to where Bestwick and some seamen were hammering at the wooden chocks securing a life raft to the deck. "What's happening?" Matt asked. "Why aren't those boats being lowered?"

"You can see for yourself, sir," Bestwick panted. "Because of the list, they just get their keels ripped out. Only one's made it to the water." Bestwick was nearly at breaking point. He had been ready to cheer when the boat commanded by the ship's barber had sailed away, only to watch it founder and sink a minute later because of the damage to its underplanking.

"There's still a lot of people," Matt said. "What do they do?"

"Since she's stopped heeling over, we could stay afloat for another hour," Bestwick assured him. "If not, they can swim to the collapsibles. Rescue ships will be here soon."

Matt nodded. The boy was doing his best, but knew no more than anyone else. The priority now was to make sure that Peter was as far from the *Lusitania* as possible before she went down, because of the suction. To imagine she could float for another hour was madness. He turned to his son and was illogically relieved to see the cord of Harry Hightree's amulet still round his neck. Peter was looking up at him questioningly, but not afraid. "We're going to have to swim for it, Chief," Matt said. "Come on." They started up toward the main entrance, to cross to starboard.

Ahead of them, higher up, the crewmen at the rope falls of the two boats were fighting to keep them level. It was a struggle, with each boat weighing over five tons and each holding seventy people.

The able seaman in charge of the top boat was standing at midships with a fireman's axe. He had seen the destruction of the other lifeboats and understood Captain Turner's order to wait. With the *Lusitania* continuing to settle slowly, his job was to cut the ropes and the restraining chain the moment the deck was awash. Purser McCubbin was waiting by the collapsible underneath to give the signal.

Isaac Lehmann came shouldering through the crowd toward them. "Why has this boat not been put down?" he demanded.

"Captain's orders, sir," McCubbin told him. "Our best chance is to wait."

"Ridiculous!" Lehmann snapped. "Anyone can see this ship is sinking!" He turned and called up to the able seaman, "Launch this boat!"

"We're under Captain's orders, sir," the seaman said.

"To hell with the Captain!" Lehmann swore. He gestured to the crowd. "Let's have some volunteers!" Half a dozen men started forward. Like Lehmann, they had not witnessed the wrecking of the first boats on this side.

"No, gentlemen! Please!" McCubbin protested.

He was startled and there were gasps around them when Lehmann pulled out his revolver and aimed at the able seaman. "Launch this boat!" Lehmann shouted. "I'll shoot the first man who disobeys!"

Seeing his set face and the revolver pointed up at him, the seaman brought his axe down, severing the restraining chain.

There was a mass of men and women standing on and by the collapsible. Because of the extreme list, the heavy lifeboat swung inboard instantly with tremendous violence, pulping thirty to forty people against the smoke room bulkhead. Lehmann was thrown on his back with someone lying across him. To his horror, he realized it was McCubbin, his head mangled beyond recognition.

Tearing free of its ropes, the lifeboat with its load of terrified passengers careered down the sharply pitched angle of the deck, battering through the hundreds of people gathered there for protection, leaving a dreadful trail of havoc. Matt was almost at the main entrance and saw the boat hurtling toward him like a giant log down a waterchute. He hurled Peter ahead of him into the doorway and flung himself after him. But the boat, slewing round on its side, passed over his legs, crushing them, before bouncing and rolling over, jamming itself between the bulkhead and the collapsible at which Bestwick was working and forming itself into a hideous barrier of wreckage and mutilated bodies.

In the anesthesia of shock, Matt felt hardly any pain. His only concern was for Peter and he began to drag himself back up toward the main entrance. His vision was blurring and he had to rest his head on his arms. When he raised it again, he saw Peter crouching at the side of the door, watching him anxiously. "You shouldn't have waited," Matt said. His voice came out as a croak and he swallowed, making himself sound more normal. "You have to get going, Chief."

"You come with me, Daddy," Peter said.

Matt swallowed again. "I can't . . . not just yet. It's every man for himself now. Understand?"

Peter hesitated and nodded. His face was beginning to crumple and he stretched out his hand.

Matt took it, and held it tightly. The pain had started to pulse through him, growing more unbearable at every beat, and made it difficult to talk. ". . .I'm counting on you, son," he said. "You have to make it—for me. For both of us."

"Daddy . . ." Peter whispered.

"Braves don't cry," Matt said. He smiled and after a moment Peter was able to smile back. "I'm proud of you," Matt said. "And I love you." He could barely keep his head up. "So long, Chief . . ." He pushed with the little that was left of his strength and Peter went sliding away, gazing back, his hand still reaching toward him. Then was gone. Matt gave one low cry as an unendurable stab of pain from his crushed legs lanced through him. His head reared and his last sight was the cloudless blue of the sky.

Peter went spinning down the slope of the entrance hall toward the lower doorway and the green water beyond it. He tried to stop himself spinning, but could not, and his forehead smacked into the pillar by the door, knocking him unconscious. He slid out into the water.

The nurse, Alice Middleton, was still lying along the pillar on the opposite side. She saw him glide down toward her and strike his head. She grabbed for him to try and catch him, but missed and tumbled after him. The water surging along the deck was high enough to carry Peter out into the swell, but Alice was heavier and was washed into the rail. She clutched it, feeling the sea break over her, tugging at her. She watched Peter's body float away, buoyed up by his life vest, yet the more she wanted to let go to swim after him, the harder her hands gripped the rail.

The passengers in No. 3 boat, in which Livvy had been placed, had seen the three higher boats being lowered and cheered when the ones commanded by First Officer Jones and the petty officer were launched safely. The highest of the three, commanded by Lewis, had followed them, although it had to be swung down nearly eighty feet. Just above the surface, it jerked on its ropes and rocked, tossing out some of its passengers. They were all lifted back on board and the people in No. 3 cheered again. Now, however, they were silent and tense.

Their lifeboat had settled gently into the water, but the hammer to release the pin of the restraining chain had been lost. Brooks and Les Morton kicked the pin and beat at it with the thick end of an oar, but it was wedged so solidly it could not be got out. Meanwhile, the *Lusitania*'s starboard deck was sinking deeper. The ropes had been cast off, but the chain was attached to the deck and inevitably drew the lifeboat's inboard side down. Water began to spill over the gunwale and, at the same time, one of the davits threatened to crush the boat in the middle. "It's a goner," Les said.

"Save yourselves, everybody!" Brooks shouted. "Swim for it!" The women in the boat were rising in fright, yet were afraid to leave. Brooks and Lauriat climbed onto seats and dived into the sea, and the women started to jump after them, hampered by their long, cumbersome skirts and restricting corsets. Some were carrying small children. Others had hatboxes and jewel cases.

Livvy was still sitting, although the water in the boat was at her knees. Les pulled her up. "Come along, ma'am!" he urged. He helped her over the side and saw her flounder away. She was still dazed, but her life vest would support her. He dived overboard, shook the water out of his eyes and set off, swimming as fast as he could.

The coldness of the water shocked Livvy back to consciousness. She remembered abruptly everything that had happened. All round her was floating debris. Many of the women who had been with her in the lifeboat were flailing and struggling, not knowing how to swim. She saw the side of the liner sweeping past her. Any moment she might be sucked back toward the huge propellers which were still churning, mincing everything that was caught in their undertow. She struck out blindly, aware of nothing but the need to get away.

On the upper bridge, Will Turner watched incredulously as water flowed over the rail of the starboard wing. Until that moment he had believed there was a possibility the *Lusitania* might not sink, that, although crippled, her honeycomb construction might keep her afloat indefinitely. That had been the boast of her designer. It might have held good for a natural accident, but was not proof against the inhumanity of man. He knew the *Lusitania* was doomed. It could only be minutes before she sank.

He suddenly thought of the quartermaster below him in the wheelhouse. He had stuck to his post, reading out each variation of the list indicator. They were the only two left on the bridge. "Can you hear me, Mr. Johnston?"

When Johnston answered, Turner called down, "Allow me to thank you. You have more than done your duty. Now you must see to yourself."

There was a pause and Johnston shouted back, "Aye aye, Captain! Good luck, sir!"

Johnston had been steadying himself at the helm, watching the water creep toward him up the observation wing. It was unnerving and he kept glancing round at a circular life buoy on the wall behind him. A dozen times he had checked that it was still there. Only the knowledge that Turner was directly above had saved him from panic. He would rather have stayed with Turner, the man he admired most in the world, but it was the captain's privilege and right to be the last to leave. Johnston released the slack helm. It was time for the life buoy at last.

Alfred Vanderbilt had been back to his cabin. It was quite an adventure, and all to fetch himself some cigarettes. He half expected Denyer to be there. It troubled him that his valet was missing and he hoped he was safe. One glimpse of the port side, of the maimed and the dead, the survivors shocked into stupor, was all he had needed. There were pleasanter memories to occupy him and he had done all he could. He returned to the entrance hall without too much trouble and perched himself on the lower corner of the sofa he had spotted earlier. It was tolerably comfortable. The young woman to whom he had given his life belt had gone. He hoped she was on a boat. And he hoped some of the others had been picked up. Virginia Loney, the babies, the Fletchers' little girl. He had not seen either Livvy or her husband since the accident with the lifeboat. The Loneys had gone, too. And he had not seen the Hubbards. He wished them all well.

Bestwick had sweated to right the first lifeboat which had thrown out its passengers. It was now in the water, forward on the port side, attached by one intact rope to its davit. He had partly filled it and was climbing higher to persuade people to make their way down to it. Passing the entrance, he noticed Vanderbilt sitting calmly and lighting a cigarette. It was extraordinary, as if the man had no sense of the very real danger facing him. Bestwick slid down and grabbed the top arm of the sofa to anchor himself. "Better not stay here, Mr. Vanderbilt," he warned.

Vanderbilt drew on his cigarette. "I'm quite comfortable, thank you."

"But we're running out of time!" Bestwick explained. "You must try to save yourself, sir."

Vanderbilt studied the end of his cigarette and tapped off a trace of ash. He looked up with the slightly crooked smile which the tabloids had made famous. "I have various skills," he said. "But one important one I lack. I have never learned how to swim." Bestwick stared at him. Vanderbilt shrugged. "No. I cannot swim, but at least I can die like a gentleman."

Rita Jolivet and her brother-in-law and Captain Scott had formed a chain and managed to haul Charles Frohman up to the promenade deck to join them. They were standing at the rail, their arms linked, supporting one another. With C.F. on one side of her and George on the other, Rita felt more secure, but each minute of waiting seemed like an hour and she knew they must both be aware of the trembling she could not suppress. "Say something, please, C.F.?" she begged. "Tell me a story."

Frohman, however, had no more stories. He was glad to be with friends and nodded when George kept reassuring them that there was nothing to fear in the water if they stayed together, but all he could think of was Maude. "Life is a bitter jest," someone had said somewhere. The supreme irony was that he was certain beyond doubt now that she had been trying to tell him that she loved him that night before he sailed. And now she would never know that he had understood, even though it had taken such a stupidly long time. He would never be able to tell her, never know the ecstasy of hearing himself tell her that he had loved her since the moment he first saw her.

Livvy had stopped swimming. Even if the current dragged her back to the *Lusitania*, she could go no farther. She had no longer the energy to lift her arms or move her legs. In two hundred yards she had exhausted herself. Yet she was lucky. She had seen other women drown round her, borne down by the weight of their saturated clothes. In her light skirt and blouse, she should have been able to swim for hours, as she had done with Matt and the kids.

Thinking of them, she stopped moving altogether. If they were lost, she did not want to live. But she felt herself rolling over and her reflexes fought against it. She could not swim on her back and she paddled feebly, keeping her face to the water. As Matt had taught her. Where was he? He had left her to look for Peter. Where were they? She had begun to weep silently, out of exhaustion and despair.

If she gave in, she knew she would be finished. It would be easy to give in, but the thought that Matt and Peter, even Diana, might still be alive gave her just enough strength to hang on. One thing Matt could never stand was a quitter. He would be with Peter, searching for her now, knowing that sooner or later they would all be together again, because they could never—never lose . . . because they were one.

Her mind was drifting like her body. She was rolling on to her back again. As she forced herself forward, she saw something in front of her, bobbing. It was something buoyant and she reached for it to sustain herself. It was a kind of basket with a cork base. But the base on which her hands were resting was on top. There was something lumpy inside. She had realized what it was even as she made herself turn it over. However, at the sight of the drowned baby in its straps, she screamed and thrust the Moses basket from her.

Immediately her instincts drove her to swim after it, but she was powerless. She could make no progress. As the basket floated away, she could feel herself canting over again and this time could not prevent it. Yet instead of drowning, she found that the roll at the neck of the life vest kept her head higher. It was even restful to lie tilted back in the water, the position which the life preserver had been designed to assume. It was as if a gentle hand was holding her up, and she surrendered to it, letting her body go limp.

Something was disturbing the water to her right. The debris was agitated as something slid through it, like a thick broom handle with a small window at the top. It was swiveling, growing taller, and Livvy's eyes widened as a second rod appeared beside the first, but much thinner, scarcely the width of a finger, then the surface eddied and bubbled and a rounded gray hump emerged. It was gray painted metal. As it rose about four feet, dripping water, she realized that it was the upper part of a submarine's conning tower. Above its rail, a man's head and shoulders became visible. The impression she had of him was also gray, dressed all in gray, apart from his cap. He was clean-shaven, his features regular, even handsome. Livvy gasped as he leaned forward, but he had not seen her. He was gazing past her with an expression she could not read.

Walther Schwieger had been observing the *Lusitania* fixedly for the last eighteen minutes. He had fully expected her to capsize when she heeled over so dramatically, and was amazed that she was still afloat. He had given Lanz and the officers each a short spell at the periscope and described for the others what was happening, the erratic course, the spouting steam and smoke, the accidents with the lifeboats.

Like him, Haupert was surprised at how swiftly she had gone down by the bows. "Why doesn't she sink?" he muttered.

"Because she's not going to," Lanz said sharply. "Not until we put another torpedo in her." It was his constant theme.

Schwieger could not bear to look at him. Haupert had taken his turn at the eyepiece in silence, shocked at what he could see. So had Scherb. But Lanz laughed. It was his moment of triumph and he had risen from the glass, grinning, yet he had never ceased pressing for a second shot. The damnable thing was that he could be right, and they all knew it. If destroyers and patrol boats arrived, the U 20 would have to get out of range, leaving the possibility of the liner being salvaged. The attack would technically have failed and Schwieger would be blamed. He had accepted that the purpose of his mission had been to sink the *Lusitania* and had given the order for the first torpedo without compunction. He had trained himself not to think of his targets in human terms. To do so would have affected his power of decision and made his duties intolerable. This time, however, the results of the attack in their sheer magnitude could not be ignored. If it meant his command, he would not fire again until he was convinced there was no alternative.

The decision could not be delayed much longer. He kept reminding himself of its cargo of contraband munitions, its naval status, its guns and the consignment of troops it carried. Yet he could not forget the chaos of the lifeboats and the flutter of women's dresses as they fell. The more urgent Lanz became, the harder it was to think. Because of the limitations of the periscope, he could form no true estimate of the situation. For that he would have to make a surface observation. It was fraught with dangers and Hirsch advised against it, but Schwieger gave the order for the U 20 to be brought up just enough to allow the conning tower hatch to be opened. He went up the ladder alone, permitting no one to follow him.

He came out onto the platform cautiously, but saw at once that there was nothing to fear. No rifleman could take aim on the liner's unsteady decks. Even if guns had been mounted, they would be useless because of the list. What struck him first was the lingering smell of oil and coal dust. He had been prepared for the *Lusitania* to be big, but seen by the naked eye, instead of through the lens, her size was stupefying. The U 20 was dwarfed by her, as were the tiny human figures jumping from her decks. There were so many of them, so many women in bright dresses. He was still puzzled by the lack of uniforms. Where were the soldiers she was transporting? The lifeboats were all gone, but he could make out very few in the water. It could not all be due to the list. The crew must have lost their heads. What he was not prepared for were the sounds that came from her, the dreadful creaking and groaning of her metal plates, tortured by the stress placed on them by the list.

Her stern was reared so high that her huge rudder and propellers were clear of the surface, while her bows had disappeared. The water was up to her wheelhouse. At first the bridge seemed to be deserted, then Schwieger noticed a lone figure standing on the forward rail, holding one of the halyards of the foremast. The light glittered on the broad gold rings round his cuffs and on the visor of his cap.

Schwieger had forgotten the telescope, but did not need it and did not want to see the master of the *Lusitania* too closely. His questions had been answered. The liner's bows had sunk so deeply that she could never right herself again and would take her final plunge at any moment. That was bound to cause a tremendous underwater disturbance to which the U 20 would be vulnerable. He had to get her to safety.

As he turned to go below, he became aware that the sea all round him was sown with flotsam, every imaginable thing that could float. And amongst the debris were people, some

671

swimming, some struggling, holding on to planks and wooden boxes, stools and life buoys. There were many drowned bodies drifting sluggishly in the swell. He could do nothing for them, nor for the living. U-boats had neither the space nor the equipment to deal with survivors.

One was much nearer than anyone else, a woman, lying so still in her life jacket that he thought she was dead until he noticed that her eyes were open, gazing at him, wide dark eyes in a pale face. Her mouth worked as though she were trying to shout something, to scream at him, but no sound came. Her arms were moving weakly and she heaved herself round, beginning to paddle away. Others had seen the U 20 and were also swimming frenziedly away. He realized with incredulity that they were afraid of him, afraid he might hurt them, perhaps shoot them in the water. The idea of it made him angry, but he found he was sweating. He could still see the expression on the woman's face, fear mixed with such loathing as he had never experienced before. He hurried down the ladder, slamming the hatch shut behind him, and shouted the order for Hirsch to submerge at once.

As he set a course for the open sea, Lanz came to him. "We're leaving?" he asked tensely. "What's happened?"

"It's too dangerous to wait any longer," Schwieger said.

Lanz's eyes narrowed. "You are leaving without confirmation of the sinking!" he hissed. "You realize she may remain afloat?"

"It is a risk I shall have to take," Schwieger told him flatly. "In any case I could not send a second torpedo into that crowd of humans trying to save themselves."

Lanz flushed. "Indeed? With the Herr Kapitänleutnant's permission, I shall quote that in my report."

"Do so," Schwieger said, showing no reaction to the implied threat. "I shall also record it in my log." He turned to the voice tube. "Can you hear me, Hirsch? As soon as we are stable. Full ahead, all engines!"

Will Turner was standing on the forward balustrade of the bridge, balancing himself by the side rope of the ladder to the signal halyards. Round him was a jungle of ropes and hawsers, the stays of the foremast, all now slanting many degrees from vertical, like the forest of stays behind him supporting the towering funnels. He had seen Johnston come out to the flooded observation wing with a life buoy round him and let the tide carry him away. He was now the last person on the bridge, as far as he was aware the last of the officers on board. He could scarcely bring himself to look behind at the carnage on the port side, or to starboard where an empty boat dangled in the air and collapsibles which should have floated off the deck remained fixed, because there had not been time to release them or it was too difficult to free them from their wooden securing blocks.

He did not blame Anderson, whose responsibility it had been to ensure with the carpenters that all lifesaving apparatus was readily available and in working order. He blamed himself for having believed so completely in the *Lusitania*'s invulnerability that he had left the responsibility for safety to subordinates. It was no excuse that he had followed the customary routine. He should have insisted on checking all boats and equipment himself, another lesson of wartime. But it was too late now. Too late for anything.

Robert Leith was still at his bench in the Marconi room. It had become impossible to sit. He had let his chair slide away and was bent almost double, his feet braced against the lower leg of the bench. He had repeated his distress call so often that his fingers were numb. Four answers had been received so far, promises of assistance. He prayed that others had picked up his call and were on their way, although maintaining radio silence so as not to betray their positions to listening U-boats. He had to believe that to make himself go on, as the water rose nearer and nearer.

He heard a voice speaking to him from the door and grunted in relief. He had seen no one since he entered the Marconi room and had begun to wonder if he was the last man on board. It was Hutchinson, the chief electrician. A passenger was with him, Oliver Bernard, the young set designer. "Getting anything back?" Hutchinson asked.

"We've had four replies," Leith told him.

"Only four?"

"At least they're coming." Leith paused. "Though none of them's within three hours sailing distance."

Bernard saw Hutchinson wince and said, "I've just been talking to one of the engineers. He told me there's nothing

673

to worry about. The watertight compartments won't give way."

Hutchinson nodded. "Some of them still won't have given way a hundred years from now. On the bottom." He started to take off his coat and tie and Bernard copied him.

Leith was transmitting again, a new, more urgent message. *"Lusitania.* Old Head Kinsale. Send help quickly. Am listing badly."

Lee Arnstein left Beattie by one of the ventilators behind the engine hatch at the rear of the boat deck. He had seen Matt being crushed, but had not told her, although she kept asking about Matt and Peter. "They're both out of it," he said. "They've got away." He went down the deck to the bodies of the people killed by the runaway boat. One was still clutching a life belt. He took it and carried it back to her.

Beattie was wearing a blue tweed traveling skirt and jacket and he asked her to take off the jacket. When his hands went to the waistband of her skirt, she protested. "Don't argue," he said. She was not a strong swimmer and heavy clothes would only lessen her chances in the water. He stripped off her skirt and linen petticoat.

People were watching in astonishment. Among them was Lady Mackworth. She had despaired of finding her father and had joined two friends of hers, Howard Fisher, a doctor from Washington on his way to work in France, and Dorothy Conner, a Red Cross nurse. "How disgraceful!" Dorothy exclaimed, shocked. Dr. Fisher looked away.

"Lee, please! No! Please," Beattie pleaded. She was acutely embarrassed, but he ignored her and ripped off her blouse and bodice. She crossed her arms over her breasts and he had to force them apart to put on the life belt.

As he tied the tapes, he told her. "We're going into the sea. We're going to swim to a boat. I'll be with you. If you get tired, you can grab on to me, so don't be afraid." He led her carefully down the slope to starboard. All Beattie was wearing under the life belt were her stockings. She was too embarrassed to feel afraid.

They went along the rail to the gap where a lifeboat had been, holding hands. Lee hooked his other arm round the higher davit while they kicked off their shoes. He drew

Beattie to him and kissed her. "I love you," he whispered. She smiled trustingly. As they turned to the water, it seemed to swell toward them and they jumped over the side, still holding hands.

The force of the wave swept them back through the midships section of the promenade deck, tearing their hands apart.

Frohman was still at the port rail with Rita, George Vernon and Captain Scott. They could no longer see the long black flank of the *Lusitania* slanting away below them. The sea had risen nearly to where they stood. George and Scott were praying. Rita was looking round, trying to find Justus Forman and Charlie Klein, but they were nowhere to be seen among the people thronging the rail and huddled together higher up the deck. Once she had taken comfort that there were so many. Now their numbers and silence terrified her. Everywhere she looked, there were horrible things. A man had just dived expertly past her from the deck above and smashed into some wreckage drifting beneath the surface. The water turned red around him as he sank.

Frohman had found the perfect answer to fear. He had filled his mind with Maude. His eyes were open and he was gazing out, but he saw only her elfin face, her serious, winsome smile. She was turning, holding out her arms, and he saw that she was wearing a short tunic and tights, the little pointed cap of Peter Pan, his Peter, the eternal boy. Her smile was for him. She was saying something, something important, and he repeated the line aloud after her. ". . . Why fear death? It is the most beautiful adventure in life."

Rita recognized the quotation and glanced up at him. To her amazement, he was smiling. She closed her eyes, trying to calm herself like him, trying to resign herself, to think of God as a sustaining presence.

"Why fear death?" Frohman said again.

The wave from starboard, a foaming wall of water crammed with debris and threshing bodies, cascaded over them, engulfing them and hurling them over the rail into the sea. Rita was suddenly alone. In the maelstrom her buttoned shoes were wrenched off. She tried to scream and water gushed into her open mouth.

Frohman was plunging down, down into chill darkness.

He was face to face with the final mystery. His only regret was that Maude would never know his last thought was of her.

The wave was caused by the *Lusitania*'s bows taking another convulsive lurch downwards. Water frothed across the upper bridge, drenching Will Turner's legs as he swung himself round onto the ladder by his powerful arms. Climbing was difficult with the ladder leaning precariously to the side and tilting forward, but in his youth he had swarmed up to the topgallant yards to reef sail in all weathers and had not forgotten his skills. Halfway to the signal halyards, he paused and looked back. The entire bridgehouse was submerged. To his astonishment, he noticed someone hauling himself up the ladder after him. It was young Dr. McDermott, the ship's surgeon, a replacement for this voyage. He was shouting something and pointing, but Turner could not make out what he said because of the clash of the water.

The sea poured over the *Lusitania*'s boat deck at midships. In the main entrance hall, Alfred Vanderbilt heard the roar of its coming and glanced round. He had been joined by several other passengers and had just surrendered his seat to Mrs. Loney. Bestwick and Allen Loney had succeeded in persuading him to accept a life belt and he had put one arm through it. He saw the lower doorway suddenly spout water like a geyser. He lost his footing and fell toward it, but the tiderace thundered over him and thrust him back up to the higher entrance. Choking and spinning, he still clung to the life belt as the wave swept him out across the port rail.

The same wave washed Bestwick off the ship. He had given up trying to get them all to make for the lifeboat he had salvaged and was heading for it himself. He had reached the doorway when the wave swirled him out, dashing him against one of the davits with such force that he was knocked nearly unconscious. The violence of the wave had spent itself and he drifted gently over the side.

Lady Mackworth had retreated to the rear of the first-class section with Dr. Fisher and Dorothy. The second-class promenade at the fantail should have been two decks below them. Instead they found themselves looking up at it, at the men and women crawling across it and hanging on to the hatch covers. In spite of the awesome height from the water, some were diving or jumping from the rail. She was sure she saw Marie Depage among them. Others were slithering down the log line used to register sailing distances, shrieking and dropping from it when the wire rope peeled the flesh from their hands.

On the deck beside Lady Mackworth, groups of people were kneeling, their hands clasped, repeating the Lord's Prayer over and over, while others muttered "Hail Mary, full of grace, the Lord is with Thee . . ."

Lindon Bates hurried out to the rear of the shelter deck below them, carrying a chair. Fisher shouted to him, but he did not hear. He skidded down the deck to the rail and leaped over.

"I think it's time we—" Fisher began, hesitantly.

"Not here!" Margaret objected quickly, shuddering.

They shuffled cautiously along the rail to starboard. Remembering Lee and Beattie, Margaret lagged behind, undoing the fastenings of her thick skirt and the tapes of her underskirts. Modestly she held them up with one hand as she continued her slow progress. The other two were waiting for her by an empty lifeboat station. One moment they were there and the next they were gone. She was suddenly very afraid and could not take the last few steps to the edge. She was terrified of the jump, but had no need. Even as she nerved herself for it, water bubbled up over the side, tumbling her off her feet. Her loosened skirt and petticoats were dragged down to her knees, hobbling her as she rolled over and over. As she struggled to release herself from them, the backwash of the water swept her into the sea.

Leith's swivel chair fell out of the door of the radio room, coasting straight down into the water that was lapping the edge of the Marconi deck. He was virtually swinging from his bench as he completed his last signal. He could not carry on transmitting any longer. Hutchinson had shouted that the liner was about to turn turtle, and he and Bernard had gone. Leith let himself slide to the door. His camera was on a hook beside it and he lifted it down.

He pulled himself round the outside of the radio room. He had been too busy to wonder much what had been happening outside, and nothing had prepared him for the shock of seeing the mighty *Lusitania* with her bows underwater and her funnels leaning over the sea. He could not resist it and knelt, focusing his camera on the submerged bridgehouse and the lone figure of the captain high on the forward halyards.

Bernard was at the top of the portside companionway ladder and shouted to him, "For pity's sake, man! Come on—there's a boat!"

Leith took his shot, grinned and hurried after him down the ladder to where the boat righted by Bestwick was floating, still tethered to a davit underneath it in the water. There were twenty or so people in it, numbed and trembling. Others were swimming toward it, frantic to climb in, even though the davit ropes seemed likely to capsize it and pull it down. Leith and Bernard helped some of the swimmers on board, while Hutchinson broke open the locker and found the fire axe. He severed the ropes just as the liner's bows plunged again.

The sea flowed over the lower end of the Marconi deck, flinging the boat ahead of it on its crest, colliding with ventilators, bumping and rasping across skylights and condensers and wedging itself between the deck and one of the steel stays of the forward funnel. Leith and the others thrust at the stay furiously and the pressure of water sucked them out to starboard.

Turner had seen Leith come from the radio room and honored him. That he had stuck to his duty was one small ray of hope. If only his distress calls were answered soon enough. He glanced down to shout a word of comfort to the ship's doctor, but McDermott had vanished. Just then the *Lusitania* had plunged by the head and instead of standing twenty feet above the water he was abruptly submerged to his waist.

He still clung to the ladder. As he watched the lifeboat shoot across from port to starboard, he realized that the way at last was off the ship. She had been gradually slowing, but now her forward movement had finally stopped. He felt a jarring shock which nearly wrenched his hands from the ropes and after a few seconds sensed that he was rising again. It was incomprehensible until the incredible truth burst on him. The Lusy had stopped because her prow had struck the sea bed. It was not twenty minutes since the torpedo, and she had rammed her bows into the mud of the bottom, two or three hundred feet down. The bulk of her colossal length continued to move forward with her momentum and her decks reared higher and higher above him, until her rudder fanned the air over a hundred feet above the surface.

To his horror, Turner saw people still adhering like flies to her stern deck. From beneath him came hideous rumblings as her cargo stacks spilled over, and the harsh sound of machinery screeching and smashing. He was being dragged down again, and he pushed off from the ladder, making for a life raft paddle which wheeled slowly past him.

Dan Connally had managed to untangle the killer ropes from his legs and had swum away from the side. With no life vest and impeded by his clothes and boots, he was soon in difficulty. The struggle to release the ropes had already weakened him, and his muscles, unused to prolonged exertion, were giving out. A length of broken wood bobbed up near him and he grabbed it. It allowed him to recover his breath, although he knew it would not support him for long. To his left, an empty collapsible was floating, too far to reach. Ahead he could see the keel of a capsized lifeboat and directed the length of wood toward it. Kicking his feet, he drove himself over to it and felt for a fingerhold on the overlapped planks along its side. The first piece of planking he touched came away in his hand, but he used the jagged hole it made to heave himself up, until he was kneeling on the wooden shelf to which the looped lifelines were attached.

He lay over the slope of the hull, catching his breath again, and when he opened his eyes, saw that four other men and a woman had swum to the upturned boat and were clinging to it. He was highest of the six and one of the men asked him, "Any sign of a ship?"

Dan looked all round. "There's a—a fishing boat," he panted. "About two miles off."

The woman sobbed. She was slipping away from the boat, unable to hold on. The man next to her caught her arm. Dan leaned down and took her other arm and, between them, they hauled her up until she was sprawled across the hull. She was one of the liner's female staff. She had lost her white cap. Her white apron and uniform dress were saturated, adding stones to her weight.

"Look!" another man croaked.

Dan had been facing outward and craned round stiffly. The *Lusitania*'s high-reaching stern was subsiding and, as she fell, she heeled over still more to starboard while a ravening wave spumed along her superstructure, seemingly against gravity, billowing over the ventilators and round the bases of the funnels. The people left on her decks were simply swallowed up, and those on the fantail of her stern pressed farther and farther back, although death was only seconds away.

Between him and the liner Dan could see many people swimming and floundering, terrified as he had been by the menace of the giant funnels bearing down on them. As he looked, he noticed one woman drifting on her back, her long dark hair spread around her. Only her face seemed to be above water and, as she turned slowly, he began to shake. "Livvy . . ." he whispered, then screamed, "Livvy!"

She made no response and the others hanging on to the upturned boat protested as he scrambled down, rocking it, splashing into the water. He called her name again and set out toward her, but he had taken only six strokes when his muscles seized up. He could move neither his arms nor his legs. His stomach cramped in pain and he sank under the surface. He came up, gasping for a moment, then sank again, spiraling down.

A hand grasped his hair and jerked him up. He was powerless, spewing seawater, not even aware of the seaman who had saved him. It was Les Morton. He had been making for the capsized boat when he saw Dan go down. He towed him back to it, but could not lift him onto it even with the man on the other side helping. They threaded Dan's arms through two loops of the lifeline, so that his head and shoulders were above water, his cheek against the hull of the boat. Les nodded thanks to the man who had helped and struck out for the unmanned collapsible.

Will Turner had abandoned the paddle and swum to the chair from the radio room, which promised greater support. Holding it, he propelled himself forward vigorously to get out of range of the foremast stays which threatened to trap

him when they came down. Once clear of them, he rested
and glanced round, treading water. As he looked, the sea
coursing in through the ventilators and after hatches reached
No. 3 boiler room and its boilers exploded like another colossal bomb. No. 3 funnel was rent apart near the base and
pitched over, spewing out clouds of soot and steam which
completely obscured what remained of the liner.

Livvy was shocked into realizing her danger by the explosion. She was being dragged backward. Through the pall
of smoke she could see the huge funnels just dipping their
lower edges under the surface. Water rushed in, drawing
with it a mass of flotsam, wreckage and bodies. She had
begun swimming desperately, but it was futile against the
irresistible suction. She was swept back at increasing speed
until all at once she plunged into the mouth of No. 2 funnel,
where the cataract formed a raging whirlpool. Whirling round
and round, buffeted by unknown objects, she plummeted
down into its vortex.

In foundering, filling with hundreds of thousands of gallons of seawater, the *Lusitania* staggered over to an even
keel. The funnels were swinging back to vertical, and the
giant air bubbles imprisoned below suddenly burst and belched
everything out of their shafts with volcanic force. Bodies
and debris rained out of the steam cloud. Livvy was pitched
out with them, hitting the surface at some considerable distance from the ship. Incredibly she was still aware of what
was happening, but when the water closed over her again,
she lost consciousness.

Turner was motionless, clinging to the chair. He had seen
the people sucked into the funnels and shot out again, although it seemed almost unbelievable. He was partly deafened by the explosion and his eyes were smarting. Through
the haze of steam he saw the great liner raise herself by the
bows, as though making one final effort to recover her balance; then she settled very quickly, going straight down.
As she dropped, the waters of the sea poured into the chasm
she created, sweeping in every living being, every floating
thing within reach, clashing together and humping up in a
boiling white mound. The sound of her passing was weird,
a hissing, lingering moan pierced by harsh pounding and the
rumble of further explosions.

Turner was drawn rapidly toward it by the undertow, then lifted and thrown away by the surge of the outflowing wave as the mound subsided. He fought with the chair to keep it upright while the shock waves rocked it.

After the moaning and the stilling of the waters, there was silence. The wisps of smoke dispersed. His eyes were still smarting, but now with his own tears. He could not stop them. He was mourning his pride, his beautiful ship, his first love.

The *Lusitania* had gone.

Chapter 33

THE MESSAGE FROM THE SIGNAL STATION AT THE OLD HEAD of Kinsale that the *Lusitania* had sunk was received at Queenstown just twenty-three minutes after the announcement that she had been torpedoed. Admiral Coke was stunned. Like everyone else, he had been counting on having several hours at least before the rescue craft would be needed. Some boats had left, but many were still at their moorings while their crews were being rounded up, and already his office was besieged by reporters and its telephone lines jammed by calls. One distressed him. It was from the commander of the squadron of torpedo boats, requesting permission to assist in the rescue. Bound by his orders from the Admiralty, Coke had to refuse. He was not a hard man, and he knew it would cost him many sleepless nights.

Admiral Hood fumed as the *Juno* crept through the long waterway of Cork Harbour. The old cruiser and her decrepit sisters took so long to build up steam that smaller craft had already outdistanced them. They would be overtaken as soon as the *Juno* was up to speed, his Flag Captain assured him. "They'd better be," Hood muttered. "It will be a damned disgrace if the Navy is not there first."

The *Lusitania*'s distress calls had been received by other naval wireless stations and were being processed for transmission to higher authority when the news came in of her sinking. A signal was sent immediately to the Admiralty in London.

The calls had also been monitored by the German listening stations at Nauen and Heligoland. Reports were rushed as they came in to Fleet Headquarters at Wilhelmshaven and a Most Secret dispatch was telegraphed directly to Great General Headquarters in the castle of Pless.

A long lunch was ending, at which many toasts had been drunk to Falkenhayn and his field commanders, whose armies had advanced more than seventy miles in five days in a spectacular rout of the Russians, to the capture of the fortresses of Tarnow and Gorlice and the overwhelming triumph of the Eastern Offensive. Grand Admiral Tirpitz, flanked by his senior officers, had joined in the richly deserved toasts, although he drank sparingly. It was an Army triumph and would result inevitably in even greater arrogance among the military staff, with the Imperial Navy pushed more firmly into the background. For the past week Tirpitz had been short with his aides, and silent at meetings, brooding and preoccupied. He's had his nose put out, the Army Staff sniggered.

He had left instructions that any personal signal was to be delivered to him at once, wherever he was and whatever he was doing. He was gazing at his champagne glass and did not at first notice the cipher officer who appeared beside him. The man repeated his discreet cough and Tirpitz stirred. He snatched the signal envelope, then, conscious that Admiral Müller, chief of the Kaiser's naval cabinet, was watching him, opened it casually and read the enclosed brief message. He nodded a dismissal to the cipher officer and read the message again, only a faint pursing of his lips betraying his satisfaction. The first part of his objective had been faultlessly attained. Schwieger, in spite of some doubts of his flotilla commander, had been the man for the job after all. The tail of the American paper tiger had been scorched. Now events merely had to take their course.

In the absence of the All Highest, his place was occupied by his nephew, the invalid Prince Waldemar of Prussia. Like the generals and admirals of the staff, he was startled when Tirpitz rapped with a spoon on the bottle in front of him to demand attention.

The Grand Admiral was rising, holding his glass. He was an imposing figure and conversation ceased instantly, the generals expecting a graceful tribute from the junior service. Falkenhayn had come to know Tirpitz well and was party to most of his plans and expectations. He had questioned that they could be accomplished, but something about the erect manner in which the Grand Admiral stood, the victorious lift of his head, caused Falkenhayn to catch his breath. His habitual quizzical smile faded.

"Your Imperial Highness, Commander-in-Chief, gentlemen," Tirpitz said, "I give you the Third Submarine Flotilla—and the U 20!"

The generals and admirals rose to their feet, puzzled. The significance of the toast was lost on them, but they had to respond and raised their glasses. "The U 20!"

Karl Scherb's attitude to his commander had changed radically in the last two days. From fairly critical disappointment, absorbed from Lanz, it had veered to outright admiration. What the older members of the crew had told him was true. The commander was not the public's idea of a romantic daredevil, but given a target or a tight situation he was decisive and ruthless, cunning as a fox. Dogfoxes, the U-boat captains were nicknamed, and Schwieger was the most cunning of them all. Scherb tried to express some of his admiration, but Schwieger cut him off. "We only do our duty," he said.

Schwieger was not as cool as he seemed. In the last half hour, while the U 20 hummed with excitement, he had moved through it as though nothing untoward had occurred. Yet he knew that in that time his life and career had altered irrevocably. There was still the nagging doubt, repeated by Lanz, that the main objective had not been achieved. If the *Lusitania* had only been crippled, her hidden guns and contraband cargo might still be saved. He was convinced that she could not have remained afloat much longer, yet he could not leave without confirmation. He gave orders to put about and return to the area of the attack.

Hirsch was infinitely cautious in bringing them up to periscope depth, but Schwieger's first glance through the lens showed it to have been unnecessary. There was nothing to be seen of the giant liner. A few lifeboats were pulling hard for shore, no sign of gunboats or destroyers or any sizable enemy craft. "Take her up to fifteen feet," Schwieger ordered, and again the U 20's conning tower broke the surface.

This time he allowed Lanz, Haupert and Kurtz to come up to the platform with him. Lanz was chuckling, full of congratulations at last, but even he fell silent when they looked around.

The sea was still almost unnaturally calm. Wreckage was strewn over miles of the surface, most concentrated near the center toward which the U-boat was slowly traveling. The sun shone out of a cloudless sky on a vast jumble of objects floating in the water, tables and chairs, boxes, toys, barrels, framed portraits, papers and bottles, boards and broken lumber, shattered lifeboats. Schwieger saw what he thought was a wax doll drifting by. It was only when it was jostled by the conning tower's bow wave that he realized it was a child, perhaps two years old, whose hastily tied life vest had slipped to its waist and driven its head and shoulders below water. There were bodies everywhere, civilians, young and old, men and women, some appallingly mutilated. Many of the pieces of debris appeared strangely shaped because of the people lying across them or clinging to them. Hundreds of people. From some came wailing cries, despairing voices calling for help. Among them was the sound of singing. Although Schwieger did not recognize the tune, he knew it was a hymn. Only two lifeboats and three canvas-sided rafts moved through the desolation, picking up the living and the dead. But even these would soon be overloaded.

"Permission to go below, Captain?" Kurtz requested thickly.

"Granted," Schwieger said, and the boatswain stumbled back down the ladder.

Haupert was white-faced, gripping the rail. Lanz turned as if to follow Kurtz down, but stopped when Schwieger looked at him. The Mate of the Reserve was ashen, chewing his lower lip. Typical civilian, Schwieger thought. They howl for the destruction of the enemy, for total war, yet cannot bear to watch the results. "Where are all the uniforms?" he asked. "Point one out to me." Lanz was silent.

Schwieger's own expression was bleak. In his worst imaginings he had never visualized such a scene. Only by thinking of it as revenge for Weddigen and Lepsius and all the other commanders and their crews lost to the enemy could he accept it. The will to conquer was everything, he told himself. Grand Admiral Tirpitz often quoted the American General Sherman, "War is hell." The Kaiser said the enemy needed a lesson in terror to force them to their knees or to bring them to the negotiating table. If this horror helped to achieve either of these objectives, it would be justified.

He heard a splashing behind him and glanced round. A woman was threshing in the water. She wore a life belt and could not be drowning, but she was doubled up, grunting like an animal. She was not aware of the U-boat or of anything but her own agony. He heard Haupert gasp and understood at the same moment. She was heavily pregnant and had gone into labor. Her baby was being born in the sea. Schwieger felt a tremor of nausea. Haupert was looking at him and he shook his head. "There's nothing we can do," he said tonelessly. He saw Lanz swallow and wet his lips. The woman's moaning was fading as they drew away from her.

Beyond the navigation lieutenant's shoulder was the open horizon, and all at once Schwieger saw the smoke of funnels rising from it, a large steamer on course for Kinsale or Queenstown. He had observed the effect of the sights surrounding them on the others and could feel the disgust in himself. If it spread to the crew, it could be disastrous. They needed to be reminded of their priorities as a fighting unit. "War is hell," he told Lanz and Haupert. "Get below." He was bending to the voice tube. Perhaps the sinking of the liner had flushed out one of the English warships at last. "Action Stations!" he called.

The lifeboat commanded by the petty officer had nearly been trapped when the *Lusitania* went down. Tossed about inside it by the roaring waters, crewmen and passengers had rowed frantically against the terrible suction. Elizabeth Duckworth had grabbed the oar from the half-fainting man in front of her and worked it with all her strength until the last outflowing wave picked them up and bore them away from the collapsing center of the vortex. The crew was badly frightened and was making with all speed for the becalmed trawler in the distance.

Elizabeth was still plying her oar, matching the plunging strokes of the men. Their escape seemed like a miracle to her and she knew she should give thanks, but there would be time for that later. The boat was heavily laden and partly waterlogged and rowing took all her energy and concentration at first. The petty officer was shouting to them, "In . . . ! Out . . . ! In . . . ! Out . . . !" as if they were at a regatta, but it was certainly easier once they had set up a rhythm.

She could look about her and could scarcely credit how suddenly quiet everything was, how swiftly the sea had become smooth again. The huge ship, which had seemed so imperishable and majestic, had simply ceased to exist, with only the ever-widening ring of floating things to mark where it had been. In a few hours even they would be gone. She tried not to think of poor Alice Scott. You're a lucky woman, Lizzie, she told herself.

Another boat had stopped not far from them, the one commanded by First Officer Jones. It was alongside No. 1 lifeboat, the first to be launched, which had spun away empty, and she could see that he was transferring many of his passengers to it. He waved and shouted, but the petty officer urged his men on without responding. Elizabeth saw that Jones was turning back to pick up more survivors. It made her more conscious of what was in the water, not just debris but people. Their boat was drawing away, leaving people drowning. She glanced round at her fellow passengers bunched together on the seats, some kneeling between them. The gunwales of the boat were dangerously near the surface, but surely they had room for one or two more?

Just then, she saw something bobbing past them. It was a child, a dark-haired boy of six or seven, lying on his back in his life vest, motionless. She was reminded of little Arthur. Suppose it had been him? "Look! The boy!" She called to the men in front of her. "Catch him!"

"There's no point, missus," one muttered.

Elizabeth was horrified. "We can't just leave him!"

"We've no room for anyone else," the petty officer said. "Forget it."

"I will not forget it. And we have room," Elizabeth insisted. She dug her oar into the water and the petty officer realized she was not going to give up. He cursed under his breath and swung the boat's rudder round. It curved nearer to the boy and, with some maneuvering, two of the crew were able to nudge him closer with their oars and pull him on board. He was inert and they shook their heads. They laid him on the bottom by Elizabeth's feet and were startled when his eyes opened. "Love us! I thought you'd bought it, young 'un," one of them exclaimed. The boy stared at them and they sat him up.

"What's your name, sonny?" Elizabeth asked.

The boy's head turned to her. His eyes were blank and she saw that he was in a state of shock, not knowing where he was or what had happened. The male passenger took over the oar again from her and she lifted the boy up onto her knees, hugging him, chafing his cold hands and legs.

"Right, can we get on?" the petty officer asked. "We've a long pull ahead."

Les Morton was still making for the collapsible when the *Lusitania* sank. He could not resist one look back, and was unable to turn away. He did not expect ever to see such a sight again in his whole life, the stricken ocean queen and the hundreds of passengers still crowding her upreared stern too afraid to jump. He saw the lone officer climbing the rigging by the foremast and recognized him as the captain by the glitter of the gold braid on the visor of his cap. That was something else to remember, but it made him think of his brother. Where was Cliff? Had he got away safely?

When the bows dropped, dashing Turner into the water, Les knew he should put as much distance between himself and the foundering liner as possible. He struck out for the collapsible and hauled himself up on it. Someone swam up beside him. To his surprise, it was his young seaman friend, Joe Parry. Les helped Joe up onto the raft in silence. There was a white, mistlike vapor over the sea where the liner had been and a whisper of sound like a thousand voices keening. It was eerie and Les shivered. All manner of things had begun to pop up out of the water. There were people among them. Some were swimming desperately for the collapsible and Les knew he should get it ready for them. He searched his pockets, but had lost his knife. Joe had his and started to cut the canvas cover off.

The first to reach them were James Brooks and Charles Lauriat. Brooks was not a good swimmer, but had stayed to help Lauriat and the others from the sunken lifeboat. Like Les he had paused to watch the liner go down, awed by her battle against the sea and the inescapable death facing so many who had remained on board. He became aware too late that he was too near and was liable to be mashed by the funnels or snared among their crisscrossing steel stay-ropes. He avoided the funnels, but both Lauriat and he were trapped by the descending wires of the radio aerial, stretching from mast to mast. He was dragged under by one arm, Lauriat by the shoulders, and they were only saved by the *Lusitania*'s last-minute attempt to right herself. All he suffered was a cut on the arm and Lauriat a painful back, but others were not so lucky. Many were drowned or lacerated by the wires.

When Brooks and Lauriat swam up to the collapsible, they found the two young seamen having trouble cutting off the cover. Brooks passed up his clasp knife to Les and they clung to the lifelines until it was possible to climb on. Without its cover the shallow collapsible looked more like a boat than a raft, but another difficulty occurred when they began to erect its canvas sides. More people had swum up and were trying to clamber in. Les and Brooks had to plead with them to wait. Unless its sides were properly set up, the collapsible could be swamped only too easily.

At last the sides were slotted in, the seats fitted and the men and women hanging on the lifelines could be helped on board. The oars had been washed away and Les and Joe paddled with pieces of plank until they could collect other oars from among the floating wreckage.

They were constantly stopping to pick up survivors. One woman died almost as soon as she was lifted over the side. All the while, Les was haunted by the voices crying for help, the sight of people striving to remain afloat, fighting one another for handholds on crates and broken planks and hencoops, drowning before they could be reached. Another woman was hoisted on board, clutching a baby. She sat rocking it in her arms, crooning to it, refusing to believe it was dead.

Whenever an oar was found, Les passed it to the fittest of the men and they started to move with more speed. After twenty minutes they had five. A middle-aged man, balding and pompous, had begun to complain. "Do you realize that we are all freezing and soaked through?" he snapped at Les. "Unless you get us ashore at once, we are all likely to die of exposure! Think of your passengers!"

690

"This boat's made to take fifty," Les told him. "We're not leaving till we have at least that many on board, maybe more. If you're cold, take a turn at the oars."

The man gaped at him.

The news of the sinking was sent to Ambassador Page by the American Consul in Queenstown. Page was shattered, although it was only confirmation of what he had expected and dreaded. Part of the blame, as he saw it, was the State Department's. The unrestricted U-boat campaign had been delayed because of the President's warning that Germany would be held to a strict accountability for any attack on American nationals. But no firm protest had been made over the *Falaba* or the *Cushing* and the Kaiser's High Command clearly had assumed that the warning was so much hot air. The direct result was this sinking. Page's only comfort was that the Consul had reported an unofficial naval spokesman as saying that all passengers and crew had been saved. He forwarded the cable at once to the President in Washington.

The news was received at the same time at the British Admiralty and taken to the First Sea Lord, Admiral Fisher. It came as no surprise to him either. He was not even particularly concerned. The once incisive and brilliant organizer had become an embittered old man obsessed with the indignity of playing second fiddle in naval matters to the civilian First Lord, Winston Churchill, who had not even been born when Fisher commanded his first ironclad. Now a storm could break, questions could be asked by those who kept insisting that the navy should risk itself in providing escorts for merchant and passenger ships, the United States could start bleating about lack of protection for its nationals, and Churchill was not at his desk, was not even in London. Officially, he had gone to Paris to sign the secret treaty with Italy. Fisher saw how he could embarrass Churchill with his cabinet colleagues. He dismissed the report on the sinking. "This is for the so-called First Lord to deal with," he said. "Get him to make a statement."

Churchill could not be contacted. He had completed his official secret business with the Italian representatives in Paris and was now unofficially en route for the headquarters of his friend the British Field Marshal, Sir John French. No one had been informed, since he had no intention of being recalled and prevented from observing the assault on Aubers Ridge on Sunday.

The message from Page was handed to President Wilson by Joe Tumulty as he came out of a cabinet meeting. Wilson was in an exceptionally good mood. In the morning he had returned from a visit to Williamstown where he had attended the christening of his first grandson. The cabinet discussion had gone well, with Secretary Bryan in an unusually conciliatory mood. The message shook him. Like Page, he took comfort from the fact that there appeared to have been no fatalities, but the presence of Vanderbilt, Frohman and other eminent citizens on board, which must have been known to the German authorities as it was widely reported, could be inflammatory. Hurriedly he summoned back those of the cabinet who had not yet left. They agreed with him that no action could be taken until all the facts were known and that all information should be passed to the newspapers through the White House press office.

The *Peel 12* was overcrowded already. The small trawler with its crew of seven men had taken on over a hundred people, more than sixty from the petty officer's lifeboat and another fifty from Les Morton's collapsible. Trained nurses and a doctor among them did what they could for the injured while the trawler's crew brought out all their blankets and spare clothes for the women and children. The dead were piled one on top of the other in the hold. The living sat on each other's knees on the deck or with their legs over the side. Elizabeth Duckworth had seen the boy she had saved laid in the crew's quarters with a quilt round him.

"Can you take some more?" Les called up.

The trawler's skipper scratched his chin. "If you're goin' for them, laddie, I'll take as many as you bring."

Les and Joe Parry and two other men turned the collapsible and began to row back the long miles to the site of the wreck.

The petty officer's boat was tied up to the trawler. Thomas Quinn, who had been portside lookout on the *Lusitania*'s crow's nest, was still standing in it and shouted, "Right, there's a boat here! Who's coming with me?"

One of the Scots trawlermen and a husky young man climbed down to join him. Elizabeth was near the side and recognized him as the young minister who had prevented the panic in the second-class dining saloon, although now he had lost his dog collar and stripped off his coat to give to someone.

"Come on!" Quinn said. "We need hands. It's a hard row."

He was looking at the petty officer, who muttered, "We're all in. It's too far. We're too tired."

When no more men stepped forward, Elizabeth said. "I'm not tired." Before anyone could stop her, she had swung over the side and let herself down into the lifeboat. Quinn and the parson cast off without another glance at the petty officer. Elizabeth had already taken up one of the oars.

In the water, the clumps of bodies, wreckage and survivors were moving steadily apart through natural drift. Will Turner found himself floating in an area where he was completely alone. A body bobbed up only a few yards away, a male passenger. Shifting the chair round, Turner steered himself over to him with the idea of trying artificial respiration until he saw that the man's throat was gaping open where his head had nearly been sawn off by a rope or wire. It was horrible. Turner pushed the body away strongly and was relieved when the distance between them increased.

Off to his left, he could make out a lifeboat which appeared to be lifting people from the water. To his right, farther, was an upturned collapsible with people lying and kneeling on its flat bottom. He considered making for one or the other, but after an hour in the sea it took all his energy just to hang on to the chair. The water had not seemed too cold at first, although he estimated its temperature at being less than 50 degrees, yet as time went on he could sense his legs growing numb. He kicked them slowly to keep the circulation going and to try to stay as close as possible to where his ship had gone down. The wreck would have to be buoyed as accurately as possible. He would not let himself think of his life's savings, lost with his command. The thought was unworthy, when so many of his friends and crew and passengers were dead and dying.

How long was it since she went down? He almost looked

at his watch, although he knew that was pointless. It had stopped at 2:20. It must be well over an hour and still no sign of a rescue ship. He prayed that Leith's calls had got through and that one or two would arrive soon, or many more would die. Perhaps the hope of rescue was as empty as the promise he had been given of an escort? He fought the bitter anger which swelled inside him. Anger used up too much energy and he might need every last ounce he possessed.

Junior Third Officer Bestwick was struggling to keep his collapsible afloat. He had still been close to the *Lusitania* when she sank and had been dragged down with her. Those two or three minutes had been an eternity of terror, twisted this way and that, battered almost senseless by the currents of the vortex, until he was thrown out into calmer water, but colder and darker than any he had ever experienced before. Not knowing which direction was up, he was afraid to move in case he sent himself deeper and forced himself to hang suspended and motionless until he felt the faint suggestion of rising. There was only a fractional amount of air left in his lungs and, as he thrust with his feet, he held his nose clamped shut, making himself count slowly. He told himself he could last out until he got up to thirty, but long before that his chest was laboring and the pressure in his throat made him open his mouth. Seawater rushed in and he spewed it out again before swallowing more. Coughing on it was like strangling and he caught his throat, squeezing it with both hands. Just as he saw blessed light above him, he bumped into something, his weakened hands fell away and he blacked out.

He came to lying on his back. He was coughing out salt water and it was the raw pain in his throat which brought him round. The first thing he thought of was the sickening memory he had taken into the vortex with him, of Alfred Vanderbilt spinning down into the whirlpool, trying desperately to pull the life belt over his head and having it snatched out of his grasp. He was beyond help. His body would be floating somewhere down there in that cold, dead twilight.

Bestwick felt a tug at his life vest. It was one of the stokers who had taken him in tow and swum with him to an empty bread tank, by which they could support themselves. His throat hurt too much to speak and he could only nod his thanks.

By the time he had regained his strength, three other men had joined them and were also feeling for finger holds on the slippery tank. Bestwick noticed an upturned collapsible not far from them and swam for it. The stoker followed him and they helped each other up onto it. Its bottom was breached, so there was no point in attempting to right it. As it was, the collapsible did duty as a serviceable if unstable raft, and they were able to haul a number of other people onto it. Among them were Robert Leith and Oliver Bernard, whose lifeboat had lost its plug and gradually filled with water until it sank under them. To Leith's sorrow, his camera with its precious shot of the *Lusitania*'s death throes was soaked and ruined. It was a more bitter blow to Bestwick. The sinking of their boat meant that not one of those on the liner's port side had survived. All his work, all Staff Captain Anderson's, and the dead and injured, had been for nothing.

The damaged collapsible was always in danger of tipping over and Bestwick was glad when they drifted into another, still intact although partially submerged under a pile of wreckage. Once cleared, it proved buoyant and navigable. As soon as the sides were up, he moved the people from the raft into it and was able to start collecting more from the water, including the three men he had left round the bread tank. Distressingly, one of them died soon after he was brought on board. He was not alone. Shock and exposure had begun to claim their victims. When Bernard opened the locker supposed to contain emergency rations and fresh water, there were no rations and the water had turned with age into a filthy green sludge.

Rita Jolivet could not believe that she was alive. She had given herself up for dead when she had been separated from Frohman and her brother-in-law. She had not resisted when she was swept below the surface and to feel the warmth of the sun on her face and hands and to be able to breathe again was astonishing. She had emerged not far from a capsized lifeboat and she dogpaddled to it, joining in the scramble of its former passengers for the loops of rope along its sides. The rope was her link with life and nothing now would make her give up her hold.

As the shoving and elbowing stopped, she looked around, but the only person she recognized was the young Washington doctor, Howard Fisher. He smiled to her and she returned his smile automatically. Oh God, she thought, I must look a mess, and she began to laugh quietly. The people next to her were alarmed in case she was becoming hysterical, but she was not. She had realized that at least she still had her vanity, the final proof that she was alive and was going to live.

Another upturned boat was wallowing a hundred yards from them with twenty or more people clinging to it, others sprawled over its curved keel. A woman in the water was holding up her eight-year-old son, begging for a space to be made for him on the keel. He was hoisted up and the boat sank even lower.

Propped against its side with his arms through two loops of the lifeline, Dan Connally was submerged to his neck and in danger of drowning. The smallest wave sent water splashing over his face. He could do nothing to save himself. His muscles were paralyzed by the chill of the sea. As more and more people reached the boat and clutched the ropes along from him, it sank lower and lower. Suddenly it heeled over, throwing off most of those who were perched on it and sliding sideways under the surface.

Dan had concentrated on his breathing, holding each lungful for as long as possible, and was not caught by surprise like many of the others. When the boat lurched back up to the surface, half of them were gone. The boy was missing and his mother screamed and screamed until she lost consciousness. A steward and the cabin maid had climbed up onto the keel and hauled her up beside them. Another man was crouching by the stern, nursing a badly scalded arm. It was the oiler, Frank Tower. He was looking down at Dan and saw how he could barely keep his mouth above water. "Hang on, mate," he panted. "Hang on." He shuffled round, shouting to the people in the water to spread out if they did not want the boat to keel over again. "Get round the other side," he told those at the ends. When they obeyed him, the list of the boat was corrected and it stopped its unsteady rocking.

Dan's shoulders were above the surface again and he could breathe normally. "Thanks," he croaked to Tower, who winked back.

With no immediate fear of sinking, people began to think of others. A child floated by within reach, a girl, and the steward called to those nearest her to lift her up. She was scarcely able to move, moaning feebly, and it was only when they stretched her out on her back on the curve of the hull that they discovered she was not a child, but a young woman naked save for her life vest and white stockings. Her defenseless near nudity created an odd touch of embarrassment and Tower and the steward turned her over onto her face to hide her femininity. She was past caring and lay weeping silently. Presently her weeping ceased.

Margaret Mackworth found the sensation of floating not unpleasant, apart from the increasing coldness of her legs. Once her trammeling skirt and underskirts had dropped away, the life belt held her head and shoulders comfortably above the surface and she was able to look around. In her first fear, she had seized the end of a length of wooden paneling and, although it was not much help, she could not let go. A man, a seaman with a yellow, tobacco-stained mustache, had shared the board with her for a few minutes, but their combined weight submerged it. He smiled to her and swam away. Within a few seconds he flung up his arms and sank without a sound, without a struggle.

The *Lusitania*'s wreckage formed the shape of a comma with a tail two to three miles long. She was near the center of the head and the slowly circling flotsam gradually closed in around her until she was surrounded by a floating island of debris and bodies. She could see over the bulk of it to the few boats and collapsibles which were taking survivors on board. She wanted to make for one of them or somehow attract attention, but found she had neither the energy to swim nor to wave her arms. She forgot her distress as she felt something burrowing under her. Something was nudging insistently at her back and buttocks. Until this moment she had not thought of sharks or other sea creatures. She had assumed the water was too cold for them, but now she began to whimper and flail with her legs and arms. Her agitated movements dislodged the wreckage pressing round her, yet whatever it was underneath her had her trapped.

She could feel herself being borne upward. Her back was rising and her hands touched something on either side of her, like a great gaping mouth. She opened her own mouth to scream, then realized that she was sitting up. A large wicker chair with a high rounded back and wooden arms had floated up directly under her. Her movements had driven her into the seat and the backrest had swung upright. How very extraordinary, she thought, and fainted.

Livvy was drifting near the outer edge of the same island of debris. She had lapsed again into the strange state of semi-coma where she was aware of what was happening around her, yet could not react to it. Twice she had forced her eyes open, to see boats which had passed her and were plucking the living from the water. She had been left to await her turn with the dead.

She could hear voices singing "There is a green hill far away" and tried to join in, hoping the singers might become aware of her. Only the faintest dry whisper came from her throat and soon stopped. She could not remember the words.

The voices were fading, confirming her suspicion that she was drifting slowly away from the mass. On her own, there was little chance of her being spotted and she knew she should fight to prevent herself becoming separated, but she could do nothing to prevent it. Her body hung, limp, her arms trailing beside her. She heard shouting, something about a ship. A ship was coming! With a tremendous effort she managed to move her right hand. She forced it up until its fingers caught in the tapes of her life vest. She rested, then forced it to move again. Her arm broke the surface and fell across her chest. No matter how she tried, she could not move it again.

In her despair, Livvy would have welcomed death. It was taking too long to come. When she had rested again, all she had to do was let her hand slip down to the tapes of the life vest and pull them undone and she would sink away into oblivion. She saw something winking in front of her face. It was the sapphire ring on her third finger, the last present Matt had given her in New York, a bright cornflower blue like the late spring sky above the marshes where she was born. She could hear Matt telling her that. "We'll be seeing it soon," he had said. Oh, Matt . . . she whispered silently. Where are you? For his sake she could not give in.

The three merchant ships zeroing in on the site of the wreck had maintained contact with one another. Among them, the captains had pinpointed the position. To an extent it was now a race among them, but Harwood in the Anglo-American Company's *Narragansett* was well out in front. He was crowding on all speed and already through his binoculars could make out clearly the promontory of the Old Head of Kinsale and dark objects in the water. "Ye Gods!" he muttered. "There's still no one else there!" Everyone on the bridge knew what he meant. Ahead of them, people were drowning. In the twenty minutes it would still take to reach the wreck, how many more would die?

The Second Officer was at the open port door of the bridge. He glanced round before coming inside, and paused. "What's that?" he wondered aloud. He swallowed. "Aw Jesus, no . . . Periscope on the port bow!"

Schwieger had been watching the *Narragansett* for the last half hour, letting only the lens of the asparagus show above the surface for brief seconds, while he adjusted his course and speed. He had been through many changes of mood in the past two hours, from exultation to self-disgust. He could accept neither and still live with himself, and had fallen back on his training. His only concerns were his command and the orders he had been given. Once again he was as calculating and impersonal as a machine.

He was disappointed that the approaching vessel was not a warship, but it was a tanker of approximately ten thousand tons, possibly of the Cunard Line, Lanz thought, from its large red funnel. It was too good a target to ignore. "It's bound for the site of the wreck," Lanz said quietly.

Schwieger nodded. He was busy with other considerations, speeds and distances, maneuvering the U-boat to use the torpedo in the No. 1 stern tube. He sent Scherb to prime it and set its depth meter, and warned Hirsch to be prepared to surface swiftly if the tanker was only crippled and needed to be finished off with the deck gun.

Lanz was silent. Like the gunnery lieutenant, he had learned several lessons in a very short time. Chief among them was that he did not have the stomach for this kind of total war. To his surprise, he found that watching Schwieger's concentration and lack of expression, he was shivering.

Once again, it was a copybook shot. The unsuspecting tanker steamed exactly on the line Schwieger had predicted. He gave the order to fire, brought down the periscope and waited, counting off the seconds to the explosion. None came. He saw Kurtz and Scherb looking at him and gestured abruptly for the stick to be raised. The tanker was heading away from them at full speed. Twisting the lens, he could trace the white wake of the torpedo, which had run straight for some three hundred yards, then curved away to port.

On the *Narragansett*, they had seen the torpedo coming, almost at the same moment the periscope was reported. "Starboard the helm! Starboard the helm!" Captain Harwood screamed, although it was a forlorn hope. The deadly wake was streaking toward them at many times their speed. Then, unaccountably, the torpedo veered away and, as the tanker's bows swung round, shot past her stern with only feet to spare. Without another thought, the *Narragansett* fled northwest for Fastnet Rock, away from the U-boat and the wreck it had used as bait.

Schwieger swore in disbelief. The angle had been 90 degrees, conditions ideal. Scherb had primed the torpedo personally and checked its insertion into the tube. At a range of only five hundred yards it had been impossible to miss. Yet it had not hit the target. If Rudi were here, he would say it was a sign. Probably Kurtz would agree. Schwieger did not believe in signs. Once again it had been caused by a simple mechanical fault, although the odds against it having happened again were enormous. The tanker was zigzagging. It was unnecessary. Even at top surface speed, the U 20 had no hope of catching up with it now.

The others had greeted the miss with mixed reactions and watched tensely as he swiveled the periscope. Off to his left he could make out at least two other ships bound for the wreck and, to his right, what might be the smoke from more funnels, the outriders of a whole rescue fleet. Among them was certain to be the warship for which he had prayed. But it was too late. With only a single remaining torpedo, which had already misfired and must be considered defective, he could neither attack nor challenge. The U 20 was restricted to her stern gun. It was time to leave the hunting ground. For all practical purposes, the mission was over.

He snapped up the spring-locked handles and stood back, as a signal for the periscope to be lowered. His mind was already turning to other problems. Ahead of him was a dangerous voyage of some twelve hundred nautical miles. The first priority was to avoid patrols. "Take her down to seventy feet," he said. A word to Haupert swung them back to the course he had set in the early morning.

The U 20 headed for the open sea and home.

Chapter 34

THE CRUISER JUNO HAD COME WITHIN SIGHT OF THE WRECK-age. Shuddering under the speed at which Admiral Hood had driven her, she had easily outstripped the armada of tugs and trawlers and patrol boats which had set out before her.

Hood was on the bridge with his Flag Captain and officers when the lookouts excitedly reported approaching wreckage on the starboard quarter. He focused his binoculars quickly on something pointed out to him about half a mile distant. It was a waterlogged life raft, hardly still afloat, with people adhering to it. "This is what we've come for, gentlemen," he said. "Ready the boats." The order was relayed and the *Juno*'s boats were prepared for immediate launching by the waiting sailors. Every available man was spread out along her sides on watch. Hood kept his glasses trained on the life raft. Some of the people in the water were waving and his pity for them was mixed with a deep satisfaction. Poor dev-ils, he thought. Well, at least they know the Navy's here.

Out of the corner of his eye he saw the Signals Officer approach and salute the Flag Captain. "For the Admiral, sir."

"Not now," Hood said irritably.

"It's marked 'Urgent,' sir."

"Oh, very well, read it!" Hood snapped, turning away. "What does it say?"

The Signals Officer read out the message, faltering when Hood spun back to face him. Everyone else on the bridge was motionless, listening.

"It's not possible . . ." Hood breathed. "Who is it from?"

"Admiralty, London, sir," the Signals Officer told him. "First Sea Lord."

Jacky Fisher had been stung out of his lethargy by a report that Hood's cruiser squadron was proceeding to the rescue of the *Lusitania* survivors. The protection of the fleets he had built up had become an obsession with him, since every unit might be needed to repel an enemy naval attack in strength. He resented every capital ship sent to the Mediterranean to take part in Churchill's Dardanelles campaign. He had given the strictest instructions that those remaining in Home Waters were not to be risked in such mollycoddling concepts as convoys and the escort of civilians. Churchill valued the *Lusitania* as showing the flag on the Atlantic run. That was an emotional and political concept and no concern of Fisher's. What was his concern was that the *Juno* and her consorts were clearly steaming into an ambush laid by a whole pack of U-boats. Hood was peremptorily ordered to return at once and at full speed to Queenstown.

There was a horrified silence on the bridge. Hood was stupefied. "Those people out there," he rasped, "they've already been in the water for over two hours!" He looked slowly round. Everyone on the bridge knew of his unjustified dismissal from command of the Dover Patrol by Fisher. For him to refuse to obey this order would be seen as defiance and rank insubordination, resulting inevitably in his court-martial.

"Am I to put about, sir?" the Flag Captain asked.

Hood was watching the life raft, which was nearer now. ". . . First we'll pick up these people," he said.

"It will mean slowing virtually to a stop," the captain objected. "It will make us vulnerable."

"I don't care a tuppenny damn if every U-boat in the Kaiser's navy is watching us!" Hood roared. "We came here to save lives, and not for any order in the world will I sail my flagship back to Queenstown without a single survivor on board!"

The passengers in First Officer Jones's boat a mile astern of the raft cheered when they saw the *Juno* halt to take up the people in the water. Their excitement faded a minute or two later when the cruiser turned and headed away. It was incomprehensible. Surely its commander knew there were many more who needed to be saved?

At almost the same moment, several miles away, the

shouting and waving of the passengers on the other boats and collapsibles were fading. Two large ships had been making directly for them, were already in plain view, but suddenly had changed direction and were steaming away.

The ships were the *City of Exeter* and the *Etonian*, which had been following the *Narragansett*. They could see each other, but not the tanker, and the captains could not understand it. As they began to signal to each other, the captain of the liner *Etonian* spotted what he took to be a periscope dead ahead. It suddenly submerged and he turned hard to port, flashing a warning to the *City of Exeter*. The question the captains were now asking was, had the *Narragansett* herself been sunk or was she fleeing for safety somewhere in front of them?

As they piled on speed, the periscope was seen to re-emerge in their wake, tracking them. They were much faster, but just as they were pulling away, a second U-boat was seen to surface to starboard of the *Etonian*. Her captain altered course again in dismay, expecting torpedoes to hurtle toward him at any moment from either bow. No shot came and, before long, the second U-boat dived out of sight. Both captains knew that submarines at underwater speed had no hope of overtaking them, but it would be madness to turn themselves into sitting ducks by stopping to pick up survivors. The two ships scampered under full steam for the safer waters farther west.

It was another twenty minutes before the first of the rescue fleet arrived, the steam-powered fishing smack *Bluebell* and the Greek coaster *Katerina* under charter to an Italian company. First Officer Jones transferred the passengers from his boats to the *Bluebell* and rowed back to the wreckage to continue the search. Elizabeth Duckworth and the three men with her hauled on board Rita Jolivet, Dr. Fisher and the others round their capsized lifeboat. There were not so many as there had been two and a half hours before. Some hung dead on the lifelines. Rita had seen people on either side of her release the ropes, unable to hold on any longer. Those without life belts sank at once. The others floated helplessly away. She herself was almost delirious with cold and exposure.

Far from anyone, in a world of silence, Livvy drifted little by little out to sea.

Will Turner was in the grip of a hallucination. To take his mind off the cold, he had made himself remember the days many years before, when he had sailed in fast four-masters for the Argentine and the South Sea islands, for Ceylon and the coast of Coromandel. He remembered the unrelenting heat and steamy monsoons, and once before when he had spent over an hour in the sea waiting to be rescued. He had been second mate on the old *Thunderbolt* on a trading voyage to Calcutta and was fishing from the bowsprit when a high curling wave knocked him off his perch. He had kept himself afloat for an hour and a half while the *Thunderbolt* came about, reefed sail and set down a boat to fetch him in. That was in the Indian Ocean. He had been fishing for shark and now they were all round him, their triangular dorsal fins cutting the surface, others gliding up from below and rolling over to snap and tear. He had kept them at bay by kicking and beating the water. One insistent brute he had stunned by a smashing blow of his fist on its nose. But now they were massing for the kill, and the ship's boat reached him just in time.

His chin struck the rim of the chair's seat and he jolted awake, taking a firmer hold of the spokes. Getting old, Will, tiring more easily, he scolded himself. Looking round, he saw more boats hunting through the wreckage. It puzzled him for a moment; then he realized with a pulse of elation that the rescue ships had come. At last . . . at last. How long had it been? Three hours? He craned his head round to where the sun was lower in the sky. Before long it would set. Anyone not found by then would drift till kingdom come.

Count von Bernstorff in Washington heard the news of the *Lusitania*'s sinking from the Swedish Ambassador, who added his congratulations. When he was informed, von Rintelen summoned an urgent meeting of his lieutenants, Steinberg, Wolpert and the Irishmen, Freeman and Mike Foley. From his manner, none of them suspected that he did not share in their jubilation. The purpose of the meeting was to call an immediate end to all sabotage operations, especially those directed at American vessels and installations. The sinking would cause untold complications and investigations. With the revelation of the liner's contraband cargo, it might even lead to an embargo on all shipments of munitions, the goal for which they had been working. Nothing must be allowed to jeopardize that. Their agents were to be thanked and instructed to lie low until further orders.

After the meeting, Koenig brought him an invitation from Papen and Boy-Ed to join them in a small celebration. Von Rintelen politely declined. He told his secretary to take a vacation, as the office would be closed indefinitely. He returned to his hotel and packed, then the Secret Service agents shadowing him lost him. He was on a train, bound for the fashionable small seaside resort of Kennebunkport in Maine, where he would register in the best hotel as Commander Brannon, a South African in the British Navy. He intended to relax for a few weeks, to swim and to flirt a little and await developments. He would not let himself think of the innocent victims on the *Lusitania*, nor of Olivia Fletcher and her family. Later, he would make discreet inquiries to find out what had become of them. And he promised himself once again that later still, when all this was over, he would wash his hands in carbolic acid.

In New York as the news spread, the saloons along the Hoboken docks filled with exultant German crewmen and, on the interned liners, the officers drank to the unknown captain of the victorious U-boat.

Vessels of all descriptions were converging on the Old Head of Kinsale, small fishing boats from Kinsale harbor, rowboats and canoes from villages along the coast, motorboats and the tugs *Stormcock* and *Julia* of the auxiliary patrol, the minesweepers *Indian Prince* and *Lady Elsie* and the Queenstown tender *Flying Fox*, an antiquated paddle steamer. All were amazed by how many people were still in the water, and sickened by the number for whom rescue had arrived too late. Most of the living had been found. Their task was to pick up the dead.

Dan Connally owed his life to Frank Tower. Their upturned boat had continued to capsize, each time losing more of the men and women clinging to it. Each time Tower and the steward and cabin maid had managed to crawl back up onto the keel and to save the near naked girl. The cabin maid had taken off her apron and tied it round the girl's loins for decency. Not really a girl. They had discovered that she wore a wedding ring. She was only half conscious and, while the cabin maid chafed her feet, the steward rubbed her hands to help her circulation after each dousing.

Tower made himself responsible for Dan. Eventually, out of the original twenty, there were only the five of them left, and he saw that Dan could not last much longer in the water. The rescue boats were working closer and he made the steward and cabin maid help him to hoist Dan up until he was lying across the keel. "Be all right now, mate," Tower told him. "As long as we don't bloody well capsize again." Dan's bones ached with cold. A good sign, Tower assured him. "Time to worry's when you can't feel nothin'.'"

The cabin maid was worried about the girl, who seemed to be having trouble breathing. They heard a splashing in the water and looked round. A man was swimming toward them, a powerfully built young man moving determinedly but very slowly.

Lee Arnstein had been swimming for over three hours, stopping only to snatch a few moments of rest, holding on to pieces of wreckage, once supporting himself by two bodies. He had traversed the area again and again from boat to raft, to every floating thing round which people had clustered. He had searched the debris and the hideous flotsam of corpses. He refused to give up, to believe that Beattie was not somewhere waiting for him, and that he would not find her. But he was tiring.

He saw the overturned boat with the steward and people he did not recognize crouching on it. He could rest there for a minute or two and he made for it. As he grabbed the side, the boat rocked and Tower shouted to him for Christ's sake to be careful, then shuffled to the other beam to balance Lee as he pulled himself up.

Lee dragged himself out of the water, hanging on to the overlapping planks while he recovered his breath. He inched up higher. He had not seen the girl who lay in the curve of the opposite beam. When he did at last, he became absolutely still and whispered, "Beattie . . ."

"Do you know her, sir?" the steward asked.

Lee made no reply. He reached over the keel and touched her hair, her bare arm, her face. She seemed to be sleeping. He leaned closer and took her hand in his, and suddenly gripped it very hard. She did not stir. He slipped his fingers under her cheek and lifted her head very gently. He was weeping. It was some time before the others realized, too, that she was dead. Lee cried out.

It was the most despairing sound Dan had ever heard. What followed next he could never forget. The young man stood up, ignoring the protests of the others and the wild rocking of the boat as he drew the girl up with him. He stood holding her, embracing her tightly, kissing her softly, and saying her name over and over, "Beattie . . . Beattie . . . Beattie . . ." All at once, he leaped with her into the sea. Neither of them came back to the surface.

Dan passed out. He revived slightly when Jones's boat bumped into theirs and he heard Tower say, "Oh, we're fine an' dandy, sir. You take this gentleman and the missy." Dan and the cabin maid were lifted over into the lifeboat and ferried to the *Flying Fox*.

Elizabeth Duckworth was nearly exhausted. She had collected over forty men and women in her boat, dead and alive, but none of them fit enough to use an oar. She and the three men with her had had to row all the way to the wreckage and all the way back to the *Peel 12*.

When they reached the little trawler, it was more overcrowded than ever and its skipper had to tell them reluctantly that he could take no more or he doubted if he could make harbor. Elizabeth's head slumped forward. She found herself looking at a man lying at her feet. His sightless eyes stared back at her, his dead mouth still bubbling mucus. Next to him, a woman with a broken jaw was trying to be brave, but was obviously in great pain. The young minister laid his hand on Elizabeth's shoulder to comfort her, and was surprised when she sat up and smiled. "Well," she said, "we'd better get these good people to shore."

Fortunately they did not have to row far. The auxiliary *Stormcock* steamed up and took her passengers and those on the *Peel 12*, which was still waiting for a wind. Elizabeth was embarrassed when she stepped onto the deck and the people on board cheered her.

Will Turner's hands were slipping from the chair. He could no longer feel his legs and could not move them. His body had become a useless weight that his arms could not sustain for much longer. A minute, no more. "Into Thy hands, O Lord, I commit my spirit," he began to mutter, "and the spirits of all those who have died so cruelly this day." Someone swam up beside him and put an arm round him, holding him up. It was a seaman from the *Bluebell*, who had spotted the glimmer of the broad bands of gold braid round his cuffs. It was obvious that he needed help at once and the sailor, Jack Roper, had dived in and held him until the *Bluebell*'s overladen boat could get to them.

Les Morton helped Frank Tower and the steward onto his collapsible. He already had some thirty people on board, but he could not stop, although his muscles ached from rowing. He still had not found his brother.

It was twilight and many of the rescue ships were heading back for Queenstown. Others, smaller craft, were still sifting through the wreckage before it became too dark, prodding at it with oars and boat hooks, still finding and picking up bodies. There was a shout from some fishermen in a rowboat who had spotted Lady Mackworth sitting in her chair, deathly pale and motionless. It was uncanny and they crossed themselves before lifting her on board. Even when they laid her down, her arms and body remained bent, as if she were sitting.

Les and Joe Parry had directed their collapsible farther out from the wreckage in case the tide had carried anyone more out to sea. Les prayed that that had not happened to Cliff. The stronger among their passengers were also on lookout. They were making one final sweep before turning for the last of the rescue ships. It would soon be dark. The sun had set and only the lingering red glow of the western horizon lit the swelling surface of the sea with shifting, insubstantial light. Lamps twinkled on some of the far-off boats. The lantern of the Kinsale lighthouse winked on.

"When you come to the end of a perfect day," Frank Tower murmured. Some people laughed nervously and he began to sing, "When the sun goes down with a flaming ray, And the dear friends have to part . . ." His voice died away with the laughter.

"Shut your mouth!" Les growled, "Shut up!"

"Look at that," Parry said. "Do you see it?"

Les looked where Joe was pointing and saw a strange

speck of light. Something was catching the last flicker of day and reflecting it, but the sparkle was somehow blue, a glittering blue, not red. He steered the collapsible toward it and soon they made out the body of a woman swaying slackly in the low waves. One hand lay across her breast and it was a ring with some kind of blue stone set in it which had caught the light.

Ambassador Page had a difficult decision to make. As always in such matters he consulted his wife. They had arranged their dinner party in honor of Colonel House for this Friday evening. Now, with the shocking news about the *Lusitania*, he wondered if they should cancel it.

She thought not, since even the most up-to-date report said that casualties appeared to be mercifully slight. Page agreed. Many influential people were invited to the dinner and none of them, after all, had backed out. With the exception of Winston Churchill. Which was perhaps a blessing, since he and the Colonel did not exactly see eye to eye. Page hoped that discussion of the motives for the attack might prove valuable, not least as a lesson to House in the true British attitude to this war. If necessary, he could explain to him his reasons for not canceling the dinner. Yes, on the whole, it was much better to carry on with it.

Margaret Mackworth came awake on board the steamer *Bluebell* as she was being carried to the bunk in the captain's cabin. To her acute embarrassment she discovered that she was naked, wrapped only loosely in a small blanket. The two sailors carrying her chuckled when she tried to tuck it round herself more securely, and one said, "That's good. Coming round, are you?"

A man was rising from the bunk and moving away to allow her to be laid in it, with her blanket spread round her. She was shivering uncontrollably and had a dull pain in the small of her back. She was lightheaded and had great difficulty in working out at first where she was. She had only indistinct memories of what had happened. It was some time before she recognized the man who had given up the bunk for her as Captain Turner.

Bestwick was nodding asleep, sitting against the wall of

the cabin beside Virginia Loney. He also had trouble recognizing his captain, who seemed to have aged and shrunk in some way. He saw several people speak to Turner, who did not reply, but sat huddled in his blanket, silent and withdrawn.

In the outer cabin was Martin Mannion of St. Louis. He was thoroughly sober now and trying to piece the last few hours together. All he could remember was the bar steward running out of the smoke room, and deciding to pour himself another drink. How he came to be here he had not the foggiest idea. Near him, Isaac Lehmann was asking when someone would have the courtesy to attend to his injured leg. The lack of proper medical provisions he considered inexcusable.

Livvy had been laid with the dead on the deck of the minesweeper *Julia*. She was next to Alice Middleton, the nurse to whom Vanderbilt had given his life belt.

Dr. Houghton, traveling to Belgium with Marie Depage, had seen her drown shortly after they had jumped from the stern. He had been unable to reach her in time. He had an idea that a list should be made as soon as possible of the survivors and of the identifiable dead. With assistance from only two of the *Julia's* crew, he was working through the bodies on the deck. The task was almost hopeless in the dark with one of the sailors holding a tiny shuttered lantern, but something about Livvy and Alice made him pause as they were moved aside. "You know," he said, "I've a notion there's a bit of life still in these two."

The sailors stripped off Livvy's and Alice's life vests and began to apply artificial respiration. It was twenty minutes before Livvy coughed and started to breathe raspingly, nearly an hour before Alice was breathing anything like normally. By then Livvy had been wrapped in a quilt and laid in front of the stove in the crew's cabin. She was weak, but recovering from an agonizing bout of pins and needles all over her body and a bruised ache in her ribs from the sailors' pummeling.

Alice was brought down and laid beside her, and managed to blurt out some of her story. She had been through a nightmare experience. When she had at last been swept from the deck rail, she had been under the overhang of the side and, when the *Lusitania* had keeled over, her head had been trapped in an open porthole. She had struggled ineffectually with bursting lungs until the rush of the liner's internal air pressure had blown her out, and she had surfaced to find herself surrounded by the bodies of drowned children. She fainted again as she was telling it.

Sleep was probably the best thing for her, Houghton decided. He was proud of Livvy's surprisingly swift recovery, but warned her against trying to do too much for several days. He held her while she drank a mug of weak tea which sent life tingling through her and he checked for her that not Matt, Peter or Diana were on board. "They'll turn up," he told her. "Don't fret."

The Queenstown waterfront was lit by flaring gas torches and many people from the town had gathered beyond the barriers to watch the rescue fleet come in. There had seemed nothing too terrible in the few survivors landed from the *Juno*, but when the smaller ships appeared one by one out of the darkness and the long procession of the living and the dead began, haggard, limping men, trembling, staring-eyed women and children and the endless chain of bodies, the atmosphere became one of subdued horror.

Some boats were delayed in docking because the pier superintendents protested they were not observing the correct procedures. Customs officials were trying to insist on declarations being filled in and signed. The Admiralty had organized nothing, leaving everything to the local Cunard manager. He and the American Consul had alerted the relief committees and medical services, arranged for accommodation in the available hotels and boarding houses and some private homes, and for emergency beds in the hospitals and nursing homes. No one knew how many of any sort would be needed, but all facilities were soon stretched to the limit.

Many of the uninjured refused to leave the pier, but waited and asked anxiously for news of relatives and friends. Women wept piteously as heaps of corpses started to pile up. When Will Turner walked unsteadily down the *Bluebell*'s gangplank, he was given a ragged cheer.

In an excess of pride, Lady Mackworth would not let herself be carried ashore. In a borrowed sailor's greatcoat and the captain's slippers, she tried to walk and finished by crawling down the gangplank on her hands and knees. On the quay, she was overjoyed to see her father, D. A. Thomas, waiting for her. He held her to him and led her to an automobile he had hired to take them to their hotel. He had watched expressionlessly as Captain Turner came ashore. A reporter recognized him as a political figure and asked for his comments on the day's events. "Individual heroism, collective madness," he growled. "The standard of human efficiency is normally far below what we are entitled to expect. Today it was ghastly."

Livvy and Alice Middleton were driven with others to a nursing home for further treatment and to rest for a few days. Livvy was agitated. She did not want rest, she told them, but news of her family. The doctors were overworked and threatened to sedate her. She pretended to calm down, but only because she had noticed on one of their lists that another temporary patient was Lady Allan. Diana had been sitting next to her and her daughters when their lifeboat toppled over. If Lady Allan was safe . . .

As soon as she was left alone, Livvy got out of bed and put on her hospital dressing gown. Walking was not easy, but she found Lady Allan's room and knocked on the door.

Lady Allan was alone and not asleep, although she had been given painkillers. Her arm was badly broken. She seemed very reserved and only shook her head when Livvy asked if she had seen anything of Diana. "It's just that that I thought, since you're here," Livvy explained.

"Yes, I'm here," Lady Allan repeated tonelessly "And my maid. But both my pretty darlings—" She closed her eyes, but could not stop her tears. She and her maid had been rescued by one of the other boats, but she had watched her two beautiful teenage daughters, Gwen and Anna, drown as the wave foaming along the liner's steep side carried them away from her.

Comforting the older woman, Livvy forgot her own grief for a while.

Walter Page was late coming home. His wife hurried to him to remind him that he had little time left to change before their guests arrived. His manner was very contained and serious, and he handed her a yellow form, the latest dispatch from Queenstown. She was horrified to read that the early estimates had been mistaken. Many more were dead than had been suspected, perhaps as many as a thousand men, women and children. Among them were many Americans.

It was too late to postpone the dinner. Colonel House arrived first with Loulie. They had not heard the news and were stunned when Page told them. Most of the other guests had already been informed, Sir Edward Grey, Captain Hall of Naval Intelligence, Sir F. E. Smith, the Solicitor-General, Wickham Steed, foreign editor of *The Times,* George Booth of the Ministry of Munitions, a cousin of Cunard's chairman, and others, all men of similar influence and background.

For them and their ladies, the evening was to have been one of sparkling conversation and challenging ideas. Instead it was almost totally subdued. Speech was kept at a level just above a whisper. Many details had now been reported and, round the table in the dining room, they discussed the inevitable conjectures and rumors that had started. The preposterous ones, that the Admiralty had deliberately allowed the *Lusitania* to be attacked, that her captain, Turner, was in the pay of the Germans. How many submarines had been involved? Eyewitness accounts varied. Some said one, some two. Certainly several had been reported in the area by other vessels, although whether they were part of one ambush or there to make sure that at least one of them sank her, no one could say. How many torpedoes had been fired at her? Again, the eyewitnesses differed, some stating positively there was only one, others three or more, though most believed she had been struck twice. One survivor even claimed to have seen a U-boat on the surface shelling lifeboats with its deck gun. And what of the larger explosion? Had it been the *Lusitania*'s contraband ammunition going off? Already the Anti-War League was claiming that the naval patrol boats had prevented survivors from being landed at other places than Queenstown to conceal those who had been disfigured by gunpowder burns. Or asphyxiated by escaping poison gas.

"Impossible," Captain Hall explained. "Because of the number of survivors. No one could induce so many eyewitnesses to lie or keep silent about such matters as exploding ammunition or poison gas."

"The rumors are spreading so quickly," Smith said, "it is

almost as if they are part of a propaganda campaign prepared beforehand."

Conversation continued muted and desultory, and every twenty minutes or so the butler brought Page another of the yellow dispatches from his Chancery, which he read out. The number of survivors, including injured, was confirmed at around seven hundred, the number of dead at well over a thousand, including over a hundred Americans. They began almost to dread the slips of yellow paper as each contained, among the dead, names which they all knew, in some cases personal friends. Alfred Vanderbilt and his valet, Charles Frohman, Charles Klein, Justus Forman, Commander Stackhouse, Mr. and Mrs. Elbert Hubbard, Mme. Depage, Father Maturin, Federico Padila, the Mexican Consul General. Booth was appalled to learn that his friend Paul Crompton was dead, with his wife and all six children. It was not only passengers. Many were dead among the crew, including the Staff Captain, Anderson. House had crossed on the *Lusitania* only a few months ago and remembered many of them well, Purser McCubbin, Chief Officer Piper.

The ladies did not leave the table when the port and brandy were circulated. They could not tear themselves away. For the same reason, the party went on afterwards in the drawing room. No one could leave. Yet there was no immediate condemnation of Germany. They asked one another what motive the Kaiser and his admirals could have for authorizing or ordering such an attack. No one could answer. They were still stunned by the sickening details which Page read out.

"What effect will it have on the future nature of the war?" someone asked.

"I cannot imagine," Grey said. "I have not yet grasped it fully. It is the greatest act of infamy which any supposedly civilized state has perpetrated since the massacre of Saint Bartholomew."

"Thinking of Vanderbilt and the others," Wickham Steed said carefully, "the question that must be asked is, what reaction will there be in America? What will Washington do?"

"More particularly," Lord Mersey added, "what will President Wilson do?"

They were all very conscious of Colonel House, the Pres-

715

ident's closest adviser. He had been among them now for months, advocating the cause of peace. But they had directed the question to their host, Ambassador Page.

Page honestly did not know what to reply. He could no longer even guess at Wilson's motives and intentions. He shrugged. "I regret, I cannot predict the President's reactions."

"You of all people should know that he will act with the utmost energy," House said. Everyone looked at him. This harrowing event, its sheer callousness and barbarity, had crystallized in his mind all the doubts about his mission of which he had been becoming aware. He had no more reservations. "The United States has been left with no option," he said firmly. "We shall be at war with Germany within a month."

Les Morton had rested on the trip to Queenstown and spent the hours since he landed searching the hotels and lodging houses for his brother, then the fish curing sheds by the docks which had been turned into makeshift mortuaries. He was not the only one searching. Men and women, nearly everyone who was fit enough was hunting, for wives, husbands, children, until late into the night. Les had never seen a dead body before. Now he had seen hundreds, but Cliff was not among them.

Then coming out of the main shed for the second time, he walked right into him. While he had been looking for Cliff, Cliff had been trying to find him. They flung their arms round each other, laughing with relief and excitement. Until they compared notes. All the cadets who had jumped ship with them in New York had been killed. They were the only two still alive.

Dan Connally had also been searching. He had been put in a room in the Queen's Hotel with two other survivors, and told to sleep. But it was impossible. He had put on his stained and crumpled suit again and gone out to walk the streets and make inquiries about Matt and Livvy and their children. And their friends. What he had learned was almost too much to bear.

He headed for the docks, but could not make himself enter the mortuaries. He had gone into a dark narrow saloon instead, and ordered a double whiskey. He had a little English money. When he laid it on the counter, the bartender said, "Are ye from *her*? From the *Lusy*?" Dan nodded, and the bartender pushed the money back across the counter. "Then ye can drink as much as ye like. I'll not be taking a penny from ye, not this night."

Dan had five whiskeys. He was not much of a drinking man, but they still had no effect. They did not help him to forget. It was certain that Matt was dead. And probably Livvy and Peter and Diana. What was almost harder to accept, so were all their friends. Out of all the Canadian volunteers, their own group and the others from Winnipeg and Toronto, he was the only one left. Barney, Larry, young Piet, all of them, all dead.

He could not drink any more and left the saloon. He was opposite the three sheds. A woman had just come out of one and was leaning against the wall by the door. She was wearing a shapeless drab skirt and some kind of gray tweed jacket, too small for her. Her dark hair hung loose to her shoulders, masking her face. It was too much to hope, but he found himself walking stiffly toward her. "Livvy?" he said.

It was her. She spun round, looking at once to either side of him, eagerness for a moment lighting her face. When she saw no one with him, she looked at him questioningly.

"Matt's gone," he told her. "He didn't make it." She sobbed, and her body jerked as if she had been stabbed. Just for a second her eyes hated him. "I know," he muttered. "I wish it was him who was here, and not me."

Livvy's eyes closed. She bent forward, leaning against him, and he put his arms round her. "Dan," she said brokenly. ". . . No, Dan." Her head was on his chest. "I'm sorry."

Secondhand clothes had been handed in for the female survivors. They were on a table in her corridor. She had dressed in the first she picked up and stolen out of the nursing home, hurrying away as fast as she was able. The names of Matt and the children were not on any of the lists of living or dead. A sympathetic cabman had given her a lift to the docks and she had forced herself to examine the bodies. In the first shed they were nearly all women and girls, but she had seen Lee and Beattie lying side by side. Lee had had a hard death, but Beattie looked peaceful. She was still naked, although someone had draped a coat over her. Livvy had been asked to identify them.

She still had two mortuaries to go through and Dan was worried. "Are you sure you want to?" he asked. "I can do it for you."

"I have to do it myself," she said quietly. He took her arm and helped her to walk steadily as they went into the main shed, where the men had been laid out.

The light of the gas jets was glaring, throwing harsh shadows over the rows of corpses on the marble slabs used for cleaning fish. They joined the line of people moving slowly along the rows. Many of them were weeping. A woman suddenly stopped and tried to throw herself across the body of a young boy. The man with her held her back and they swayed together until she collapsed against him, sobbing. Another man, elderly and more dignified, was kneeling in prayer, unaware of the shuffling line as it bent round him.

Some of the bodies were discolored and bloated, grotesquely disfigured, and they had to look at one or two quite carefully. Fortunately Matt was not among them. Charles Frohman was, however. He alone seemed largely untouched. He lay as if asleep, almost smiling.

Livvy was growing tired. The American doctor had been serious when he said she would have to rest, but she could not give in now. There was still the last shed, the worst of all. It was filled with children and babies.

The smallest were crammed together, bare or partly dressed, some still wearing bibs or lace bonnets and sundresses, like broken and discarded toys after a halfprice sale. A pair of distraught parents were being helped out. Like others they had complained, but no other arrangements could have been made in the time, for lack of room. There were so many. Out of the thirty-five babies on board, only four had been saved. There had been a hundred and twenty-nine children. Ninety-four were dead. Only a few hours ago they had been playing and laughing, carefree, sulking, hiding, fighting, teasing one another. Livvy had nerved herself, but nothing could have prepared her for this.

The older children were heaped in the middle and along

the opposite side. There was only one adult among them, a young mother so disfigured she could not be identified, still holding a child to her for protection in each bent arm. The shadows of the gas jets wavered over them. Some of their faces were green, smeared with bloody mucus. Livvy recognized Peter's playmate, John Crompton. And the bigger boy he had beaten in the race on sports day. She could not see Peter anywhere.

The first children to be delivered had been laid out more neatly at the far end. That was where she found Diana.

Like Frohman, Diana's eyes were closed and she seemed only to be sleeping. She was wearing her sailor dress. It was stained and sodden and she had lost one shoe. Her hands were folded on her chest. Her long dark hair was tangled and still retained a trace of the frizzy curls over which the Allan sisters had taken so much trouble that morning.

Dan was puzzled that Livvy showed hardly any emotion, but Diana appeared so peaceful it gave her a strange feeling of calm. She brushed aside a thick tendril of hair that lay across her daughter's forehead. She was so pretty, no one would ever think she had been such a tomboy. All at once Livvy gasped and trembled, and Dan put his arm round her again in case she broke down. But she did not. She had seen, still pinned to Diana's breast, the *Lusitania* badge. She had been so proud of it, she said she would wear it always.

The Secret Service men on duty at the White House were congratulating themselves on having an unexpectedly quiet evening. The projected dinner party had been canceled because of the news and the President had dined alone early. They were startled when the policeman guarding the main door rushed in and told them that the President had just gone out. "He's on his own!" the policeman panted.

Grabbing their coats, the agents ran from the office and through the parking area, in time to see the President cross Pennsylvania Avenue and head north up Sixteenth Street. They hurried after him. There was a light drizzle falling and, although he wore no hat, the President appeared oblivious to it. The four Secret Service men turned up their collars and dropped into step a short distance behind him.

Wilson was stunned. The first dispatch from Queenstown

was bad enough, but he had been relieved by its assurance that no lives had been lost. He had surprised Tumulty and the members of his cabinet by his coolness, even when Secretary Bryan castigated them for not having listened to his warnings. "I have been expecting this," Bryan told them. "England has been using our citizens to protect her ammunition." Everyone knew, he said, that the *Lusitania* was armed. Wilson telephoned Lansing to check on that and on the contents of the liner's manifest with Malone, the Collector of Customs in New York. Yet those were legal wrangles, essentially. They might prove a minor embarrassment to the Administration, but as long as everyone had been saved after the attack, America could not be vitally involved.

He dined alone. And Joe Tumulty had brought in Lansing's preliminary report that the *Lusitania* carried no guns, certainly none that had ever been seen mounted, and her cargo was mainly foodstuffs. It was clear, however, that she had also contained a large amount of cartridges and unfilled shrapnel shells. That was more tricky.

He had scarcely considered the implications when the more detailed telegrams had begun to arrive from the Queenstown Consul, Wesley Frost. He regretted the inaccuracy of the early reports. The *Lusitania* had not remained afloat for several hours, but had sunk in twenty minutes. By nightfall, only five or six hundred of her two thousand passengers and crew had been landed safely at Queenstown. Of these, some had later died of their injuries. Would the President like him to prepare a list of the American survivors? Survivors . . .

Newsboys were running along the sidewalks shouting and Wilson cut west off Sixteenth Street to avoid them, but he could not blot out the sound. "Extra! Extra! *Lusitania* latest! Americans among the dead!"

There had been no possibility of holding back the news. The press had its own sources, local agencies, eyewitness stories. When the details were printed, nothing could prevent the tidal wave of indignation and revulsion which would sweep across the United States at the sinking of the world's premier passenger liner. The lack of warning, the prominent Americans lost, the women and children would far outweigh any talk of contraband or war zones. The German Embassy's announcement on her sailing day would be seen as the most callous advance self-vindication. Already ex-President Teddy Roosevelt was calling the sinking "not merely piracy, but piracy on a vaster scale of murder than old-time pirates ever practiced." The nation was roaring its agreement. The *New York Times* thundered that there must be sent to Berlin "a demand that the Germans shall no longer make war like savages drunk with blood."

Wilson sympathized with those feelings. He was haunted by the images of drowning children, of whole families wiped out, of men searching the dark and rocky shores of Ireland for the bodies of their wives and daughters. What had man come to that such a crime could even be plotted, far less executed? He had shed tears for the innocent, reading the dispatches. Already he could hear the insistent clamor of voices howling for war.

And yet—and yet. He could not afford the extravagance of emotion. Two things had guided his whole attitude, that the bulk of people in the country counted on him to keep them out of the war, and that it would be a calamity for the world at large if the United States should be drawn actively into the conflict and so deprived of all disinterested influence over its settlement. There was another factor. He could have no influence over the outcome whatsoever if he were no longer President. The election was coming closer and he would have little chance of winning it without the help of Bryan and his pacifists, and the millions of votes of Democratic supporters in the Midwest, of German, Austrian and Hungarian origin. He could not let such a consideration dictate his policy, yet it would be politically inept not to recognize its existence.

He had become aware of the Secret Service men following him, and he felt a spasm of irritation. He was suddenly conscious of the cold and the drizzle. At least he had worked off some of his agitation. He walked back to the White House by the shortest possible route.

Joe Tumulty was waiting and said, "We were anxious about you, sir."

"I felt like a walk," Wilson told him brusquely. "To clear my head."

Tumulty watched him continue up toward his study. He

had no love for the English, but the dispatches from London and Queenstown had shocked him. For the first time all the talk about a war to preserve civilization made sense. Now the war had come right up to their front door, but the President seemed determined not to see it.

Wilson had noticed the look in his secretary's eyes and understood it. He had no need to justify himself to anyone, yet Joe was almost one of the family and he turned back. "I suppose you think I am cold and indifferent," he said slowly and seriously, "and a little less than human. But my dear fellow, you are mistaken." He paused. "You are mistaken." He carried on up.

For a moment Tumulty had been allowed to glimpse the uncertainty and pressure and distress behind the mask of detachment. He had never seen the President look so careworn.

Up to the sparsely lit quays and through the dark streets the grisly procession went on, the last gleanings of the night's harvest of the dead. The little ships tied up and the bodies on their decks were transferred to carts to be trundled off for identification. Others arrived from the temporary casualty wards and operating rooms.

The town had not gone to sleep. Many survivors had fallen in a stupor of exhaustion on the beds and mattresses provided for them, but many were still searching, unwilling to abandon hope. Livvy and Dan waited with others outside the sheds. He was increasingly worried about her. She was scarcely able to stand, yet the only sign of real distress she had shown was when he had suggested taking her back to the nursing home. The pain was deep inside her, too deep for anything as simple as tears. Worst of all was the uncertainty. If Matt and Peter had been lost too, she had to know and forced herself to look at each body as it was lifted from the carts and carried inside. By morning she would know if there was any reason left to live.

In another part of the town, people were searching for the boy Elizabeth Duckworth had saved. He had seemed physically unharmed, but was still in shock and had not spoken, not even to tell them his name or age. A room had been found for him with the family of an understanding

Methodist minister. He had been given warm milk, undressed and put to bed. An hour later, when the minister's wife went in quietly to make sure he was asleep, she discovered that he had dressed himself again and had gone. The minister and his wife and neighbors had spent hours hunting for him.

Crowds of silent townspeople were still watching at the docks. They did not notice the boy move among them, searching silently himself. He had reached the street with the wharves and sheds where the crowd was densest, and heard men talking about the terrible tally of bodies and how more room would have to be made for the hundreds still to come. He could see the sheds. A flat brewer's cart was drawn up in front of one, the dray horses stamping and restless as heavy bundles were handed down and taken inside. He stepped forward and the light of a gas lamp caught the birdlike shape of the wooden amulet on a leather cord round his neck.

The cart jerked and moved off, and he started across the cobbled street. A man noticed him and waved him back, knowing what was over there was not for a child, but the boy did not see him. The cart had rolled away, revealing the knot of people by the door of the main shed. The boy stopped. He was standing rigidly erect and his mouth opened soundlessly. He was trying to speak and at first could make only a croaking whisper. "Mummy . . ." He tried again and this time his voice was stronger. "Mummy?"

Dan felt Livvy stiffen against him. Her head turned. He had heard nothing and did not understand when she took a step toward the street. He made to follow her, but she pushed him away. She took another unsteady step. "Peter . . ." she breathed.

Peter was running toward her. She was swaying and dropped to her knees on the wet cobbles, and he threw himself into her arms, hugging her, rocking himself against her. "Mummy," he said again brokenly. "Mummy, Mummy . . ." She laid her cheek on his head and the releasing, healing tears came at last.

723

Chapter 35

WILL TURNER ARRIVED AT THE OLD MARKET HOUSE IN Kinsale with First Officer Jones and Junior Third Officer Bestwick. Looking round, he saw faces he recognized, the crow's nest lookout, Quinn, Second Engineer Andrew Cockburn and the Marconi operator, Robert Leith, Chief Electrician George Hutchinson and a young seaman, hardly more than a boy, whom Jones told him was Morton, who had been starboard lookout. They were all standing out of respect for their captain and Turner nodded to them as he moved to his seat.

Watching him, they were shocked. He had aged by ten years. It was not merely the uniform, shrunken out of shape by hours in the sea, nor the ill-fitting temporary cap replacing his own which had been ruined; his step was unsure and his whole body seemed to have shriveled. The foursquare erect carriage had gone. His shoulders were bent and the set of his jaw had altered. Most noticeable of all, his eyes, which only the day before were so clear and penetrating, had faded. They were the eyes of an old and disillusioned man.

John J. Horgan had observed the hum of sympathy when the captain came in and took his seat in the front row, opposite the jury. He made a mental note not to let himself be influenced by it. It was a time, if ever there was one, to deal in facts and not emotions.

Horgan, the Kinsale coroner, had been tipped off by legal friends that instructions were on the way from the Solicitor General in London. All inquests on the *Lusitania* were to be held in Queenstown, and no public statements were to be made by Turner or anyone else until the Board of Trade had carried out an official inquiry. The move was partly directed at Horgan himself, a notorious Republican sym-

pathizer, but he was not an easy man to silence. He realized
the intention was to censor anything which might embarrass
the British government and the Admiralty. Naturally they
wanted everything kept under wraps until they had found
out for themselves what had caused the explosions on board
and how the passengers had died. That was why the auxiliary patrol had insisted on survivors being transferred to
its own vessels and taken to Queenstown, even though it
meant that more had died through having to wait longer for
treatment. But bodies had been washed ashore at Kinsale
during the night and others brought in by local fishermen.
Horgan had hurried to Queenstown in the morning and summoned Turner, his remaining officers, members of the crew
and a number of the fitter passengers to attend an inquest
that afternoon. Twelve shopkeepers and fishermen of Kinsale made up the jury.

"This is not a trial," he had said. "It is an inquest into the
cause of the death of these persons, apparently as a result
of violence. The jury is empowered to ask any questions it
chooses and witnesses are under oath to answer, to establish
that cause and any guilt which may appertain to person or
persons unknown."

Doctors' evidence confirmed that the deceased had died
from exhaustion and prolonged immersion in the sea. Listening to the legal phrases and medical jargon, Turner could
feel himself becoming more and more detached. His blunt
fingers knotted together in his lap. What did this makeshift
rigmarole have to do with people, real people who had died?
One thousand, one hundred and ninety-eight, blown to pieces,
drowned or dead of exposure. Not all of them accounted for.
All along the coast, corpses would be left by each tide for
many days. There'd be precious little fishing done. Not with
Cunard offering £1 a body, and more for officers and VIPs.
And the grand first prize, £1,000 put up by the family lawyer
for Alfred Gwynne Vanderbilt.

Evidence had been given on the *Lusitania's* course and
speed. He heard the foreman of the jury ask Quinn if the
captain might not have avoided the torpedo if he had been
going faster or had changed direction. "I don't think she
could have escaped," Quinn replied, "not if she was going a
hundred knots an hour."

It was not a trial, but Turner suddenly saw how every

thought and action of his was going to be analyzed and dissected, now and at the official inquiry, how quickly and easily he could find himself in the pillory. He tried to think back through the sheaf of Admiralty orders he had to obey and the advices he was supposed to follow. Unless they conflicted with his judgment of the circumstances. He had obeyed his instructions, but not followed all the advices. Some did not apply, some were not practical. He had been given to believe he would have an escort, but had already been told the Admiralty's answer to that by the Senior Naval Officer at Queenstown. He had been in a patrol area, and so did not need a specific escort. To complain would sound as if he were excusing himself. He had been advised to avoid headlands, but it would have been criminally negligent not to fix his position before attempting the dangerous run through St. George's Channel at night. It was sheer chance that he had picked the Old Head of Kinsale. If he had not, would the *Lusitania* now be at dock in Liverpool? Perhaps. Perhaps not. No one could know for sure. The truth was the only answer he could give, the simple truth.

What is the truth? he kept asking himself when it was his turn. He was impassive, speaking very quietly, hunched forward. He heard himself speak and it was like listening to someone else, to someone behind glass. "I gave the order at once to lower the boats down to the rails, and directed that women and children should get into them. I also gave orders to stop the ship, but we could not stop as the engines were out of commission. It was not safe to lower boats until the speed was off the vessel." None of them, surely none of these self-conscious ordinary people in the jury could understand the horror contained in those words.

Question after question, then the foreman asked, "Were you going a zigzag course at the moment the torpedo took place?"

"No, it was bright weather and land was clearly visible."

"Was it possible for a submarine to approach without being seen?"

"Oh, yes, quite possible." He could tell they were puzzled. But no one had remotely expected the *Lusitania* to be attacked, certainly not without warning. As soon as he was challenged, he would have fled at top speed, obeying the

726

advice to zigzag. However, any sudden alteration of course caused damage and brought complaints from the passengers. Even the Admiralty could not have seriously intended him to stagger his way across the whole war zone. A thirty-odd-thousand-ton liner carrying many more thousand tons of cargo could not be hurled about on the surface like a destroyer.

"Was the course of the vessel altered after the torpedoes struck her?"

"I headed straight for land, but it was useless. Previous to this, the watertight bulkheads were closed. I suppose the explosion forced them open."

"Was any warning given you before you were torpedoed?"

"None whatever. It was suddenly done and finished."

"Was a warning given to the lower decks after the ship had been struck?" Coroner Horgan asked.

Turner was a long time in answering. "All the passengers must have heard the explosion," he said slowly. He was thinking of Archie Bryce, old Archie with his beetling mustache and infectious chuckle, trapped in the forward boiler room, of Piper and Hefford giving their lives to buy another minute of time for the passengers, of Anderson working like a man possessed right up to the end, and poor little Purser McCubbin on his last voyage before he retired. And two-thirds of the crew, all gone.

Horgan asked another question for clarification. Receiving no reply, he repeated it more brusquely.

There was total silence in the Market House apart from the tick of the clock on the wall behind the coroner's chair. Everyone was looking at Turner, the man of iron. Shockingly, he had lowered his head to his hands and was weeping.

Walter Page and his Chancery staff collected reports and comments from all sources, and Page sent them direct to Woodrow Wilson. He did not need to add anything of his own. House's cables did that for him. At last the shameful period of waiting was over. He had lived in hope of the United States coming into the war as the best means of ending the slaughter and the only chance of giving his country standing and influence when the reorganization of the world finally began, and the President would need ammunition against the Hyphenateds, the fainthearted and the pro-German lobby in the Senate.

There were reactions the world over.

From Sweden, "The Swedish nation is practically unanimous in its policy of strict neutrality. Yet a large section is anything but neutral in its feelings at the methods of warfare which have been adopted in this terrible war."

From Denmark, "Whenever in future the Germans venture to speak of their culture, the answer will be, 'It does not exist: it committed suicide on May 7th, 1915.' "

Dispatches continued to arrive from Wesley Frost in Queenstown, the picture becoming more and more harrowing as the details built up. Out of one hundred and fifty-nine American passengers, one hundred and twenty-four had died. From the consul, Page learned that many victims were to be buried on Monday in mass graves. On the same day the first survivors were to reach London, having taken the mailboat from Ireland to Holyhead. He rose at five in the morning and was at Euston Station before six-thirty. Many relatives of passengers were already on the platform with reporters and Cunard officials. Others and a restless crowd were behind the barrier. Page was allowed through. He felt alien, an intruder on the grief of the people among whom he stood, waiting to receive the handful of American survivors.

When the night train pulled in, there was hardly any movement on the platform. The chattering crowd hushed as the survivors began to come from the train. Some were limping and bandaged. Others had to be helped off by the attendants and appeared confused. All were listless, their faces without expression, their eyes blank, like so many refugees in their borrowed and bedraggled clothing, a hundred or more living ghosts. Even the reporters were numbed and did not insist on responses to their questions, although the survivors who replied did so only in monosyllables, and some not at all.

Among the people watching, some were crying, others praying. The crowd beyond the barrier had come to cheer, but was silent as wives met and clung to their husbands, as small bands of relatives suddenly saw those they had been waiting for and surrounded them, sobbing, bearing them away. A few bewildered children were led out by nurses.

Most pathetic of all were the men and women searching the faces of the survivors and repeating the name of someone who had been reported missing, hoping against hope that one of those who heard would have news.

Page spoke to one or two identified by the sleeping-car attendants as American. They were grateful to him for coming, but had little to say. Only Lehmann was bitter at the lack of care taken of them since they landed. He intended to sue Cunard and the British government. Dr. Fisher was continuing directly on to France as soon as he had reported to the Red Cross. Rita Jolivet wanted to return to New York, but was terrified of crossing the ocean again. All Page could do was to remind them that the Embassy was at their service. Words of comfort were inadequate and impertinent.

A couple paused near him, a serious fair-haired man and a woman who was strikingly beautiful, although gaunt with suffering, her pallor emphasized by her dark hair and huge dark eyes. There was a boy with them, very manly, with a strong, square jaw and dark hair falling over his forehead. The man's suit was stained and torn at one elbow. The woman's dress and coat were mismatched, obviously secondhand. The boy was better dressed than either and wore round his neck an odd kind of Indian sign in wood, shaped like a bird. "Pardon me, sir," Page said to the man, "are you American?"

Dan Connally shook his head. "No, we're Canadian. From Alberta."

Page raised his hat to them and smiled to the boy, who looked back at him with a slight frown, as though puzzled that anyone could still smile. It saddened Page inexpressibly. It would be a long time before that boy learned how to smile again, and Page was ashamed to be part of the adult world in which such things were possible.

Dan took Livvy's arm and led her on. She had not even noticed the Ambassador. Matt's body had been found in a bay to the north of Kinsale. She had seen him carried in, pale and still. It was her dream made real, although he had not died in battle and the fisherman who found him had closed his eyes. She had wanted to stay with him, but Dan had arranged for a coffin and her father insisted on her bringing Peter home. Matt would follow them and be buried in the churchyard in the little town of Winchelsea, where

729

they had first met. Later, after the war, she might take him back to Calgary, where his grave would be on a hill, in sight of the Rockies.

Page watched them go. Although he knew nothing about them, they summed up the whole tragic business for him. An older, kindly looking man was standing at the gate of the barrier. The woman stopped and gazed at him. They did not speak, but Page saw the man's eyes fill with tears as he drew her to him and led her away. The fair-haired man put his arm round the boy's shoulders and followed them.

Walther Schwieger checked that the horizon all round was clear and brought the U 20 up to the surface. With the opening of the hatches there was a relaxation of tension in the crew and the men on watch swarmed quickly up the ladders into the fresh air.

The U 20 had continued her homeward voyage along the west coasts of Ireland and Scotland well out to sea to avoid patrol boats. The cooling system of one of the pistons had jammed beyond the power of Hirsch to repair it, and she had had to be kept below eleven knots. With favorable wind and weather and at restricted speed, the voyage had become almost like a cruise. The crewmen were not able to hide their pride in their captain and in having sunk the giant munitions carrier. Unlike Lanz and a few others, they had seen none of the hideous details of the sinking, and so were not troubled by them. With the ability of fighting men everywhere to snatch at moments of leisure and put all memory of hardship and danger behind them, they laughed and gossiped and sang. They celebrated Bibermann's twentieth birthday with an impromptu party, but it was more in celebration of the *Lusitania*'s sinking than of the young machinist. Afterwards Lippe had taken his concertina on watch with him, and had only stopped playing when it was threatened with confiscation.

The war had abruptly returned on the fourth day, when they approached the channel between Fair Isle and Ronaldsay, rounding the north of Scotland from the west, and detected the smoke of destroyers on guard. They had submerged just in time to avoid being spotted and crept by underneath at night, listening to the vicious whir of the propellers crossing and recrossing above them. They traveled submerged for five hours. Rightly suspecting that the hunt was for him, Schwieger came up very cautiously and saw a second screen of destroyers and torpedo boats farther out. Beyond them was a third, even more thinly spread, and the slow underwater progress had continued. There was always a possibility of a new enemy minefield or trailing nets, and it was a relief to surface at last, when the wasplike destroyers were safely behind.

They were in the North Sea with a straight run home to Emden, and Schwieger gave Lippe permission to let Hansel and Maria and the puppies scamper about on deck for a few minutes while the radio mast and aerial were being rigged. It was another fine day, not much cloud, good visibility.

Schwieger could see Lanz standing at the base of the conning tower, alone. The Mate of the Reserve had lost much of his aggressiveness in these last days. He seemed subdued and was certainly avoiding conversation. Nor had he joined in the crew's celebrations. Central Control was undoubtedly more pleasant without his sniggering laughter and intrusive comments, but his withdrawal and nervousness had been noticed. To Schwieger it was obvious that he was suffering from a mixture of delayed remorse and anxiety over reaction at home to so many civilian deaths in an attack in which no warning had been given. Schwieger could have put his mind at rest. Lanz's function was merely to be pilot and adviser. Sole responsibility for an attack was the commander's. It was difficult to suppress one's feelings of sympathy for the victims, a hard lesson. He did not consider that Lanz deserved his help in learning it.

He had no doubts that they had been sent to sink the *Lusitania*, and that it would have profound political effects. They were not his concern. The decision had been taken elsewhere. What did disturb him was that his target had been set out so obliquely. If a storm of protest developed, he would be at its center. Any adverse consequences would fall on him. He had formulated his answer: he had done his duty, and would do so again.

He had given the radio operator their coordinates and a brief report of their patrol to relay to the advice ship *Arcona* at Heligoland and was waiting in his cabin when the man brought him an urgent signal. "They've asked for an immediate acknowledgment, sir," he said.

Schwieger took his copy of the naval cipher from its lead covers and decoded the signal. It ordered him not to return to Emden, but to proceed without delay to the main base at Wilhelmshaven, where he was to report to Naval Headquarters. "Acknowledge," he said. "The U 20 will comply." There was no use speculating what the order signified. In three days he would either be a made man or his career would be over.

Colonel House walked briskly across the south side of the traffic island at Hyde Park Corner, the lightness of his step an indication of his new sense of purpose.

Even for someone with his phenomenal patience, the last months had been dispiriting. He had come to Europe for one great humanitarian purpose, to end the war. Whatever effort it involved, the Governor and he were determined to lead the warring parties to the negotiating table. Yet over and again, each time a tiny advance had been made, it had been set back or blocked by a change of policy or fresh objections from Berlin. He had persevered against the odds. However, the sinking of the *Lusitania* without warning and the large number of American lives lost had ended at one stroke any attempt to arrange an armistice, any hope of reconciliation.

He had often explained to the Ambassador in confidence that he had no partisan feelings. The cost of the war meant that England would lose her place as first among nations, whether or not she defeated Germany. The United States would come to the forefront all the more quickly, and he meant her to be ready to accept her destiny, ready to lead and reconstruct a world torn apart by imperialist struggles and national jealousies from which she had nobly stood aside. For that, he strove to protect his country's interests and the prestige of the President, whom Page and he had helped to create. "The problems of England and Germany are of their own making," he frequently said. "Apart from the humanitarian aspects, we have no connection with this war." In the last few months, however, he had been reluctant to admit a change in himself. It was a question of values. Those truths and rights which America was pledged to uphold were the very ones for which England was fighting, and it was becoming increasingly difficult not to recognize that publicly. The destruction of the *Lusitania* made it impossible.

In his cable to the President, he had advised that a note should be sent to Germany with a demand for an immediate assurance that such a horror would never happen again. If the assurance was not given and war followed, it would not be a new war, but an endeavor to end more speedily the old one. Their intervention would save, rather than add to, the loss of life. "America has come to the parting of the ways, when she must determine whether she stands for civilized or uncivilized warfare," he had said. "We can no longer remain neutral spectators." Wilson was touchingly grateful for his support at this difficult time.

He had just written again to the President, pressing for an even firmer ultimatum to Berlin. The Kaiser's generals laughed at America's minute standing army and lack of preparedness. "If, unhappily, it is necessary to go to war, I hope you will give the world an exhibition of American efficiency that will be a lesson for a century or more," he had written. "In the event of war, we should accelerate the manufacture of munitions to such an extent that we could supply not only ourselves but the Allies, and so quickly that the world would be astounded."

Now he was heading for the Chancery in Grosvenor Gardens to have the letter sent in the diplomatic pouch. It was an undeniable relief to be able to talk unguardedly to Allied statesmen at last, and to walk through the streets of London and be able to look everyone in the eye.

He was waiting for a gap in the traffic to allow him to cross the road and did not notice the placard at first, as the newspaper seller partly obscured it. Just as House was about to move on, the man turned aside. House stopped as the words printed on the placard seemed to leap at him. WE ARE TOO PROUD TO FIGHT—WOODROW WILSON.

Fifteen minutes later, he was shown into the Ambassador's office. Page looked up and smiled. One good result of these last five days had been that he had at last come to a better understanding with the President's friend and adviser.

733

House did not return the smile. He pitched a newspaper onto the desk and said, "Read that. I did, coming down Constitution Hill. I felt as though I'd been given a kick at every lamp post."

The afternoon edition headlined a report of a speech made by President Wilson the previous evening to a group of newly naturalized citizens in Philadelphia. As he read it, Page felt a chill settle over him. He could see the Stars and Stripes and the crowded Convention Hall, the people eager to know the path the President had chosen. He could see Wilson on the podium, the autocratic head raised, eyeglasses catching the light, and hear the dry, moralistic voice. The speech concluded, "The example of America must be a special example, and must be an example not merely of peace because it will not fight, but because peace is a healing and elevating influence on the world and strife is not. There is such a thing as a man being too proud to fight. There is such a thing as a nation being so right it does not need to convince others by force that it is right."

Ambassador James W. Gerard's post in Berlin had become very difficult. The news of the *Lusitania* and the death of so many American passengers had been accompanied by such roars of triumph in the German newspapers and such open hostility to the United States that he had advised the Embassy staff to pack their bags and had made inquiries about hiring a special train to evacuate them to Switzerland.

Von Jagow, Zimmermann and the Foreign Office assured him that no precipitate action was necessary and that they regretted the accidental deaths, but at the same time it had become dangerous for himself and his staff to be overheard speaking English in the street or in restaurants.

Gerard gritted his teeth and guarded his temper, and at last the note of protest he had been expecting came from Washington. It was all he had hoped for. While most of the nation was relieved that the President had opted to stay out of the war, Roosevelt and the Republicans and sufficient numbers of others had protested so vehemently that Wilson had thought again. From all sides he was reminded that he had warned Germany she would be held to a strict accountability, and must stand by it or be discredited. He had kept House's cable and read it to the cabinet, together with the

734

draft of a strong note to Berlin prepared by Lansing. The cabinet willingly endorsed it, with the exception of Secretary of State Bryan. Finally, however, on a promise that a similar note would be sent to England to prove to Germany that the United States was defending her rights against aggression from both sides, Bryan reluctantly signed it.

The *Lusitania* note declared that attacks on merchant ships by submarines must inevitably lead to violations of the principles of justice and humanity. It reasserted the right of American citizens to travel wherever they wished on the high seas, and demanded that the German government repudiate the actions of its U-boat commanders, take immediate steps to prevent any recurrence, and pay compensation. "The Imperial German Government," it said, "will not expect the Government of the United States to omit any word or any act necessary to the performance of its sacred duty of maintaining the rights of the United States and its citizens." Gerard hurried to present the note formally to the Foreign Minister.

After two days he still had not had a reply, nor any indication of what it might be. As the situation remained critical, he called in person on the Foreign Minister and was told that von Jagow was unavailable. Instead he was led to the office of his Deputy.

Zimmermann did not look up from his desk when Gerard came in and bowed. He went on reading through a file of dispatches. Basic snub number one in the diplomatic manual, Gerard thought. It really ought to be reserved for clerks and undersecretaries. "You seem pretty busy," he said. Zimmermann glanced up and saw to his amazement that Gerard had sat down facing him, without invitation. "Not interrupting, am I?" the Ambassador inquired easily. "I just thought I'd drop in and see if your government was ready to give us an answer."

"An answer to what?" Zimmermann asked blandly.

"Our note. It is considered fairly urgent."

Zimmermann shrugged. "I should not have thought any answer was expected to such a piece of impertinence."

"Impertinence?" Gerard's voice was quiet. "May I remind you, Herr Zimmermann, that you are speaking of an official note of protest from the President of the United States?"

"And may I remind you, Mr. Ambassador," Zimmermann

735

retorted, "that the Imperial German Government is not accustomed to being addressed in such terms and treats all threats with the contempt they deserve?"

"And that is your answer?" Gerard said. "That is what I am to convey to Washington?"

The Deputy Foreign Minister saw that he was preparing to rise and leave. "Not precisely," he replied after a pause. "His Imperial Majesty and the Government are still considering what form their official answer should take. What I have said is unofficial, off the record, but I do not believe their reaction will be any different from mine."

"Also off the record," Gerard told him, "I sincerely hope it will be. Mr. Wilson is not a poker player. He's not bluffing."

He rose and bowed, but Zimmermann was not to be halted. "I have no animosity toward you personally," he said. "In all friendship I counsel you to warn your President to soften his tone."

"Such a warning would be inappropriate from me," Gerard pointed out. "Or from anyone else."

Zimmermann's face darkened. He was working himself up into a passion which he could barely control. "He had better take care! Inside his own borders he will have enough to occupy him if he does not!"

Gerard shook his head. "Don't count on it. Whatever he decides, our people will back him one hundred percent."

He nodded again and made for the door, but Zimmermann stopped him by rapping on the desk with his fist. "Back him? The United States does not dare to move against Germany, and he knows it! We have five hundred thousand German reservists in America who will rise in arms against your Government if your Government should dare to take any action against Germany!"

For a diplomatic discussion, it had become a pretty good impersonation of a barroom brawl, Jimmy Gerard thought, with the Deputy Minister shouting and thumping his desk. He paused by the door and scratched gently under his left ear. "Well now, Herr Zimmermann," he said, "let me just assure you that we have five hundred thousand and one lamp posts in America, and that is where your German reservists will find themselves the morning after they try any uprising."

* * *

An escort met the U 20 and took her through the minefields round Heligoland and protecting the approaches to the naval bases at Cuxhaven, Bremen and Wilhelmshaven. She saluted her escort and proceeded alone up the channel of the Jade estuary toward the huge basin and the home of the High Seas Fleet.

For the last three days of the voyage, the U-boat had been scrubbed and cleaned from prow to stern under Boatswain Kurtz's personal supervision. Whatever else was waiting for the U 20, he did not want her to be criticized for her appearance. The crewmen had washed their clothes and dried them in rotation. They were all shaved and wearing their best uniforms. Only Hirsch and essential crew were below. On Schwieger's orders, the petty officers and their sections were spaced out on the deck and along the rail. Haupert, Scherb and Mate of the Reserve Lanz stood with him on the conning tower platform. The Imperial Ensign floated at the stern, and on the forward wire of the radio mast hung the pennants for a sailing ship, two armed freighters and an auxiliary cruiser. The U 20 rounded the sandbanks at the entrance and sailed into the bay.

Schwieger heard the gasps of the crew as the view unfolded before them, and the barks of the petty officers for silence. Ahead was a sight he knew they would never forget, the massed ranks of battleships, dreadnoughts and destroyers, and the outlying squadrons of cruisers and auxiliaries, stretching all the miles to the mighty docks and quays of the base at Wilhelmshaven. With ferryboats and smaller craft plying across the fairway and the sun shining, nothing seemed to him to have changed since that day of the Kaiser's review.

Lanz was trying to talk to him confidentially and he looked away. He had nothing to say to the Mate, not since the morning when Lanz came to his cabin and blurted out nervously, "We have to agree what we are going to tell them."

"I have nothing to add to what is in my log," Schwieger said. "And I presume you have written your report."

"But there may be an inquiry!" Lanz insisted. "Good God, we sank a passenger ship—a liner!"

"We sank an auxiliary cruiser," Schwieger reminded him. "You identified it yourself from the British manuals. There

737

is nothing more to discuss. I shall commend your invaluable assistance."

Although he ignored Lanz himself, Schwieger was aware that the man's anxiety had communicated itself to his officers. Scherb was pale. Haupert alternately bit and licked at his lower lip. Neither could blot out the memory of what they had seen through the periscope or from the platform. It was impossible not to link that to the U 20's summons to Headquarters. They could not understand how the commander could appear so calm.

Schwieger had kept to his decision not to speculate. There were so many possibilities that he would only worry himself into a state of being unable to function, and as always his first concern had to be for his command. As they made toward Wilhelmshaven, he did not know what to expect. It was as well, he thought, for nothing happened. No additional orders were received. They were passing the first tiers of the anchored fleet and no one paid them any attention. Compared to the massive dreadnoughts, the U 20 was quite insignificant.

He felt Scherb shift beside him and, looking ahead, saw a group of four U-boats heading for them, two abreast. For a moment, it almost seemed as if they intended to run the U 20 down, then the group parted in the middle and passed her, wheeling to come up on either flank. The maneuver puzzled Schwieger until all at once he recognized the leading boat to starboard as the U 38, Max Valentiner's. Max was stepping up onto the platform and ratings poured out of her hatches to line her deck. At almost the same moment the crews of the other three U-boats filled their decks and others of his friends appeared on their conning towers. Captains and crews were saluting, and Schwieger brought his own crew to attention to return the salute, realizing at last that the Flotilla was according the U 20 an escort of honor.

The sailors on the battleships, becoming aware that the boat they had been waiting for had arrived, rushed to the rails, cheering. Guns boomed out in tribute, horns blared and the civilian craft joined in with their whistles and klaxons until the entire deepwater basin rang with sound. The reception was staggering, all the more so for being completely unexpected. Schwieger saw Lanz gaping round in astonishment. Scherb's cheeks were wet, and Schwieger felt the prickle of tears himself. "For us?" he kept wondering. "All this for us?"

Their route to the U-boat pens did not pass the flagship, but their escort curved aside to lead them under her towering sides and Schwieger brought his crew to attention again. On the wing of the *Friedrich der Grösse*'s bridge he could distinguish a row of flag officers. Her rail was packed with sailors, cheering in disciplined unison. Schwieger saw Lippe, as irrepressible as ever, tear off his cap and wave to them. Within a minute the rest of the crew had copied him and the men on the flagship were waving and shouting too, irregularly now, but louder than ever.

At the pens, a band and a guard of honor were drawn up on the dock, with the commanders of the Flotilla, newsmen and press photographers. There was nearly an hour of speeches and posing for photographs and interviews until Schwieger was driven away in a staff car to Naval Headquarters.

The aide who had accompanied him relieved him of his logbook and ushered him into the same office in which he had met Tirpitz. He was left facing the Commander-in-Chief, Admiral von Pohl, and the Chief-of-Staff, Reinhard Schoor. Von Pohl congratulated him and added the personal congratulations of Grand Admiral von Tirpitz, who had been detained unavoidably at Pless. Schwieger was bemused and confessed his amazement at the reception by the entire High Seas Fleet. The admirals smiled approvingly, then realized that he genuinely did not know of the intense worldwide reaction to the *Lusitania*'s sinking. For the first time he heard the extent of the loss of life and was appalled until they also told him of the immense amount of contraband ammunition she was carrying. "We have verification of that," Scheer said. "So you can comfort yourself in the knowledge that by slaying twelve hundred of the enemy, you have undoubtedly saved several hundred thousand of your fellow countrymen."

Schwieger was given quarters for the night and his kit was fetched from his cabin. The U 20 was to be refitted here, but he had been ordered to report at once to the offices of the Naval Cabinet. He was to leave by the first train in the morning for Berlin.

That evening he dined with Max and Georg and two others

at the Officers' Club. He was under the strictest orders not to speak of his trip to Berlin, yet found that it was an open secret. His friends envied his good fortune. With one sinking, he had shot to the top of the list of aces and the U 20, next to the U 9 and Hersing's U 21, had become the most famous of all submarines. Not only that, now he had been singled out by the Kaiser's naval cabinet, and what honors that could lead to were anyone's guess. He was still troubled by the loss of life, but they assured him that only a very few who did not understand the necessity for the unrestricted campaign had commented on it unfavorably. The U 20's exploit was applauded by the whole Reich. They would not let him go until he had described the attack in as much detail as he could remember. "Singlehanded," Max said, toasting him, "you have taught the treacherous Yankees the meaning of total war, and what it signifies to trade with and arm our enemies."

In the morning Schwieger had a pleasant surprise at the station. Rudi Zentner was waiting for him and sat with him until the train left. Rudi had brought the morning papers and a bundle of others which he had been saving. "Here you are. You can read all about yourself. Very flattering," he said, and grinned. "You won't recognize yourself." He sighed. "I knew I should've been with you. I've missed my only chance of fame."

"Whatever they say," Schwieger told him quietly, "you were well out of it."

He had a compartment to himself and fell asleep as soon as the train pulled out. He was bone tired, but he came awake with a start an hour later. He had had a dream. Not the old one, where he was choking, yet it left him almost as disturbed. He had been telling his mother and sisters and Anneliese about the sinking and had watched them recoil from him and run away. Their reactions had seemed so real. He was still calling to them and stared round at the drawn corridor blinds, the empty seats and the green, sparsely wooded fields streaming past outside. He breathed out slowly, reassured that it had been a dream. He would not let himself think what it meant. Dreams go by opposites, he had often told himself. He lay back in his seat, grateful to be in a private compartment.

He wiped his forehead and palms with his handkerchief and rang for coffee. The attendant when he came was all fingers and thumbs, apologizing for his clumsiness. He would not let Schwieger pay. He had only presented the bill, he explained, to request the honor of the Herr Kapitänleutnant's autograph. When Schwieger signed it, he stammered his thanks, bowing himself out.

Schwieger poured a cup of coffee and opened one of the newspapers. His photograph was on the front page beside one of the U 20, her number carefully blacked out. The accompanying story was embarrassing in its fulsomeness. He had certainly never uttered any of the heroics attributed to him. The other papers were the same, although some had reported him more accurately. He began to smile. In one photograph of the U 20, there was a smaller insert of Lippe cradling Maria and Hansel and the puppies. How many letters would that bring from ladies recognizing the father of their children? He laughed. One photograph was of Lanz standing proudly with his hand on the deck gun.

The other papers were ones which Zentner had collected from all over the country. Reading them, Schwieger was staggered. "We rejoice over this new triumph." "The news will be received by the German people with unanimous satisfaction, since it proves to England and the whole world that Germany is in deadly earnest over her submarine warfare." The *Kölnische Volkszeitung* said, "With joyful pride we acclaim this latest deed of our Navy." The city of Magdeburg proposed to honor the entire crew with the Freedom of the City. Lithographs and illustrated postcards of the U 20 and the *Lusitania* on the point of sinking were on sale. A commemorative medal had been struck. There was rejoicing throughout the Reich. Even Weddigen had never earned a tribute like this.

When the train arrived in Berlin, another staff car was waiting and rushed him to the Imperial Naval Secretariat. It was hard to prevent his excitement from showing when he was hurried past the guards, through the corridors and anterooms, directly to the office of the Chief of the Naval Cabinet, Admiral von Müller.

Müller was by the window when Schwieger was ushered in. When he turned, Schwieger saluted, took off his cap, tucked it under his left arm and stood to attention. Müller nodded and they were left alone.

"You were given an ecstatic reception yesterday at Wilhelmshaven," Müller observed. His voice, like his manner, was dry and detached.

"It was an unexpected honor, sir," Schwieger said.

"Unexpected?" Müller's eyebrows lifted. "Were you not informed that you would return from this patrol a hero?"

Schwieger did not grasp his meaning. "It was a routine patrol, sir," he answered carefully. "One sets out only in the hope of doing one's duty."

"One's duty to whom, eh?" Müller rapped. "Duty to whom?"

Something was wrong. Schwieger kept his voice as toneless as the Admiral's. "To His Imperial Majesty and the Fatherland, sir."

Müller's look was skeptical. "Come with me," he said acidly. He turned and Schwieger followed him to a door in the rear wall.

The room they were entering was a kind of inner office, its only windows narrow slits near the ceiling. A man was seated at the leather-topped table, wearing a uniform, a plain gray tunic without insignia. He was reading a newspaper. Other papers were scattered on the table. When he looked up, Schwieger caught his breath and his heart hammered in his chest. He snapped to attention, clicked his heels and bowed. He was in the presence of the All Highest, Kaiser Wilhelm.

"Kapitänleutnant von Schwieger," Müller announced.

Schwieger was gazing straight ahead, but could feel the eyes traveling over him, assessing. "You are the commander of the U 20?" Wilhelm asked.

The voice was rougher and more hoarse than Schwieger remembered. "Yes, Your Imperial Majesty."

"Can you read English?" Wilhelm asked.

Again, Schwieger did not understand the reason for the question. "A little, Your Imperial Majesty," he said.

"Try this," Wilhelm suggested.

Schwieger bowed and took the newspaper the Kaiser was holding out. As he did so, he saw the All Highest properly for the first time, the lines of strain round the eyes, the sagging cheeks. The newspaper was from England. LUSI-

742

TANIA VICTIMS INQUEST, Schwieger read slowly, piecing out the words. Conscious of the All Highest and Admiral Müller watching him and waiting, he jumped to the section at the end marked by the red pencil with which the All Highest was tapping the table. A verdict had been reached. "The Jury finds that this appalling crime was contrary to international law and the conventions of all civilized nations, and we therefore charge the officers of the submarine and the German Emperor and the Government of Germany, under whose orders they acted, with the crime of willful and wholesale murder."

Schwieger's mouth was dry. "Well?" he heard the Kaiser demand. "What do you have to say?"

Schwieger laid the newspaper on the table. "It is a most effective piece of propaganda, sir," he answered.

"You dare to speak to me of propaganda?" the Kaiser roared, his hand slapping down on the table. "Because of your actions I am accused of murder before the tribunal of the civilized world and you speak to me of propaganda?!"

"Answer!" Müller ordered.

Schwieger tried to pull himself together. "If a gunner fires a cannon, killing a number of the enemy, it is an act of war, sir, not of murder. Because the enemy chooses to consider it so does not make it so."

"Do not bandy words with me," the Kaiser hissed. Müller and others of his personal staff had warned him of a plot by Tirpitz and his clique to assume total control of the war effort and to embroil the United States. He could not accuse Tirpitz or provoke a confrontation at this time of crisis. Yet he had to know. The treachery, the implied disloyalty of his highest officers and some members of government made his mind reel. Later, when Germany's European enemies had been crushed, America would be dealt with as she deserved, taught an ineradicable lesson, but not now! Tirpitz was loudest among those who claimed that the *Lusitania*'s fate would lead America to impose a ban on all shipments of arms. But that was only a first step. He knew the Grand Admiral's insidious methods.

Kaiser Wilhelm stared at Schwieger. He remembered him, had decorated him personally. That his hawks, his U-boat commanders, might be involved in the plot horrified him.

"You were sent to sink the *Lusitania*," he said. "By whose orders?"

"With respect, Your Imperial Majesty," Schwieger replied, "I was sent to a general patrol area, with no specific target. I was not hunting the *Lusitania*. It was the purest chance that our paths crossed."

"How fortuitous," the Kaiser commented sardonically. "And having met her, you sank her."

"She had been identified by my civilian pilot as armed, carrying contraband and possibly troops, sir," Schwieger said.

"By the traditions of your Service," Kaiser Wilhelm rasped, "any other commander would have challenged and given her passengers time to take to the boats, or allowed her to proceed. You torpedoed her without warning!"

As Schwieger hesitated, Müller ordered sharply, "Answer!"

"It would have been futile to try to search her, sir," Schwieger said. "At the speed she was traveling, I had only one opportunity to attack, only seconds to carry it out. Not to do so would have been a dereliction of duty."

Kaiser Wilhelm sat erect. "Was it your duty to kill neutral passengers? To bring the Fatherland to the brink of war with America?"

"Answer!"

"I had no knowledge of the passengers, sir."

"And no compassion for them, either!" Kaiser Wilhelm ranted. "You drowned hundreds of civilians, hundreds of helpless women and children. Such conduct is an insult to your Creator! Such conduct besmirches the honor of your uniform!"

Schwieger's cheeks were flushed with the effort not to protest. The Kaiser had forgotten, or never understood the meaning of, the unrestricted campaign which he himself had proclaimed. Schwieger would not betray himself or the Flotilla by making excuses. He held his tongue and accepted the injustice of the reproof.

"You have still not answered the All Highest's question," Müller said. "By whose orders?"

Schwieger swallowed. "My orders were from Flotilla Headquarters. To sail to my hunting ground and attack all enemy warships, merchant ships and troopships."

"And where did your secret orders come from?" the Kaiser asked.

"I had none, sir," Schwieger said firmly. "Only the general patrol orders from the Fregattenkapitän." He paused. "I carried them out to the best of my ability, and performed my duty as I saw it. And would do so again."

It was the formula he had rehearsed. There was sufficient defiance and pride in it to make the Kaiser bridle, yet it presented him with a dilemma. He could scarcely discipline the U-boat commander whose deed had made him the current hero of the Reich. He would antagonize millions of his subjects and risk forfeiting whatever loyalty remained in the Navy. He recoiled from the thought, his mind revolving again. Perhaps Müller had been oversolicitous? Perhaps there was no plot. Certainly there was nothing more to be drawn from this boy.

Wilhelm caught himself up sharply. Weakness was a betrayal of what was required of him. Yet he already felt a twinge of regret for the reprimand. He had not altered his opinion of the sinking, but it could be amply demonstrated by simply not promoting or decorating Kapitänleutnant Schwieger and his crew.

As he glanced at Müller to indicate that the interview was over, there was a soft tap at the door. Massmann, a Privy Councillor and member of the Naval Cabinet, came in and bowed. He hurried to Kaiser Wilhelm, bowed again and spoke quietly, turned away from the others. Wilhelm rose quickly, signed to Müller and they went out, leaving Schwieger alone.

Schwieger was trembling and it was minutes before he had steadied himself, nearly sick with shame and shock. And disappointment. And he was angry at the way he had been used. He could only assume it was by the intention of the Grand Admiral, and that the Kaiser had not been informed. He could not defend himself without being squashed flat between two millstones. In self-preservation, the only course was to remain silent. But what had become of his career? If only that fog had not lifted . . .

He had to admit that he had been angered, too, by the Kaiser's attitude. That the All Highest, who had called for all-out war, could be squeamish about its results was disillusioning. It was only possible to do what one had to because of the knowledge that the Kaiser willed it and approved of it. But if the All Highest himself was uncertain, what justification was there for any of it? The line of thought was too dangerous and Schwieger would not follow it.

On the table in front of him was the newspaper with the Irish jury's verdict. He pushed it away. Other English language newspapers were lying underneath, some from America. Passages had been underlined. "The civilized world stands appalled at the torpedoing of the *Lusitania*." "This act is wholesale, deliberate, cowardly assassination." "Germany surely must have gone mad." "Nothing in the annals of piracy can, in wanton and cruel ferocity, equal the destruction of the *Lusitania*."

He was afraid to be caught reading and stepped back to his place. He had not been dismissed, and as he waited he thought about the comments he had read. He could not accept them. Those people had forgotten they were writing about a war. The Kaiser should have recognized that, although they certainly helped to explain his outburst.

The door behind Schwieger opened at last, and someone walked round him and stopped by the table. It was Kaiser Wilhelm and he was alone. He was holding some sheets of paper.

Wilhelm was torn. His anger had subsided and had been replaced by exhilaration. His nature was to share it, but he could hardly do so with a junior officer whom he had just reprimanded. Even though the situation had changed. He had just received several pieces of news, one of which meant that the American threat had been defused in an unexpected and unquestionable manner. Another flash from an Intelligence source in London was even more gratifying.

Following a stormy debate in the English House of Commons over the inadequate protection provided for the *Lusitania*, the First Sea Lord, Fisher, had resigned. Better still. His resignation was mainly to emphasize his disapproval of Churchill, perhaps the most dangerous man in the British cabinet, but combined with mounting criticism, it had brought down the Liberal government. That had been succeeded by a coalition with the Conservatives, who before agreeing to it had demanded the expulsion of their pet hate,

Winston. So in one week both Fisher and Churchill had been removed. And it was all as a result of the *Lusitania*.

In spite of himself, Wilhelm could no longer look on the sinking with such revulsion. He could admit also to himself that his first reaction to it had been one of gratification. The loss of life was still regrettable, but the responsibility was the British government's, due to its blockade, which forced retaliatory methods on Germany.

He had also read something which changed his attitude to Schwieger. He sat at the table and reread the typewritten pages he had brought, underscoring some lines with his red pencil. He looked up. "You are aware that your actions have created an element of tension in our relations with the United States?"

"I have realized that, sir," Schwieger said tautly.

"For reasons which I do not intend to go into, that tension is no longer of such concern," Wilhelm told him. "However, it is desirable for us to prepare a reply to the absurd charges made by other neutral nations. Do you understand?"

"I believe so, sir," Schwieger said. To his astonishment, the Kaiser's manner was completely different, not friendly, but no longer accusing. He was holding out the sheets of paper, and Schwieger took them. He was bewildered when he saw that they were a typed transcript of pages from his log covering the day of the sinking.

"You recollect writing this, I presume," Wilhelm said.

"Yes, sir."

Wilhelm nodded. "Very well. Using it as a basis, you will submit a report on the *Lusitania*. It will be confidential, but may be shown to interested parties. You will not alter whatever I have underlined, particularly the passage where you say you could not fire a second torpedo."

"Yes, sir."

"For the rest, you will make it quite definite that you did not know the identity of the ship until after you had fired. That the second explosion on board was most likely caused by gunpowder. And you will stress your surprise at the rapidity with which she sank and that the loss of life was largely due to the inefficiency of her crew. Is that clear?"

"Yes, Your Imperial Majesty."

"You will be assigned temporary quarters. Until the report is finished, you will communicate with no one. Afterwards you will mention it to no one. Is that also clear?"

"Yes, Your Imperial Majesty."

Wilhelm paused. "Very well. That is all. Carry this out satisfactorily, and no further steps need be taken."

Schwieger clicked his heels and bowed. Remembering in time not to turn his back, he retreated to the door, bowed again and went out.

Wilhelm had watched him, wondering if he should perhaps have said something more. But no, there had been enough of a hint of absolution in his final remark. All the same, he could not help smiling when he thought of Fisher. And Churchill, thrust into political outer darkness. He laughed. Who could have imagined this sorry business could have such gratifying side developments? Poor President Wilson, the dried-up ex-professor. And the yelps of the neutral curs. He swept the foreign newspapers contemptuously off the table to the floor.

Woodrow Wilson sat with his fingers on the keys of his old typewriter. This past month had stretched everyone's nerves. Hysteria had increased rather than diminished, although few of the protesters went so far as to shout outright for war. At the same time, it was clear that the bulk of the country was largely indifferent to events in Europe, while the German reply to the *Lusitania* note was almost insulting in its disregard of the issues raised. And now it appeared that William Jennings Bryan had assured Germany, through the Austrian Ambassador, that America had no intention of ever going to war.

It was tantamount to treason and Wilson had been dazed with shock. Bryan had blustered that he had said no such thing, but no one was convinced. It had taken all the power of the White House to save the Secretary. Wilson unrolled his draft of a new note from the typewriter and read it through carefully. Again it was trenchant, but it was still well short of being an ultimatum.

As he expected, the Cabinet meeting was almost a carbon copy of the last dozen or so. Wilson had a fundamental respect for Bryan, and the Secretary of State was the only other man in the room who could have been President. He might have been, too, but for the rash policies into which his passion led him. Wilson's fingertips traced a spiral pattern on the table top in front of him.

"We claim it is a question of our national sovereignty," Bryan was saying. "Is that sovereignty not more wantonly disregarded by the enforced ban which the British have placed on our legitimate trade with Europe than by the accidental damage caused by a handful of German submarines fighting? We should bring all pressure to bear on England to remove the great cause of friction and all the smaller ones will dissolve. Mr. President, I appeal to you. Is that not so?"

Wilson glanced up. He shook his head. "With the warmest regard, Mr. Bryan, I cannot agree with you."

Bryan's neck had turned red and he appeared to be laboring for breath. He glared round the room. "You people are not neutral!" he suddenly blurted. "You are taking sides. You are all pro-Allied!"

There was a chorus of angry exclamations, cut off when Wilson rapped sharply on the table. His voice was as cold and cutting as a lancet. "Mr. Secretary, you have no right to make that statement," he said. "We are all honestly trying to be neutral against heavy difficulties."

Bryan subsided, muttering an inaudible apology and taking no further part in the discussion. The President ended the meeting.

Back in his study, Wilson continued his deliberations alone. He was more and more conscious of his responsibility. He had made up his mind that the second note must be sent. He knew basically that his decision was right, and yet his confidence in his own opinions had been thrown into confusion. He was torn by uncertainty and conflicting emotions. Through the clamor of jingoism and pacifism, of hatred and factional propaganda, it was hard to detect what the people really wanted. They had an unerring, inarticulate instinct for what was right, and he would soon know if he had misjudged it. They insisted on the strongest protest being made. Did they realize it meant war if Germany did not give way?

The fire had burned low, but Walter Page did not stir even to drop another log on it. He was seated in the high-backed chair in his study, wrapped in his old dressing gown. For several hours his only movement had been an occasional shake of the head or flexing of his interlaced fingers.

The ripples of the *Lusitania*'s sinking had continued to spread, an endless series of shock waves. It had brought an end to Colonel House's mission to Europe. The "too proud to fight" speech had damaged his credibility as a spokesman for the President, and he agreed with Page that his best course was to return to the United States, where his influence with Wilson could end the dangerous delay in America joining the struggle against German militarism. Then, while he was still at sea, the news came of Bryan's resignation over the dispatch of the second note to Germany. Contrary to Bryan's expectations, his resignation had the very opposite effect to that which he had intended. His countrymen did not find it so easy to make excuses for Germany and a hurricane of abuse descended on him. He was denounced as little more than a traitor and his popular appeal was wiped out, while the new note was acclaimed by the great majority.

House arrived home to be told he was being offered the post of Secretary of State. Wilson needed him, but true to his self-effacing code, he declined. The next choice was Page himself. Yet even as he debated whether or not to accept, word came that the President had decided he was too closely identified with one side in the war to be acceptable to many factions in the nation. The final choice, to many people's surprise, was Robert Lansing.

Page was relieved and delighted. Yet he could not believe what was happening. He had lost all his former respect and admiration for Woodrow Wilson. The quibbling and constant backpedaling and twisting to maintain a precarious neutrality had made American diplomacy seem ludicrous. He even doubted Wilson's sincerity, since his eyes were so unmistakably fixed on the 1916 presidential election and the votes of the uninformed, self-sufficient majority who still believed in peace at all costs and isolationism. The President could have awakened them to the inevitable and joined with the Allies to put a swift stop to the slaughter and the threat to their future, but Wilson did nothing. His moral scruples combined with his sense of political expediency to prevent him.

Colonel House, as Page might have anticipated, had re-entered the ranks of the appeasers. He had had an unpleasant shock on his return to discover that his role as President's confidant had been largely taken over by the unknown Mrs. Galt. He was no longer the closest to the throne. If he had accepted the State Department, he might have retrieved his position, but now it was too late. The President did not ignore him, but obviously their minds were not as attuned as he had imagined. There had even been a hint of criticism from London, something to which Wilson could never take kindly. House had to do some fancy footwork to stay in the ring, and he now counseled a diplomacy of wait and see. As he wrote blandly to Page, American interests must as always come first. "I need not tell you that if the Allies fail to win, it must necessarily mean a reversal of our entire policy."

So much Page might have considered inevitable. His most unlooked for disappointment, however, was in the new Secretary of State. Instead of becoming more incisive, the *Lusitania* notes, with Lansing's participation, had become more pettifogging and legalistic. Page had waited in vain for any sign of the opinion which Lansing used to express in private of the necessity to America of an Allied victory. "Quite apart from any emotional ties or considerations, in our own interests we cannot afford to let England and France go under." Now he was as temporizing and mealymouthed as House.

The Ambassador's whole anxiety was somehow to preserve the friendly relations between the United States and Great Britain. He had watched impotently while they were eroded, and in their place an atmosphere of distrust and suspicion began to develop. Bryan might have lost his position, but his spirit still dominated the White House. Page had hoped against hope for a positive move by Lansing. At last it had come, and it was the most bitter blow of all.

Page had written to the new Secretary, asking despairingly for some precise guidance on how he was supposed to deal with the British government. Now the answer had arrived, a lengthy indictment of the trade restrictions imposed by England's blockade of Germany, a mass of legal complaints and allegations under thirty-five headings with three appendices. Page felt as though he had been poleaxed. He had asked for something to help him to preserve a friendship between nations. Instead he had been sent this thing, without a word of courtesy or hint of a possible compromise. To present it as it was could lead directly to a severance of diplomatic relations, and yet he was instructed most particularly that every point must be gone into thoroughly, nothing could be sidestepped, full and true replies had to be provided for each of its many charges.

Page went over it in his mind for the hundredth time. Woodrow Wilson had reached the stage when anyone who argued with him was suspect, and whatever Lansing's private opinions were, he would not last long unless the advice he gave chimed exactly with what the President wanted to hear. Thinking again of the admonition to ensure that not one point was to be neglected, Page slowly began to smile. Perhaps Robert Lansing was the smartest of them all.

The note to England was too long and too complicated for anyone but lawyers to understand. There were no vital issues in it, only quibbles. It had taken months to prepare and would require many more months to answer. Clarification was needed on many points and communications would pass endlessly between the lawyers of the British government and of the State Department, yet no result could be achieved until every single point had been analyzed and agreed on, and even then Lansing could raise additional topics. But it was no rallying call for action. Lansing had trusted him to see that. He could keep it going until the inevitable day when the German mask dropped, when the one provocation too many was offered, and the American people had had enough. When they rose in their righteous anger and forced the high-principled, moralizing, indecisive Man in the White House to draw the sword which should have leaped from its scabbard on May 7, 1915.

Walther Schwieger came out into the street and paused. To be outside again was like being released from prison. The transcript was in the manila envelope under his arm and rooms had been booked for him in the Hotel Königshof in the Neue Wilhelmstrasse. It was odd to be in Berlin and not to be going home, but his orders were explicit.

As he looked around for a taxi, a driver in naval uniform opened the rear door of a limousine and saluted. "Kapitän-leutnant?" Schwieger returned the salute. The curtains at the limousine's rear windows were drawn. Climbing in, he hesitated, seeing someone already seated in the opposite corner. But the door was closing behind him and he sat.

The driver got in behind the wheel. "Where to, sir?"

"Hotel Königshof."

Schwieger curbed his bitterness as they moved off. His unnecessary escort was a naval captain. As Schwieger looked at him more closely, he suddenly remembered where he had seen him before. In the entourage of Grand Admiral Tirpitz.

"Did you have a pleasant meeting with a certain gentleman?" the captain asked. Schwieger did not answer. "Not too unpleasant, I hope?"

"Not too unpleasant," Schwieger agreed.

"Good."

Schwieger took out his cigarette case and offered it to gain a little more time. He had an uncomfortable feeling that it was beginning all over again.

"Were any specific points raised?" the captain asked casually.

"Only that the British have accused us of murder."

The captain flicked his hand dismissively. "They would. Don't let it bother you."

"I won't," Schwieger said. He lit his cigarette. It would do no harm to tell them what they were bound to find out. "And I've been asked to rewrite my log."

The captain tensed. "For what purpose?"

"As a report. To stress that everything happened by pure chance."

"Ah." The captain thought for a moment. "And where are you to submit it, this report?"

"I really don't know, sir," Schwieger confessed. "That was not mentioned."

"In that case," the captain said, "you will submit it to the Admiral Staff, to the office of Grand Admiral von Tirpitz." He paused. "Do you understand?"

Schwieger understood only too well, and nodded. "Yes, sir."

The captain smiled. "The Grand Admiral thinks very highly

of you. I can see why." He considered Schwieger. "To rule a nation at war is very difficult. The All Highest, for example, has been under immense strain. It is unwise to burden him with extra problems, details. Indeed, his mind is so quick that sometimes he forgets things in his haste. He may perhaps have forgotten to reward you sufficiently for your exploit. The Grand Admiral, however, wishes me to assure you that he is not ungrateful. As he will prove when the opportunity arises."

Schwieger's overnight case was already at the Königshof. He opened it, uncorked his hip flask and took a draft of brandy. His lips and palate stung as it burned away the sour taste. Damn them and their intrigues, he thought. He had heard rumors of the Kaiser's instability, but had seen no trace of it until today. Tirpitz had always seemed like a rock on which the Reich sat securely, immovable, unswervingly loyal. It was naive at his age, Schwieger told himself, to mourn for fallen idols. Yet it was inevitable when his whole career had been an attempt to be worthy of them.

He took another drink. To hell with them, he thought again. He had not been lying when he said his only wish was to do his duty. In the long run, or the short, that was all there was. He toasted himself and the U 20. His loyalty was to the Service and to his command.

The hotel room was stifling. He knew what it was. That dream on the train had unsettled him. Until he had seen his parents and sisters for himself, he could not be certain of their reaction. And there was Anneliese. She hated the war, the killing, and his part in it most of all.

She had taken a small apartment in Bremen while waiting for her next engagement. It meant he could be with her whenever he had a day or two. He had promised to call her as soon as he got back from patrol. There could be no harm in that. He picked up the telephone and asked the operator to put him through to her number.

The concierge answered. "Fräulein Anneliese? She's gone, sir."

"When do you expect her back?" Schwieger asked.

"No, she's gone, sir," the concierge said. "Left the apartment."

"When?"

"This morning, sir. She packed her bags and went."

"Where to?" Schwieger asked. "Where did she go to?"

"I don't know, sir. I'm sorry. She didn't leave a forwarding address."

Schwieger replaced the receiver. He knew exactly what had happened. None of the announcements had said who sank the *Lusitania*. Not till this morning. She had opened the paper and seen his photograph and the U 20. She would have cried maybe, for both of them. Then she had packed and left the apartment before he could call her. Anneliese had gone. No forwarding address.

Walther Schwieger crossed to the bed and began slowly to undress. He hoped he would not dream.

About the Author

David Butler is the author of EDWARD THE SEVENTH, LILLIE, and DISRAELI, novels on which the British television series were based. He has numerous film and television credits. He lives in London with his wife and two daughters.